The Choice

Vampiris Bloodline - A Paranormal Vampire Romance Series Book 1

V. P. Nightshade

Sohmer Publishing

Contents

EPUB ISBN: 978-1-7374885-1-4

Kindle ISBN: 978-1-7374885-3-8

PDF ISBN: 978-1-7374885-2-1

Paperback ISBN: 978-1-7374885-0-7

Hardback ISBN: 978-1-7374885-4-5

First edition

The Vampiris Bloodline Series Universal Links

The Choice: A Paranormal Vampire Romance
(Vampiris Bloodline - A Paranormal Vampire Romance Series Book 1)
https://mybook.to/TheChoice-VPNightshade

Now, Always, Forever: A Dark Paranormal Vampire Romance
(Vampiris Bloodline - A Paranormal Vampire Romance Series Book 2)
https://mybook.to/Now-Always-Forever

The First Time In Forever: A Paranormal Vampire Romance (Vampiris Bloodline - A Paranormal Vampire Romance Series Book 3)
https://mybook.to/TheFirstTimeInForever

Growling In My Bed: A Paranormal Love Story, A Vampiris Bloodline - Shifters of Diamond Wolf Ranch Series, A Novella (Vampiris Bloodline - A Paranormal Vampire Romance Series Book 4)
https://mybook.to/Growling-In-My-Bed

Forever Blood: A Dark Paranormal Vampire Romance
(Vampiris Bloodline - A Paranormal Vampire Romance Series Book 5)
https://mybook.to/Forever-Blood

Growling In My Dreams: A Paranormal Werewolves and Shifters Romance, A Vampiris Bloodline - Shifters of Diamond Wolf Ranch Series (Vampiris Bloodline - A Paranormal Vampire Romance Series Book 6)
https://mybook.to/Growling-In-My-Dreams

Growling In The Dark: A Paranormal Werewolves and Shifters Romance, A Vampiris Bloodline - Shifters of Diamond Wolf Ranch Series (Vampiris Bloodline - A Paranormal Vampire Romance Series Book 7)
https://mybook.to/Growling-In-The-Dark

Growling In My Soul: A Paranormal Werewolves and Shifters Romance, A Vampiris Bloodline - Shifters of Diamond Wolf Ranch Series (Vampiris Bloodline - A Paranormal Vampire Romance Series Book 8)

https://mybook.to/Growling-In-My-Soul

My Immortal Passion: A Steamy Vampire Romantic Fantasy (Vampiris Bloodline - A Paranormal Vampire Romance Series Book 9)

https://mybook.to/MyImmortalPassion

More By V. P. Nightshade

A **T̲w̲i̲s̲t̲e̲d̲ ̲F̲a̲i̲r̲y̲ ̲T̲a̲l̲e̲ Obsession, Steamy Fairy Tale Retellings**

Step into the enchanting world of A Twisted Fairy Tale Obsession, where our reimagined timeless fairy tales have a spellbinding, mesmerizing, steamy twist, offering readers a fresh adult perspective on beloved stories they thought they knew. Each installment in this captivating series transports readers to fantastical realms where love, sacrifice, and destiny intertwine in unexpected ways. From the ethereal forests of Beauty's Beast to the mystical depths of the Mer Kingdom, prepare to embark on an unforgettable journey through the interconnected threads of each narrative, where revelations linger like the echoes of a fairy tale's magic.

With each turn of the page, prepare to be swept away by the allure of these reimagined fairy tales, where love defies boundaries, sacrifices shape destinies, and the echoes of magic linger long in your heart after the last chapter ends. Embark on a journey unlike any other, where each enchanting tale weaves the essence of love, magic, and a steamy twist into its very fabric. Use the universal links below to get to your local Amazon Store to order yours today!

Coming June 1st, July 1st, and August 1st respectively:

Held Within His Fangs: A Twisted Steamy Beauty And The Beast Retelling Book 1

Beneath The Beast's Heart: A Twisted Steamy Beauty And The Beast Retelling Book 2

Beauty's Beast Forevermore: A Twisted Steamy Beauty And The Beast Retelling Book 3

Coming December 14, 2024

To Love The Goblin Prince, A Vampiris Bloodline Standalone

Dedication

This series is dedicated to everyone who ever gave me inspiration and who will never read it!

For Ivy ~ wherever you are!

*A Special Thank You to my Readers ~
without you,
the hardback version wouldn't have been possible!*

Acknowledgement

Writing and publishing a work of fiction is both harder and more rewarding
than I imagined!
But it would not have been possible if not for a few people.

I want to thank specifically my friend,
and partner in crime,
Romana Disrud
for your untiring support while I struggled with the
planning, plotting, writing and the completion of this book.

To Rick Trimmer: I hope Mansuetus turned out to be the decent guy that you
wanted him to be!
Thank you for his inspiration!

Last but not least, thank you to my family and specifically my husband
who paid the bills and allowed me to create
and FINISH this project
despite being a non-believer in the subject matter!

Epigraph

"I have found the one whom my soul loves."
~ Song of Solomon 3:4, The Bible, King James Version

"The sweet, fragrant curves of your body,
the soft, spiced contours of your flesh
Invite me, and I come.
I stay until dawn breathes its light and night slips away."
~ Song of Solomon, 4:6-4:7,
The Bible, The Message Version

"If there ever comes a day when we can't be together,
keep me in your heart.
I'll stay there forever."
~ A. A. Milne

Prologue

APRIL 1995

"Y OU ARE HERE." Coming from the darkness, the melodic voice seemed surprised, but pleased.

She turned a full circle, glancing around to the dim corners for the sound of that voice, feeling lost and off-balance. It was musical, that voice. It pulled at her, and she was desperate to find its source. The room appeared richly furnished, illuminated only by a small fire in an immensely colossal fireplace. The sofa facing the fire had an archaic shape, draped in red velvet and gold brocade, while the armchairs on each side were equally opulent with green and gold upholstery. The walls themselves were paneled in dark wood, with paintings thrown into shadow by the dim firelight. Everything that you could possibly imagine being placed in an old mansion on the stage of an old movie set; this was what the room was. To her, it was a peregrine place; and she wanted badly to know where she was and how she had got there. She still didn't see the source of the voice.

"Where are you?" She asked the room, turning full circle again, opening all of her senses in her search.

Out of the shadows stepped a beautiful man. He was lean and powerful, but neither tall nor short; just shy of six feet. She thought he might be mid-thirties in age. He had lovely, loose golden waves of hair that curled at the ends and brushed the bottom of the collar of his shirt. The waves were neither true blonde, nor true brown, but like the burnished gold of a ring. His hair looked so soft and silky; her fingers ached to run through those waves. His eyes were large, thickly lashed, bright amber, just marginally darker than his curls, and gleamed with knowledge. His skin shown lightly tan in the firelight, and it looked like he hadn't shaved in a day or so. He moved gradually and cautiously towards her as if she might vanish or run from him.

"Are you ready?" he asked her softly, hopefully, moving slowly toward her.

"Ready for what?" she replied with a question of her own, curiosity in her voice. She took in his garments. A modern dress shirt, crisply white, expensive, unbuttoned, cuff-links long removed, loose and pulled from his pants, to hang from his broad shoulders, exposing the fact that he wasn't wearing an undershirt. It was as if he had quickly thrown it on. She glimpsed the tanned skin of his chest with its light golden hairs through the gap, and a well-defined, muscled abdomen. Ebony dress slacks, and incongruously bare feet. He was relaxed, and his relaxation was infectious.

"Ready to come to me." He stated simply, softly, his voice a soft tenor that vibrated through her body, setting off a wave of desire; she smelled cinnamon, ginger, and a hint of sandalwood. He now stood an arm's length from her.

She looked up into those gorgeous amber eyes, reflecting the flames of the fire, and burst out laughing. His surprise was palpable, and he blinked in confusion.

"This is a dream," she chuckled. "I am dreaming." She expressed, suddenly relieved, emphatically nodding in agreement with herself, and then nodded more forcefully, looking at him and smiling, as he shook his head negatively.

"No." He slowly shook his head at her. "We are communicating. Our souls are speaking..." He said, gradually reaching towards her, obviously to pull her into his arms; the gap in his shirt widening to show a larger expanse of his well-defined chest and flat stomach, sparse golden hairs trailing into the waistband of his pants drawing her eyes downward.

"Yep." She giggled. "A sex dream."

"No, i psychí mou. I am not a dream." He told her softly, touching the bare skin of her arms and his eyes widened in wonder and discovery.

As he ran his warm, soft, but lightly calloused hands cautiously up her arms, she was shocked into a state of apperception, and went quite still.

Her teal-colored eyes widened also and locked with his amber ones. She was confident that she had never set eyes on him, but she was sure that she *knew* this man. Like she knew herself.

The Beginning

CHAPTER ONE

L EILA WOKE TO THE sound of the radio, not wanting to leave the comfort of the bed, excuses she could use to not go to work floating through her mind. Lingering as the music droned on, she took her pillow and covered her face, trying to recover the dream that she had been having. It was a mistake.

She heard Michael's voice as he gave her a rough shove. "Get up and turn that damn thing off!"

Get up and do it yourself, asshole! She thought, but did as she was told. *If I didn't set the alarm at night, your ass would be late every morning!* Her inner voice expounded silently.

She remembered the night before. Michael went to bed earlier than herself, as usual, not wanting sex. The only time he ever stayed up as late as she did was if he wanted to have sex.

She had come in after doing laundry, making sure he had a clean uniform for the morning. As she lay down, she glanced over at him and realized that he was pretending to be asleep. She then asked softly, "Did you set the alarm?"

He had snapped, "No! Leave me alone, I am trying to sleep!"

She had gotten up and set the alarm; knowing that if she didn't, they would both be late to work, and he'd make her pay somehow. It had been another mistake to have even asked him. They went through the same routine at least four nights a week. Maybe she was hoping he would finally do something for himself, that something would change. She knew that doing the same thing over and over and hoping for a different result was a sign of insanity, but there you have it. It kind of summed up her current relationship status!

Her body ached. It was getting harder and harder to get up in the morning. She knew something was wrong with her. She was sure it had to be a mental or physical problem, because in the evenings she felt wonderful; like she received a second boost of energy.

Even being around Michael in his normally bitchy moods each evening, she felt like she had more energy than ever! But when it came to getting up and facing another day, she just wanted to sleep and sleep. She had tried changing several things to feel better.

She tried going to bed early and force herself to sleep. She would sleep restlessly, until the early hours of the morning, and even with nine straight hours of rest under her belt, she still could barely force herself out of bed. She knew it had to be some sort of depression, or maybe it was a chemical or hormonal imbalance? If the problem kept on much longer, she would be forced to see a doctor, and she hated going to the doctor!

Turning on the light above her vanity, pain flashed behind her eyes as she squinted them against the glare. She looked over her right shoulder at the form of her husband on the bed; blankets pulled over his head, thinking, *Lord knows I have a right to be depressed.*

Running a brush through her short chestnut curls, she thought about the disappointments of her four-year marriage. She had high hopes for them in the beginning, but secretly, she had harbored fears. It seemed that her fears were coming true.

She had never thought of marrying again.

Her first marriage had occurred for all the wrong reasons. She had been young, not twenty-one, and wanted to be on her own, to escape from the confines of her family. Her first husband, Evan, had been in the Navy, and he was so handsome he made her hands sweat. But he was shallow, had no morals, and even less intelligence. She never truly loved him but had been blinded by his beauty and the exciting aspect of moving away and traveling the world; that excitement overshadowed everything else, and she had never bothered to get to know him well before she married him. The whole thing had been a mistake.

She had known Michael for almost 8 years now. He had been a friend of her ex-husband, and when they had lived in Connecticut in the same apartment complex, she had even introduced her girlfriends to him. He had been so nice and so smart; and when Evan started seeing other women,

Michael was there for her. He became her best friend. Her anchor in a lonely, choppy sea.

Despite Evan's infidelities, she made one last ditch effort to save her marriage and had moved to Georgia when he got stationed there. They bought a house, and she genuinely tried to work on her marriage and to forget the painful past, but it never ended, as the ever-increasing line of women just didn't stop. She couldn't bring herself to care anymore. At the end, it was on her.

She walked away, despite Evan's earnest protests to stay together and work through it. Against her lawyer's advice, she gave Evan everything except a few mementos and pieces of furniture in exchange for absolving her of the responsibility of her half of their marital bills. She figured that since he had created the whole of the debt and she couldn't afford even half of it on her small salary, he could just have everything: debt included. She just wanted to pretend that it had never happened.

Then she met Michael again.

It's a fact that if you are around the military long enough, sooner or later you run into the same people; though spread out worldwide, it is still, after all, a small community. Michael had made rank since she last saw him. He was now a First-Class Petty Officer. She didn't find out until after she started dating him that their getting together wasn't accidental.

Evan had seen Michael at a base softball game and had told him about their divorce. Bitter, in his own nasty way, Evan had told him, and everyone else within earshot, that he had always known that Michael had wanted to fuck Leila, and here was his opportunity to have her. After all, he was sure that she wasn't fucking anyone else, and now that Evan was through with her, she was available; Michael should look her up. Evan never guessed that Michael would do just that.

Only after Leila started dating Michael did she find out that their meeting in the parking lot of the base Off-Crew building had been no accident. Michael had waited around an entire week hoping to "bump" into her, either coming to or from her job in the administration building next door.

Leila wondered if she had been a pawn in a "get me-get you" game between the two men. She'd been upfront with what she thought was a truth at the time, telling Michael that she would never remarry. She wouldn't go through that again with anyone. It was a childish statement. She was only twenty-five at the time; and she was far too young to be so cynical. Then she became pregnant.

Early in her marriage to Evan, she had found that birth control pills had made her violently ill. So, they had used other forms of contraception, or often, no contraception at all. She had secretly hoped having a baby would settle him down, but by the time her five-year marriage had ended, she was convinced that she couldn't become pregnant. An aunt on her father's side was barren, and she just assumed that she was like her. Michael had been convinced she was wrong.

Leila told Michael that even though she felt she couldn't have children, she wasn't taking any chances and she wanted to use protection, anyway. He kept telling her; he wanted to have kids, and at every opportunity would make spontaneous and enthusiastic love to her. She truly hadn't been concerned about getting pregnant, even when he would fail to use a condom, and would smile sadly when he would whisper in her ear while they were making love, "Give me a baby."

She remembered going to the walk-in Medical Center, after Michael had gone to sea for a three-month tour, to find out what was wrong with her 'this time'. The staff and doctor were used to her coming in as she had developed two yeast infections and had been treated for a urinary tract infection over a three-week period. When the clinic doctor had suggested doing a blood test to see if she was pregnant, she had laughed out loud. "Go ahead, but I really don't think that's the problem!"

She had fainted as soon as the nurse had taken the blood sample. When she came to, she told the nurse, "I'm pregnant."

"Dear," the nurse replied. "We haven't even done the test yet."

"I don't care. I know I'm pregnant! I never faint when I give blood." Leila had said to the nurse with wide eyes.

Sure enough, she was pregnant. She was halfway between depression and elation. After believing that she couldn't have children, the opportunity of bringing her child into the world was wonderful, but on the other hand, she didn't want to remarry. Her divorce had only been final for a couple of months, even though she had been separated for nearly two years, and she was not ready to get remarried.

Her parents wanted her to come home to Iowa. Especially her father.

"You can come home, and we will help you," he had told her when she called them with the news.

She couldn't bring herself to do it. A fighter throughout her life, she wasn't used to tucking tail and running. Besides, with Michael out to sea, she hadn't even had the opportunity to tell him. Even though she expected him to be supportive of her, she still had a small doubt in that secret place in her heart. Telephone service being impossible on a submarine. She couldn't come right out and tell him she was pregnant. But the limited communication messages, called family-grams, were not private.

After all, he was a single man. The ship's captain could decide that this type of news to one of his single crew members might be unreasonably stressful for him and hold the family-gram until the end of the cruise. She and a girlfriend devised a code to indicate to Michael that she was pregnant. In one family-gram, she had written that she had quit smoking. In another, she had written that she had started a walking program. In yet another, she had stated that she had started a health food diet. All the while hoping that he would read between the lines.

Feeling totally unprepared, she bought several books on pregnancy and child rearing. Having never been the 'babysitter' type of teenager; she knew her experience was lacking. With no family in the state, she was doing her best to educate herself on what to expect.

She was reading her books one evening when the phone rang. "Hello," she answered, expecting it to be one of her friends.

"Hey babe, we came in early." Came Michael's deep voice.

"Hi." Her voice was almost frozen with nervousness.

"Well, come get me. I am at the Explosive Handling Wharf."

"Okay." She said quickly, hanging up the phone with shaking hands, forgetting to even tell him goodbye.

Heart hammering in her chest, her thoughts flew. Did he receive the family-grams? Did he pick up on the messages and realize what she was trying to tell him? What was his reaction going to be? She drove the mile and a half to the back gate of the base and showed her employment badge to the guard there. Driving through the gates, she headed toward the lower base and the restricted area.

Due to her job duties in the Communications-Information Technology Department, she had access to get clear down to the submarines themselves.

Showing her badge again to the gate guard at the controlled area, she drove her red 1991 Mustang through to the EHW. Michael, standing with three other sailors, was dressed in blue dungarees, the working uniform of a submarine First Class Petty Officer and below. Leila always thought that the uniform made them look like prison convicts.

Leaning in the car's window, Michael said, "Pop the hatch."

She did, and he and the other men loaded their 'sea bags' into the back. Well, at least he doesn't seem like anything is wrong, Leila thought, watching as they packed themselves into the car.

"These guys live in the apartment complex next door; you don't mind if we give them a ride, do you?" He asked as he leaned over and kissed her warmly.

Shaking her head, she turned the car around, heading off the base, not saying anything for the short drive back to the apartment. She couldn't even bring herself to greet the three men in the back of her car, as she was becoming more nervous by the minute.

The men all thanked her as she dropped them off at their building. She and Michael still didn't speak as she drove toward his apartment building. When she had parked the car in front of the building and turned off the engine, he finally spoke.

"Well, are you pregnant?" He had asked softly.

"Yes." Taking a deep breath she replied simply, facing forward with her hands gripping the steering wheel tightly, awaiting his reaction.

"I guess you'll have to marry me now." He had stated victoriously, almost like winning a contest, and wrapped his arms around her, pulling her close. He still didn't know how much that statement had rankled her.

Back in the present, she looked at her reflection in the mirror, smiling wryly. That had been almost four years ago. Since then, their son Zachary was born, then came their second son Devin, now nine months old. Michael made the decision that he didn't want any more children, since he had his 'heir and a spare', and regardless of Leila's thoughts and desires, had gotten a vasectomy three months ago.

Since marrying him, Leila found Michael to be cold, uncommunicative, easily angered, and totally dismissive of her thoughts and desires. He could often be downright nasty.

She tried excusing his behavior due to life's pressures. After all, they had been married the day after her 26th birthday in a small ceremony at the justice of the peace, with little fanfare and a short weekend honeymoon to Orlando, FL. Then they had bought a house together a month later, and he returned to Sea Duty less than a month after that. Leila gave birth to Zachary, a small curly-haired, blue-eyed, smiling baby via an emergency C-section a few months later.

Leila's mother was there with her, but he wasn't. Michael found out about the birth of his firstborn via family-gram – the same way that he had found out about her pregnancy. He was angry that she had named their son Zachary David, when he had *told* her that he had wanted to name him Brian after some cousin that she had never met.

After everything that she had gone through with her C-section, she felt that she had the right to name the baby. But, most especially after he had made the two months that they spent together before Zachary was born a nightmare for her. He bullied and tried to control every aspect of her pregnancy, from her diet to her maternity clothes. Nothing she did was ever good enough. For the first time, she was happy to have him leave for the sea.

So many things had happened throughout their marriage. It seemed throughout the four years that they were together that he was rarely around on any of their marital milestones. He was always out at sea.

Before Zachary was a year old, Michael was promoted to Chief Petty Officer. With the promotion came more responsibility and the transfer from the sea environment to a shore environment at the Submarine Squadron. Though he frequently rotated with another Chief at the Squadron, he still spent a minimum of one-week per month at sea riding one of the eight Trident submarines to perform inspections.

She then became pregnant again and had their second son Devin, a bright-eyed little demon of a baby, exactly thirty months and a week after Zachary had been born. Devin was active, colicky, and was the polar-opposite of his brother! Zachary laughed and smiled and knew no strangers! They could take him anywhere and everyone loved him. Devin, on the other hand, hated everyone and everything except for his Mommy, and made any outing a miserable occasion! Leila frequently joked with her mother on their weekly phone call, "If we had Devin first, we would not have had two!"

Last month, Michael had come up for promotion to Senior Chief Petty Officer, but surprisingly, wasn't promoted. Being so smart and working so hard for perfection in his job, Michael's ego had taken a blow. Leila wasn't concerned at all because he had been making rank ahead of schedule, but Michael was miserable to be around most days now and was determined to live at the job to make Senior Chief, regardless of the pressure it placed on Leila to basically raise their two sons by herself.

Overall, there had been a whirlwind of activity for Michael in the last four years, and she believed he had a right to be edgy. Having a new family, children, new home, job promotion worries, in such a short period of time were all stress factors in anyone's life.

But the winds of change had been whirling around her also, and despite everything, she was positive that she had never intentionally treated him shabbily, while he seemed to take every stress or disappointment out on her.

Shaking her head, she moved to put these thoughts out of her mind. She knew if she didn't control her expressions, he would take offense in some way and make sure her day got lousier before she made it out the door to head to work.

After showering, she finished curling her chestnut-colored hair, and applying makeup to her lightly freckled face, and shadow and liner to her teal-blue-gray eyes. While her head was starting to throb, the skin on her arms started itching like crazy, so she applied some skin cream thinking that she must be getting a bad case of dry skin. She took a couple of aspirin to head off the headache and watched Michael get out of bed in the mirror. His naked body could still make her heart race, even with all the bad things that had passed between them.

She quickly looked back at her own reflection. He didn't like her to look at him that way and if he caught her at it, he would make a nasty remark to her. He was self-conscious about his body. At thirty, he was slightly overweight and well on his way to being bald, but she still thought he was sexy.

After two children, she wasn't perfect herself. Who is? Unless you have the money and time for a personal trainer and surgery. Still, she would have given almost anything to have him look at her the way she looked at him; the way he *used* to look at her.

She dressed herself in a beige skirt and a flowered faux vest with short, capped sleeves, patterned in soft pink roses with khaki green leaves on a cream and beige background. There was a lace inset with a deep V for a neckline and faux pearl buttons set off with a gold tone braid border around each one.

She had made some dramatic changes in the past couple of months. Her clothing was one of them.

Everyone in her office was surprised at this change. She had worn casual clothing, made for a much older woman for so long that people had almost forgotten what a pretty young woman she was. Now she dressed in more age-appropriate clothing with a dressy business sense. Part of the changes were because she wanted a promotion *very badly*.

She had been due for a promotion since she had transferred to the Information Systems side of the Department three years before and had taken on greater responsibilities. But even she had to admit that no matter how exemplary her performance was, her dress and attitude didn't warrant a higher grade.

Being so tired, and even restless, much of her time, she had felt an overwhelming need to change her life. To become something different. Though she wasn't sure what or why. Still, she felt like there was something inside struggling to get out, like a butterfly battling to break free of its cocoon.

Many times, throughout her life she had felt the need to be free, but until recently there had been too much fear, too much shyness, too much reluctance to draw attention to herself. She had been too afraid that what made her feel good would be mocked by other people. Mostly by Michael.

Now, she just didn't care what other people thought. She had been doing things to give pleasure to herself and it made her feel good to have people notice her, both professionally and personally. She never got any compliments at home, only criticism, so the compliments from her fellow employees made up for that.

It appeared that she had gained more influence at work as well. She wasn't sure if it was the clothes or the attitude, but that felt good, too. It was as if she were more intuitive of other people and better able to make decisions that both were right and satisfied others in the process.

Well, almost everyone. Leila thought as she packed Devin's diaper bag for the trip to daycare. *I can never really catch a break with Michael. He's absolutely never satisfied.*

Unbreakable in his opinions, Michael was always critical of others, though never critical of himself. Sometimes the silence between them after the kids went to bed was deafening. She desperately wanted to tell him about her feelings. Maybe talk to him and in the talking figure out why she had the overwhelming need to change in the first place. But anytime she tried to talk, he was busy, or in a bad mood, or was watching some sort of sports broadcast on television and couldn't be bothered. When she tried speaking to him about not taking part in their family life, he always turned the conversation around on her and acted like she was crazy and needy because he wouldn't make any time for her or the kids. Somewhere after the marriage vows, he had become her husband but was no longer her friend.

After she made major changes in her dress and appearance, Michael started to watch her closely. Even going so far as to accuse her of having a boyfriend. She had scoffed at him. Like she had time for a boyfriend while basically being a single parent!

Smirking to herself, she remembered the look on his face when she had dramatically cut her hair short. In all the years he had known her, she had never gone shorter than a few inches below her shoulders. Now her thick hair was short and curly, layered away from her face, and just brushing past the collar of her shirt. Her hair was a deep auburn-chestnut, with a touch of flame in her highlights. She loved her shorter hair. She felt right, lighter somehow, more herself; not like she felt before, like she was at a masquerade; forever trying to satisfy someone else's thoughts and desires.

Walking into the garage to put the diaper bag in the car, she noticed the glow of the rising sun. Moving to the front of the garage, she paused to admire the golds and the pinks. She loved sunrises and sunsets. Standing just at the edge of the open garage door, when the light touched her body, she experienced the most searing, blinding, intense heat, and the pain staggered her. Thrusting her hand out to steady herself, she clutched at the trunk of her charcoal gray 4-door sedan, her new sensible 'Mom' car that Michael had insisted that she buy, selling off her cute Mustang. It was just another of one of her compromises that she had made to maintain the peace in her household.

As more of the light from the rising sun crept up the driveway, touching more of the exposed skin of her body, agony flowed over her, driving her down. The last thing she thought as she watched in slow motion the pavement coming closer was, *Dummy, you should have been wearing your sunglasses*. She attempted to catch herself with her hands as the blackness inked out the flaming pain.

The Beginning

CHAPTER TWO

S HE OPENED HER EYES, seeing that she was in a hospital room, wallpa- pered in a blue-gray striped pattern, lying in bed, a pillow underneath her head. She saw Michael pacing back and forth in front of her bed, clearly agitated, with his arms crossed, dressed in his khaki uniform. Noticing that her eyes were open, he moved to stand at the end of her bed and gripped the foot board tightly.

"How do you feel? What happened?" He questioned.

"I don't know." She replied tiredly.

"I found you passed out behind your car. What the hell happened?" He sounded irritated and thoroughly put upon, which was his normal attitude.

"I just told you I don't know." She said, getting angry herself. "I just suddenly found myself in blinding pain and then I couldn't stand up. It...it was...it just happened so fast. I'm not sure." She stammered, thinking hard about it.

"Well, they've been running tests since you've been here." He said gruffly.

"What time is it?" she said, cutting him off.

"I don't know. Early afternoon, maybe one or one-thirty."

"What? Where are the kids?" She demanded anxiously.

"Gary and Ellen came and picked them up. They have them, don't worry. I called your office and told them you're in the hospital. I took care of it." He said roughly.

"I can't believe it's early afternoon. I can't believe that I slept this whole time. What in the world happened to me? What does the doctor say?" She said, firing questions at him.

His irritation grew as he answered. "I haven't talked to him yet. When I brought you in this morning, they did some blood work and hooked you up

20

to that machine," he said, pointing at the box next to her which was emitting soft beeps.

She glanced over and noticed that she was hooked up to an EKG. The heart monitor was beeping, it seemed to her, quite slowly; of course, she wasn't a doctor, so she didn't really know. She felt alright now. Trying to push herself into a sitting position, she felt a little dizzy, and she braced herself on one forearm, putting her other hand to her forehead.

Michael looked worriedly at her. He came over, adjusting the bed until she was sitting upright, and then handed her the remote, which was fixed to the bed with a cable.

Well, at least he seems worried about me, she thought.

"I need to call Ellen and find out how the kids are. I'll be back in a little bit." He walked out the door.

"Well, there he goes. Running away." She murmured to herself as she leaned back against the bed. *God, I am thirsty.* She thought as she ran her tongue around the inside of her mouth, looking for some moisture. Looking at the remote that Michael had given her, she pressed the on-call button for the nurse.

A young, very fit nurse with a slightly turned-up nose and blonde hair came into the room, smiling at her. "Mrs. Sutton, you are awake, excellent! How are you feeling?"

"I'm okay. Really thirsty, though. Can I get something to drink?" Leila asked.

"Absolutely." The nurse, whose name tag proclaimed her to be Andrea, took the bedside table next to the wall, wheeled it over to the bed, and adjusted it so that it became a table over Leila's lap. Taking the empty pitcher, she said, "I will be right back with some ice water and will let the doctor know that you are awake."

Leila thanked her as she walked from the room.

She glanced at the IV attached to her arm, noticing it for the first time. It looked to be connected to a saline solution. Well, at least she knew she wasn't dehydrated. It felt like she was catheterized as well. *How convenient.* She thought in irritation.

This would mark the third time that she had been in this new local hospital this year. The first time when she had delivered Devin. The second when she had to have her gallbladder removed, and now with this 'mystery illness'.

This was becoming a habit! Sighing, she wondered where the doctor was. The less time she was here, the better!

Michael stood at the pay phone, impatiently drumming his fingers as he waited for someone to pick up at Gary and Ellen's house.

"Hello." Rang out Ellen Greene's voice. Ellen was a nice, quiet woman married to his shipmate Gary Greene.

Michael liked her very much. A stay-at-home mom, she was one of the few people he trusted with his boys. Though she was much plainer than his Leila, Michael felt Gary was lucky, as she never gave Gary any hassle when Gary wanted to go out and get a couple of drinks with the guys after work or complained when Gary played computer games with the guys. Leila would not think twice about some sort of sarcastic comment if Michael spent as much time outside of the house as Gary did. To tell the truth, he was quite envious of Gary's freedom.

"Hey, Ellen! It's Michael. Leila finally woke up!"

"Michael, that is great! How is she feeling? Do you know what is wrong?" Ellen sounded worried.

"I haven't seen the doctor yet, but she seems to be weak, and she looks kind of pale. How are the boys doing? Devin isn't giving you any trouble, is he?" He asked concerned. He knew that his youngest son could be a handful.

"Well, he was mad after we collected him this morning, but he is off trying to catch up to our cat now. I am going to get him down for a little nap in a few minutes. Zachary has been simply perfect. He is in watching Sesame Street." Ellen said, and then in the background said, "Devin! Stop that!"

"Ellen, I am so sorry to impose on you like this," Michael started.

"Nonsense! He is just a busy little guy." She chuckled. "You can leave them here as long as you need to."

"Thanks so much. I will let you know more after I speak with the doctor. Thank you again."

"You are welcome! Let Leila know I hope she is better soon!" Ellen said, hanging up the phone.

Michael placed the phone in the receiver and sat down on the bench next to the phone bank in the hospital lobby. Putting his face in his hands, he rubbed his eyes. God, he was tired! It seemed as if it wasn't one damn thing; it was another! He stood up and hoped that the doctor was on his way to Leila's room. He needed to find out what was wrong with his wife. He wasn't sure what he would do if this were something serious! Exactly how he was supposed to take care of two small kids with his wife sick was a daunting task that he just wasn't ready to think about just now. *One thing at a time.* He thought, standing to head back to the room.

As he entered the room, a nurse was pouring ice water for Leila, who took it and immediately started gulping it down.

"Slowly, Mrs. Sutton." Andrea said. "Sometimes if you drink it down too quick, it will just come right back up."

"Sorry," Leila murmured. "I am just so thirsty." She said, taking a smaller sip.

"Dr. Lambert will be here soon to talk to you."

"Thanks." Michael told her, as Leila still had the straw in her mouth.

"Oh, Mr. Sutton. I didn't see you standing there. Why don't you take a seat? I am sure the doctor will be with you any minute." Andrea said. "How about if I open the blinds for you?" Pulling open the blinds with a smile.

Leila immediately put a hand up to shade her eyes. "No. Please don't. It's too bright."

"All right. Don't hesitate to hit the on-call button if you need anything, Mrs. Sutton." She re-closed the blinds and left.

"How are the kids?" Leila inquired, looking at Michael.

"Fine. Ellen has everything under control." He looked at her. "The light hurts your eyes? Do you think this is a migraine?" He questioned, almost hopefully.

"I don't think so. I don't particularly have a headache. But, yeah, the light seems overly bright." Leila settled back against the pillows, closing her eyes. "I am just so tired."

"Well, don't go back to sleep! The doctor is going to be here in a second, and I am sure he will want to talk to you." Michael said impatiently.

"I'm not. I am just resting my eyes." Leila opened her eyes to look at Michael sitting in the chair next to the bed. "I didn't do this on purpose, you know."

"Nobody said you did," he said defensively, with just as much impatience as before.

"Well, it is not the way you are acting!" Leila started, when an extremely beautiful young man in his thirties came walking into the room.

"Hello, Mrs. Sutton, my name is Dr. Dene Lambert. How are you doing this afternoon? You gave us all quite a scare!" He said with an easy, sexy smile.

Leila looked at him in wonder and thought. *Oh, my God, I could be on a soap opera right now!* She took in his black hair, ice-blue eyes, and pearly white teeth. It was a killer combination with his sultry, sexy voice. She actually swallowed.

"Well, Doc, I have definitely been better!" She smiled at him in return. She couldn't help it; his smile was infectious.

Michael was less than pleased by her reaction. "Do you have any idea what happened?" He was blunt, eyeing the handsome doctor.

"We are waiting for the labs to come back, and I have them on rush. But, Mrs. Sutton, why don't you tell me what exactly occurred?" He pulled over a wheeled stool to sit next to her bed, glanced at the EKG machine and then took her wrist in his soft, warm, long-fingered hands, looking at his watch as he took her pulse.

"Well, I was tired when I got up this morning. Almost like I hadn't slept. I have been feeling that way in the mornings for a while." She replied, with a quick look at Michael, as the doctor stood and pulled a small penlight out of his pocket and shined a light in her eyes; she winced, flinching.

"That was uncomfortable?" He asked, feeling around to the back of her head. "Do you remember hitting your head when you fell?" He looked inquiringly at her.

"I don't think I did. I remember trying to brace my fall with my hands." She looked at them as she spoke, seeing they had some minor scrapes and a light bruise or two on them. Dr. Lambert also checked them over. He looked at the nurse, who wheeled over a tray with some antiseptic and cotton balls. He applied some antiseptic to the cotton and soothingly washed her hands.

"Please continue. So, you were tired?" He washed as he spoke. Moving her small fingers gently, looking for injuries.

"Yes. I have been feeling tired lately. I have a toddler and a 9-month-old at home, and it is kind of par for the course. So, you know, you just get sleep when you can. But last night I slept through the night. I didn't wake up at all, so I know I got a good rest."

"One of your pupils isn't reacting as well as I like, but you don't seem to have any indication of a head wound." He spoke clinically. He pulled the light from his pocket once more. "Let's try this again?" He inquired with a soft smile. She grimaced and nodded her head.

He again looked into her eyes. She winced, but remained still.

She spoke as he looked. "I have an eye condition called Adie's pupil. My left pupil is weak occasionally. I pretty much always wear sunglasses during the day to prevent migraines."

"I see. Well, that could definitely cause what I am seeing." He leaned back and looked at her intently, so she continued.

"This morning was a little different, in any case. I wasn't experiencing a migraine; I was only very tired. It was dawn, so it wasn't exceptionally light out, and I was getting my car ready to take my kids to daycare. Suddenly, I just felt this extreme sensation of pain. My skin was tingling, itching all over, like I was over-heated, then I lost my balance and felt myself just going down. It was really weird, and all very slow-motion." She stammered a little as she struggled to remember and describe to him what had happened.

Dr. Lambert nodded as she spoke, looking at her intently.

"Well, I don't see any external physical cause at this moment. But I want to keep you overnight for observation. It is strange to lose consciousness for as long as you did, with no apparent physical cause. But we are waiting on labs, and I would like to get you in for an MRI today, or tomorrow at the latest." He glanced at the nurse, who nodded and left the room. He glanced once again at the EKG.

"So, she has to stay overnight?" Michael spoke directly to the doctor.

"Yes, I recommend she does. Depending on when we are able to get her in for the MRI and get the test results, maybe another night as well." Dr. Lambert said to him.

"An MRI? Is that where they pump you full of that stuff and take x-rays? I had one of those tests in 1987 when they were looking for a cause with my eye condition. Before they figured out that it was Adie's pupil. That test is awful! It made me really sick," Leila told Dr. Lambert.

"No, an MRI uses magnetic fields and radio waves to scan the body. It is basically painless. The nice thing about this hospital being brand new is that we have some of the best equipment right here in-house. We will be able to scan every part of your body to detect any anomalies that may give us a clue as to what caused this episode and help us determine a treatment to make sure that it doesn't happen again." He said, smiling his toothy-white movie star smile at her and included Michael in the smile too.

"Fine," Michael said gruffly, "if that is what you recommend."

"I do." Dr. Lambert said with authority. He looked at Leila. "So, it is a little early for dinner. But I would like you to eat a little something before dinner for me if you can. I would like to take another blood sample about an hour after you have eaten to compare it with the one taken this morning. Mr. Sutton stated you hadn't eaten or drank anything, correct?" He glanced at her chart as he questioned her.

"I don't think so. I don't normally eat anything in the morning. I took a couple of regular Tylenol with a handful of water to just to head off what I thought might be a mild headache coming on, but I hadn't had any coffee or anything to eat," Leila said softly.

"That's actually good in this case. We will have a good comparison for the two samples and can do a full workup." Dr. Lambert smiled at her again. "I specialize in hematology, so you are in good hands." He chuckled at her as if he had made a joke.

She thought as she smiled at him. *Pretty, but a bit of a dork.* Then she said, "Ok, I can try to eat something. Do you think I can have this catheter and IV removed? I would prefer to be able to move around a bit. Especially if I have to stay here for a night or two."

"That will be fine. I will instruct the nurse to have something to eat sent up as soon as possible, and to remove the catheter and IV as I don't think looking at your vitals, that you are in any danger at this time of having another episode happen soon. But," and here he paused, "I want you to rest. Think of the next couple of days as a vacation. Rest, relax, no worries. We will get this all figured out for you." He stood up to go. "I will check back in a few hours."

"Thank you, Dr. Lambert." Leila said gratefully.

"Yeah, thanks, Doc." Michael reached out his hand toward him.

Dr. Lambert gripped his in return. "Mr. Sutton."

Leila gave a mental sigh as she watched him leave the room. Then she glanced at Michael, who was eyeing her. *Here we go. Out comes Mr. Jealous.* She thought.

"So, he was something." Michael said with a strange look on his face.

"He wasn't the ER doctor?" She asked innocently.

26

"No. I was listening to the nurses earlier. He is some hotshot new attending physician here at the hospital. He's from Detroit, is new to the area and hasn't really set up a private practice yet. One of the nurses said that she wasn't sure if he would, as he talks like he will only work here for a couple of years. They are all hot for him." Michael said with a smirk.

"You seem to be quite well-informed!" Leila said, impressed.

"Well, I have been bored waiting for you to wake the hell up!" He said frustrated.

"It's not like I am here by choice, Michael! You know how I feel about hospitals. This is the last place I want to be!" She snapped.

"I know, sorry." He mumbled.

"Would you go get the kids?" She asked, and he gave her a terrified look. "Seriously, Michael. I want to see my kids."

"Well, I will go get them, and bring them by after you have eaten something. They will not be able to stay here long. You know how Devin can be," he said in a helpless voice, "and besides, you heard the doc. You are supposed to be resting."

"Fine." She replied as a couple of nurses came in.

"Mrs. Sutton, the doctor has given instructions to remove your catheter and IV and to get you up and moving around. This is Nurse Macey." Nurse Andrea said as she and another young woman started removing the blankets.

"That's my cue to leave." Michael said with a grimace, and headed for the door.

"Coward." Leila thought as she watched his quick exit.

Once the nurses had thankfully gotten everything disconnected from her, she slowly swung her legs over the side of the bed, as Macey used the remote to lower it closer to the floor to make it easier for her to stand. Andrea let her use her arm to steady herself as she slowly stood.

"Dizzy?" Andrea inquired.

"No, just feeling a little unsteady from laying down for so long. Could you help me walk to the bathroom?" Leila asked.

She slowly walked with Andrea's steadying arm to the bathroom.

"I will give you some privacy, but you give me a shout if you feel dizzy at all, you hear?" Andrea's Georgia twang came through. She nodded and closed the door. Sitting on the toilet, she let her head fall into her hands.

She didn't feel particularly dizzy. But it was a little strange to feel this fragile and kind of disconnected from reality. She appreciated Andrea's help and thought about how much nicer this hospital was compared to the hospital in Brunswick, where she had delivered Zachary. Everything here was very new, and with it being such a large facility in a small community, she had never had another patient in the room with her. Which was genuinely nice. The nurses had always been extremely sweet, too.

Getting up, she washed her hands thoroughly and looked at herself in the mirror. She had some circling under the eyes, but a quick wipe with a washcloth revealed it to be mostly smudged eyeliner and mascara. After washing her face, she was pleasantly surprised to look quite healthy. Lack of makeup let the light freckles on the alabaster skin of her cheekbones and nose be exposed. But, at this moment, she was okay with that.

Opening the door, she found that the nurses had made short work of making up the bed with fresh linens. Feeling a little stronger, she slowly made her way over to the bed, climbing in without any needed assistance.

"Thank you very much." She said to them sincerely and they both beamed at her.

"Absolutely, Mrs. Sutton. I wanted to let you know that I was able to get you on the MRI schedule for first thing in the morning." Andrea said with a smile. "So, I will be here to wheel you down about 7:45 am."

"Great." Leila said with a bit of a sigh.

"Now, don't you worry! You are in the best of hands with Dr. Lambert." Andrea said, looking at Macey.

"Yes, he is wonderful! So, smart! He will get you sorted right out." Macey chirped, smiling.

"Thanks so much, I am sure that he will." Leila said, thinking that Michael had hit the mark.

Just then, an orderly arrived with a tray. On it was a cup of tomato soup, an egg salad sandwich on wheat bread sliced diagonally, cherry jello, and a pint of whole milk. Leila smiled at him as he arranged it on the rolling tray across her lap.

"Well, Mrs. Sutton, now you eat up and I will come back in about an hour to take that second blood sample for the doctor." Andrea said. She and Macey left her to her lunch.

Just as Leila started eating her soup, Michael returned. "Oh, egg salad!" He said and stole half of her sandwich.

"Would you like half my sandwich, Michael? Don't mind if I do, honey!" Leila said sarcastically.

"You never eat the whole sandwich anyway, and I am hungry!" He said, sitting down with his pilfered half and munching on it. "How are you feeling now, by the way?"

"Well, I am able to move around by myself with no dizziness. So that is a plus." She responded, taking a small bite of her sandwich.

He reached over, grabbed her milk carton, opened it, and took a drink. She looked at him. "Sorry, had to wash it down!" He said wiping his mouth with the back of his hand. "Well, that's good, right?"

"Yes. If I were dizzy, they would have found a way to keep me in this bed, and I cannot be stuck in this bed for two days." She said, taking another spoonful of soup. "I am just hoping to be able to sleep tonight. I don't like being away from the kids."

"Don't I know it..." He mumbled under his breath.

"What?" She asked.

"Nothing." He said, grabbing the remote, turning on the television and flipping through the channels. "Wonder what's on television during the day?"

"Probably nothing worthwhile." She replied, finishing her soup and the sandwich. She opened the jello container, took a bite, and said, "I think I have had enough." She handed it to Michael, who scooped it out of her hand as he found a sports station on the hospital cable. She gave a wry smile and settled back, closing her eyes to rest.

"You are back." The voice said.

"Lord, am I back to this dream?" She said, willing herself to wake up.

"This is not a dream." The man said softly as he again emerged from the shadows of the room.

"Sure." She said, not facing him this time. Instead, she looked around the room with curiosity. She seemed to be more aware in this dream than she was last night. She noticed she was standing on a Persian carpet laid on a flagstone floor. The carpet intertwined the red, green, and gold in a floral motif, complementing the other furniture seen in the sitting area. She wiggled her toes.

I swear I can feel the wool in this carpet! She thought to herself, surprised.

"Yes, it's wool. I purchased it in Kashan, an exceedingly long time ago." She whirled around and found he was standing directly behind her. His appearance was unchanged from this morning.

"I didn't say anything!" She said, looking up into his amused amber eyes.

You don't really have to. Not between us, anyway. He thought at her.

She widened her eyes at him. "I *heard* you!" She accused, still disbelieving this possibility.

You're having a problem with the whole 'we are communicating thing', aren't you? He thought at her with a small smile.

"I am losing it." She said to herself, raising her fingers to her temples. "I have to get out of this nightmare! Wake up, Leila!" Her voice rose in pitch as she panicked.

He took her hands gently in his warm, lightly calloused palms, exuding that bewitching scent of cinnamon, ginger and just a touch of sandalwood, which seemed to soothe her. "I psychí mou. Be calm. I am arranging to be with you soon." He spoke, his smooth voice like an angel. He led her to the couch, as if she were under a spell. Pulling her gently but firmly down to sit next to him, while continuing to soothingly stroke her hands. She allowed this attention, though she wasn't sure why. Then confusion once more set in as she noticed she was in a long, white silk nightgown, knotted at her shoulders, and gathered tight with a red silk bow beneath her breasts, leaving her arms quite bare.

"This is just a dream." She told him softly.

"Fine." He said simply. *If it will make you less apprehensive, I will indulge you in this dream notion.* He thought at her, then smiled softly at her as her eyes widened. "And we will 'speak' to each other while here if it will ease your fears." This time, the harmonious voice came from his sensual mouth.

Looking at him, she realized she didn't fear him, and that he was trying to set her at ease. She felt a sense of satisfaction from him as she thought this.

"You have no reason to be afraid of me." His melodious voice, soft, gentle, soothing. "I have contacted your aunt and she will join you this evening. She is closer to your location than I am, so you will have a familiar face as you go through this transition. I am working to join you both as soon as I am able to make the necessary arrangements."

"My Aunt? Which Aunt?" She asked, confused. Her mother had five sisters and she couldn't think of any that would be here quicker than her own parents could be, or that one of them would even bother to make the trip. "You know I am in the hospital?" She said to him.

"Hmmm." He said with some surprise and seemed slightly displeased with her news. "You are unharmed? I am not sensing any physical injuries. Did you have an accident?" He looked at her with great concern and slightly tightened his hold on her hands. She noticed that his voice and actions conveyed greater concern than her own husband.

"No, not really," she replied. "I passed out this morning, and they don't know what caused it. They are running some tests and keeping me here for a day or two for observation." She actually patted his hand to comfort him, then thought to herself, *Why am I telling him this? I don't even know who this guy is. He is just some guy I have made up in my dreams.*

He looked at her with narrowed, impatient eyes. "I am *not* your imagination." He spoke, a small amount of steel creeping into his tone. She raised an eyebrow at him, not appreciating his sudden change in attitude. "Nevertheless, this hospital stay could cause some issues. I will make sure that Mansuetus attends you both and that he leaves a message for your aunt upon her arrival. Testing isn't usually a good thing with our kind." He mused almost to himself, obviously deep in thought.

"Man, who?" She sounded like an owl in her confusion.

"Mansuetus." He pronounced it, man-sue-A-toos. "My servant."

Her eyes fluttered open as she felt Michael take and shake her arm urgently. "Babe, wake up!" He said loudly. "The nurse is here to draw your blood."

"Okay. I am awake." She said to him and shook him off. "I'm awake." She said again, sitting up a little straighter.

As she helped Leila straighten the pillows behind her back, Andrea said, "I am going to be using a 'baby' needle in your right arm to take this sample."

"Can't you just take it from the arm that I had my IV?" Leila said to her, looking at her left arm and then frowning at the dark deep blue bruising in her elbow joint. It covered the whole inside of her left elbow in at least a three-inch circle. It was like a hand had reached around her arm and given her a vicious squeeze. That had not been there earlier, she was sure.

"Not this time. Unfortunately, sometimes bad bruising occurs when an emergency IV is done." Andrea said, as she watched Leila look at her arm. "But I promise you, I will be very gentle, and there should be minimal to no bruising. You shouldn't have to look like a pincushion!" Andrea said gently.

Leila nodded her head and Andrea quickly and efficiently took the sample, drawing blood for five different collection tubes. "Wow, I don't think that I have ever had so many tubes done at once," Leila said in surprise.

"Yes, Dr. Lambert has ordered a complete series of tests for you. He wants to make sure that we diagnose you correctly and quickly. He is very efficient!" Andrea said with a smile. "He is sure that you want to get back home to your babies as quick as can be."

"Well, that's true!" Leila said appreciatively. "Speaking of my babies," she looked at Michael as she spoke this last.

"Okay, I am going!" He said, exiting the room with Andrea.

She settled back and thought, *What weird dreams I am having today?!* The beautiful man notwithstanding, no way was she going back to sleep for a while. Her dreams had become too confusing. She took the remote from where Michael had put it on her bedside table and started flipping channels. "Oh, *Jerry Springer*!" She said, settling on one. "I haven't seen him for ages!" She thought and settled back to watch the show's racy topic for that day, sure that Jerry's antics would keep her solidly awake.

It was about 20 minutes after Jerry had ended, and she was starting to doze off, when she heard a child's voice in the hallway say loudly, "We are here to see MY Mommy!"

"This way buddy, right through there!" She heard Michael's voice and then Zachary came walking through the doorway.

32

He stopped and looked at her. "Mommy?" His little brows furrowed in fear.

"It's okay, baby. Come here." She said and held out her arms.

He ran to the bedside, and she reached down to help him on the bed. He threw his small arms around her neck and squeezed hard. She hugged him in return. "My, that was a big hug from my big boy!" She said with a catch in her voice, tears coming to her eyes. Her love for her children always overwhelmed her.

"Mommy, you sick?" Zachary said, taking her face in his small hands. His pale blue eyes boring into her teal ones. He then noticed the large bruise on her arm from where her IV had been. "Ow!" He said loudly.

"Shhhh, baby, I am okay. Just a little owie. But you have to be quiet because there are people here who are trying to rest." She told him softly.

"Sick people?" He whispered loudly, always a curious child. He asked a lot of questions and obviously his father had told him she was in the 'sick people' place.

"Yes." She whispered in return, fluffing his caramel-colored curls and waves away from his face, as he smiled sweetly at her.

Michael maneuvered around the corner, pushing the double baby stroller through the door, looking a little haggard with the diaper bag thrown over his arm.

Devin, who was waving his chubby arms around like a cheerleader at a Friday night football game, his pecan-colored hair both darker, thinner, and much straighter than his brother, little flips at the end of his longish locks giving him a slightly devilish appearance, was making little squawking noises of interest as he looked at his new surroundings.

He saw her in the bed with Zachary next to her, and started yelling, "Da, da, da, da, da, da" as his father hurriedly extricated him from the stroller belt.

They learned early on, as Devin became 'mobile', that he had to be strapped into the stroller or he would invariably escape! Michael picked him up, the stream of yelled Da da's never stopping once, and he gratefully plopped him down on his mother's lap.

Devin immediately stopped and looked at her with accusation in his clove-colored eyes; almost like he was angry that she hadn't seen him all day. She looked at him and said, "Momma."

He looked at her, said, "Da, da" once more, and placed his fist in his mouth, gnawing at it, looking around with interest as he settled on her lap.

"Devin yelled all the way here." Zachary whispered to Leila, so as not to wake the 'sick people'.

"It looks like he is teething again." She said to Michael, as she placed her face in Devin's hair, giving him smooches. He waved her off with his arm. "Did you bring his Binky?"

"Yes, it is here somewhere." Michael said, digging through the diaper bag, looking a little helpless. "Teething again? He already has four teeth! Is that normal? He's just nine months old!" He said with exasperation as he dug through the bag some more. One of the things that seemed to stress him out was that Devin outpaced any normal child his age. He had crawled early, got his first baby teeth in early, wanted solid foods, knew a few rudimentary words, and was almost walking. He was a definite handful, causing major parenting changes in their household, whereas Zachary, who was laid back, was quite easy to parent. "I know it's here somewhere!" Michael said helplessly.

"I don't have *normal* children. I have *extraordinary* children." She said, giving them both a big hug. Zachary giggled and Devin wiggled at the attention. She noticed that Michael had changed out of his uniform into a Cincinnati Reds t-shirt, a pair of jeans, and tennis shoes. She admired his profile for a second. "Check the stroller." She told him.

"Oh, yeah! Here it is." He said, handing it to her.

She replaced fist for pacifier and settled Devin against her body and he relaxed against her as she held him. She placed her 'owy' arm around Zachary, who leaned against her as well.

"I see you got changed." She stated.

"Yeah, I stopped at the house to let the dog out and changed before I picked up the kids from Ellen's. That's why it took me a bit." He settled down in his chair next to the bed. "Seen the doctor again?"

"No. Just watched some TV. He should be doing the evening rounds, though. The nurse checked in about a half hour ago and said that they have the same shift schedule, and he is on the 7 am – 7 pm shift with her. I guess they do 12-hour shifts, 4 days per week. Just think of it. Work 4 days on, 3 days off. That would be cool, wouldn't it?" She said softly to him, making conversation, as the kids settled down with her.

"Sure." He said, focused on flipping channels, as he had commandeered the remote again.

She leaned back as he found ESPN and started watching sports news. As she relaxed with her children cradled in her arms, she thought, "This is my family," as she hugged both of her children, who were unusually quiet, to her. "This is my purpose." She smiled softly to herself, closing her eyes to rest.

At 5:00 pm exactly, Dr. Dene Lambert walked into the room. Despite having her eyes closed, she knew it was the doctor and found it strange. She was sure that she heard him say in dismay, *"Oh my gosh. Children!"* But she must have been mistaken because when she opened her eyes, he was greeting Michael calmly.

He took her chart, glanced at it, and then said to her, "Mrs. Sutton, I see you have some company! Also, good, you are scheduled for your MRI bright and early at 8:00 am." He smiled at her with his wide, sexy smile.

Devin took one look at him, spit his pacifier out and started screaming bloody murder! Much to the horror of Dr. Lambert and Michael's embarrassment.

"Shhhh. Devin, stop! This is the doctor." She said to him softly to no avail as his shrieks took on the pitch of a fire alarm! "Michael, please!" Michael came over and scooped up his screaming youngest son and headed out of the room. Yells, reverberating from the outside hallway.

"I am so sorry, Dr. Lambert." His ice-blue eyes were wide with shock and consternation. She knew immediately that he had little to no experience with children. "Please don't take it personally. He *hates* strangers! It comes and goes too. The next time you see him, he may not react to you at all." She told him in embarrassed explanation of her youngest son's behavior.

Dr. Lambert bravely tried to laugh it off. Though Leila could see that the incident had shaken him. He looked at Zachary in apprehension, who was sitting next to his mother, observing the doctor quietly.

Zachary said to him calmly, "Devin bites."

Both Leila and Dr. Lambert chuckled. Dr. Lambert, still chuckling, chart in hand, rolled his stool over to the side of the bed.

"Doctor, this is my oldest son, Zachary. Zachary, this is Mommy's doctor, Dr. Lambert." She said to the two of them.

Blue eyes met blue eyes as they considered each other. Zachary held out a small hand to him, and Dr. Lambert in surprise, took it, and shook it once. Zachary said, "Hi!" in his chirpy voice.

"Hello, young man." Dr. Lambert said in return and smiled at them both. "So, Mrs. Sutton, how are you feeling this evening?"

"Better actually, as the day goes on." She said with a smile.

"Well, I have received some preliminary results from your blood work this morning. Everything looks fine. I even had them run a pregnancy test, and that is negative." He said, looking at the chart. She was getting the feeling from him that he felt she had 'dodged a bullet,' after his experience with Devin.

"Well, I could have told you that. My husband has recently had a vasectomy. So, no worries there." She told him bluntly.

"You can never be too sure about anything." He said with a laugh. "Though I am glad you are feeling better and up and about! We still need to diagnose what actually happened to you."

"I agree. It was frightening." She nodded her head.

"Yes, I am sure." He said, looking at her. "Your MRI is scheduled for tomorrow morning. I will oversee the lab work myself from the sample that we took from you this afternoon." He told her, as if that would make all the difference. "I don't want you to wear yourself out this evening and it may seem difficult after all the sleep you have had, but I would like you to rest."

"Okay. But I am kind of feeling like I am getting my second wind."

"Yes, I thought you might. Sometimes a day of rest makes us feel that way. But until we figure out what caused your episode, I want you relaxing as much as possible." He said, patting her arm that she had wrapped around Zachary. He looked at it strangely for a moment and turned it over to look at the large, black, and blue, IV injection site. "Hmmm." He said and wrote something down on her chart.

"What?" She asked bluntly.

"Well, frankly, I don't really like the looks of this. It could always be because you were brought in under ER circumstances and the IV was placed hastily, so they weren't incredibly careful when they did it due to expediency. But this bruising to me seems excessive. I just want to monitor that."

"Nurse Andrea took my blood for the second test from this arm," she held out her right arm for the doctor to look at. "It's not bruised hardly at all." She said to him to prove a point.

"Yes. Andrea is exceptionally good at her job. This looks better. Hardly any marking at all," he agreed, investigating the slight pinprick on her arm. "We will keep an eye on it all. Hopefully, your test results from tomorrow are promising and we can figure out exactly what happened to you. That way you won't have it happen again. But you get some rest, and I will see you sometime tomorrow after your MRI."

"Thank you very much, doctor. I really appreciate everything that you're doing for me." She said sincerely.

"You're very welcome Mrs. Sutton. I hope to find out your diagnosis soon so that we could put your mind at ease and treat the cause for your fall this morning. I will see you tomorrow and you have an exceptionally good night too, young man," he said to Zachary, and gave him a small smile as he left to see the next patient.

"Bye-bye." Zachary said.

Leila hugged Zachary to her, and he wrapped his little arms around her. She buried her nose in his soft, sweet-smelling hair. She always loved it when she was able to hold her babies and they were so sweet. She tried not to let what Dr. Lambert told her worry her. She would do her best to get some rest tonight and, if not sleep, at least relax.

After about ten minutes, Michael showed back up carrying Devin, who had stopped throwing a fit, at least for the time being. He gave her a big mischievous smile, all four teeth, two up and two down, showing, when he saw her and Zachary in the bed. She smiled back as she shook her head. He was so impish and cute that you just couldn't hold it against him for his mercurial attitudes.

Michael packed up both boys, getting them both strapped into the stroller to take home. He gave her a quick peck on the cheek and murmured something about being back around lunchtime tomorrow. She smiled a little sadly as he wheeled the carriage out of the room and settled in to flip through the television channels for a few minutes, bored without her family with her.

A hospital volunteer came into the room with a book cart. Which piqued Leila's interest, as she was a voracious reader. She selected a 'bodice ripper'

romance and thanked the volunteer sweetly. *This is much better than TV.*
She thought to herself as she turned off the television and settled in to read.

A little after 6:00, an orderly brought in her dinner. Tonight, they were
serving meatloaf with mashed potatoes and gravy, green beans, a pint of
milk and, of course, a side of strawberry jello. It looked like a dinner
that was designed to put you to sleep after you ate it. Comfort food and
sleeping, she was sure, were partnered when staying in the hospital.

Surprisingly, she found that it was tasty, and that she was hungry, so she
almost finished it. Well, her constant life of dieting was now shot for the
day, but she sure didn't feel sleepy! She felt surprisingly good. She picked
up her book again to read for a while. At about 7:45, she felt a little restless.

She got up and moved around the room a bit. Opening the vertical
blinds to look out into the Georgia night. The darkness had fallen hard
and fast. She looked out into the dark parking lot of the hospital. The light
poles lit up, a slight fog rolling in from the Atlantic Ocean. She thought
it odd that she had seen no one since the orderly came to take her dinner
tray away. Not one doctor, not one nurse. She opened the small wardrobe
in the room and saw her outfit from this morning hanging up, and an
over-sized hospital robe and some slippers were also there. She gratefully
pulled them on. This morning seemed so far away and long ago. It seemed
unbelievable that it was still the same day.

It was so quiet. Not like the daytime. She didn't hear any sounds from
the hallway.

She peeked her head out the door. Having arrived unconscious, she
wasn't positive what floor she was on, but from looking out the window,
she guessed she was on the fourth floor of the five-floor hospital. She
looked at the number outside of her room, posted to the wall by her door:
4E-10.

From her recent stays, she knew that the nurse's station on the patient
floors was near the middle of each floor next to the elevator banks. Each
floor was a rectangle, with patient rooms on the outside and administrative
functions like nurse stations, offices, labs, operating rooms, all located inside
and between the patient rooms. The only floors that didn't house regular
patients that she knew of were the first floor, where the ambulatory care,
emergency room area and ICU were, and part of the second floor where the
cafeteria and gift shop were. She knew that her room overlooked the main

parking lot. So, she would have to be the 5th room from the middle of the hospital, and nurses' station facing East.

It wasn't an exceptionally large hospital, but neither was Kingsland, Georgia, where it was located. Slightly less than 60 regular beds, it was a huge benefit to this community and was also the third largest employer in the area, only behind the Naval Submarine Base and the paper-mill.

Feeling physically stronger than she had all day, restlessness drove through her, and she stepped outside her room into the hall and looked to her left toward the nurse's station, the floor still eerily quiet, listening hard for some sort of sound.

She took a step toward the left, looking curiously around as she did. Suddenly, her senses were bombarded with a cacophony of sound staggering her. She placed her left hand on the wall, leaning and trying to steady herself, concentrating hard on keeping her balance.

"God, you are such a bitch! There is no way I am letting them put me on this floor with you once more. You make this shift long and miserable!" She heard loudly above the other conversations. She focused hard on distributing the noises that were coming at her in differing volumes and strengths. Separating the noises seemed to help. Focusing on the loudest again, she let that voice overpower the others and, as she did, she was able to block out the rest, enabling her to regain her balance. "Fine bitch. Sit there and don't say a word. What a miserable person!"

Curious to see what in the world was going on. Leila stood again on her feet, stronger than before, and made her way tentatively toward the nurse's station, wrapping her arms around her midsection as she did so. She couldn't believe that this person was speaking so loudly at after 8 pm at night in the middle of a hospital. She distinctly heard the voice coming from the nurse's station and couldn't believe that they were speaking to each other like that where the patients could hear! No wonder everyone else around was whispering and talking. They must be as shocked as she was.

A few steps from being directly in front of the nurse's desk, but still on the room's side of the hallway, she craned her neck up, expecting to see some sort of confrontation going on. Instead, she saw two women, both in their thirties, backs to each other. One facing the west side of the floor, the other the east side, one seemingly concentrating on paperwork, the other looking at a computer screen. The one viewing the computer screen was the east side nurse; the nurse who handled the care of the patients of the east side of the 4th floor. She glanced up at Leila in surprise and then irritation.

Brows drawn, the nurse said to Leila sharply, "What are you doing out of bed?" The other nurse turned to find out who she was speaking to. Eastside stood up to come around the corner of the nurse's station. "Where do you belong?"

Leila started to answer her as the nurse took her by the arm when she heard, "Jesus Christ, you would know where she belonged if you had bothered to do your rounds! You lazy, nasty cow!" That was shocking enough, except she had a clear view of both nurses when it was said, and her ears were positive that the West-Side nurse had verbally expressed the sentiment, the look on her face was such that she had to have said it, but the West-Side nurse hadn't moved her lips, and the East-Side nurse acted as if nothing had been said by West-Side at all.

Leila felt like the atmosphere was sucking her in. She reached up and placed a hand to her eyes, feeling disoriented. East-Side took her other arm, not harshly, but not gently either. "Come on." She said, leading her back in the direction of her room. "Which room are you in?" Annoyance flooding her voice. "Do you remember?"

"Ten. I am in room ten." Leila said softly. Letting the nurse lead her slowly in the direction of her room, her hand still pressed to the side of her head.

"Don't you pass out!" Leila heard the nurse say sharply.

"I won't." Leila said, sniping in return.

"What?" East-Side said, tightening her grip, almost painfully, on her arm.

"I am not passing out!" Leila said to her harshly, pulling her arms from the nurse's grip, shocking herself. "I got it!"

East-Side put both of her hands up in surprise, and guided Leila to her room with those hands out to steady, but not genuinely touching her. Leila got in bed without her assistance and the nurse pulled the chart from the holder at the end of the bed.

"Mrs. Sutton." She said after reading the chart. "You have to stay in bed at night. You can't be wandering the hallway, it isn't safe!" East-Side said curtly.

"I am not wandering the halls. I was just a little restless and wanted to stretch my legs a bit." Leila said, trying to remain calm. She could feel a real anger building up inside of herself.

"I am going to put up the rails on your bed." East-Side said moving to do just that.

"No, I don't need to be 'railed in' here. Dr. Lambert said I could be up and about a little bit." Leila said simply, thinking what a pain it would be to get out of the bed to go to the bathroom if those damn rails were up. The nurse ignored her and proceeded to commence messing around with the rails. Leila looked at her hard, "I said, *No.*" With the word came a feeling of power rushing throughout her body, unlike anything she had ever experienced.

East-Side stood up stock straight, suddenly wooden in her movements. She said, "Fine. I will bring you some ice water," grabbed the pitcher from Leila's rolling table and quickly exited the room.

Leila stood up, and as if in a trance, removed her robe and hung it in the armoire where she had found it. She went into the bathroom and closed the door behind her, flipping on the light. She examined herself in the mirror. Her eyes were radiant; a light neon teal. Her pupils seemed to be immense. Closing her eyes, she shook her head slightly, then investigated the sink and turned on the cold-water to watch it splash in the basin in slow-motion. Feeling thoroughly detached from everything, a stillness overcame her body. Slowly she washed her hands, splashing water on her face. This seemed to slightly revive her, settling her nerves, and when she faced herself in the mirror again, her eyes were back to their usual dark teal color and her pupils normal sized.

Opening the bathroom door, she saw a new pitcher of ice water had been brought and was surprised that the nurse hadn't checked on her while she was in the bathroom. Picking up her watch from the table where Michael had placed it earlier, she checked the time. 8:45 pm. She must have been in the bathroom at least thirty minutes! West-Side was right. The East-Side nurse was terrible. She could have been unconscious on the floor of the bathroom, for Christ's sake. Feeling anger start to come over her once again, she got back into the bed, pulled her legs up to wrap her arms around them, and rested her forehead against her knees. Trying to soothe herself, she blew all the air slowly out of her lungs and took a slow, deep, calming breath.

"What the hell is wrong with me?" She whispered softly, analyzing herself. She was never so quick to anger, especially toward strangers. Still, she felt mentally and physically stronger this evening than she had in what seemed an eternity! She knew she had heard those voices, and she knew she had heard another nurse talking, even though she knew she hadn't spoken aloud. She *knew* it. Didn't she?

Hearing a soft tap at the window, she glanced up to see two red glowing orbs floating outside of her window.

"What the hell is that? A bird?" She spoke the words out loud just to hear the sound of her own voice; to make sure that this wasn't another dream. Feeling no fear, she struggled to see the form behind those orbs, but the light of the room reflected against the glass of the window, obscuring everything but the orbs. Being on the eastside of the hospital, in this darkness, those orbs could be from a far-off ship in the Atlantic, she supposed. But a strange feeling was coming over her; her body tingled all over, raising goosebumps on her arms and lifting the small hairs on the back of her neck.

Getting up from the bed, she turned off her room light as if to prepare for going to sleep, partially shutting the door, only allowing about eight inches of light from the hallway to penetrate the darkness. She walked slowly to the window, her eyes quickly adjusting to the darkness of the room.

Approaching the window, she saw incongruously clinging to the outside of the hospital wall, a woman. She continued the few steps to the window. The woman, the night breeze brought in by the ocean causing her hair to swirl about her head in a riot of dark curls, looked at her with recognition.

Leila searched her memory, and recollection swam to the surface of her mind. She knew this woman, but the last time she had seen her, she had been thin, sickly, her hair thickly streaked with silver. This woman was at least 20 years younger than that version. The impossibility of it all burned through her. "Aunt Iris?" She whispered. Younger, healthy, *ALIVE*, and clinging to the wall of a hospital, looking at her from outside of her window *FOUR STORIES IN THE AIR!*

The woman nodded her head with a smile, placing her left hand against the glass.

Leila automatically started to place her hand to hers on the other side of the glass when she noticed the long lethal looking talons on that hand. Leila slowly lowered her hand, feeling no fear, only a shocking numbness. She reached over and slowly drew the vertical blinds against the sight as the woman clinging to the wall, who shook her head in denial, saying mournfully through the glass, "Leila!"

Leila felt a presence, a light rapping insistence, right at the edge of her mind like someone was trying to get in, as she looked at the closed blinds, trying to deny what she had seen with her own eyes. She shut it out, like slamming a door to close off the pitter-patter of the beginning of a rainstorm.

"No," whispering to herself as she automatically turned her back, shaking her head in refusal and walked slowly to climb into her bed, "no, no, no, no, no, nope!" Pulling the covers over her body, huddling in them, she felt a coldness come over her. Reaching out of the blankets for the bed remote, she lowered the bed flat, pulling one of the pillows over her head. "I am going crazy!" She whispered aloud. Squeezing her eyes shut, she turned her back to the window to lay on her side, pulling her knees to her chest, and clutching them hard, willing herself to go to sleep. "Crazy, crazy, crazy," she whispered over and over to herself, softly rocking her body back and forth.

Feeling his presence behind her, he greeted her with a soft accusation, as if he were deeply disappointed in her behavior. "Your Aunt is terribly upset. I have never heard her cry before in all the years that I have known her now!"

"Just fucking great! *You're* back! Obviously, you are all a part of my insanity!" She turned, yelling at him; she would show him behavior!

His amber eyes widened in offense, as if there wasn't ever a time anyone had ever yelled at him in such a manner. He straightened up to his full height as if she had slapped him, which she was considering doing just that.

"You will stop this!" He started with command; his voice pitched strangely.

"Don't you *dare* tell me what to do!" She snapped shocking him further. "You don't get it! I can't allow myself to be insane! Michael will have me committed and take my kids from me! I will never see them again!" Her voice rose as the panic set in. She had to get it together or she would lose her children!

"Michael?" He questioned softly, reaching out to her, that scent of cinnamon, ginger and sandalwood trying to overcome her senses. She was having none of it!

She jumped out of his reach, keeping her distance and then ran behind one of the green and gold armchairs, putting it between them and clutching the back of it for dear life, gripping it tightly to keep from losing her mind. "Don't you touch me!" She held up a finger in warning, her eyes flashing fire at him.

"I psychí mou," he said softly, dropping his arms, his mellifluous voice pained. One beautiful hand touched his chest over his heart as if she had stabbed him. He looked at her like he was the most innocent, least dangerous creature in all the world.

She didn't believe it for a hot minute!

"And stop saying that!" She said angrily. "I do not know what you are saying to me! Oh, my god, I am speaking to myself in tongues!" She grabbed herself by her head with both hands, willing herself to wake up from this nightmare.

Instantly, far too quickly for a normal person to move, he had rounded the chair to pull her into his arms. She fought him like a devil, cursing and screeching for all that she was worth, hitting, punching, and kicking him over and over. It was like beating herself against a steel beam or a boulder.

He held her tightly to him as if she were nothing more than a struggling child, saying over and over softly, sadly, "Se parakaló agápi mou, se parakaló agápi mou, please my love," until she collapsed against him in exhaustion, only his arms kept her from sinking to the ground. He braced her petite, five-foot, two-inch frame with one sinewy arm, then bent to put the other under her knees; standing tall to scoop her up and hold her high against his chest as if she weighed nothing. She started to struggle in his grasp once more.

"Ochi, agápi mou. No, my love." He said softly, sadly into her ear, his soft lips brushing her cheek. She wrapped her arms around his shoulders and sobbed heart-wrenchingly into his neck. She felt him sigh deeply as he walked over to the couch and reclined into a sitting position against the large pillows propped up against the arm, stretching out his long muscular legs, still cradling her as she sobbed against him. He stroked her from the base of her neck, down her back, over the curve of her hip and ass, to the back of her knee and then back up again. Over and over, he soothed, as she cried and breathed in his soft, calming scent. The strength and warmth of his hand over the silk of her gown lulled her tears, until finally they were just small, exhausted, hiccupping sounds.

"You make my heart break, agápi mou." His perfect voice was sad as she looked up at him with reddened eyes. Suddenly, his lips were on hers. Soft and tender, and oh, so warm. His warm stroking of her body never ceased, still soothing, still comforting.

Gently, she felt his tongue enter her mouth as she felt a soft tug at her shoulder and one side of her gown's bodice was pulled down and open to the warm air and his exploration. She felt his warm hand cup her breast, his lightly calloused thumb softly caressing her nipple into a hard bud as she leaned her head back against his shoulder and closed her eyes in exhaustion and surrender, exposing her throat to his lips. "Panemorfi, beautiful," he whispered softly, kissing her offered throat gently.

She felt so drained and weak as she relaxed herself back into his shoulder, closing her eyes, as he went back to soothing, stroking, and massaging her body with one hand, holding her tightly against his warmth with his other, occasionally she felt his lips softly kiss her on her mouth; her throat, her shoulder blade, her collarbone. Breathing in his cinnamon, ginger, and sandalwood scent, she had never felt so thoroughly relaxed in a man's arms. She wrapped one of her arms about his shoulders softly, not returning his massages, just holding him in return.

She felt his hand on her bare ankle, which would have normally startled her, but he used just the right amount of pressure. Too soft it would have tickled; too hard. It would have alarmed her.

He softly kneaded the muscles of her calf, working his way up her bare thigh. Massaging, kneading, slowly, up, and down, up, and down. "Glykó," he whispered softly in that melodious voice of his, "áse me na se agapíso."

She didn't know what he was saying to her, but at this point she was beyond caring, so it just didn't set her off in a frenzy as it had before. She simply was tired. It felt so good to be held like this, so warm, so comforted, so cherished, so loved, and she couldn't fight against it even if this wasn't her husband.

Before that traitorous thought could take root, she felt him cup her sex with just the right amount of pressure, and his mouth covered her breast, his tongue licking at the hardness of her nipple. She started to give a token resistance, squeezing her thighs around his hand slightly to stop him, but the heel of his hand pushed against the curls of her sex and her clitoris, which was hard and ready, causing her to moan in response.

"Open. Epitrépste mou na sas dóso efcharístisi. Allow me to give you pleasure" He whispered against her nipple.

As if his words were magic, she parted her thighs slightly for him, and he slid a finger tentatively inside of her slickness. She felt waves of satisfaction come from him at her wetness. Wetness that he had caused. Pleasure rolled through her body as she opened wider for his exploration.

He pulled his finger from her, gathering her wetness and rubbing it against his thumb, then slid the two middle fingers of his hand into her body, filling her and simultaneously sliding his now slick thumb over her clitoris.

"Oh, God!" She gasped softly as his head return to her breast, sucking her nipple into his mouth. She felt his hard cock rub against her ass as he held her tight, suckling and slowly working his hand between her legs, in and out, over and over. Reaching up with both hands to run her fingers through the softness of his wavy hair, something she ached to do from the very beginning, she pulled his head to her breast, burying her face in his sweet-smelling hair arching against his hand.

"Mmmmm." He moaned softly in pleasure, rubbing his cock against her faster, as she began to actively participate in her own pleasure.

Letting her exhaustion and her body take her over, she tightened against his fingers, as he stroked her clitoris with his thumb in time with his fingers, sliding them in and out of her drenched pussy. She couldn't remember the last time that she was so wet and needed this type of release so badly. She bucked against his hand, riding his fingers, and he tongued her nipple hard, rubbing himself against her ass even harder, holding her tightly against him. Their friction doubling the warmth of their bodies.

"Please don't stop," she moaned against his head and softly into his ear. "Please don't stop, I am going to cum." Her pussy tightened as he moved his fingers faster in response, his thumb applying just a small amount of more pressure on her clitoris, his own hips pumping his cock against her hard. He groaned deeply as he felt her body grip his fingers and the sound reverberated throughout her body, starting with her nipple, which he still suckled, licking ever harder. When the vibrations reached her pussy, she exploded in orgasm with a sharp yell, convulsing against him. His corresponding yell of orgasm was muffled against her breast, setting off another smaller but no less intense orgasm throughout her body.

The last thing that she remembered hearing was him whisper, "Yes," against her breast as he held her gently in the aftermath, resting his head against her chest, and wrapping her in his arms.

She knew Andrea was pottering around her room, though her head was still buried beneath the pillow.

"Mrs. Sutton, it is 7:00 a.m. It is time to get ready for your MRI appointment this morning. Also, your breakfast is here."

Leila groaned. She had never felt so tired in her life! She removed the pillow from her head, only to recover it as a blinding light from the window hit her. "No, light!" She said sharply, painfully.

"Oh, I am sorry, Mrs. Sutton." Andrea said, and she could hear the contrition in her voice as she hurried to re-close the blinds. "There, all better."

Leila tentatively removed the pillow and then sat up. Andrea adjusted the bed to a sitting position, rolling her breakfast on the bedside table across her lap. Leila looked at it with a grimace.

"Are you sure I may eat breakfast before this test?" She asked.

"Oh, yes," Andrea said cheerfully, placing a fork where she could easily reach it.

Leila was not sure how much cheer she could manage this morning. She herself was feeling quite surly, not being a morning person until she had her coffee. She grimaced as she looked over the tray, feeling queasy. Scrambled eggs, two thin strips of turkey bacon, she knew from experience, a ridiculously small can of orange juice and...she perked up, a small cup of coffee on the tray. "Do I have to eat?" She asked, looking at Andrea's happy face.

Andrea frowned, checking her chart, "Well, no."

"Great!" Leila said reaching for the cup. "Coffee it is." Hopefully, a cup of coffee would help to wake her up a bit.

"Mr. Sutton, dropped off a bag for you with toiletries this morning." Andrea said. Placing the small duffle in the bathroom for her.

"That's great!" It actually paid to have a husband who wanted a clean woman around, and she was sure she was a fright. "He is expecting to get to take me home today." Leila said sipping her coffee. It wasn't the best coffee that she had ever drank, but it wasn't the worst either. She got better at work, she thought.

Just then, a very tall woman with huge breasts, flamboyant clothing, and a headful of wild bushy orangish brown hair that would have done the 80s justice came into her room with a small flower arrangement.

"Jackie!" Leila said in delight.

"Hey, girl!" She said loudly. There was only one volume to Jackie, and that was loud. Leila loved that about her. Jackie loved life, and it showed.

"Shhhh. Ladies, it isn't even visiting hours yet!" Andrea said sternly.

"Sorry!" Jackie said in return. "Just two minutes, I promise," Jackie said and Andrea nodded begrudgingly. "I just wanted to drop these off from the office." She put the flowers on the bedside table. "Are you getting out today? We are all so worried! Are you okay?"

"We don't know yet. I have an MRI in a little while. But, according to the doctor, the one thing that I am *not* is pregnant." She said, knowing that Jackie would pick up on the joke.

Jackie burst out laughing! Quickly covering her mouth with her hand as Andrea gave her a glare.

"Well, duh! You have to be *exposed* to catch that!" She said in a loud whisper. "Do you get to come home today?"

Jackie was one of Leila's favorite people. Smart, funny, wild, and raunchy, and Leila thoroughly enjoyed being around her. "I don't know yet. The doctor is still running some tests and wants to look at the MRI before making that decision."

"Well, I got to go. I will let everyone know you said 'hi'!" She said, heading to the door.

"Yes, tell them that, and thank you so much for the flowers." Leila said, smiling and waving after her. She leaned back against her pillows, thoroughly exhausted already.

She drank the rest of her coffee before getting out of bed. "I just want to take a quick shower and get cleaned up some. I am sure I must be a mess!" She said to Andrea, trying to shake herself out of her lethargy. "Do I have ten or fifteen minutes?"

"Plenty of time. I will get you a fresh gown and robe."

"Do you know if I have to be nude for this test?" Leila said tentatively, self-consciously, worriedly.

"No, they will do the test with your gown on. Panties are fine, no bra though. No metal of any kind. They will have a tray for your wedding ring in the exam area. You will just slip it off before the test, and you can have it directly after. No worries!" Andrea said, smiling. "Just keep the bathroom door unlocked, just in case, and I will check back in with you in fifteen minutes." She said, giving her some privacy.

Leila hurried into the bathroom. Turning the open shower on, noticing that there was a little sitting area in the shower and a small bar of soap, shampoo, and conditioner available.

It's like hotel service, except it's not as nice and costs ten times more. Said a snarky little voice inside of her. "Ain't that the truth!" She said out loud to herself.

Stripping and throwing her hospital gown into a cloth hamper, she stepped into the shower. The Georgia water was warm, and she could tell that it had some sort of central processing done, but it was still harder than the softened water at her house. In any case, it helped to revive her slightly. She quickly washed herself, foregoing washing her hair since she had just washed her hair yesterday morning. Had she been here for only a day? It seemed forever, and she was quite ready to go home.

Turning off the water, she wrapped her body in a bath towel and stepped out of the shower. She had forgotten to turn on the exhaust fan, so the mirror was fogged. She dug through the small duffle that Michael had dropped off for her and found her toothpaste and toothbrush.

She wiped the condensation from the mirror, and over her shoulder, shirtless, and looking at her with satisfaction, a small smile on his sexy lips, was the man from her dream! Immediately blushing, she whirled around, almost losing her balance in the process, to see the back of the bathroom door. She was totally alone!

"No, no, no, no..." turning around to face the mirror, no one was in the reflection behind her. "This is NOT happening today!" She said to herself and brushed her teeth. Thinking the whole time, "no, no, no, no" trying to lose herself in the mundaneness of her actions.

She had just slipped on the fresh panties that Michael had thought to include in her duffle bag when a knock at the door startled her. "Mrs. Sutton, are you okay?" Came Andrea's voice from the other side of the door.

"Yes," she said, cracking the door to peek out around it.

"Great. Here you go." Andrea handed her a fresh hospital gown and robe.

"Thank you, Andrea! You are a lifesaver." She said, pasting a smile on her face. There was no way she could let anyone know how discomfited she was right now. The fewer questions, the better, until she was able to figure out what the hell was going on with herself. "Just give me a minute and I will be right out and ready to go." She spoke in a chipper tone.

"Will do."

Donning the gown and robe, she stepped into her slippers, opening the door. Andrea was waiting patiently with a wheelchair.

Leila looked at her skeptically.

"Sorry, Mrs. Sutton, hospital policy I am afraid." Andrea said in apology, patting the back of the chair. Leila sighed, getting into the chair and adjusting her feet on the footrests and they were off.

"So, where is the test taking place?" She asked curiously as Andrea efficiently wheeled her from the room.

"First floor. Good news, also! Dr. Lambert has finished his rounds and will be attending the procedure with our on-staff radiologist, Dr. Kathleen Grant. She's brilliant!" Andrea said to her in her happy voice.

"That's good. Not that you haven't been wonderful, but I am ready to go back home." Leila said to her as she wheeled her into the elevator.

"I understand completely, Mrs. Sutton." She said with a smile. "No one likes to be sick."

Leila smiled at her in return. *And I am a great actress, since I seem to be losing my mind,* she thought as they arrived on the first floor. "At least this will be over with today, and I can get back to my boys." She said out loud instead.

They navigated back to the testing facility and into a room. Leila's first thought was that the machine in the inner room looked like a science fiction coffin from the future. She wasn't feeling as secure about this process as she had moments before. Dr. Lambert had a chart open and was standing next to an attractive, studious woman in her late forties with mousy-brown hair and horn-rimmed spectacles. It was obvious that they had been discussing her as they both looked up.

"Mrs. Sutton, how are you doing this morning?" Dr. Lambert greeted, flashing his sexy smile. "Are you ready for your MRI?" He approached her with his hand out and helped her to extricate herself from the wheelchair. He braced her by the elbow, as the lady came to introduce herself.

"Mrs. Sutton, my name is Dr. Kathleen Grant. I am the radiologist here. Dr. Lambert tells me you had an unusual episode yesterday morning?" She inquired.

"Yes. I had some sort of fainting spell." Leila said, slightly intimidated by the straightforwardness of this doctor.

"Yes, and you were unconscious for several hours after. Why don't we get you checked out and see what is going on, shall we?" Dr. Grant asked. "Are you steady enough to walk?"

"Yeah, I am good. I had a fairly good night, and I am feeling much better today." Leila said, lying through her teeth.

"Very good. This way." She led her into the room behind the glass window to the large tubular machine, Dr. Lambert following along behind.

"Why don't you remove your robe and step up here and take a seat?" Leila did, handing her robe to Dr. Lambert, who hung it on a hook on the wall. "So, tell me exactly how you felt when this spell first occurred. As much as you can remember." Dr. Grant said.

"Well, as I told Dr. Lambert. It was dawn, and I was in my garage getting ready to take my kids to daycare. Suddenly, I felt this extreme pain throughout my body, kind of a burning or itching sensation. Then I felt dizzy, disoriented really, and everything seemed like it was in slow motion. I could tell that I was falling. I remember trying to break my fall by catching myself against the back of my car. The last thing I remember was putting my hands out to catch myself from hitting the pavement. Then that's it until I woke up yesterday afternoon here in the hospital." Leila told her story to Dr. Grant.

"So," she said, making some notes in the chart. "You were walking? In motion?" She glanced up at Leila.

"No." Leila replied.

"No? What were you doing?" Both doctors looked at her.

"I was at the end of my garage, standing next to the car, waiting for the sun to come up. I like sunrises and sunsets." She said simply.

"Were you holding one of your children?" Dr. Lambert inquired.

"No, I went to the garage to put the diaper bag into the car. My husband was putting their shoes on in the house. Once I put the bag in the car, I walked a couple of steps to the end of the garage to wait for the sun to come up. I wasn't in the garage more than a minute or two before it happened. The car wasn't on yet. My husband had the kids. I was just standing."

"Did you have a headache? I see here that you had taken two Tylenol that morning." Dr. Grant said to her.

"Not particularly. But I felt some throbbing pressure, like I had one coming on and I was cutting it off before it got to a full-blown headache." Leila stated.

"Do you often have headaches?" Dr. Grant asked.

"I wouldn't say 'often', but I have had migraines in the past. I used to take Elavil when I was getting them frequently. But I haven't had a major migraine for months. I have learned the signs for my body, and that morning thought that I might be getting ready to have a headache."

"It also says in your chart that you were light sensitive when you regained consciousness after the episode yesterday. Do you have that issue this morning?" Dr. Grant asked.

"Yes." Leila said simply.

"On a scale from one to ten? One being the lowest." Dr. Grant fired the question at her.

"I can't really say for sure. I had the nurse close the blinds again right away. It was not comfortable. Not a one, but not a ten either." Leila said thinking this lady knew her stuff.

"Alright. Let's get you settled on the scanning table." She patted the table for Leila to lie back. There was a small pillow to lay her head on. "Now don't be alarmed, Mrs. Sutton. This table will slide into the tunnel here. If you would please give your wedding ring to Dr. Lambert, to take into the observation room. You can have it back when the test is over, okay?"

Leila shook her head nervously and handed her ring to Dr. Lambert, who smiled reassuringly to her. He slid it into his front breast pocket on his lab coat, patted it and said, "I've got it safe and sound right here, okay?" She shook her head at him.

"Now, being in the tube can be a little claustrophobic." Dr. Grant told her, and Leila looked at her with wide eyes. "But don't be nervous. You can just close your eyes and that will help with that sensation. You will hear several repetitive sounds from the device throughout the test. These are all normal. We will put on some music for you to listen to. What kind of music do you like?" She said smiling at her.

"Eighties." Leila said softly.

"No problem. We have some great mixed tapes here." Dr. Grant nodded to Dr. Lambert, who went over to speak with the technician sitting in the outer room behind the glass in front of a computer screen. "Now the test itself will take about 30-45 minutes. Just keep calm. This won't hurt at all. You also have access to this call button here if you feel like you need to call us for anything." She said this like she knew it wouldn't happen. "You will need to lie as still as you can. That way, we can get a good look at what is going on. Would you like a light blanket? Are you feeling cold?"

Leila shook her head, still looking extremely nervous.

"I will tell you a secret, shall I?" Dr. Grant said with a smile, and at Leila's nervous nod continued. "Lots of patients actually fall asleep in here." At Leila's incredulous look. She continued, "It's true. It can be very peaceful, and the humming sound of this machine can be very relaxing." She smiled, and Leila gave her a small smile in return. "Ready?"

Leila nodded, and they began.

She knew where she was immediately. The glow from the fireplace lighting the room softly. She sighed in resignation. This dream just wouldn't leave her. "Where are you?" She called out. He stepped out of the shadows. This time he was wearing a silk collar-less shirt of emerald green and soft fawn-color pants. He was Mr. Ultra-Relaxation today, she thought.

"I change my clothes everyday like most people do." He told her simply, reading her thoughts.

She looked at herself and she was still wearing the white gown, knotted at her shoulders, gathered beneath her breast with a scarlet-colored silk ribbon. She held her arms out as if to say, "Well?"

"I thought you had determined that this was a dream? Well, this is your dream." He said with an impish look in his eyes.

"Don't get on my nerves. I am not having a great day." She said to him, but with no real heat, and tiredly sat down on the couch.

He came and joined her. "You seem distressed, Glykó." He said, not touching her, though she could feel that he wanted to; badly.

She thought for a moment. "I am tentatively hopeful," she said.

"Hopeful?"

"Yes. They are doing a test on me right now that will hopefully tell me what is wrong with me, and then they can fix me."

He rolled his eyes, scoffing. "There is nothing *wrong* with you!"

"You know nothing about it." She said irritably.

"I know everything about it." He said assuredly, reasonably. "After all, I am your dream, aren't I?"

He leaned back against the couch, stretching his legs out to place his bare feet on the coffee table and crossed them at the ankle. He interlocked the fingers of his hands together to rest them on his lap, directly above the bulge at his crotch. She couldn't help but stare a moment. She glanced up at his face and he was giving her a 'come fuck me' look. She realized he had been trying to get her to look there all along.

She sighed, then said, "Stop it."

"You have been neglected, Glykó. I intend to 'fix' that." He said softly, sensually, using her word.

"You know I don't understand you, right?" She asked simply. "What language are you speaking?" She figured that would throw her mind for a loop, since this was a dream.

"Greek." He said immediately.

"What?"

"Greek."

"But I don't know Greek. I *only* speak English." She said forthrightly.

"Well, I know many languages. But my native language is Greek." He told her simply.

"So, what does Glykó mean? In English." She questioned, then clarified.

"Sweet one." He said, giving her his 'fuck me' look.

She ignored the look. "So, what was it you were saying to me last night?"

He slowly raised his golden eyebrows impishly and leaned toward her slowly, half reclining remarkably close to her without touching. "Oh, many, many things. Would you like me to..." he paused for effect, "repeat them?" He looked up at her with thickly lashed eyes that glowed a light amber in the firelight.

"Not right now." She could feel herself flush. She leaned back slightly. "Was I dreaming about you this morning?" She said instead, seeking to distract him and thinking of his reflection in the mirror.

"No."

"Oh," she said softly. *So, her mind was attempting to manifest her dreams during waking hours? That couldn't be good,* she was thinking.

"I was attempting to come to you this morning." He said simply. "After all, you left my arms so abruptly it woke me." He looked at her with curiosity. "But my appearance in your bath this morning clearly alarmed you, so I decided that retreat was a more strategic move. You looked nóstimo wrapped in your towel." He looked at her with hunger.

"Nóstimo?" She questioned as he leaned farther toward her.

"Delicious." He said capturing her lips with his and wrapping his arms around her, taking her down with him to lie on the couch.

"Stop." She said half-heartedly, as he pulled her against his body, and his delicious scent enveloped them.

"You don't want me to stop." He smiled, suddenly playful, and kissed the tip of her nose as he rolled her beneath him. He leaned down to whisper in her ear, "I would love to put my tongue where my fingers were last night."

"Stop!" She said more forcefully, bucking her entire body against his to dislodge him, as she felt her pussy give a twinge at the thought. Suddenly, she sagged in his arms. "I feel so tired." She whispered, as he rained light kisses on the side of her neck.

"Yes, i allagí mou, my changeling. I know. Sleep and rest." Wrapping her in his arms, he held her tenderly.

"What is your name?" She asked softly.

"Nichola." He whispered.

"Nichola." She breathed and fell into a deep slumber.

"Mrs. Sutton! Mrs. Sutton!" Dr. Lambert was shaking her slightly by the shoulders. "That's it. Wake up, Mrs. Sutton!" He said in relief as her eyes fluttered open. He fixed her with a hard-blue-eyed stare. "Can you sit up?"

"Yes. I am okay. I was just sleeping. Are we done?" She said tiredly as she sat up unsteadily. The MRI technician was there to help her with her robe, looking worried, and to help her down from the scanning table. "Truly, I am fine." She said to him sharply, patting his arm to offset the tone. She sensed that they all were extremely worried and stressed. "Okay, doctors," she said to Lambert and Grant, "you might as well tell me. What is it?" She said as the technician helped her to sit in the wheelchair. "That was a quick test."

"Actually, the test took us a bit longer to conduct." Dr. Grant took a step forward. "We had you in the MRI for 75 minutes."

"Okay," Leila took a deep breath, steeling herself for bad news. "Tell me what's wrong."

"Nothing. We've found nothing with the MRI that would indicate why you passed out yesterday, Mrs. Sutton." Dr. Grant said definitively.

"But," Dr. Lambert looked at Dr. Grant sharply. "We couldn't wake you for a full ten minutes after the test. I thought that you may have slipped into unconsciousness again."

"No, it did not show that on the MRI, doctor. This patient was definitely in a dream state." Dr. Grant stated bluntly.

"It is science that unconscious patients can dream." Dr. Lambert started.

Leila put up a hand. They can argue without her, she had decided. "Fine." They looked at her. "MRI was good. No brain tumors, no cancer, no whatever." Leila waved her hand. "Nothing to indicate why I lost consciousness. Is that correct?" She demanded.

"Yes, that is correct." Dr. Grant said.

"Well, for me, that is good," Leila said reasonably.

"But we still don't know why it happened yesterday and after this incident, I would like to keep you and observe you for another night." Dr. Lambert said.

"Fine." Leila said to him directly, but obviously not happy. "One more night. That's it. I want to go home tomorrow."

"Yes, I agree. I would like to take some blood again right away, and I will spend the night here tonight to observe you personally." He said to her doggedly.

She could see a light in his eyes, as if he were on a crusade for the truth.

"Thank you, Dr. Lambert. I genuinely appreciate your concern. Can I go back to my room now? I am feeling very tired all of the sudden." She told him softly.

He nodded his head and motioned to Andrea, who had just arrived to take her back. "Nurse, please take another full screening sample from Mrs. Sutton, stat."

It was a silent trip back to her room on the fourth floor. When they arrived back. Leila got into bed without assistance and took a drink of the ice water on the rolling table. Andrea left and returned with a table full of tubes and a small syringe. Leila sighed deeply as she drew more blood vials from the same arm that she had the day before. The other arm was still black and blue, but showing signs of yellowish healing.

Both were silent throughout the procedure. Leila because she was worried, and Andrea because she respected that her patient was worried and needed quiet.

"Andrea, could you flip off the light? I am going to sleep for a while," Leila asked quietly, as the nurse gathered the vials and testing syringe.

"Absolutely, Mrs. Sutton. Just give me a buzz if you need anything else," Andrea said softly.

"Thanks. I appreciate it." Layla said, using the remote to lower her bed flat and rolling over on her side. Andrea nodded, flipping off the light and closing the door behind her slowly.

Leila closed her eyes and fell into a deep sleep almost immediately.

Aunt Iris

CHAPTER ONE

R ECLINING ON HER BED in her room at the Spencer House Inn, Bed
and Breakfast in downtown St. Marys, Georgia, Iris' long legs were
outstretched upon the flowered coverlet, her back supported by mounds
of pillows. A mauve silk nightgown clung to her curves.

Dressing for her rest was one of the few things she had yet to give up
since her crossing. Her heightened vampire senses reveled in the silky
feel against her skin.

She had been a rebel as a human, and that hadn't changed since she
became a vampire. No one was her Master. She owed her existence
to no one, she came, went, and did as she pleased. Being a 'blooded'
vampire versus a 'made' vampire was an advantage. It gave her a standing
even higher than those 'made' elders, almost like royalty. No matter her
comparative youth, she had the powers and the senses of an elder.

It came with the bloodline.

The ability to fly and shape change had been hers within five years
of her crossing, whereas made vampires, and even genetic vampires like
herself, sometimes took centuries to develop these powers. If they ever
did. If they survived long enough. The pattern of her rest was like that
of an elder as well. The need for actual sleep was minimal.

She spent most of her days watching talk shows. She had become an
expert on Oprah and abhorred the decline of The Donahue Show.

The notion that humans went on these shows to tell the nation about an
unfaithful spouse or reveal that they had sex not only with their wife, but her
mother, sisters, and cousin amazed her to no end. The thought of vampires
going on the talk show circuit to reveal their 'secret' made her giggle. The
technical issues alone would be amusing as 'made' vampires would never

show up fully on camera; that power and curse reserved only for elders and those few 'blooded' vampires in existence.

Her very favorite host was Phil Donahue, but Jerry Springer intrigued her. Flipping through the channels looking for Jerry, she knew she liked him because he brought out that raunchy human side of her that was still buried deep. Liking his radical and offbeat shows, she realized that his bespectacled, intelligent, soft-spoken appearance stirred a hunger in her that was more akin to sexual desire than blood-lust.

She had stayed away from Leila's thoughts since last evening. Her niece was not taking her change very well, and Iris was unsure of how to handle the situation. Iris had expected her to welcome her last night, but instead she had shut her out. Almost as if she didn't believe her eyes.

Changing could be difficult to accept. She herself had fought her change for years; only succumbing when there was no one else who mattered. Francisque, her husband, had died prior to her actual change. But she had made a promise to watch over the children of her deceased sister, Dolly, and for them Iris had fought hard to stay human as long as possible.

Jamie and Jack had grown up into strong young men. Neither had lived with Iris, but she had kept an eye on them throughout the years. Jamie had lived with his paternal grandmother, and when older with his own father, while Jack had lived with her oldest brother, James. Watching them for any sign of the change that had taken over their mother, Dolly, had been difficult with the boys living apart.

Jack never showed signs of changing, and now that he was fifty, Iris knew he never would. Jamie, on the other hand had exhibited the usual extra sensory signals early on; quiet, introspective, and highly intelligent; with the ability to keenly sense the emotions and thoughts of others quite easily.

When Iris reached her mid-forties, she found that she too had begun to change, like her sister had almost 20 years before. It was very unusual that two children from the same set of parents would develop the vampire condition and her own change came as a shock to her. She hadn't been paying attention to herself as an individual due to her focus on Jamie and Jack. She never thought that she would turn, especially when her little sister had started to turn in her early twenties. But, then again, the twenties were a rare turning age. Most 'blooded' vampires turned in their third decade. Iris would have welcomed her vampire state if she had noticed it early on, but she had been taking care of her terminally ill husband, Francisque.

Her childless marriage to Francisque had never been a 'love' match, at least on her side, and there had been many affairs throughout the years. But she had liked him throughout much of their marriage, and he was wealthy. He offered her the opportunity for a better life, and she had grasped it with both hands.

When Iris was 45, Leila had been born to Jamie and his wife, Evelyn, who had married almost two years before. As soon as Iris saw her, she had loved her with her whole being. After keeping such sharp eyes on the development of Jamie and Jack throughout her life, she had never really bemoaned her childless state, but she felt the loss when Leila was born. Leila made up for that.

Jamie and Evelyn's little chubby, red-haired cherub had stolen her way into her heart. Jamie eventually had two other daughters, but Leila was by far Iris's favorite. There was no way she was willing to never see her again. Then, as Leila had started to grow up, she started to exhibit the signs just as her grandmother and father had.

Jamie started to change in his early 30s, but by coaching and extreme control, he had the vampire in him at bay, refusing to leave his family and his wife Evelyn, whom he loved dearly. He once again needed her, and she stayed to help him; living through the winter after Francisque' s death with him and his family. Leila had been ten at the time.

Iris feeling the pain of Jamie changing, and their combined denied hunger, made the struggle to combat the change much more difficult and she could see the change taking its toll on her physical body. For the first time, she cursed the part of her blood that made her what she was.

Iris was so lonely that next winter by herself. But Jamie had taken control of his condition like a prizefighter and being together only made it more difficult for them both. Iris asked Jamie to bring Leila down when school was out to spend the summer with her. He had reservations about doing so, but Leila had been so excited about the prospect he had let her go despite his misgivings. Leila had spent Iris' last human summer with her, in her summer home, on Lake Viking.

It had been a wonderful summer for both. Iris felt better than she had felt all winter! By then, denial of her natural tendencies had started to show a marked effect on her physically. She had grown thin, her loneliness and denial driving her body to waste away. As soon as Leila arrived, along with her energy and girlish laughter, Iris began to bounce back.

They had long talks, more like friends than great aunt and niece. Iris noticed, though, that Leila would need time alone and would take long walks down to the lakeside. The sun would burn her fair skin till she blistered and then Iris would make her stay in the house, only letting her out when the sun went down. Leila though, seemed to enjoy this more than being out in the sun. She would tell Iris after coming home from her walks in the dark, "The night speaks to me".

Then Nikolaos arrived, in the dead of night like a demon, introducing himself as a long-lost relative and telling her their family history. He sensed Leila's presence in her home, like a bloodhound sensing its prey.

"There is another vampire here?" he had asked with curiosity burning in his amber-colored eyes.

"No, my niece is sleeping in the other room. She's not a vampire!" Iris had said emphatically. "She is just a child!" Iris said quickly, as Nikolaos focused on her panic with curiosity.

Nikolaos' eyes had sparkled, sensing something that she herself did not. "Well, let's look at her, shall we?"

He had moved so fast it was like he had disappeared. She had run down the hall as fast as her infirm body could into Leila's room after him, feeling breathless. When she arrived in the doorway to the spare bedroom, he was sitting on the edge of the bed next to Leila, holding her small hand in his, and looking down on her face with what could only be termed as bemused wonderment.

"No, you're right, not yet one of us. But she is strong in this form, nonetheless. When she does cross, I will make sure I am there." He reached down and caressed the soft freckled skin of her cheek softly.

"Don't you hurt her!" Iris said sharply, protectively, startling Leila awake.

"My dear, I wouldn't dream of harming this child." Nikolaos said to her, while he looked deeply into Leila's wide, teal-green eyes, softly stroking the curve of her face. They looked like they were both entranced for the briefest of moments, and then he smiled at Leila's sleepy expression, briefly showing strong white teeth against the light tan of his handsome face. He then turned to lock eyes with Iris.

"You are killing yourself." He stated bluntly. "There is no purpose to you being mortal any longer. Your body knows this. Take a long hard look at yourself and you would see that. Stop fighting yourself and stay out of the sun!" He was suddenly standing directly in front of her, moving so fast it was like magic. "Think of me and I will be here for you to lean on, cousin." He briefly touched Iris's shoulder in understanding, then with one last long enigmatic look at Leila who had sat up in bed, her long chestnut-colored hair framing her face and small body. He was gone, like he had never been there.

"Aunt Iris?" came Leila's frightened voice out of the darkness. "Who was that?"

"You are dreaming, my love. It's nothing more than a dream." Iris had said, using the *voice* for the first time in her existence, and willed Leila to sleep.

She had called Jamie to arrange for Leila's departure. Iris didn't feel that Leila was safe there any longer, not with Nikolaos hanging about. She didn't trust him. Less than two weeks later, Leila was gone, and Iris was more alone in the world than she had ever been. Iris packed up the summerhouse, and moved back to her house in Kansas City, and uncharacteristically shut out the world.

It took six months, but her starving body overtook her mind and had finally driven her to seek out and drain the blood of a wino in a filthy downtown alley. The act was so totally out of character with whom she was, the disgust and guilt almost drove her to suicide. With the partaking of blood came knowledge, and one major weakness. Knowledge that at this early stage, she would be unable to survive on her own. An infuriating prospect to her and her independent nature.

The weakness being that she could no longer stand the light of day, not even a small amount. It wouldn't outright kill her. She didn't burst into flames or anything dramatic. But the pain was unbearable, and she was still so physically weak, now far weaker than a human, and would lose consciousness if not careful. Humans are a diurnal society, and she could no longer function in it without assistance. She summoned Nikolaos. He and his companion servant arrived in the night and took her to Toronto, to his winter residence.

She had called her sister Lystel. Lystel, like all her siblings, was aware of their family's peculiarity. Lystel took care of the mock funeral arrangements, everything to make her death look legal. Her lawyer transferred the now enormous amount of money that Francisque had invested over the years of their marriage and had left her upon his death in a Canadian bank.

She left a legacy of both her residences and $50,000 cash to her nephew Jack, knowing Jamie would always be able to take care of himself. She had also sent a letter to Jamie, telling him of her fears for Leila. She never thought he would ignore her instructions to educate Leila; to prepare her for when the change took hold of her. To prepare her for what lay in her future.

Iris remembered her own funeral, which had been held in Missouri on a misty and cold April day. She had argued endlessly with Nikolaos; wanting to attend it.

Nikolaos had been against her flying down for it as she was a newborn, a fledgling, and it had only been two weeks since her complete physical transformation. In the end, he had relented and flown her down in his jet and patiently waited at their hotel while his servant Mansuetus had taken her in a black limousine to the graveyard. Its windows were tinted blacker than the night itself.

Bundled in the back of the limousine, she was dressed in black with a black wide-brimmed sunhat, complete with a heavy lace veil and dark sunglasses to protect her eyes. The black glass of the limousine protected her bundled form from the weak sunlight of that day. Iris had needed to say goodbye to her human life. Something Nikolaos had seemed to have forgotten about in the years since his own change.

She remembered seeing her sister Lystel and her greedy children crying tears that, with her new vision and insight, were so obviously fake. She could easily pick up their thoughts of money that they felt would be coming to them at the reading of the will. She had smiled at the thought of their anger when her will was read. There were no tears from Jamie, only a deep sadness for her. His wife Evelyn was the one that shocked her the most. Her tears and grief were real. Iris had never thought that Evelyn had ever really cared about her when she was in her human existence. She was ashamed that she had been so wrong.

Upon her return to the hotel, Nikolaos had asked, "Well, are you satisfied?" His eyes were dark and unreadable, the shadow of his three-day beard dark gold against his tanned skin. She had nodded her head and lay down and rest. They left town that night and she had never told him of her feelings about that day and he had never asked. That had been in April 1978.

Since then, Iris took what knowledge Nikolaos offered and when she finally reached her full strength and powers ten years later, she had left for her own domicile and to make her own way in the world. Their parting hadn't been bitter, only inevitable. Never lovers, only companions, Nikolaos had never tried to control her, only guide. It was as if he had a duty to a family member; and she supposed that since they shared the same bloodline, this was true. He checked in with her a few times per year.

He had taught her how to hunt when the need arose. When to stop before death arrived. But mostly he taught her that the taking of human life was dangerous. A vampire at the height of their powers need not feed off the blood of humans, as if they were cattle. True Vampire Elders, able to exist off the emotions of humans, rarely fed off human blood unless they had a willing host. It was just too dangerous to hunt, feed, or kill in today's world.

Discovery meant death, that was certain. If it were serious enough, The Vampire community would step in to stop the discovery, or there loomed the danger from other factions. There were several organizations throughout the world that still 'hunted' those things that they didn't understand. Fortunately, modern society regarded them as crackpots, but still, it was of the utmost importance that new vampires were trained to not bring attention to the community. Animal blood, cow or pig's blood was a favorite for its taste, would keep a vampire at full strength; unfortunately, drinking human blood was still the sweetest and intoxicating of all elixirs. Some vampires would occasionally take an unwilling or unknowing human for various reasons, then use the "voice" to convince them that it had all been a dream, but that was still a risk, and occasionally, it drove the human to insanity.

Since coming into her full powers, she had not been overwhelmed with the need to drink human blood or to connect with human beings at all. That is until she started watching Jerry Springer. That was the desire that he awakened in her; that need to partake of human essence, so much more than blood really, and all the emotions, physical sensations, and memories that filled the vampire's body and mind during the feeding. It truly was the best sex. Ah, there he was. She had finally found him on Channel 12.

The title of his show today was *My Pimp is Ruining My Life.*

She smiled as he came into view, and she got up and went to the small refrigerator in the room that Nikolaos' man had seen was stocked for her; unused to having a daytime companion. Though she couldn't call Mansuetus a true companion. He said extraordinarily little, only enough to convey needed information to her, but he was better than no one while traveling, and skilled at taking care of a vampire's daytime needs.

She removed a green-colored glass bottle, uncorked it with a long sharp nail on her right hand, and poured herself a glass of rich red liquid. Sipping from the glass, she grimaced: cold cows' blood. Well, at least it would soon become room temperature and would then be almost tasty. She knew what she would like to be doing now though, as she ran the tip of her tongue over one sharp fang and watched Jerry talking to his guests.

Finishing the show and the now warmer blood, she flipped off the television with a sigh, feeling lonely. Vampires, by nature, were solitary creatures, rarely pairing up for longer than a century or two and then usually only for protection. Human beings had enough trouble being with one partner for twenty or thirty years, let alone with the same person for all eternity.

She needed companionship, someone to share her time, but wasn't ready to settle down with a partner yet. This life was still too new, too exciting. Vampires think of themselves as above human standards; most elders had forgotten that they had ever been born human, that underneath all the powers that Vampirism brings, they are still part of the human condition. That basic core of humanity gives vampires the ability for deeper loves and passions than a normal human being can ever experience. It also gives them the ability for a more frigid remoteness than any human being could ever endure.

Iris felt it was these emotional highs and lows that were the danger to a vampire's existence. Any total lack of, or overexposure to, emotions usually is the downfall of humans. This is more so in the case of a vampire. Too much emotion, either hate or love, can cause mistakes to occur. Any lack of conscience in a vampire also causes mistakes. Nikolaos always told her that their kind had the capacity to be the most dangerous serial killers or the most ardent poets in existence. Either extreme was dangerous, and as such, both should be avoided.

The feelings of loneliness she was experiencing, along with her deep maternal feelings for Leila, had to be resolved or she could adversely affect the way Leila handled her change. Iris was intelligent enough to know this. Her last mind connection with Leila had been for information purposes only. She hadn't intended Leila to sense her presence, but she had anyway. Iris had underestimated Leila's abilities. She had not meant to upset her more than she already was. Not only was Iris hurt when she had closed the blinds against her, she was shocked when Leila blocked her attempt at a mind connection.

Last night when she hovered outside of Leila's window at the hospital, watching as she instinctively used the 'voice' magnificently with that bossy nurse; she had been extremely impressed and maternally proud of her niece. Iris knew then that Leila had the capability of great power. She would make a magnificent vampire and would most likely attain her full powers quickly, probably quicker than Iris had herself.

Iris attempted another mind connection, tentatively. Because they were related not only by the vampire state but by remarkably close blood ties, it was easy for her to bridge the few miles to the hospital to connect herself with Leila's mind. She searched for that faint presence that other vampires gave off and found that Leila had shut herself off to any further outside interference.

Iris was shocked and impressed again. Such defined power in a fledgling, much less a changeling, was unheard of. More so because Iris was convinced that it was instinctual and not a purposeful mind block. Nikolaos was right; she was immensely powerful in her present form indeed. What should she do if Leila continued to block her out?

Iris remembered how out of control she had been when she made her first kill. The change had taken its toll on her body, and she was almost skeletal: starving, hurting, raging, in and out of consciousness. If a human had seen her at the end, they would have encountered a horrifying creature of terror.

The night it ended was one that she would never forget. By fighting the change all those years, by using the crippling sunlight to maintain her humanity, she had not understood that she had made it harder for the change to finally take hold. One minute she was laying in her bed, sweat pouring from her pores, writhing in pain, wondering when, or if, it would stop or if she would just die. Then the next minute she was walking down the street barefoot in her nightgown! A horror show for anyone who saw her.

Thank God it was so late that no one was around. Even the streets were almost deserted of cars. Of course, she had found herself in the 'wrong' part of town where rapes, murders, and robberies often occurred. Night brought locked doors and closed shutters to these streets. She remembered even now how blithely unconcerned she had been about the possible dangers of the neighborhood. If she had been fully human, she would have said that she had a death wish.

She remembered hearing a scratching noise, like rats in a box, down a side street and how she followed the sound, unafraid. It was astounding for her to experience the scents she detected, initially overwhelming her and leaving her staggered. It was as if her whole body and not just her nose smelled the rot, the filth, the garbage, the underlying poverty, and hopelessness of Kansas City's ghetto area. Then she smelled the blood. Blood, she sensed blood! Smelled the coppery tang, knew it instinctively, tasted it across the cells of her tongue; and like a hound on the scent, she immediately proceeded down a dimly lit alley.

There she found a bundle of rags huddled against the cold air of the night using the cracked wall of a rundown brick four-story building as a windbreaker. As she approached the bundle, it grew in form, revealing itself to being a grizzled, filthy old man who lifted his blood-shot eyed head to gaze at her.

Words spoke out loud to her that barely registered with her brain; the blood scent so overwhelmed her faculties, "Hey lady! What are you doing here? You're not even wearing any clothes! This is MY home, and I ain't sharing it! Get out of here!"

The stench of sour wine and hostility rose to jockey with the blood scent as the words were hurled her way. As she knelt next to the man, he flung out a bandaged hand toward her. Waving her off.

"Get the Fuck Out of Here! You crazy old bitch!" He had yelled at her.

She sensed his hostility as a façade and tasted his underlying fear, sharpening her desire and causing her mouth to water.

Iris captured his waving hand and brought it to her face, smelling the dirt and wine, and then the blood seeping through the bandage. Sinking her teeth into the bandage like a snake would a struggling mouse, he screeched in pain and shock, a sound that hurt her now sensitive ears; and in a millisecond her teeth were on his filthy, sweaty throat, ripping through flesh and muscle and lodging in his carotid artery, as her body worked to pull his coppery scented blood into her body. As the blood filled her stomach to spread throughout her veins, she almost reeled in orgasmic throws, quite like as in great sex and she sucked ever harder at his throat, gorging herself in his fluids and his life, as pleasure rocked her body and wiped her mind of all else.

Thoughts of her first victim always filled her with a fascination at the mindlessness of it all; and disgust at herself. What she had not known at that time was that she didn't have to kill to feed. Her grief and guilt were great when she found out, and like the memories of that kill, still haunted her, and she suspected always would.

Iris wouldn't let that type of pain be visited upon her Leila. She must do something!

Visiting Leila in the hospital had not been totally planned last night. She had only meant to check in on her. After all, there were certain things that she needed to do, certain information that she needed to have, to get her out of that hospital quickly. After that fiasco at the window, she had snuck into the hospital to read Leila's chart, finding out that she was scheduled for an MRI the next morning, and who the attending radiologist was. That was something that needed action and she had quickly taken steps to ensure that the test would be considered 'normal'.

She was also curious after Leila had used the voice so well. That act alone, to Iris, was a sign of advanced transformation, and it scared her. Iris wasn't afraid of Leila; she was afraid *for* her. After all, her sister Dolly, Leila's grandmother, had been killed in a hospital. To Iris, hospitals were places of death.

Dolly had been so beautiful. Leila resembled her in size, shape, and coloring. Leila's hair was that same shade of auburn-chestnut, it even had a natural wavy curl like Dolly's.

There had always been a strong streak of the vampire bloodline in Iris's family from the maternal side. Originally from an area in the northern region of Greece, called Katerini, there were family members as far back as memory who had made the change to vampire. In each generation, there had always been at least one who made the change, and the family overall was both accepting and protective of this fact.

Her mother's brother, Martin, had transformed to vampire before her birth.

When she had been small, like all children do from time to time, Iris would often hide and listen to the adults talking in the late evening when she was supposed to be asleep. This is how she had learned about vampires.

In the year of her birth, 1920, her uncle Martin changed. Her mother's family was supportive; after all, Martin was blood. He was *family*. His secret they would take to the grave. This was the way her mother's family had always been with members who had been 'afflicted'. She remembered now, with some contempt, how the 'human' members of the family had talked about Martin's condition as if he were diseased. A manageable disease with needed adjustments, but a disease none-the-less. They had been such peasant fools.

Her father allowed Martin to spend his days in the large root cellar of their farmhouse. Martin would take his rest and then build beautiful pieces of furniture that her family would either use or sell in town. This additional money made the family one of the wealthier farm families in the region.

Her father, though, barely tolerated this arrangement, and did so distrusting Martin every day. Regardless of the additional large income that it brought his large and extended family, which kept everyone fed and clothed well, if not richly; the fact that he even tolerated the arrangement was only due to her mother's sake. Her father had grown up a German in Central Europe, the first of his family to come to the United States. His upbringing had made him a hard man and given him a distinct mistrust of all things that went bump in the night, even if one of those things was his brother through marriage. Iris remembered the amount of backbreaking work her Uncle Martin would do throughout the night on the small family farm in Central Missouri that they had owned, and she felt her uncle had more than paid his share for the benefit of the family. There was only one time she had ever feared her Uncle Martin, who usually was a soft-spoken, kind, calm type of man.

She had come upon Martin in a devouring fury when she was ten years old, and it had terrified and enlightened her knowledge beyond what her close family members ever realized about what it could possibly be like to be a vampire.

She remembered going out to the barn to play with the rabbits that they raised for both food and fur. She came upon Martin with one of them, its throat torn open wide. The blood matting its soft white fur as Martin had drained it of its life. The bodies of a half dozen more were scattered throughout the floor around his crouched form as he buried a bloodied face into the animal. The one thing she would never forget was how the rabbit's legs had kicked and clawed futilely against his hands and face, opening small wounds that healed within seconds. She remembered Martin's face buried in the rabbit's wound, sucking loudly, how the kicks had slowed and slowed, then finally stopped altogether, as Martin drank every drop of blood, leaving but a husk of bone and fur.

She had stood marble-still while her uncle fed. When he had finished, he sighed deeply then all at once seemed to sense her presence and raised his head from the rabbit's corpse, facing her full-on. She had watched in horror and fascination as the blood had run from his fanged mouth and down his chin to drip, drip, on the little furred body he still gripped tightly in his hands. Then she had looked into his glowing red eyes, saw the unsatiated hunger still there and ran full speed back to the house.

She had never told her mother about that episode. The next day, the family had taken their harvest to sell at the county fair. Her father, insisting that the whole family needed a break after a successful growing season, even took her mother's elderly parents, Iris's grandparents, who also lived with them and helped with their life on the farm. Her grandparents rarely left the farm except to attend the occasional church service. Their whole lives were wrapped around their son, Martin, their daughter Iris's mother, and their grandchildren.

Normally, a trip to the county fair would be too expensive for the whole family to attend, and they would have gratefully stayed behind to keep an eye on the smaller children. For the first time, they took both farm trucks and her grandfather's sedan, loaded with children and women, for a grand family outing to the fair. It was going to be quite the adventure and the excitement amongst all was palpable!

Returning to the farm late that night, they found the house had burned to the ground. Martin had been inside. The charred remains of the main timbers had collapsed through the ceiling of his root cellar, and the smoke from them still drifted on the late-night air as the family, all except their father, stared in disbelief.

The next morning, their farming community, and her father's brothers all arrived to give support and help them rebuild their home. If the family ever mentioned Uncle Martin again, they did so out of earshot of Iris or the other children. From that day forward, her mother and father, kept separate bedrooms and, as Iris would learn later in life, separate company.

In 1944, when Dolly, her youngest sister, and the baby of her siblings started transforming, there had been no one in the family locally who was "afflicted". Her parents and grandparents were dead, and Iris herself, through her flamboyant nature and lush beauty, had married very well by capturing the attention of the older Francisque, and had moved to Kansas City for a life of adventure.

Dolly, who was living with her mother-in-law on a distant small farm, had a husband who was fighting the Second World War on the European front, two small children, and as such, had no one to learn from. No one who may have remembered what the signs were. As her siblings had grown up and moved away, there was no one left who might have remembered Uncle Martin.

Dolly had passed out, much like Leila had, by being unprepared for the sunlight. She had been rushed to the hospital with a high fever and was unresponsive; where unguided by anyone, an unknowing, inexperienced doctor had performed an unnecessary appendectomy, triggering a hemorrhage that the doctor was unable to conquer before it took its final toll on Dolly's life. Being in the middle of the change, she had been vulnerable. The loss of blood was too much for her unnourished body to manage. Unreasonably, Iris had never gotten over feeling guilty about her sister's death. She had always felt if she hadn't been so eager to escape the small farming community that had been their home, she may have been able to have done something. At least something to protect her baby sister.

Iris couldn't let Dolly's fate befall Leila. Her Leila. The child of her soul, if not her body.

She would need to take drastic steps to make her niece understand what was happening to her, but first she needed to get her out of that hospital so she could speak with her.

The Beginning

CHAPTER THREE

D r. Dene Lambert followed Dr. Grant into her office, unable to believe that she had proclaimed that nothing was abnormal with Leila Sutton's MRI test. "What exactly are you saying, Kathleen?"

"What do you mean, Dene?" She calmly questioned in return as she sat behind her desk.

"What I mean is that I watched that test being performed. That MRI was not normal." Dr. Lambert stated as he stood looking down on her in irritation, his hands on his hips.

"The Sutton MRI was absolutely normal." Dr. Grant said, as if remembering her grocery list. "The results are absolutely normal." She repeated.

"You yourself saw how we couldn't wake up the patient after the test!" Dene exclaimed.

"Dr. Lambert, the patient's MRI was normal." She said, as if stating it again would make it true.

"What about narcolepsy?" Dene asked her.

"What about narcolepsy?" Dr. Grant queried in return. "The MRI that we conducted excluded those rare causes of symptomatic narcolepsy. There were no structural abnormalities of the brain stem, nor various abnormalities that would correspond to any type of underlying cause of narcolepsy. Her MRI was normal." Dr. Grant said calmly shuffling through some papers on her desk.

"Kathleen, people are not just unresponsive for no reason!" Dene Lambert started again.

"Dene, you are brilliant, but you are not the radiologist on staff here. I am. Mrs. Sutton's MRI was completely normal. Have you thought it could be another issue?"

"Such as?" He inquired testily.

"Such as a mental cause? Depression, anxiety, insomnia, or other psychologic/psychiatric disorder? How about obstructive sleep apnea? Or a genetic issue?" She responded to his question with her own.

"Oh, please! You are right, I am not a radiologist. But her episode, her scans, and her reaction to the MRI machine itself, was not normal!" He stopped suddenly, as an idea came to him. Abruptly he turned on his heel and left her office.

Dr. Kathleen Grant wasn't surprised at his reaction. He was passionate about his patients and dogged in pursuit of diagnosis. Picking up some more papers on her desk, she shuffled through them absently. "The Sutton MRI was absolutely normal." She whispered and began to do her paperwork.

Dr. Lambert headed for the fourth floor. He wanted to check in with Mrs. Sutton. Besides, he realized, he still had her wedding ring and needed to return it to her. He had to admit, so far, she was the most interesting case he had come across in this little Podunk military town. When he had agreed to do a two-year stint in this small hospital to repay the government for his medical student loans, he never realized how truly boring it would be here. He had been thinking of Florida beaches, not Georgia swamp, when he agreed to this location over the other two backwater towns that they had offered him.

There was little to do, except drink, and everything that they had in the restaurants here was fried! No one understood the importance of consuming organic vegetables and eating a healthy diet. That had given him the idea of doing a study on the blood of the local Georgian. He was sure that by studying their blood and atrocious diet, he would find a correlation to any number of blood-born cancers. Which, when this stint in hell was over, was what he really wanted to focus on. His goal was to be a head researcher for a large pharmaceutical company and be the one who ultimately finds the cure! He was a genius in the lab and knew he was destined for great things in this life! Probably a Nobel! If only his parents hadn't died, he wouldn't have had to take out all those student loans to finish his schooling and provide his living expenses while in school! At least it was for a short time, and he figured he might as well take advantage of his environment to study the natives.

After almost a year, the case of Leila Sutton just fell into his lap. He summarized the Sutton case in his mind, thinking hard about the details. Her husband brings her unconscious into the emergency room, where they fail to rouse her using all means possible. After more than 6 hours, she comes to on her own. There are no injuries, no apparent physical cause, to have put her in such a state to begin with. Blood tests are all *normal*.

At 34, he might be physically young, but he also had a head start on most in the field of medicine. Considered a genius, he graduated high school at fifteen, and immediately attended college to become a doctor of hematology. He knew his goal and was single-minded in his pursuit of it. He spent the next fifteen years honing his exceptional skills throughout school, residency, fellowship, and post-fellowship, becoming both a brilliant internist and a pathologist. He spent the next three years working to get out of his crushing student debt, barely surviving. That's when he made a deal with the government to wipe that debt clean.

In all his years as a researcher, he had never seen blood samples on a general level be so perfect as Leila Sutton's. Not only normal, but perfect for range. If the White Blood Cell count reference range is 4.8-10.8, Leila Sutton's was normal at exactly 7.8. If the hemoglobin reference range is 14.0-18.0, Leila Sutton's was normal at exactly 16.0. The same for Red Blood Cell, Hematocrit, MCV, MCH, Platelet count...all of it! All blood tests! Thinking that he had some idiot lab tech, he ran those tests again and additional tests, only to obtain the same results. In his experience, no one is range 'perfect'. Not before eating and after eating, not when it comes to blood, nor should they be. Combined with her strange bouts of unconsciousness, to him *that* ultimately was what made Leila Sutton's case abnormal, so remarkably interesting and, he was determined, to find the cause.

He stopped at the nurse's station to speak with Andrea Hobbs. He, Andrea, and the other nurse with her today, Macey Russell, usually played a game or two of tennis every week at the Osprey Cove Club, which was a few miles from the hospital. He smiled his sexy smile at them. He stood tall, up to his full 6'1" height. He knew he was extremely handsome, in good shape, and that women found him and his black-haired, blue-eyed looks to be both charming and sexy. He frequently used his gifts to get his way and knew that he could have either or both Andrea and Macey, if he so chose. But he wouldn't mix sex and his work with other employees at the hospital for anything. He was careful, he wasn't stupid, and he knew that could be a disaster for his future career. They both seemed to be genuinely nice, and he liked them very much, but he had no intention of settling down anytime soon and he felt they deserved someone who wanted what they did: marriage and kids.

That was *so* not him. But still, he wasn't above using his gifts to get his way.

"Nurse Hobbs, Nurse Russell. How is everything up here on the fourth today?" He asked smoothly.

"Very good today, Dr. Lambert." Macey Russell gushed at him with a slight blush as Andrea handed him two charts.

He looked them over. "Mr. Jones can be discharged today." He said, signing the chart. "Please make sure that his prescription is called down to the pharmacy for him." He glanced at Leila Sutton's chart. "Mrs. Sutton will be with us for another night. Were you able to take those samples as I asked?"

"Yes, doctor. I have them right here. I am about to send them to the lab," Andrea said, smiling at him.

"Don't bother, Andrea. Set them aside for the moment. I will run those tests myself and will take them with me this evening to my lab. Please leave a note for the evening shift so they know in case I don't return until their shift. I will pull an overnight for observation on Mrs. Sutton. Did she eat breakfast this morning?" He said, making a note in Leila's chart.

"No, doctor. She had coffee but wasn't hungry." Andrea told him.

"Hmmm." He said and made another note. "I will check in with her. I want you to make sure that she eats her lunch and dinner today, Andrea." He said, making several notes, and walked toward Leila's room.

"She's sleeping doctor." Andrea said. "Poor thing seems like she is exhausted."

"Sleeping again?" Dr. Lambert said with a frown. "It doesn't say here in her chart that she had trouble sleeping, or a restless night."

"She didn't as far as I know," Andrea replied calmly. "She was sleeping soundly when I woke her up this morning at 7:00 a.m. to prepare for her MRI appointment. She said that she had an early night and slept well."

"Okay." Dr. Lambert said deep in thought, carrying Leila's chart to her room.

He opened the door almost silently. Though the blinds were drawn, the room wasn't totally black, the Georgia sunlight was strong enough to illuminate around the blinds, which lightened the room enough to see. He could see that she was sleeping on her side, facing away from the blinds. He walked to the end of the bed and replaced her chart in its holder.

"Hello, Dr. Lambert," came her voice softly, startling him. He was sure that she hadn't opened her eyes to look at him.

"Hello, Mrs. Sutton," he said just as softly, getting his rolling stool and rolling it over to her bedside. "I am sorry for waking you."

She opened her eyes to look at him, and in the half-light of the room they were a light teal.

He looked at her, transfixed by those eyes. "I came to return your ring," He said, smiling at her, pulling her wedding rings from his breast pocket.

She took them from his hand and put them back on. "Thank you." She said simply. "So, did you and Dr. Grant come up with what is wrong with me?"

He was forthright with her. "Dr. Grant wants us to look at your anxiety levels. Do you have a reason to be anxious or depressed?"

"So, *you* think it might be mental?" She countered, not answering his question.

Her gaze was boring into him with those hypnotic eyes.

"No. I don't." He said simply, honestly. "I think that there is a medical cause, a physical cause, for what is happening to you. I just don't know what that is yet," He said, shocking himself; he couldn't remember a time when he had ever admitted to a patient that he didn't know something. "I will not rest until I know what is occurring here, Mrs. Sutton." He told her resolutely.

"Good." She told him.

"I am going to be unavailable for a few hours today, but I will be back this evening to look in on you. I will run your labs personally, and will stay tonight to keep you under observation." He tried to reassure her; to tell her he would find out what was wrong with her.

"That nurse that was here last night was horrible, you know." She said to him with a yawn and closed her eyes; effectively releasing him from captivity.

"We will see what we can do about that." He said with a smile. "Mrs. Sutton?"

"Mmmmm?"

"Make sure you eat your lunch and dinner. Would you do that for me?" He said coaxingly.

"Okay." She said softly and dozed back off.

He quietly exited her room and finished his rounds on the fourth floor, deep in thought and on autopilot. The floor was sparsely populated with no critical patients, making it a swift sweep.

Stopping back at the nurse's station. He said to Andrea, "Nurse, I will be back this evening to check in and pickup Mrs. Sutton's samples. Dr. Johnson is working on three, so if there are any emergencies, please page him. Though everything looks well, and it probably won't be necessary."

"Yes, doctor." Andrea said, making a note.

"You and Macey have a good shift." He told them, flashing his sexy smile.

Their smiles in return were blinding.

He headed to his large personal office/lab space on the fifth floor. It housed a small but complete lab, private bathroom, and shower, as well as a separate private office with plenty of space for his personal medical tomes, a large desk, computer, and an amazingly comfortable sofa and chair arrangement. The sofa he had used several times in the last year, as he had a habit of researching or running lab work late into the night. This space was the one thing that he had requested from the hospital, and they were so pleased to have someone with his experience and education on staff they jumped at the chance to fulfill that request.

He removed his white lab coat, hung it up and laid down on the sofa to think about the strange case of Leila Sutton, his 'blood-perfect' patient who couldn't seem to stay awake. He himself soon dozed off.

A short while later, he was awakened by a soft pair of full lips around his flaccid penis.

He opened his eyes to watch her bleach-blonde head of curls bob up and down, using the suction of her mouth to pull him erect. He grabbed her by the hair and thrust up, in and out of those plumped lips, willing to spill himself into her mouth, if that was the way she wanted it.

She shook him off, to quickly straddle his erect cock, her jean mini-skirt hiked up around her waist, her platform, silver, high-heeled sandals looking deliciously vulgar on each side of his legs.

He watched with a detached interest as she gripped him with expertise and worked her shaved pussy up and down his length, moaning her pleasure softly, the tops of her large tits almost bursting from her black lace push-up bra she was wearing under her scarlet tank top.

As she rode him, she threw her head back, whispering "yes, yes, yes" to him as he responded to her by thrusting his hips ever so slightly. Her act was almost perfect.

He reached up and pulled the bra down roughly, stretching the top of her tank top from her shoulders, freeing her tits to fall, overflowing into his hands. He gripped them tightly, not tight enough to be painful, but tighter than a lover would.

After all, as far as he was concerned, he wasn't her lover.

Bobby Rebekah Patterson, 34, local bartender, wasn't lover material. Extremely attractive and sexy in a trailer trash kind of way, she clearly thought she was lover material, and that he was her meal ticket.

He knew better.

As far as he was concerned, her conversation was vapid, her mind ignorant, and her singular pursuit of him using her body, foolish; but he sure did like to fuck her. There, she clearly excelled. But he knew her better than she knew herself. The more he held back, the more she threw herself at him; and as such, he was never undersexed.

He could tell from her pussy gripping him she was close but trying to hold back. She had been working on this seduction game with him for six months now. She wanted a response from him. Something that told her she had some sort of control over him, that he couldn't get enough of her, her body, her pussy. A sound, a noise, a shout.

He always refused to give her one. To do so would give her too much satisfaction. He had too much sense to let her have the upper hand with him.

He also sensed that she could become unruly if she thought she controlled him.

But his cock was now rock hard, and he was close himself. Time to take control of this situation.

Giving her left breast a tight squeeze with his right hand, he distracted her small thrusts slightly and put his fingers in his mouth, gathering saliva, and reached between them to stroke her clitoris, as if it was a small penis.

Her eyes flew open, and she made a soft keening noise as she involuntarily orgasmed around his cock, fighting it the whole time.

He stiffened his jaw, clenching his teeth, lips closed, holding back for all he was worth, still stroking her clitoris. He reached up, grabbing her by the shoulder, as her hips faltered, pushing her pulsating pussy hard down on him, whispering to her, "Don't you get lazy, Bobby! You move that ass and make me cum!" He ordered.

She did as she was told, sliding up and down, as he continued to control her orgasm, until finally he felt her muscles slowly loosen. Then and only then did he let go of his own control and, silently breathing through his nose, he closed his eyes and shot his cum deep inside of her.

She collapsed on top of him, face in the crook of his neck, spent.

"I hope you locked the door," he said calmly, coldly, his cock still hard and buried in her.

She leaned up and looked at him in wonder with her brown eyes. "Yes, both doors."

"Good." He patted her hip, indicating that she should get off him. She complied. "So, to what do I owe this pleasure?" He said calmly standing up and walking into the bathroom.

"Well, I expected that you would come by for lunch." She explained in her soft southern Georgia girl twang, looking lusciously disheveled as she pulled her skirt down, pulled her bra over her ample bosom, and retrieved her thong panties from the floor.

He suspected that her accent, like much about her, was completely contrived.

"I am working today." He said from the bathroom sink, washing her from him with a wet, soapy washcloth and putting himself to rights.

"You didn't look like you was workin'." She pouted as he came out of the bathroom. Patting her bleached curls into place. "Since when don't you get a lunch break?"

"I get a lunch break. But I am working all night, as I have a patient that needs observation, so I was catching up on some sleep."

"Well, I brought you a sliced turkey sandwich." She said with a wink. "Just like you like. Lettuce, tomato, lite mayo. Toasted, not grilled. Steamed veggies instead of fries." She beamed at him.

"Thank you. What do I owe you?" He said with his sexy smile.

"Well, I think you already paid me, sugar." She said with a giggle.

"Mrs. Sutton, wake up." Leila heard the nurse's voice. Her eyes fluttered open. Andrea had turned on her room light. Leila struggled to comply, using the remote to raise her bed to a sitting position. Andrea helped her adjust the pillows to support her back. "Dr. Lambert has given specific instructions to make sure that you eat both your lunch and dinner." She told her.

"Yes." Leila said sleepily.

Andrea rolled her lunch tray over to her.

Leila looked at it with interest, if not appetite. A cup of what looked like Garden Vegetable soup, a baked Fish Sandwich, the typical sugar-free Strawberry Jello, and what looked to be Iced Tea. She reached out to taste it. Unsweetened. *Yuck,* she thought, grimacing, as she searched the tray for some sugar or sweetener. Unable to find any, she looked at Andrea.

"Sorry. I will see if I can get you some sweetener." She smiled.

"The blue packets, if you can find it, please. It's way better than the pink stuff!" Leila returned her smile gratefully.

"I agree." Andrea said. "You eat up while it's warm, and then I will come back, and we will take some notes for Dr. Lambert. How you feel now, and how you feel after lunch. How's that sound?"

"Good," Leila said as Andrea left the room.

She looked at the tray. Though it looked and smelled good, she had absolutely no appetite. She sighed, and using the butter knife, proceeded to cut the fish sandwich in half. Taking a small bite, she started to chew slowly, reaching for her book to read while she ate. Though it looked like she was reading the words on the page, her mind was going a hundred miles per minute.

"I am not sure that I believe Dr. Lambert when he says he is sure that it is a physical condition and not mental. After everything I experienced last night, hearing things, seeing dead Aunt Iris hanging from the side of the building, having a recurring dream of some strange guy...could I really be having a breakdown? At least I didn't see my dream guy after the MRI test. That's got to be good." She thought. "Though I must admit, I kind of missed him." She blushed, thinking of the way she had surrendered herself to him. It was a heck of a time to ask for his name *after* a sexual encounter with him. "Nichola. What a strange name. How the hell am I coming up with this stuff?"

She took another small bite of the sandwich, eyes totally unfocused on the page, absorbed in her own thoughts.

"Why are you still in bed?" Michael said irritably from the doorway.

She looked up from the book, thinking, "I do not feel like putting up with your crap right now." She answered instead, "The doctor is keeping me another night for observation."

"Why? What happened with the MRI? What did it say?" He asked, coming to sit in the chair for visitors next to her bed.

"Nothing. But they kind of freaked out this morning because they couldn't get me to wake up for a few minutes after it was over." She took another small bite of sandwich. "They took another blood test after."

"This is crap. If they can't find anything wrong with you, they should let you go home." He grumped. "They just want to charge the military another night to stay in the hospital! I want to talk to that doctor!" Michael ranted.

"I don't think so, Michael. Dr. Lambert went home for a little while but is coming back to stay overnight for observation. He is running some more tests. I have already told him I am staying one more night and that's it." Leila told him firmly.

"You didn't think to discuss this with me?" He looked at her, offended.

"Well, you weren't here to take charge, were you? So, after consultation with *my* doctor, I decided." She snapped at him.

"You know I have to deal with the kids!" He started.

She cut him off. "And now we come to the real issue! You must do something for your own children! I manage everything for the kids, by myself, all the time. If I can do it, you can do it for a couple of nights while the doctor tries to figure out what the hell is wrong!"

She could feel herself getting angrier by the second. She rarely spoke back, not wanting it to be a constant battle zone, but she had just had it with him.

"Fine." He snapped. "I will be back to talk to the doctor tonight. I have to go back to work!" He got up and stomped from the room in a huff.

Andrea came in as Leila was pushing her tray away, basically uneaten. She placed two blue packets of sweetener on the tray.

"Mrs. Sutton, are you okay?" She asked softly as she noticed her crestfallen look. "I saw that Mr. Sutton left abruptly."

"Yeah, I am okay. He's just mad because I have to stay another night. He'll be back tonight to speak to the doctor."

"People react differently when their spouse is sick. Their reactions can be based on many things, fear usually being the driving factor," Andrea explained softly, trying to comfort her.

"I am sure that you are right." Leila responded, refraining from telling her that her husband was just a self-centered prick too used to being catered to.

"I know that you probably don't feel like it, but you have to eat a little more than this. We want to get you strong right?" Andrea said with a soft smile.

"Okay," Leila replied, sighing, pulling the rolling tray back to her.

Michael sat in his truck in the hospital parking lot, gripping the steering wheel hard. His emotions roiled through him; anger at his own helplessness, fury at Leila's defiance and smart mouth, outrage that she would question his dedication to his kids, fear that something could seriously be wrong, worry that his career would be screwed if he couldn't perform his job well.

He hated to depend on other people, and to him, asking for help was a sign of weakness.

"Fuck it!" He blurted harshly to himself.

He would call Ellen from the office to see if she could take the boys for the evening so he could be there when the doctor came back. He wanted to speak to him personally, and he needed to get his wife home where she belonged.

He had things he needed to get done.

Leila finished eating as much as she could. No appetite and Michael's hissy fit not helping anything, just making the food that she was able to eat sit in her stomach like a rock.

Andrea came back, grabbed her chart from the end of the bed, and sat down next to her. She asked her an array of questions, which Leila answered to the best of her ability.

"Do you do this often?" Leila asked her. At Andrea's inquiring look, she clarified. "Ask questions and take notes for the doctor?"

"Yes, quite often, actually. I will tell you a secret," she said with a smile. "Every time a nurse asks you, 'how are you feeling today', they will make a note for the doctor if anything is out of the ordinary. In your case, Dr. Lambert has left me a list of things that he would like to know when he checks back in this evening." Leila looked at her doubtfully as she talked to her. "He really is brilliant, you know. Dr. Lambert. This hospital is so lucky to have gotten him, even if it probably is only for a short time." Andrea said, to reassure Leila.

"Why do you say that? Only for a short time?" Leila asked.

"Well, I didn't tell you this," Andrea said, suddenly all gossipy, "but...he was sent here by the government to help with this hospital. Being such a small area, with not a lot to do, we have a problem attracting and keeping good physicians. It's not like New York, or Chicago, or some other big city, so the well-educated ones never want to move here to little Nowhere, Georgia where the pay's not that great, and there are few attractions.

With the military here, but no military hospital close to the submarine base, the government has a vested interest in retaining good physicians in the area." She continued making some notes in Leila's chart. "So occasionally we will get a doctor in here to do a certain amount of time on staff in exchange for a forgiveness of all or some of their student loan debt. It is some doctor program that the government has. It is great for the hospital, great for the doctor, and if we are lucky, they will love the area and settle down to stay.

Dr. Grant from this morning is one of those. She got here as soon as the hospital opened, and lucky for us, has no plans to leave. She even bought a house over in Osprey Cove a few months ago, so it looks like she is staying for the long haul, and that is good for the community." Andrea said, smiling brightly.

"That's great!" Leila smiled. "Are you from here?" She asked, feeling that it was relaxing to talk to someone.

"Yes, ma'am. Born and bred in St. Mary's! My Daddy owns the building that the Magic Mart is in over on Osborne, and my mama's a real estate agent."

"Oh, I know exactly where the Magic Mart is," Leila told her.

"He's owned it forever!" Andrea said with a smile.

"So, am I allowed to go back to sleep? Or should I try to keep myself awake?" Leila said tiredly.

Andrea checked the chart. "You can rest all you want."

"Great, I think I am going to relax a little and maybe nap some more."

Dr. Lambert arrived at the nurse's desk just as Andrea returned.

"So, how is Mrs. Sutton?" He inquired, gathering up the tray of blood vials from the last blood draw, marked Sutton/Dr. Lambert and making sure that they were all accounted for.

He had decided after his visit from Bobby Rebekah that his nap was shot, and he might as well get started on the blood work.

"I was able to coax her to eat most of her lunch, but she is still tired. A little depressed as well." Dr. Lambert glanced up to pay more attention as Andrea explained, "Mr. Sutton stopped by and was not happy that she was staying overnight again. He took it out on her, I think." Andrea said with a sad shake of her head.

"I will never understand why some men are not interested in the health of their wives." He said in return. "Pulling them out of an observational environment without proper diagnosis after an episode like Mrs. Sutton's is tantamount to asking for it to occur again. In any case, I am going to start on these tests, and see if we can figure out the problem for her. Please page Dr. Johnson if necessary, but I will be in my lab upstairs if any genuine emergency occurs." He said, heading toward the elevator bank with the tray of vials in his hands.

"Yes, doctor." Andrea smiled, thinking that he was the most dedicated doctor ever.

"Oh, no," Leila whispered to herself as she found herself in the familiar room, "and I was so proud of myself for getting past this dream, too."

She walked over and sat on the sofa, put her face in her hands, her elbows on her knees and stayed that way for several minutes, just trying to quietly calm her mind. Just when she thought she might be alone in this dream; she felt the cushion dip as someone sat down next to her. She glanced up to make sure that it was him; after all, you never could tell who you would dream about.

He looked at her with worried eyes. "You are distressed?"

"Yeah." She nodded her head.

"Why?"

"Because my life sucks? Because my marriage sucks? Because I feel like I am spiraling out of control, and I can't stop it? Take your pick." She whispered miserably.

"You are still in the hospital." He stated. When she nodded her head, he asked, "Why?"

"The test from this morning was normal." She told him.

"This is good!" He exclaimed, and she shook her head 'no' at him. "This is not good?" He asked, bewildered. "How is this not good? A normal test should have secured your release."

"You would definitely think that, right? Well, it seems I had some sort of episode, and they couldn't get me to wake up for several minutes after the test had concluded. So, we are back to step one: my medical mystery disease." She said sadly. "So, now I have to spend another night in the hospital for more tests and observation."

"More tests are not good." He said adamantly.

As she looked at him doubtfully, he took her by the shoulders and pitched his voice melodiously, saying firmly, "There is nothing wrong with you!"

"You keep telling me that, and yet, here I am still in the hospital. I think I am in denial. I am losing my mind and am too afraid of the repercussions to just own up to the fact that I am hearing things and seeing things. I should just tell Dr. Lambert. But, if I do, Michael will send my children away to live with his parents, which would be disastrous for the kids. He will have me committed and I will end up in a psychiatric hospital. I will never see my boys again." She whispered to him, fearfully.

"That scenario would definitely complicate this situation. But fortunately, it doesn't quite work that way." He said with authority. Then glanced at her as she looked at him curiously. "We don't have time for a discussion on that subject. Just believe me when I tell you I know what I am speaking about. You should know that we realize now that you are totally unprepared for what's happening to you." He began, but she cut him off.

"We?"

"Your Aunt and me. I will send her to you again tonight. You must speak with her. She will set things right for you. She will explain everything." He said, looking deeply into her eyes, his voice pitched in that melody that she found so fascinating. "We must get you out of that hospital before..." he stopped as she was shaking her head affirmatively with a look of growing anger in her eyes.

"That's right. You are the part of my mind that sent my dead aunt to me! Thanks so much for sending that delusion! The dead aunt hanging off the outer wall of the hospital. The dead aunt with the clawed hands. If I had screamed my bloody head off, I would be in a fucking straight jacket now! Lucky for you," she paused. "Lucky for me? Whatever! I know that my dead Aunt Iris would never hurt me, no matter what form of delusion she comes to me in. She loved me, the old battle-axe. More so than anybody. But, truly, thanks, but no thanks! Don't do me anymore favors!" Leila said, sitting up straighter, crossing her arms in irritation, and turning away from him to stare into the fire.

"Your Aunt isn't dead." He stated flatly, looking at her angry profile.

"Yeah, whatever." She said, staring straight ahead. "I believe they had a funeral for her!"

"Can you not tell that I am not lying to you, i psychí mou? I couldn't lie to you if I wanted to." He said in frustration, as if he wished that weren't the case.

She continued to stare straight ahead without responding.

He slid over next to her and wrapped an arm around her stiff, unyielding, crossed-armed shoulders.

She could feel the heat from his body warming her; his scent, calming her, comforting her.

"Your Aunt once accused me of not remembering what it was like to change. I let her think what she wanted. But it is different between you and me, and if you let me, I will tell you a secret." He said softly, sadly, and she turned to look at him curiously as he had hoped she would. "I never forgot my change. No one ever does. It is a curse and a lesson. So, please..." here he paused, looking at her with sad amber eyes that reflected the glow of the fire, "please, let me help you. I want your memories to be sweeter than mine."

"Change?" She could feel his sincerity despite not understanding what he was talking about. She looked at him for several seconds stonily, and then she realized if she looked deep enough, she could see the reflection of the flames in his eyes. She felt herself relax, as if he willed her to do so.

"Do not be frightened, allaxiéra. There are those who love you. Keep your secrets from this doctor just a little longer. You will be free from this hospital, and soon I will be with you." He promised as he laid her back on the couch.

"I thought you said that you are here with me now?" She said to him, childlike, exhaustion taking over, as he covered her with a soft blanket.

"I am, and as much as I would like to join you right now, I have preparations to make, and you need to sleep and gain your strength." He said softly stroking the side of her face, giving her a sense of déjà vu, as she slowly closed her eyes.

She felt his lips softly kiss hers as she fell asleep.

Dr. Dene Lambert looked through the microscope, lifted his eyes, a look of deep thought crossing his handsome features. Then he turned his eyes back to the ocular lens, adjusting the coarse and fine adjustments as needed. His new light microscope was the highest possible for a lab outside a university setting and he could see samples at 400X magnification.

He didn't believe what he was seeing.

It was as if Leila Sutton's blood cells were being attacked and altered, but not destroyed, by what looked like an unidentified enzyme. The enzyme didn't look like it was killing the cells, but instead modifying them, changing composition as he watched. He knew at 400X it was impossible to be conclusive. But if it were conclusive, a new type of enzyme being produced in her body? It would have to be some sort of genetic mutation.

His hypothesis, though yet untested, was that enzyme deficiency would indicate a genetic defect, and genetic defects could cause blood-born cancers. This, on the other hand, looked to be like a production of a whole new enzyme by her body, which in turn was attacking and *changing,* or *metamorphosizing* the cells of her blood.

To his way of thinking, this type of enzyme production would show either an autosomal recessive, or X-linked recessive genetic defect. Something that would have been passed down through her family, possibly over generations.

This could be the cause of her symptoms. He needed to get these samples sent up to the Biomedical Research Center in Atlanta to a former colleague for an analysis through their electron microscope, to see if he was really seeing what he was seeing.

His icy blue eyes sparkled with discovery; this could send his career skyrocketing!

Leila slept until Andrea awakened her for dinner. It was on the lighter side, for which Leila (and her waistline) was grateful: Herbed Chicken Breast with Broccoli and Squash Medley, the normal Strawberry Jello, and Unsweetened Iced Tea.

Andrea had been kind enough to bring her two packets of blue sweetener, which Leila was thankful for. Her appetite was better, and so was her mood after her sleep. She was once again feeling better, stronger. It seemed the excessive sleep was at least helping something.

After she ate, Andrea questioned her, recording her answers as she had before after her lunch. Then it was time for Andrea to go. She had to do a turnover with East-Side, the unpleasant night nurse.

Though not verbalized, she picked up the thought that Andrea to felt that East-Side was a substandard nurse and had no business being around any of what Andrea considered 'her' patients.

Leila figured that Andrea and West-Side probably had a lot in common.

It was almost 7:30 pm. She had yet to see either Michael or Dr. Lambert. She wasn't that surprised by Michael. He might not even show up. He often had passive-aggressive tendencies, especially where she was concerned. But she was surprised that she hadn't seen Dr. Lambert yet, at least for a check-in, and wondered if he had found something in her latest blood tests.

With nothing but her thoughts to keep her company, she wondered if she could be dying? Maybe this was just the beginning of something profoundly serious? What could she do? What would happen to her boys if she were to leave them to the world so young? Who would be there to guide them?

Michael? Doubtful. With his schedule, how would he? He would probably send the boys to be raised by his parents, both of whom were several years younger than her own parents.

That would be disastrous.

Though she loved Michael's mother dearly, his father had two emotions, angry and angrier. In fact, the only person in their family, including Michael, that he didn't bully outright was Leila herself; and she felt that was only because she absolutely would not allow him to. Much to the delight of both her mother- and sister-in-law.

They absolutely loved it when she didn't take his garbage. Still, he was passive aggressive with her, much like his son. While she was thinking about it, Michael's whole family was passive aggressive to varying degrees.

There was absolutely a reason why Michael was the way he was. He had grown up that way. According to his sister, Michael had never wanted to grow up to be like their dad. But whether or not he realized it, he was losing that battle, and Leila was determined that her kids would not grow up to be the same way.

If Leila had known more about Michael's family and the way he had been raised before she had married him, she was not sure that she would have gone through with it, pregnancy or not.

Leila knew she loved Michael. She did. There was not a doubt about that for her. But he frequently made life much more difficult than it had to be with his cold and hot moods and his unreasonableness; where he constantly kept her guessing about what would or wouldn't make him happy.

Leila wanted her children to have a stable life; stable home, stable income, two parents who were together in one household; and she provided that for them by staying with their father, but she knew in her heart that she wouldn't stay with Michael if he was in their lives full-time; not like he was now.

It only worked for now because he wasn't around a lot. She was determined that she wouldn't raise Michael 'clones'. She wanted her sons to be better men than their father was now.

With Michael being gone so much of the time, that was what she did. She provided the stability and love that they needed and she would make sure that they grew up polite, kind, and caring; not angry and bitter.

If she were seriously sick, she would fight and do anything to stay and raise them for as long as possible, until her body gave out.

They were hers! She would die protecting them.

At 7:45 exactly, Michael arrived and sat down in the chair without a greeting; coldly giving her a look.

She thought, *This pouting is going to stop now!* She said instead, "Who has the kids?"

"Ellen." He answered after hesitating just long enough to let her know he didn't really have to answer her but was choosing to do so. "I can't stay long. Have you seen that doctor yet?" He asked coldly.

"No. But I expect him any time. Nurse Andrea said that he would pop in after the second shift started. It started at seven o'clock." She said just as coldly.

He gave her a dirty look at her tone, and they both sat in silence.

A few minutes later, Dr. Lambert arrived, took one assessing look at the situation, and pulled his wheeled stool over to her side of the bed to sit with her. He took her hand and looked at her IV injection site, which seemed to be healing better, but was still unusually bruised. He shook his head. "I have found something with your blood work, Mrs. Sutton." He said calmly.

"What is it?" Michael said to him sharply.

"I believe that Mrs. Sutton's body is producing an additional enzyme caused by a genetic mutation." Dr. Lambert looked at him hard for his interruption.

Leila looked at his ice blue-eyes, stricken, and gripped his hand hard.

"Nothing to worry about too much at this point," he looked at her and patted her hand in a reassuring manner, "as it's not definitive, at least with the equipment that I have here at this hospital. It could simply be a virus that is hard to identify and may pass in due course." He tried to reassure her. She could tell that he didn't really think that. "I will send your samples to Atlanta for additional testing and analysis. But I have some questions for you about your family history."

She nodded and stole a look at Michael, who was sitting very still, listening intently.

"Okay." she said, still gripping his hand.

"Good." He said with his smile. "So, tell me. Do you remember this type of illness happening to any member of your family? Either your mother's or your father's side? Where they would faint, pass-out or lose consciousness at any time?"

"No." she whispered.

"How about any premature deaths? Before the age of 50, maybe from unknown causes?"

"My grandmother died when my dad was three years old. But..." She stopped, frozen in shock, as she noticed movement over the doctor's shoulder, and she saw who was standing in the doorway.

Aunt Iris

CHAPTER TWO

"**B**UT THAT WAS DUE to an idiot of a doctor doing a hatchet job of an appendectomy." Came a sultry voice from the doorway. Dr. Lambert looked over his shoulder, just in time to hear and see the most luscious, beautiful woman he had ever beheld walk through Leila Sutton's door.

She was of an indeterminate age, and only his expertise in women told him she was in her early forties. But he could be wrong in either direction. Maybe 5'7", her hourglass shape was truly exquisite, wrapped in a curve hugging red and gold patterned dress, classy, not too low cut with just a hint of cleavage, and cut just above the knee; her form pumped high with red four-inch stiletto heels, all of which looked stunning against her skin, which was a creamy olive with a warm, golden undertone. Her black hair was piled in a riot of curls on top of her head, and her black eyes were lined like a queen, and snapped with intelligence and something more. A bit of danger? Dr. Lambert could feel himself grow hard under her piercing regard; he self-consciously crossed his legs and realized that she had absolutely fascinated him.

"Baby?" The woman said, looking at Mrs. Sutton.

So much love was in that one word it hurt.

"Oh, Aunt Iris, you're really here!" Leila said and wept softly, putting her hand over her mouth, clearly distressed.

Dene Lambert watched the woman come around the opposite side of the bed, totally ignoring Mr. Sutton, who stood in stunned confusion as she sat down on the edge of the bed gently embracing her niece. She gave an unreadable look to him, placing fault for Leila's distress on his shoulders as she cradled her against her body.

"No, doctor. This has never happened to anyone on either side of Leila's family before." Her voice was like a melody he could listen to for hours.

"Why don't I come and give you some more...details," and that one word held such promise it stopped his breath for a heartbeat, "in your office on our family history in a few hours. That way, my niece and I can catch up a little bit." She gave him a soft, predatory smile. "I have already explained to that horrid creature at the front desk down the hall that I and my driver, will attend Leila this evening. That's all right with you, isn't it?" She asked sweetly.

"Yes, oh absolutely, that would be good," he felt himself stammer just like a schoolboy. He stood up, still half hard. His partial erection was thankfully hidden by his long lab coat. "I will speak with the nurse's desk and make sure you have no further trouble." He noticed for the first time a large, powerfully built man in a nondescript beige suit and brown tie unselfconsciously holding what looked to be a red overcoat and a clutch purse that matched those red stilettos perfectly. He hoped he wasn't ogling someone's wife so openly, "My office and lab are on the fifth floor, Room N5-16, Mrs. uh..."

"Ms., honey." She looked at him with a knowing smile on her full, dark red lips. "Ms. Iris Gauche. I will join you in a few hours." She finished and then ignored him completely to give all her love and attention to her niece. He left in a daze and headed in the direction of the nurse's station.

Michael stood looking down at the pair, as his still sobbing wife wrapped her arms around this stranger, who she claimed as an aunt. He had never heard of an Aunt Iris before. He approached the large man who was with her and extended his hand. "Michael Sutton," he said.

He looked up as his hand was engulfed and shook firmly, but not crushingly so. *This guy has got to be at least six-four,* he thought, impressed, *and 220 pounds of solid muscle!* He took in his close-cropped light brown hair, a nose that had obviously been broken a few times, swarthy weathered skin like some of the old sailors that he knew, and hazel eyes. He had to be close to fifty or a little older. "This guy could be scary, I bet."

"Mansuetus Smythe," the other man said, pronouncing his name in a deep bass voice, Man-sue-A-toos Sm-eye-tha.

"That's an unusual name, Mr. Smythe." Michael said, making conversation, trying to place his accent. His English was perfect, but he would bet that he was foreign. "Where are you from?"

Mansuetus then gave him that very scary smile, showing squared, white teeth. "Everywhere."

"Now don't you mind Mansuetus, Michael." He heard a feminine drawl. He turned around and 'Aunt Iris' was standing directly behind him. He thought, how the hell did she sneak up on me in those damn heels? "He just hates attention!" Aunt Iris continued. "Besides, he is only here to squire me around your little burg until his boss shows up. Give your Aunt Iris a hug!" She said, hugging him to her and Michael's whole body stiffened.

He hated hugs! Especially from strangers!

He stepped back out of her embrace. "So, did Leila call you?"

"Why no, honey. Her Daddy called me and since I was closest, well, here I am!" She said with a smile, hands in the air, mimicking the look of a magician's assistant. Michael turned to look at Leila in accusation.

"I must have forgotten to tell you I called Dad yesterday while you were gone." Leila said looking guiltily, lying for all that she was worth.

"Yeah, no problem. I probably should have called your parents myself; it's just been crazy." Michael said, accepting her answer. After all, they both knew that there was no love lost between them. Michael still hadn't figured out that her parents would like him better if he'd been on his best behavior on the few occasions that they had met him. Frankly, he really didn't care. He intentionally acted like a total asshole to her whenever they visited, knowing that Leila would be reluctant to defend herself and fight with him while they were around. It irritated her mother to no end, because it was so obvious that he was acting this way on purpose, and she constantly bitched about him to Leila whenever he was out of earshot, which had placed Leila squarely in the middle. It had put a strain on her relationship with her parents, which was fine with him, because they all needed to know who was in charge of his house.

"So, where do you live, Iris?" Michael asked politely, a little leery of Mansuetus, who now stood behind him.

"Call me Aunt Iris, sweetie! Oh, I have several homes. I was in South Carolina when I found out what had happened and came as soon as I could." She smiled.

"So, do you need a place to stay?" Michael asked, again politely.

"Lord, no! I would never impose. Mansuetus and I have a guest suite over at the Spencer House Inn. That charming little bed-and-breakfast in downtown St. Marys." She smiled. "We will move when Dr. Tsoukalous arrives in a few days."

"Dr. Tsoukalous?" Michael inquired, a little confused. He kept losing his train of thought as she talked to him.

"My personal physician. Yes. He and I are related, in a way." She looked at Mansuetus.

"Distantly, through a marriage." Mansuetus smirked at her.

"Yes, well, we are cousins of a sort. I have asked him to come and check out our Leila. I want her to have the absolute best of care." She said, nodding at Michael. "When he has completed his current business, I believe he intends to take a house for us in the area close by."

"That's good!" Michael said sincerely to Iris, turning to Leila, who was surprised at his answer. "Babe, I got to go pick up the kids from Ellen and take them home. It's getting late. Do you want me to come pick you up tomorrow? Do you think that Dr. Lambert will let you come home?" All the sudden he was the solicitous husband.

"Don't you worry about that, honey." Aunt Iris said to him. "Dr. Lambert will let her come home tomorrow. I guarantee it." Aunt Iris said softly, in her melodious voice to Michael. "Mansuetus will take her to your house when the doctor releases her tomorrow. If you would be so kind as to drop off and pick up the children at your sitter? I am sure that he will have her all settled in by the time that you get off work."

"Sure, thanks, that's awfully nice of you," Michael said feeling overwhelmed by this take-charge aunt, but glad to leave Leila's care in someone else's hands.

"Well, you are welcome, sweetie." Aunt Iris said with a small smile.

"Michael, do I have a change of clothes?" Leila said.

"Yeah, I got them in the truck. I will go get them." He said relieved.

"I will come with you," Mansuetus said surprising Michael. "One trip. Let the ladies get reacquainted."

Michael nodded in response, stepped over, and gave Leila a quick kiss goodbye. "I can leave the back door unlocked for you, Leila. I didn't bring your purse, so you don't have your keys." She nodded to him, surprised that he was so accepting of all of this. Normally, he was such a control freak.

Mansuetus motioned for Michael to lead the way, shutting the door behind him as they left.

Aunt Iris quickly put her finger to her lips as Leila started to say something to her, listening intently.

"Aunt Iris, your alive!" Leila said in a whisper. "It's impossible! How can this be? And you are so young! You would have to be in your seventies by now." She said calculating in her head.

"Yes, I am alive, and I just turned seventy-five." Iris said softly and sat on the bed next to her.

"How?" Leila asked.

"Well, it's a long story," Iris replied as she poured Leila some ice water and handed it to her. "You may need this. It affects you too, so let's have a little heart-to-heart. Try not to be afraid."

"Aunt Iris, I am not afraid of you." Leila said looking at her aunt with affection.

"You've never had to be, honey! But it is a bit shocking. You see, I grew up knowing this, so it wasn't really a shock to me when it happened. What's shocking is that your dad didn't tell you when you came of age that this always was a distinct possibility." Iris said in irritation.

"Dad?" Leila asked.

"Yes. But that's for you to discuss with him." Iris said, inhaling deeply and exhaling a little breath of soft nervous laughter, "Now that I am here with you, I am not sure where to begin. I guess I should just come out and say it. I am a vampire." She waited for Leila to react.

Leila gave her an unreadable look, reached out, and touched her arm several times, the last time quite firmly. "Okay, you don't feel like a hallucination. But obviously, I am in the middle of some sort of breakdown." Leila said talking out loud to herself. "Of course, crazy people don't think their crazy, do they? I am sure that I read that somewhere. I don't understand. Obviously, I am loony toons. Maybe I am not even conscious? Maybe this whole thing is some sort of comatose dream state?" She said babbling to herself.

"Leila Marie Kelly!" Iris said reaching out and pinching her on the upper arm, hard.

"Ow!" Leila said grabbing her arm.

"You stop that right now! You are not crazy! You come from a long, long line of vampires!" Iris whispered loudly with some anger.

"You just said that you weren't dead! I can feel you! You are warm!" Leila responded, speaking in a normal voice.

97

"Hush!" Iris said listening, and then continued whispering. "I am not dead. Dead is *always* dead. I don't care what you are, and baby, believe me, there is more out there than even I know about, but if you are dead, you are truly dead, and I am not dead. I am Vampire."

"Fine. How? Were you bitten? Is it like a sexually transmitted disease?" Leila said, looking at her suddenly and strangely concerned, whispering loudly.

"I am a 'born-vampire'. It is in my, *our*, genes. Though there are what are called 'made' vampires. It takes much longer, several attempts, and does include a transfer of blood and venom..." Iris attempted to continue.

"Venom? Like a snake?" Leila said with raised eyebrows.

"Yes. I guess so. But only the oldest of us can do it. So, while born vampires are rare, made vampires are even more rare. There is some risk involved also, I have been told." Iris said.

"Risk?" Leila said.

"Well, they could die throughout the transformation process, or go crazy." Iris said.

"So, you weren't bitten?"

"No." Iris said firmly.

"Ok. Let's see your teeth. Do you have fangs?" Leila asked bluntly, almost rudely.

Iris gave her a look and begrudgingly showed her teeth, and as Leila watched, Iris's upper and lower canine teeth extended about a centimeter in length.

Leila said, "That's impressive." Her tone said otherwise. "Why all four?"

"I truly don't know." Aunt Iris said, her teeth slowly receding. "Probably so that you get a better grip."

"Okay. So, bite me." Leila demanded, holding out her arm.

"No!" Iris told her, shocked.

"Why not?" Leila pressed; her arm still extended.

"Because I choose not to bite people!" Iris said offended, pushing her arm back to the bed.

"So, you have never bitten anyone?" Leila said.

"I didn't say that. I said I *choose* not to. The taking of blood is part of the final transformation." Iris said with a sideways glance.

"So, can you eat real food?" Leila said.

"I can. But it doesn't taste the same as it did when I was human." Iris said.

"So, if you don't bite people, and you don't eat normal food. What do you eat? You are alive, so you must eat. Am I getting this right?" Leila questioned intensely.

"Yes. I drink animal blood. Usually, cow or pig, as it is easily available." Iris paused to let Leila absorb it all.

"So, what about garlic or the cross?" Leila questioned.

"What about garlic or the cross?" Iris said, starting to get irate.

"Do they repel you?"

"Of course not. Except for the bad breath with garlic. I love going to evening mass, even now!" Iris shrugged.

"Would you die if someone put a stake through your heart or cut off your head?" Leila said.

"Leila, anybody would die if they were staked or decapitated." Iris said, giving her niece an irritated look.

"What about the sun?" Leila asked.

"Leila, why are you asking me all of these questions with this tone?" Iris said, raising an eyebrow at her niece.

"Well, you wanted to have this 'heart-to-heart', Aunt Iris. I am just waiting for you to drop the other shoe." Leila said giving Iris a harsh look.

"The shoe?"

"Yeah, that you think I am becoming a vampire?" Leila threw the question down like a gauntlet.

Iris answered instead, "Direct sunlight doesn't kill me, Leila. But it does hurt, and it can incapacitate me until I can get out of it. It weakens me, so I avoid it or protect myself from it, but I don't burst into flames."

Leila sighed, wearily, and leaned back in bed. "So, how did this all start with our family? Does everyone have this happen?" She asked.

"No, baby. Not everybody. Not even half. Probably less than five percent in total." Iris said, getting up on the bed and sitting next to her and putting her arm around Leila comfortingly. "I will try to tell you what I can. As far as anyone knows, vampires have been around as long as humans have existed. No one knows how we came into being, if we are an offshoot of the human species, or a totally different species unto ourselves. There is debate on whether it was a virus that changed our genes, or our genes create a virus that in turn mutates our genes as we mature. Regardless, here we are."

"A debate?" Leila questioned.

"Yes. We are an extremely small community relative to regular humans, but we are a community, nonetheless. I can't give you thousands of years of history in a few short sentences, Leila. Let me give you as much as I can then, after you have had a chance to think about and absorb what I tell you, I promise I will answer as many of your questions as possible. I am not going anywhere for the foreseeable future. Yes?" She looked at her niece, who nodded her head and waited for her to continue. "There are two types. Born and made. Our family is born. Our family carries a gene that mutates, and a very few of us 'transform' into vampire." Here she paused as Leila started to speak, putting up a hand to stop her.

"We have traced our family's history back about a thousand years to one central ancestor. A woman in Greece called Ursula Tsoukalous. We know she was infected while she was pregnant, but did not change. The virus, or what have you, changed her twin sons, one of which eventually became a vampire, the other twin did not, and that brother passed the gene down through our family line. Our family line is not vast. But it isn't small either. For the moment, it really boils down to this. I don't *know* if you are changing. But I believe you are, yes." She felt Leila breathe deep, but she didn't ask any questions, so Iris continued. "It is different for everyone. Sometimes it happens quickly, sometimes partially, but many times not at all."

"I am having pain and tiredness during the day. I passed out the other morning. I was relatively fine until the sun came up." Leila said tiredly, worriedly, and Iris nodded her sympathy.

"Yes, that is my understanding, and you are in the age range where it seems normal for us to turn if we are going to do so." Iris said.

"Normal?"

"We usually start the transformation anywhere from mid-twenties to late-thirties. It is different for everyone. My Uncle Martin was in his thirties. Though there are the occasional late bloomers, like me and occasional early bloomers like your Grandmother Dolly, who was in her very early twenties." Iris said with a small, sad smile.

"Grandma Dolly, Dad's mom?" Leila asked softly.

"Yes."

"But...she died!" Leila said with wide eyes.

"Yes. But she shouldn't have. She passed out, just like you. The idiot that operated on her did so unnecessarily and she died from blood loss. Vampires are durable, but we are vulnerable during transition; our temperature can spike quite high at times, mimicking infection, and we experience pain, tiredness, and, on occasion, unconsciousness. Doctors who don't understand what is going on attempt to treat us in many ways; that's why it is imperative that we get you out of this hospital and into the hands of an expert." Iris said firmly.

"Aunt Iris, do you know Dr. Lambert has found something in my blood? He doesn't know what it is. But he is going to be sending my blood to Atlanta to be evaluated using better equipment than he has on hand." Leila said with a worried glance at Iris.

"I heard him from the hallway, baby." Iris said softly holding her niece to her closely. "Aunt Iris is going to take care of it."

"What are you going to do, Aunt Iris?" Leila said, leaning away from her and fixing Iris with a hard look. "I like Dr. Lambert."

"Nothing like what is running through that overactive imagination of yours! If you are transforming, you cannot be here in this hospital. It is dangerous for you and all vampires. The world is unaware of us as anything other than myth. The community needs to keep it that way. None of us would like to become guinea pigs or prisoners." Iris said, then saw the terrified look on her niece's face. "Baby, I am going to secure your release for tomorrow, get you some much needed time away from work, and I am going to get my hands on your samples. Right now, you need to rest in your own environment. Mansuetus is going to help us with that, and we can then assess the situation in a few days when the doctor gets here. Okay? I promise, I have got this."

Iris looked at her as Leila worriedly shook her head. "Right now, I want you to rest and conserve your strength while I meet with Dr. Lambert. Mansuetus will be in here to sit with you while I am gone. I am here for you, baby, and come what may you are going to get through all of this, okay?" She kissed her softly on the forehead, just like she used to do when Leila was a small child, getting up from the bed. "Just try to relax now and maybe get some sleep."

"I get the impression that Dr. Lambert likes you very much, Aunt Iris." Leila said softly as Iris headed toward the door.

"I hope that he does." Iris said, pausing slightly and then left the room. She already knew, Mansuetus was waiting for her in the hallway, and she closed the door to the room softly.

"You didn't tell her the half of it!" He said sternly to her under his breath, much more silent than Leila and Iris' whispers had been. Giving Iris a hard look, he stood there holding Leila's bag.

"How could I? She thinks she is delusional as it is." Iris said to him, matching his volume. "You let me handle my niece. I know her. She will come to accept this in time if we give her the time to accept it at her own pace. When was the last time a new vampire occurred in our family who had no clue what was going on?" She challenged him.

"*He* will not be pleased!" Mansuetus said in the same tone.

"Well, then, Mansuetus, *he* will have to get the hell over it!" Iris said in irritation, whirling and heading for the elevator bank.

Mansuetus gave his offended look to her back. He breathed deeply and schooled his features. He was aware that he could present a frightening visage to some humans, and this changeling was so young, small, and unaware that he had no wish to frighten her. She was too important a figure. Her predicament and circumstances reminded him of another important person, and the last thing she needed was fear. He knew that would not help her. He softly opened the door and carried her small bag into the room.

She obviously had been deep in thought as she looked at him calmly from the bed, where she was sitting up with her arms wrapped around her bent knees. Her teal eyes sparkled at him as she gave him a soft smile. "Thank you so much, Mr. Smythe. That was truly kind of you to bring me my things and to give my aunt and I some time alone." She said to him politely, sweetly, and immediately endeared herself to him.

"You are welcome, Déspoina." He looked at her in inquiry as he held up the overnight bag.

"Please, just put it in the bathroom. Hopefully, I am out of here tomorrow and will need it in the morning." She smiled at him, softly, as he did as she requested. "Déspoina. Is that Greek?" He nodded. She indicated the chair next to her bed, and he eyed it skeptically. "Please sit with me, Mr. Smythe. I find I am not tired and require some companionship this evening." She said softly.

He said to her as he sat, placing his hand on his chest, "Mansuetus."

She looked at him curiously, "What does Déspoina mean?"

He considered it carefully, obviously trying to translate it for her. "Lady." He said in his deep bass.

"So, it is a title?" She asked. He nodded his head once more, smiling slightly. "Are you a vampire?" She asked directly, which so shook him he choked; his coughing and sputtering caused her to inquire, "Do you need some water, Mansuetus? I have an extra cup!"

He recovered enough to say, "No, Déspoina, no thank you! No, I am not a vampire."

"Good. I don't think that I am either, despite what Aunt Iris thinks." She told to him bluntly.

"Hmmm. You are very direct, aren't you, Déspoina?" He said with a smile. "Aren't you afraid of me even a little?" Deciding that he would be just as direct.

"When I was a small child, my Great Grandma Kelly told me, 'Fear no man, only God.' Now even though I am not a churchgoer, I am honest, and I try to live that way as best as I can. So no, I fear no man." She smiled.

"Fearless." He said softly with a small chuckle as if laughing at a private joke. He took in her small form, short naturally curly chestnut locks, lightly freckled nose and high cheekbones, teal eyes, and alabaster skin, thinking that she wasn't statuesque or glamorous like her aunt. Instead, she was impish and beguiling in an entirely bewitching way – and he knew in his old bones that she was going to lead his Kýrios on a merry chase. At least it would never be boring!

Iris stood in the hallway outside of N5-16 thinking hard at the light-colored wooden door. First and foremost, she needed to get her niece out of this hospital. Everything else was secondary for the moment and could be managed in different ways. Her initial read on this doctor was that he was extremely ambitious. She could tell that he was looking at Leila's case as some sort of means to an end for him. Her arrival on the scene had certainly distracted him. She stood tall, thrust her shoulders back, displaying her firm bosom, and decided on a frontal attack on that weakness. She sharply rapped twice on the door.

Her enhanced hearing brought the sound of a chair scrape on the floor, then quick footsteps towards the door, where they paused; she imagined him putting himself to rights, as she pasted a sultry smile on her lips.

The door opened and Dr. Dene Lambert faced this woman who so fascinated him. He breathed deep as he took in her beauty, touching briefly on her perfectly rounded bosom before he remembered himself, looked up, and got sucked into the blackness of her eyes. He swallowed hard, incapable of speech.

"May I come in, doctor?" She asked softly.

"Oh, I am sorry. Yes, please do, Ms. Gauche." He said, standing to the side and swept his arm inward indicating that she enter.

She sashayed in, passing close to him on her spike heels, a soft sway to her hips, giving off a soft scent of lavender. And was that pumpkin pie that he smelled? She threw softly over her shoulder, "I'm not your patient, doctor. Please, call me Iris, and your given name is?" She invited, turning to face him, looking him squarely in his ice-blue eyes, her hand extended.

"Dene. Dene Lambert." He said, taking her hand in his. A shock of arousal hit him again, making him thankful that he had kept his lab coat on. He shook her hand once, then dropped it, thinking, "This lady is dangerous!"

She turned away, looking around with interest. "So, this is your lab?" She asked in her sultry voice.

"Yes. This is my personal lab. I am a hematologist." He said in wonder. He had never had a woman ask him about his lab.

"A hematologist? That means that you are a specialist?" She said looking closely at his lab tables in curiosity.

"Yes, I study blood." He said, thinking well she will lose that curiosity now. Most women weren't turned on by his field of study he had found.

"Blood? Really? That's fascinating, actually." She said sincerely. "What does that entail?" She looked at him with interest.

"Well, I specialize in diagnosing, treating, and preventing blood diseases." He said to her, unused to any beautiful, elegant woman taking an actual interest in his work or his professional mind. Most were like Bobby Rebekah, interested in him as a way out of their current lifestyle, or husband-material like Andrea or Macey.

"What do you look for?" Again, she walked up and down his lab, looking at the sample refrigerators and at his main lab table with interest, which was full of test tubes, solutions, slides, and his microscope. Bobby Rebekah had always referred to his lab as she passed through as 'his mad-scientist get-up'.

"Well, iron-deficiencies like anemia, hemophilia, which is a disease that prevents your blood from clotting, sickle-cell anemia, leukemia and lymphoma are types of cancers. Any condition that involves either your blood cells, platelets, blood vessels, bone marrow, lymph nodes, even your spleen." He said, warming to his subject. "I can diagnose sepsis, which is an infection of the blood itself, or thalassemia, which is a condition in which your body doesn't make enough hemoglobin. Blood disorders can affect almost all areas of the human body! Of course, there are transfusions, marrow transplants, and there has been a fairly new discovery of stem cells..." He stopped himself, looking down at her. She had moved closer to him and fixed him in her gaze. Once again, he smelled the soft scent of lavender and pumpkin pie, which was surprisingly intensely erotic. "Sorry, I can get a little carried away when talking about it." He said flushing.

"Not at all, Dene. I am quite fascinated! I love a man who gets passionate...about his work." She paused and gave him her sultry smile. "So, how did you come to be my niece's doctor?" She asked softly.

That's right! He thought, feeling like an idiot. This woman was his patient's aunt, and she had come to discuss her niece. He said instead, "Well, I was the attending physician on duty when Mr. Sutton brought her into the ER."

"Well, how lucky for us." She said softly, very sincerely. "So, my niece tells me you think she may have a problem with her blood?" Iris said.

"Well, I am not 100% mind you. I do have to send her labs to be reviewed under a better microscope than I have here. I need your niece's samples to be reviewed under an electron microscope in Atlanta, to be sure." He said softly as he gazed into her eyes, fascinated by the depths that he found there. It was like looking directly into a still body of water in a starless night. Black but with its own special gleam.

"Would you show me?" She asked softly in her melodious voice.

"Show you?" He replied just as softly, thinking that there were many things that he would love to show her, losing his train of thought.

"Yes, would you show me her sample? Do you think I could see it?" Looking into his eyes.

He was surprised and noticed that she was awfully close to him; her rounded breasts were only inches from his chest as she looked at him. He once again breathed in lavender and pumpkin pie. "Okay. I don't see any reason you can't."

"Thank you, this is very interesting!" She said smiling winsomely.

Pleased with himself that he made her smile, he quickly prepared a slide for her, placing it on the microscope for her to view. He showed her how to adjust the lens and watched her bend slightly to look with both eyes open to look through the ocular lens, admiring her shapely ass while she looked. "So, would you tell me exactly what to look for?" She asked.

"May I?" He said, moving in close and she moved slightly away from him, but he still felt like they were occupying the same space as he looked through the lens. She sure set his libido off, and his arousal was apparent if she only glanced down at him. He moved away slightly, and she again moved closer, still looking through the lens. He felt like he had never had a more fabulous and luscious lab partner. Standing this close, breathing in her scent, he realized he could see the pulse in her throat throb slightly, slowly and he ached to take her exposed earlobe gently between his teeth. God, what the hell was wrong with him? He resisted her pull and stepped away.

"With this equipment it is difficult, but if you concentrate, you will see what looks to be small cells 'swimming' around her platelets. It looks to me like these are enzymes; enzymes are created by amino acids in our bodies. Now, an enzyme is a special protein that transcribes or unzips a specific segment of our DNA in our bodies. It's complicated, but the unzipped portion of the DNA makes RNA, and RNA is used to make proteins, and this sends instruction to our cells. As you can see, it looks like these enzymes are affecting her platelets. Not truly attacking or destroying them, but entering the platelets and altering them; transforming them into something new. That, in and of itself, is unknown to anything I've ever seen." He said as Iris looked. "Her other tests are perfect." Iris glanced up at him in wonder, whether at his explanation or what she had been viewing on the slide. He was unsure which, but she was looking at him with a sense of wonder. That look brought him once again close. "Iris," he said softly, using her name for the first time, "when I say perfect, I mean perfect. With the human body, that's impossible. Nobody's perfect."

She licked her full red lips, drawing his attention to her mouth. "I am a little thirsty. Do you have something to drink? Maybe in your office?"

"Oh, absolutely. We need to talk about your family history, after all." He said, taking her softly by the elbow and gentlemanly leading her into his office. "I have water, Coca-Cola, or if you are adventurous, bourbon or Chianti." He waited to see what she would say.

"Chianti? Is it chilled?" She asked softly with a smile.

"Perfectly." He said as if she had passed a test.

"Then that will do." He opened a built-in cabinet to reveal a small refrigerator and several types of glasses on the shelves. He poured them both wines, intentionally being liberal in his portions. He knew he was treading the waters of inappropriateness with her already and even though his earlier encounter with Bobby Rebekah had left him physically satiated, his reaction to Iris was baffling, exciting and a little frightening. It had been so long since he had any interaction with an intelligent, sophisticated, and extremely beautiful woman; one who seemed genuinely interested in him and what he was all about. He realized that he just didn't want this encounter to end just yet.

When he turned around with their glasses, he had expected to see her seated in front of his desk, instead he found that she had slid out of her heels and had curled up to lean her arm and much of that fabulous bosom across the armrest of his sofa, with her bare legs tucked up under her and the material of her dress riding about mid-thigh, showing her exquisite legs. She was elegant, yet relaxed. She propped her head up with her right hand, reaching for a glass with her left. He suddenly realized that he had totally forgotten about the wine as he looked at her. He handed her a glass three-quarters full. If she noticed the large amount, she didn't comment on it, but instead brought it close to her lips and breathed deeply. She took a small sip, and he felt slightly overheated. "I am sure that you must be warm, after such a long day, Dene. Why don't you relax a little while we talk about my family history? After all, it is quite late." She said softly taking another small sip of her wine.

He realized that it was pushing midnight. The time had flown! She had been here for over an hour already! He sat his glass down and removed his lab coat, hanging it up on its hook. He realized he was nervous. It had been a long time since he had spoken with or entertained a woman like her if ever, and never one that was so interested in his field. He joined her, sitting in the oversized but comfortable chair closest to her, barely two feet from her end of the couch. Despite his nervous mind, his body was totally relaxed and comfortable as he responded to her casual and easy manner.

"So, where to begin?" He said to her, unbuttoning the top button of his shirt and unconsciously loosening his tie. "Earlier, you said that no one in your family had ever exhibited these types of symptoms. Are you sure? What side of Mrs. Sutton's family do you come from? Paternal or Maternal?" The questions came second nature to him.

"Oh, her father's side of the family." Iris said softly.

"But you are familiar with both sides of the family?" He asked just as softly.

"Oh, yes. I am a family history buff, you see, and have enjoyed learning about my family extensively throughout my life." She smiled at him with her knowing smile. "Are you confident that this isn't just some sort of virus? Some strange case of a flu?" She asked suddenly.

He blinked at her. "In my experience, a virus will attach itself to a cell, any type of cell, which is usually far larger than the virus. They have a membrane called a capsid that fuses with the cell membrane and that's how a virus usually merges with a cell. The interesting thing is that when they get into a cell, they will release their genetic material into the cell producing proteins, and they hijack the cell processes, which start killing the normal proteins of the cell. Then it uses the cell's own mechanisms to replicate itself.

With my equipment I am not seeing that, but with the discovery of HIV in America just 10 years ago, I cannot rule out that this is a wholly new virus either. What I am not seeing is a destruction of the platelets, and the spreading of a virus, but instead a modification into a whole different type of platelet, something I have never seen and don't recognize. I understand that for you and your family, this is an emotional time, but as a scientist, to me, this is extremely fascinating to witness." He said, unconsciously baring his personal thoughts to her. "What I am seeing is a modification of the blood. I have never seen this before. But I will concede that without better equipment, I cannot rule in or out a whole new type of virus.

In addition to my not thinking that this problem is viral, is the fact that your niece doesn't have an increase in white blood cells." He said softly watching her as she put the wineglass on the small end table next to her. Shifting to a sitting position, she placed her bare feet on the floor, showing her blood red painted toenails of her shapely feet. Her movements were fluid and hypnotic. He thought he had never had a more beautiful or attentive audience to any discussion he had on his craft. She leaned toward him as if she were enraptured by his explanation, giving him a wonderful view of her beautiful cleavage, and another opportunity to breathe in her scent. He swore he was smelling lavender, pumpkin pie, and was that freshly baked doughnuts? His libido responded accordingly, and his erection was suddenly high, tenting his dress slacks. He was too enthralled to even try to hide the evidence of his arousal.

"White blood cells?" She softly questioned, her eyes never leaving his. Like magic, she was on her knees in front of his chair. Slowly taking his wineglass from him and putting it next to her own. He paused, surprised, wondering how she had gotten there, then her tongue dabbed at the corner of her mouth, perhaps to catch a drop of wine, further entrancing him.

"Yes." He suddenly continued, almost as if on scientific autopilot. "Your niece's white blood cell count is perfectly normal. Not too high or too low. Perfect." He said softly. He felt her hands run across the tent of his erection and move on their way to his belt buckle, and still, he couldn't stop looking into her eyes. He could feel pre-cum wet the head of his penis, and his testicles grow and rise. He continued with his explanation robotically, still engaged on scientific autopilot, as he couldn't tear his gaze away from the blackness of her eyes.

"If this were a viral infection of some sort, we would expect to see one of two things. Either an increase in white blood cell activity as her cells attacked the virus, or a decrease in white blood cell activity because the virus would be attacking her white blood cells." He could feel her unknotting his tie and removing it. Still, she captivated him with her eyes. Her hands quickly unbuttoned his shirt, lying his chest wide and bare for her exploration, as her hands moved to pull down his pants clear to the floor, baring his body for her full exploration if that was what she so chose.

He continued, unabated with his explanation. Bewildered that he couldn't stop talking, or stop her, or help her. Instead, he desperately clutched the arms of his oversized chair. He could feel his heart rate increasing, and his blood pressure rising. His breath was coming quicker. "White blood cells are created by the body, in the bone marrow, in response to infection, either viral or bacterial. I am seeing no indication of this with your niece's case."

He had finished. He was still staring into her eyes. But he was meeting them over the largest, most swollen erection he had ever experienced in his entire life. His penis stood straight up, away from his body, as if held in invisible hands and throbbed with blood in time to his heartbeat, and the pupils of her eyes were so large. Her gorgeous red lips were no more than a half inch from its swollen head.

She smiled softly, knowingly, full red lips turning up. Hunger shined in her eyes.

"I think it is just a virus, Dene." She said softly. He shook his head 'no' in disagreement, even as he felt her breath soft and gentle against his cock. "Yes," she said simply and intentionally blew on the ridge of his cock.

"Yes!" He said to her, sucking in his breath, as a shock of electric current went from the head of his cock to his scrotum, pulling his testicles up toward his body tight.

"Yes. Just a virus." She looked deeply into his eyes, his soul.

"Just a virus," he whispered. "Yes, just a virus!" He said louder in a strangled voice, as an impossibly long tongue extended from her mouth, through incredibly white teeth to lick a drop of pre-cum from the head of his cock. Another shock flew through his body, heating the space between his anus and his testicles.

"You will release my niece tomorrow. Because she has a virus, she should be off work for a while. She needs time to rest and recover. Don't you agree?" Her voice was a melody in his mind. The scent of her making him intoxicated.

"Yes, time to recover." He agreed softly. Her tongue darted from her mouth once again to wrap itself fully around the head of his cock, wetly massaging softly, and he felt himself getting ready to explode in orgasm. "Two weeks off of work." He gasped out. Then watched her tongue slide back into her mouth. Disappointment flooded his features as he stumbled on the brink of orgasm. Had he displeased her? The thought of displeasing her almost crushed him.

"Now we wouldn't want her to go back too soon tiring herself out, would we? She will need time to rest after her ordeal." She said reasonably, shaking her head no and then yes as she spoke, and he mirrored her movements. He felt himself leaking pre-cum down the sides of his raging cock, lubricating himself, readying himself for her lips; he was dying for release, and he would give her anything for it. "Yes, let's say a month. Yes, a month should make sure she is fully recovered." She said. Her mouth waited above his cock, waiting for his answer, partially open, breathing softly against his glands. The irises of her eyes, now ringed in red, never leaving his, exuding a promise of more pleasure than he had ever experienced before. His breath was now coming in gasps, and the pupils of his eyes were so dilated that there was only a sliver of ice blue iris showing. He felt enveloped in lavender, pumpkin pie, and that elusive scent of fresh doughnuts, not overpowering, but wrapped softly in her scent.

"Yes, she will take a full month from work. To insure full recovery." He whispered, gasping in anticipation, shaking his head yes, begging her with the tone of his voice, if not with his words.

Her eyes were so large, her lips so red, her teeth so large and white. Large and white?

Just then she swallowed his entire cock without hesitation, clear to the base, and proceeded to fellate him with the strength of her long tongue. He tried to hold back, to fight her, like he fought Bobby Rebekah, so that this would be just an act, one that he controlled, and he would truly give none of himself. But after just a second sweep of her muscular tongue up the full length of the back of his cock, sweeping around the ridge of his head, he felt the contractions begin in his pelvic floor muscles. As she touched him with her hands for the first time; her fingers pushed firmly against the space between his balls that were bunched high, and his anus, causing his erection to grow even larger than before, setting off a soul crushing uncontrollable orgasm.

His hips left the chair in spasm thrusting high and he felt the head of his cock spurt cum in the back of her throat, and as his orgasm took him to stratospheric heights, he felt her bite down on him and *suck hard*, and he gave Iris something he had never given another woman, a scream of pleasure.

The Beginning

CHAPTER FOUR

W HEN IRIS RETURNED TO Leila's room well after 1:00 am, Mansuetus was concerned.

Leila had chatted with him until almost midnight, telling him about her children, the stress of her job in the information technology department, finally sleepily telling him about how hard it was to care for her sons basically on her own, and how often her husband seemed to choose his job over his children and his wife. It worried and hurt her that they didn't seem to come first in his life. How he never seemed to be happy with everything that he had been blessed with. How they never seemed to be good enough for him, how he always demanded more, no matter how much he received.

Mansuetus was a good listener, having years, or rather centuries, of experience to perfect this skill, although Leila didn't know that. Usually, she was reticent about sharing anything with anyone, and he could tell that normally she was the one that everyone else in her circle leaned on and took from. Over time, this had made her weary. His quiet acceptance and non-judgment of her was what she needed to help with the stress that she was experiencing, both physically and emotionally. She literally talked herself to sleep, thanking him very sweetly, as she closed her eyes in exhaustion, for being such a kind person to listen to her troubles.

His conscience twinged over that remark as he sat guard next to the bed watching over her. The small light, which she insisted stay on for his benefit, from the partially opened bathroom door dimly illuminating the room. It had been an exceptionally long time since he had thought of himself as kind. He was obedient and loyal to his master, a pragmatist who went through time doing what needed to be done to keep his Kýrios safe; his role had changed over time, warrior, protector, strategist, sounding board, always ruthless when needed, and a murderer if necessary. This small, sweet lady trusted him with her thoughts and thought him kind for taking the time to listen to them. He shook his head in wonder.

When Iris leaned into the wall in the doorway of Leila's room, he narrowed his eyes at her, and knew immediately what had occurred, thinking, *Young ones! They never learn!* He quietly stood up, gathered Iris's coat and purse from the other chair, then took her by the arm, pulling her gently into the hallway, closing Leila's door silently behind him, leading Iris past the nurse's station to the elevator quietly. In the elevator, Iris leaned into him, and he noticed that she had something stuck in the front of her dress. He knew that they were more than likely under elevator security cameras and placed his arm around her shoulders, patting her gently like any human would any sleepy female who may be sad and in need of comfort.

As they exited the elevator to the virtually silent first floor, he almost wished for a bustling big city hospital. The more people in attendance, the least amount of attention they attracted. Well, there was no helping it, he thought. He nodded to the security guard at the front desk, with a sad look pasted to his face, as he led Iris, who stumbled like a person who was sleepy and under some emotional stress. The security guard nodded back to him in some sympathy, thinking that they were there to visit an extremely sick relative.

He opened the front passenger door to the black 1995 Lincoln Town-car Executive Limousine he had secured for its trunk space and blackened back windows, and loaded Iris in. He was too irritated with her to load her into the back and then pull her back out. She was going back to the suite, where she could sleep it off, but first he had a few questions for her! He opened the driver's side door, slid in, and started up the car, gently pulling out to take her back to the bed-and-breakfast.

"I have never seen you blood drunk before, Iris." He said bluntly. "Is he still alive?" He questioned, wondering how he was supposed to get the doctor's body out of the hospital undetected. Disposing of bodies in a public building wasn't as easy as it used to be!

"La!" Iris giggled tipsily. "Of course he is! He is also extremely happy," she said with a silly smile on her face. "Don't worry, it is done. Leila will be released tomorrow, and these," she said, removing blood vials with Leila's name on them from her bodice and placing them in the console, "are no longer a concern."

"That news will at least please *him*." Mansuetus said to her, pleased that he could at least be able to report back on some positive progress. He glanced over at Iris when she didn't respond; seeing that she was sleeping softly. "Young ones!" He said again under his breath, shaking his head slightly as he drove down the almost empty streets of the small town to deposit her in her bed and call his master.

Nikolaos Tsoukalous hung up the phone. Neither pleased nor displeased with Iris' progress of the evening. After all, it was the least she had been expected to do. Though he was slightly surprised that Mansuetus was unusually vague about details and the progress of Leila's education that was taking place in Georgia. Soon, he would be able to join them and assess the situation himself. His lawyer had almost secured him the property he had chosen on the East River. Location and security always being more important than price where he was concerned, the lawyer just had to come to a final agreement with the current occupants of the residence, transfer the funds, and secure the typical non-disclosure agreements and record the deeds under one of their shell corporations. Unlike many of his age, he understood the modern world and the processes necessary for these transactions to move forward and had patience where many did not. He imagined being approached by a lawyer for the purchase of your property when it wasn't on the market for sale was a shocking thing. Some people may be resistant initially, but he had found in his years that *everyone* had their price. He also preferred private sales in general regardless of the complications and costs, because, as to be expected, he valued his privacy above all things.

He had already arranged for his personal car to be commercially flown to the Jacksonville International Airport and then transported to the St. Mary's municipal airport to await his arrival by private jet as soon as the lawyer had completed the cash sale. He realized that a small-town airport was a little more public than he may care for, and a private jet may cause a bit of local stir, but there was no way his movements nor activities would be hampered by being dependent on Mansuetus, who he was sure would have his hands full while they were there.

He required independence of movement, and privacy, for the activities that he had planned. He also did not know what the length of his stay in the tiny Georgia town would be, but strangely, overall, didn't resent it like he had in the past when he was required to help a young one make the transition. His excitement for this adventure was large. After almost twenty years, finally, *she* would be with him. Only the thought of *her* had been what had kept him going.

He looked at the clock. At least with their locations there were no time zone issues, though he was concerned that he hadn't heard from her in over 12 hours. He missed her. Already. But the transition could be taxing, and he didn't want to startle her with reaching out to her like he had this morning. She was correct. She could have had a more adverse reaction to him showing up in her bath. There was no sense in taking chances while she was in the hospital, no matter his desire to connect with her. He had waited this long; he was willing to wait longer.

Dr. Lambert woke with the dawn. He was fully clothed and stretched out on his couch. He knew he had spoken with Leila Sutton's aunt the previous evening, but couldn't quite recall all the details. What an attractive, intelligent woman she was, he thought; missing the sight and sounds of the big city, knowing that he was still stuck in this tiny town in southeast Georgia with its backwoods inhabitants. It was a shame that he was unable to meet anyone here with such sophistication. He got up and showered and changed into his spare shirt and slacks he kept on hand in his office. When he arrived on the fourth floor to take up his rounds, he was greeted by Andrea and Macey who were just arriving also for the seven am shift, pushing all thoughts of Iris Gauche from his mind as he chit-chatted with them over coffee as they reviewed the notes in the charts made by the night shift nurses.

"Mrs. Sutton can leave today as soon as she is ready." He told Andrea.

"Oh, that is wonderful, doctor. She will be so pleased." Andrea responded with a smile. "So, it is nothing serious after all?" She asked happily.

"No. Just a virus." He said automatically, robotically. "But I am going to fill out a work release for her for a month. That way, she will have plenty of time to rest and recover. I also don't want her driving." He added as an afterthought, but didn't know why. "If she has any further issues, she can contact me here at the hospital. Otherwise, she is free to go."

As Andrea headed to Mrs. Sutton's room, Dr. Dene Lambert felt a niggling thought pull at the back of his brain. He massaged the back of his neck, thinking that he needed a good night's sleep in his bed instead of on the couch of his office, and turned his focus back to the patient charts in front of him as he prepared to do his rounds.

Leila was awake when Andrea came into the room. "Mrs. Sutton, good news! Dr. Lambert has released you! As soon as you are showered and ready, you are free to go home."

"Oh, thank goodness!" Leila said happily. "Did he say what's wrong?"

"You have a virus, but it's nothing to worry about. He is writing you a release from work for thirty days, no driving, and wants you to rest and recuperate. If you have any further issues, please contact him here at the hospital."

"Wow, thirty days! That's a long time." Leila said in wonder, not sure if she wanted to be off work for a whole month. She could afford it. She had plenty of sick time on the books, having taken most of Devin's maternity leave in an unpaid status, but still the work would pile up.

"With viruses, you never can tell." Andrea said sensing her hesitation. "They can take their toll if you don't take appropriate care of yourself, and you wouldn't want to inadvertently spread it. Though there should be little risk of that since you aren't running a fever. I understand from the night nurse that your family was here with you most of the night and left quite late?" She asked as Leila got out of the bed, heading for the shower.

"Yes. Mr. Smythe will be here to take me home today sometime."

"Mr. Smythe is here," came a deep bass voice from the door to the room. Both women looked up, startled.

"Mansuetus, you move very softly!" Leila said breathlessly.

"I find it of benefit to do so, Déspoina." He replied with a small chuckle.

"Andrea, is there a place that Mr. Smythe can wait while I am getting ready to leave?" Leila asked.

"Yes, at the end of the hall just past the stairwell is the waiting area for the floor, Mr. Smythe, if you would care to wait there." Andrea said to him.

He ignored her completely, his focus on Leila. "I could pack your bag while you shower, Déspoina." He said to her.

"No. I would be more comfortable doing that myself, but thank you for offering." Leila said to him, heading into the bathroom.

"As you wish, Déspoina." He said, bowing slightly, hand to his chest and smiling as she closed the door softly.

"Maybe he is a little scary in the light of day." Leila thought to herself as she turned on the water in the shower to let it run and heat up, overall thankful to be gone from the hospital.

Outside the door, Andrea smiled at him. "Would you like me to show you to the waiting room, Mr. Smythe?" She asked, thinking that he was an exceptionally large, robust, but handsome man.

"No, thank you, I will find it." He said, smiling at her in return, asking. "You will let me know when she is ready?"

"Absolutely!"

He left the room just as quietly as he entered for such a large man, Andrea thought as she stripped Leila's bed.

Less than an hour later, Leila was being wheel-chaired into the waiting room, her two small overnight duffle bags filled with her clothes and personal items on her lap; her release and work release papers in hand, to see Mansuetus perusing a copy of *People Magazine*, which she found humorous in a way. He exuded this whole soldier of fortune attitude with his brown sports coat over a tight green t-shirt, jeans, and casual boots and here he was reading *People*. He noticed her amused smile as he put the magazine down, looked curiously at her for a second and spoke to nurse Andrea. "You would like me to take her down?"

"Oh, no Mr. Smythe, I have to go down to the curb with her. Hospital rules." Andrea said with a smile.

"This is good. I will take bags and pull the car to the curb." He turned to Leila, who realized he had a plastic drawstring shopping bag in his hands. "From your aunt." He handed her the bag, taking her paperwork from her and putting it in one of the small duffels and removing both from her lap.

Leila looked inside to find a wide brimmed beige sunhat with a green ribbon, and deep black heart-shaped rhinestone sunglasses. "She's kidding, right?" She looked at Mansuetus, deadpanned.

"Oh, what an excellent idea!" Andrea said appreciatively. "This will solve your sensitivity to the sun for your trip home."

"I will look like Elton John!" Leila protested.

"No vanity, Déspoina." Mansuetus took her bags from her lap and headed for the stairwell. "Must protect you from the sun."

"You know we will beat you by taking the elevator, right?" Leila challenged.

"Mansuetus moves silently and quickly when needed, Déspoina!" He said with a slight accent, teasingly, returning her look of challenge.

"We shall see! Quick Andrea, let's get to the elevators!" She laughed.

By the time they waited for the elevator, stopping once at the second floor to add another passenger going down, had stopped in the lobby for Leila to put on the sunhat and sunglasses and went through the automatic doors, Mansuetus was pulling up to the curb at the end of the canopy.

Andrea said, "Wow," as she took in the limousine.

"It's not mine," Leila said to her. "It's my aunt's. She's kind of a high-flyer." Leila said with a bewildered look, thinking, *You would think that Aunt Iris would like to keep a low-profile.*

"It's cool!" Andrea said as Mansuetus bounded out of the driver's seat to open the back door for her.

"Do I have to sit in the back?" She asked Mansuetus.

"How do you feel?" He asked with concern.

"A little itchy." She said, feeling the blistering sun along her arms exposed by the t-shirt that Michael had packed to go with her jeans.

"Back." He said decisively, helping her into the back seat of the limousine with its blackened windows.

"Thanks so much, Andrea! You have been wonderful! You are a fabulous nurse," Leila told her sincerely.

"You are quite welcome, Mrs. Sutton. I am so glad it wasn't serious." Andrea was sincere.

She waved goodbye and Mansuetus closed the door between them. Leila sank back against the soft leather of the seat, feeling very tired and Mansuetus got into the front seat to slowly drive away. He lowered the glass partition that separated the front from the back portion of the car.

"You good?" He questioned.

"Yes, do you need me to give you directions?" She asked.

"No. I have already scouted the area." He said simply.

She hooted. "Scouted the area! You are killing me back here."

"Déspoina, in order for me to do my job, I must know any potential issues or threats with your safety." He stated matter-of-factly.

"Mansuetus, you are giving me a ride home from the hospital, for which I thank you, but it is my neighborhood. We live in the suburbs of a tiny town in Georgia. We don't have any crime to speak of, so there are no threats to my safety. In fact, I lead a tedious life overall." Leila laughed softly. "Once you drop me off, I will just climb into bed and then you can take the rest of the day off if you promise to bring Aunt Iris back out later tonight. She and I need to talk."

"I agree that you and your aunt need to speak in-depth. But I must stay while you are alone in case an emergency arises." He stated simply.

"Are you also a nurse?" Leila questioned. "Aunt Iris said that you don't really work for her. You work for a Dr. Tsoukalous."

"I do not function as a nurse now, but I have in the past. I am definitely qualified to manage any emergency that occurs." He said quite vaguely, Leila thought.

"Fine. There is a small grocery store to the right when we exit the interstate onto Harriet's Bluff Road. If you could stop, I can pick us up something for breakfast and lunch. Damn, I just remembered! Michael didn't bring me my purse." She said irritated, thinking that she would have to go out again depending on what she had at the house; she hated not having her purse with her.

"No need. I have been to the grocery and have items in a cooler in the trunk." He said simply as he merged onto the interstate.

"Thank you, that was very nice of you, but you must allow me to repay you, Mansuetus." She was grateful that she didn't have to go out again. She was starting to feel tired.

"No." He said simply.

She ignored him, thinking she would slip him some money sometime or buy him a special gift once she got to know him a bit better. She knew how to get around stubborn men.

Less than ten minutes later, they were pulling up in front of a cute 3-bedroom, 2 bath ranch home with brown-stained cedar siding trimmed in forest green on a corner lot that was close to an acre large. Leila really loved her home and was proud of it. She and Michael had added an exceptionally large sun-room addition to the back side of the home before Devin was born, which she loved to sit in and read and play with the kids. They were out of Michael's way, and it kept him from being irritated that they were making too much noise when he was trying to watch a ball game. Michael and she had installed a hot tub when they first built the room, and they had often joked that Devin was a 'hot tub' baby. They hadn't used the hot tub for a while now, though Michael kept it in good condition. They had added new tile flooring in the large eat-in kitchen and new carpet in the living room that better matched the floor to ceiling stone wood-burning fireplace, and she was pleased with the overall effect.

The driveway was long enough to accommodate three vehicles parked nose to tail on each side, which was a big selling point for Michael when they bought the house, though they rarely, if ever, had enough people over at once to fill those spaces. It was perfect, and then some for the limousine.

"Please park on the right side of the driveway, Mansuetus. Michael parks his truck on the left-hand side of the garage. That way, he can get in and out easily."

Mansuetus grunted and complied with her request.

She got the distinct feeling that he could not care less about what was easy for Michael. He turned to her after he turned off the car. "The back door is unlocked?"

"Yes, I am trying to figure out how I am going to get around the house to the back of the sun-room. It is quite a distance." She said, thinking. "Oh, I forgot to ask. Do you like dogs and cats?"

"Yes, I do. I could carry you." He stated.

"I am not sure I am comfortable with you carrying me in broad daylight. Most of the women in the neighborhood are stay-at-home moms. They might get the wrong idea." She said, knowing that there were at least four sets of gossipy eyes on the car right now.

"I will go in and open the garage. We will enter through the garage. Does the dog bite?"

"No, she's very friendly. Her name is Pepper. The cat's name is Gladiator. Neither are afraid of strangers, but Glad might door dash on you. The back door is on this side," she said pointing to the left side of the house, "once you enter the house it is the doorway to the left of the hot tub, left through the kitchen, right through the laundry room and you will see the door to the garage immediately. The garage door remote is just to the left of the door as you are coming out. Just hit it and I will come on in."

"Stay in the car until I come to assist you. Please." His voice was firm.

"I am okay. I feel fine," she said in return.

"Please." He said, looking at her.

She knew it wasn't a request.

"Fine. Only because you were so thoughtful and bought groceries." She said to him, smiling. Less than five minutes later, both Mansuetus and Pepper, a white and brown spotted English Setter, were exiting the open garage door. Pepper was dancing around his feet like she had found her new best friend. Leila thought to herself, *Thank God I don't need a watchdog!*

Leila opened the back door and Pepper transferred her dance of love to her, putting her paws up on her knees, licking her face profusely, preventing her from getting out of the car.

"Sit!" Mansuetus said firmly, and the dog sat rigidly, though her tail thumped a hundred miles a minute. He reached inside and she took his arm.

She was feeling itchy and weak again.

He got her out of the car, closing the door, and with a firm arm around her waist supporting her, and the dog following a few steps behind, moved her into the darkness of the garage.

She immediately felt better, if not one hundred percent. Standing on her own, she and the dog preceded Mansuetus into the house.

He got her situated at the dining room table, closing the blinds, and then went to bring in her bags and unloaded the groceries.

While she petted the dog and was watching Mansuetus thinking how efficient he was, a large black form landed in front of her on the table. Startled, she looked into huge slanted yellow eyes. "Are you supposed to be on my table?" she asked the 30-pound panther-like feline, who was giving her a narrowed look. The question started a deep loud purring in the cat's throat, and he rubbed his head none-to-gently against her face. "Yes, I missed you guys, too." She said, giving him little butterfly kisses on his massive head.

"Mansuetus, I am going to let the dog out the back for a few minutes," she said, standing up and walking into the sun-room. To her surprise, all the blinds were drawn, dimming the room against the strong Georgia sunlight. She turned and Mansuetus was directly behind her.

"I will do this, Déspoina." He instructed. "You must stay out of the light. It will only make you feel ill."

"I know you are only being polite, but please call me Leila." She requested sweetly. "I am not an invalid. I can open the door and let the dog out. She doesn't leave the yard and I will sit right here until she returns to the door. I can see that you are concerned about me. I won't give you any trouble."

He nodded once and returned to the kitchen. Where she heard, "Cat! Down!" making her chuckle slightly.

She let the dog out, thinking about what she really needed to be doing, but unsure of how she should go about it. After a few minutes she heard the soft tap, tap, tap of Pepper's nails on the screened security door and she let her back into the house. The sunlight struck her arm, causing a sharp intake of breath and a burning sensation up her arm. She gritted her teeth against it and closed the door after the dog.

She walked back into the house, grabbing her small duffels. Mansuetus was making something in the kitchen. "Mansuetus, I'm going to my bedroom to unpack my things." She said softly and he looked at her with concern.

"You need to eat something." He said in a tone that left no room for argument.

"Oh, yes, I am going to. I just want to get this taken care of first. I will be back in a few minutes." She assured him as he nodded at her.

She entered her large master bedroom, another selling point for Michael, as it was large enough for their queen bed, a large dresser, a chest of drawers, two nightstands, an entertainment center with a twenty-five-inch television that he had run cable to, a rocking chair and an exercise bike. She put her duffels down on the small bench at the foot of their bed. Luckily, they had blackout shades in the master. A by-product from her many migraines, Michael had installed them so that she could rest comfortably in peaceful almost darkness during the day if need be. A few months after he had done so, her migraines had stopped as suddenly as they had started, but they had left them up as he had found them useful when he had to work the night shift on the submarines when they were in port. She walked over to Michael's side of the bed, sat down, and picked up the phone. She dialed a number, trepidation and something more gripping her chest.

"Kelly here." She heard a strong male voice answer the phone.

"Hi, Dad." She said softly, then with more strength. "Do you have a minute?"

"Well, hello, number one daughter!" He chuckled. "What are you up to?" Usually, she smiled here and chuckled. She did neither. "Why are you calling me at my office during the day? Is everything okay?" He asked after her pause, with a shade of worry.

No sense beating around the bush, she thought. "Aunt Iris came to visit." She said simply.

"During the day?!" He said voice rising slightly. "What happened?!"

"Of course, not during the day. I just got home from the hospital. I had a bit of an episode." Leila said with a sinking feeling in her stomach. "Why didn't you tell me, Dad?" She asked softly and she couldn't prevent the hurt and betrayal in her voice. Mansuetus came into the bedroom, looking at her with concern. She glanced at him, then said to her father. "Dad, we need to talk. But not now."

"Yes, we do. Listen to me. I will be there tomorrow night. Don't *do* anything until we talk, *don't make any decisions, until we have had a chance to talk*!" He said with a touch of desperation in his voice.

"Okay. I can do that." She replied quietly and hung up the phone, looking at Mansuetus.

"Come," he murmured. "Get some food in you. It will help."

She nodded her head, following him from the bedroom.

She was pleasantly surprised upon returning to the dining room to see the table set for two and a small repast of cold thinly sliced rare roast beef, a small skillet of scrambled eggs, sliced apple, peaches, pomegranate seeds, apricots, and iced-green tea.

"Wow! Mansuetus, this looks...delicious!" She said appreciatively.

He smiled in pleasure and held the chair at the end of the table for her.

"I thought you were a nurse; I didn't know that you were a chef!"

"I have learned to be many things throughout my life, Déspoina." He said, then when she looked at him, "Leila," he acquiesced with a nod and then seated himself. He served her a small amount of everything. She had rarely had time for fresh fruit since she had children, and never as a main portion of her breakfast, a meal she usually would forgo and told him as much.

"You will need to eat breakfast throughout this time. It will help you keep up your strength. These fruits, rare beef, and eggs all help your body to build and circulate blood. Green tea widens your blood vessels and increases blood flow." He said simply as she started to eat.

"How do you know so much about this?" She asked. "You said that you are not a vampire."

"I am not. But I have been on hand for many transformations." He said simply, honestly. She stopped eating to look at him and he continued. "There are no textbooks available, as you can imagine. So, in the beginning, it was trial and error." He said with a strange look. "But you learn." He intentionally paid attention to his own plate.

"Do I make you nervous?" She questioned softly.

"No. I am not sure how much I should tell you. It is not my place." He said simply.

"If no one tells me, I would be doomed to learn everything on my own. Through trial and error, as you say. If you know the answers and do not tell me, how fair is that to me? Why should I have you here?" She questioned.

"I agree, Kyría! Why indeed? Therefore, I answer questions." He smiled widely.

"Kyría?" She asked.

"Lady," He mumbled around a mouthful of scrambled eggs.

"Incorrigible." She mumbled in return, biting into the pomegranate seeds, savoring the tarty-sweet taste.

After she had finished eating, she had to admit, she felt surprisingly good. Not normal, but stronger, less weak. She helped Mansuetus clear the table and put the leftovers in containers, then into the refrigerator. She loaded the dishwasher while he washed the skillet and then dried it and put it away when he was done. They performed all these domestic chores in a companionable silence. Not stilted, like she was used to. His silence was not ringed with hostility and so was not unwelcome. In fact, she found it soothing.

"Would you like to watch some television? Or we could play cards?" She asked, at a loss as to what she could do to entertain this big man who was still really a stranger, and therefore she felt a guest in her home.

"You don't have to entertain me, Kyría. I am here to serve you. But if you would allow me a favor, I would like for you to take this time to rest. One good meal feels good to your body, but in truth, the best thing for you is to rest." His voice was gentle.

"Are you sure? I would feel bad about deserting you."

"Yes. That would make me happiest. Besides, I have business phone calls to make, so I will not be bored." He said, pulling out a new Nokia 2142 cell phone and a charger, which he plugged into the wall next to a chair at the kitchen bar.

"Oh, you have work to do." She said in relief. "Okay, I will nap a little. Thank you so much for breakfast. It truly was delicious. I really appreciate you staying with me, after all." She said with a smile and headed for the bedroom. Once there, she changed into a pair of loose lightweight cotton shorts and a t-shirt, then gratefully climbed into her own bed, quickly falling into a contented sleep.

Mansuetus, though not a vampire, was attuned to them and felt the vibration of her falling into slumber; he smiled to himself as he plugged in the phone and touched a key on the phone pad.

"She has been released?" Came the anxious question without greeting.

"Yes, Kýrios. I am here at her home with her. She has eaten, and she now sleeps in her own bed."

"Excellent," came the reply. "Tell me about her. How does she live?" The question was more hesitant and curious than Mansuetus had heard in a long time.

He smiled to hear the curiosity in that voice. "Above average, but not wealthy by today's standards. Neatly. She is very neat. Everything has a place. There are many books here, of all types. Like at home. She is kind, sweet, polite, honest, intelligent, and fearless."

"This is high praise coming from you. So, you like her then, my friend?" Came a chuckle.

"I do. Very much so. But I also fear she may be a handful. It's the bloodline, I think." Mansuetus teased.

"Hmmm. I will keep that in mind." Came the reply. "I am waiting for word from the lawyer. It will only be a few days until we are able to take possession of the house I have chosen. I am having my car delivered to the local airport in town. It should be there tonight. I will call you when I know my arrival schedule."

"Good. Something I did not tell you last night and you should know. Iris, either through necessity or not, obtained her release by feeding from the doctor. She took much from him, so much so that she was giddy and blood drunk last night. This concerns me. I checked on him this morning, and he seemed fine, functioning. But it may be something that bears watching." He warned.

"I could tell there was something you weren't telling me last night. Monitor the situation. Iris's powers aside, she still is a fledgling in many ways."

"Yes." Mansuetus agreed.

"Overall, I am pleased, Mansuetus. The immediate danger is behind us. But as we both know, there are many hidden turns ahead. Is it just you two in the house?"

"Yes, for a few hours at least," Mansuetus replied, hearing the eagerness in his voice.

"Excellent," and then the line disconnected.

She smelled him first. That cinnamon, ginger, and sandalwood combination which was so intoxicating to her senses. Then she felt the bed beneath her. She opened her eyes to stare at her own reflection in a gilded mirror on the ceiling.

"What in the world?" She started. Noticing in the reflection that Nichola was next to her on her left, lying on his side facing her, her head pillowed on his muscular arm, his lightly tanned body dark against the cream-colored sheets that covered him from the waist down. She noticed a decadent looking chocolate brown fur blanket at the end of the bed. She turned to look at him and when she did, he opened his eyes, looking triumphant.

"It worked!" He said with a delighted smile, his strong white teeth pearly against his tanned skin.

"What worked? Where are we?" She asked curiously.

"Always with your questions, i psychí mou. Can you not just accept what is?" He said in return. She stared at him in silence, and he sighed in resignation. "We are in my bedroom, more specifically, you are in my bed," He said with a soft smile.

"Really?" She said sitting up to look around in curiosity, only realizing as the sheet slipped from her, baring her breasts, that she was totally naked under the soft sheet that covered her. "Woah!" She said, grasping the sheet to her chest.

She looked down at him as he rolled to his back, pulling two pillows under his head, then placing both hands behind his head and interlacing his fingers, giving her a wondrous view of his muscular bare chest and flat abdomen. The sparse hair of his underarms was also golden, like the sparse hairline that ran from the middle of his chest directly above his heart over his muscular abdomen toward his...she swallowed hard as her eyes moved lower. Then he quickly grabbed the sheet as it started to slip below his waist, reaching over him to grab some excess from the side of the bed and to tuck it quickly under his side opposite her to keep it securely in place.

He gave a proud, jubilant chuckle. "You are very 'virginal' today." He teased.

She looked at him in irritation. "That has nothing to do with it." She said and looked around the room in curiosity, still clutching the sheet to her chest, presenting her back to him. *She did not know where she was coming up with these dreams!* She thought, as she took in the whitewashed stone and brick walls, the occasional marble column, the high ceilings. While not dark, like the living room, it was just as comfortable and elegant. The white and gilded fireplace opposite the bed was flanked with comfortable looking white and gold brocade sofas, and sported a small burning fire, which was reflected in the mirror above the bed; further lighting the room. The floors were made of a dark mahogany covered with the occasional white and gold patterned rug. The windows were covered with heavy gold drapes.

She felt his fingertips on her bare back, and she knew what he must be investigating. She said self-consciously, "That's my birthmark." Thinking, *why am I being self-conscious in a dream about something so silly?*

"In my day, we would have called it a witch's mark," he said, rubbing it softly. "I think that is what I shall call it, too."

She faced him with hurt eyes. "Why?"

"Because," he said, pulling her swiftly to collapse across his chest, causing her to lose her hold on the sheet. "You have bewitched me, glukó mou."

She propped herself up on her forearms on his chest to look him in the eye, very conscious that there was nothing separating her breasts from his warm chest.

"These dreams I have of you," she said, then continued as he raised a tawny eyebrow in invitation, "are they real? Do you exist?" She questioned, afraid of the answer.

"We are not physically together." He replied enigmatically and his hands held her lightly.

"I feel you." She said in wonder, tentatively running her hand over the silkiness of his skin on his chest. "You are warm." His eyes dilated slightly at her touch as he watched her. His scent once again enveloped her. "And I *smell* you!" She said breathlessly.

"You smell me?" He said with a strange look. "What do I smell like?"

"Cinnamon, ginger, and sandalwood." She said breathlessly as he rolled them over, with her beneath him, one of his legs wedged intimately in between hers, and she could feel his substantial erection against her hip.

"I smell you as well." He said simply as he placed his forearms on each side of her, kissing her lips tenderly.

"You do?" She said self-conscious again once he had lifted his head from her. "What do I smell like to you?"

He slid down her body, removing the sheet as he moved down to put his nose against her skin right in between her breasts, making her breath catch in her throat. "Mmmmm. Licorice...and," he paused.

"And?" She asked.

He crawled down her body, removing the sheet as he went breathing against her skin, taking her scent into him. She watched the muscles of his back ripple in the mirror and as he moved down her body, it was the most erotic sight she had ever seen.

He stopped to place a small, soft kiss at her waist. "Mmmmm. Jasmine, and," he continued to breathe in her skin to her navel, pausing to dip his tongue lightly into the indentation. "A hint of peppermint and," here he settled himself in between her thighs, his broad shoulders pushing them wide. His tanned skin was darker than her alabaster, a contrast that was entrancing. She closed her eyes against the sight of his tawny head above her sex. There was no way she was stopping him now.

"And?" She gasped.

"And woman," he said softly, placing a tender kiss on the curls of her sex.

"Oh." She said breathlessly as desire rushed through her veins. "How does that all make you feel?" She would never have asked such a question to anyone other than this dream lover.

"Hard." He said simply as he gently parted the lips of her pussy with his long fingers. "Do you remember where I told you I wanted to put my tongue?" His voice vibrated throughout her entire body from where he spoke against her, clear to her fingers and toes.

"Yes." She whispered in anticipation.

"May I?" He was giving her a choice. "Do you want me?"

"Oh...please, yes," her voice was a hoarse whisper as her body ached for him.

He was surprisingly gentle as he touched her, as if he knew how much she ached and any overt pressure on her clitoris would have been a shock setting back her desire. Instead, he ran his tongue up and around to softly circle her, occasionally dipping into drink of her juices, barely touching her clitoris until she didn't think that she could stand it anymore. She clutched his hand, which he had rested against her stomach as he lay between her legs, holding them wide with his shoulders and he loved her with his mouth. She ran a hand through the silky waves on his head and he took her engorged clitoris into his mouth to gently suck and run his tongue gently over her, gently stroking her length.

She had never felt anything like it as her hips involuntarily moved to meet the actions of his mouth. "Oh, Nichola!" She gasped out in pleasure.

He quickly moved to place his hips where his head had been. She moaned out her disappointment. "Ochi, agápi mou. No, my love," he translated. "Prépei na eímai mésa sou me ton éna í ton állo trópo; I need to be inside of you one way or the other before I lose control." He whispered, and he stroked his cock against her pussy, not entering. She moaned in surprised delight at how good that felt and wrapped her arms around his shoulders and brought her legs up above his hips. This was not her most favorite position, as she found it difficult to achieve orgasm, though that had rarely mattered to any partner in the past. She found she did like him stroking his cock against her though. Maybe he would bring her close before he entered her.

"No, my sweet." He said softly. She opened her eyes and looked up into his. They were large and dark, and his amber irises were ringed in red. "I am extraordinarily strong; I can still love you properly if you wrap your legs around mine. You do not have to be in any position that doesn't please you." As he spoke, she noticed that his teeth had grown long and sharp. She moved her legs lower and wrapped her legs around his with a sigh of pleasure, and he showed her why his movements against the cleft of her pussy with his cock had been more than pleasure as he slid wetly into her tightness, more than filling her. She lifted her hips to meet him with a gasp and reached her hands down to grip his ass, pulling her closer to him, as she kissed him, finding herself wholly unafraid of his teeth.

He paused in his movements so that she could adjust to his size, though she could tell it was difficult for him to do so.

"You are so very...tight," he whispered with his eyes closed in pleasure, against the side of her face, as he slid his arms around her, clasping her hips.

"Sorry." She whispered, once again self-conscious.

He chuckled softly, and she felt small butterfly kisses against her shoulder and the side of her neck as he started to move slowly, gently, "I'm not," came his whispered moan.

She watched him love her in the mirror above the bed. Fascinated by the flexing muscles of his shoulders and back, the slow strokes of his hips which tightened his ass, and she ran her hands up and down those muscles being rewarded by soft moans of pleasure, and whispered Greek words that she didn't understand, "Pio agapiméni mou, áse me na se agapó gia pánta. Ela gia ména."

Soon, she was responding to each thrust of his hips as he slid his cock in and out of her. She could feel herself growing tighter around him, thrusting upwards to meet each stroke. Holding his ass tight as he moaned his pleasure softly in her ear, urging her on, "Ela gia ména".

Never having a lover who responded to her needs like this before, she found herself moaning and whispering to him when he rubbed against that perfect spot, "Yes, Nichola, there. Right there!" When she did, he changed his rhythm to half strokes, intentionally rubbing the head of his cock on the area that she wanted him to, and she nearly came undone.

He felt her pussy tighten in response and moaned softly, "Yes, come for me, i psyhí mou, come for me!" He urged her softly, whispering in her ear, as her grip on his ass tightened urging his hips on.

Several short strokes later, he felt the spasms in her pussy grip his cock and run throughout her body as she began loudly moaning her orgasm, tossing her head back exposing her throat to him and he fought against his very natural urge to bite down on her shoulder. Instead, he continued to stroke her special place with the head of his cock, riding out her orgasm and as the first ended he was shortly rewarded with a second, louder, unexpected orgasm, causing him to give a purely male, low, growl of satisfaction. No longer being able to hold back, he pumped his cum inside of her body, losing himself.

As he recovered, still buried deep inside of her, he realized her arms were still holding him tightly, and he worried he may be crushing her into the mattress. He rose onto his forearms and looked at her to find her looking at him in teary-eyed wonder. He knew his eyes were red, and his teeth still ached, so they hadn't receded yet. He probably was a fright and hoped he wasn't scaring the hell out of her. He had been so careful to make sure that she hadn't been able to see his transformation the last time.

"This isn't a dream, is it?" She asked softly, touching the side of his face gently, unafraid.

"No, i psyhí mou. It isn't." He said simply, kissing her lips softly, taking her hand and kissing her palm and then her wrist as he slid from within her body, then moved to hold her close to his side, so his weight wouldn't crush her.

She sighed softly, closed her eyes, and fell asleep, held tightly in his arms.

She woke up to some sort of commotion going on in the living room. She heard several things at once.

Michael's voice, "Hey, man. How's everything going?" A low bass reply that she couldn't make out which had to be Mansuetus, and then "Who are you?" in Zachary's loud chirpy three-year-old voice. Then the louder, "Da, da, da, da, da, da, da," of Devin calling for her. She got out of bed, kind of surprised that she was still dressed in the loose short outfit, and threw on a lightweight robe. Taking a quick look in the mirror, she was surprised that she looked so well, and she had to admit she felt great. Then she remembered everything and flushed guiltily. She walked out into the living room.

Zachary was the first person to see her, screaming "Mommy!" and running to her to fling his little arms around her legs.

Michael had put Devin in his walker, and he had been silently contemplating Mansuetus' tall form.

Leila thought, *He's probably trying to decide if he should start screaming or not.* Upon the completion of that thought, he changed his attention to come flying over to her once he saw Zachary had a hold of her. Leila quickly scooped up Zachary and moved to the side, knowing from experience that to avoid severely bruised shins that was what was required. Devin had one speed in his walker, ultra-fast, little to no concept of braking, and could frequently be dangerous.

Zachary screamed "Wheeeee!" as she swung him over the back of and onto the loveseat. Leila grabbed hold of the walker and pulled Devin's shrieking "Da, da, da, da, da," body into her arms.

"Momma!" She told him automatically.

"Da, da, da, da, da!" He yelled.

"Yes, I am right here now. I am not going anywhere." She said soothingly to him. She noticed that the Daycare had secured his pacifier to his wrist with some sort of string and elastic wristband, and she said, "Binky." He compliantly opened his mouth, and she popped it in.

He was a mess today. They sent him to daycare primped and pampered, and more importantly, clean, and he frequently came home a dirty mess. Today, she saw that he obviously had spit more food on his shirt than usual and they had done a lousy job of cleaning him up again. He had a smudge of dirt on his nose today! She gave him a look of irritation and he mirrored her look back at her. Then she smiled at him, and he crinkled up his nose and eyes and smiled around his pacifier, waving his arms around and looking like the little demon he was. With Devin secured to her side, she walked around and sat next to Zachary, who hugged her hard.

"You got off of work early," she said to Michael, standing next to Mansuetus, who seemed to be taking in this domestic scene in stride.

"Well, it's actually after four o'clock, so no, not that early. You look flushed. You okay?" Michael asked.

"Maybe a little overheated." She said not meeting his eyes to smile down at Zachary, who was pulling at the sleeve of her robe.

"Mommy, who that?" He whispered pointing at Mansuetus.

Mansuetus came around the end of the couch to kneel directly before Zachary on one knee as he sat on the loveseat. "I am Mansuetus, young Master." He said very formally, a fist to his chest. Leila, put out with him, realized they had more discussions to be had, and he glanced at her out of the corner of his eyes.

All the sudden, Devin spit out his pacifier and yelled out, "Man!" Both surprising and irritating the hell out of Leila. Holding his arms out to Mansuetus in demand.

"I am Zachary!" Zachary chirped to him. "That is my brother, Devin. He bites." He said in warning.

"I have been around many biting creatures before, Master Zachary." Mansuetus told him with great solemnity and confidence as he plucked Devin from Leila's arms with practiced ease, as if he had been around children his whole life, and stood up in one fluid motion, much to Devin and Zachary's delight.

"You are big, Man!" Zachary's voice was in awe.

"I eat all of my food, Master Zachary." Mansuetus said to Leila with a secret smile. Leila couldn't help herself and smiled back at him. This was the softest she had seen the big man, and he seemed genuinely happy.

"Oh!" Zachary said, as if he had imparted some great wisdom to him.

"So, where's your aunt?" Michael said to Leila, jealous of his children's attention.

"Iris has the night shift." Mansuetus said in response.

"That's great!" Michael said. "You guys have it all worked out. I have some bad news," he said and didn't sound like he felt it was bad at all.

"Really?" Leila said curiously. "What's going on?"

"I have to go to sea," He said simply.

"For how long now?" Leila said in stunned disbelief, and Mansuetus even looked at Michael in surprise. Michael returned a guilty look to the other man as Leila continued. "You just got back a week ago!"

"I will be gone for at least a month. In and out of AUTEC. We are performing testing on multiple systems and multiple ships." Michael said, trying to sound important.

"Does your command even know what is going on *here*, Michael?" Leila said quietly. She never thought that she could be so angry.

"I will take the children for a walk," Mansuetus said gently. "This is acceptable, Kyría? Do you have a carriage for the small one?"

"Yes, that would be truly kind, Mansuetus. Thank you so much. We have a double stroller. Let me get it for you." Leila headed for the front closet and pulled it out.

She turned around and Mansuetus handed her Devin. He took over getting it unfolded and set up, while Devin yelled, "Man, man, man, man!"

Mansuetus looked at him and said softly, "Hush, Master Devin!" Devin quieted right down and watched him while he got the stroller set up properly.

Michael escaped past them to head into their third bedroom at the opposite end of the hall, which they used as his computer-game room and, on occasion a guest bedroom. She could see him toss his seabag on the daybed.

Michael headed back into the kitchen to grab his briefcase just in time to see Mansuetus stand up from securing the boys into the stroller and to put a shoulder holster with a Glock 17 on over his t-shirt. He also picked up a double-sided tactical knife from the table that he secured in a hidden back sheath along his belt. He met Michael's eyes calmly as he pulled his sports coat on.

Michael said quietly, "I thought you were a driver?" giving Leila a strange look.

"I am a driver, I am a nurse, and occasionally I am a bodyguard." Mansuetus smiled his scary smile at Michael. "I am versatile." He said with a very European shrug.

"Any particular instructions, Kyría?" Mansuetus asked in deference to Leila.

"Just be careful if you go over to the pond on that side of the neighborhood," she said, pointing north. "It seems a small alligator has taken up residence to munch up the neighborhood ducklings."

"Would you young masters like to see Mansuetus wrestle an alligator?" He said to Zachary.

"Alligator!" Zachary yelled.

"Man, Man, Man, Man!" Yelled Devin.

"Mansuetus!" Leila scolded, following him to the front door, with Michael trailing behind, watching the whole scene suspiciously.

"Do not worry, Kyría," he chuckled at her. "My life before theirs." He assured her softly and wheeled his young charges through the front door.

Upon closing the front door, she wheeled on Michael and said hotly, "What kind of bullshit is this that you are pulling on me, Michael?"

"Who the hell is that guy?" He questioned in return.

"Mansuetus is not the problem."

"What the hell was it he called you? Kyría? What the hell does that mean?" He yelled, trying to deflect her attention.

"It means, Lady or missus. It's fucking Greek! Who the fuck cares? What the fuck are you doing? I can't go back to work for thirty fucking days, Michael! I'm not allowed to drive! What the fuck!" She yelled following him as he stormed into the office to start packing his sea bag. "Look at me." He turned and looked at her coldly. "How long have I worked for the military?" She asked him. Her voice had calmed, but her stance was anything but as she faced him straight on, feet shoulder width, and her arms crossed tightly.

Startled, he blinked. "I don't know. Seven years."

"Right, almost eight years now. How many assistants have I had working for me over the years?"

"I don't know," he said in bewilderment. "A few."

"Five. Let me tell you how I ended up with five different military service members, three of which were submarine sailors, who reported directly to me. They had some sort of family issue. Their wife or one of their kids was ill.

It was always a temporary situation until their family problems were resolved. The military doesn't want their personnel on a ship when their minds are elsewhere. It's bad for morale, it's bad for operations. People make mistakes. When people make mistakes, people can get hurt." She said, crossing her arms, and her eyes flashed at him. "They wouldn't put you, a chief, working for some civilian. They have a lot of chiefs at the squadrons. They would rotate a chief or two around, and you would pick up their rotation after I was able to return to work. Why on earth wouldn't you tell your command what is going on with me?"

"Your family is here. You don't need me here too. You're just bitching!" He ground out through clenched teeth.

"You knew nothing about my family being here until last night. *I knew nothing about my family being here until last night.*" She stressed to him.

"You know, I need to make Senior Chief! There is so much to think about, so many things can happen. I am working my ass off for us!" He yelled in her face trying to intimidate her.

"You are so full of shit!" She screamed back. "You have never done *anything* for us! You have only done shit for yourself. What would I have done if my family weren't here?" He turned his back to her to continue packing his bag. "Look at me and answer me, asshole. What would I have done if my family weren't here?"

He turned and looked at her calmly. "I am not sure that I can do this anymore."

"Really?" She said just as calmly with a strange contemptuous look in her eye. He had never seen her look at him like this and was floored by her reaction.

"Yeah, I need to decide whether or not I want to stay married." He had done this a few times with her in the past, and she always buckled. He knew how important her family was to her.

"You are going to pull this crap on me now?" She said calmly. Frost could have formed on her words. "Because you can't handle the truth?" Again, she gave him that strange disdainful look he'd never seen from her before. As if he were nothing.

"Obviously, I don't see you begging me not to divorce you!" He said in exasperation. Throwing more things haphazardly in his seabag. "If you gave a crap about me, why aren't you crying or something?" He said, looking at her furiously.

The look she gave him was derisive, and her words were like ice, spoken so cold and smooth, "So, you want me to *beg* you to be a decent husband? No, you *need* me to *beg* you to be a decent husband." It was a statement as if she had just realized something for herself, something about him. Something that disgusted her.

He zipped up his bag, grabbed it, and pushed past her, infuriated with her and with himself. "I am going to stay at the barracks. The ship has an early departure time tomorrow morning. I will leave the truck in long-term parking, and just drive myself when I come back. You won't have to worry about it." As if he were doing her a favor.

"Whatever! You do you, Michael. That seems to be what you are truly best at." She stated calmly, coolly, in a patronizing way.

She followed him to the connecting door going to the garage, thankfully in shadow, and calmly watched him take out the kid's car seats from the back seat of his truck to put against the wall of the garage and then throw his bag in. He turned to look at her and realized that the fading light in the open garage made her eyes seem to glow. Her look of calm nothingness had not changed. He'd never seen her so cold toward him before, and this shook him to the core.

"We'll talk about this when I get back." He said to her softly. Desperate now for a reaction from her other than her looking at him like a piece of shit to be scraped from her shoe.

"Life is about choices, Michael. You made your choice, and I will make mine." Her voice had changed into something unemotional and remote, alien. It lacked all warmth and passion, either of love or anger, and was not like his Leila at all.

He got into the truck and started it up, and to his utmost surprise, she turned her back on him, walked into the house, closing the connecting garage door behind her softly as if she could not care less.

He made a couple of sweeps of the neighborhood, looking for Mansuetus and the kids. He found them on their way back and he pulled up to the big man pushing the stroller. Mansuetus stopped and looked at him. "You are leaving?" He asked calmly.

"Yeah, we pull out really early tomorrow. It's best that I spend the night on the base." Michael said as Mansuetus fixed him with a stare. "Hey, man, I just want to thank you for everything that you are doing to help. I know Leila appreciates it, and I do too. Please let her aunt know that as well."

"I will. Leila is family. Family is everything." Mansuetus said simply.

"Well," Michael said to him, clearly at a loss for words. "Thanks a lot. I will see you guys in a few weeks."

Mansuetus nodded.

"Bye guys!" He said waving to the boys.

"Bye Daddy!" Zachary said, unconcerned, looking at him.

Devin squinted at him with his clove-colored eyes quietly.

He pulled away. This was the first time he had ever felt a tightness in his chest about leaving his family; an uncertainty of the future. He hoped like hell he hadn't fucked it all up.

When Mansuetus wheeled the boys back into the house, he found Leila in the kitchen, setting up a highchair at the table. Leaving the children secured in the stroller, he helped her silently.

"I need to get the kids fed and bathed." She said simply, calmly.

Mansuetus glanced at the clock. 5:30 p.m. "The sun doesn't set until 7:47 p.m. today." He said matter of fact. "I will leave to collect your aunt at 7:30." He immediately started removing things from the refrigerator, while Leila grabbed a washcloth and washed up Devin, while he was secured in the stroller, much to his displeasure.

"No!" He yelled.

"You know two words. 'No' and 'Da'." She told him conversationally, as she wiped.

"Man!" He said as if he were yelling for rescue.

"I am sorry, three words now. Why won't you say Momma?" She looked at him. He fixed her with a stubborn look. "I know you can say it if you really tried. Momma." She smiled, coaxing. He smiled in return as she cleaned the smudge of dirt from his nose. Suddenly, her large black cat stood up next to the carriage to see what she was doing, putting his huge black head into Devin's face purring loudly much to Devin's delight. Pepper stood on her other side, giving Zachary kisses as he laughed hysterically.

"Where have you two been?" Leila said.

"Sunroom." Mansuetus said softly, passing behind her. He kneeled on the other side with a washcloth of his own, moving the dog and her kisses aside, and cleaned up Zachary, unfastening him and pulling him from the stroller. He put him in his booster seat at the table.

"Man, man, man, man." Devin yelled, waving his arms.

"Yes, Master Devin. I am coming." Mansuetus said, performing the same function and putting him in the highchair securely. Getting his tray secured to the seat. Mansuetus put a handful of banana slices on the tray and Devin immediately scooped up one to bite it.

"Me!" Yelled Zachary.

Mansuetus sat down a plastic child's plate in front of him, one of several to be found in Leila's cabinets, filled with banana slices, seedless grapes sliced in half, sliced blue berries, and sliced mango pieces. Mansuetus added a few small, sliced mango pieces to Devin's tray, who proceeded to gobble them up. He then added a few small cut squares of what looked to be buttered bread with the crusts cut off to Zachary's plate and two small ones to Devin's tray. Leila sat at the table and watched them in stunned silence, as her kids munched up their food happily.

"Mansuetus, when did you have time to do all of this?" She said in awe.

"While you slept, Kyría." He said simply.

"You have a lot of experience with small children, don't you?" She asked softly.

"I do." He said simply, setting a plate in front of her that she hadn't even realized he had been preparing, so preoccupied with the sight of her children eating happily and healthily. Not a processed food in sight.

She looked down and saw the rare roast beef from earlier warmed, buttered bread and a variety of fruits and sliced cooked vegetables. She watched as he added a few sliced cooked carrots to the tray and plate of her children. He had obviously cooked them earlier and let them cool. They usually refused to eat carrots; today, they ate them right down. Causing her to pick up her fork and spear one, which was larger and warmer, and pop it into her mouth. It was cooked to perfection. As she ate her food, she watched Mansuetus give a little of the ultra-tender beef to the kids. Devin was not a meat eater. Of course, with the way baby food meat smelled, she couldn't blame him much, but he gobbled his small pieces down with gusto.

Zachary, who liked meat, said, "Mmmmm. Good," and Mansuetus added a few more pieces to his plate, cut simply perfect for Zachary.

Her eyes filled with tears, and she said to Mansuetus, "Mansuetus, I can't thank you enough for this. I don't know what I would do if you weren't here right now." She said and hurriedly wiped a tear that spilled over. Suddenly he was there kneeling by her side.

"No, Kyría, it is my privilege to be here," clearly distressed by her tears, taking her hand in his. "It has been an exceptionally long time since I have had the pleasure of taking care of children. I truly didn't know how much I had missed it myself." He smiled reassuringly.

"You are a very good man, Mansuetus." She said softly and smiled.

"It touches me you think so, Kyría. Why don't we get them bathed and ready for bed and I will retrieve your aunt?"

She nodded her head to him.

With the kids well-fed, bathed, and dressed in their pajamas, Leila settled down with them, into her oversized blue loveseat recliner, a Disney video popped into the machine. This was their quiet time, just before bed. Zachary on one side and Devin on the other, everyone wrapped in one of her mother's handmade throw quilts that dressed up the soft blue cloth furniture of the living room, watching and listening to the songs on the video. Gladiator lay stretched out along the back of the loveseat, loudly purring, as was his habit during quiet time. It was hard to believe it was only Wednesday night. To Leila, it felt as if at least a week had passed since she had woken up in the hospital.

At 8:30 p.m., Aunt Iris, hair loose, dressed in a light jacket, pair of jeans, t-shirt, and tennis shoes, walked quietly into the house, followed closely by Mansuetus. Pepper lifted her head from the couch where she had been laying, to give a soft 'woof'. She jumped from the couch to come and lay on the loveseat next to Leila and the children protectively. A soft, low growl coming from her throat. Glad stopped his purring to fix her aunt with a narrow-eyed glare, the hair starting to rise on his back. He landed in Leila's lap to lean against her protectively, a warning growl reverberating throughout his body. Leila was shocked by their actions.

"Shhhh. Pepper, Glad, stop it!" She said softly.

Aunt Iris said to them steadily in a mellifluous voice, "Hush beasts, your charges are safe from me." Pepper stopped growling but kept a protective eye on her. Gladiator stopped growling likewise, but the hair on his back didn't fully go down. He too, kept a yellow-eyed stare on her aunt.

Leila asked softly, "Dogs and cats don't like you anymore, Aunt Iris?" She felt sad for her as she knew her aunt loved animals.

"It's not really a matter of 'like', I think. It's more a matter of 'trust'. One predator always recognizes another." She said softly with a small shrug, but Leila could see that it bothered her. "So, these are my nephews?" She asked softly, sitting at the far end of the couch, so as not to excite them, giving them a smile. "They look like you, my love."

"Zachary," she nodded toward him, curled up on her left side, "and Devin," nodding toward him on her right.

"Hi," Zachary said sleepily.

Devin watched Aunt Iris as he sucked on his pacifier. He didn't make any noise until he saw Mansuetus standing behind her. Pulling out his pacifier, he said sleepily, "Man!" holding his arms out to the big man.

"Should I get them down for the night, Kyría?" He asked softly.

"Yes, it is almost time for their bedtime." She said quietly.

"No!" Zachary said loudly.

"Hush, young master, and do as your mother wishes and I will tell you a bedtime story." Mansuetus said.

"'Kay. With dragons?" Zachary asked. His new favorite cartoon had dragons, and he loved them.

"I know about dragons, Young One. They are mighty and wise beasts." Mansuetus said scooping a child in each arm, Devin rested his head on the big man's shoulder, and he took them down the hall toward their room.

"I gather you have had a rather trying evening." Aunt Iris said to her, and Leila nodded her head back at her in return tiredly. "Your husband is gone?" Aunt Iris asked directly.

"So, Mansuetus told you?" Leila said.

"No, he would never break a confidence. He didn't have to. Michael's truck is not here, and I do not sense him in the house. It's elementary, my dear." Aunt Iris tossed a hand, doing a Holmes impression. Leila smiled softly at her as she continued. "So, for how long?"

"Forever, maybe." Leila said with a sad smile.

"Men are bastards sometimes, aren't they?" Aunt Iris leaned forward in confidence. "He'll be back, then he will be more trouble than he is worth." She reassured her.

"It doesn't make much difference," Leila said, "it has come to my attention that I am having a wildly intense love affair in any case."

Iris looked shocked. "No! Beasts see to the children." She waved her hand, and the animals headed toward the boy's room where they could hear Mansuetus' voice softly speaking. She reached over, grabbed the remote and turned the television off, slid to the end of the couch closest to Leila and, giving her full attention, she continued softly, "Tell me all about it! Is your lover handsome?"

"He's beautiful. Extremely sexy." Leila said with a smile.

"Is he smart? But that doesn't really matter! In fact, and take my word for it, it's preferable if he isn't smart, the smart ones become difficult quickly. Is he married? Jealous women are always a problem!" She said, chuckling quietly in remembrance.

Aunt Iris' affairs had been legendary throughout the family.

"No, I don't believe he is married. He seems to be highly intelligent." Leila smiled at her.

"Oh, that's too bad," Iris said sadly.

"But the sex is fabulous! The best I have ever had," Leila said softly as she watched her aunt's eyes light up. She remembered how much her aunt loved gossip and how much Leila had loved to listen to her conversations when she was a quiet child. The things that she had learned from Iris and her sister Lystel's conversations would raise hairs on her mother's neck!

"Oh, in that case, that overcomes the intelligence. Lord, you didn't tell your husband, out of a sense of guilt, did you? Is that why he is gone?" Iris asked, slightly scandalized.

Even she had never 'admitted' about her lovers to Francisque, not that he and the world weren't perfectly aware of what was going on. Iris was never very discreet. They had a very strange relationship, Leila thought.

"I am not a fool, Auntie." Leila said, looking at her fondly, teasingly.

"Did you meet him through your job?" Aunt Iris questioned.

"No, I only met him a few days ago." Leila said.

"A few days ago?" Aunt Iris inquired. "But you have been in the hospital for the past few days." She said guiltily, "Please tell me it's not that young doctor!"

Leila wondered what had happened between her and Dr. Lambert to make her say that in such a manner and tone. "No, Auntie. It isn't Dr. Lambert."

"Phew! That's a relief!" Iris expressed with a small, guilty laugh.

"Why?" Leila asked suspiciously.

"Oh, no reason. No reason." Iris said quickly brushing aside the question, along with an imaginary speck of dirt from her jeans. "So, who is it?" She inquired, not meeting Leila's eyes, still brushing her jeans.

"His name is Nichola." Leila stated, looking at her aunt's reaction.

"Nichola?" Iris quickly looked up. "What does he look like?" Iris demanded with suspicion.

"A golden, amber-eyed, Greek god," Leila said simply. "That occasionally has red eyes and extremely sharp teeth."

"No! He is here?" Iris asked, confirming Leila's suspicions.

"No, Auntie, he is coming to me in my dreams. He has been since the first day." Leila said.

Iris put a hand to her forehead. "That's how he knew!" She muttered. "And your dreams are sexual in nature?" Iris asked, looking at her strangely.

"Sexual in nature is not the way I would describe it, Iris. Unless you call full frontal penetration, and multi-orgasmic, 'sexual in nature'." Leila said hotly in a low voice.

"I have my bags in the car. I want to stay here with you for the next couple of days." Iris said, changing the subject so quickly Leila was shocked.

"What? That's not possible, Aunt Iris!" Leila said.

"Well, why ever not?" Iris inquired.

"This is your response to what I just told you?" Leila asked hotly.

"Ladies," Mansuetus said, coming into the living room. "The children are asleep. Please speak lower." He said quietly in his bass voice.

"I can help you with the children." Iris said to her softly.

"Aunt Iris. I don't have a room that's light tight. Unless you want to share my bedroom with me?" Leila said. "And that's not totally light tight, either."

"No. You have a little room in the back. I can rest in there. Mansuetus, can take care of the window. Correct?" She inquired.

"Yes. I have the necessary supplies to do that." Mansuetus said.

"Aunt Iris, I don't want to seem indelicate. But can I really trust you with the children?" Leila said.

"Darling, you know I would never! I don't feed from humans." Iris put the guilty pleasure of Dene Lambert from her mind.

"Well, what about the dog and the cat?" Leila said, giving her a look.

"Leila, I promise I won't eat your pets! Or your neighbor's pets, either." She said, as Leila started to speak. "I am perfectly safe. I have my own food. I would feel better if I were here with you, and Mansuetus would not have to bring me back and forth if we are both here."

"Where will Mansuetus sleep?" Leila said.

"Couch is fine. Or I can make a pallet in children's room. Large room." He said reasonably.

Well, he was right about that, Leila thought. The boy's room was twice the size of the normal sized third bedroom and had a larger walk-in closet than she had. It was where they stored Michael's uniforms, most of his clothes, and the boy's toys. She did appreciate the help.

"Fine. But I must go into the base early tomorrow morning. We will need to stop and obtain Mansuetus a thirty-day pass so that he can take the kid's to and from daycare, if we need a day sitter. I really don't want to get them too much off schedule, just because I am sick. I also need to stop in at work and give them my medical leave pass, so they can process the paperwork. I don't want to lose my job. I worked hard to get it." She said, entirely missing the look that passed between Mansuetus and Iris. "That will not be a problem, will it, Mansuetus? You have a license and insurance, correct?"

"Yes." He said simply.

"Great. I can just show Pass and ID my medical excuse and explain the situation to them and it shouldn't be a problem getting the pass. We can then take the kids to daycare, get you set up with permission to drop them off and pick them up, and go do what we need to do with human resources. Does that sound like a plan?"

"Yes." Mansuetus said.

"Wonderful!" Aunt Iris said happily. "This situation will only be for a few days at most anyway, sweetheart. Dr. Tsoukalous will be here..." she looked at Mansuetus.

"Friday night. He should be here by midnight, if not earlier." He provided for her.

"Great." Leila said, seeing that the time had flown, and it was already closing in on ten o'clock. "Do you need me to help you with anything to secure the room, Mansuetus?"

"No, Kyría." He said softly.

"We should try to get some sleep, you and I," she said to Mansuetus, then looked at Iris, at a loss for words. Iris smiled sweetly at her, and Leila looked at Mansuetus again. "You, me and the kids, should leave here around six to beat the worst of the sun. We will need to get the kid's seats in the limousine. They must be secured in the backseat. It is the law. They are in the garage where Michael left them."

"I will take care of it, Kyría, you do not need to worry."

"Ok, let me get you guys some sheets and blankets." She got up and headed for the large linen closet in the back hallway.

"We need to talk!" Iris said to the big man in a low whisper.

Mansuetus nodded in return. He knew he was going to get an earful from the young, flamboyant vampire and didn't relish this conversation.

Leila had gone to bed after making up the daybed for Iris and making up the couch for Mansuetus. Iris followed Mansuetus outside into the driveway as he carried the car seats out to the limousine and climbed into the back to belt them in. She joined him in the back and then closed the door. She did not know how to belt in the car seats, so had no intention of helping, but she also didn't want their conversation to be overheard by Leila or anyone who may walk their dog at night.

"What the hell is *he* about? She will be furious when she finds out." She said to him. "You don't know my niece when she decides she is going to set her mind to something. Either for or against!" Iris started.

"You walked into that conversation. She can manipulate almost as well as you do. I can't believe that you would encourage her to take lovers! *He* will not be pleased!" Mansuetus said, aghast.

"Oh please! It's good for a woman to have a lover now and again. It keeps your husband interested, and he doesn't take you for granted, and besides, she is becoming a vampire. There will be many lovers for her. But you are right. I should have known. Leila has a great sense of loyalty and a high moral attitude when it comes to her personally, even as a child." She eyed Mansuetus, thoughtfully. "As for manipulative conversations, out with it. No more misdirection. Why is he visiting Leila in her dreams? *How* is he visiting Leila in her dreams? He never came to me in a dream state while I was changing."

"You were already known to him, through Martin. He too, blames himself for the loss of your sister. He wasn't paying attention. So, he made sure to be paying attention with you and the rest of your siblings. But even his powers don't include being able to visit unknown humans in their dreams. *He* didn't visit her the first time; *she came to him*. As a human changeling, she initiated and made the connection. So, now he can visit her as well. As to how, he has his theories." Mansuetus said as he secured the first seat, not looking at Iris.

"Oh, please! That old vampire wives' tale?" Iris sat back in disbelief.

"It is not a wives' tale, Iris. It is just extremely rare." Mansuetus said firmly, working on the second seat.

"How many have you met over the years?" She scoffed.

"Two." He stated softly. "Two pairs."

"What?" Iris said. "How do you know?"

"Together, they can do extraordinary things. Communication across great distances is said to be one of them. You have not been a vampire for two decades yet. You have much to learn." Mansuetus said to her as he completed the second seat. "You need to tell her what is happening to her. You need to tell her she is becoming a vampire." Mansuetus said to her. "You need to explain to her what that means. There are many things that she needs to know and prepare for. *He* will teach her about everything else. But she will not be able to understand *that* until she understands she is becoming a vampire."

"Mansuetus, she does have choices." Iris said softly.

"Yes, she has two choices. Accept what is or fight it and end up changing later in a painful manner. Maybe hurting someone. Is that what you of all people want for her?" He asked angrily.

"Mansuetus, her father, still hasn't crossed. He is doing well." Iris said, trying to sound reasonable, but with a small doubt in her heart.

"Is he?" Mansuetus asked rhetorically. "You forget who monitors the family, Iris. His struggle is valiant, but it is arduous. By the way, prepare yourself. Your nephew Jamie will be here tomorrow night." He said to Iris' stunned face as he exited the limousine, leaving her to get out by herself.

In the morning at exactly 6:00 a.m., Mansuetus and Leila loaded the kids into the back of the limousine as Iris waved them goodbye in the dark. Mansuetus was not happy, because he did not understand, or like that they were fed their breakfast at daycare. He did not trust daycare to take care of them properly and proceeded to lament about taking them to daycare in the first place.

"Mansuetus," Leila asked, not being a good morning person herself, "do you drink coffee?"

The question threw him off his rant. "No, Kyría." He answered automatically.

"Well, you need to start." She sniped.

They rode to the base in relative silence after that.

Twenty minutes later, they were pulling up to the Pass and ID office outside of the front gate. Mansuetus parked the limousine and Leila went inside to discuss getting a thirty-day pass for both Mansuetus and the limousine. Five minutes later, she came back out and sent him in with his license, registration, and insurance card, while she waited in the car with the kids. In less than ten minutes, he was back in the car, taping a temporary pass on the inside of the windshield, and clipping a badge on the lapel of his jacket.

Easy-peasy. They proceeded through the main gate, and she directed him to the daycare facility.

Mansuetus grabbed the diaper bags in a huff, and Leila grabbed Zachary as Mansuetus took Devin and into daycare they went. It was simple to get Mansuetus onto the pickup and drop off list for the kids. Which did not improve his mood, as he felt this was substandard security, and how could the boys possibly be safe with substandard security? He also didn't hesitate to tell her so in a low whisper. Leila wasn't sure what he was expecting. Maybe a strip and body cavity search? After all, she was their mother, and she was there putting him on the list. Of course, both boys threw an absolute fit, screaming at the top of their lungs "Man!" when they dropped them off with their daycare workers in their respective age group rooms, and the more upset Mansuetus became, the more 'Greek' he became.

"Sýnchrones gynaíkes!" He said in frustration, stomping out as they left the daycare center.

"Don't you 'modern women' me! It's modern men that force us to have to work outside of the home! We must make a choice between providing a home for our children or a hovel! I don't like this anymore than you do, probably less, but it is what it is!" She said to him sharply.

"You understood me!" He said, shocked.

"Don't ask me how because I don't know how! All I know is that it is almost 7:00 and sunrise is at 7:11! Human resources opens at seven. We need to get there, get parked, and get inside as quickly as possible." She said feeling agitated the closer to dawn it got and climbed into the front seat.

"I am sorry, Kyría." He said pulling out, as she pointed the way.

"We both need coffee," she grumbled.

They got the car parked, taking two spaces, which should please some-one, she thought, and got into the building by seven. She saw Mansuetus grab her sunhat, glasses, and an umbrella but thought little of it. She stood in line, gave the girl at the front her medical excuse, which they made copies of, and then gave her the required form, which she filled out. Thank God her main offices, and Bart Crispin, her Department Head, was upstairs on the second floor. Now she just needed his signature, and they could be on their way, heading back to the relative quiet of her home. She was stressed out and exhausted already!

She and Mansuetus walked up the stairs and she nodded hello to several of her co-workers, who seemed incredibly happy that she was out of the hospital. Mansuetus flanked her, and his large frame garnered many an appreciative look from her female co-workers. She noticed he was scowling. She smiled at them waving tiredly at a couple, and said softly to him, "You are being intimidating."

She got a low grunt in response, thinking, "Okay", with a sigh.

At the end of the hallway came a loud shriek, "You're back!" and the tall, big-breasted form of her friend Jackie came rushing at them. Jackie's outfit today was a gregarious, flowing, low-cut, long-skirted, purple, and green outfit that only her wild-haired self could pull off and still look incredibly attractive. She stopped to gently hug her as if she might break, "Girl, you look peaked!"

"Yes, I am a bit of a mess. I need to get this into Bart. Is he in yet? They have let me out, but I can't work or drive for thirty days." She said tiredly.

"Oh, honey, what is wrong? Bart's around here some place, probably getting coffee." Jackie said in sympathy.

"Some sort of mystery virus. Kind of like mono I guess, extreme exhaustion, sensitivity to the sun, headaches. That sort of thing. I'm not dying or anything though, so silver lining." Leila gave her a half-hearted smile. She was getting good at this lying thing, she thought, looking up to see Mansuetus absolutely transfixed by Jackie.

Jackie noticed his attention and at about 5'9" flat footed, in her three-inch heels, she was almost able to look at Mansuetus straight in the eyes. So, she fixed him with her chocolate brown eyes, batted her long lashes, and flirtatiously said. "And who do we have here?"

"Jackie, this is Mansuetus Smythe. Mansuetus this is my particularly good friend Jackie Guilliams. Mansuetus works for my aunt's personal physician. My Aunt is here to help me out for the next few weeks."

"Mr. Smythe, very nice to meet you." Jackie said with an enormous smile holding out her hand.

Mansuetus took it in his, bowed and bestowed a kiss on it, saying, "Gracious Lady, I am your servant."

Leila thought to herself, "Oh, no! I guess he has decided to not be intimidating anymore!"

Jackie just about fainted. "Oh, my!" She said loudly, giving Leila an impressed look.

"We both need coffee, Jackie." Leila said and just let the inevitable occur, figuring that's what he gets for being a grump, and for being such a flirt first thing in the morning!

"Well, let's fix that, shall we, while we help Leila track down Bart!" Jackie said wrapping her arms around one of Mansuetus' muscular arms and pulling him along, while Leila walked sedately behind them, smiling. "My! You are very well built, Mr. Smythe!" Jackie said, smiling and throwing a look back at Leila, who smiled right along with her.

"Thank you. You look quite lovely in those colors." He said sincerely, giving Jackie a huge smile. Making Jackie giggle loudly.

Leila shook her head. Who would have thought he liked wild women? At least he wasn't being bitchy about the kids anymore.

They rounded a corner and there, sitting next to the coffeepot looking through some paperwork, was Bart Crispin. Bart was a decent looking, kindly older gentleman, whom everyone in the department considered to be their father figure. Leila really liked Bart, but everyone knew he was counting the days until he could retire, so while everyone liked him, he wasn't the most effective Department Head on the base.

"Oh, my god! You are back." He said with a smile. "We were so worried!"

"Hey, boss! Yeah, they released me from the hospital, but I have some bad news. I can't work or drive for thirty days." Leila said, giving him her paperwork and grabbing a Styrofoam cup.

"What's wrong?" He asked worriedly, looking over her paperwork.

"Some sort of mystery virus. Kind of like mono, but without the transmission rate. The nurse said I shouldn't be contagious if I am not running a fever. Exhaustion, sensitivity to the sun, headaches, a general feeling of yuck, basically. Eric has my password to the training program, and all my newest slides are completed and uploaded. You just need a body to present the material, so it shouldn't be an enormous deal with my being out. But you know that you guys can always call me if you have any questions." Leila said sincerely as she handed Mansuetus a cup of coffee. "Here, try this." He took it from her and took a sip.

She poured herself a small cup also and sipped it. Now she was starting to feel a little human. Bart looked at Mansuetus curiously. "Sorry, Bart, for my rudeness, I haven't had coffee since yesterday morning. I am not feeling quite myself, either. This is Mansuetus Smythe. He works for my aunt's personal physician. Mansuetus, this is my Department Head Bart Crispin. Mansuetus and my aunt are going to be helping me out while I deal with this illness."

"You sure you are okay?" Bart said sincerely, worriedly, looking at Mansuetus and shaking hands.

"Yeah, I am going to be okay. It's just a virus. It's got to run its course, I guess. I just need to stay out of the sun and get some rest."

"Follow doctor's orders." Mansuetus said, and Leila thought she detected a slight lilt to his voice.

"Yes, I am going to do that." Leila said grouchily drinking down her coffee. "Speaking of which, can I get your signature on this, Bart? I will drop it back to HR on our way out. I am not feeling too great right now. I will have them put a copy of it all for you in your box downstairs."

"Absolutely! Leila, you need to follow your doctor's orders, so don't worry about us here. I want you to concentrate on getting well, okay?" Bart said, signing the paperwork and standing up and giving her a gentle hug.

"Thanks, I will do my best." She said with a small smile as Mansuetus said goodbye to Jackie, taking Leila by the elbow and walking her downstairs to HR with her paperwork. At the door to the building, Mansuetus made her put on her hat and sunglasses, then opened the umbrella to shade her. Putting a muscular arm around her, he supported her as they made their way over to the parking lot and then loaded her into the back of the limousine. Little did they know, but they had an audience.

"My, that's not good!" Jackie said to Bart, watching how Leila had to be supported to get into the car.

"Make sure you check in with her in a couple of days. If he works for a doctor, that guy is a nurse. I want to make sure that she is okay." Bart said with worry.

"You did not come to me last night." He said softly behind her, kissing her shoulder.

"I have a lot of stuff going on right now." She replied, rolling over to face him. They were back in his bed, both naked again. "A lot of things to think about. Besides, you scare me." She said honestly.

"I would not harm you for the world." He spoke as if she had wounded him.

"Not the teeth, not the eyes. Those don't scare me. *You* scare me. It's one thing for a person's subconscious to take over and to dream about having sex with someone, who doesn't exist and who's not your spouse, it's quite another to want to have sex with a person who from all indications is real. Not only that, but also someone I am communicating with in a, I don't know, supernatural way." Trying to explain her thoughts to him was hard when she could feel the heat coming from his body. She sat up suddenly, moved to the bottom of the bed, grabbed the fur throw and wrapped it tightly around herself; trying to put some distance between them so she could think. He watched her with sad eyes.

"If we were not soul-mated, we could not be doing this together. What we have is incredibly special. Exceedingly rare." He said, propping himself on his forearm, bending a knee to rest his other arm on it, giving her a full-on look at his muscular tanned body in its altogether.

She swallowed heavily. God, he was the most beautiful man she had ever seen. "You are being deliberately provocative!" She said hotly, blushing, indicating him with a hand.

"Am I?" He questioned, raising an eyebrow at her, a small amount of steel in his voice. "From my perspective, you are being unreasonable."

"How so?" She questioned, astounded.

"We are soul-mated; this is natural. You are fighting what we are to each other instead of accepting what is," He said in the same steely tone.

"How can I accept something that I don't understand?" She said with a frightened catch in her voice, getting up from the bed, moving to stand by one of the sofas flanking the fireplace.

"What is there to understand, i psychí mou? Come back to bed," He coaxed, patting the mattress. "You want me to give you pleasure; I want to give you pleasure. You receive strength from me and, almost more importantly, control from me every time you have allowed me to do so. Do not run away from me; you need me; you need my strength. Besides, you cannot outrun me in any case." His voice was sad, but determined.

"I cannot do this! I have a family! I have children! I have a husband! This is not right!" She exclaimed, panicked, shaking her head, denying what she feared in her heart could be true. She turned her back to him.

He was behind her in a breath, pulling the fur from her, wrapping his arms around her from behind. "What does being a human wife have in comparison to being my soul-mate?" He questioned jealously, whispering in her ear. The steel in his voice could have cut through stone. He held her tightly against him as he touched her body intimately. She tried to stop him by pushing his calloused hands away, tried to stop his exploration. It only angered him further. "You were mine years before he entered your life. I have waited a long time for you." He told her as he easily lifted her into his arms, carrying her back to the bed to lay her there.

She rolled over and tried to scramble away from him across the mattress. He simply grasped one of her ankles, and with the other hand, flattened her to the mattress, belly side down, following his hand with his whole body to hold her in place. She could feel his erection in the cleft of her ass. "Stop it, Nichola!" She said to him angrily. She tried to buck him from her and get away. She was angry with herself for wanting him, despite her own words.

"Stop fighting me, Leila!" He commanded, stilling her. She didn't think that he had ever called her by her name before. "I want to be patient with you, i psychí mou. You are my other half. I want to show you the love and patience that you lack in your life. I do. Please believe me when I say I do. I remember and I understand what you are going through." As he spoke, he slowly rubbed his cock along the cleft of her pussy from behind, occasionally rubbing the head against her clitoris. "Feel me. Feel my words for the truth that they hold. Let me love you and give you strength. It will make your transition much easier to endure." He spoke huskily in her ear, holding her tightly.

"You just want to fuck me," she said into the mattress, so angry, at him, at herself, at the world, at this situation, even as her body betrayed her.

"No." He whispered softly, her words making him angry, and she could feel his anger through her body. "I *also* want to fuck you, as you so inelegantly put it. I want it all. As you come to know me better, agápi mou, you will frequently realize that I want it all." He said arrogantly, supremely angry at her denial of him.

My love! She thought, scoffing mentally, then hesitated for a moment, realizing that she had understood him.

In her hesitation, he easily, quickly, pulled her hips up, tilting against him, pressing her shoulders into the mattress, moving between her legs, as she felt his legs spread her own wide. His scent enveloped her, and her traitorous body betrayed her even more as her need for him rose, wetting the velvet of his cock. She could feel her own anger boiling inside of her to fight the need that he created in her. She felt his hand grasp her hair to pull her face from the mattress and turn her head to the side. She gasped in the fresh air and took in more of his scent. This all happened so quickly that she had no time to fight him. She could feel his hips rubbing the head of his cock against her. He wasn't hurting her, but he was easily holding her in place with his superior strength, which she resented. She opened her eyes to meet his angry red eyes and sharp white teeth as he bent over her to intentionally look her in the face, ensuring that she got a good look at his face and what he was. What she feared she was becoming, too.

"Yes. You understood me. You understood me because we are soul-mated." He stated. "Also, understand this," he pushed his cock slowly, carefully, into her unresisting body. As her eyes widened to the sensation, she saw a gleam of anger, jealousy, and triumph in his red eyes. "You are mine. You belonged to me before anyone else and we will belong to each other long after all others are dead and buried." Here he paused, clearly fighting his anger hard for self-control, and partially withdrew his cock and then thrust himself deep inside of her, eliciting a gasp of passion from her throat and a further widening of her teal eyes. "And yes, I do like to fuck you." He said with a growl.

He let go of her hair and taking both her hips in his hands, thrust himself in and out of her body deeply causing her to bury her face into the mattress, to try to suppress the cries of passion that he was eliciting from her, and she could still feel his tightly leashed anger. He suddenly stopped and withdrew, and as he did, he felt her sob once in need beneath him, vanquishing his anger and jealousy.

He rolled her over gently onto her back, to see a tear of frustration, need and anger escape the corner of her eye to roll down her face. Kneeling over her, a knee on each side of her thighs, his back was straight, his erection resting wetly against her stomach unabashedly. He looked down at her and sighed deeply. "But, mostly, I want to love you." He placed his right knee in between her thighs and pulled her left leg to wrap around his waist, leaving her right leg straight between his legs. Laying back against the mattress, she looked up at him in confusion. Taking a hold of her hips, he raised and tilted her hips up, sliding his right knee under her ass to move her up and support her as he easily pulled her forward, sliding his cock deep inside of her.

She gasped in surprise and pleasure.

"Ase me na se agapíso. Let me love you." He said softly to her, withdrawing and again thrusting deeply.

She raised herself slightly on her elbows, to watch him slide in and out of her body in wonder.

"Epitrépste mou na sas dóso efcharístisi. Let me give you pleasure." He said, loving the expression on her face as her jaw dropped open, and her eyes widened in pleasure as he tilted forward to grind his pelvis softly against her clitoris, burying himself to the hilt in her tight sheath.

He held her hips securely as he watched her expressions change and he kneeled at the altar of her body, sliding in and out of her. Loving the sight of her as he learned about her body's reactions. Her nipples were hard pebbles, and her breath was coming in gasps and groans. He knew where he should be, but he wasn't ready to give her release just yet; wanting instead to watch her as her passion built and burned. He was so fascinated with watching her he almost missed his own warning signs.

Suddenly he withdrew slightly from her and changed his tempo. Thrusting the head of his cock softly against an awfully specific spot; *her* spot. She looked him in the eyes for just a moment before collapsing back on to the mattress; his eyes were dilated and red and knowing.

"Ela gia ména, Glykó. Ela gia ména. Come for me, sweet one. Come for me." He coaxed her.

And she did.

She woke up around three o'clock. She didn't remember the trip home, let alone going to bed. Mansuetus probably had to carry her here, she thought in embarrassment, as she was still dressed, but her shoes had been removed. Aunt Iris was sitting in the rocking chair next to the bed, reading a book. How she could read was beyond Leila's understanding as the room was basically dark, just enough light for her to make out the furniture in her own bedroom and Iris rocking in the chair.

"Baby, how do you feel?" Iris asked worriedly, putting her book aside as Leila sat up slowly and propped herself against some pillows to sit up against the headboard.

Leila considered the question carefully. "Good. Strong." She said with a sigh and put her face in her hands in misery, knowing why she felt that way.

"Oh, honey!" Iris said, moving to sit with her on the bed, wrapping an arm around her, misinterpreting her reaction. "The change is hard on everyone. You'll get through this."

As if on cue, Mansuetus came into the room carrying a tray with food and a glass of iced green tea. Placing it on the dresser, he turned to secure the bedroom door against the dim light of the hallway. Leila watched him, wondering what he had done to the windows of the other two bedrooms to get them so dim. He placed the tray on her lap. She gratefully drank the tea. Her mouth was surprisingly dry.

"So, how many people saw you carry me into the house, do you think?" She asked, after a moment, wondering how shot her reputation was at this point. "Thank you, by the way."

"Couldn't have been many, Kyría. I backed the limo into the garage." He said with a smile. "You are not getting enough to eat. You need to eat on a more regular basis." He indicated the tray. "May I go and pick up the children?" He said eagerly.

"Yes, I would like to visit with my aunt for a while. Thank you, I appreciate you, Mansuetus." She said dutifully eating the light repast he had brought her of what he considered to be super blood building foods. Today he had added sliced beets to the repertoire. As they were one of her favorite foods, this was a nice addition.

They heard the car start up and Mansuetus leave.

"I need to know, Auntie. Has anyone successfully stopped this change?" Leila asked.

"I tried. When I faked my death, I had been fighting my change for a long time. But eventually it was too much. Exposure and lack of blood were killing me." Iris remembered; her eyes shadowed.

"I don't want to bring up painful memories, Aunt Iris." Leila said softly, seeing her aunt's expression. "But I have to know."

"No, honey. It's okay. You do need to know," Iris said in understanding. "The only other person who I know who has successfully kept the change at bay for longer is your dad."

"Dad?" Leila asked, shocked.

"Yes. It has been almost twenty years now for him. I am surprised that he never educated you on the possibilities. I sent him a letter telling him that I thought that you might have the gene too." Iris declared. "I don't understand why he didn't prepare you for any of this. I am so sorry. I know that not knowing what to expect has to make it so much harder." Iris said, taking her hand.

"I don't understand, Aunt Iris. Why did you think that I had the gene? How did you know?" Leila asked. "I haven't seen you since I was twelve. What exactly about me made you think that?" She asked, worrying about her own children.

"You were always more comfortable at night, baby. Stronger and more alert than in the sun. You sensed what others were feeling, even if they tried to hide those feelings, even when you were incredibly young. You were so smart. So, quick to figure things out," Aunt Iris said, remembering Leila as a child. "That last summer it was like you knew what everyone was thinking. Vampires sense each other, too, but, truthfully, I wasn't even honestly thinking about you, because I was concentrating on what I was going through myself. At least until Nikolaos arrived and told me you would be like your dad and me. Initially, he had even thought you were a vampire. But once he looked at you, he realized you were still only a human."

"I don't ever remember meeting him." Leila said softly trying to remember.

"Well, honey, you were just a child. He showed up in the middle of the night basically to tell me to get on with it; to let it happen, because fighting it was killing me at that point. You were sleeping. He, I don't know, sensed you somehow. He rushed into your bedroom. I am the one that accidentally woke you up. I thought he might hurt you. I was being overprotective. Nikolaos would never hurt a child. You saw him for maybe a minute at most. I put you back to sleep. I told you that you were dreaming." Iris told her.

"Well, who exactly is he? How old is he?" Leila asked.

"He is a distant relation, honey. He's not real forthcoming about most things on a personal level. So, I don't really know a lot. He is an elder, so he's old. Incredibly old. But, frankly, I just don't know, other than we are distantly related through a Tsoukalous ancestor."

"He helped you when you transitioned? You were lovers?" Leila asked, with a sinking pit in her stomach.

"Lord, no!" Aunt Iris said emphatically. "He helped me transition, though. He taught me many things about my nature and how to get on in this world as a vampire, and frankly, I probably would have never made it if it weren't for him. So, I owe him a lot. But we were never lovers. He's too much of a cold fish!"

"Aunt Iris!" Leila said, laughing at her.

"Seriously. I made a lot of mistakes. He never got mad or happy, truth be told. We only argued once, and that was in the beginning when I wanted to attend my own funeral; and it was hardly an argument. I don't think he was against it per se, I just don't think he wanted to fly me back down to Missouri after he had just picked me up!" Iris said with a smile.

"But in the end, he relented. He even went so far as to go with me and stayed in the hotel while I attended my funeral from the back of the limousine that Mansuetus had bundled me into. Mansuetus is the one who drove me to the cemetery. I think Nikolaos realized it was something that I needed to do to make the break. Leaving your whole life behind is frightening, after all. Truly, I don't really think he cared one way or the other, except I was dragging him all over the country. They are funny that way. The old ones. Very unemotional." Iris said with authority.

"Unemotional." Leila mused. That didn't sound like her, Nichola, thinking of his jealousy, anger, and passion. Maybe she had been mistaken in her thinking, and the Nikolaos that her aunt referred to and Nichola were not one and the same. "What is a soul mate?" Leila finally asked.

"It's a vampire myth. Mansuetus probably knows more about them than I do. He claims he's met two soul-mated vampire couples. I have met none, and I know I have never met mine!" Iris said with a laugh.

"Well, what is the myth?" Leila wanted to know.

"Well, kind of the way it sounds. You only have one. You know them when you see them. You are supposed to be able to know what they are thinking or know their emotions or some such nonsense. There are no barriers between you. Not language, not race. None of that matters. You gather strength from each other. Communicate on a spiritual level. You are mated forever. I find it kind of daunting, personally. I mean, after all; we are kind of immortal. Could you imagine spending forever with just one person? Knowing where they are at and how they are feeling all the time? Talk about a ball and chain! It's all very 'metaphysical' hippy bullshit, if you ask me." Aunt Iris said, waving the thought away.

Leila smiled at her. She could see that Iris had changed truly little as a vampire. She had always been one for 'if I can't see it, and it hasn't happened to me, I don't believe it'. In a way, it was funny, considering that she was a vampire. "So, what would be the benefit of having one, then?" Leila wanted to know.

"Well, even if you were separated by long distances, you would never be alone." Iris immediately responded.

"Why is that important?" Leila asked, confused.

"Baby, think about it. You are almost an immortal creature. It is lonely. Very lonely. Every mortal creature around you will eventually die. It isn't for everyone. There are always rumors about vampires who just can't cope anymore. They find a way to kill themselves or find someone or some group that will do it for them. The thought of an eternal soulmate, someone to spend the centuries with, I am sure, is comforting to some. I can see the advantage of having a companion myself. Nikolaos has had Mansuetus around for years. He's does a lot of legwork for me also, even though I no longer live in Nikolaos' home and have basically gone my own direction. If I ever need help, he will send Mansuetus to help me. That's why he's here now. Nikolaos, personally, I think, is bored, and that's why he will be here tomorrow night."

"Why do you say that?" Leila inquired.

"Well, he has kind of made it his business for a long time now, to help his family members, and I mean all of his family members, to transition if that seems to be in the cards for them. He and Mansuetus keep tabs on as many of us born to the Tsoukalous bloodline as they know about, and if they get any inkling that one of us is turning, they go to their rescue, so to speak. It has kind of been a project of Nikolaos' for a while now, I gather."

"Really?" Leila said. "I wonder why."

"Like I said, I think it is boredom. Gives him something to do. When I first met him, I used to think of it as collecting something. You know, a hobby. Like people who collect stamps or antiques. But the longer I know him, it's like he's on a mission. He's extremely wealthy, and amazingly in tune with everything modern, which for most elders, is very unusual. He doesn't let the grass or the years grow beneath his feet. He is always learning and keeping up with the newest technology. He has the resources to do it, and so he does. But vampires are few and far between. So, if it's his hobby, it doesn't assume a lot of his time."

They both heard the connecting garage door open at the same time. Leila looked at the clock. No way could that be Mansuetus. She could see her aunt was agitated. "I will be right back, Aunt Iris. Don't worry."

Leila walked into the living room, just as she heard, "Leila, are you here?"

"Dad!" She walked into the kitchen. She was extremely happy to see him. It had been almost a year, and she realized she needed him more than ever right now, hugging him tightly. "Is Mom here?" She looked around his shoulder and through the garage, noticing a rental parked behind her car.

"No, it's just me." He said, looking at her with sharp eyes. Pepper and Gladiator jumped down from the couch to greet him and he kneeled to pet them both. "Hey guys. Are the kid's here?" He asked.

"No," she said a little sadly. She would have figured that her mother would put aside her animosity for Michael to come and visit her in this situation.

"Oh, Michael took them to work with him?" He asked.

"No, Dad. Michael should have left for sea this morning. Mansuetus went to pick them up at daycare." This news seemed to stun her father.

"Michael went to sea and Mansuetus is here? I thought you said that you wouldn't make any decisions until we could talk." He gave her a hard look.

"I haven't. Michael abandoned me as soon as he possibly could. Mansuetus and Aunt Iris have been here almost the whole time, and I appreciate their help. Come on." She said to him, leading him into her bedroom, telling the dog and the cat to stay, closing the door behind them. Her eyes quickly adjusted to the dark room.

Her father and his aunt were looking at each other strangely. Leila realized this must be the first time that her dad had seen his aunt since she had faked her own death. Suddenly they were hugging.

"Aunt Iris, you look great!" He whispered, giving her a kiss on the cheek. "You look just like you did when I was a kid!"

"Well, I can't say the same to you!" She said, laughing. "My, how you have aged!"

Instead of being insulted, he laughed. "Well, that's what happens when you get old!" He said chuckling. "How are you doing? Really? I have always wondered how you were doing." He told her, hugging her again tightly and giving her a kiss on the cheek. Leila suddenly remembered that Iris had been his favorite aunt. Just as she had been Leila's favorite aunt.

"I am good. Incredibly good. But, Jamie, I can't say the same for our little girl here. Why didn't you prepare her that this could happen like I asked you to?" Aunt Iris, ever direct, demanded.

"And, Dad," Leila said before he could answer, "why isn't Mom here?" She couldn't keep the hurt from her voice.

Her Dad sat down on the edge of the bed and Leila joined him. Aunt Iris settled back into the rocking chair. Iris and Leila could tell that he was trying to gather his thoughts, and they gave him a moment to do so.

"Honey. Mom doesn't know that I am here. She thinks I am on a business trip. I actually have a red eye flight back tonight at midnight." He said softly and she felt he sounded like he had something to be guilty about.

"What? Why wouldn't you tell her what's going on?" Leila said in disbelief.

"Because she knows nothing about this, does she, Jamie?" Iris asked.

"No. I have never told her. I couldn't. It would have scared the shit out of her, and she may have left me and taken my kids." He said, looking down at his hands in his lap.

"That's why you never told Leila." Iris said.

"How could I?" He said with some passion. "I didn't want to believe it! I did this! This is my fault! I passed this along to one of my kids. You don't know what that feels like." He told Iris hotly.

Leila immediately jumped in. "Don't you dare criticize her! You should have told me! If you would have told me, maybe I would have made different decisions!"

"Leila, honey, you don't get it. I stayed for you girls and your mom. What would have happened to you if I had just taken off and abandoned you?" He asked softly. "I go through every day, working really hard to fight this."

"Dad, you are out in the sun. You golf! You live a normal life! How are you doing that?!" Leila demanded. "I can't tolerate the sun at all. I pass out at daybreak. It's been horrible the last few days."

"Honey, do you remember when I passed out in the shower when you were a young girl?" He asked.

"You mean that silly story that Mom always tells where you were calling for her, and she walked into your bedroom to find you flat out on the floor naked, and she at first thought you were screwing around with her for taking so long to come and see what you wanted? After she figured out that you weren't faking, she ended up taking you to the hospital and they couldn't find anything wrong with you?" He shook his head at her. "So, you are saying that's not the truth? You knew what had happened the whole time! That it was you passing out from this," Leila said, motioning with her hands to include the three of them.

"Yes. It was one of the times that I passed out. There weren't many. I was able to figure it out quickly. Iris helped a lot. Remember when she stayed with us for the winter? She distracted your mom." Jamie looked at Iris and smiled.

"Yes, many times. I think she hated me after that winter." Iris said with a wry smile of her own.

"She didn't really hate you. But she did think that you were needy and whiny." Jamie chuckled.

"So, great, you two concocted this scheme to keep this from Mom and Dad, you kept it from me. Why? Because you thought I might tell Mom? I needed to know this. Who knows if I have passed it on to my kids?" Leila asked, feeling herself getting so angry.

"Leila," Jamie Kelly said to his oldest daughter. "I am so sorry. This anger that you are feeling is part of the transition. Everything is magnified until you get this under control."

Leila breathed deep, attempting to calm herself. Getting angry at her dad right now wouldn't help, she needed answers. "So, how do you do it? How do you go back to tolerating the sun and living a normal life?"

"You will never live a normal life again." Jamie said bluntly. "I make myself endure the sun. It hurts like hell at first, but after a while, the largest part of the pain goes away. It also helps to keep the cravings at bay most of the time."

"Cravings? For what? Blood? I don't have any cravings for blood." Leila said simply.

"Not yet," Jamie said, enigmatically.

"So, what else do you do that helps? Are you telling me that you drink blood?"

"No. In addition to spending time outside in the sun every day. I take a ton of vitamins. Iron, Vitamins A, B, C, and E, and Copper. I also eat a lot of red meat. Also, I play golf. It's good exercise, and I get out in the sun. The sun, I think, kills this thing. It hurts, but I have learned to tolerate it and I wear the highest level of sunscreen I can find, and always a hat and sunglasses. I rarely drink alcohol. I never let myself lose control. Ever."

"So, the eyes, the teeth, the claws." Leila said, indicating Iris. "They never happen to you?"

"You know that's just rude, Leila." Aunt Iris told her.

"Sorry, I don't really have a lot of patience right at this moment." Leila said to her. "It doesn't happen to you?" She faced her father.

"No. It doesn't. I am not a vampire." He said simply. Iris rolled her eyes.

"Yet, you mean." Leila said.

"No. I mean ever. I'm not ever going to become a vampire." He stated emphatically.

"Oh, please," Iris said to him. "In this room right now, we are all vampires. In one phase or another."

"No, I'm serious, Iris. This is not a philosophical discussion. As far as I am concerned, I am never becoming a vampire. I am not a vampire now. I am a human being that has a livable physical disease. I'm going to die a normal death. I am not going to crossover and become what you are. Not that I am saying what you are is horrible. But I won't live my life that way." He said emphatically.

"Well, Jamie, that's ridiculous. It's eventually going to happen. Whether you want it to or not!" Iris said. This topic clearly upset her.

"Not to me it won't." Jamie Kelly said to them both. "I'll take my own life before I head down that path. I do not want to live forever; I do not want to be separate from other humans. I won't live an existence, eventually losing everyone and everything that I love. I don't want to do it; and I'm not going to. It's my choice. It's always been my choice in the end. It's hard and I truly don't know how all of this is affecting me, physically, but it is my choice." He turned and looked at Leila directly. "Leila, honey, we all have our choices. We all must do what's best for us, but I promise you, if you choose to stay human, I will be here for you from now on. I will always be here to listen to you and to guide you."

They all heard the connecting garage door open and Zachary yell. "Mommy! Where you at?"

"Right now, I want to see my grandsons." Jamie Kelly said and left the bedroom.

Leila looked at Iris, who looked terribly upset and followed her dad, closing the bedroom door softly, leaving Iris with her thoughts.

It was evident that her father had met Mansuetus more than once over the years. Mansuetus was quiet, taking a backseat to Jamie Kelly playing with his grandsons, but he was watchful.

Gathering the boys for their bath after dinner, Leila and Mansuetus got them into their pajamas. Iris emerged from the bedroom at dusk to join in and both boys warmed to her, pleasing her immensely. All-in-all it was quite the domestic little scene.

Around 9:15 pm Mansuetus took the boys into their bedroom for a continuance of their dragon story. Jamie quickly gathered his few things for his trip home. At 9:30 pm, Leila walked her father to his rental car as it would take at least an hour for him to return to Jacksonville, FL International Airport to catch his red-eye flight back to Iowa. Neither spoke about her situation after the kids had come home.

"Dad, I could tell that you know Mansuetus. Why is that the case if you have decided to fight this thing?" She asked, standing with him in the driveway.

"He checks in periodically to see how I am doing." Her father told her evasively.

Trying another tact at gathering information, she asked, "So, do you know this Nikolaos Tsoukalous that Aunt Iris has talked of?"

"No! Why?" He asked harshly, almost as if he were afraid.

"Why ever not?" Leila asked, shocked.

"It's my understanding that Nikolaos, only meets with family members who are in true transition. He wouldn't have either the time or the inclination to meet somebody like me," He said, not looking at her and she sensed he was hiding something. "I made my decision a long time ago and I am sticking with it. I work hard to maintain who and what I am. The fact that Mansuetus shows up a few times a year is bad enough."

"Okay." She said, giving him a quick hug, deciding that she would not tell her father about Nikolaos' impending arrival. She sensed it would freak him out even more than he already was.

"Remember that I love you, Leila. I am your father; I will always love you and be here to support you. You are one of the strongest people that I know. You can conquer this. You have two beautiful little reasons to conquer this. Just remember that." He said, giving her a quick kiss. "Don't forget to call your mom this weekend."

"Okay. Drive careful and have a good flight home."

"I will." He got into the car driving away.

Sighing deeply, Leila looked up to see Iris standing in the garage with Leila's tennis shoes in hand.

"I thought you might want to take a walk with me? Stretch your legs a bit? It's an awfully pleasant night for April." She said softly to Leila.

"Yes. That would be really nice." She smiled, quickly slipping on her shoes.

"You know," Aunt Iris said, wrapping her arm through Leila's, "the best thing about living basically in a little neighborhood in the country is this right here." Leila looked at her quizzically. "Take this neighborhood, for instance," Iris continued. "Large lots, average-size houses. So, though it's a large neighborhood, there's not a lot of people. Traffic is basically nonexistent in the evenings. No street lights. Just the odd occasional light coming from a house that leaves their porch light on, or maybe a yard light out front." She said, indicating one of the neighbors across the street. "Quiet. Peaceful."

"I've always loved this neighborhood." Leila agreed.

"I can see why. It's a perfect place for one of us." Iris' voice was soft.

"Really?" Leila asked, looking at her. "I figured that a big city would be the place to be."

"Maybe to hunt," Iris whispered. "But, not to live. You would be surprised how many of us reside in suburbia." She laughed softly, quietly. "Privacy is the key. Quiet and peaceful, fewer people are easier than fast and hectic and many people. There are still people and groups out there who believe in us, who believe that we must be destroyed. That we are evil. Thankfully, most of them also think that we reside in the big cities."

"So, what you are saying is that there is some danger...for you?" Leila's voice was quiet and worried.

"On the whole, no. Unless you draw attention to yourself, to what you are. There are all kinds of crazy people in all walks of life. Occasionally, one of us goes off the deep end. Just like any other population. We police our own. None of us normally want to draw attention to what we are. Who would understand us?" Iris replied quietly, walking sedately along.

"I wondered that the other day when Mansuetus took me home from the hospital. Why would you draw attention to yourself with a limousine, Auntie?"

"Am I really though? Or am I Leila's wealthy aunt here to take care of her in the middle of a health crisis? It's all in the presentation and the backstory that you give to people. The car helps protect us; it also gives us an excuse for Mansuetus. Our driver. Our nurse..." Iris looked at her.

"Our bodyguard." Leila finished, beginning to understand a little better.

"Yes. People generally believe what is right in front of their eyes. If you don't give them any other reason to believe something different, they won't. At least the general populace."

They continued sedately around the block.

"I want you to know something, my love." Iris said quietly.

"Yes?"

"I too will support you in your decisions. Just make sure that those decisions are, well, your decisions. We are not all the same. I am worried about your father. Though he seems to be successful in holding his transition in check, if he were to ever lose control, it could be dangerous for those around him, and ultimately, dangerous for him. I can see why Mansuetus checks in with him from time to time."

"But he is doing well." Leila replied quietly.

"Yes, he seems to be on the surface. But this is not a disease to be managed, Leila. He's wrong about that. It is not something that can be cured. Fought for a time, obviously, yes. Even in my case. But eventually everyone succumbs. It is who and what we are. Take it from me, my love. Guilt is a hard thing to live with." Iris said sadly.

Leila patted her aunt's hand. Trying to give her comfort. Comfort from her past, comfort from her worry about her father. They continued to walk in silence. Each wrapped up with their own thoughts. Soon they were back home.

Walking back into the house through the garage, Leila noticed how clean everything was. Mansuetus was sitting on the couch in a pair of gray sweatpants and a blue long-sleeve t-shirt stretched tightly over his chest. His nose in a book. The big man had obviously been waiting for them to return before going to bed.

"We are sorry for keeping you up, Mansuetus." Leila said softly, sitting next to the big man on the couch.

"No, Kyría. I am fine." He said, smiling.

"I have to ask, but only because I am a concerned mommy. Where are your weapons?" She wondered.

He smiled at her, pulled a steel box from beneath the couch, sat it on the coffee table and punched in a combination. The box sprang open. "Secure from children. Easily available if needed." She peeked inside to see his pistol, several full ammunition clips and two double-sided knives. She briefly wondered where he kept the second knife, then put it from her mind. The fact he felt he may need two was a little disconcerting.

"Thank you. I'm sure you won't need them." She smiled.

"Better safe." He replied with a scowl.

"Yes. If it makes you feel better." She said soothingly.

He smiled.

She knew her next sentence would not make him happy.

"You know that the boys have to go to the daycare tomorrow." She said to him softly and, sure enough, the scowl returned. "I know you don't like it. Despite how it was this morning, they genuinely like it there. They have other little children that they play with. But I promise you, we will have them with us all Saturday and Sunday and by Monday morning you will be ready to take them back to daycare." He gave her a doubtful look.

"Can we not keep them to break the fast?" He asked. He was genuinely concerned with their diet, it seemed; or maybe, just looking for a way to keep them a little longer, Leila suspected.

"Yes, if you would like. But they have to be there no later than eight o'clock." She smiled at his smile. She heard an exceedingly small noise in the kitchen. Mansuetus immediately had her on the floor next to Iris's feet and had placed himself in front of her, his Glock in his hand as if by magic.

Iris, who was sitting on the loveseat calmly sipping something that Leila would rather not think about, said. "Well, you are early!"

Leila looked up into the amber eyes of her dream lover.

"You are getting old, Old Man!" Nichola said calmly focusing his attention on Mansuetus with a good-natured chuckle.

"Kýrios!" Mansuetus exclaimed softly, straightened from his crouch, putting the gun down in the steel box, securing it, and approached the younger man. They gripped each other's right forearms in greeting, smiling broadly. Mansuetus gripped him by the shoulder as he said, "Not too old to realize that Iris' young doctor is parked down the street at the other corner with this house under observation."

"What!" Both Iris and Leila exclaimed loudly.

"Ladies," Mansuetus murmured softly. "Children are sleeping."

"Yes, I noticed that too when I scouted the neighborhood just now." Nichola said. "Should we kill him, do you think?" Sliding a look at Leila.

Leila gasped in horror before she realized he had said that for her benefit, then narrowed her eyes at him. He gave her a playful smile in return.

Iris, on the other hand, thought he was totally serious and said softly, "Oh, please, don't Nikolaos! I do like him very much!"

"Aunt Iris! I knew it!" Leila said in a loud whisper.

Nichola looked at Mansuetus in doubt. "Should we keep an eye on him and try to determine if he is out for love or blood? What do you recommend, old friend?" Ignoring them both to consult Mansuetus.

"Easier to kill him." Mansuetus said with a shrug. "We can dispose of his body by feeding him to the alligator. There is one right around the corner in the pond."

Iris looked stricken. They were teasing her! Making Leila's hackles raise.

"Stop it, you two!" Leila scolded them in a loud whisper. "Auntie, they aren't killing anyone! Especially Dr. Lambert." She patted her leg comfortingly.

"As you wish, Glykó." Nichola said softly, looking down on her where she sat next to Iris' legs.

"As you wish, Kyría." Mansuetus said with a small bow.

Nichola walked around the back of the couch into the living room and offered her his hand to assist her up from the carpeted floor. She looked up at him, hesitating. He was wearing a brown bomber jacket, an expensive white button-down shirt, a pair of boot-cut jeans and casual brown boots. Which fascinated her for a second as she realized this was the first time she had ever seen him with shoes on. He gave her a smile as if he knew what she was thinking, and she reached up to take his hand. He pulled her up to hold her against him lightly.

It was the same warm skin; same light callouses that she remembered. His skin in a full light was still tan, he was clean shaven tonight, but the shadow was still slightly visible, his hair was still dark gold, like a well-burnished ring, the only difference being that in a full light she could see a hint of auburn in the highlights making it more of a tawny color; more like it had been with the additional mirrored firelight in his bedroom. His eyes were the same amber that she remembered, and he looked so incredibly pleased to see her.

"Well, do I look different?" He asked softly smiling down into her eyes.

"No," she replied. "Do I?"

"No." He whispered, unable to take his eyes from her.

"You two need to get a room." Iris smiled.

"Yes." Nichola replied to Iris, his eyes never leaving Leila's. Then, suddenly, he was all business, "Later. Now, Iris and I need to invite the young doctor out for a drink."

"What?" Came Leila and Iris' duo response loudly.

"Ladies, please." Mansuetus implored.

"Iris," Nichola looked at her, "what have I taught you? Face your issues head on. We cannot have the young doctor stalking this house. It, at the very least, will bring the attention of the local constabulary when a well-meaning neighbor calls to report a suspicious car in the neighborhood at night."

"What will we say to him?" Iris said nervously.

"Let's try a version of the truth, shall we? You and Leila walked right past his car on your walk. You will tell him you didn't acknowledge him because you didn't want to draw attention to him. We will refrain from saying that truly was because he was ducking down in the seat attempting to not be seen, and both of you were not paying attention, as you should have been. You will say instead that it was because you were attempting to get Leila in the frame of mind to lie down and get some needed rest.

Since I, Dr. Tsoukalous, your personal physician, have just arrived, you would like to discuss her case with me, and how wonderful a doctor he must be to make a house call. What dedication he has! Does he know of any drinking establishment in the area that would be open this late and would he like to go with us, at the very least, to show us where it is?" He looked at Iris.

"You lie well. Even I might believe that," Leila said to him, crossing her arms and giving him a look.

"Many years of practice, glukó mou," he said, looking at her warmly. "Also, you will go to bed, because you do need to rest."

"Are you even a doctor?" Leila questioned.

"I am! I have doctorates in both medicine and psychiatry." Nichola said with a touch of arrogance.

Mansuetus came in carrying what looked to be a bedroll of some sort. "Where?" He said to Nichola.

"Suggestion?" Nichola said.

"Master bedroom closet is fairly large, and is the most light-tight space, against even an accidental breach."

"Does it smell like him?" Nichola said with a touch of jealousy.

"No, it smells like the Kyría. His clothes are in the other two closets." Mansuetus said with a small smile.

"That is good, then. Iris, when we return, you will need to sleep in Leila's bedroom."

"Why?" Both Leila and Iris said again in unison.

Mansuetus just rolled his eyes at their volume, shaking his head, and headed for the bedroom as Nichola said softly, "Because Mansuetus will leave the house tomorrow during the day to do several things. He will take the children to and from.." here he looked at Leila for clarification. "School?"

"Daycare." She supplied.

"Daycare. He also will meet my lawyer to pick up the keys at one o'clock to my newest property, at this address." He pulled a sheet of paper from the inside of his brown bomber jacket and handed it to the big man as he started to pass, heading back out to bring in another bag. Mansuetus nodded briefly as he glanced at it. "The lawyer will assist you in overseeing the crewmen with the necessary modifications to the place throughout the weekend. If all goes well, we should be able to move in Sunday evening." Then he continued to Leila and Iris.

"But, while Mansuetus is gone during the day, I must be able to protect both of you. It is easier if we are all basically in one room."

"Hey, hey, hey." Leila started. "This is my house..."

"And as such, you are queen," Nichola replied.

"No, I am not locking my kids down in the dark during the day on this or any other weekend. They are home with me on the weekends. Daycare is not available." She started.

"I am sure that we will come up with a workable solution to keep everyone safe, agápi mou. But at this current moment, Iris and I need to deal with the good doctor." He interrupted her talking by kissing her cheek quickly and he and Iris walked out the door. She was flabbergasted.

"Just the overnight bag for tonight, Mansuetus." She heard him say from the garage.

"Did he just come into my home," she said following Mansuetus when he walked back in and proceeded through the house, heading for the master bedroom with the bag.

"Of which you are queen..." Mansuetus chuckled softly.

"And take over and start giving orders?" She fumed, ignoring his chuckle. "I will tear him up!" She said, getting loud. "I will toss him out of here on his vampire ass!"

Mansuetus put the bag down quickly. "Kyría, quietly, the children sleep." The big man took both of her hands. "Have patience with him. He's been in charge and responsible for everything and everyone around him, basically the whole of his existence. This doctor's situation worries him. Frankly, it worries me too. He only wants to keep you and his family safe. He will learn that you are not without your own resources. That you are a sýnchrones gynaíkes." Mansuetus said.

"Yes, I am a modern woman, with two small children and I am not locking them down during the day, Mansuetus. That is not healthy for them. They are not vampires. I am not a vampire." She said to him in a softer, more reasonable tone.

"No, they are not vampires." He said in agreement and turned to go into the closet. She watched him from the doorway to see what he was doing. He looked to be rearranging the few pairs of shoes that she owned to one end of the closet and setting up some sort of thin mattress, using a small quiet pump to inflate it. Well, at least Nichola wasn't planning on sharing the bed with her, since it seemed that her bed-mate was going to be Iris for the next couple of days. Or did vampires consider it their nights?

"How long have you worked for him, Mansuetus?" She asked quietly.

"A very long time." Mansuetus said evasively and continued to quickly and efficiently set up what looked like an amazingly comfortable looking temporary bed.

She noticed it was almost eleven o'clock. "I am worried about you, Mansuetus." She told him with concern.

That got his undivided attention. "You worry about me, Kyría? Why?"

"Well, with everything that you are doing, are you getting enough to eat and sleep for one thing? It has got to be hard to keep the schedule that you have. Day and night, after all. I am not trying to be rude, and I am not saying that you are old, but you are no spring chicken after all. It must be exhausting to take care of children and sick people. I also notice that you have so kindly been cleaning my home, for which I will find a way to properly thank you." She said softly.

"You are right, I am 'no spring chicken'. Kyría, I get plenty of rest and food." He said with a chuckle. "In fact, I promise you I will rest as soon as you are in bed resting." He giving her a pointed look.

"Fine." She said, going to get a pair of cotton shorts and t-shirt from her pajama drawer and headed into her bathroom to shower and change for bed.

When she returned, she saw Mansuetus had placed Nichola's deodorant, hairbrush, toothbrush, toothpaste, and shaving items on one side of her double vanity. Looking at these items, she found it strange that vampires even used them. Then she realized how strange it was that her own husband had never moved anything more in here except for the barest of necessities into this bedroom, but instead had taken over two other closets and a separate bathroom for himself. She had never really found Michael's habits singular or strange before and had merely accepted it as one of his idiosyncrasies, but she realized how they were now. That he had never fully joined with her, having always kept himself separate.

She noticed that Mansuetus had laid out men's black cotton pajama bottoms on the bed he had made up and had hung up some shirts, another pair of jeans, and a thin, black, man's cotton robe that looked to match the pajama bottoms, at the end of the closet. These must have been packed in the overnight bag. Also, there were several pairs of socks and silk boxer shorts folded neatly and stacked on the floor, a pair of boat shoes, and what looked to be soft casual black leather boots, below the hanging items. He had made her bedroom closet into a small, comfortable little room for Nichola, like it was an everyday occurrence to care for him.

This man, Nichola, whom she had only known intimately in a dream state, was now physically present. It was strange, irritating, intrusive, and yet, somehow, seemed right.

She poked her head into the living room to find Mansuetus lounging on the couch once again with his nose in a book. He had turned off the overhead light, and only the small reading lamp on the end table behind his head was on. He looked up when she entered, watching her run her fingers through her still barely damp hair to further dry it.

"Everyone taken care of?" She asked softly.

"Dog, cat, children; all is in order, except you, Kyría." He softly returned.

"You're going to wait up for him, aren't you?" She asked quietly.

"It is an old habit of mine." He smiled. "Rest assured he will not be gone longer than is necessary."

"Can I wait up with you?" She asked, shyly, not wanting to intrude on his quiet time, but wanting to find out about the situation with Dr. Lambert.

"If you wish to lie on the loveseat and rest, I know he will wake you when he returns." Mansuetus said.

She smiled happily, lay down on the loveseat, covered herself with one of her throw quilts and in minutes was sound asleep.

He smiled as he went back to reading his book.

Less than thirty minutes after they had left the house, Dr. Nikolaos Tsoukalous, accompanied by Ms. Iris Gauche, was parking his raven black 1969 Q-Code Cobra Jet Convertible Mustang in front of J's Tavern and Sound House in Saint Marys, Georgia.

Iris had chatted at him instead of with him, since she required little to no response, all the way into town about how Leila was probably throwing his things into a burn barrel in the backyard for treating her so highhandedly, that he had started to get a little worried about it himself.

Silently he contemplated. *Surely, she must understand that he only wanted to keep her and their family safe?* Of course, she also might be remembering their last encounter. Though ultimately, pleasurable for them both, her anger, which was a by-product of her change, had also affected him. He was unused to the deeper emotions after his centuries of holding himself in check and tamping down emotions he felt were detrimental to his survival or the survival of others. The longer he was in contact with her, these foreign emotions continued to creep into his behavior, surprising him; and he admitted to himself that he hadn't handled their last interaction as well as he would have liked.

"You know he left her, don't you?" Iris asked during her monologue.

"What?" He said, focusing his full attention on her. "Who?"

"Yes. Her husband. He told her basically that he couldn't handle their marriage anymore and was considering divorcing her."

"Then he's a fool!" Nichola said immediately, then quickly added. "Though it is best in the end, I would hate to have to kill him after all." He said seriously in a dangerous tone, feeling jealousy rise in him for this unknown human.

"She would not like that," Iris warned softly.

"Does she...love him?" Nichola asked, stone-faced.

"What does that have to do with it?" Iris said simply, bluntly, she after all, had never loved Francisque; yes, she had liked him very much sometimes, but she had never had a great love throughout her human life. "He's her husband, and he is the father of her children. I know his leaving hurts her."

They noticed Dr. Dene Lambert waving at them. They pasted on friendly smiles, parked, and got out of the car. "What a beautiful car, Dr. Tsoukalous." Dene said.

"Please call me Nick. Thank you! It belonged to my father. I rarely have a good climate to drive it in, so when Iris said this likely may be a long-term situation, I had it shipped down." Nichola indicated Dene lead the way.

"So where is your practice at, Nick." Dene said as they walked into the bar and restaurant.

"I've stopped practicing regular medicine for the time being, except for private patients. Currently, I am teaching a class every other semester at the St. George campus in Toronto. But my long-term plans are to open a private psychiatric hospital, like my grandfather." Nichola smiled.

"Really? Where did you go to school?" Dene said, trying to find out his qualifications.

"Harvard." Nichola smiled, knowing he was being reviewed.

"Great school!"

"Yes. It was a good experience," Nichola said, sensing envy, but it wasn't coming from Dr. Lambert.

A voice floated from the bar. "We were just getting ready to make a last call, Doc."

Dene looked up and Nichola sensed more so than heard a groan. Iris raised her eyebrows, sensing the same thing.

"Hello, Bobby Rebekah, we are here on business. Can we get one round, please?" Dene requested. He had been avoiding her phone calls and hadn't even given her a thought when he had suggested his own watering hole, when the other two had invited him to join them.

"Well, for you anything honey!" came the vivacious reply from behind the bar.

They headed for a table midway between the sunken dance floor and the bar. Being Thursday night, the place was quiet. Which was good as far as the vampires were concerned; since they had a distinct purpose of figuring out what Dr. Lambert was up to. He had been a little bashful when they matter-of-factly approached his car and Iris had related their story as they had discussed in the house. Nichola was fairly convinced that the doctor's focus had been on Iris, but he also was picking up interest toward Leila that he didn't care for.

Bobby Rebekah came around the bar and approached the table herself instead of sending over the lone waitress, smiling at Dene broadly in a predatory proprietorial way. Her platinum bleached-blonde hair was done up in an elaborate ponytail of escaping ringlets, her V-neck, mid-drift t-shirt cut so low it showed the lace at the top of her push-up bra, her short black miniskirt barely covering her ass, she walked seductively over to their table in silver high-heeled ankle boots to take their drink order.

"So, what will you all be having? Our kitchen has unfortunately closed." She stated coldly. Obviously, she was feeling neglected by the doctor, Nichola sensed.

"That's alright." Nichola said, turning on his charm as he realized Iris was giving the bartender a murderous look. "We would just like one drink and then we will be on our way. It's been a long day for everyone." He flashed his toothy white smile at her. She was immediately entranced.

"Doc, what nice friends you have! Sure honey, what would you like?" She fluttered her false lashes at Nichola, trying to make Dene jealous. Unfortunately for her, he only had eyes for Iris.

"I will have a vodka and water on the rocks with lime. The lady will have the same. What would you like, Dene?" Nichola inquired. Dene tore his gaze away from Iris to look at Bobby Rebekah, and Nichola gave Iris a swift kick in the ankle to get her attention. She quickly schooled her expression.

"Don't tell me, Doc. I know what you like." She said with a purr, turning and heading back to the bar with an exaggerated swing to her hips. Nichola watched her appreciatively as any human male would be expected to do, giving Dene an inquiring look, which he in turn pretended not to understand, especially since Iris was glaring in her direction. Which Nichola could feel pleased the young doctor.

"Humans." Nichola thought, though he was surprised by Iris' reaction. "So, let's talk about Leila; shall we before our bartender throws us out?" He said, bringing both of their attentions back to himself. "Since I just arrived this evening. If you could fill me in on her physical issues, Dene. Iris told me on the way over that she is concerned about her mental health."

"Well, she has a virus." He said woodenly. Nichola glanced at Iris. This was obviously something that she had planted in his subconscious. "I have prescribed lots of rest, no work for at least thirty days. I have also told her I don't want her to drive until she has fully recovered. It wouldn't do for her to pass out while behind the wheel." He said worriedly.

"Not a problem, Dene. I have prescribed my nurse to her care."

"But I am concerned about her mental health. A poor mental state may impede a full recovery. Iris, why are you concerned about her in this way?" Dene asked, taking her hand in his. His voice perceptively softened when he said her name. Just then, of course, Bobby Rebekah chose that time to return with their drinks. She sat them down with a plunk and sat a bourbon and water on the rocks down in front of Dene, slopping it slightly over the side and onto his sleeve.

"Sorry about that Doc!" She said hotly.

"That's quite all right, my dear. I am sure that you have had an exceedingly long day." Nichola said soothingly using his *voice*. "For your trouble." He held up two twenty-dollar bills for her, and she took them from him with an avaricious look, smiling broadly.

"Why thank you!" She said with a smile and sashayed away from the table throwing a speculative look at Nichola.

"Well, it seems her husband has left her." Iris told Dene with a sad sigh.

"When?" Dene said, befuddled.

"After she was released from the hospital yesterday."

"Some people!" Dene said. "I mean, I knew he wasn't happy with her stay in the hospital, but I didn't think it was as serious as that. She's such a nice young lady."

"Yes. This could definitely be a cause for concern in her physical recovery." Nichola said and took a sip of the drink in front of him. The bitter alcohol wouldn't affect him, but blending was important right now. He stepped on Iris' toe slightly and she too took a small sip of her drink.

Dene took a napkin from the table and attempted to dry up the spill in front of him and his sleeve. Finally, picking up his cocktail and taking a deep restorative drink as if he had decided. "I would like to partner up on Mrs. Sutton's case if that's not a problem with you, Nick. Just to check in really, to make sure she doesn't backslide."

"That is truly kind of you, Dr. Lambert." Iris said.

"We agreed it was Dene and Iris, didn't we?" He murmured, giving her an enamored look as he held her hand.

"Yes, we did." Iris smiled softly in return.

Nichola inwardly sighed. So it was love, after all. Who was he to deny Iris pleasure? Especially since he would pursue his own? As long as she was careful, the diversion would keep her occupied. "That would be helpful. Thanks, Dene."

"I am off of work tomorrow." He was telling Iris. "Perhaps I could call you? You are staying at Mrs. Sutton's home?"

"Yes, for a few more days, at any rate." Iris said, looking to Nichola for help.

"Yes, I too will be in residence until my own place is set up. How about if you give Iris your number? Then you two may contact each other." Nichola said helpfully.

Iris was surprised, and Dene pulled his card from his pocket and a pen to quickly write something on the back of the card for her. "This is my personal number, and my beeper number also, in case there is anything that you may need me for." He told her softly, emphasizing *anything*.

"Thank you, Dene." Iris said seductively, putting his card inside her bra, patting her heart.

Nichola sighed deeply inwardly, only wishing to get back to his i psychí mou to hold her in his arms. He drank down his drink. "Well, it's a plan, then. I look forward to consulting with you, Dene. But Iris and I really should get back now. I am sure that my nurse would like to get some sleep and I am tired myself."

At 12:40 am, Nichola and Iris quietly entered through the connecting garage door, as he had parked the Mustang next to Leila's Honda accord. One less car in the driveway overnight to draw the neighbor's attention. He pushed the automatic garage door button, watching the door slowly and completely close, realizing that he was happy to be home. "Home," he thought, "home because *she* is here."

He saw her sleeping on the loveseat as he entered the family room from the kitchen and smiled softly. He looked down at Mansuetus, stretched out on the couch with his book.

"She wanted to wait up for you." Mansuetus whispered.

"I see that."

"Do you want me to take her to bed?" Iris whispered.

"No, I will take her in shortly." Nichola whispered in response.

"Well, what about the young doctor?" Mansuetus murmured.

"Love, I believe." Nichola sighed in response. "He wants Iris. I believe she has gained her first human lover."

"Really?" Mansuetus' voiced quietly in disbelief.

Iris stuck her nose up in the air, sniffing in offence, responded in a chilly tone, "I am going to get ready for bed!" heading into the secondary bathroom.

Nichola and Mansuetus both chuckled softly as she left. "Well, she has good taste, I must say. He's extremely good-looking by today's standards." He whispered to Mansuetus. "Iris almost had me convinced that Leila may have burned my things while I was gone."

"Well, it hadn't quite come to that, Kýrios. But she spoke about dismembering you and throwing your 'vampire ass' out of her house." Mansuetus chuckled quietly. "Never fear though, I convinced her you needed a patient hand."

"Did you now?" Nichola replied in return. "Well, you will have to teach me this gift of yours. I fear I will need it in the future." He smiled. "I will be back for her in a few minutes."

He entered the master bath and took a quick shower, using the same towel to dry himself that Leila had used earlier, breathing in her scent. He put on the pajama bottoms that Mansuetus had placed on his bed. Now that he was here with her physically, he was slightly trepidatious. Nervous that she may not enjoy his physical body as well as she had his mental body. He was very sure, and worried about it, that loving her physically would entail more control on his part, both as a lover and as a vampire, and he didn't want to hurt her or disappoint her.

He entered the living room and removed the small blanket that covered her. Easily lifting her sleeping form, he cradled her in his arms like a small child. He nodded to Mansuetus goodnight. He noticed a light on under the door in the room at the end of the hallway. He silently thanked Iris for this privacy that she was affording to him, knowing that she would retire at daylight to the master bedroom as he had requested. Iris understood his reasoning for security, even if Leila didn't.

He gently lay her on his bed in the closet. He then closed the large accordion doors to the vanity area between the bedroom, and then turned on the light in the small bathroom, and quickly partially closed the door. He then entered the closet, closing the accordion door to the closet behind him. Mansuetus had been right. With both the outer door and inner closed, no sunlight would even accidentally be able to enter this closet. It was the most secure space for a vampire in the whole house. With the small bathroom light softly coming in through the wooden slats in the door, he could see her sleeping form as if it was full daylight. He had turned the light on for her, knowing that she would be able to see him, even if it wasn't as brightly as his vision. He wanted her to know exactly who was loving her, and that he wasn't a dream.

He quickly slipped off his pajama bottoms, and gently removed her shorts and slipped the t-shirt from her sleeping body. She was just as sweetly beautiful as he remembered her, maybe more so he thought as he gently touched her skin, which seemed to glow in the light. He held himself over her, and lowered his head to softly kiss her lips, then to kiss and suckle at one of her nipples, which hardened under his lips. He performed the same action for the other and kissed down her body to taste her. She sleepily responded as he hoped she might, and he knew the precise moment when she fully woke.

"Nichola." She sighed deeply as she ran her fingers through his hair. He moved further down, reaching up and softly cupping her breasts in his hands as he licked her clitoris softly and gently. She pulled his face from her to look at him. "No." She said simply.

"No?" He said in disappointment, supreme disappointment.

"Come up here." She said softly. He came up to lie next to her. Curiosity in his eyes.

She rolled him over to lay him on his back. "Am I not queen here in my own home?" She asked him softly, taking his hardness in hand.

"Yes," he breathed. He didn't remember her ever touching him like this before. She stroked him and he groaned.

"Say it, please." She whispered softly to him, stroking him expertly with her soft hand.

"You are a queen in your own home." He whispered, thinking, *please don't stop.*

"Remember." She said in a voice he had never heard before, and her eyes glinted their teal color. She then quickly slid down his body to take him into her mouth. His eyes widened. She had never done this to him before; and he realized immediately that she did it very well. Just as he was on the verge of orgasm, she stopped and looked up into his eyes. His eyes were dilated and his breathing heavy. "Promise me you will remember." She said to him softly.

"Ypóschomai." He said desperately, aching as she gently caressed his testicles.

"In English, please." She said softly. Her eyes glowed with a light that was not quite human as she looked into his eyes, awaiting his response.

"I promise." He said, begging.

She returned her mouth to him taking him all the way down into her throat and ran her tongue up and down his length, only the shock of what she was doing kept him from coming immediately as he watched her take him in, then she returned her lips to the head of his cock to suck at the head only, moving her head up and down quickly several times fondling his testicles at the same time and try as he might he couldn't stop himself as he exploded in her mouth, still she didn't remove her mouth, and instead, drank him in, swallowing him down. "O Theé mou." He whispered with a groan.

She then straddled him, holding his still hard cock in her small hand. "You will not go soft on me now, will you?" She said in that same voice.

"God, no," he said in wonder at her command of him.

She slid down his length, impaling herself on him. His nerves were on fire directly after his orgasm and he gasped out, "Please, my love."

"Yes. I know." She said to him, all but ignoring him as she slid up and down his shaft, riding him, gripping him over and over with the muscles of her body. She leaned forward, placing her hands on either side of his body, to dip her head to lick at his nipples, which he could feel harden in response to her tongue. As she did so, she squeezed him over and over with her muscles, riding his cock slowly up and down, focusing her squeezes on the head of his cock and he struggled desperately to suppress his moans of pleasure.

He could feel her grow ever tighter around him and found unbelievably that he too was close to orgasm again as he watched her sit up and throw her head back, using his cock to bring herself to orgasm. She was the most beautiful creature he had ever beheld, and he held her hips tightly as she ground herself around him, trying to keep himself quiet, knowing that if he weren't careful, he would alert the whole household to the fact that he was literally being taken by her. More taken than he had been in many centuries, if ever, like this.

Just before she came, she whispered to him softly, simply, "Come *with* me, Nichola. Come *with* me."

And with a soft shout of release that he could no longer hold back, he did.

She collapsed on top of him and fell into a deep, exhausted sleep, and he held her against him tightly for a long time. Wide awake, wide-eyed and in awe of what had transpired between them. He had always been afraid to show himself to her, fearing that he would frighten her, but in the end, she had never been afraid of him. Tonight, with her physically in his arms, his teeth hadn't grown, and he knew his eyes hadn't reddened. She had loved him as a man, not as a vampire, and he had responded to her as a man. He knew it wouldn't, couldn't, be like this between them forever, but he would cherish this moment, this gift from her while he had it. He realized that his heart was full. "Efcharistó, glykó mou, Se agapó."

"I love you, too, Nichola." She murmured in her sleep against his chest.

He kissed the top of her head gently in response and held her while she slept, wrapped in her arms.

The Beginning

CHAPTER FIVE

L EILA WOKE TO FIND herself sleeping across Nichola's body. She stayed perfectly still and listened to the slow rhythm of his heart and the deep breaths that he took that told her he was sound asleep. Slowly, she raised her head to look at him. Surprisingly, she was able to see in the dark. He looked younger in slumber, the slight growth of his tawny gold beard notwithstanding.

She knew that it was still dark, and she slowly, silently slipped out of his arms. She wanted to see the boys before Mansuetus took them to daycare and she was sure that was what had awakened her. The movement in the house, telling her they were up. She grabbed her t-shirt and shorts and exited the closet, softly closing the accordion door behind her to get dressed in the vanity area of the bathroom. She turned out the light in the small bath and slipped out of the vanity area silently. Closing that door behind her as well. She could see her aunt sleeping in her bed, thinking to herself that it was strange that the vampires had retired so early. Then she looked at the clock. It was nearly 7:00 am. Not so early, after all.

Silently, she exited the bedroom, closing the door behind her, to tiptoe into the kitchen where the boys and Mansuetus were eating breakfast.

Zachary started to yell, 'Mommy', but she quickly shushed him with a finger to her lips and moved to give him a quick kiss.

Devin was eating a banana slice, and waved his arms at her, "Da, Da," he said once and then ignored her to continue eating hungrily and she bent over giving him a quick kiss to the top of his head.

Smiling good morning at Mansuetus, she made herself a quick cup of coffee, sipping it while the boys finished their breakfast and then she and Mansuetus got them cleaned up, surprisingly with a minimum amount of noise. Slipping on some house shoes next to the back door. She grabbed their diaper bags to check that everything was in order with diapers, pull-ups, baby food in Devin's bag, and an extra change of clothes in each bag that was all required for daycare. She followed Mansuetus to the limousine as he carried out and got the boys belted into their car seats. She quickly loaded their bags into the car and gave them a quick kiss each goodbye.

Mansuetus quickly closed the door, saying to her, "You must go in now, Kyría." He said pointedly looking east. She smiled at him, patted his forearm in thanks, and went back into the house. Watching him pull out of the driveway sadly just as the sun was rising.

She walked into the kitchen, cleaned the dishes, wiped the table, and put the leftovers into the refrigerator. While in the refrigerator, she noticed Mansuetus had once again went shopping while she must have been sleeping yesterday. He had bought some ribeye steaks, russet potatoes, some tomatoes, and other items for salad, and obviously had plans to cook them for dinner. He had also replenished the thin, rare roast beef that she and the boys really liked.

What had her full attention right now was what was next to the steaks. Next to them was a pint container of what was labeled bovine blood. She picked it up to look at it in wonder. Who knew that you could purchase blood from the butcher department of the local Publix? She shut the refrigerator and took the pint container to the counter. Curiously, she opened it. Looking at it. Yep, it was red. She sniffed it and raised her eyebrows. *It smells good;* she thought in surprise. She reached up, got a small orange juice glass down from the cabinet and poured about a half inch into the glass. She put the pint top back on the container and replaced it in the refrigerator.

Looking at the orange juice glass on the counter. She looked through the side of the clear glass at the blood for a few minutes. She suddenly picked up the glass and swirled the liquid around to watch it run in a reddish film back down into the bottom, studying it closely. *In for a penny,* she thought, tipping the glass sharply and shooting the small amount of liquid into her mouth.

She had been expecting a thin liquid tasting of salt, copper or some other such metal. The truth was so far from her imagination as to almost put her over the edge of sanity. To her it was thick and fully coated her tongue, with an apple crisp honey-like sweetness with a hint of cherries. She could feel heat running through her body to her stomach, and then she felt dizzy, almost intoxicated. She tightly gripped the counter to keep her balance. She most definitely did not like this feeling!

The sun was fully over the horizon by the time that she made it back into the bedroom. She was shocked that she didn't wake up Iris. Slowly to keep her balance, she removed her clothes in the vanity area, gripping the edge of the sink for support and then returned to Nichola's bed, moving as quietly as possible to keep from waking him. She moved in to lie next to him, hoping that the room would stop spinning soon. She closed her eyes, breathing deeply, trying to regain control.

Nichola woke to the smell of blood. Leila was curled in a fetal position next to his side. He rolled over to spoon himself against her, unsure of what had happened. He was positive that what he was smelling was cow's blood. He knew that she hadn't harmed anyone or anything, and though it had been centuries since he was forced to partake of blood to survive or even to keep himself strong, he still wanted it. Once an addict, always an addict.

"What happened, i psychí mou?" He asked gently.

"Curiosity happened, I guess." She breathed deeply.

"Curiosity?" He questioned.

"I wanted to see what the big deal was about. Besides, it smelled good." She whispered, not moving.

"How did it taste?" He asked, curious himself about her personal experience and reaction.

"Indescribably even better than it smelled. But now my head won't stop spinning. It's like I am standing topside of a ship in a storm. I don't like this at all." She whispered.

He lifted himself up to his elbow to look at her, to see that she had tightly squeezed her eyes shut against the sensation. He rolled her onto her back. "Relax, it will pass." He stroked her body soothingly and she gradually relaxed to lie next to him. "I would suggest to not experiment."

"But neither you, Aunt Iris, or even Mansuetus will really tell me anything about what is going on with me." She said slowly, her eyes fluttered open for a second, before she closed them again to breathe deeply to try to still the sensations rushing through her body.

"It is like the most potent of drugs." He said softly to her, remembering. "Different types of blood can be considered different drugs. Humans are the most potent of all. The ultimate of highs."

"Yuck." She said at the thought, making him smile. "How do you do it?" She whispered.

"I don't." He said simply.

She opened her eyes to focus on him, which helped calm the spinning quite a bit. "How is that? How do you survive then? I thought you had to?"

"I am incredibly old, Leila. My time for needing to drink blood to survive passed long ago. I feed from the human emotions around me. That doesn't mean that I don't desire blood, it just means that I don't have to have it to survive, or even thrive in my life. When I was young like you, I needed blood to survive. Blood-lust can be extremely hard to control, and I don't like that feeling any better than you do."

"I know that you have wanted to bite me." She whispered to him. "Is that why you didn't? Because you were afraid that you couldn't control yourself?"

"No," he said, smiling at her wickedly. "I don't want to bite you for food. I want to bite you because it is a perfectly natural response to my having sex with you. Having an orgasm while inside of you is fantastically wonderful, my biting you at the same time would probably be evangelic." He told her, and his eyes glowed at the thought.

"Then why haven't you gone for it?" She wanted to know, and he smiled at her broadly. "What?" She asked.

"Nothing. I love the way you speak to me; and the reason why I haven't 'gone' for it is because neither you, nor, I will admit, probably myself, are quite ready for that yet. I am not interested in rushing you. You are my soulmate, and I want you to develop at your own pace." He told her.

"Why?" She asked.

"Because I know others who haven't with disastrous results." He said cryptically giving her something to think about. "I have waited for you a long time, and I will not risk you. So, for us, we will go slowly."

"I don't feel like we are going slowly." She whispered to him.

"How do you mean?" He questioned.

"Do you realize it has only been a week? Really, only five days? I was just in the hospital on Monday." She explained. "To me this," and here she pointed first to herself and then to him, "is all overwhelming."

"To me, it has been seventeen long years of waiting for you." He said softly stroking her stomach.

"Seventeen years?" She asked in amazement.

"That's when I first became aware of your existence, and what you were to me." He said softly, kissing her mouth gently.

"Stop; don't distract me." She said to him.

He smiled at her. "I really am not trying to distract you. When I look at you, I want you. It's just that simple."

"Well, I want to know why, if you knew about me seventeen years ago, you waited so long?"

"I waited for you to be ready for me. For your transition to begin. I am not human, not in the strictest sense of the word at any rate. I am vampire, but I am *not inhuman*. You were a twelve-year-old child, and while child brides were common in my time, Mansuetus convinced me that stealing you away would not be beneficial to you. I didn't want to wait." He said with an unidentifiable emotion in his voice. "But you deserved an opportunity for a normal life, normal experiences. So, I have waited." He rolled onto his back. She could see that he was struggling with some feeling. It was her turn to perch herself on his chest to look down at him.

"What's wrong, Nichola?" She asked in a whisper.

"Doing what is right is not always the easiest thing to do." He said, touching her face.

"Why don't I remember you? Is it because I only met you the one time? When I first felt your touch, it seemed like I had known you for a long time. But I don't remember you. How is that? When you touch my face like it gives me such a sense of déjà vu."

"It's because I have touched your face. After I first met you at Iris's home and realized what you were to me. I did not stay away. When you left the house to walk to the lake at night, I was there. We spoke on many subjects before you left. You told me of your dreams for the future," he smiled at her. "I remember everything about that night, and I am the one who removed those memories of me, at Mansuetus' insistence, I may add.

So, what is wrong? I have regrets. Regrets for not taking you away with me. Regrets for not being the first man to make you gasp in passion. Regrets for not being your first lover, for not being your first and only love. But those are *my regrets*. I do not regret letting you grow up human. For becoming a mother. For experiencing the sun and life and everything that comes with it. No memories of me stopped you from living your human life." He said a little sadly. "So, for me, we are not moving too fast. We are still moving terribly slow."

"Well, what now?" She asked.

"Well, Mansuetus and your children won't be home for several hours, and Iris is still sleeping." She could see he was listening to something intently. "There doesn't seem to be anyone stalking the house, and your dog and cat are also sleeping. So, right at this moment," and here he flipped her over onto her back, eliciting a little giggle from her, "I want to make love to you again." He kissed her deeply, then he lifted his head to say, "I also may want you to perform that service for me you did so very well last night."

"Oh? You liked that, did you?" She said, laughing softly in a highly feminine way.

"Very much so." He said quietly with a gleam in his eyes.

"Well, why don't we save that for another occasion?" She whispered as his lips closed over one of her nipples. She gasped in response and ran her hands down his back.

"You are queen," he murmured, kissing his way down her body.

Soon she was the one clutching his head to her and softly begging for release as he sucked softly on her clitoris, flicking her with his tongue. As happened earlier, he didn't feel the need to bite her this time either, so for the first time, he felt safe enough to bring her to orgasm with his mouth on her. As he had suspected, she was delicious in her desire.

When he slid into her, she gave a small gasp. He immediately stopped. "I have hurt you?" He asked in concern, moving to withdraw.

"No, I just think that I am not used to this much activity in such a short amount of time." She whispered. "And you are a little large. Try going a little slower."

He did as she asked. Soon she had wrapped her legs around his and had him wrapped in her arms and he was moving slowly inside of her, holding her tightly. They were forehead to forehead, and he was whispering "Oh, God!" against her lips as he stroked in and she whispered in reply, "Not yet, Nichola, not yet."

"There." She said suddenly to him, grabbing him by the hips.

"Yes?" He said, following her direction.

"Yes, there." She whispered.

"Oh, God!" He said as she tightened around him, and he fought his own need. "Now?" He groaned.

"Almost." came her soft reply.

He could barely hold back as her muscles tightened around him even stronger. Still he thrust, closing his eyes, concentrating.

"Now, Nichola, now!"

As he felt her orgasm around him, he stroked in hard and thrust deep, letting go with a loud groan, hearing her yell out in pleasure, and in turn feeling pleasure throughout his entire body, clear to his toes. When they had ridden the waves and it was over, they both collapsed in a heap, only to hear Iris yell from the other room, "You two are killing me out here!"

They both erupted into laughter and as he felt the laughter throughout both their connected bodies, he felt Leila's lips seek his in a soft gentle kiss, and thought to himself, *This was worth waiting for.*

Leila got up a few hours later, showered and got dressed in a pair of jeans and a light sweater. Nichola was up and sitting in the rocking chair, while Iris lounged in the bed with a book.

"Where are you going?" He asked her softly. His tone was disapproving.

"Well, I am going to get Aunt Iris something to drink from the kitchen." She looked at him sharply. "I will not leave the house, so don't get in a snit." She left the bedroom.

"You cannot think to hold or keep her with an iron fist." Iris said to him softly. "She is not the type of woman to respond well to that."

"I am aware." He replied, irritated with himself.

The phone rang while Leila fixed her aunt a glass of the cow's blood. "Hello?" She answered.

"Mrs. Sutton?" Came a male voice.

"Yes?"

"This is Dr. Lambert. How are you feeling today?"

"I am feeling good doctor, better now that I am in my own home. How are you doing?" Leila smiled, knowing that he really wanted to speak to her aunt.

"That's good to hear. I am good. Is Iris there?" He asked shyly.

"Sure. She's in the other room. Hold on just one moment and I will get her for you." Leila put the phone down, grabbed the glass of cow's blood, and went back into the bedroom. She handed Iris the glass, picked up the bedroom extension, and then handed it to Iris, mouthing 'It's your boyfriend' with a smile.

Iris smiled widely. "Hello?" She asked seductively. "Oh, hello, Dene. How are you?"

Nichola rolled his eyes in disgust and headed for the shower.

Leila smiled and headed back into the main house. Stopping in the boy's room, she grabbed their laundry basket, hung up the kitchen extension to give her aunt some privacy as she passed through and headed into the laundry room to do their laundry. She figured she would get a head start on the laundry while she had the opportunity. Sorting through the clothes and creating a couple of loads, she got the first started, and she glanced at the clock. Mansuetus should be meeting with Nichola's lawyer right now, picking up the keys and walking into his new house. Leila was curious about how all of that occurred, and she wondered where it was.

She moved back into the kitchen to unload the dishwasher and maybe fix herself something to eat, as she was feeling a little out of sorts. She had finished unloading the dishwasher and had pulled out several containers and placed them on the counter to decide what to eat, when she happened to glance out of the kitchen window into the backyard.

Outside in the grass was one of the large gray squirrels that frequented her yard. She soon became totally fascinated by watching it move. It dug and then stopped. Stood up and looked around. Sat up, head high, ears perked and flicked its tail, on alert, sniffing the air. Then it returned to digging in the yard.

In the next instant, she was in the sun-room and had opened the door to the backyard. As soon as the sunlight hit her body, a burning sensation flared through her and she cringed away from it. Pulling her arm up and over her eyes to shield them, she pulled the door closed quickly.

"Jesus! What the hell is wrong with me?" She thought as she lay down on the carpet in pain and exhaustion. She soon felt herself being lifted. She opened her eyes. And it was Nichola. He was dressed, his hair was damp and fluffy, and he had on a pair of dark Ray-Ban Classic Black sunglasses.

As he was carrying her back into her bedroom, he whispered to her, "Glykó. Let me tell you what the best thing about being soul mates is. It's experiencing when your partner feels pleasure. The worst thing about being soul mates is experiencing when that partner feels pain."

"What happened?" Iris asked worriedly as Nichola laid her on the bed next to her, perching himself next to her on the other side.

The dark of the room felt wonderful after being exposed to the sunlight and she opened her eyes, looking over at the clock. It was almost two thirty! She had been gone from the bedroom for almost two hours!

"Leila, what were you doing?" Nichola asked her in a reasonable tone. She knew that despite his tone, he was not happy with her. She decided to go on the offensive.

"How were you able to leave the bedroom?" She demanded.

"I can move about, even in indirect sunlight, just like you can. It is more a matter of sight for me." He removed his sunglasses and held them up to her in explanation. "As with Iris, the darker it is, the more comfortable it is. My age allows me a greater degree of tolerance. Now, what were you doing?" He again asked reasonably.

"I don't know." She looked away, embarrassed.

"So, you would attempt to lie to me?" His voice was bitter.

"Well, if you know what I was doing, why do you ask?" She said, getting angry.

"I don't know exactly what you were doing! But I know you are attempting to lie to me." He said, looking hard at her, and she could feel him getting angry at her in return.

"I think I was hunting a squirrel!" She yelled in self-disgust, quickly covering her mouth with her hands.

Iris looked shocked.

Nichola took the statement more in stride and looked at Leila closely.

Iris looked at him in inquiry.

He shook his head. "No. She's just not getting enough to eat," He said to Iris.

"Right here!" Leila yelled, pointing at herself.

"Alright." He said to her. "Leila, when was the last time you ate any food?"

She thought about it hard. "Yesterday, dinner. I had a cup of coffee this morning, and that sip of cow's blood. But you already know about that." She said softly.

Iris looked at Nichola.

He shook his head back.

"If you want to stop having cravings for small animals, you will need to eat more." Nichola said, putting on his sunglasses and leaving the room. Leila rolled over and put her head on her aunt's lap, like she used to do when she was a young child.

"It's okay, honey. He's not angry with you. When you got hurt, he felt it and it simply scared him. Men get angry sometimes when they get scared." She patted her shoulder gently.

"He's right. I don't want to really think that this is true, so I haven't been taking it as seriously as I should be. I have got to learn to control this thing. I can't be going after the dog or the cat next! What about the boys? They are the most important things in my life. I can't take care of them properly if I don't get this thing under control." She wrapped her arms around Iris's waist. "If I can't take care of the kids, should I tell Michael what is going on?" She sat up to look at her aunt.

"Baby," Iris said, putting her hand on her cheek. "There are plenty of people to help you take care of the kids and to learn control. The bigger question is what's being gained or lost by telling Michael, especially if your marriage is over?"

Michael

NOBODY HAD TO TELL Chief Gary Greene or Senior Chief Andy Thompson that there was something going on with Chief Michael Sutton. Gary had known Michael for four years, and Andy Thompson had known him for more than eight years ever since Michael had been a brand-new Second-Class Petty Officer and Andy had been his Department Chief. They knew how smart he was, and how dedicated he was to his job and the Navy. Neither had ever seen him like this before.

The past day and a half, he had been functioning just as well as he always did. Sharp and in control. That wasn't the problem. The problem was that he was too quiet. Always a man's man, Michael had always been comfortable being onboard ship, putting the systems through their paces. He excelled at his job, knew it, and was usually friendly with his shipmates. So far, during this training exercise, he had barely spoken to anyone, beyond what was necessary for the job, even Andy, whom he looked on as a surrogate father.

The three of them climbed from the submarine aboard a tugboat to take them to the Atlantic Undersea Test and Evaluation Center, on Andros Island in the Bahamas, more informally known as AUTEC. Usually, testing occurred on a three-two rotation: three days of testing onboard a submarine, two days off. But due to some major test failures, they were coming in a day and a half early to let the ship make repairs before going back out.

Gary and Andy were both looking forward to the extra time at AUTEC, where there was little to do except eat and drink while the ship was making those repairs. Michael acted like he couldn't care less.

Once they disembarked from the tug, they headed to the bachelor enlisted quarters to check in and change into civilian attire. From there they grabbed a cab to The Beach House, a casual bar on the beach, to get a sandwich, play some pool and drink the night away.

Gary and Andy chatted with one another while Michael sat in silence. After the first beer was gone and they were on their second, Andy had had enough.

"Michael, what is up with you, man?" Andy said in his southern drawl. He was a good-natured man, twelve years Michael's senior, and was looking at retirement in two years. He really liked Michael, and his behavior over the last two days had him deeply concerned. Gary and Andy looked at him.

Michael looked at them, took a drink of his beer, and said quietly, "I think Leila and I are getting a divorce."

"Oh, no." Andy said. He was a man who took marriage and family very seriously, and he was a rarity in the Navy, as he had been married since he was nineteen to the same woman. "That's terrible."

Gary, who was married to Ellen, his second wife, said immediately, "Oh, man. Is she seeing somebody else?"

Both Andy and Michael looked at Gary like he had three heads, said in unison, "What?"

Gary held up both hands, one with a beer in it, and said, "I'm just asking. That's usually the case."

Andy gave Gary a look of disgust. Looked at Michael and said, "I don't believe it! Not Leila."

"No. It's me. I want the divorce." Michael said.

"You're having an affair?" Gary said incredulously with raised brows.

"Knock it off, Gary!" Andy said. "Nobody's having an affair! You aren't having an affair, are you?" He said to Michael as though that would break his heart.

"No!" Michael said. "You know she was in the hospital on Monday and Tuesday, right?"

"Yes. Well, you are here. She's okay, right?" Gary said.

"Yes, she's got some sort of virus going on. She's going to be off work for the next month and can't drive, but her aunt, who I had never met before, came into town to take care of her. The aunt's got to be loaded too, since she's got a personal physician who's coming into town to keep an eye on Leila. There's also some big-ass freaking airborne ranger looking dude who drives the aunt around and is supposedly this doctor's nurse who is there for 24-hour care. It's good that they are there with her, I suppose though." He stopped talking as a waitress brought them another round of beers. Michael took a deep drink of his.

"I still don't see what the problem is." Gary said, looking at Andy.

Andy, who knew Michael better, motioned Gary to keep quiet. "Keep going." He said to Michael.

"I realized that it's just too hard." Both Andy and Gary looked at him and he continued. "You know, the Navy, Leila, the kids. She doesn't pay any attention to me. She's always focused on the kids, or her job now. She demands so much. I work my ass off! If I want to go out and have a drink with the guys, she bitches, or she makes a snide comment. Like I am gone all the time, and she feels like she is carrying most of the responsibilities. She just doesn't get it. Look at Ellen," here he looked to Gary, "you have it made. Ellen never bitches at you. She doesn't give you nearly the shit that Leila gives me, and you come and go as you please."

Gary looked him straight in the eye and said low so only the three of them could hear, "Michael, you are a fool! I have never seen a woman look at a man like Leila looks at you! Ellen doesn't give a shit if I leave because she is fucking the next-door neighbor!"

Andy was quiet.

Michael looked at Gary and said, "What?"

"Yeah, Pete, the yardbird." Gary said in disgust.

Pete Lebowski, Gary's neighbor, was a retired chief petty officer, and he was now a civilian supervisory electrician who worked on the submarines when they were docked in port. All three of them knew him well. He seemed to be a quiet, soft-spoken guy, who was even-tempered and dependable.

"Come on! Not Ellen!" Michael said in disbelief. "How do you know? Did you catch them?"

"No. I don't need to catch them. I know my Ellen. You know, I am going to tell you something. My first wife was the opposite of Ellen. She left me for another guy. Said I wasn't ready to settle down, and she wanted something more. I married Ellen specifically because she wasn't hot. She wouldn't drive me to distraction or make me crazy. I know my Ellen is a plain Jane. I figured she would be a good mom, and I knew she wouldn't put a lot of pressure on me to stick around the house, stay sober, or gripe at me. She's not hot or pretty like your Leila. But she don't look at me anymore like your Leila looks at you. Hell, she never looked at me like your Leila looks at you. You know who she looks at like that when she doesn't think I am paying attention? Yeah, Pete, the yard-bird. And guess what? He looks at Ellen the same way." Gary said, taking a long drink to finish off his third beer.

They stayed silent for a minute while the waitress brought them another round. Gary continued after she had left.

"So, that's why she doesn't give a shit whether or not I am there. Here's another thing. All the guys envy you, Michael. Leila is smart, pretty, and she works her ass off. She makes good money too. Did you know I saw her teach a class about a month ago?" Michael shook his head. Gary continued. "Yep. I missed my IT security punch because of a dental appointment, so the squadron sent me over to the Subase to take the class with one of the off crews. Guess who was teaching? Yessiree, your Leila. There she was in the auditorium, up on the stage in one of her business suits, giving a class to 250 submarine sailors on the importance of information systems security and how to properly secure computers and classified information. Confidence rolled off her. She had them eating out of her hand. Another surprise? She knew her shit, too.

Here's something else you probably don't want to hear, but I have had enough beers that fuck it. I am your friend, and you just need to hear it. You have two healthy boys who are smart as shit and cute as hell, just like their mom. You *are* gone all the time. It's the nature of the job. If she bitches because she wants you around more for those boys, when you are in port, who are you to complain? At least she wants you around! Another thing," Gary was now on a roll, "you treat her like an asshole! In front of other people! You don't see me treating my Ellen that way in front of other people, and I know she is fucking another guy!" He was getting loud.

Andy looked at him, "Go take a piss, Gary." He said softly.

"I am going to take a piss," Gary said, getting up and heading to the bathroom.

Michael sat back, looking pissed-off, and took another drink from his beer.

"I have a question or two." Andy said, his southern voice soft. "Did you tell her you wanted a divorce?"

"Yeah, I guess. Kind of," Michael said, taking another drink.

"So, just so I can get this straight, you have a sick wife, who doesn't know if she's seriously ill, and you decide that what you need to do is head to sea?

The day she gets released from the hospital that evening, before you leave for a month, you tell your wife that you think you want a divorce?" He looked at Michael, who closed his eyes and nodded. "Michael," Andy said, "I love you like the son that I never had, but just how stupid can you be?"

Michael leaned forward, putting his head in his hand. "Andy, she didn't even care when I told her I might want a divorce! She just got all cold. I have never seen her like that." He said, feeling miserable.

"You are such a hothead, son! How did you expect her to react? She's been working for the military the whole time I have known her. She knows bullshit when she hears it. You may come back to nothing." He said as Gary sat down looking calmer, with three shots of tequila in his hands. He sat down, one shot in front of Andy and one in front of Michael.

Andy continued, "Do you really want her to leave you, or are you just trying to control her? That should be your question to yourself. Do you want another man to raise your boys?" Michael looked at him sharply. "Because Gary is right about one thing," he said, looking at Gary and Michael looked up at Gary as well. "Being married to somebody who does what we do is a hard existence for most women. A woman like Leila won't be alone for long. You need to get home as soon as possible and take care of your family before you don't have one to take care of!"

Gary raised his shot glass, Michael and Andy did the same. "Women!" Gary said.

They all drank it down, making the same faces that everyone in the world who has ever done a shot of tequila makes.

Gary made a motion to the waitress for another round.

It was early when they got back to the bachelor quarters, only eight o'clock at night. But, with five straight hours of nonstop drinking under their belts, they were all three very drunk.

Michael staggered into his room and picked up the phone next to his bed. He made a collect phone call to his house.

He heard the operator connect. "Collect call from Michael. Will you accept the charges?"

"Yes." He heard a male voice say on the other end.

"Go ahead caller." The operator said, and he heard the click patching him through.

"Can I speak to Leila?" His words were heavily slurred.

"No." Came the calm reply.

"Is this Man...Man...Mansootoos?" Michael asked, laying back on the bed as his world started to spin.

"No."

"Oh, is this the doctor?" Michael asked curiously.

"Yes." The reply was ice cold.

"How is Leila doing?" Michael could hear Devin in the background now yelling "man, man, man, man," Zachary's laughter and the dog playfully barking. He became very homesick.

"She does...extremely well." Came the enigmatic reply.

"Is she getting any sleep?" Michael said, feeling a little awkward and dizzy. This doctor didn't seem to be very forthcoming.

"Very little." Came the reply with a soft note of laughter, which set the hair up on the back of Michael's neck, though it did nothing to sober him up.

"Well, you will take good care of her, won't you?" Michael said, feeling sick to his stomach.

"I shall. My life for hers." Came the soft reply, then the line went dead.

Aunt Iris

CHAPTER THREE

L EILA SAT WITH HER aunt in the far-left-hand corner of the sun-room as Mansuetus, both boys, and the dog played on the floor.

The huge sun-room itself was thirty feet long and fifteen feet wide, and three sides comprised of large windows. Michael and Leila had designed the room and a friend of Michael's had added it to the home for them at a discounted rate since Michael took part in helping with the construction. The large space of the room was perfect for big get-togethers, card parties, and the use of the full-size hot tub that was at the opposite end of the room from Leila and Iris. It had two large ceiling fans and two skylights with shades, and it was a wonderful room for the boys to play in. It also gave the ladies the benefit of being private while still being part of the family unit. It was Leila's favorite room, and she spent most of her time there when she was at home.

Nichola came back into the room from answering the telephone in the kitchen.

"Who was it?" Leila called to him over the noise from the kids and the big man wrestling around in the middle of the room.

"Someone who wouldn't take 'no' for an answer." Nichola said as he sank back into the high-backed chair at the opposite end of the room to watch the kids with a smile on his face.

"I hate those telemarketers!" Leila said to Iris. "The calls get later and later all the time."

"Yes." Iris said enigmatically as she looked at Nichola.

"So, why did you finally accept this life, Aunt Iris?" Leila asked suddenly as she watched Devin crawl over to Nichola.

"I had nothing to hold me back anymore, honey. There was nothing in my daily life to keep me grounded. Not like you have. Ultimately, I had prevented my full change for many years, without ever really knowing that I was doing it. When I finally allowed it to just happen, the pain and the need were terrible! Imagine my surprise when I completed the change and ended up being in my early forties again!" Iris replied animatedly.

Iris had her hair pulled back with combs, which highlighted her elegant high cheekbones and large gold and diamond earrings. She was dressed in a cute black and blue patterned blouse and black slacks outfit, and she wore a pair of low black walking pumps. Dene was supposed to stop by soon and they were planning on going out for a while.

"How does that occur?" Leila said curiously.

"Well, according to Nikolaos, the changed gene maps the body at transition. As our genes change, they freeze our aging process. That's my explanation for it. He says what really occurs is that our body is constantly repairing itself to the time of transition. Cell by cell. Maintaining a constant state of existence."

"How does he know, though, Auntie?" Leila said, watching as Devin pulled himself up Nichola's jeaned legs to grip his knees.

Nichola bent over to pick him up and place him on his lap.

"I gather he has studied our existence for a very long time." Iris said, looking over as well. "Well, who would have thought? He likes your children." She said, smiling.

"But you were aging. I remember. Dad is also aging." Leila said.

"Yes. But we also exposed ourselves to the sun daily. Exposure to the sun slows the transition process, maybe cripples the renewal process in a way. I am not sure. Maybe that is why the sun is so painful? But it never stopped the initial gene mapping, and our genes remember."

"So, then Nichola showed up at your house?" Leila asked softly.

Nichola glanced her way briefly when he heard his name.

She was sure that he was listening intently to their conversation.

Devin was standing on his legs, balancing himself on his lap, little arms outstretched, smiling around his Binky at him while Nichola gently steadied him.

"Yes. I don't know how he knew. But he knew. He has resources and abilities due to his age that the rest of us don't." Iris said. "Luckily for me, he did."

"How exactly old is he?" Leila asked.

"Honey, make him give you specifics if you really want to know. He's worse than a woman who doesn't want people to know that she is over forty. Anytime I have ever asked him, his answer is 'incredibly old'." Iris said with a smirk.

The doorbell rang and Leila started to get up to answer the door.

Nichola shook his head, picking up Devin, and went to answer the door. He soon came back with Dene in tow.

Dene was dressed in a nice button-down shirt of soft blue that set off his eyes and navy slacks.

Pepper gave a soft 'woof' and approached the doctor, who was looking at Nichola like he was the bravest person on earth for tackling Leila's youngest son.

Zachary, who was sitting astride Mansuetus' chest, chirped "Hi," giving him a wave before erupting into giggles as Mansuetus tickled him.

Dene reached down to pat the dog softly, earning him a wag from her tail.

Leila thought, *Well, there's a plus for you, Doc*; knowing any man who likes dogs is a plus in her aunt's book. He also had a small bouquet. *Two pluses*, she thought, and she whispered, "Your boyfriend is here," to Iris with a smile.

Iris ignored her as she gave him a bright smile, getting up to receive him. His eyes lit up as she approached him. "Hello, Dene. My, what a pretty bouquet!" She said as he handed the flowers to her.

"Not as pretty as you look tonight, Iris." He said appreciatively.

She smiled shyly at him and then said, "Leila, show me where the vases are."

Leila got up, smiling her welcome to Dene, and went into the kitchen with Iris.

"Have a seat, Dene." Nichola said, sitting back in his high-backed chair, perching Devin on his lap in the crook of his arm.

Dene sat in its twin, a small coffee table in between them. He gave Devin a skeptical look. Devin looked at him calmly.

"He likes you; you know," Nichola said with a smile.

"Really?" Dene said in doubt. "The last time he saw me, he screamed bloody murder." He said apprehensively.

"Well, he reads the room. It's his environment as well. Everyone here likes you; he feels that, and you don't seem to be a threat. Small children are often good at that. They can often know how you feel about them. It's an ability that many people lose as adults." Nichola said in explanation.

"So, how is Mrs. Sutton doing?" Dene said.

"Leila is doing well. She's not eating as much as I would like to see her eat. But we are working on that." Nichola said, specifically using her first name.

Dene looked quickly out the door of the sun-room listening for Leila and Iris, who were still in the kitchen looking for just the right size of vase for the flowers. "Has she spoken to..." he said softly, letting his sentence trail.

"No. It is best for a clean break in these cases sometimes. I am endeavoring to keep her mind focused on other things." Nichola said, smiling.

"Good thinking." Dene said in agreement.

"After the children go to bed, I believe I will take her to see my new property. It will not be ready for me to move into for a few days, but it should take her mind off things. Do you think she is physically healthy enough for small evening excursions?" Nichola asked him in a consultatory manner.

"Yes. I think it would be good for her to get out in the evenings for a few hours."

Just then the ladies came back in with the flowers prettily arranged in a vase and heard the tail end of that conversation. Both looked at Dene.

"Mrs. Sutton," Dene said.

"Leila, please." She smiled.

"Right, Leila." He said, returning her smile. "I was just telling Nick that I think it would be good for you to spend some time out of the house in the evenings if you feel up to it."

"Really?" She asked looking at Nichola.

"Yes, I was telling Dene that I would like to take you to show you my new property after the children go to bed tonight. If you are up to it?" His eyes were warm.

"I would love to. I have been very curious about it since Aunt Iris mentioned it." She smiled.

Iris walked to the other end of the room to place her bouquet in the middle of the large octagonal table and four chairs that Leila used as a card table when she and Michael had friends over to play cards.

"It looks lovely, Aunt Iris," Leila told her with a smile.

Dene stood up. "I thought we could take a walk down by the riverfront and stop for a bite to eat and a couple of drinks at Seagles." He told Iris as she came to join him.

"That sounds lovely, Dene." Iris smiled sweetly.

Nichola gave Iris a pointed look behind Dene's back, which she ignored.

Iris grabbed a small black handbag from the kitchen counter that matched her shoes.

Nichola and Leila walked them to the front door, Nichola carrying Devin along, who watched everything with great interest.

"Now you have my phone number programmed in your phone in case you need it?" Leila asked Iris quietly, as Nichola was asking Dene about Seagles.

"Yes, do not worry. I will call you if I am not home by dawn!" Iris said with a small laugh.

"Gosh, I would hope so!" Leila whispered worriedly, giving her a hug. "Have a good time. I will leave the front door unlocked for you. Dene, there is a lot of wildlife out here on this road. Please drive careful." She said to him. "Have a good time."

"Yes, I will. Don't worry and relax and get your rest!"

"I will, thank you."

Nichola, she and Devin watched and waved from the front porch as Dene opened the door for Iris to a red 1990 4-door Buick Skylark Sedan. Leila took Devin from Nichola's arms, and he turned them both with a hand on the small of her back to go back into the house.

"I am worried." Leila said to Nichola as he closed the door behind them, and he lightly wrapped his arms around her and Devin in the foyer.

"She's an adult." He said, giving her a small kiss.

"No!" Devin said to him.

"Kiss." Nichola said to him, giving him a small kiss on the forehead, which elicited a laugh.

"You don't know what I know about Aunt Iris! She was a wild thing in her day, and she doesn't seem to have changed much over the years." Leila said, heading back out to the sun-room where both Zachary and Pepper were sprawled on top of Mansuetus. All three looked exhausted, and Gladiator had jumped up on the table to bury his head in Iris's flowers. "Glad get down from there!"

The big cat ignored her.

"Cat! Down!" Nichola said and Gladiator jumped down from the table. "Say it with authority, agápi mou, or he will not take you seriously."

"I will remember that the next time I am telling you to get down." She told him with a look which elicited a broad smile across his handsome face.

Iris hated to admit it to herself, but she was feeling a little nervous. It had been decades since she had been on a real 'date'. Not since she was a young girl. She didn't count her many extramarital affairs as 'dates'. Meeting someone specifically for sex couldn't be considered a date after all. This night could end with sex, or not. It was kind of empowering, but still a bit nerve-wracking.

She and Nikolaos had a bit of a heated discussion while Leila and Mansuetus were bathing the children and getting them into their pajamas for the evening. Of course, heated with Nikolaos tended toward the quiet rational end of the spectrum, at least where Iris was concerned.

"You need to be very careful with your doctor friend, Iris." He warned.

"I do not know what you mean!" she said to him innocently.

"Please, we do not have time to play these games, Iris. You need to think about this rationally, and you need to think about what you did to him by feeding on him. I must say that I am surprised at you," giving her a perplexing look, "after all this time, you broke your own rule: never feed from humans. I also know that he is not a knowing or willing donor. So, you had to have altered his memory deeply. You know how dangerous this can be."

She sighed, deciding to not deny it further, obviously Mansuetus had told him. "He is so young, sweet, and intelligent, and he admired and desired me so much, I just couldn't help myself. It's been decades since I felt that coming from a beautiful young man. Did I have a moment of weakness? I will admit it: yes. Overall, my weakness solved an immediate problem." Shrugging her shoulders.

"Iris, you need to watch your step! You put us all in danger. Whatever you did to him caused him to park himself down the street and watch this house in the hopes of..." he paused here, "who knows what? It could be anything.

He doesn't seem to be the stalker type to me. Nor does he seem to be the type of human who easily falls in love. He seems to be the type of man who takes his sex where he wants, with no internal conflicts. So, he may even be confused by his own actions and emotions towards you.

Maybe he fancies himself, infatuated with you? At this point, it would seem so. On the other hand, maybe, you are new in the area, and it is just sex he is looking for; when he gets that, he will move on like most men. But even that could trigger any number of things. If you bite him again, you could make him remember everything! Who knows what that will do? It could drive him to madness or homicide.

Right now, we have Leila to protect and get her through her transition, and these children have no father to take care of them. They are our family. I know you love them and would not want to put them in danger through foolishness! We cannot take Leila with us until the children's father returns." Nichola's hard look was accompanied by a lecturing tone.

"I understand, Nikolaos! I will do nothing to jeopardize my family. But I believe I know my niece much better than you do if you think she will ever leave her children." She said, looking at him incredulously. Shaking her head, she walked into the bedroom to finish preparing for her date.

"A penny for your thoughts..." Dene said to her as they exited the interstate to head into the small town.

"Just worrying about Leila." Iris gave him a small smile.

"Not tonight." He instructed, reaching over to hold her hand. "Tonight, we will let Nick take care of Leila, and I am going to take care of you."

"Really?" She tested laughing softly, squeezing his hand gently. "Do you think I need a doctor?"

"Oh, no. I think you are one of the liveliest people I have ever seen. I think you need a friend, a confidant...a dance partner?" He gave her a small lift of his eyebrow in inquiry.

"Oh, it has been a long time since I have been dancing." She mused.

"Well, that ends tonight." He grinned at her.

Nikolaos

CHAPTER ONE

L EILA SNUCK AWAY WHILE Mansuetus was tucking in the boys and
telling them another bedtime adventure story, about Bartimaeus
the Dragon, whom Zachary immediately dubbed Bart. Mansuetus begrudgingly accepted the name change to Bart the Dragon. She smiled at
his patience and waved softly goodbye to him from the doorway, after
she had given them their kisses. He nodded at her to acknowledge her
wave. She had to admit, he seemed to love playing with them.

She walked out into the garage to find Nichola wiping down the
interior of his beautiful black Mustang with a soft white cloth. Though
a rag-top convertible, he had the top up. She walked around the car,
looking it over closely. As a former Mustang owner herself, she appreciated its beauty.

He was in the passenger's side of the car, putting something into the
backseat. She approached him and he got out and wrapped his arms
around her.

She quickly looked out into the dark to see if anyone was watching
before looking up to meet his wicked amber eyes. "You are one of those
guys, aren't you?" She questioned. He raised his brows at her in inquiry.
"You know, one of those guys who loves his car."

He nuzzled her ear softly, "I loved my horses too when I rode them."
He said with a soft laugh, motioning for her to get into the car. He closed
the door behind her, and she buckled her seat belt. It was too dark for
her to see what he had put into the backseat. He got into the driver's
seat and started it up.

The engine purred; not a knock, not a tick. It was perfect.

She closed her eyes, shaking her head. Loves his car, check.

He put the car in reverse and slowly backed out of the garage and down the driveway. Once they were on the road, she asked, "How far away is the house you bought?"

"Very close." He said and then took a left onto Sheffield Island Road.

She was shocked. "You bought a house here?"

Sheffield Island Road led into a gated community called London Hill Bluff. It was a little more than 3 miles from her own home and right off Harriet's Bluff Road like her own neighborhood. This is where the similarities ended. London Hill Bluff was extremely exclusive and incredibly expensive. Most of the homes were right on the East River.

He nodded his head with a smile as he punched in a numbered gate code.

"I didn't realize that any of the homes out here were for sale." She declared, surprised.

"This one wasn't, and then it was. I had my lawyer work the deal. I prefer private transactions. There are fewer questions. Less disclosure." He explained simply.

They drove for another mile down London Hill Road. He pulled the car into a short drive up to a set of gates, punched in another code, and the gates opened. All the external lights were on. The house itself was on the marsh, private, and surrounded by large trees draped in Spanish moss. The lower section was made of concrete block and housed the four-car garage, and more, she was sure. The upper section was surrounded by a wrap-around porch, with gray and white vinyl railing. He parked the car in the driveway in front of the first garage bay. Each of the four garage doors was black. She got out to investigate. Both the lower and upper sections looked to be covered in a grayish white coquina. The upper section had black shutters on each window, and a black double front door. It looked like it had a black metal roof, and it was huge! Easily three times her own home.

He was looking at her, watching her reaction. "Do you like it?" He probed softly.

"It's beautiful," she smiled. "Very Georgian."

"Good. I thought so too when the lawyer faxed me the pictures on Monday evening."

"You made this purchase happen since Monday?" She asked in awe.

"I have a very good lawyer." He told her softly, pulling out a sheet of paper, reading to her, "It's over two acres, completely fenced on three sides, the fourth of course being the marsh, four bedrooms, four full bathrooms, one half bath, on the second level with an elevator connecting the first and second levels. Hardwood floors throughout the second level, the wet areas, and the first level all have slate tiling, large kitchen, with a breakfast room, a formal dining room, a library, walk-in pantry, wine room, two wood-burning fireplaces, one in the family room, one in the master suite. The master suite is twenty feet wide by forty feet long." Here he raised his brows.

"A sun-room off the kitchen overlooking the backyard with citrus trees, a pool, and hot tub system under a glass house. I am not sure what Mansuetus means by that. There is a recreation room including a bar, pool table, smaller second kitchen, additional bedroom, and bath, as well as a workshop on the other side of the garages on the lower level. It has central heat and air conditioning." He continued, quickly scanning the rest. "It would seem that Mansuetus loves the house and is overly excited about one thing." He looked at her, smiling as she held up her hand.

"Don't tell me. I know. It has gas heat and cooking." She smiled in return.

"How did you know?" He asked surprised.

"Did you know he talks to himself sometimes?" She smiled. "That's his complaint about my house, that it has electric cooking. I think that's why he bought steaks for dinner tonight, just to use the grill." She laughed.

"Well, your house is also exceptionally clean, which is a compliment coming from him." He looked down at the paper again. "This purchase was supposed to be made with most of the furnishings included. So, let's walk the place and find out." He said, handing her a set of keys, opening the passenger side door and removing a picnic basket and a furry throw blanket from the backseat. She raised an eyebrow at him. "Always be prepared, Glykó. Contracts are contracts, reality is reality. I hate to sit on the bare floor." He smiled.

They climbed the front double staircase to the front doors. Unlocking and opening the door, she felt something from him and noticed that he was on alert behind her.

"What are you doing?" She asked.

"Just making sure that we are alone." He said enigmatically.

"How?"

"I am able to sense the presence of others. It's an extra sense or feeling. You will develop it also as you and I spend time together. The presence of an elder always helps changelings and fledglings develop their abilities. More so than lone vampires, at any rate."

"How do you know that?" She asked him.

"Time and experience. I also have made it my business to learn as much about our kind to assist my bloodline over the years." He looked at her patiently, knowing that she had more questions.

"So, this ability it's a defense mechanism?" She questioned hesitantly, opening the front door for him.

"No." He walked into the house with her following close behind.

The lights in the foyer were on. Mansuetus had obviously expected him to inspect the home this evening and had left lights on in every room. Or maybe he had left the lights on for her? She knew that they had spoken several times on the phone throughout the afternoon, before Mansuetus had returned with the children that evening. Each room they passed through was pleasantly furnished. Most of the furniture was a few years old. But it was clean.

"You know you will have to explain these things in detail to me? I need to have answers, Nichola." She said, looking at him directly as they had found the kitchen toward the back of the house.

Placing the basket on the granite of the kitchen island, he draped the throw over the back of a high-backed counter chair.

She saw what must have sent Mansuetus into spasms of pleasure; what looked to be a Wolf sixty-inch six burner gas range with a twenty-four-inch griddle and double oven. He probably thought he had died and went to heaven after using her plain electric stove and oven. She couldn't blame him; she herself preferred to cook on a gas appliance. Shaking her head, she looked to Nichola again, as he had not answered her.

She realized this was truly the first time that they had physically been together without anyone else in the same house. It seems he had too and was giving her a predatory look. "No." She told him as he continued to look at her with growing desire. "We are talking. You and Aunt Iris keep promising me answers, and I have gotten extraordinarily little from either of you."

"Yes." He said as if making a final decision. "Come." He grabbed the basket, taking her hand to pull her out of the back of the kitchen and into an elevator. He pushed the down button and then continued to hold her hand as they moved down one floor. 3

210

They stepped into a recreational room with a bar, pool table, and poker table. Giving her no time to look around, he pulled her through the area and out through a set of French doors to the large, in-ground pool. It was at least fifteen feet wide by twenty-five feet long. It had a separate round in-ground whirlpool. "So, he meant solarium." He said, looking at the glass enclosure. "Remind me to tease him. At least this area will not have to be treated." He said with a smile. The glass pool enclosure was domed, and the glass looked to be heavily tinted. She looked at him quizzically, and he motioned the area with the sweep of a hand. "It is treated to block out UV rays. Which is what the rest of the house's windows will have to go through before we move in." He explained.

"We?" She asked in bewilderment.

"Yes. We. Despite the appearance that I have a one-track mind when it comes to you, I have actually brought you here to talk." He placed the basket down on a lovely slate covered table next to the pool. Reaching into the basket, he removed a bottle of wine. Taking a corkscrew from the basket, he expertly opened the bottle to breathe while he found glasses in the basket.

"I am not much of a wine drinker." She told him doubtfully as he handed her a glass, looking at the straw-yellow colored liquid with its light bubbles. She could feel the chill through the glass.

"You will like this; it is an after-dinner wine and extremely sweet." He said with confidence. He grabbed the bottle and sat on a chaise lounge by the pool, motioning her to take a seat in its twin next to him. He placed the wine bottle on the small table between the two chairs.

He looked at her with a strange look on his face, not nervousness, not apprehension, but maybe somewhere in between.

Usually, he seemed incredibly open to her, and she realized she was having difficulty knowing his emotions, almost like he was trying to prevent her from doing so.

"So, what do you know? What has Iris told you?" He asked.

"She says that we are from a long line of 'born' vampires. She says that we have a connected ancestor. Her name was Ursula Tsoukalous. What changes us into vampires is a defective gene that only some of us are born with. If we have that genetic defect, we transform into vampires. My father is one," here he rolled his eyes, "and Iris is a full vampire. It is a choice. I can learn to deal with it like any other illness. I can accept it, or I can choose to fight it. I have choices." She said softly.

"Well, I am going to tell you the truth." He was blunt and irritated.

"That's not the truth?" She questioned.

"Frankly, it's not. The situation is more complex." He sat up, placed his feet on the ground and faced her, as if bracing himself for a negative reaction. "Over the years, I have spent much time and spared no expense in studying our condition. We, our family, do not carry a defective gene. We have an evolutionary trait in our genes. Most times it remains dormant, other times it becomes active. But every single one of us born to our line has this gene. Every single one of us has the capability of turning vampire. It is one of the reasons I have worked long and tirelessly to keep track of our bloodline."

"So, Zachary and Devin could..." She said softly, fearfully.

"Yes, they definitely could. More likely than not, this evolutionary trait may be dominant in them because their mother is becoming a vampire herself." He replied, not unkindly.

"How do you know? How do you know that I am becoming a vampire? How do you know that this will not just pass away? Like it did with my dad?" She grilled him, becoming upset.

"I have never lied to you about my real name, i psychí mou. Out of necessity, I have gone by other names over the years, but with my family, I have never lied about what my real name is. For some reason, none of them ever seem to want to grasp the concept or connect the dots. My name is Nikolaos Tsoukalous. I was born to Ursula and Nikephoros Tsoukalous in the Katerini Province in Macedonia, what you know as Greece, in the year of our lord 1028." His voice was soft as he watched her closely, putting down his wineglass on the small table next to the bottle.

"But that would make you..." She said, trying to do the math in her head and failing to grasp it.

He rescued her wineglass from her suddenly numb fingers to sit it next to his own, still watching her intently as he felt shock-waves coming from her.

"That would make me nine hundred and sixty-seven-years old, in the early spring; sometime last month, I believe."

She felt lightheaded, and a little sick to her stomach. Shaking her head, she slowly put her trembling fingers to her temple.

He reached out to give her shoulders a small shake. "Don't faint on me, Leila." He said sharply. "You wanted the unvarnished truth. I am giving it to you."

"You are my great, great, great, whatever...grandfather?" She asked in disbelief and shock.

"I am not!" He said with an incredulous look on his face. "You amaze me, Leila. This is what you take away from my statement? I made my own transition at thirty-four. To my knowledge, I never fathered any children when I was fully human, and I know I never fathered any children since I became vampire! We are at most *extremely* distant cousins of a sort. You are descended from my fraternal twin brother, Philippos." He said clearly irritated with her.

"How?" She questioned, the shock still lacing her voice.

He gave her the glass of wine back. "Drink." He commanded.

She took a drink, then downed the glass.

He refilled it, giving her a highly irritated look.

"Don't look at me like that, Nichola. You are telling me I am having an affair with a nine hundred and sixty-seven-year-old man, who happens to be a distant relative?" She said, drinking another gulp of wine.

Suddenly he was kneeling before her, a hand on either hip, looking at her rakishly from his amber eyes, his touch immediately soothing her. "What bothers you most, agápi mou, that we share a little DNA, or that this old man can make you scream in pleasure like no man ever has before?" He gave her his most provocative smile.

With his hands touching her, she couldn't help herself; she gave him a small smile in return. "Just tell me. I want to know everything. Was one of your parents a vampire?"

"No. Neither. My mother, while she was pregnant with my brother and I, was raped and bitten by a vampire. This vampire, as far as I understand our physical nature, most likely released a large amount of venom into her bloodstream that affected our development in the womb. That same vampire killed my father, who was attempting to protect my mother." He said emotionlessly.

"Nichola, I am sorry." She said softly, touching his face.

"It happened before I was born, agápi mou. There is nothing for you to be sorry about. Besides, I was raised by an exceptionally good man. He

213

taught me good values and brought me up to believe in myself and to love my family." He smiled.

"Mansuetus." She said in sudden clarity.

"He told you? What magic you must hold! As far as I know, he's never told anyone." He said with wonder in his eyes.

"Actually, no. He never did. It was a wild guess on my part. But he is not a vampire. How is he alive after all this time?" She asked.

"Well, that is a little more complicated and I will get to it in due time." She could tell he was remembering. "But, from the beginning. My mother was a reputed beauty, and a strong woman. I still remember her honey blonde hair and green eyes. A Lady, you would call her. We were landholders, Noblisse, minor nobility. As first born, I was brought up to be a Lord of the land. Mansuetus was a freeman from Delphi whose family served my mother's family, and he came with her when she married my father. When my brother and I were born, he was seventeen. He was given the responsibility of looking after us. Without my father, the ruling of our lands fell to my mother, until my majority.

Mansuetus taught us everything that he knew. As well as our bodyguard, he guided us into becoming men. He taught us swordplay, how to fight, how to drink, all about women. My mother had much responsibility in running our lands, but she employed many masters for our education. Language, the arts, mathematics, science, she worked to teach us the politics that we needed to know to survive and to protect our people. She died when I was seventeen." He spoke softly remembering.

"Did you ever marry?" She asked.

"No. I resisted marriage. Don't get me wrong. I loved women. Much like our Iris's young doctor. People in my position didn't marry for love, we married for power and politics. But we were always in such political unrest in Macedonia. If we had been a more noble family, I am sure I would have had to make an alliance somewhere down the line before I became a vampire, but as it was, the political landscape always seemed in upheaval." He said, shrugging his shoulders.

"What do you mean?" She asked curiously.

"For instance, when I was born, Constantine VIII was emperor, he died before I was a year old, his daughter became empress, and it was understood that the first two of her three husbands were murdered by herself. Her third husband ruled after her death, with a brief four-month rule in between by her adopted son, who was the son of her second husband. They forced him into a monastery, making way for her third husband to fully take over, and upon his death, her sister became empress for a year. There was a full three years of upheaval where everything was undecided, and when I became a vampire in 1062, Constantine X was emperor, and he was the first and last of his dynasty.

I was just extremely glad to be of minor nobility and far enough away from the capital to never have to set foot in court. As it was when I took full power of my lands, I worked hard with Mansuetus and my brother to protect my people and to make us prosperous. I always tried to be a good and fair lord. My brother married though." He remarked, looking at her.

"How did it happen to you?" She asked him softly.

"My becoming vampire?" He asked, and she nodded. He sighed deeply as his eyes lost focus as he remembered what had happened almost ten centuries before. "I began having problems being in the sun. Spells. Like you. It was 1062. We, my people that is, were very superstitious. We were basically Orthodox Christian, but we were also an ancient people, and many followed in the old beliefs and secretly worshipped the old gods of Mt. Olympus. My brother specifically felt that I had been cursed, most likely by a witch." Here he stopped, deep in thought. Considering those past events. "I have thought back on it many times throughout the years. I still do not know whether he really thought that I had been cursed or whether it was an excuse to kill my lover, Artemisia, while I was in a weakened state. Philippos could often be a proud, arrogant man." Here he stopped, obviously disturbed by his memories.

"Nichola, why would you think that?" Leila asked.

"Well, simply put, he wanted her. She had rebuffed him several times before I took her to my bed. As I said before, men in my position, and in my brother's position, did not marry for love. We married for lands, politics, and power. My brother, Philippos, had married for lands and money. His wife, Cynane, was not a beauty, but I found her to be a pleasant woman, intelligent and a good mother to my brother's children. Overall, I liked her and felt it was a good match. As far as I know, he never treated Cynane ill. Still, my brother had many women besides her.

Maybe Philippos thought Artemisia had too much of a hold on me? Maybe he really thought she was a witch? Maybe he thought I would marry her? If so, he was mistaken. She would have been entirely unsuitable to be my Déspoina." Nichola was quiet for a few seconds as he considered questions for which he had no definitive answers.

"Did you love her?" Leila asked softly.

"Oh, not in the sense that you mean. Not romantic love. I enjoyed having her in my bed. She was very, 'inventive' in my bed." Here he smiled rakishly at her, and Leila gave his shoulder a small shove, feeling a tinge of jealousy for a woman long dead. "But I also liked her outside of my bed. I respected her and liked her as a person. I found her to be intelligent and kind. She was our main healer and midwife. She passed her skills to several apprentices, and as such, she had power amongst my people.

Artemisia truly tried to help me when the transition took hold of me, but she clearly did not understand what was happening to me until it was too late. Maybe Philippos thought she would alert the people to what I was becoming? I think he suspected. As I said, he claimed to have thought that I had been cursed by Artemisia. I will never really know that truth." He said with a shrug. "What I do know is that my brother had her murdered."

Leila looked at him in shock.

"I actually killed her attacker. That completed my transition." His voice was simple, direct, and emotionless.

"What happened?"

"She was attending to me at night. I was raging in fever. She had sent Mansuetus for cool spring water and herbs from her home. While he was gone, her assassin entered my bedchamber and slit her throat." Leila was silent and horrified at what he must have witnessed. He faced her and continued in a solemn voice. "The scent of the blood transformed me, and I attacked her killer, ripping his throat out and drinking him dry. Mansuetus and Philippos found me covered in blood and transformed.

Mansuetus knew immediately what I was. Philippos had a choice at that point: kill me, which Mansuetus obviously would not allow him to do, or banish me. I could not stay as vampire; my own people would turn against me as soon as they found out what I was. My brother said he was convinced that Artemisia had cursed me. It was then that I knew he was the one behind her murder." He stopped, deep in thought.

Leila had many questions but held them in; waiting to hear what else he would tell her.

After a minute, he continued. "I loved my brother, agápi mou. He was not the best of men. But he was my brother. He, in his own way, loved me, too. He banished me, but he also banished Mansuetus with me, to care for me. I think he realized that I would not survive without him. He was at least giving me a chance. Even though my brother and I both felt like I was a monster, he gave me the best chance I could hope for. You see, we'd both depended our whole lives on the wise council of Mansuetus. It hurt my brother's power structure as Despótis to lose him, his support, and his council."

"So how is Mansuetus not long dead?" Leila asked him softly.

"As a young vampire, you are always hungry. Always." Here he looked at her with empathy. "Mansuetus and I did not realize in the beginning that animals were almost as good as humans. I hated the thought of taking a human life to feed what I considered at the time to be the monster inside of me, and often refused to feed, until the blood-lust became a rage. I fought myself constantly and many times, countless times, Mansuetus fed me with his own blood. He taught me control. He taught me that I could survive on but a little blood at a time. By the time we finally figured out that animals were a good human substitute, it was too late. It was a while before we realized that Mansuetus had picked up several of my vampiric abilities from my biting him and inadvertently injecting him with my venom over the years, and at least a decade before we realized that Mansuetus had stopped aging all together."

"No!" Leila said.

"Yes." Nichola said, with some guilt.

"So, what is he?" Leila asked.

"Other vampires would call him a companion, which is just another name for a compelled servant. You see, Mansuetus is different from other companions. I have never compelled him to do anything. I have never had to. Everything that Mansuetus has done for me has been done out of love. Mansuetus still thinks of himself as my servant, but we have always been closer than that. To me, he has always been more than a servant; he is my companion, my friend, my confidant, my advisor, my protector, my father.

Without him, I would have never taken on the project of helping the rest of my bloodline during transition, I would never have tried to learn as much as I could about our condition, and frankly, if not for him, I would have ended my existence long ago. Even with him, I had found a way to end it all. He is the reason I lived long enough to meet you." He told her with a look akin to shame.

"You were going to commit...suicide?" Leila said, wholly engrossed in what he was telling her.

He refilled her wineglass, which she hadn't realized she had been drinking throughout his tale.

"Well, suicide by vampire hunter organization at any rate." He said with a gleam in his eye. "But that is a separate story. Suffice it to say that it is lonely being immortal, watching everything and everyone around you die, being a wanderer, never having a permanent home. Never allowing yourself to love, because then you would have to bear the pain and the loss. Many of us eventually go mad. Then one of us elders must take matters into our own hands and kill those who have gone mad before they alert the rest of the world to our existence.

I understand why they go insane. I never stay in any one place longer than twenty or thirty years and often come back to the same area as my own son or grandson after a few decades. Even my work with my fledglings, they eventually leave me; like Iris eventually did, for their own lives and their own existence.

If I hadn't been alerted by Mansuetus about Iris's impending turn, I would have never met her, nor would I have realized your existence. Once I knew of your existence, my thoughts of death changed. Finally, after almost a thousand years, I had found my soulmate." He looked at her lovingly.

"I think that one of the reasons that vampires rarely meet their soulmates is that they do not have the patience enough to wait for them to enter their lives, nor do they seek interaction with each other enough to actually discover them." He said, holding her hand in both of his slightly calloused ones. He brought it to his lips to kiss her tenderly, reverently.

Feeling those calluses, she turned his hand over to touch them softly. "How do you have these?" She asked.

"They are from a time when I swung a sword as a human man. I have been a Lord, a warrior, a monk, a crusader, a physician, a soldier, a scholar, a businessman, many, many things throughout my long life." He smiled.

"I don't remember you; I don't ever remember meeting you. Though I can't deny that there is in me an overwhelming pull toward you. Incredibly, I do things with you I would never have imagined doing." She blushed deeply, thinking, there, she had said it, and it was out in the open. "I still don't understand what you mean by 'soulmate'. Iris said that when you contacted her, she didn't introduce me to you. She said that you came after I had gone to bed." Leila had to know. She realized she needed to know.

"I sensed your presence first. When I was in Iris's home for the first time, it was like there were three vampires: Iris, me and one other. When you sensed me scanning the area here, and you asked me if it was a defensive mechanism. It is not. It is an attack mechanism. Everything about being a vampire is offensive. We are an apex predator at the top of the food chain. We have no natural enemies. The older we get, the more of a predator we are. I automatically scan my immediate area without ever thinking about it." He said, looking at her.

"So, you thought I was a threat?" She questioned. He shook his head negatively. "Well, how did you know I was your soulmate?" She asked softly.

"I felt the overwhelming need to see you, and then I saw you sleeping. The sight of you set my whole being to vibrate. I couldn't help but touch you, and when I touched you, I felt this electricity, an overwhelming sense of knowing; knowing that I knew you as well as I know myself. Looking into your eyes that first time was like seeing my other half; my better half. I never realized that I had only been half a person until I saw you and realized that only with you would I be truly whole.

You made me feel emotions I hadn't felt since I was human, more emotions than I had ever felt as a human. I must admit, I was afraid of you." He said, meeting her eyes. "It took all of my strength not to steal you away as I watched you sit up in bed that first night, especially when I saw you, with your long hair enveloping your body. I have never felt a desire for children, that is not the type of man that I am, but I desired you that night with an overwhelming need that terrified me, and I had to escape to the shadows to keep from frightening your aunt, and I am sure, yourself.

I stayed in the area because I had to know; I had to be sure. I had to be sure that you were my soulmate. I had to know that I wasn't losing my mind and becoming a stalker of children. I needed to know that I wasn't becoming even more of a monster than I already was, and that wanting you, a child, was not just another reason it was a good idea to end my existence. The next night when I saw you and spoke with you, I realized you were truly my soulmate. Only Mansuetus kept me from stealing you away." He looked at her tenderly, touching her face and her jawline, giving her that sense of déjà vu again.

"Nichola," she said after a moment, "I want to remember. Would you give me my memories back? Can you do that?"

He looked at her wide-eyed, in trepidation. Then he sighed deeply in resolve and nodded. He stood, reaching out to help her to stand.

She staggered slightly and realized that she was more than a little drunk.

Wrapping a strong arm around her waist, he helped her into the house, and they took the elevator upstairs. He guided her into the master bed-room. One long wall comprised French doors and windows leading out onto the wrap-around porch.

"Why are we in here?" She asked him, her suspicion growing, especially when he turned off the lights, which did nothing to stop the moonlight from flooding in and lighting the room.

He suddenly lifted her into his arms and carried her to a stripped down four-post bed to lay her on the bare mattress.

"Are you attempting to distract me again?" She asked him in frustra-tion.

"No. I am thinking of your comfort right now. I must admit that I do not know how you will react when I do this." He told her, removing his shirt and hanging it from one of the posts. He sat on the edge of the bed and removed his shoes. She lay on the bed behind him and watched him sigh deeply, nervously. "Please know that I wouldn't have done it. I wouldn't have taken your memories from you if I had realized the effect it would have on you. The future you." He said, suddenly turning to face her anxiously.

"What does that mean?" She demanded.

He pulled her into a sitting position and quickly stripped her shirt over her head. He was very methodical and disciplined.

"What are you doing?" She demanded as he expertly unfastened her bra and quickly removed it from her, hanging both from the headboard. "Stop it!" She ineffectually pushed his hands from her.

He quickly wrapped her in his arms. He was not lover-like; his voice and manner were cold, efficient. "I am going to bite you, Leila. I am sure that you don't want to get blood on your clothes."

"WHAT!" she yelled in alarm. He had *never* bitten her before. "No!"

"Leila, it is just going to be a nip. I have to if you want to remember." His eyes were red, his teeth were long, and his voice was very controlled.

"Not like this." She pushed against him, leaning away from him.

"Well, how else would you like me to do this?" He said in frustration, pulling her close as she scrambled to get away from him.

"Not like this. You are being so cold, and you are scaring me!" Pushing against him with all her might, becoming more alarmed by the second. "Don't!" Her voice became loud with an edge of panic.

"Easy." He said gently, his movements changing. He held her loosely, letting her push him back. He stroked her back softly. She smelled his scent as it enveloped her, relaxing her. "I am sorry. We will take it slowly." He stroked her arms softly, leaning forward to place his forehead against hers. He touched her breasts, his caresses expertly tender.

He kissed her lips tenderly. She could feel his fangs against her lips and unlike before, she did not ignore them; they made her apprehensive.

"I always make mistakes with you, i psychí mou. I always forget that you are still so human." He murmured softly, lovingly, against her lips as he squeezed her nipples gently, bringing them to peaks. He laid her gently back against the mattress, following her down. "You see, I do not want my fangs to be part of our sex play. I always want to love you like a man."

Moaning as he kissed her lips, she breathed in his scent, as he used his *voice* and his hands softly stroking to give her pleasure. She wrapped her arms around him.

Moving to take one nipple into his mouth, he felt her tense up. Willing her to relax, he ran his hand over her, taking her other breast in his hand, delicately caressing her. He licked gently, relaxing her. Feeling her fingers through his hair, he smelled her getting wet, and he hardened in response.

Biting quickly, he barely punctured the top of her breast. Feeling her stiffen slightly, he heard her sharp intake of breath. Shaking with repressed need, he took just the smallest sip. Then he ran his tongue over the puncture wounds, sealing them, healing them with his saliva. Rolling the few drops of her blood around in his mouth, he savored the taste of her. He swallowed a few drops, which made him want to lose control; if he hadn't been so ancient, he may have. She was his ambrosia from the gods, and he could drink her day and night. He felt his venom relax into his mouth. Still stroking her breasts lightly, to keep her relaxed, he move to kiss her gently, tenderly, then entered her mouth with his tongue.

Leila could taste blood and something more in his kiss. Slightly drunk and highly aroused, she was unprepared for her reaction. It was like fireworks had been set off in her veins. Her body convulsed, and he held her to him, wrapping her tightly with both his arms and legs so that in her convulsions she wouldn't do herself harm.

Her back arched, and still he held her tightly, kissing her neck tenderly, whispering in her ear, "Do not be afraid, my sweet. It will shortly run its course. Do not fear, I am here with you. I will not abandon you. Ride it out and remember."

She could feel her body slowly return to normal, but it was like her mind was outside looking down. She could physically feel him holding her to him tenderly, like she was the most important thing in the world to him. For the first time ever, she could feel his emotions like it was a physical sensation, could feel his love, she could feel his apprehension, she could feel his desire for her.

Then it was like she was being sucked into a tunnel of lights; snippets of memories were returning to her.

Opening her eyes, he was there, his hair a little longer, his beard slightly darker. His eyes were wondrous as he looked at her, amber and gold, like the purist form of tiger's eye. He touched her face softly, reverently, sending ripples of recognition through her, like sparks of electricity. Holding her breath, she was sure that he was an angel.

"My dear, I wouldn't dream of harming this child." He said to someone, as if it were such a ridiculous notion it shouldn't even be spoken aloud, and she resented that he would think she was a child! All the while, he continued to look deeply into her eyes, softly stroking the curve of her face, making her want to touch him in return. Then he smiled briefly showing strong straight white teeth against the light tan of his handsome face. He then turned to look at her Aunt Iris.

"Stop fighting this change! It is useless." He stated bluntly. "You are killing yourself. There is no purpose to you being mortal any longer. Your body knows this. Take a long hard look at yourself and you would see that." She felt an overwhelming need for her from him and he was suddenly gone, and she was bereft. He could not just leave her, she thought and sat up in bed.

"Think of me and I will be here for you to lean on, cousin." Briefly touching Iris's shoulder, he looked back at her; she felt his almost overwhelming desire for her, and she sensed he was puzzled, bewildered, and frightened. She felt an irresistible need to go to him and reassure him; to be with him, and just like magic, he was gone; he was gone, like he had never been there.

"Aunt Iris?" she had asked. "Who was that?"

Then she was waking up the next day. She took a shower and washed her long hair, brushing her teeth, and getting dressed in a light sun dress. She had gotten sunburnt again two days ago and knew her aunt wouldn't let her go outside today, but she would take her walk to the lake tonight in the dark. She preferred the dark in any case. She liked to watch the lightning bugs light up the yards of her aunt's neighbors and listen to the whip-poor-will sing its song and look at the moon and starlight being reflected in the dark waters of Lake Viking. It was quiet and peaceful, and no one bothered her, and she could let her imagination take hold.

She could tell that her aunt was upset about something, so she didn't bother her. She just went into the music room and played the record player. She loved her aunt's records. She had a complete Elvis collection, her blues records, like Savoy Brown, Righteous Brothers, and Derek and the Dominos, where they would sing 'her' song to her.

In the next memory that came to her, she was walking down the lane; lightning bugs lighting up the large expansive yards around her, heading to the lake. The screeching of the crickets and the song of the whip-poor-will were all around her. There were no clouds in the sky, and the stars and moon gleamed. She happily left the lane to skip down the path through the large old trees, no fear in her heart or mind, heading for an open area by the lake where she loved to sit and watch the water. It was community owned, and the senior citizens in the neighborhood association had it well-mowed and planted with neat little flowerbeds. She loved to smell the scent of the flowers as she looked out over the lake.

She walked through the enormous trees, heading for the area. Not a care in the world. She had seen no one else on her treks to the lake at night. Most of the lake residents were like her aunt and elderly, and she had never even seen another young person like herself or even an older teenager.

She had no expectation that she would tonight either. She was wrong. She was almost out of the tree line when she sensed him. She stopped on the barely illuminated path. She could barely make out his shadowed form in the moonlight. He was leaning back against the trunk of what she liked to think of as the enormous Grandfather Tree, which was a huge ancient oak.

It was a tree that she would have loved to climb, but it had been pruned back sometime in its history and its nearest branch was slightly higher than six feet from the ground, which even though she was tall for her age at five feet, two inches, she still couldn't reach it even when she jumped.

"I see you; you know." Calling to him; fearless. "Come out." She demanded. As she watched him step out onto the path, she realized it was the angel man from last night, her aunt's friend. She walked to him slowly.

He looked at her in silent contemplation.

Smiling up at him, she beamed, "Hello. My name is Leila."

Swallowing as if he was afraid that she was a mirage, he placed his hand over his heart. "Nichola."

"Would you like to look at the lake with me?" She asked, and he nodded silently. "Well, it is down this way." Moving around him and heading along the path, she told him, "We are almost there."

Following her silently, he thrust his hands in the pockets of his long thin leather duster to keep from laying them on her.

"Aren't you hot in that coat?" She asked curiously without turning around.

"No." He stated sincerely. "Aren't you cold in that sun dress?" He asked, smiling at her back.

"No." She replied, shaking her head with a smile and then explained. "I got sunburnt a few days ago and though it doesn't really hurt anymore, it still makes me feel hot."

"You are too fair to be in the sun. You will ruin your pretty skin." He said softly in a strange, aching voice.

"That's what my aunt says, too. How do you know her?"

"So, you remember me?" He evaded her question.

"Of course." She said simply as they left the trees behind to enter the secluded clearing. "Here we are."

Watching her twirl around the clearing, he found himself chuckling softly at her, thoroughly bewitched.

"Are you one of my aunt's lovers?" She asked while laughing at him in return.

His chuckle turned to a choking cough.

She came to him worriedly. "Are you okay?"

"No, I am not one of your aunt's lovers." Gasping out as he looked down at her impish face.

"Oh, that's good." Leila smiled, skipping to the water's edge to look out over the lake. "Maybe you will be one of mine one day." She looked down into the water with interest.

Shocked by the statement, he reached out to her with his mind and felt nothing but innocence coming from her. "Maybe I will." He said softly. "Does Iris have many lovers?" He asked, just to keep hearing her sweet little voice.

"Not anymore," she replied, still studying the water. "She says she used to have dozens when she was younger. Though she says the man next door would like to be her lover." Turning, Leila looked at him. "She doesn't care for him, though. I don't blame her. He is incredibly old, much older than Aunt Iris." She wrinkled her nose in distaste.

Chuckling to himself, Nichola sat on the iron high-backed bench that faced the lake, which was almost directly behind her, crossing his legs in a relaxed manner.

He smiled softly at her conversation. "Leila, come sit with me for a while." Looking at him with a friendly smile, her hair floated about her shoulders as she sat next to him. "Do you know what a lover is?" He asked, looking intently at her.

"Of course, I do. It is a boyfriend. Aunt Iris says I should have a great many lovers throughout my life." She stated to him matter-of-factly.

"Does she now?" That didn't sit well with him. "Why?" Was all he could think of to ask.

"Because she says that only men who are your lovers treat you well. They buy you nice things and take you to nice places, and if they are mean to you, you can just get another one." She said simply.

Well, he thought, he could hardly argue with that logic. "How old are you, Leila?" He asked softly.

"Twelve, going on thirteen now." She said, smiling brightly. "How old are you?"

"Very old." He said, sighing as he looked into her eyes, wishing for just a small amount of her child-like innocence.

"I don't think that you are very old," she told him gently, "and I am not a child." She looked at him with a directness that most adults didn't have.

"No, perhaps you are not." He whispered, looking into her teal-colored eyes.

"Where do you live?" She asked.

"Not here. I live in an exceptionally large house in Toronto, Canada." He had not meant to tell her that, he realized too late.

"Were you going to lie to me just then?" She asked, displeased.

"Yes. I had thought to." He said honestly in his bewilderment.

"I thought so." Giving him an annoyed look again.

"So, what would you like to do with your life when you get older?" He tried to steer their conversation in another direction.

"I think I would like to be a writer! Or a doctor. A brain surgeon, maybe." She said matter-of-factly. "Do you have a job?"

"I do."

"Well, what do you do?" She urged.

"I am a doctor." He said simply.

She looked at him sharply, irritated with his less than forthcoming answers. "Well, what kind of doctor are you?"

"I am a psychiatrist. I help people who have emotional problems or mental disorders." He said again, unable to resist her pull for honesty.

"Oh." She seemed disappointed, and he suddenly realized that he was distressed to have disappointed her. "Well, for a minute, I thought you might be able to help my Aunt Iris." She continued sadly, tears filling her teal-colored eyes as she looked at him. "She's extremely sick, you see. She doesn't want anyone to know. But I know."

He reached out and touched the curve of her jaw. "Do not be sad, Glykó. Your aunt will be fine." He wanted so badly to reassure her and to see the sadness leave her eyes.

"Do you promise, Nichola?" She gave him a look filled with hope.

"I promise. I will make sure of it." He told her, pulling her close to him to ease her distress. "I will help her." He only meant to comfort her as he hugged her, to ease her sorrow.

It was a mistake.

She laid her head against his chest and wrapped her arms around him, returning his hug.

He felt the softness of her long hair around them. He suddenly breathed in her scent: licorice, peppermint and just a hint of jasmine and immediate desire roared through his body.

Her next memory was that she was on top of his coat in the grass and his scent was all around her: cinnamon, ginger, and sandalwood.

"O Theé mou, se parakaló voíthisé me." He whispered pleadingly. His body was wracked with spasms, and he was clearly distraught as he held her tightly against him, fighting for control. His face was buried against her, and they were both wrapped in her hair.

"It's okay, Nichola. I will help you." She told him kindly as she put her small hand gently against his face, pushing him up to look at her.

He gazed down at her in shock with tear-filled red eyes and sharp teeth.

She blinked up at him in surprise, then smiled tenderly at him. "I will help you." She reassured him in a whisper, smoothing his hair back from his face.

He took her hand and kissed her palm reverently. "You understand me? You do understand me?" He asked in disbelief.

"Of course, I understand you." Her voice was soft and reassuring.

"I psychí mou," he whispered, and then repeated in disbelief, "i psychí mou." He then kissed her lips gently, in awe of her.

The next minute, he was thrown into the middle of the lake and a large man was in between them.

"Do not do this, Kýrios! You will hate yourself for it!" The big man said in a low bass growl.

"I will tear you to pieces, Mansuetus! She is mine!" Nichola said furiously, swimming back to shore. His strong arms cut through the water silently, expertly. As he stepped one foot on the shore, the large man hit him once, hard, in the chest, sending Nichola flying back into the water at least thirty feet from shore.

"That may be one day, and if she is your Kyría, I will serve her as well and as loyally as I do you, but currently she is a child!" The big man told him angrily.

She jumped up from the ground to place herself between them, while Nichola, who was still in the lake, glared back at the big man on the shore. "Don't hit him!" She ordered the large man with a glare. "Please don't hit him again!"

"Mansuetus, she is mine. She understands me, she defends me, I cannot lie to her. We *know* each other. She is mine." Nichola's voice was sincere and close.

She turned to Nichola, who had swum back to shore, and now stood directly behind her.

He was soaked, his shirt and pants clinging to him wetly. His red eyes and sharp teeth were gone, and he met her gaze tenderly with soft amber eyes.

"We can take her with us. We can take her home with us." Nichola looked at the big man who was now behind her.

"To what? Live with a vampire? How long would it be before she would be in your bed? A day? Less? How long before you would take blood from her? When her monthly menses comes, and you went insane with blood lust?" Mansuetus said with some anger. "Would she even last a month? Would you deny her a human life?" The big man asked softer, but not unkindly. "And what about your new friends that you think I know nothing about?" Nichola looked at him, stunned. "Do you think they will spare her if they find out about her existence? If she is yours, you must give her what you can, you must protect her. If she really is yours, she will be yours forever."

"I would never harm her or bring harm to her." Nichola told him. Looking deeply into Leila's eyes, he reached out to touch her along the jawline as she gazed up at him.

"I will go with you if it will help you, Nichola." She whispered, and he looked at her stricken.

"You would never intentionally mean to cause her harm, Kýrios. I know this. But if you steal her away to live in the night right now, you know you would be harming her." Mansuetus said, his voice soft but with conviction.

"You must wait for her to mature. You must wait until she is ready to live in the night."

"No." Leila whispered to Nichola, clutching his hand to her face. Nichola looked at the big man behind her, and she could feel pain, heartache, and acceptance flow through him. "Why do I know what you are feeling?" She asked, bewildered.

"Mansuetus will take you back to your aunt," he told her gently, sitting on the bench and pulling her to stand between his knees, holding her loosely.

The heartache that she felt coming from him was breaking her.

"No. I want to stay with you." She told him, taking him by the shoulders, willing him to understand her, as tears flowed down her cheeks unabated.

"That is my dearest wish, agápi mou." He told her, and she felt his heart breaking. Pulling her close once in a tight embrace, he swiftly kissed her.

Shocked, she felt his tongue demand entrance and automatically opened for him. She tasted a spicy sweet flavor flow throughout her mouth as their mutual tears mingled. She felt herself falling.

He held her close, sobbing, and whispered to her in his *voice*, "Forget, until you are ready, i psychí mou."

Slowly coming back to the present, she was lying flat on her back, and he was lying next to her, his head propped up with one hand, the other hand resting gently on her stomach, looking down on her with concern. "What did you give me?" She inquired.

"A few drops of my blood, and one of my venom."

"What did it do to me?"

"Well, you grew no taller. You lost your drive to be either a writer or a doctor. You forgot about me, my promise about your aunt, and most importantly, that vampires were real."

"Yet you kept your promise to help Aunt Iris."

"I did," he said softly.

"You waited for me to come to you."

"I did," he said again.

"Did you never check on me?" She questioned.

He shook his head, replying, "Mansuetus did, frequently, and reported back to me your progress."

"You didn't? Why didn't you, personally?" She was surprised to be hurt by his reply.

"I wanted to, if only from a distance, but I didn't trust myself not to steal you away. Mansuetus didn't trust me either. But, once you reached the age of majority, I knew I would never let you go again. Do you regret having your children?" He asked her.

"Never." She replied fiercely.

"If I had come for you, you would not be a mother; I cannot give you children. I had to let you experience a real human existence. All of it. The love and pain. I want you having no regrets. It was the most difficult thing I have ever done, knowing you were in the world and choosing not to come and take you." He stated, stone-faced.

With her memories now intact, she could feel him fully, and was overwhelmed by the many emotions coming from him: pain, regret, need, desire, love. The sensations made her dizzy, and she didn't know how to stop it. She wasn't sure where he ended, and she began. Was this the way he has always felt her?

"Yes, i psychí mou, it is." He said, answering her unspoken question.

"I want to go home, Nichola." She said, reaching for her bra and her shirt.

He let her go and his sadness brought tears to her eyes.

Aunt Iris

CHAPTER FOUR

I T WAS ONE O'CLOCK in the morning, and their drive home was quick and silent.

Leila didn't wait for Nichola to come around and open her door once he had parked the car in the garage. She quickly got out of the car herself, escaping into the house.

Mansuetus was awake and waiting for them; he knew right away that something was wrong. He got up from the couch and she walked up to him, wrapping her arms around him, giving him a fierce, tight hug, shocking him. He briefly hugged her back.

Stepping back to look up at him, she said, "Thank you, Mansuetus."

"For what, Kyría?" He asked in confusion.

"For being such a good man." She simply and sincerely said, then went into the master bedroom to softly close the door behind her.

Nichola didn't follow, but instead sat on the loveseat heavily, leaning his head back, closing his eyes.

"What has happened?" Mansuetus asked worriedly.

"I gave her memories back to her." Nichola's voice was solemn.

"Why?" Mansuetus asked, bewildered that Nichola had done so.

"Because she wanted me to. Because she needed me to."

"How is she feeling?" Mansuetus asked hesitantly. "Angry?"

"I don't know." Nichola said, looking at him with sad eyes. "Confused. Jumbled. But now she is doing an extremely good job of shutting me out."

Mansuetus returned his look, puzzled. "You? But you are her mate!"

"It seems my changeling has some strengths of which I didn't realize. I must admit to not challenging her on those strengths. I am not trying to hammer down her walls, at least for tonight. She needs me to be patient and I am willing to try to give her time and my patience."

A few minutes later, Leila came back into the family room dressed in soft cotton shorts, t-shirt, and robe. "Mansuetus, I am sorry. But could you sleep in with the boys tonight? I would like to wait up for Aunt Iris."

"Of course, Kyría." He said, gathering his bedding.

"What time do you have to meet with the contractor tomorrow?" She asked.

"Not until one o'clock. The lawyer is overseeing them in the morning." He replied.

"That's great. May the boys and I go with you? I would love to take them swimming. Nichola says the solarium is UV protected, so I am guessing I should be okay there. Is that right?" She asked, looking to both Mansuetus and Nichola.

Both nodded their heads yes.

"May I go with you?" Nichola asked, unsure of his welcome.

"Sure." She said and his eyes flashed with happiness. "After all, it's your house."

At first, his eyes turned sad, then he turned impish. "Of which I am King?"

"Of which you are king." She said with a look.

***

Dene and Iris pulled into the driveway after 2:00 am. Iris had a wonderful time with him. They had talked about everything, about her being widowed, about why he was in Georgia, about his thoughts on blood-borne diseases and her interest in such things. They found that they shared many things in common, including a love of classic literature and, of all things, seventies rock and roll. They had danced and flirted until last call at Seagles. The drive home was noticeably quiet, and both were nervous.

"I had a wonderful time, Dene. I would invite you in for a nightcap, but..." Iris said as Dene turned off the car, looking at the foyer windows and the small light behind them indicating that someone was waiting up for her. The porch light beckoned. She looked at him with dark liquid eyes, and he slid his arm along the back of her seat.

"I understand." He said, giving her a hungry look.

Oh, my. She thought and said instead, "Yes, it's a bit crowded in there now. I am actually sharing Leila's bedroom."

He gave her a soft kiss on the cheek and said, "I am surprised at that actually," and then trailed his kiss down her throat, pulling her close to him.

"Mmmmm?" she said, lightly wrapping her arms around him as he kissed his way back up.

"Yes, I get the distinct feeling that Nick has an interest in Leila." Kissing her softly on the lips once and then trailing down the other side of her throat.

"Oh, he does. But these things are complicated." Iris tried to explain, but was distracted by his soft butterfly kisses.

"Yes." He agreed. "I really want to see you again, Iris. Soon. I am off tomorrow, or is it today?" He chuckled against her throat.

"I don't know what our plans are. I know that Nikolaos' house will be ready to move into sometime this weekend. How about if I call you in the afternoon?" She told him breathlessly, just as he kissed her mouth again, deeper this time, pulling her closer, running his hands up and down her back. She could feel his chest hard up against her breasts.

"God, you smell so good." He whispered against her throat, brushing his hand against the side of her breast, not quite cupping her, but awfully close to it.

She thought, *Oh, lord! Down tiger!* Instead, she said, "How does that sound? I will call you and let you know my schedule?" Pulling away slightly to give him some distance.

He clearly struggled as he sat back. Then he gave her a boyish lopsided smile, slid out his door and came around to open hers, holding his hand out to help her out. She was surprised to find herself a little wobbly, and it had nothing to do with blood lust, only plain old desire. He held her hand as he walked her to the front door, turning to pull her against his hard body. He molded her hips to his, and she could feel his hard erection against her. Her eyes widened as his ice-blue eyes smoldered into hers, "Promise me, you won't forget to call me, Iris." He said softly and then kissed her deeply, sliding his tongue into her mouth.

She hadn't been kissed like that in years! "Oh! I promise!" She whispered to him as he pulled gradually away, reached over, and opened the screen door and deliberately opened the front door for her. "I promise." She said to him again and stepped into the house. She waved as she watched him walk back to the car and backed it out of the driveway, pulling away.

She gently closed the door with a sigh, and came face-to-face with an irritated Leila, who was looking at her with crossed arms.

"That's what gets everyone in trouble, isn't it?" She said quietly to her aunt.

"What?" Iris said, bewildered and startled.

"That smell! You know, that 'come fuck me' smell. It gets us plain old humans every single time, doesn't it?" Leila whispered.

"I can normally control it. But he pounced me in the car, and I was a little unprepared for him. Sometimes it just happens when our desire is stirred." Iris said, skirting her niece and heading for the refrigerator to pour herself some much-needed cow's blood.

"So, I am assuming from what I saw through the window sheers that your date went well?" Leila asked.

"Oh, honey! I had the best time." Iris said, smiling, then grimaced as she sipped the cold blood.

"Why do you drink it cold, if you don't like it that way?" Leila said, taking it from her aunt, popping it into the microwave on low for thirty seconds and stirring it with a spoon. She handed it back to her aunt, who sipped it and raised her brows, impressed. It was now about room temperature and still not clotted, much better in Iris's opinion. "I know you should see me with a bottle. Mommy of the year!" Leila whispered, smiling at her, then turning and heading back into the dim living room to sit on the couch.

"Did you just 'read' me?" Iris said, following her, then looked around. "Where are Mansuetus and Nikolaos?" She whispered, scanning and sitting on the couch as well.

"Yes, I did just 'read' you, and Mansuetus is sleeping with the kids and Nichola is pouting in the bedroom." Leila whispered simply. "Did you know? Did you have any idea that he and I were *really* 'soulmates'?"

"Not until the other night when Mansuetus told me that Nikolaos believes you are." She whispered back honestly. "Why is he pouting in the bedroom?"

"Because right now, I have him blocked out, and he doesn't like it," Leila whispered.

"You have blocked him?" Iris asked, impressed.

"His emotions are overwhelming my own, and I need some time to think without him trying to manipulate me." Leila whispered, then she concentrated a second, "but he is absolutely listening to everything we say."

"So, how did you read me?" Iris asked again, even more impressed by her niece's abilities.

"I find that now that he has returned my memories to me, I am experiencing abilities I didn't know that I had, and I am not sure if I like them or not."

"He returned memories to you?" Iris asked in a soft whisper. "What memories?"

"That's why I waited up for you. Did Mansuetus ever bring me home to you? Like the day after Nichola was at your lake house?" She asked quietly.

"Well, no, not to my knowledge. I found you asleep on the small couch on the screened-in front porch the night after he had been there, though. But that wasn't abnormal." She said delicately thinking about it for a second.

"It seems I had a run-in with them both, where there was some debate on whether or not Nichola would take me home with him. Thankfully, Mansuetus's cool-headedness won out on that debate. Though I must admit, I, in my naivete, didn't make it easy, and Nichola was not in a good place at the time." She said truthfully.

"Take you home, as in steal you away?" Iris demanded, getting angry. "You were twelve years old, and wholly human!"

"Yes. Well, be that as it may, it didn't occur. But having those memories blocked probably put my transition back a few years." Leila stated, considering the matter.

"You think so?" Iris asked, surprised.

"Yes. I would say it did. I seem to have some abilities that I shouldn't have, or I am picking up these abilities through my connection to Nichola, I am not sure, but they are playing havoc with me, and I am finding it hard to concentrate now."

All the sudden Nichola was kneeling before her. He was shirtless and dressed in his black pajama bottoms.

"Parakaló agápi mou, Lypámai," he implored.

"Please go back to the bedroom, Nichola. I cannot think rationally with you battering at me with your guilt," Leila whispered sharply, and just as quickly, he was gone as if he had never been there.

"My love, you realize he is an elder and will not tolerate that for very long," Iris warned.

"I understand exactly who and what he is, Aunt Iris." Leila's voice was sad. "He would never hurt me. But his emotions are overwhelming, and I must think through this rationally right now. Which means I need some distance from him to do that."

"His emotions?" Iris queried. "He's not an emotional guy."

"I know it seems that way to you. But he blocks everyone else out, quite effortlessly. Right now, he is extremely emotional, and with my memories restored, and as his soulmate, it is making my headache! He feels extremely guilty, which, considering his options at the time, is probably ridiculous, because I do not blame him for anything." Leila paused for a moment. "He feels much better now." She said to Iris with her hands in the air.

"I can't pretend to even understand what being connected to another person like you two are must feel like." Iris felt helpless. "I don't know how to help you, baby, and I really want to. Is he speaking Greek to you and now you are wholly understanding him, I take it?"

"Thank you for being here to discuss this with me, Auntie. I need a sounding board. He doesn't like being separate from me. But right now it is overwhelming and tiring for me to continuously shield him in this way, and yes, he is speaking Greek to me, and I understand him. He speaks Greek to me when he feels emotional, or," and Leila smiled, "horny." Pausing as if she was hearing something. "Now, he is evaluating that statement and he is not happy with my analysis. True though it is." Leila sighed.

"Maybe," Iris offered, "he should try just shielding himself a small amount, and you would be able to have him in the same room with you?" She spoke reasonably as if speaking to the air.

"That might work if he will try to control himself, because it is really hard for me to hold most of his emotions at bay. I also wanted to tell you I am taking the kids swimming tomorrow at Nichola's new house at one o'clock. The pool is covered by a solarium. Would you like to come?" Leila asked.

"Well, I do have my suit. It is already UV blocked?" Iris asked, and Leila nodded. "That's right, you went and saw it. Did you like it?"

"Yes, it is very pretty, and just huge!" Leila smiled.

"Nikolaos does like his space." Iris mused.

"What does his home in Toronto look like?" Leila said curiously. "I understand that you have been there?"

"It is actually an extremely large old mansion, with extensive grounds. Very elegant. I believe he has had it for a few centuries now. How do you know about that property?"

"He originally told me about it years ago, but it must also be the place where I sought him out when I began my transition, and I can't believe I am going to say this Monday morning. It seems like it was ages ago, so much has happened to me in the last week. In and out of the hospital, my marriage in tatters, finding out about vampires, taking a lover, gaining a soulmate, feeling all these emotions as I transition, regaining memories that I never realized I was missing, it is so overwhelming, is it any wonder that I am stressed out, exhausted, and my head throbs?" Leila leaned her head back on the couch, closing her eyes tiredly.

"Well, I think there is someone here who, now that they are in the proper frame of mind, can help you with that." Iris said lightly. "Goodnight, honey."

"Goodnight, Auntie." Leila said quietly, as she felt Nichola's hands gently grip her shoulders, bringing a sense of comfort as he began to softly massage and knead the knots from her muscles and neck.

The constant barrage of emotions that had been overwhelming her were almost gone, and she relaxed. As she was able to relax, the pain in her head decreased, and she sighed in relief. She felt the couch dip, and he held her closely against him.

Not saying a word, he slipped her t-shirt from her and removed her shorts. She opened her eyes and looked at him, and he kissed her deeply and lifted her body to straddle him as he sat up against the couch. With her straddling him, he was free to continue his back massage and to suckle her breasts, which she suddenly realized he loved to do. He loved touching her and tasting her, and then she realized he was 'reading' her too, and he knew she loved this position. She gently pushed him back so that his head was against the couch. He looked at her, still running his hands gently up and down her back.

How much, she thought at him, gently, tentatively, as she ran her fingertips over his forehead and through the silken strands of his hair, *how much can we do?*

I don't know; he thought back at her, surprising her. *It's new for me too.*

She realized this was true. They both only had each other in this way. *Try to be totally silent. I don't want to wake the kids or Mansuetus.*

I have shut their door, just in case. He thought at her with a smile, stroking her softly as he went back to suckling her. Soon he was sliding his cock against her, using her wetness to lubricate himself for her.

She slid slowly down the length of him, and heard him think, *Oh, God!,* just over halfway down his length.

Is this your 'spot', Nichola? she thought at him in discovery, and rose again to slide down him once again slowly.

Just one of many, my love. Came his thought back to her, as his head fell back against the couch as she reached his 'spot' once more. *With you, just one of many.* Gripping her hips, he let her set the pace.

Soon, she was ready to come, but he wasn't quite there yet; that changed when she reached behind her to gently massage his testicles while she rode him, as he thought *Jesus,* in response.

What's my name? She thought to him, as they came together.

O Theé mou, Leila. He thought at her. A few moments later, he opened his eyes to meet hers.

She had propped an elbow on each of his collarbones to hold her head up while she stared down at him with a self-satisfied look in her teal-colored eyes.

"You look so very triumphant to have gotten the big bad vampire to think Greek at you!" He whispered to her out loud.

"You love me." She whispered in return, giggling.

"Very much so," he said sincerely, touching her jawline and kissing her tenderly.

For My Children

L EILA WATCHED HER CHILDREN playing in the pool with Nichola, Mansuetus, Iris and, of all people, Dene Lambert, who had shown up around 2:30 p.m. at the request of her aunt. She slowly wrote in a small leather-bound journal. She decided to write down her experiences, including those with her father, and even those personal experiences with Nichola, so that if anything ever happened to her, her children would have an account of everything she had gone through and learned about herself, soul mates, and vampires over the last week.

She was determined to make sure that they at least had some idea of what happened to her and what could happen to them over the course of their lifetimes. Her father had done a horrendous job of preparing her for anything and losing her memories through Nichola's venom had been a detriment to her development, and regardless of her understanding and acceptance of why, she felt resentment.

She would never leave them so wholly unprepared for anything the future may throw their way, even if she weren't around to prepare them for it. So, anything and everything, including her soul connection and intense affair with Nichola, as well as their father leaving them, was being dutifully recorded. Frankly, writing everything down was good for her soul, and if she never disappeared from their lives, they would never read all the juicy details in any case.

She had shielded exactly what she was writing from Nichola, when he had become curious, and she had explained that she had felt an uncontrollable driving need to write ever since she had regained her memories, though she never told him what the subject of her writing was. His guilt over what he had taken from her was enough to cause him to not dwell too closely on her little writing 'project', and he basically gave her privacy over the details of the matter, though she was quite sure that she probably was breaking some 'super-secret vampire taboo' by putting to paper her knowledge about becoming a vampire.

She didn't care, not when it came to educating and protecting her children, so while the vampires, Mansuetus, and Dene were busy splashing around and having a grand time in the pool with the kids, she was relaxing by the poolside sitting at a slate covered outdoor table in a comfortable chair, writing. Though April, it was still Georgia and Georgia sunshine; under the UV protected glass of the solarium, it was very warm in the pool house area and the water was warm as well.

Mansuetus, who was infrequently interrupted by the occasional question from the crew foreman that was running the window modifications and cleaning crews upstairs, was doing a good job of keeping the kids at the shallow end of the pool. Devin had taken to the water like a fish, and they had outfitted him with inflatable 'floaties' on both of his arms, and one around his chest. Zachary, who had spent his first two summers with his grandma and Grandpa Sutton, who had a large in-ground pool at their home, had experience in and around a pool already, also had on a little life jacket.

Both Mansuetus and Nichola were strong swimmers, and Nichola was attempting to teach Zachary the breaststroke, after he realized that Zachary already knew how to float on his back and could tread water very well for his age. She had just delved into explaining what had happened during her summer with Aunt Iris as a child when she 'heard' it.

I wonder how old she is? A century? Maybe older?

Leila sat stock still. She surreptitiously glanced up, Dene and Iris were remarkably close together in a corner of the deep end of the pool, he was whispering something in her ear, and she didn't even want to think where his hands were, and what made her aunt give him such a hot, seductive look. Iris was luscious looking after all in an emerald-green one piece that pushed her full breasts up into a deep cleavage; and Dene hadn't been able to take his eyes from her cleavage since he had arrived. Leila had good-naturedly rolled her eyes at his apparent lust for her aunt, and she knew Iris loved the attention.

These thoughts, though, were another matter entirely, and there was no one else in their little group who would have thought them.

She had been intentionally blocking most thoughts from Mansuetus, Iris and Nichola since last night. None of their thoughts that she had accidentally received had given her cause for any alarm or concern, and Nichola, knowing how overwhelming his thoughts were for her, was trying his best to keep his 'shields up' toward her to help. Though many of his thoughts that she had picked up tended toward concern for her, he did have a little bit of a mental meltdown when she took off her swimsuit cover to reveal a pink polka-dotted two-piece.

As far as two-pieces went, she found it quite unrevealing since it had a moderately high-waist and noticeably short, skirted bottom and a scooped neck top so that it revealed extraordinarily little cleavage or bared midriff.

Nichola, on the other hand, initially had done mental back-flips over her suit. At least until he decided she was 'almost naked' in front of other people and then was constantly scanning for workman at the windows from the second story who might look down into the pool area at his 'woman'.

If she had been any attraction at all for Dene, which thankfully she was not, she would have found herself back in her swimsuit cover in no time flat. She found Nichola's possessiveness a little irritating, and kind of cutely endearing at the same time, especially since he worked ridiculously hard to hide it from her.

Having lost her train of thought, she placed her pen in the journal and closed it. Standing up and bending over to put it in her beach bag to come back to later. It was time to have the kids take a short nap before dinner. Both were looking tired after being in the pool for almost two hours.

The downstairs of the house had no windows to speak of, apart from the French doors going into the pool solarium itself, being wholly made of concrete cinder block and set up for the possibility of a hurricane. Mansuetus had called the attorney early in the morning and the cleaning crew had started in the downstairs, so the downstairs was now spic and span and the bedroom and separate bath had been cleaned and the queen bed made up with cute new navy-blue bedding. She and Mansuetus had early-on decided that this is where they would put the kids down for a nap after getting them in the tub to wash off the chlorine from the pool.

Leila had learned that a lawyer and a few of his assistants had personally flown down with Nichola and were housed at The Spencer House with their rental cars. They had been doing all the shopping and had engaged the necessary crews for modifications and cleaning, as well as overseeing everything while Mansuetus was unavailable. She knew that this must be a huge expense for Nichola and, though not a cheap person; she was thrifty, and had said so to him. She questioned why he would retain an attorney and three assistants to handle these types of particulars when he could have easily just secured the less expensive services of an executive assistant or two and got the same job done and paid less money.

He had given her a look and just replied that he was not without 'resources', whatever that meant.

Sensing movement close to her, she glanced up to her right. Nichola stood next to her and was holding her swimsuit cover, which she accepted with a small sigh. He himself was dressed in short simple maroon and gold swim trunks, which currently clung wetly to his muscular legs, though she got the distinct feeling that this was still too much cover to swim in for his personal tastes. Admiring his lithe, muscled body, especially his muscled abdomen, she smiled at the Dragon Ball Z themed beach towel around his neck; that Zachary had insisted that he use. Glancing over his shoulder to check on Zachary, she saw Mansuetus was getting both kids out of the pool.

"I am responsible," he said, giving her a slightly offended look in reaction to her checking that he hadn't left Zachary in the pool to drown.

She gave him a half smile. "I know you are. But I am a mommy." She said, making a mental note to ask Mansuetus to take her to the bank on Monday. She thought intentionally at Nichola, *We may have a discussion about Dene very soon.*

Concerning what? He thought in return.

I am trying to form my opinion on something. I am reluctant to reveal more currently in case I am incorrect. Let me do some more information gathering and I will let you know. She thought as she gathered the boy's things.

If anyone had looked at them, they would have thought that he was waiting patiently for her to gather her things to take the boys into the house. He almost imperceptibly nodded his head at her, but she could read the curiosity coming from him.

"Aunt Iris, we are going to take the kids in for a bath and a nap." She called.

Her mind was met with two thoughts: Dene, who thought he might convince Iris of having a quickie in the pool, and Iris, who was determined that they weren't having a quickie in the pool.

She smiled quickly, then schooled her features as Iris called. "Okay, darling, we will come in shortly ourselves."

Once she had the kids bathed, she and Mansuetus dried and dressed them. She turned around and saw that Mansuetus had a disposable camera in his hands. Zachary, who was quite the ham, wrapped his arms around Devin, who saw Mansuetus at the same time and just as she was stepping out of the way, they both smiled for the camera and Mansuetus took their picture. She looked inquiringly at him, and he looked a little bashful.

"We have an agreement that if they are good for their baths, we will take picture. I will get them developed this week and we will see how they turn out." The big man smiled.

"Well, make sure that you get a double set. I would like one as well." She smiled in return.

Mansuetus sat in the rocking chair to tell them a story for their nap. She listened as he told them about Bart the Dragon's adventures on Mt. Olympus. It seemed that currently Bart was very hungry and hunting for a golden fleeced goat to eat.

She felt Nichola wrap his arms around her from behind. "Could you imagine what he would have been like if he would have been able to take pictures of my brother and I?" He whispered in her ear, giving her a small kiss on the side of the neck.

Did he never have children of his own? She thought to him.

No. I think he found that my brother and I took up his life. He always seemed to be content with just us. As it was, he was a good father to us. He showed us love, patience, and discipline. Which, given our circumstances, we needed. Nichola thought in return, and she could feel his love and respect for Mansuetus in his thoughts.

They left the bedroom, closing the door behind them and returned to the recreational room. Both Iris and Dene were there, and she could feel the sexual tension between them. They were trying to figure out the stereo and find a decent radio station to listen to. They found a local station that played pop and rock music.

"Not too loud, please. The kids are going down for a nap," Leila told them.

"Who is up for a game of cards?" Nichola asked, looking through a basket on the bar that had several card decks and games in it.

"I am not playing cards against you and Leila," Iris said. "You two are bound to cheat!" She said with a laugh.

"I would never, Auntie!" Leila said, offended.

"Well, how about the men against the ladies, Iris?" Nichola said in challenge.

"How about we play Uno? That means we are all playing for ourselves." Leila said, investigating the game decks. "Do you play cards, Dene?" She inquired.

"I haven't for years," he said with a laugh, thinking that he would love to play strip poker with Iris. Just then, his beeper went off. He checked the number and then ignored it.

"Is it the hospital calling?" Iris asked, thinking sadly that he may have to leave.

"No. I am not on call this evening." He said vaguely. Leila got a thought of a blonde woman flashing through his mind. "So, how do you play Uno? I don't think that I have ever played it." Sitting down at the card table and looking at the box, Iris, who had played Uno with Leila's parents years before, sat down next to him to explain the game rules.

So, who is the blonde that just flashed through his mind, do you think? Did you catch that? Leila thought at Nichola as they sat down at the card table.

No. You are picking up on him better than I am. I am doing my level best to shield myself from you, so I am not focused on him. But probably the bartender that we had the other night. They have been intimate. If he was interested in her, I doubt it was much more than just sex. She doesn't seem to be the type that would interest him intellectually, and he actually does seem to be interested in, and like, Iris. Nichola thought in return.

"Are you two paying attention?" Iris asked them, and Leila knew she was in a competitive mood.

"Absolutely." Nichola told her.

"Mansuetus, would you like to play?" Leila said as the big man came through the recreational room.

"No. I want to check on the contractor's progress and see what I can do about preparing dinner, Kyría." He said, heading for the elevator.

"Do you need help?" Leila asked, starting to stand.

"Oh, no! I have this all handled, Kyría." He said, grinning. Leila realized he was eager to get into the kitchen to check out the appliances and get cooking. She smiled as he quickly got into the elevator.

"Why does he call you Kyría? Is Leila your middle name?" Dene asked her conversationally as Iris dealt out the cards.

"Because he refuses to call me Leila." Leila said with a shake of her head. "Kyría is Greek. It means missus or something."

"Actually, it means lady or mistress. He's old-fashioned." Nichola said as he looked at his cards.

"He doesn't call Iris anything but Iris." Dene said, looking at Iris.

"Iris is an unattached female. In his mind, Leila has a higher standing and is deserving of a designation or title." Nichola explained with a shrug of his shoulders.

"Well!" Iris huffed, causing Leila to give her an enormous smile.

"Don't worry yourself over it, Auntie. Unattached females have more fun," Leila laughed.

"Do they?" Nichola asked with a sharp, slightly jealous look. Leila quickly smiled down at her cards.

"Yes," Iris said, looking at Dene with a sultry smile, which he returned.

Later, they all sat down in the eat-in area of the kitchen to eat a wonderful meal that Mansuetus had made. The work crews had finished with almost the whole back of the house. It was now UV protected and spotless. Since the elevator exited in that area, there were no problems in bringing up the party from downstairs. Leila realized that had been intentional on Mansuetus' part, which was good because they all needed to remember that Dene was an unsuspecting human, Nichola nor Iris needed any deep scrutiny, and Leila wasn't up to any sunlight without protection.

Leila was sure that the vampires, though they ate, didn't enjoy it as much as Dene, she, the boys, and Mansuetus did. He had made a wonderful moussaka, Greek salad, steamed vegetables, and revani topped with ice cream. The adults all drank Retsina wine, which Leila found delicious, and Mansuetus had milk for the boys. She could tell that Mansuetus was incredibly pleased with the compliments he received over the meal. While she took care of the boys, she watched Nichola, Iris and Dene help Mansuetus with the dishes. She was surprised to find that she was quite content and relaxed after their family meal, more so than she had been in an exceptionally long time, even before her transition.

Is Mansuetus lonely, do you think? She intentionally thought at Nichola.

I wouldn't think so. After all, he has me and now he has you. Nichola thought arrogantly back.

But is this all he does? Take care of other people? What about a girlfriend? She questioned.

Glykó, I believe Mansuetus has as many women as he chooses. She could hear the humor in Nichola's thought as he dried a plate and put it away. *Why are you worried about Mansuetus? He is quite content; I assure you.*

She answered: *He's been truly kind to me and my children. This has been a difficult week for us, and I would like to do something for him.*

Glykó, he would not want you to fuss over him. It is not his way. Nichola thought, smiling.

"What are you smiling about?" Iris questioned him.

"Didn't you know, Auntie? Nichola loves doing housework, especially dishes!" Leila giggled.

Mansuetus burst out laughing, earning him a disgruntled look from Nichola.

"It really isn't that funny," Nichola said a tad grumpily.

"It is just a little funny." Mansuetus said with a chuckle and a shrug.

"Okay, let us in on the joke." Leila smiled.

"Kitchen duty was the most effective punishment for Kýrios when he misbehaved as a child. He hated to work in the kitchens." Mansuetus smiled, remembering.

"At least until I was about thirteen and became interested in a couple of the cook's daughters." Nichola's smile was devious.

"Yes, it seemed he was misbehaving more frequently than usual, until I realized sending him to the kitchens was no longer a punishment, but a treat! I had to come up with something else to curb his wild ways." Mansuetus chortled.

"So, you helped raise Nick?" Dene asked curiously.

Both Mansuetus and Nichola sobered; Dene had been so quiet and observant, it seemed that they had all forgotten about the 'human' in their midst.

Leila knew Dene was very curious about all their relationships and she, in turn, was very curious about Dene.

"Yes, I have worked for the Tsoukalous family for a long time." Mansuetus remarked neutrally coming to help Leila with the kids.

Dene's beeper went off again. Again, he checked it, squinting his eyes in annoyance. Leila got a clearer picture of the blonde that she had seen earlier.

"Mansuetus, would you please take me and the kid's home? I think the boys will be wanting to turn in early tonight..." She said and was hit by a chorus of 'No's' from Zachary, Nichola, Iris, and even Dene.

"We haven't even finished our game yet!" Iris said.

"Swim, Mommy!" Zachary yelled, causing Devin to start yelling in response.

"Glykó, Mansuetus and I can take the boy's back a little later. I can then pick up the Mustang. There is no reason to cut our evening short. Unless you are feeling unwell?" Nichola asked above the noise.

She looked at Zachary, who looked back at her imploringly. "Okay, I suppose..." He gave her a huge smile and a big hug. She hugged him back tightly.

She found that it was hard to say 'No' to him right now. They'd all done a good job of keeping the boys occupied, but she had expected Zachary to ask about his dad by now. He was used to his dad being around and always asked where he was if he didn't come home after a day or so. This time, he seemed to accept that his dad wasn't there. She was unsure of how she felt about it.

She didn't know how she would really answer Zachary's question when it eventually came, other than to tell him that his dad was 'out to sea'; even though her marriage was over, she had expected that Michael would call by now to check on the boys at the very least; he always had before when he was running tests out of AUTEC. It saddened and pissed her off simultaneously.

Even if he didn't want to be married to her anymore, he still was the boy's father! Surely Michael would want to be involved in the boy's lives, wouldn't he? Maybe she had given him too much credit after all? The only thing that she was totally sure of was that she didn't want her children to hurt any more than they would be, considering the circumstances.

Some of these conflicting emotions must have made their way to Nichola, since the next thing that she felt was his hand on her shoulder as she held her oldest son tightly to her. A sense of comfort came from him. She looked up, giving him a small smile. He gave her an unreadable look in return, shielding his innermost thoughts heavily from her. She knew then that no matter how he felt, he never wanted to see her in pain. She held his hand briefly in gratitude.

"Okay, well, we have to wait a couple of minutes before we can get back into the water." She said to Zachary. "How about if I take you downstairs and get you guys back into your suits?" She asked him with a smile.

"Yay!" Zachary said.

Nichola scooped up Devin, following her and Zachary while Mansuetus finished cleaning off the table.

After they had finished getting the boys back into their swimsuits, they were heading through the recreational room to head back out to the pool when, unexpectedly, Nichola put both boys on the couch. Kneeling before them, he asked, smiling, "Would you like me to show you how to dance with a lady?"

"Yeah!" Zachary said loudly, clapping his hands. Devin gave a toothy laugh to his brother.

Nichola stood and, turning around with his vampire grace, quickly pulled Leila into his arms as she realized that *I Love the Way You Love Me,* by John Michael Montgomery, was playing on the radio.

"Now pay attention," Nichola instructed the boys, who laughed at him as he moved her around. "Ladies love it when you sing to them."

Nichola sang out loud in a perfect key as Zachary and Devin roared with laughter. Leila, smiling, rolled her eyes at him.

The twang in his voice would have done a real southerner proud, and he gave her a large smile and spun her around. As she laughed, he continued singing loudly in his perfect voice, swaying her to the music and moving her around the room. The boys continued to laugh loudly and clap their hands as he smiled at her as the song ended, slowly turning her out of his arms to bow over her hand.

The boys were still yelling and laughing as the elevator doors opened and Iris, Dene, and Mansuetus exited. "Well, are we late for the party?" Iris smiled.

"Nick was dancing and singing to my Mommy!" Zachary told her, laughing. "He is funny!"

"Yes, we heard him clear upstairs." Dene said, looking at Nichola and laughing. "You should take that on the road, man. You were pretty good!" Smiling, he held open the door to the pool for Iris.

Picking up the boys, Mansuetus headed toward the pool, smiling at Nichola, shaking his head.

Nichola quickly pulled Leila into his arms with a smile, "Did you think I was 'pretty good', agápi mou?" He asked her tenderly, holding her against him tightly and kissing her lips.

"You were perfect." She murmured, wrapping her arms around his neck, returning his kiss.

Nikolaos

CHAPTER TWO

A S NIGHT FELL IN the Georgia sky, Nikolaos watched Leila playing in the shallow end of the pool with Devin. As the sun sank below the horizon, he could feel his full powers returning to him. It had taken a good part of his strength to keep himself shielded from his soulmate during the daytime, but now, with the passing of the sun, it was easier. He reached out with part of his mind to the good doctor, who was with Iris in the adjacent hot tub, to find out what had distracted Leila so much about him today. He sensed nothing more than his single-minded desire to get Iris to have sex with him and Iris' determination to not have sex with him, at least not tonight. This caused him to smile wryly as he considered women and their silly thoughts when it came to sex.

He considered Leila in a predatory manner as she bounced up and down with Devin in her arms, laughing as the child yelled in laughter. It was good that they had quickly gotten past such games, because he desired her more and more each day. She glanced his way, and he quickly schooled his features into a bland expression, stretching his legs out in front of him as he seemingly relaxed in a poolside lounge chair. She narrowed her eyes suspiciously at him and he gave her a come-hither smile. She rolled her eyes at him in response, causing him to smile broadly. He had every intention of keeping her here in his bed tonight until she begged for mercy and could hardly wait for some much-needed privacy to have his way with her.

She would be surprised to know that as much as he wanted to have un-limited patience with her, his patience only went so far. As much as he had enjoyed their occasional sexual experiences together since his arrival, he knew she had felt constrained because they were not truly alone. He wanted to experience her when she had no such inhibitions, and had hoped to do so last night, but unfortunately that hadn't worked out as planned.

Since he had tasted Leila's blood, he had an overwhelming need to be close to her and had fought himself several times throughout the day just to keep from continuously touching her. He knew that at this moment he needed to continue to shield his emotions from her to keep from overwhelming and frightening her, as she didn't have control over her own abilities yet.

He was determined that tonight would be a more successful campaign. As such, he would go with Mansuetus when he took the children back to their own beds, pick up the Mustang, and then return, and if needed, give Iris many hints to vacate the house with her young doctor. As far as he was concerned, they could play their games with each other elsewhere. He wanted his house to himself and his mate.

"You are looking very fearsome, Nichola. What are you thinking about?"

He looked down to see Leila gripping the side of the pool nearest to him, looking up at him.

"I am surprised that you don't know, Glykó." He said, looking at her with hunger, to which she widened her eyes.

Mansuetus had both children in his arms and Nichola got up to follow him.

"Where are you going?" She asked quickly.

"We are taking the children home, Kyría." Mansuetus answered simply.

Leila started to pull herself from the pool.

"No. I will make sure that everything is well and will return with the car. Stay, enjoy the peace, and quiet." Nichola ordered and his tone brooked no argument.

"But..." she started.

Nichola knelt next to her at the pool's edge. "Leila," reaching down to touch her face as she gripped the edge of the pool. "They are safer with Mansuetus than anyone. You need to take some time for yourself. Do not worry. Why don't you explore the upstairs while I am gone and see if you like the way the house has been furnished today?" He stood and followed Mansuetus into the house.

Leila swam over to the steps of the pool in the shallow end and got out. Wrapping a towel around herself, she looked up as she noticed a movement to her left. Iris was standing next to her.

"What are you doing, child?"

"They are taking the boy's home." She told her aunt.

"Yes, just as they agreed to do after dinner, remember?" Iris said to her. "You are supposed to be relaxing after all, Leila. Why are you worried?"

"I don't know." Leila admitted softly.

"Honey, I don't think that you ever give yourself time to relax or any time for yourself. Why don't I take Dene and have him take me for a long drive, and if he is lucky, some heavy petting?" Iris said softly with a sultry smile in Dene's direction. He looked at them questioningly from the hot tub, unable to hear their conversation.

"Aunt Iris, you are bad!" Leila whispered with a small laugh, looking at Dene herself.

"He's been after me all day long to touch certain things. Shall I make his wish come true?" Iris chuckled softly. "I'll have him drop me at your house when I am done with him. Why don't you go in and take a nice, long, hot bath and enjoy the peace and quiet?"

Nikolaos gently laid Devin in his bed and covered his sleeping form as Mansuetus did the same for Zachary. Both boys had quickly fallen asleep on the way home, wore out from their day in the pool. Mansuetus nodded his thanks and closed the door behind them as they both went into the living room.

"Kýrios, I would like to speak to you before you leave." Mansuetus's voice was muted.

Nikolaos's mind had been on returning as quickly as possible to Leila was surprised. "What is it?" He asked distractedly.

"I want to know if you realize Kyría will never leave these children?"

"What?" Nikolaos asked sharply.

"I said she will never leave these children. No matter how long her transition takes. Even after she is a vampire. She will never leave these children. She will never give them up." Mansuetus' voice was soft.

"Vampires don't raise children, Mansuetus. It is not a healthy environment for them. You have pointed out this fact to me in the past." Nikolaos said heatedly. "She will do what is best for these children."

"Kýrios, you are mistaken if you genuinely believe that. She is their mother. As far as she is concerned, being with her is in their best interest and she will never abandon her children." Mansuetus said sadly.

"She's my soulmate! She will take her place by my side, where she belongs." Nikolaos said dismissively.

"If it is a choice between you and her children, she will choose her children, Nikolaos, no matter how much it hurts her to do so," Mansuetus warned.

Nikolaos scoffed, irritated because it had a ring of truth, and started walking around the big man to leave the house.

Mansuetus continued louder to get his attention. "I want you to consider something; remove the children from the equation."

"What the hell are you talking about?" Nikolaos growled, whirling, grabbing Mansuetus to push him against the wall, fear twisting his insides.

"Don't misunderstand me, Kýrios. You know I would never advocate harming any child, let alone these children. What I am saying is that we could take them all with us. Kyría and her children. There is nothing holding them here. Their father cares more about himself than he does his family. You could be their father and would probably be a better father to them. We could have a family again, with children. We could raise them together; you, I and Kyría. You and I don't live too differently from humans now. We interact with humans all the time. Kyría could take all the time that she needed to make her transition." Mansuetus told him in a pleading voice, laying out his case.

With a profound sense of relief, Nikolaos suddenly embraced him. "I am sorry, my friend. I should not have doubted you. I will think about it. I give you my word." Troubled by this conversation, he left the house and got into his Mustang.

As Nikolaos started the Mustang and backed down the driveway, Mansuetus' words floated through his mind. He stopped the car, placed it in neutral, and engaged the emergency brake, resting his head against the steering wheel.

Could it be possible? Could he claim her children as his own? He never thought of being a father. Neither as a human nor as a vampire. After everything that he had done, all the havoc and death that he caused in his long existence, did he even deserve to raise children?

He tried to make amends for all the evil that he had done. He was under no disillusionment about his existence. He knew that a large part of his actions were selfish and evil, and he had tried to make amends for those actions over the last couple of centuries. He tried to guide his family's descendants in a better direction. After all, what happened to these descendants was no more their fault than what had happened to him. He, at least, was there to guide them; something that had been unavailable to him. But did that make him good enough now to be a father?

He looked out the rear-view mirror as he put the car back into reverse. He needed to calm himself before he returned to Leila. He drove the short distance to his house. Passing Iris and her doctor leaving as he entered the community gates. He automatically returned Dene Lambert's wave as he passed them, thinking to himself that at least one issue was resolved.

Pulling into the property, he scanned the area, seeking out Leila's presence. Parking the car in the garage, closing the garage door, he entered the downstairs. He sensed her upstairs and after locking the French doors to the solarium; he rode the elevator up, seeking her out. Walking through the house ensuring that all the doors were locked; thinking that he would need to teach his allaxiéra the importance of safety and security, especially when she was alone.

Opening his senses to her he found she was laying in the bathtub, relishing the heat and sound of the water as it washed over her body, he realized she was tired, body and soul, and wondered if he had a hand in this exhaustion. Was it too many late nights and not enough sleep, or was it because he wasn't giving her enough of himself to sustain her through her transformation?

He then realized that she did not know that he was even in the house. She wasn't scanning for him, nor had she sensed him come in. She had worked so hard to shield herself from him. She was exhausted and now that she was relaxed; she was just a human woman enjoying her bath.

Silently moving through the master bedroom, he gradually opened the bathroom door to lean against the doorjamb, watching her.

Laying back in the tub with her eyes closed, she pointed a small foot under the faucet to feel the hot water flow over her skin. He could almost feel her moan in pleasure, and with his senses totally open to her, that pleasure vibrated throughout his entire body. This shared connection was stronger and deeper since her memories had returned, and he was both surprised and grateful for it. Her enjoyment in just this simple act of bathing was profound and highly erotic. Allowing himself to be totally open to her, he realized that being immersed in her feelings was an intense experience that battered at his self-control, and he understood better why she had shielded herself from him. If she had felt half last night of what he was feeling right now, it was no wonder that in her inexperience she felt overwhelmed.

He silently closed the door between them, giving her privacy, and looked around the master bedroom to see how his legal team had decorated the large space. His lawyer had made sure that it was light and airy, just like he liked his personal space. The walls in this room were now a pale yellow-green, and the wood of the furniture was a honey walnut. They had placed an oversized and comfortable-looking pale-yellow and white striped chaise lounge and two solid yellow wing chairs in front of the white fireplace. The wall of windows and French doors overlooking the pool and marsh at the back of the property had been covered in UV blocking window film and was now decorated with white sheer curtains. They had purchased a king-size sleigh bed, whose curved headboard and foot-board were upholstered in white fabric, and it was now made up with pale yellow cotton sheets and comforter.

He was pleased with the overall effect, but he expected no less from his employees.

He noticed the stereo against the back wall and moved to turn on the local station. Listening to the soft notes of music, he stripped his clothes off and walked barefoot to pull the window sheer aside and stare out over the marsh. His sensitive vampire eyes easily pierced the darkness to look out on the beauty of the marsh as it was bathed in the light of a half-moon.

He thought intently about what Mansuetus had said about the children. From everything that he knew and had seen about vampire soulmates, he knew Leila was essentially his other half. But that didn't mean that she wasn't her own individual person, and he was just beginning to realize how different they were.

A thousand years was a long time and even though he worked awfully hard to keep up to date with the way the world had changed, he realized that their way of thinking was profoundly different.

He had been surprised when Leila had offered her opinion earlier on the cost effectiveness of having executive assistants perform the same work that his lawyer and his team frequently did for him. He at first was offended, and then amused when she had made her recommendation, but shielded those thoughts from her, as he quickly realized that she was only trying to protect him, and he didn't want to anger her. She didn't realize that he used a legal team because he didn't like to be bothered with details or matters of funds, and he gave his lawyer control over both and trusted him implicitly.

He almost told her that he needed to trust his staff as he didn't like to murder them unless it was absolutely necessary and was therefore incredibly careful with their selection; but he didn't, because he wasn't sure if she would see the humor in that funny, but fully accurate statement.

There were many things that, even with their soul connection, she didn't know about him. She didn't yet understand that he, after almost a thousand years, had amassed enough money to do as he pleased. Nor did she understand that loyalty, security, and performance were far more valuable than money, and a trustworthy staff were worth their weight in gold. Being able to trust his small staff was also one of the reasons why he had survived for so long. Still so very innocent, she had never had to worry about trust and survival.

He wanted her, cared deeply for her, needed her with him, but he also needed to remember that she wasn't a full vampire yet, and was still very much a modern human woman. He had quickly realized that she didn't respond positively to his edicts, and in turn had strived for her cooperation. He knew she wanted him, cared deeply for him, and needed him in return, but he also knew that she could be very stubborn if she thought someone was trying to control her, even if that guidance was ultimately to her own benefit.

Nichola blamed her husband for this attitude. He knew from reading her that she had to fight for even a measure of individuality with her husband. She frequently felt that she had to give up even that small measure to keep her sons from living in a battle zone. Nichola knew she felt that her husband was controlling and manipulative; he also did not want her to believe that this was a male trait.

It had been obvious from her husband's drunken call to the house that he didn't want to give Leila up, and had hoped that she had been cowed by his threat of divorce into compliance. In Nichola's opinion, any man who used such threats to control his woman or bend her to his will was not a real man. Being connected to Leila as he was, he knew that her husband's manipulative treatment infuriated her; but he also knew that she would go to any lengths, put up with anything, even swallow her pride, to give her children the best family life possible.

Deep in thought, and focused on looking out over the marsh, he didn't acknowledge her presence, even though he knew she had come out of the bathroom. He felt her wrap her arms around him from behind. He held her hands as she rubbed her cheek on his back, like a small, loving cat.

"You know you are always naked in your bedroom." She stated, giggling.

He turned to wrap his arms around her towel clad form. "Well, at least I am not naked in the other parts of my house, and I am glad to see that you are not attempting to clothe me this time." He smiled down at her.

"I think that somewhere deep down inside, you have a nudist streak in you, so I have decided not to waste my time trying anymore." Leila smiled. "As long as you remain clothed in public, I can put up with it in private, I suppose."

"You realize we are born nude, and man has performed many tasks nude. The ancient Olympians competed naked. There are also many religious sects that practice nudism." He told her with a tone of instruction in his voice.

"Really?" She asked, raising an eyebrow in amusement.

"Yes." He stated emphatically. "In fact, it is only this current century that has seen a rise in American Puritanism when it comes to the human form. It is probably why my naked form causes you so much unease. You are of this century and country. Europe and much of the rest of the world for centuries have been more accepting of the human body."

"Wow, how serious! Here I thought it was because you just didn't want to be bothered to take the time to take off your clothes when you wanted to make love to me." She said tartly, with an impish gleam in her eyes. "And for your information, your 'naked form' doesn't cause me any 'unease'."

"It doesn't?" He teased, holding her tighter to him.

"No. To tell you the truth, I find you incredibly beautiful." She said softly to him, resting her hand on his tanned bare chest. This simple touch caused his desire to flare.

"Hmmm. I can see why you would. I *am* beautiful, after all." He stated simply, then smiled down at her.

"Yes," she rolled her eyes at him, "and very modest too." Laughing softly, shaking her head.

"I also find you beautiful, agápi mou." He murmured softly as he bent and kissed her shoulder, kissing his way up the side of her neck, to gently nibble on her earlobe as he removed her towel. As the towel slid from her body, his hands followed it down, gripping her hips and pulling her close to him, pressing her to him as she leaned into him for a deep kiss. "Open up to me, Leila." He whispered against her lips.

She pulled back from him with wide eyes. "What?"

"Drop your walls and open up your senses to me." He whispered, holding her face in his hands.

"No. It's too hard. It's too much." Shaking her head.

He felt her trepidation. "It is just the two of us, Leila. No one else is here. I will help you; I will protect and guide you. Feel me. I am open to you." He whispered, caressing her body gently, purposefully pulling her tighter to him and enveloping her with his scent. "Trust me. Give yourself over to me." He bent and lifted her, wrapping her legs around his waist.

She quickly clasped her arms around his neck tightly to steady herself. "Nichola! What are you doing? You are going to drop me!" She said breathlessly.

"You know I would never drop you, Glykó." Chuckling softly as he held her to him and walked a few steps to the nearest wall, leaning her back against it to brace her with his body, his hands steadying her. "And as for what I am doing? I believe you know what I am doing." He slid into her body with a groan.

She gasped in response as he slowly thrust into her. She held him tightly in return; she had never felt more exposed to anyone before in her life. She could feel the strength of his arms, shoulders, and back as he slowly moved within her. Braced between the wall and his body, with his arms and hands supporting her, securely holding her as he thrust in and out of her, she was unable to move and the only thing that she could do was hold on tight as he moved within her. Impaled on his cock, and subject to only his movements, she started to feel trapped, like an animal in a snare. Then his delicious scent wrapped itself around her once more, making her feel lightheaded.

"Relax. Trust me, glukó mou. Open up your senses to me, feel what I feel." He whispered against her throat in a husky voice.

She breathed him in and buried her face in his hair as she held him tightly to her. She could feel him pressing on the walls of her mind as he gently moved inside of her. His physical and mental nudging was difficult to withstand, and she sensed that if he wanted to, he could easily overpower her, but he wanted her to make the decision.

"Give yourself to me, Leila, my love, and let me in. I am already open to you. Surrender." He coaxed softly as he claimed her lips; and like Jericho, her walls tumbled, and sweet bliss flowed through her veins.

She could feel the smoothness of her own skin where his hands held her, and the heat and slick tightness of her body as he thrust within her. She then felt a sense of deep satisfaction, tenderness, and love. The feelings were so strong that she started to mentally pull away.

"Ochi agápi mou. Stay with me. We are almost there." He whispered with a groan, and she tightened her legs around his waist as he thrust faster and harder.

Pleasure flowed throughout her body as she arched against him, seeking release. She wrapped her arms tightly around his neck and ran her fingers through his hair to clutch at him as he took her; feeling that sense of triumph and satisfaction flowing through her again as she felt her own velvet softness tighten and pulsate around him. "Oh, Nichola!" She cried out as she experienced both her orgasm, and his, through him.

Then she felt his teeth pierce her shoulder and experienced a mind-blowing euphoria take her to the edge of sanity, as if it were, she, that tasted the sweetest of elixirs. She heard herself scream in ecstasy as she lost consciousness.

Leila woke to find herself lying on the bed with Nichola's arms and legs wrapped around her, holding her to him. He was breathing deeply as if asleep. But she knew he was awake and feeling quite intoxicated. Turning her head, she looked at his face next to hers to see that he was watching her intently. The pupils of his eyes were very dilated, showing only a thin ring of amber iris.

"You bit me." She said simply looking at him in bewilderment.

"Yes."

"Why?"

"You felt what it was like, and you need to ask?" He smiled lopsidedly, gently caressing her breast.

She held his hand to stop the caress. "But..." she started.

He put a finger on her lips, silencing her, as he read her mind. "Leila, when you get your fangs, I will let you bite me. Hell, I will probably beg you to bite me. You are perfectly fine; I only took a few sips. You know I would never harm you, o ómorfos ángelos mou, my beautiful angel." He replaced his finger with his lips, kissing her deeply as his hand made its way over her belly. As he thrust his tongue between her lips, his skilled fingers parted the folds of her punani for his exploration.

She clutched at his wrist as she involuntarily thrust herself against his fingers. She turned her head away from him, pulling away from his kiss. "Again?" She gasped out, feeling his emotions flow over her once more.

"I want to hear you scream and feel you come around me again, my angel." He whispered as he took her nipple into his mouth to suckle, sending a jolt of ecstasy throughout her body.

Leila woke to the smell of coffee and muted light flowing through the window sheers into the room. She turned her head to watch Nichola place a cup of coffee on the nightstand next to her. Looking incredibly sexy, he was bathed, clean shaven, and dressed in a light blue button down, long sleeve dress shirt, dark blue jeans, and boots. She suddenly sat up, clutching the sheet to her breasts. "Oh, my god! What time is it?" She asked.

"Almost noon." He told her, smiling. "We should get you something to eat."

"I have got to get home to the kids." She told him with a blush as she swung her bare legs over the side of the bed. She couldn't believe that she had been here all night and felt a huge amount of guilt wash over her for having spent the entire night away from her children to frolic in bed with her lover.

"Stop." He said and sat down next to her, wrapping an arm about her shoulders. "Mansuetus has already brought the children over. They have been playing outside in the backyard and are now in the kitchen, getting ready to eat their lunch. You," he put a finger under her chin and moved her so that he could look into her eyes, "are a good mother. A wonderful mother. But even mommies need a break and time to themselves."

He reached over her, picked up the coffee, and handed it to her with a tender look. She realized he was remembering the previous night, in detail. She blushed again, sipped the coffee, and looked away. "I need to get showered." She said softly.

"Well, I am clean. But I could join you if you like." Leaning over, he kissed her bare shoulder, sending a frisson of excitement up her spine.

"No, I just need a little privacy, please." She choked out as the blush reached her chest. Then a thought suddenly occurred to her, and she looked at him. "Oh, please tell me that Mansuetus brought me some clothes. The only things I have from yesterday is my bathing suit and cover."

"I believe he did. He gave me a bag for you, which I have placed in the bathroom." He again looked at her and softly kissed her lips.

She knew exactly where his mind was heading.

"No. Go, go, go!" She pulled away and shooed him with her free hand, her blush returning.

He smiled rakishly at her and left the bedroom, softly closing the door behind him.

Placing the coffee cup back on the nightstand, she fell back onto the bed in astonishment and a little embarrassment.

The things that they had done last night! She hadn't even realized there were so many positions to make love. She couldn't believe that she had been so abandoned with him, much more so than she had ever been with any man; and that he now knew every inch of her intimately as she did him. She had never felt so loved, no worshiped, by any man as she had last night.

Walking into the kitchen, dressed in the jeans and t-shirt that Mansuetus had thoughtfully packed for her, carrying her now empty coffee cup, she saw

Nichola sitting at the kitchen table, a newspaper open before him, with the boys and Mansuetus.

Zachary saw her and yelled out, "Mommy!"

This caused Devin to yell, "Da, da, da!"

She quickly came to give them both hugs and kisses. She noticed Devin had a new highchair, and Zachary had a new booster seat as well. She looked at Mansuetus in inquiry. He met her gaze innocently, as he got up from the table and took her coffee cup from her. The boys were eating homemade macaroni and cheese.

"He didn't do it." Nichola said without looking up from his newspaper. "I gave instructions to my staff to provide them with everything that they needed for this house."

She could hear the work crew at the front of the house as she sat down at the kitchen table. "Are they almost done with the house?" She asked, trying to see what he was so intent on reading.

"They should be complete by the end of the day." He answered, still engrossed in what looked like the business section of the Sunday newspaper.

Mansuetus sat down a plate with a small grilled tuna steak, Brussels sprouts, wild rice, and a glass of iced green tea in front of her. "Wow. This looks wonderful, Mansuetus. Thank you." Grateful that this blood building diet he was feeding her would help keep her weight under control.

"That is not something that you need to worry about," Nichola murmured, still engrossed in his paper. "You are a very beautiful woman just the way you are," He added, glancing up to give her a smoldering look, causing her to blush again and focus on her food.

When the boys and she had finished eating, she helped Mansuetus clean up the kitchen, and then they took them downstairs, leaving Nichola to his newspaper.

"Mommy, come look." Zachary said to her, taking her by the hand and leading her outside to the solarium. He was pointing outside the glass wall to the fenced backyard.

She noticed two men putting the finishing touches on an A-frame swing set. They had dug out the ground around it and were spreading fine sand around the bottom. She looked at Mansuetus, who was carrying Devin, and he gave her a large smile.

"Mansuetus, you bought them a swing set?" She spoke.

"Kýrios." He replied, smiling.

"Nichola bought them a swing set?" She wondered softly looking through the glass.

"What's going on?" She heard Iris say from behind them.

Leila turned to look at her. "Auntie, I didn't know that you were here."

"I came over this morning with Mansuetus and the boys. I was resting in the bedroom down here; my bedroom isn't quite complete yet. Oh, look, a swing set!" Iris ruffled Zachary's curly hair. "You guys are going to have fun with that."

Zachary smiled at her and gave her leg a big hug, and she smiled down at him.

"How was your evening?" Leila asked, smiling impishly. "Is Dr. Lambert happy this morning?"

"Not nearly as happy as he would like to be, I am sure." Iris replied with a small smile. "Your evening must have gone well. You look well rested."

Leila blushed lightly and before she could respond, she felt Nichola in her mind. She looked up through the roof of the solarium to see him looking down at them from the breakfast nook windows. "Nichola wants to speak with me. Would you mind watching the boys for a few minutes, Mansuetus?" She asked.

"Not at all, Kyría. Take your time. Now that Iris is up, I am going to put them down for a nap." He said with a smile, taking them back into the house.

"No!" Zachary said to him with a yawn.

"Come now, Master Zachary. We will swim again after you take your nap," Mansuetus said coaxingly and took him by the hand.

"Okay." Zachary replied, letting Mansuetus take him into the bedroom.

Leila took the elevator upstairs with Iris. As they went into the kitchen, Iris waved in Nichola's direction and headed to the refrigerator to make herself a glass of cow's blood.

Nichola took Leila by the hand and led her into a study that had obviously just been completed, closing the door behind them. He pulled her down to sit with him on a brown leather loveseat.

"Thank you for getting the boys a swing set." She said to him before he could speak.

"They are welcome. I want them to be happy here." He replied. "In fact, this is what I want to talk to you about," He said, leaning forward and taking her hands in his. "It's probably become obvious to you this morning, but I do want to tell you, to make it clear, I want you and the boys to move-in here with me."

"I don't think that's a very good idea, Nichola." She said immediately.

"Why not?" He sat back, giving her a straight look.

Leila could feel him getting angry. "It's complicated. I have a dog and a cat. I have a job. I have a reputation to think of. I have a life, a human life. I have a house. I worked hard for my house. I like my house." She explained, but could tell that he wasn't buying any of it.

"You have a husband." He added angrily.

She felt him put a wall between them, cutting her off from his thoughts.

"I do have a husband." She admitted. "You don't have to say or think it. I know I'm not a particularly good wife. Ever since you have come into my life, I positively suck as a wife. It's not your fault, it's entirely mine. I want to be with you; I can't help it and I'm not fighting it. So, I suck as a wife. I feel guilt over breaking my vows. I have never been unfaithful to my husband before. What's worse, despite everything, despite feeling this guilt, I'm not sorry for being with you." She reached out, grasping his hand resting on his leg. "That's probably the worst of it. It's what really makes me a bad person. I'm not sorry for wanting you. But no matter how much I want you, it's too soon for me to be moving in with you. I am going through a lot of change in my life. There is only going to be more, and I'm not ready to make that kind of move right now. I am not willing to put that change on my children. I can't make such a serious decision and not take them into consideration. Right now, I wouldn't know whether it is the right decision for both me and them." Leila told him, wishing that she could explain it better. "Please don't be angry. Please understand."

He pulled away his hand, gazing at her with unreadable eyes. With the shield that he had erected between them, she felt nothing. Her heart ached, but she could not give him the answer he desired.

"Leila, you understand you can't run away from what you are, don't you? There's no going back. You can't escape what we are to each other." His voice was gentle.

"I'm just trying to take things one day at a time, Nichola. My whole life has shifted and upended in just one week! I'm feeling things and doing things that I never in a million years thought I would. I've been riding the wave of all these changes. Being with you has helped. I'm not denying it, but it's so much to handle, and I'm working so hard on just controlling everything that I'm feeling. I just can't take anymore change right now. I just can't!" She stopped as she heard the frightened note of panic in her own voice.

He sighed deeply, leaning forward, gripping her by the back of the neck and placing his forehead against hers. She immediately felt calmer, though she still couldn't feel his emotions through the wall that he had erected.

The Life of a Modern Vampire

NICHOLA DISTANCED HIMSELF FROM her for the rest of the day. Even with the wall that he had erected between them, she could tell that he was upset. His stand-offish behavior hurt her feelings and then irritated her. Believing that he was sulking, she in turn ignored him just as much as he ignored her.

That evening, Leila, Mansuetus and the boys went back to her house.

Iris, who was perceptive enough to realize that something was going on between Leila and Nichola, stayed behind with Nichola now that her room was finished.

Mansuetus was unusually quiet but still played with the boys and helped her as he had been for the last several days. After putting the boys to bed, they watched television in companionable silence until he went to bed in the spare bedroom around ten o'clock. Leila, who had become used to the late nights, was surprisingly tired and went to bed not long after Mansuetus. She fell immediately asleep.

About half-past eleven, she was startled awake to see Nichola standing next to the bed looking down on her. She sat up quickly gasping. "You scared me!" She scolded. "How did you get in here?"

"After almost a thousand years, I believe that I have learned some burglary skills." He replied bluntly, his eyes never leaving hers as he proceeded to unbutton his shirt, pulling it from his pants.

"I know you are angry with me, Nichola. Just go home. I am too tired to get into this with you tonight." Avoiding looking at his body, she lay back down, presenting her back burrowing under the covers.

As she started to relax, the blankets were ripped from her body, and he landed on top of her. He held her pinned under his naked body with clawed hands. She gazed up at him in shock, and he stared down at her angrily with piercing red eyes and extended teeth.

"Why do you persist in treating me like a human man, i allagí mou? Have I spoiled you? Should I show you the fire that you play with?" His voice was a deep, frightening growl.

"I am not afraid of you, Nichola!" She replied, though she didn't fight him. She turned her head, closed her eyes, to expose the side of her neck to him. "Just take what you want and go." She whispered, hoping to shock him into leaving.

Instead, after a slight pause, she felt his teeth deeply pierce the curve of her shoulder and his clawed hands lift her nightgown to tear her panties from her body.

Truly frightened, she fought him in earnest, starting to yell, but found his hand covering her mouth.

"Stop, Leila." Came his rough growl in her ear as tears filled her eyes. "You told me to take what I want. Do not invite things you do not mean."

"My shoulder hurts!" She cried softly as he removed his hand from her mouth.

"Hold on." He said simply and she felt his tongue lap at her shoulder as the pain disappeared.

"How bad is it?" She whispered tearfully.

"It was hardly a bite! I barely pierced your skin!" He scoffed angrily at her reaction. "Besides, was there a mark on you this morning?" He asked her irritably. "Has there ever been a mark on you?"

She thought hard for a moment, working to calm herself. "No." She said softly looking at him quizzically.

"Our saliva heals our bite wounds. It can heal even deep bites. This is especially helpful in certain cases, like Dr. Lambert's. Remember, Iris bit him and made him forget he was bitten? She could hardly have been able to do that if there had been a wound for him to ponder over." Nichola explained, paused for a few seconds, then whispered to her. "I am sorry for biting you in such a way, i psychí mou. I did it because I *am* angry. I am angry and disappointed and...hurt." He admitted. "Your rejection hurts and has made me beastly." His voice was gruff as he pressed her body into the mattress with his, holding her close and burying his face in the crook of her neck.

She breathed deeply, irritation replacing her fear. "If you do not want me to treat you like a human man, you need to stop behaving like one!" She grabbed him by the hair and pulled his head up so he would look her in the face. He squinted his eyes at her in irritation. "I am not rejecting you! I just need time to adjust to everything. I need *my* space to do that. This house, my life; it's my space. It doesn't mean that I don't want you. It doesn't mean that I am rejecting you. I am just not ready to take on anymore change right now."

He buried his face against the crook of her neck again, holding her tightly. "I want you with me. I can't protect you if you aren't with me." He said into her shoulder.

"As I keep telling you and Mansuetus, there is nothing to protect me from. I live a very peaceful existence. The only thing that I need help with is getting the kids back and forth to daycare and driving me around during daylight hours occasionally. I am safe here in my home."

"So, you don't need me?" He whispered stiffly.

She tried to read him but ended up blocked by the wall that he still had erected. "Nichola, of course I need you." Leila wrapped her arms around his shoulders. "I don't know what else is going to happen or when. I am afraid. Afraid for myself, for my children. You make me less afraid. You give me strength. Of course, I need you." She whispered.

He disentangled himself from her arms and sat up on the edge of the bed, reaching for his clothes. She tried to read him again, only to fail.

"Where are you going?" She asked softly.

"Get some sleep, Leila." He replied quietly.

"What do you want from me, Nichola?" She asked with a catch in her voice.

"I want you to need me. Not because I make you strong or make you feel better, but because you want me, because you want to be with me." His voice was bitter as he sat with his back to her to jerk on his shirt.

She was silent for a moment, shocked. "Nichola, you can read me. You keep telling me we are soul mates. I am not the one that has put up a wall between us! Can't you tell that without you I am a disaster? Please stay, don't leave yet." She reached out and touched him on the back.

He initially stiffened under her touch, and then she felt his muscles relax. He pulled his shirt back off and laid down beside her. She rolled over, pillowing her head on his shoulder. He stiffly wrapped an arm around her, though didn't touch her in any other way. She wrapped her arm around his chest, snuggling against him. Eventually, she could feel him relax, and the last thing she remembered was him placing a small kiss on top of her head just before she fell asleep.

She woke up about six-thirty and he was gone. She sighed in disappointment.

She attempted to scan the house. It was extremely difficult, and she wasn't sure if she was doing it right, but the only people she sensed were Mansuetus and the boys in the kitchen. She got up, threw on some clothes and headed in to see them.

Both boys yelled when she walked into the kitchen. She quickly gave them a kiss and proceeded to get herself a cup of coffee and sit down at the table. Mansuetus sat a plate of blood-building food in front of her.

"Good morning, Mansuetus. Thank you." She said quietly.

"Good morning, Kyría." His voice was soft.

She realized he knew Nichola had been there last night. "So, how many of my neighbors do you think saw the Mustang parked in the driveway last night?" She asked him with a sigh, thinking that her reputation would soon be in tatters, and it would be the *only* night that she hadn't gotten laid that would do it.

"He didn't drive here last night." Mansuetus said softly. "He would not harm your reputation. He realizes it is important to you."

"How the heck did he get here, then?" Leila asked in astonishment.

"It's not far." Mansuetus said vaguely, then changed the subject. "Will you be coming with me to take the boys to daycare?"

"Yes, I had thought too. I was wondering if you could take me to the bank after we drop the boys off, unless you need to be somewhere this morning?" She asked hopefully.

"I am at your service, Kyría." He told her sincerely.

Over the next few days, she, the boys, Mansuetus, and the vampires got into a routine. Mansuetus was her constant companion throughout the day. He and she took the boys to daycare every day, then they would run errands like grocery shopping or other mundane things such as laundry and cleaning the house. She took his advice and wore a wide-brimmed sunhat, long sleeves, and dark sunglasses. She felt she looked silly, but at least she was able to function.

Mansuetus even mowed the lawn and trimmed the bushes, which needed it, since Michael hated doing yard-work and the grass had been long when he had left. She explained to Mansuetus that she would hire someone to come do the lawn after she had found him in the garage tinkering with the lawn tractor; to not worry about it. He had looked at her like she was crazy and told her unceremoniously to go back into the house. She then watched him from the windows as he sped around the yard on the tractor.

Leila knew her house had never looked better, and Mansuetus seemed to be wholly enjoying himself.

Nichola and Iris came over every night. While she enjoyed visiting and reminiscing with Iris, Nichola usually got on her nerves. He spent the nights in near silence, staring at her contemplatively, especially when he thought she wasn't paying attention. When she stared back at him, he would relax back and stretch his legs out, daring her to look at his body with a come fuck me look that would make her heart race. Her reaction to his body always irritated her and she would then pretend to ignore him, which would, in turn, irritate him.

The wall that he had erected between them remained firmly in place, and he hadn't shown up in her bedroom since Sunday night.

On Wednesday night, she and Iris went for a walk, leaving the boys with Mansuetus and Nichola. Iris told her that Dene wanted them all to come out and see a band on Friday night. Leila told her she wasn't sure that she was in the mood to go out, and she didn't think that it would be fair to Mansuetus to leave him with the boys.

"Then get a babysitter!" Iris exclaimed. "You need to get out of the house and enjoy yourself. Besides, I don't know what is going on between you and Nikolaos, but you two need to kiss and make up! He has been miserable to be around the past couple of days. He's even more cold than he normally is, which I didn't think was even possible!"

"It's not my fault, Auntie! He is angry and has walled himself off from me because I will not move into the London Hill house. He refuses to even try to understand why!" Leila said angrily.

"Leila, the fact that he hasn't forced you to move-in is actually saying something for him!" Iris said, exasperated.

"He can't force me to do anything!" Leila replied hotly.

"Leila, he is a vampire elder. He could compel you! He hasn't tried to compel you to do anything, as far as I am aware." Iris tried explaining.

"He better not try, either!" Leila exclaimed, anger flashing in her eyes.

"Leila, listen to me. Your emotions are everywhere. That is a large part of transitioning. He has given you total free will. He doesn't have to, and I am not sure that he even should." Here, Leila looked at Iris in shock. Iris continued. "During transition, changelings can often be a danger to themselves just because they are so emotional. He isn't trying to control you at all. Despite that fact, for the last couple of nights, you seem like you resent his very presence!"

"That's not true, Auntie!"

"Leila, as soon as we walk in the door, I read resentment from you towards Nikolaos. It's no wonder he has walled himself off from you. Your connection seems to spark powerful emotions in him. If you threw that much resentment and anger at me every night, you and I would be fighting. Closing off your connection is probably the only way he's able to keep his cool around you. So, give him a little credit for giving you and Mansuetus, who by the way seems to be having the time of his life playing house with you and the boys, enough trust to keep from compelling you and packing your ass up and taking you to the house." Iris said, exasperated. "Not only are you acting stressed out, but you also *look* extremely stressed out. You need a break, and you need to relax. Believe me, I have been there."

Leila walked along with her in silence, considering Iris' words.

When they got back to the house, she approached Nichola, who was watching *Sliders* on television with Mansuetus, and sat down next to him on the couch. He looked at her with unreadable eyes, and she reached over and took his hand. He felt warm and strong. She hadn't touched him since Sunday night and sparks of desire flew from his hand throughout her body, making her catch her breath and bringing a tightness to her chest. She could feel herself flush. "Would you like to go out on Friday night?" She asked him, slightly breathless as she fought her reaction to the desire flowing through her body.

He held her hand gently looking at her with soft knowing amber eyes and replied, "Yes."

"Aren't you even going to ask for details?" Leila asked him curiously, surprised at the short response. Even with the wall, she could feel his happiness.

"No." He smiled at her warmly.

Mansuetus, who was sitting on the loveseat watching them, spoke up happily, "I will watch the children."

Leila looked at him. "Oh, no, sir. You are going with us." Then she got up and headed for the phone.

Shortly before midnight, she walked into her bedroom to go to sleep and turned on the light. She gasped as she saw Nichola sitting in the rocking chair. Clutching her chest, she said, "Jesus! I thought you had left."

"I did. Now, I am back." He said simply. "You are always so startled when I return, and you wonder why I am concerned with your safety. Do you not even attempt to scan the house for threats before you retire?"

"I have only tried doing that once. I find it difficult to do." She said lamely, feeling chastened without knowing quite why. She immediately felt resentful toward his criticism. "Why are you here?" She asked, more bluntly than she had intended. She immediately felt regret for her snappish tone, but remained silent.

"I hunger for you." His voice was low and gruff, and there was a light red sheen to his eyes.

"I thought that you were angry with me." She said cautiously.

"It doesn't change the fact that I hunger for you." He gracefully stood and slowly stalked towards her.

"It's exhausting to be at odds with you." She said with a weakness that she hadn't realized that she felt towards him, watching as he approached her.

"You could always just give in." Nichola's eyes gleamed as he reached to gently pull her into his arms.

"I can't do that..." she started to say as he took her mouth with his, thrusting his tongue deep, holding her head still with both hands to prevent her from pulling away from him, sending shivers of desire throughout her body.

"What can't you do, i psyché mou?" He whispered softly against her lips and his scent enveloped her, caressing her senses. His hands were then under her shirt, expertly unfastening her bra while one hand cupped her breast, and his thumb teased her nipple into a rigid peak, causing her to catch her breath.

He quickly lifted her into his arms, and she once again marveled at his great strength. He placed her on the bed, pulling her shirt over her head and divesting her of her bra. He put his hand on her chest, over her heart, and pushed her back slowly with his palm to lay on the bed. She looked at him helplessly as uncontrolled desire flowed like lava through her veins. His eyes were a deep blood red. He lay down beside her, still fully clothed, and his hand caressed down her body to work at the buttons of her jeans as he took one of her nipples gently into his mouth. Her body involuntarily arched as if electricity flowed through her as she felt the points of his sharp teeth graze her skin.

"I thought you said that you don't have to drink blood!" She gasped out.

She felt his chuckle throughout her body, causing goosebumps on her flesh.

"I don't." He murmured as he licked her hard nipple.

"But you said that you are hungry." She whispered as she felt a fire building inside of her lower belly as he pulled her jeans and panties from her hips and knelt beside her to pull them from her legs.

"I am not hungry. You have been feeding me your anger for days now and I feel positively fat with it. If you were just another human, feasting on your anger wouldn't affect my personal emotions. Your anger, while nourishing to my vampire-side, in turn makes me bad-tempered. I much prefer to feast on your desire. It is sweet and delicious, and I hunger for you and the feeling that it gives me. I want to drink in your desire." He kneeled over her, whispering once again against her breast, kissing her softly as his fingers parted the curls in between her legs to softly stroke her wetness.

She quickly reached for the buttons on his shirt, feeling an overwhelming passion to touch his skin. She burned with the need to touch his bare skin. She parted her legs for him as a painful ache blossomed inside of her.

"Please, Nichola. Please." She whispered to him desperately, not really knowing exactly what she was asking of him, only knowing that this painful ache was overwhelming her body and her senses.

Fortunately, he knew exactly what she wanted. He quickly undid the buttons on his pants, opening them to free his erection. He was long and hard and more than ready for her as he felt her desire and scent surround him as she wrapped her legs around him. More dressed than undressed, he slid into her hot, wet, tight body and paused to enjoy the silken feel of her with a low groan. He felt her hands run up his back underneath his open shirt, urging him on as she raised her hips hard to meet him and his cock rubbed against the entrance to her womb.

He was trying to stay still and was holding her tightly fighting for both his physical and mental control, when the wall that he had erected between them suddenly collapsed and she was awash in his feelings. Desire, anger, fear, need, love swept over her with the force of a hurricane as he began to move within her. She had managed to rip the buttons from his shirt, exposing the muscles of his chest and abdomen. She wrapped her arms around his shoulders tightly pulling herself against his skin. She just knew that she needed to feel his skin against hers to stop the ache within her.

His movements were too slow for her, and she slid her hands down his body to clutch at his ass as she ground herself against him, crying out slightly in frustrated need. He stopped moving again to hold her tightly to him. She wrapped her legs tightly around him, rocking urgently against his rigid body.

"Stop, i psyhí mou, or you are going to unman me, and I am going to cum!" He groaned into the curve of her neck, sounding desperate for control.

"I need you to fuck me, Nichola!" She demanded urgently, as the ache inside her throbbed painfully.

"I am going to. Just give me a moment, you are so hot and tight..." He groaned softly as he moved one of his hands in between them to stroke her clitoris, causing her to cry out in need. Her sweet soft cries continued as he stroked her, kissing and sucking at the curve of her neck, careful not to mark her with his fangs. She could feel herself grow ever tighter around him. Finally, after what seemed like forever to her, he began to move slowly again within her.

She gripped his ass tight again and thrust up to meet him hard, squeezing her eyes shut tightly, groaning "please, please" throwing her head back, and arching her back as she tried to vanquish the throbbing and painful ache inside of her body.

"Fine." She heard him groan out in a strangled voice as he lifted his upper body with his arms and began to thrust himself in and out of her with long, hard strokes, almost withdrawing from her body only to return deeply. She met each of his thrusts with small sounds of joy as she opened her eyes to watch him.

His eyes were closed in concentration, his long full lashes dark against his skin, as he moved in and out of her and she realized she loved the look of him. Right now, at this moment, she loved the way he looked. As liquid desire ripped through her veins, she felt intense throbbing spasms begin where they were connected and spread throughout her body, banishing the ache as she cried out loudly in pleasure. He thrust harder and faster, riding the waves of her orgasm, and a look of ecstasy came over his face as he found his own release deep inside of her.

Leila woke late the next day to a note on her pillow.

"I psychí mou. You were sleeping so soundly tonight that I didn't have the heart to wake you. By the time that you read this, I will be going to Toronto on business. I will return early Friday evening and will meet you and Iris for our evening out. I worry about you, my sweet. Please rest and make sure that you eat while I am gone. I will try to connect with you on Thursday night to check

in. Mansuetus is at your service and will take care of you until my return. I will be thinking of you. Yours, N."

Yours. Yes, as the wall had crumbled between them last night, she knew he was hers. What would she do with her vampire? She wanted to be with him as much as he wanted to be with her. She sighed. Perhaps it was time to face the reality of what was happening to her and the impact it would have on her children. Could she stop it like her father had? Did she really want to? Would it even be possible to stop something that she didn't want to stop? It was hard for her to remember a time without Nichola being such a force in her life, and she couldn't imagine being without him now. She didn't want to imagine ever being without him.

The ring of the telephone startled her out of her thoughts. She rolled to the edge of the bed to answer it.

"Collect call from Michael. Will you accept the charges?" The operator asked.

Shock made her pause a long moment, and then she answered "Yes," woodenly.

"Leila?" She heard his deep voice come down the telephone line.

"Yes." She responded.

"I have been trying to get a hold of you now for almost a week!"

"Really?" She responded doubtfully.

"Well, I got a hold of that doctor last Friday. He didn't give me any information about how you are doing. Then I called Saturday, and no one answered and then I called again Tuesday during the day, and no one answered. Where have you been? How are the kids?"

She ignored his questions. "So, you talked to the doctor? When on Friday?"

"Friday night. He accepted the collect call from the house. Were you really that sick? Why was he there so late?" He asked.

"I am better." She said, not feeling that she needed to answer his questions in detail anymore. After all, he had lost that right.

"How are the kids?" He asked again quietly.

"They are good." She responded.

"Are they there? Can I talk to them?"

"Mansuetus takes them to daycare every day. We are trying to keep them on their schedule."

"I miss them. I miss all of you." Michael replied unexpectedly, softly.

"Well, you've always missed us when you were gone. But you always came home to treat us like shit, regardless." Leila told him bluntly, no longer wanting to paint a rosy hue over the truth.

"Leila, I am sorry. I am an asshole!" He started.

"You won't get an argument from me about that."

"Leila, I screwed up!" He again started.

"Listen, Michael, it's not the first time."

"What is wrong with you?" He asked in bewilderment, unused to her strong attitude with him.

"Nothing is wrong with me. I just won't live under the threat of you leaving us if you don't get your exact way all the time. My life will not crumble without you in it, and neither will the boys. I will make sure of that." She stated firmly.

"What the hell is that supposed to mean?" He was starting to get angry at her attitude.

"It means that they don't need a man in their lives that is angry and critical all the time. They need a good, strong man in their lives to teach them how to be good, strong men. If you won't be that man, so be it. I will make sure that they have a good man in their lives to teach them everything that they need to know. Someone who loves them."

"I am sorry, Leila. I do love them. I love you. I know I am a jerk. I will do better. I can be that man." He said lamely, like he was lost.

"I am tired, and I don't want to fight, Michael." Her voice softened, as a little of the ice around her heart melted at the imploring tone of his voice.

"I know. I don't want to fight anymore, either. Are you still feeling sick?" He questioned.

"I have my good days and my bad days." She responded as her door slowly opened, and she saw Mansuetus with a tray full of food. She smiled kindly at him as he approached the bed. "I have to go. I just got up and I haven't eaten yet. Mansuetus just came in with some food. Everyone keeps telling me that I am not eating enough."

"Well, make sure that you do what you are supposed to, so that you get better." His voice was concerned. "I go back out for testing again tomorrow, but I should be back home in a few weeks. I really do miss you and the boys."

"I know. We will talk when you get back." Her voice quiet as she heard the loneliness in his. She felt a twinge of guilt piercing her icy barrier.

"Okay. Get your rest and get better. I love you." He said sincerely.

"I will see you when you get back." She told him, hanging up.

When the boys went to bed in the evening, so did she. Having never intentionally or consciously tried to dream-walk before, she was determined to try. Concentrating ridiculously hard to control her body and her mind, which seemed to be humming with agitation and anger; she worked to calm her breathing and her soul in the darkness of her bedroom. Almost immediately, she felt like she was swimming through a thick soupy fog, though she knew that her body was still in her bed. She focused all of her mind on Nichola.

Before long, the fog thinned, and as it did, she found herself in the original living room where she had first met him. Alone, she didn't see or hear him, and frustration reared its ugly head inside of her. Confused about what she had done wrong, frustration turned to anger. She had focused so hard on finding him! Now, she was unsure what to do, since he was not here. She was sick and tired of not knowing how to control her abilities! Deciding to search the rest of the home for him, she started to head out a large arched entrance into what looked like a large foyer when Nichola entered the room. Seeing her startled him and he froze in place.

"I psychí mou! How are you here? Are you in distress?" He moved to her in concern.

"Am I only allowed to be here if I am in distress?" She demanded sharply.

"Well, no." He blinked, surprised by her tone. "But you are untrained..."

"That is so true! So far, the only thing that you have trained me to do is to be in your bed, while giving me extraordinarily little knowledge about my abilities as a vampire." She growled furiously at him.

"Well, you are not a vampire yet." He responded angrily in return, glaring down at her.

"Why did you hide that Michael had called the house?" Her angry look met his, but her words effectively took the hotness from his posture.

He coolly turned away from her to put down a stack of papers on a table that sat against the back of the sofa; papers that he had been carrying when he walked into the room, throwing over his shoulder, "I didn't hide it." He said quietly, not looking at her.

"Oh, please!" She exclaimed in disbelief. "We are not supposed to be able to lie to each other. Right?"

"I was very specific that it was someone who didn't want to take no for an answer." He replied again, cool and quiet, not meeting her eyes. "Besides, he was very intoxicated. I figured you had more than enough to deal with, without dealing with an intoxicated man!"

"That is the lamest excuse that I have ever heard!" Stepping aggressively toward him to get him to face her. "It was a collect phone call. You accepted the charges! I am surprised that you identified yourself as a 'doctor'." Here she actually used air quotes, causing him to raise his eyebrows in astonishment at her. "I am *incredibly* surprised that you didn't bother to tell him the 'truth'," air quotes again, "that you were just some guy that was fucking his wife." Sarcasm and anger drenched every word.

He peered dangerously at her in return, as he mirrored her actions and aggressively stepped close to her. "One, I am a 'doctor'." It was his turn to use air quotes. "Two, I am not just some 'guy'." More air quotes. "I am your mate, and you will respect me!" He warned her in a low, scary, growl.

She was unimpressed.

"Pffft!" The sound she made caused him again to widen his eyes in surprise. "Respect? That goes both ways, Nichola! You should have told me he had called. It was my choice to speak to him or not. You may be my soul mate, Nichola," here she practically spit out his name as she pointed at him, "but you don't rule me! You don't get to take my choices from me!" Sharp anger rolled off her words.

"Take your choices from you? We all have very few choices in our lives, Leila! I will tell you mine. I 'chose' not to tell you he was on the line. Because. He. Hurts. You!" He said, pitching his angry voice low as his gaze bore into hers. "I also 'chose' not to tell him I was, as you so elegantly put it, 'fucking' you. Though I sorely wanted to. If only to hurt him in a small measure for the pain and neglect that he has caused you since your marriage. The only thing that stopped me was the fact that he would find a way to come back as soon as possible and then I would gleefully kill him. But, according to Iris, that would not be a good idea."

Leila looked at him in shock; fear and concern evaporating her anger as she realized he was telling her the stark truth. He genuinely wanted to kill Michael. "You can't kill him, Nichola! He's the boys' father!"

"That is what Iris said." He looked at her harshly. "But I will not have this fight with you again. I do not like it. I do not like the way *his* name makes me feel. And while I am on the subject, I do not like you describing what we do as 'fucking', Leila." He swiftly pulled her hard against him. It was like his body was made of concrete; heavy and unyielding. She looked up at him in apprehension as his eyes bore into hers. "What we do together is not 'fucking'." He snarled in her face. "I do not like you to use this word while we are fighting. What we do is not dirty or impersonal. It is so much more than that." His face was alien and devoid of all emotion as he looked down at her.

"You don't get to tell me how to speak or what words to use!" She said hotly, anger swiftly returning. "I will do and talk whatever way I please!" She tried to pull out of his arms. It was useless. "Besides, what are you going to do? Beat me?" Exclaiming in sarcasm as she struggled hard against him for freedom.

"Leila," he tightened his hold cruelly. "I am a one-thousand-year-old vampire elder! Born in a time when men frequently beat their disobedient women. I am starting to lose my patience with you, so do not tempt me!" Growling into her ear, he pulled her close, giving her a small shake.

"You wouldn't!" Her voice was a frightened squeak, like a mouse in the claws of a cat.

"I might!" He ground out, nipping her earlobe with his fangs.

She woke up, quickly sitting up in her bed. Relief and fear making her heartbeat fast and hard. She reached up to her earlobe, which actually hurt a little. She felt no wetness that would indicate that she had received the wound that he had inflicted with his teeth, though the memory of pain was there.

Well, that conversation hadn't gone as I had planned! She thought to herself as she laid down; breathing deeply and slowly, attempting to slow the rapid beating of her heart, she wearily tried to find sleep.

Hours later, she was woken by the bed dipping under his weight behind her, and his arm pulling her back against his chest. "Did you think to escape me, i allagí mou?" He breathed quietly in her ear.

"No. It just happened." She murmured sleepily.

"Yes. I thought as much." He delicately sucked the earlobe that he had bitten earlier into his mouth, startling her. "You have such power, i allagí mou. But absolutely no discipline or control over your power or your emotions." He sighed. "That sometimes makes our conversations on both our parts a little dangerous."

"Well, whose fault is that, Nichola?" Her sleepy voice held an edge of hostility.

"The fault lies squarely with me. I have been neglectful of your education because of my own selfish pursuits." This was said quietly, but simply.

She rolled over to suspiciously look at him in the dark, surprised by the amount of night vision that she now had.

"I always admit my mistakes and wrongdoings when they rarely occur, so there is no need to look at me like that. I love to spoil you. I do not feel guilty about it and take great pleasure in giving you your way and making you happy. But you are right, I need to teach you about vampires. What and who we are. I need to help you conquer and control your powers and discipline your emotions so that they are useful to you, and not dangerous. My love for you is making me neglectful as your elder." He acknowledged.

She looked at him, a question almost coming forth, as he softly put a finger on her lips, silencing her.

"Rollover, so that I may hold you for a short while." He said softly in command, pushing her back onto her side. "I will be leaving soon for the airport. We will talk more later on the subject." He spooned his body around hers, holding her close and softly kissing the side of her neck. "Sleep o ómorfos ángelos mou, my beautiful angel." She heard him say as her heavy lids involuntarily closed over her eyes and she slumbered in his embrace.

A Night on the Town

THE LIMOUSINE PULLED UP in front of a small, cute, one-story cottage in the center of St. Marys, just as the sun had set. Jackie Guilliams rushed out of the front door of the small home dressed in a pink and purple paisley print dress and black heels, her curly orange-brown hair cascading down her back. The bodice of her dress was tight, plunging over her large breasts, while the rest of the dress was flowing and very feminine.

Mansuetus sat still, in shock, for a moment in the front seat of the car before turning around to meet Leila's Cheshire grin, then he hurriedly exited the car to open the back door for Jackie.

"Well, it is ever so nice to see you again, Mr. Smythe." Her voice was sweet, and she batted her heavily lashed brown eyes at him, eyeing him up and down, taking in his jeans, casual boots, and white, button-down dress shirt.

"You, also, miss." He gazed at her, entranced.

Getting into the back seat of the car, she quickly hugged Leila to her. "I am so glad you invited me tonight, sugar! You do look tired, though!" Leaning back, she asked, "How are you feeling?"

"Well, I feel okay. I have been told that I need to get out of the house for a while and relax. So, this is therapy." Leila smiled at her friend. "This is my Aunt Iris. Aunt Iris, this is my dear friend Jackie."

Dressed in a beautiful red silk top, with long sheer red sleeves and black miniskirt, hose, and four-inch spiked high heels, Iris wore her black curls long and loose. Her perfect red lips returned Jackie's smile, and she inquired. "So, what do you think of our Mansuetus?"

"Well..." Jackie began, catching his eyes in the rear-view mirror. She flashed him a smile.

Mansuetus put up the window partition between the back and the front compartments, causing all three women to roar with laughter.

"I hope we have fun tonight." Leila said after it quieted down. "I need some fun in my life about now."

"Yes, you do, sweetie." Jackie said, grabbing and holding her hand. "I cannot believe Michael abandoned you like this. What the hell is his problem?"

"He's a jackass." Aunt Iris chimed in.

Leila smiled at both of them. It was comforting to know that other people had your back when bad things happened in your life. "Yes, he is. But, despite that, I am putting him from my mind for tonight and am going to endeavor to have a great time. It's been years since I have been out dancing. I hope the band is as good as Dene says it is, Aunt Iris."

"Who's Dene?" Jackie asked.

"He's my Aunt Iris's boy-toy." Leila smiled at Iris, who returned her smile with one of her own.

"Well, he wants to be my 'boy-toy' anyway." Iris laughed as the limousine pulled into the crowded parking lot of J's Tavern and Sound House.

Mansuetus exited the car and opened the back door. The ladies got out of the car, giving him a look as they all got a case of the giggles. He tolerated this emotionlessly and then fixed all three of them with a firm stare. "Before we all go in, I will have your word that you will all be on your best behavior." They looked at him innocently for a moment, then looked at each other.

"Why, whatever do you mean, Mansuetus?" Iris asked sedately, giving him an innocent, inquiring look.

"I can sense that you all are in an extremely celebratory mood, Iris. So, I would ask that you do not cause problems in this establishment that will cause me to have to intervene. I would prefer not to get into a bar fight attempting to save you from your own devices, and I do not wish to explain to Kýrios the details of what led up to that happening." He was blunt. "I would request moderation tonight. Remember, Kyría needs a relaxing evening, not an exciting evening."

"Relaxing doesn't have to be boring!" Iris exclaimed, drawing out the last word. "You are just worried about how Nikolaos will react if we are having too much fun," Iris said irritably.

"He shouldn't be," came a cold steady voice from the darkness. "Because Nikolaos is here."

Iris rolled her eyes. "Fine. Moderation. But my niece needs to let her hair down. So, don't either one of you be killjoys!" Linking her arms through Leila and Jackie's, she led them in the door, leaving the men to trail behind them.

While Nichola paid their cover charge, Leila, who had never been in the Sound House before, was entranced with the atmosphere. The interior was large and fairly dark, with dim lighting behind the bar and over the two pool tables in the corner, but the main lighting came from the lit dance floor and band area. The place was large, with a huge bar that could seat thirty, had many tables of various sizes, noisy, smoky, and currently packed with people. She was surprised that there were so many people in this one establishment, since the town itself was so small. While she was getting her hand stamped by the bouncer at the door, she and Iris noticed Dene stand-up from a large table right next to the dance floor and wave at them to come over. Nichola took her by the elbow before she followed the others over to the table that Dene had secured for them.

He guided her to the bar, leaning against it, resting one of his booted feet on the brass-rail footrest, waiting for one of the two bartenders' attention. While he patiently waited, he looked her over slowly, taking in her satin teal colored, short-sleeve blouse and miniskirt, admiring the color contrast against her creamy skin, and then focused with interest on her silky hose and brown flats. He pulled her gently against his open body and leaned over to speak into her ear. "Your outfit matches your beautiful eyes, Glykó."

Noticing that he was wearing a lightweight taupe-colored canvas duster, white button-down dress shirt, black jeans, and his soft, casual black leather boots, she gave him an admiring look.

"Aunt Iris picked it out. I've had it for a while but have never had the occasion to wear it before." She responded, smoothing down the soft fabric of her skirt. "But I think us girls are a little overdressed for this place." She disclosed with a small self-conscious smile, looking around to see that most of the other patrons were wearing jeans.

"You look beautiful. That's what matters," he complimented.

She looked down the bar to see what was taking a bartender so long, when one of them walked towards them, her eyes focused on Nichola. Leila thought to herself, *If 'dressed like a hooker' could be looked up in a dictionary, this chick's picture would be right next to it.*

285

"Well, Hi Honey!" The platinum blonde bartender said to Nichola with a sultry smile, leaning over the bar and giving him an ample look at her breasts which were almost escaping from her V-neck cropped t-shirt, while completely ignoring Leila's presence where he held her lightly. "You've come back!"

Leila experienced his mental groan, and she looked at him with narrowed eyes.

He smoothly answered the bartender, "Yes. Hello again. I would like to open a tab for that front table over there." He pointed to the table where Dene, Iris, Jackie, and Mansuetus were sitting and chatting. Jackie was obviously regaling them with some sort of story, as Leila noticed she was gesturing wildly with her hands and laughing uproariously. Mansuetus couldn't seem to take his eyes from her.

Leila gave a little smile.

Bobby Rebekah said with a little moue of distaste to her mouth, "Sure, honey. I will send a waitress right over."

"Thank you very much." Nichola's voice was smooth.

Leila looked at her, "Yes, thank you. Could I get a whiskey sour in a tall glass, please?"

"Coming right up. Anything for you, honey?" She addressed Nichola with a purr.

"Vodka and water on the rocks, please." He replied, smiling at her, only to feel Leila intentionally step on his foot. He glanced down at her as Bobby Rebekah turned away to make their drinks, and she subtly, but not gently, poked him in the ribs. He rubbed the spot and smiled down at her.

What have you been doing in this bar? She thought at him, scowling.

I psychi mou, I have only been here one time. That is the woman that I believe our young doctor has been avoiding ever since he met our Iris. He thought back to her in all innocence.

Well, that is just great! Leila thought in return, staring into his eyes. *Now I know why we were being warned outside by Mansuetus. This will not go over well with Aunt Iris. Things could very quickly get out of hand.*

Yes, hopefully the bartender's attention will be distracted by all of these people, and we will have no issues. Though I believe the brunt of her displeasure will be directed at the Doctor, it would be a mistake for her to confront Iris in any way. He nodded to her, then leaned over and spoke in her ear, as they seemed to draw attention by staring into each other's eyes. "So, who is this friend that you have brought?"

"That's my friend, Jackie. We work together. She is in the financial services division, and I am in the information technology division, but we are in the same department under the same boss." She smiled.

"You have hopes of a 'match' between her and Mansuetus?" He looked in the table's direction.

"He likes her." Leila said with confidence, giggling as she stood on her tiptoes to speak into his ear.

"And you know this how?" Nichola asked.

"I introduced them last week." She said, as if that explained everything.

"Well, he certainly seems transfixed by her." He said, again looking in their direction. Leila followed his gaze, and he was right. Jackie had Mansuetus' full attention as she animatedly spoke to Iris and Dene. She also had the full attention of several of the other male patrons near their table, but they were giving Mansuetus' large frame looks of apprehension.

Leila glanced around the bar and noticed that the male-to-female ratio in the place was about six or seven to four. Which she guessed was not too out of place in a military town.

She heard Nichola's voice in her head as Bobby Rebekah placed their drinks in front of them. *Yes. There are not enough women here.*

Leila looked around and noticed that she was getting her fair share of admiring male attention as well. As he handed the bartender his card to start their tab, she felt him run his hand over her ass lightly in full view of everyone there, while she heard his voice in her mind, *Don't forget who you are going home with.*

She glanced up at him, shocked that he would do such a thing in public. He released his hold on her to retrieve his card, put it in his billfold, and take their drinks in hand, indicating that she lead the way to the table. Whatever emotion he was exuding as they walked toward the table caused them to get a wide berth and she easily made her way through the crowd to the table, with him following closely. They got to the table just as the waitress arrived to take everyone else's drink order.

Nichola caught Mansuetus' eye and made a surreptitious glance around the area. Mansuetus turned, looked around, noted the attention the women were receiving and nodded his head once.

Leila sat down next to Iris to watch Mansuetus lean back in his chair and place his arm along the back of Jackie's chair. Jackie was so absorbed in her conversation with Iris and Dene that she took no notice of his subtle movement. Dene already had his arm around Iris.

Looking at Nichola, she thought to him, *Are you able to communicate with Mansuetus in the same manner that you and I communicate?*

Not to that detail; but, after almost a thousand years together, he and I do not need to communicate like this at all. We know and read each other very well. He thought to her bluntly.

Well, what are you two doing? She demanded, silently staring hard at him.

We are giving subtle hints to these neighboring gentlemen that we will brook no interference with our women tonight. She could hear the threat in his thought.

Well, stop it! She ordered him.

Why? Are you interested in them? He thought in return forcefully, looking at her sharply.

Don't be ridiculous! She thought back, exasperated. *Neither one of you is being very subtle!*

His eyes suddenly crinkled in a small smile as he sat at the end of the table next to her and slid his foot across the floor and behind her leg so that her calf was resting against his jean clad shin. "Perhaps we are not." He said out loud to her as he leaned over to place her drink in front of her.

Shaking her head, she rolled her eyes at him, thinking he found the strangest things humorous. She took a small sip of her drink, grimacing slightly at the strength of the drink, as she waited for Jackie to quit speaking. When the others had ordered their drinks and she had obtained Jackie's attention, she introduced her to Nichola.

Jackie intentionally leaned across Mansuetus, brushing her breasts against him, and offered her hand to Nichola. Mansuetus seemed to take this contact in stride.

"So, you are Leila's doctor?" Jackie asked loudly.

"One of them," he replied, gesturing to Dene on the other side of Iris and directly across from Jackie with his drink. Dene raised his glass in return.

"Both of you?" Jackie asked, looking between the two, and as they nodded at her, as she addressed Leila. "Honey, how sick are you and where can I get some?!" She laughed loudly, causing them all to chuckle with her.

As the band got on the slightly raised stage to play, Nichola leaned over and said into Leila's ear, "Mansuetus tells me you have secured a babysitter for the children for the entire night. He wasn't pleased about it." He chuckled.

"I figure if I have to take a break, so does he. Besides, I so rarely go out. I didn't want us to have a curfew tonight." She explained, smiling. "The children are safe. My sitter is my next-door neighbor's daughter. If anything happens, her parents are close by. She's a really good kid. She is eighteen and has been watching them since they were born. They love her." She leaned close to say softly in his ear, "I don't think that he is thinking about them right at this moment."

They both looked at Mansuetus, who was leaning toward Jackie, still with his arm behind her chair as she was speaking to him. He had little need to respond to her as she chatted away to him. He was watching her intently.

"You play Cupid, Glykó." Nichola's gentle voice in her ear sent shivers down her spine.

"Not really. They are both adults, and they are both lonely. I care for them both and if introducing them makes them happy, so be it. It is ultimately up to them."

"Your friend is lonely? She doesn't seem the type to be," Nichola observed.

"Well, she tends to be wholly attracted to totally inappropriate and often married men. There is one now who works in our office who plays with her emotions frequently. Believe me, I know the type, and he is never leaving his wife for Jackie. Much as she would like to believe that he will. If Mansuetus distracts her from that self-destructive pursuit, as far as I am concerned, that is a bonus." She replied quietly in return.

"You have a tendency to try to take care of everyone, don't you?" He asked, looking at her strangely.

"Not everyone. Only those people that I care about. Besides, you can only help people who want help. Jackie would love to break free of Chase's mental prison. She tries to very often, but unfortunately he keeps reeling her back in." Speaking into his ear, over the bar noise. "That's what I mean by lonely. She wants someone to love her so badly that she often finds herself alone; waiting for a man who will ultimately never follow through on his word. Even though deep in her heart she knows he is lying to her, still she wastes her life waiting." Noticing movement to her right, she saw Dene and Iris getting up to dance.

She realized the house band was playing *Live Forever* by Oasis. She looked back to Nichola, who was looking at her contemplatively. "Would you like to dance, i psychí mou?"

"You really dance?" She asked, surprised. "But this isn't a slow song."

He smiled broadly at her and took her by the hand to lead her to the dance floor.

She was laughing and gasping for breath when she finally pulled him back to the table after a solid half hour of non-stop dancing. He pulled back on her gently to try to get her to return to the dance floor. "No, please," chuckling. "I need to drink something. You are wearing me out!"

Sitting down, she stirred her drink to mix in the water from the melting ice to take a large sip. *At least it doesn't taste as strong now*, she thought at him as he sat down next to her, placing his hand on her stocking clad leg possessively.

Her smile, laughter, and impish looks, as well as the sway of her slight body, had drawn a large amount of attention from the large number of unattached males in attendance. While Iris and Jackie were both tall, beautiful, flamboyant and their bodies stimulated a man's sexual fantasies, they seemed unattainable to an average male. His i psychí mou's pretty impishness exuded joy, laughter, openness, and innocence, which he loved about her, but in his opinion, these were not good traits to keep pushy men at bay in a nightclub, and their attention made him protective of her.

Iris and Jackie came in from the dance floor, grabbing her arm, pulling her out of the chair. "Where are you going?" He asked, realizing they were moving away through the crowd.

"We are going to the ladies' room." Iris laughed back at him as she moved Leila along.

He looked at Mansuetus, who started to follow after them.

"No. You guys stay here. We will be fine." Leila declared. *No eavesdropping from you!* She thought, pointing at Nichola as she laughed with the other women as Jackie pulled her by the arm.

Dene reassured the other two men, who were looking with concern at the departing women, as he sat down to sip his drink, "It's Saint Marys. They will be okay."

You will call to me Leila if I am needed. Nichola thought at her in command.

I promise. She thought back.

With so few women in the club, they didn't have a long line to wait in. As Jackie headed into a stall, Leila and Iris checked their lipstick in the mirror, and Iris fluffed around with her hair. Leila leaned back against the wall in relief to be away from the loudness of the main club for a little while. Jackie's voice came from the stall. "Oh my God, Leila! Where did you get these guys? They are sexy as hell and all three of them can dance their asses off!" She laughed boisterously.

"It's a long story," Leila chuckled.

"That Nick wants you so bad, too!" Jackie tittered as she came out to wash her hands.

"You think?" Iris smiled in Leila's direction as she headed into the stall.

"He's burning the place down with it!" Jackie effused as Leila flushed in embarrassment.

"Well, I think that you have made yourself a conquest with Mansuetus." Leila replied as she watched Jackie adjust her bosom in her dress.

"Manny is so sweet." Jackie replied, her smile large, as she looked at Leila in the mirror's reflection.

"I'm not sure that I would classify Mansuetus as 'sweet'," Iris stated, returning. "But to each their own."

"Iris, Dene is very hot for you too," Jackie giggled. "You've got to put him out of his misery, girl!"

"I believe I shall." Iris smiled wickedly as she washed and dried her hands. They looked at Leila pointedly, then at the open stall.

Leila held up her hands. "I am just along for the ride." Laughing, she headed out the door to run right smack into Bobby Rebekah's chest, thinking to herself, *What is up with all of these tall women?* Realizing who it was she thought loudly, *Nichola!*

"Excuse us." She smiled brightly and Bobby Rebekah stepped back into the hallway and out of the way to focus a hot glare on Iris. Iris returned her look coolly, with calculation.

Nichola rounded the corner to the hallway leading to the ladies' room, just as all four women were together in the hallway. He took one look at the situation and stridently said, "Ladies!" Theatrically throwing out his arms.

Having gained everyone's attention, he proceeded to say boisterously, "I am here to escort you back to the table." Smiling broadly at them, as Iris and Bobby Rebekah threw visual daggers at each other over Leila's head. He realized Leila had maneuvered herself to stay between the two. "Make me the envy of every man here and join me on the dance floor!" He continued jovially in a slightly tipsy voice. Only Leila and Iris realized it was a lie, as Jackie took him by the arm and grabbed Iris' hand to pull her along. Leila followed in their wake, feeling Bobby Rebekah's glare on their backs.

Feeling like she had escaped a dodgy situation, she sat next to Dene, who had faced their chairs toward the dance floor as Nichola led both Iris and Jackie out onto it. Nichola motioned to her to join them, and she shook her head slightly giving him a gentle relieved smile.

"Nick just took off like a bat out of hell all of the sudden! Now here he is with both of them! I hope he knows what he is doing!" Dene laughed to her as he watched Nichola dancing with both women. They had him sandwiched in between them. Leila smiled and rolled her eyes at them as she took another long swallow of her drink. A waitress came to the table, and Leila motioned for her to bring them another round.

"Please make my whiskey sour in a tall glass. Thank you." She smiled at the girl, who returned her smile as she watched Nichola twirl both women in a circle. As the waitress walked away, Leila leaned over to Dene, fixing him with an intense direct stare. "You need to do something about your bartender bimbo before you proceed any further with my aunt."

"What?" He asked, startled by her look and low tone, which to him bordered on dangerous.

"You heard me. If Nichola hadn't arrived when he did, we would have been in the middle of a fight in the hallway outside of the ladies' room, and Dene, your bartender, would have lost. I don't want my aunt to be put in that position, and I would be extremely disappointed to think that you would want that for her." Suddenly, she knew, she just *knew*, that Dene knew Iris was a vampire. "We don't need that type of attention. I believe you understand what I am talking about." She stated softly.

"She's not my girlfriend, or even my ex-girlfriend." He started in an apologetic voice.

"Well, whatever she is, she is a threat to my aunt." Leila smiled at the antics occurring on the dance floor.

If she had been a jealous person, she would have been perturbed to watch Iris and Jackie running their hands all over Nichola's body as they danced with him in between them. Their antics had gathered a huge audience, and they now had most of the dance floor to themselves as the crowd laughed and clapped.

Hearing a small *help* in her mind, she quickly sent a giggling thought back to Nichola, *That's what you get for taking the hoydens out onto the dance floor!*

Then she shut him down for a brief moment, to finish her conversation with Dene; thankful that the dance floor antics actually provided her with a bit of privacy, noticing that Mansuetus was at the edge of the dance floor cheering them on and clapping loudly.

"I would make another strong suggestion, Dene." She told him sternly. He returned her look apprehensively. "Tell Iris what you know. Or at least think that you know. If you care about her, and I think you do, be honest with her."

"I do and I will. Tonight." He told her sincerely.

"Good." Leila nodded her approval.

As the song ended, Leila watched in satisfaction as Mansuetus pulled Jackie into his arms for a slow dance.

Nichola was before her, taking her by the hand, pulling her into his arms, with what she felt was relief on his part, as the band started playing *Now and Forever* by Richard Marx. He pulled her close, holding her hand over his heart, and wrapping his other around her waist. She wrapped her other arm around his shoulder and as she was enveloped by his scent, she rested her head against his chest, and he started singing softly in her ear in his perfect voice as he turned her around the dance floor.

As he sang, a sense of safety and love overcame her, wiping away the worry that she had been dealing with for the last few weeks. The pain, sorrow, and betrayal that she had been feeling due to Michael's abandonment disappeared, too. With as many angry outbursts as she had been having, she hadn't realized that she had been bottling up any emotions, but now it was obvious to her that she was.

With every turn around the dance floor held firmly in his arms, it was as if his beautiful voice was weaving a magical spell of peace, security, and love around her. Helping her to heal, helping her to be strong.

She knew she could trust him to keep her and the boys safe. He would die before he'd allow anything to happen to them.

She finally realized what he and Mansuetus meant when they said, 'My life for theirs' and she was overwhelmed by it. To willingly give your life for someone, even someone you love, is no small thing.

She gazed up at him in wonder as the music stopped and the band left to go on a break, and he smiled down at her, still holding her. They were the only two people still on the dance floor. To her, they were the only two people in the world. "Should we make our own music, agápi mou?" He smiled tenderly.

Giving him a little shake of her head, she smiled in return, taking his hand to lead him back to the table.

She noticed Mansuetus had disappeared somewhere, and that Jackie, Iris and Dene had decided to do tequila shots. *Oh, no.* She thought, looking at Nichola in concern.

Well, it won't affect Iris much, if at all. Nichola thought back, looking at them, smiling indulgently.

Well, it will Jackie and Dene. Leila thought worriedly.

Mansuetus and Iris will take care of them. He thought, and she could almost see his mental shrug.

And us! We will have to take care of them, too. Leila thought in return.

He gave her an enigmatic look, and the lead singer announced, "Before we start our next set, we have had a special request." They started to play a song slowly that was almost middle eastern in sound. Nichola looked up, suddenly glancing in the direction of the band.

She followed his gaze to see Mansuetus on the dance floor. He held his arms out to him, almost in challenge. He started snapping his fingers in time to the music. Nichola exclaimed, "Ha, old man!" and walked out onto the dance floor to join him.

The two men stood side-by-side and then gripped each other's shoulders and started to dance in time to the music.

"Oh, my! I haven't seen that in years." Iris beamed, watching them.

"What? What are they doing?" Leila asked, bewildered. It seemed her low-key vampire had decided to make a wild night of it.

"They are dancing the Hasapiko. It is an ancient Greek folk dance. Your Great-Great-Grandfather and uncles used to dance it when I was a small child." Another good-looking young man, somewhere in his late twenties, obviously military by his haircut, joined them from the crowd, gripping Mansuetus by the other shoulder and quickly matched his steps to theirs. "You can always tell who the Greek men are when they start playing this music." Iris said with a slightly melancholy smile, remembering something from long ago.

As the tempo increased, their steps kept pace, soon they were stepping and lunging in synchronicity.

Leila at first thought it looked incredibly complicated, but then decided it was beautiful and somewhat sexy. The large crowd around the dance floor were enjoying it too, because they were clapping and stomping their feet in time to the music.

Suddenly, Nichola yelled, "éla na to párei, come on, pick it up!" and all three men moved extremely fast as the music was set at an accelerated pace. Soon it was over, and all three men started clapping and laughing. Both Mansuetus and Nichola gripped the young man by his forearm as they had done to each other on the night that she had first met him.

As Nichola came and stood before her with a large smile on his face, she beamed at him. "That was wonderful! You never cease to amaze me."

Pulling her to him, he kissed her quickly on the mouth before she could self-consciously pull away. "I feel young tonight." Holding her close, he gazed down at her. "You make me feel light and young."

"I think it is the atmosphere in the bar, honey." She murmured smiling, looking at him, believing that he was punch drunk with the festive, drunken emotions that he had probably been taking in all night.

"No, it is you." He replied, staring deeply, hungrily into her eyes.

"Jesus," Jackie declared in awe to Mansuetus as he sat down next to her, watching them. He moved his arm across the back of her chair possessively. "I have never seen a man look at a woman like that in public. If he could spontaneously combust, he would." She giggled a little drunkenly, leaning into him.

Mansuetus glanced down at her, getting a fabulous view down the front of her dress. "You have not known enough real men to say that Young One." He told her smoothly in his deep sexy bass voice, speaking gently into her ear, giving her his own hot look.

She looked up into his face, startled, blinked her thickly lashed eyes a couple of times, and simply said, "Wow!"

"Iris, I want you to come home with me. I want you to spend the night with me. In my bed," Dene told Iris softly, knowing that she would hear him over the loud music, even when no one else could, as he danced close to her on the dance floor.

She looked at him with sharp, thoughtful eyes, not answering.

At 11:30 pm, Nichola stood up and announced, "I am taking Leila. She is tired and needs to sleep."

"Oh, no! It's early, and I have a sitter for the whole night!" Leila exclaimed in disappointment.

"No!" Jackie said. "It's so early!"

Nichola gazed at Leila, holding her eyes with his and stated softly, "You are tired, glukó mou."

Leila suddenly felt absolutely lethargic as he pulled her to stand. "I guess I do feel tired." She told Jackie, a little wobbly, as Nichola draped his duster around her shoulders. It came close to brushing the ground on her. "But you guys stay and have a good time."

"Yes, stay." Nichola smiled. "Mansuetus will escort you home. We brought two cars in case of this."

Jackie stood to give Leila a gentle hug. "Feel better, honey, and get some sleep. It was so nice to see you. I hope you had a good time."

"Oh, I did! It was so nice to get out!" She returned her hug, smiling.

"The bartender took my payment information, so the bill is paid for, Mansuetus." Nichola told him.

"I will take care of everything when I get home, Kýrios. Godspeed." Mansuetus replied softly for his ears alone, gripping Nichola's shoulder, while Iris was giving Leila a hug goodbye.

As Dene gave Leila a hug goodbye, he whispered to her worriedly, "You are feeling okay?"

"Yes, I am just really tired," giving him a smile. "Keep your promise." She whispered softly.

"I will." He told her with a slightly nervous smile, and she patted his arm reassuringly.

Nichola escorted her from the bar and to his car with a supporting arm around her waist. Unlocking the car, he turned her around to help her put the duster on her arms, pulling it close about her as she gave him a tired look. "I don't wish for you to be cold." He said in his *voice*.

"I do feel a little chilled." She replied sleepily, yawning.

He helped her into the front seat, helping her to wrap his coat and intentionally wrap his scent around her. He secured her seat belt, tilting her face up for a sweet, tender kiss.

"Thank you."

"For what, i psychí mou?" He inquired; his eyes crinkled slightly at the corners in humor as he smiled.

"For such a wonderful evening." Her eyes closing of their own accord as she felt him recline her seat to make her more comfortable.

"You are welcome. Sleep. Rest." He said in his *voice*, touching her along the jawline ever so soothingly.

At 1:00 am, Mansuetus, Jackie, Dene and Iris headed into the parking lot. Mansuetus helped Jackie, who was laughing and somewhat drunk, into the

back of the limousine like she was the Queen of Sheba. He leaned in and fastened her seat belt around her, and she ran a hand down his chest to hook a long finger behind his belt buckle, smiling wickedly at him. He in turn gave her a steamy look as she leaned back on the seat, theatrically waving herself with her hand and giggling sillily. He gave her a crooked smile, closed the door, and headed around to the driver's seat. He looked in Iris' direction, who waved him off as she headed to Dene's car on his arm. Nodding at her, he got into the car and drove away.

Dene opened the car door for Iris, as he shut it to head around to the driver's side, he heard a brassy voice several feet behind him say, "Hey, Doc! Don't you think you should be man enough to talk to me before you take off with that old whore?"

He turned to face Bobby Rebekah, who stood about ten feet from him; angrily gripping her own hips with her garishly long-nailed hands on her rounded hips. "I figured you would take the hint by now, Bobby." He replied coldly.

"Does your old whore know that you have been fucking me?" She yelled at him, walking up to face him and looking around him to glance in Iris' direction. He stepped into her line of sight.

"One, Iris is a lady, not a whore. Two, yes, I *was* fucking you, past tense, but frankly, who hasn't?" Bobby slapped him hard, jerking his head back, leaving a bright red palm print behind on his face. "Are you done, now?" Glaring at her coldly out of ice-blue eyes.

"You'll know when I am done..." she started, only to be cut off by a female voice from the door yelling her name.

"Bobby Rebekah, Marcus is looking for you! He wants to know why you aren't behind the bar!" Their waitress was yelling as she stood in the entrance doorway, letting the loud music from the band escape into the parking lot.

"This ain't over, Doc!" Bobby Rebekah yelled at him stomping back to the entrance, "Just take your old whore and get the fuck out of here!"

"Yes, it is over, Bobby! Stay the hell away from me and quit calling me." He yelled in return.

Holding up her middle finger in the air, she walked up the two steps to the front entrance.

He angrily turned around and walked to the driver's side of his car and got in. He fastened his seat-belt and looked at Iris, who was staring straight ahead, cold, and emotionless. "I'm sorry to have put you through that, Iris. I should have taken care of that before I ever brought you here." He said sincerely.

"Yes, you should have." Iris stated emotionlessly.

He started the car and slowly left the parking lot. They drove in silence for about five minutes until they reached a small, isolated cottage on the shore of the St. Mary's River. When Dene came around and opened the car door for Iris, she got out and silently, curiously, looked around.

"It's very private, isn't it?" She noted, looking at him.

"Yes."

"Do you rent it?" She asked, looking out over the river and the beauty of the reflected moonlight on the waves.

"No. It comes with the job." He moved to stand close beside her, also looking out over the water. "I have never brought anyone else here, Iris. I just want you to know that." His voice was gentle as he looked at her perfect profile, watching the soft breeze from the river ruffling her black curls.

He took her hand and walked up the front steps to the porch, unlocked the door, stepped over the threshold, and turned around to face her, hesitating only a moment.

Smiling softly at him, she reached across the threshold, and placed her hand on his chest, moving him back as she stepped over the threshold uninvited, much to his amazement.

"So how long have you known what I was?" She inquired softly, stepping around him to look at the combined small living room and kitchen. She heard him close the door behind them.

"Since the day that Leila was released from the hospital." He stated softly in surprise, watching her walk to the back window of the living room to again look out over the river. "I didn't know right away, of course. It came to me in bits and pieces throughout the day. Once my memory had returned to me in full, I couldn't get you out of my mind." He remarked.

She seemed calm, relaxed. "Well, don't believe everything that you have read." She stated matter-of-factly. Then asked, "So, what was your first inkling that something wasn't quite what it was supposed to be?"

"I couldn't get you out of my mind." He repeated. "I've never had a problem putting aside all other thoughts when it came to my job. I'm usually so singularly focused when it comes to my professional life. That ability to focus everything that I am, is what makes me an excellent doctor, Iris. But as my mind kept running over Leila's case, all I could remember were your eyes." He turned on a small light by the door.

"And once you remembered, you decided to follow us home?" Iris turned her eyes and body toward him, leaning against the wall next to the window. "Do you not see how foolish that was? Insinuating yourself into our lives."

"How long have you known that I knew you were a vampire?" Asking in return, he finally said the word out loud.

"I realized it tonight when you stepped across the threshold and didn't invite me in." She said with a slight smile and a shake of her head. "I read it all over you."

"Oh. I thought you might have overheard me with Leila tonight." He said softly.

"No, I didn't. So how long has my niece known?" She asked.

"I don't know. Maybe a while." He answered. "I didn't tell her. She just knew."

"She tends to keep secrets. Well, it's not surprising that she knows. The rest of us underestimate her because she is so young. Obviously, a mistake on our part."

Moving into the kitchen, he took out some ice, glasses, and a bottle of whiskey. She followed him silently. "Would you like a drink, Iris?" He asked, dropping cubes and splashing whiskey into a tumbler.

Smiling, she was amazed at how calm he was. Surely, he knew what kind of danger he was in? "Sure. Why not?" She replied.

Handing her the glass, he made himself another drink, then walked into the living room to sit on the couch.

Iris followed him, sitting as well.

"So, I gather Leila is becoming a vampire? That is what was occurring while she was in the hospital? Is it because Nick bit her?" He asked, looking straight ahead, swirling his whiskey around in his glass.

Iris burst out laughing.

Startled, he looked at her sharply, failing to see the humor in his questions.

"I do apologize, Dene. You just seemed so serious. Leila is still becoming what she is meant to be. She was born this way, as I was. So, you needn't worry. You won't become a vampire." She chuckled. "You also shouldn't dwell too closely on Nikolaos. He wouldn't like it." She advised, sipping her drink. "I think we can safely assume that neither Nikolaos nor Mansuetus know you realize I am a vampire, or we wouldn't be sitting here speaking with each other right now." She calmly took another drink as he watched her. "You know you were right about some of it. It is mostly genetics."

"So Leila really is your niece?" Dene asked.

"Oh, yes. She is my great-niece. But she has always been like a daughter to me."

"But I am sure that when she was brought into the hospital that she did not know this is what was happening to her." Dene said in bewilderment. "Why didn't you just tell her?"

"I hadn't seen her for almost twenty years!" Iris said defensively. "Her father was supposed to tell her years ago! Her being in the hospital was not my fault!" She finished her whiskey to sit the glass on a coaster on the coffee table with a sharp sound. "But right now, the larger question is, now that you *know,* what am I to do with you? Why shouldn't I kill you now and protect me and my family?"

"Because Iris, I care about you! You know I do. I would not harm you or your family! I am not a threat to you!" He stated, simply taking her hand. "I wanted to be honest with you. That's what I told Leila tonight. That I would be honest with you because I want to be with you. Because I want to make love to you. That's why I have brought you here tonight. Because I want you. I want you in my bed." He stood up, pulling her close to him. "What's more, Iris, I believe you care about me, too. I believe you want me as well."

"Dene! You really don't know what you are talking about. I am a monster! I am from a family of monsters!" She pulled away, looking at him like he was crazy.

"Come on, Iris." He ignored her protests, grabbing her hand to pull her toward a small hallway.

"This isn't a good idea!" Trying to reason with him, she allowed him to pull her into the only bedroom in the cottage. *He's behaving just like a foolish human!* she thought.

Closing the door behind them, Dene looked down on her, pulling her into his arms to kiss her deep, thrusting his tongue between her lips. She tasted the whiskey in his kiss. Moaning against him, she felt herself relax as her scent wrapped around them. He groaned in return, grinding himself against her, gripping her ass tightly with both hands.

She suddenly pushed away from him. "Dene! Stop!" She demanded, gaining some distance. "Do you smell this scent?" She gasped out, gesturing with her hands. "It's me!"

"I know." He growled at her with desire, reaching toward her as she danced further out of reach.

"Dene, listen to me. I exude this scent to attract prey! I am a predator. I have not done this with a human since I became a vampire! You are not a vampire, and I am so much stronger than you. So much! You have no clue how much stronger. I could hurt you, and I don't want to hurt you! I have never wanted to hurt anyone, and I couldn't bear to hurt you!" She yelled at him, ending with a small sob, wanting to get through to him.

He stopped stalking her and changed to a less aggressive stance, speaking gently. "You won't hurt me, Iris. I know you won't. You could have hurt me so many times, and you never have. I trust you."

"You shouldn't, because I don't trust me, Dene." She whispered, wanting him so much in so many different ways, but wanting to protect him more.

Dene slowly walked to a tall dresser, pulled open the top drawer, and pulled out four silk neckties. He slowly approached her, as if she might bolt, and gently took her by the hand to stand next to the side of the bed.

"Do you trust me?" He asked softly, looking down into her black eyes.

Parking in Jackie's driveway, Mansuetus got out, opening the backdoor to assist her. As he reached into the back to unbuckle her seat-belt, she grabbed him by the shoulders, pulling him off balance to yank him in, slamming the door behind him.

Pushing him to the floor, she straddled him, placing her soft hands upon his chest. She looked down into his shocked expression in speculation.

"Manny, have you ever had sex in the back of a limousine?" She asked, smiling wickedly.

He returned her smile with a smile just as wicked. "Never with a goddess such as yourself." His deep voice was almost a purr as he ran his large hands up under her skirt, loving the feel of her stocking clad legs on either side of his body. His hands stopped when he came to her garter belt. He sat up holding her to him and placed his face in her cleavage to breathe deep of her scent and licked in between her breasts to taste the slight saltiness of her skin, while his hands moved from her legs to her back to lower the zipper of her dress. He thought she smelled and tasted like the ocean on a bright, sunny day.

Jackie moaned softly, wrapping her arms around him, pulling his head tightly to her as he loosened her dress.

Leaning back, he pulled her dress over her head as she reached behind her back to unfasten her frilly white bra. His hands stopped her. "Allow me, i theá tis omorfiás mou." He told her gently. She looked at him in confusion. "My goddess of beauty." He whispered to her, his eyes hot with desire.

"Oh!" She softly exclaimed, taking his face in her hands to kiss him hungrily while he quickly unbuttoned his own shirt, pulling it from his body. Her hands were everywhere, stroking up and down his back and through his hair. As he kissed up and down her throat, she felt him moving under her body. Suddenly, he easily lifted her to sit her back on the seat, staying in between her legs. She was not a small woman, and his strength impressed her.

Startled by the dim overhead light when he turned it on, she attempted to cover herself with her hands. "No." He commanded, capturing her hands in his to gently place them on either side of her body, as he kneeled between her stocking clad legs. "I want you to see me as I see you. Do not move." His deep voice was quiet as his eyes captured her wide brown eyes with his own.

Moving to sit on the bench seat across from hers, he looked at her body in her frilly white bra, garter belt, panties, nude colored hose, and black pumps.

Her breath caught in her throat as she felt branded by the hot look in his eyes. His eyes never left hers, as she watched the large, lean muscles of his chest and abdomen ripple as he leaned back to slowly unfasten his belt. Watching his slow movements as he slid his pants off of his muscular hips and legs, she realized that somewhere in the dark he had removed his boots and socks. Sliding naked from the seat back to the floor, to close the distance between them on his hands and knees, she was reminded of a big cat and realized that he was almost totally hairless and bronze; an all-over bronze color with no tan lines, and everything about him was so much larger than she had expected.

Looking at him with wild desire and a small amount of trepidation, she whispered, feeling very sober. "Manny, I am not real sure about this."

As he moved slowly up her body, he ran his hands very gently over her skin as if she were the most precious of objects. Giving a small gentle laugh, he kissed the tops of her breasts that spilled over the top of her lacy bra, as he slid his hands around her to unclasp it.

"I promise I will take very good care of you, my young goddess." He murmured against her lips as he slid the straps off of her shoulders and arms to release her breasts into his large hands. Gently rubbing his thumbs over her nipples, he placed soft kisses on her lips, and was rewarded with a tremor of desire throughout her body.

Alone, tied naked and spread-eagled with Dene's silk ties to his bed, Iris tested her bonds and was fairly certain that she could shred them if she transformed. Her problem was that she couldn't see him, and without contact or sight, she was unable to read his intentions, and she had no idea what he was doing.

God, she thought, *how stupid would Nikolaos think I was if I got myself staked right now just so that I could have sex with a human!* "Dene, if you hurt me, you do realize that Nikolaos will devise a way to keep you alive for the longest of tortures!" She warned the room at large.

"Iris, you said that you trusted me!" His soft voice came just out of her eyesight. "You know I would never harm you." He walked around to where she could see him.

Even naked, he was still one of the most beautiful men that she had ever laid eyes on, human or vampire.

Looking down at her, he let his eyes run over her body from head to toe.

She could feel her body respond to his gaze as her nipples hardened into tight pebbles and her scent of lavender, pumpkin pie, and donuts permeated the bedroom.

Breathing deeply, his eyes dilated, and his erection grew as he climbed on the bed to lie beside her, to run his hand softly over her, from the tip of her breast to hip. "God, you are the most beautiful thing that I have ever seen in my entire life," he whispered, taking her nipple into his mouth.

She arched into his mouth and, gripping the ties binding her tight, she felt her fangs descend.

As Mansuetus removed Jackie's silky white panties from her body, sliding them down over her hose, he saw she was hairless and had a small heart tattoo just to the left of her pubic bone.

He thought to himself, "sýnchrones gynaíkes," deciding he liked it as he moved to spread her legs with his broad shoulders, holding her hips, he gently nuzzled her nether lips with his nose and dipped his long tongue inside, bringing a cry from her throat.

Iris raised her head from the bed to gaze down at him, as he loved her with his mouth.

Her mouth was parted, her fangs were fully distended, and her eyes were red. She was so close to coming. The muscles of her stomach quivered as she clutched her silk bindings tightly, a deep groan escaping her lips.

Dene looked up from her, smiling roguishly, unfazed by her eyes and teeth, and pushed two fingers into her as he sucked her clitoris into his mouth and flicked her with his tongue.

She squeezed her eyes shut and saw stars as she came.

Jackie was still in the throes of one of the best orgasms that she had ever experienced when Mansuetus kissed his way up her body to kiss her hard on the lips. Tasting herself on him, her eyes fluttered as he rubbed the head of his rod between her legs to gently guide himself inside.

"Oh, God." She gasped, amazed at the sheer size of him as he entered her slowly.

Whispering to her as he withdrew slightly, "Páre me sto glykó sou sóma, take me into your sweet body." He coated himself with her slick juices and slowly returned to go deeper. He moved her long stocking clad legs to his shoulders, pulling her to the edge of the seat and gripping her hips.

"Oh, Jesus! I don't think I can." She gasped loudly and her whole body clamped down on him.

"Breathe, my beautiful goddess." Gently stroking in and out of her slowly. "You feel so good, so wet, so tight. Breathe." He whispered to her in his deep voice, thrilling her with his words.

She breathed out and her body relaxed.

"Yes, that's it, panemorfi, beautiful." Whispering again, he felt her grip his waist as he leaned over to suckle her breast. "Mmmmm. You taste so delicious. A wonderful, sweet wine."

All the while, his hips moved slowly back and forth, pushing himself deeper as she moaned in pleasure.

"Manny, oh, god, Manny." She kept whispering over and over as he slowly plundered her body.

"There, my sweet goddess." He breathed heavily, pausing when he was buried to the hilt. "You've taken all of me. Now I will show you what real pleasure is."

Dene settled himself between Iris' legs, laying on top of her body. Reaching up to take her face in his hands, he gently kissed her lips, carefully avoiding her sharp teeth.

Lethargic after her orgasm, her red eyes were languid. "You are a foolish human, Dene."

"I love you, Iris." Smiling, his charming lopsided smile at her as he slowly penetrated her body with his.

Her red eyes widened, and she arched under him with a moan, as he braced himself on his arms over her, avoiding her teeth.

"Sweet, sweet, Iris." He whispered with a moan of his own as he began to move.

Jackie's breath was coming in gasps after her second orgasm, but he was still long and hard inside of her. Looking up at him as he looked down on her with a tender smile. She whispered with a small helpless moan, "Manny, I can't anymore."

"My goddess, of course you can," he encouraged, gently moving her legs from his shoulders to the floor on each side of him as he retained his hold on her hips.

"Oh, God." She groaned out as the change in position shifted the place of her pelvis, altering the way her body held him inside. Wrapping her legs around his, she gripped his hips with her hands.

Whispering, "Yes, my sweet goddess, yes." He began moving inside her once again.

Closing his eyes in concentration, Dene fought to hold back his orgasm. Feeling that she was close, so close, he stroked steadily in and out of her body. As she began to tremble beneath him, he felt her arms and legs envelop him to pull him close.

Whispering, "Yes, Iris." He felt her lips in the curve between his shoulder and his neck, kissing him and licking him so tenderly, as she moaned in ecstasy beneath him. Pumping himself harder in and out of her body, he loved the way she pulsed around him. "Yes, baby, yes." He whispered, his own mouth biting gently on her shoulder as she ground her pelvis against him. "Almost, baby, almost." Groaning louder and pumping harder, he wrapped his arms around her, gripping her ass tightly. As her hips rose to meet his, he drove his cock deeply into her with a moan; faster, harder, and deeper than he had ever done with any woman before.

Still, her kisses were so gentle and sweet and her teeth so sharp. Knowing what was going to happen, he wasn't sure if he would survive.

As her orgasm gripped his cock tightly, he plunged himself deep, coming hard, and she bit down on him simultaneously. When he screamed in pleasure, survival was the last thing on his mind.

The windows in the limousine were fogged over, and the car rocked as he drove himself into her. Mansuetus could feel her reaching hard toward that pinnacle. He just needed to hold out for her. He could feel his skin glisten with sweat as she gripped his ass hard, driving him on. He held her still with one large hand gripping her hip and one hand braced on the back of the seat.

"Oh, Manny, please." She begged, so close. "Please."

He withdrew a third of his length to stroke her in short, searching strokes. She moaned in pleasure loudly over and over. Suddenly, she gasped out.

"Yes?" He growled at her, stroking the head of his cock over the spot once more.

"Oh, god, Manny!" She yelled, gripping him tightly.

"Yes." He said in triumph as he continued to stroke her over her spot exactly as before.

Soon she was screaming her release and her body was contracting around him.

He drove her on and on until he felt her loosen slightly and then he buried himself deeply once, twice, and on the third time he too gave a shout of release as he came deep inside of her body, and as she held him tight, his shudders rivaled hers.

Leila opened her eyes briefly when she felt the car ascend up the on-ramp of an interstate.

She heard Nichola's *voice*, "Sleep, rest, allaxiéra, my changeling. I will wake you when it's time."

As her eyes closed once again, she never noticed that they were driving in the opposite direction of her home.

An Introduction into Vampire Society

L EILA'S EYES FLUTTERED OPEN. Feeling drowsy, it took her a moment to realize that she was not in her own bed. One, it was too comfortable. The mattress was soft and cradled her body perfectly. The brushed cotton sheets were luxurious and cool on her naked skin. Two, there was muted sunlight coming in from a direction where a window just didn't exist in her bedroom.

Sitting up, she looked around.

She was obviously in an awfully expensive hotel suite. The furnishings all seemed to be opulent. The walls displayed original art. A large executive desk occupied one side of the spacious bedroom, while a reading chair and a couch with a loveseat combination occupied the other side. A large television faced her directly, and a full-length mirror adorned the back of the closed door that led to another room. She noticed she was in a King bed with a fluffy brushed cotton down comforter on top of her and at least six down pillows surrounded her.

Breathing deeply, she asked whatever gods that existed for patience.

Where is that vampire and just exactly who the hell did he think he was making off with me like this? She thought. She had no fear for the boys; she knew Mansuetus would take good care of them. But Nichola needed to know that he just couldn't do this to her. He couldn't just drag her off whenever he felt like it!

Looking around for her clothes, she noticed a beautiful cream-colored satin robe with peach-colored flowers laying across the end of the bed and got out of bed to tie it around her in sharp jerking motions. Learning a lot more about her vampire than she really wanted to at this point made her furious.

Obviously, he had done something with her clothes and left this thin robe for her to wear. He probably had some sexual fantasy in his mind that he wanted to play out with her! What he was going to do was to take her home immediately! Looking down, she noticed there were a beautiful pair of what looked to be hand-stitched satin slippers on the floor next to the bed. Putting them on, they fit perfectly, making her groan with frustration.

She walked into the bathroom and wiped the makeup smudges from under her eyes, ran her fingers through her hair so that it wasn't sticking up all over, and did little else, preferring to immediately find him and make him take her home. She had to make him understand he couldn't just do things like this! She had responsibilities!

Marching over, she opened the bedroom door entering into an enormous, beautiful, black-tiled open living room area equipped with a full-size bar and white baby grand piano that matched the luxurious white furniture. The room ran parallel to a sunken garden area of approximately the same size, filled with large potted plants and small trees that was enclosed by a solarium. She headed that direction, sensing him there.

"Nichola!" She spoke sharply as she rounded the plants. "You can't just kidnap..." she stopped short, standing very still to grasp the neck of the robe close about her.

Seated around a large circular rattan glass-topped coffee table were six men in business suits seated in comfortable looking rattan chairs. She knew immediately that they were all vampires.

"Tsoukalous, a human to warm your bed? How unusual for you." A man with average features, dark green eyes, and dark auburn hair said, giving her a smirking glance.

I psychí mou, come give me your hand. Hearing his voice in her mind, she realized Nichola was sitting with his back to her. Bending forward, he put what looked to be a portfolio of documents on the coffee table, and then he held out his right hand.

Walking slowly over to him, she placed her left hand in his, her right still clasping her robe. *What's going on here?* Sending the question back to him silently, apprehensively, she finally appreciated this ability that they shared.

A business meeting. He thought vaguely in return.

"Not a human. A changeling." A ruggedly handsome man with black eyes, long black hair pulled into a ponytail and the dark looks of a Spaniard said in a soft, calming voice.

"A changeling?" Another exclaimed with a British accent, looking at her with amazed cornflower blue eyes.

She met his eyes calmly, reassured by Nichola's touch.

"Gentlemen," her vampire said smoothly, stressing the word slightly, and never taking his eyes off of the men. "Allow me to introduce my mate, Leila."

The surprise in the air was thick, and then they all stood to give her a slight bow. She nodded in return.

"Es will be here momentarily, Nikolaos." The black-eyed man said to him.

The rest of the vampires came closer to gather around them, and she was forced to either relinquish Nichola's hand or release her robe. She dropped his hand and extend her left hand when each of them extended theirs.

"Forgive me, my crudeness, Fraulein." The auburn-haired vampire said to her with a smooth sincerity that didn't meet his eyes as he bowed over her hand.

"This is Beutel." Nichola, who was now standing protectively next to her, said with boredom.

"It is a pleasure to meet you, my lady." The Brit, who had sandy blonde hair and those lovely cornflower blue eyes, said, taking her hand gently. "I have never met a changeling before." He said with interest and a shy smile.

His smile was infectious, and she returned his shy smile with one of her own.

Nichola said with a sharp scowl, "This is Peake."

"Please feel free to call me Charles." The vampire said to her shyly, then quickly let go of her hand and moved out of the way for the next man as he noticed Nichola's now slightly dangerous look cast in his direction.

The next man had skin the color of a creamy espresso and light golden eyes. His black, very wavy hair was well-oiled and combed back from a broad and intelligent forehead. He was different from the other two that she had met, as he was the only man so far over six feet in height. Not quite as tall as Mansuetus, but close. He was lean and powerful. Taking her hand, he bowed low over it. "Lady Tsoukalous, I am your servant."

Leila was surprised to hear a very neutral accent, with maybe a small hint of middle eastern descent on the crisp syllables.

Nichola was actually smiling in a friendly sort of way at him. "This is Prince Khaldun."

"You are a prince?" Leila asked, looking up at him in wonder.

"Well, that's his story, in any case." The black-eyed man with the ponytail stated with a sharp smile as he took her hand from him to bow over it himself. "My lady."

"This is Romulus." Nichola told her and she heard actual warmth in his voice.

"As in Romulus and Remus?" She inquired, wide-eyed, looking at him.

He laughed in delight. "Intelligent as well as beautiful, my friend." He told Nichola, then looked back to Leila. "No, my lady, I am not quite that ancient, though I do hail from that area."

The last man to step forward was different from the others in several ways. While the others looked to be in their thirties, this vampire's change had obviously occurred later in life. If Leila had met him on the street, she would have put him at around fifty. He had a full dark mane of hair veined with silver at his temples, and dark dancing eyes. He also was the shortest man in the room at about five feet eight inches tall, but she could see that all the others respected him.

As he took her hand in his strong weathered hands, hands that had known years of hard work, she felt a connection. Then she realized that the sensation was coming from him, that he was intentionally trying to make her feel at ease.

"Glykó, this is Ostrovsky." Nichola told her in a respectful tone.

"Call me, Aleksei, child. Have we overwhelmed you?" He asked with what she thought was a slight Russian or Eastern European accent.

"No." She shook her head, and he laughed in delight, holding her hand gently.

"Nikolaos, you have the rarest of luck to have the most fearless, beautiful women in your bloodline." He said, his eyes still locked with Leila's. "Do you know your kinswoman, Iris?"

"She is my Great-Aunt." Leila told him.

"Ah, the loveliest of women! You have her look about you, even if your coloring is different. She has quite stolen my heart, you know." He smiled at her as if sharing a confidence.

Leila smiled in return, then turned as she heard the door to the suite open. Within seconds, the most beautiful woman that she had ever seen in the flesh came around the plants. She was dressed in a lovely sea-blue colored silk robe and slippers that matched her gorgeous eyes, her long curly white-blonde hair a sharp contrast to the blue of the robe. Not much taller than Leila herself, this gorgeous vampire smiled a truly welcoming smile at Leila, ignoring the men who bowed in her direction.

Romulus stepped forward and took the beauty's hand to lead her to Leila. "Lady Leila, this is my mate, Esmerelda."

Leila held out her right hand automatically and Esmerelda took hers in welcome. "I am so pleased to meet you, Lady Leila! I have heard so much about you. I have a wonderful day in the spa planned and a fitting at the dressmakers for us. We are going to have so much fun!" The vampire goddess was absolutely giddy.

Leila smiled at her and then gave Nichola a cold look. "Nichola, I really would like to speak with you privately." She said to him extremely politely.

"I psychí mou," he said, taking her arm gently and Esmerelda took her other, leading her out of the garden area. "I have business that will take up most of my day. Go with Es, she will be lonely too as Romulus is also required to be here."

I am not lonely, and you know it. I want you to take me home right now, Nichola! She thought angrily at him.

I can't do that at the moment, even if I had an intention of doing so. It is ten o'clock in the morning. In any case, we will speak about it this evening. He thought calmly at her in return.

"Oh, Lady Leila, I heard you were working for the military. You will have to tell me all about it. That must have been exciting." Esmerelda was saying to her as she pulled her out of the suite into a luxurious hallway.

"Please make sure that she eats, Es." Nichola requested as he closed the door on them.

Leila thought at him in anger. *Coward!*

"Please, just call me Leila, Esmerelda," she said to the beautiful vampire. "I am no lady."

"Thank god!" Esmerelda laughed in relief, flashing a gorgeous smile. "I am not either! Please call me Es. All of my friends do."

Leila found herself in an elegant open dining room with Esmerelda and at least a dozen other women scattered throughout the large room, dining singly or in pairs. All were dressed in exquisite robes, like themselves. Leila guessed that about thirty percent were human. Esmerelda was ordering breakfast for them from the human waiter, who was a young, handsome man with a winning smile.

"Yes, and we will have mimosas and coffee to drink." She looked at Leila, who nodded at her.

"I had the impression that this was a vampire establishment." Leila whispered when he left.

"Oh, it is. All the windows are UV protected and bullet proof. But the day staff are human, and many are voluntary donors. But I assure you, security is top-notch here; everyone is thoroughly vetted." She looked in the direction of several men scattered about the large space that looked to be private security.

"Donors? Oh." Leila said, realizing what Esmerelda was saying.

"I understand from Rom and Nikolaos that this is all very new to you," Esmerelda continued.

"Rom?" Leila asked, feeling a little lost.

"Yes, my mate. Romulus is such a mouthful, don't you think?" Esmerelda said, smiling. "There are so very few of us, you know."

"Vampires?" Leila asked, feeling out at sea.

"Oh, yes. Those too. But I am talking about soul mates." Esmerelda continued in a chatting manner. "I know others exist, but I had never met another pair until now. I am so happy that Nikolaos has found you. It is exceedingly rare that we ever do."

"How long have you known Nichola?" Leila asked.

"Over a century, just short of two now." She paused, thinking about it. "I am not incredibly old myself, you understand. Not like Nikolaos and Rom are. Indirectly, Nikolaos brought Rom and I together. Without him, it is unlikely that we would have ever found each other." She smiled and Leila realized that her accent was British, though not as pronounced as the man that she had met earlier. "I wanted to meet you last night when Rom told me you had arrived, but Nikolaos explained you were sleeping and didn't even wake up when you got here. Oh, that means that you missed seeing the grounds when you got here last night. You will love the grounds of the hotel! It is so beautiful lit up at night, it reminds me of Vauxhall during the season. When the sun sets, we can take a stroll through the gardens."

Struggling a little to keep up with the conversation, all of a sudden, Leila realized why Nichola wanted her to spend the day with Esmerelda. She would answer many of her questions.

"So where are we, exactly?" Leila asked.

"We are at the Château les Ténèbres in Ponce Inlet, Florida. It is so beautiful here. There are several establishments that cater to our needs throughout the world, but in my opinion, this is one of the prettiest ones. There is a very private beach, gardens, even an animal menagerie. Of course, there is always musical entertainment and dancing every evening. And the services at the spa and salon are second to none! There is a small clothing store and also an extremely talented dressmaker that we will see as soon as we have finished our breakfast. She needs to get your final measurements for several items that you will need while you are here. Then, after we are finished being pampered in the spa, we will have our hair and makeup done. Nikolaos has arranged everything for us, so don't let yourself be held back by any thoughts of cost. He owns this hotel, after all."

Esmerelda continued to chat on about how luxurious and comfortable the rooms always were and how welcoming the staff was, and all Leila could think about was that Nichola owned this hotel.

Her thoughts were flying around in her mind. Exactly what did 'I am not without resources' mean to him! Just from the small amount of what she had seen so far of this hotel, he was obviously richer than God! She felt like she didn't know him at all, and she was not happy about it.

"Esmerelda." Leila said calmly when Esmerelda had stopped for breath as the waiter was putting their breakfast before them on the table and making their mimosas table side for them.

"Oh, please call me Es." She smiled sweetly.

"Es." Leila smiled in return. "So, who were all of those men in the suite this morning?"

"Oh, they didn't introduce themselves? How rude!" Es said in surprise.

"No. They did. But who are they? What were they meeting about?" Leila asked.

"Oh. Thank God! Sometimes the elders forget their manners. That is the small council." Es said cracking open her soft-boiled egg.

Leila looked strangely at her.

Es raised an inquiring brow at her.

"You don't have to eat if you don't like to. You know, just because I have to." Leila said. Taking a bite of her fluffy omelet, closing her eyes briefly at the taste. It was heavenly!

"Oh, I love to eat!" Es laughed. "Who told you we don't eat?"

"Well, Nichola told me it doesn't taste the same for vampires."

"Maybe not to him." Es said with a giggle. "But I am not nearly as old as he is. Rom doesn't eat much either, come to think about it. Though he is a little crazy about milk chocolate. The amount of chocolate that man consumes is beyond me. I on the other hand, love to eat! When I was human, I always had to watch what I ate. My figure was particularly important in my profession. So, I always felt like I was hungry all the time. Now, I am able to eat anything that I want without that worry." She said, taking a bite of her egg and following it with a bite of ham.

Leila looked at her briefly and tried some of the tender ham as well. For a hotel that catered to vampires, the food was delicious! "So, what did you used to do?" She asked, popping a strawberry half into her mouth.

"I was a ladybird." Es said, taking a sip of mimosa.

"A ladybird?" Leila asked.

"A professional mistress. Or a courtesan if you prefer. I was not a prostitute. My favors were highly sought after, expensive, and my arrangements were always for longer than a night or two and always with extraordinarily rich men," Es said, taking a bite of the sliced strawberries the waiter had left.

"I had no idea that such a thing existed." Leila said, holding her arms out for the seamstress to take measurements of her body. Upon Es announcing their arrival in the dress shop, they had been moved quickly and efficiently behind a partition and divested of their robes. Leila had been shocked and embarrassed to find herself quite naked in front of strangers, but Es had absolutely no self-consciousness about her beautiful body and absolutely showed no shame about her human life.

"What?" She asked, glancing at Leila's body standing next to her with interest as she held her own body perfectly still so the seamstress's assistant could take her measurements.

"A professional mistress."

"Oh, yes. But don't be too shocked. I was much better off than most women. I also enjoyed a greater degree of independence and freedom than even titled ladies did. It truly wasn't a bad life for me. At least not till the end."

"Why? What happened at the end? Did someone abuse you?" Leila asked, genuinely curious.

"Not in the sense that you mean," Es said. "You see, I was in-between protectors and had been casting my lure for this delicious-looking young viscount. He had arranged a late dinner with me after the opera and on my way to our assassination, I was kidnapped by my maker." She said with a look of remembered pain. "Do you know about 'made vampires'?" Es asked.

"Yes." Leila said, shocked. "Rom forced you to become a vampire? And Nichola helped him?" She couldn't believe that Nichola would do such a thing! *What the hell is wrong with him?* She thought.

"Oh, lord no!" Es giggled. "Rom is not my maker! I didn't even meet the two of them until I had been a vampire for a few years. The both of them saved me. My life was so horrible after I had been made a vampire. My maker forced me to do the most horrific things. I don't even want to think about them." She shuddered and there was a short look of remembered pain on her lovely face.

"I am sorry, Es." Leila put on her robe after the silent seamstress signaled she was done.

"Oh, it's alright. It's been a long time in the past. Nikolaos brought me my Rom and my life has been so much happier since." She praised with a smile. "Just to clarify, I said happier. Not necessarily easier." She chuckled. Tying her own robe around her, Es linked her arm through Leila's, then glanced at the little seamstress who stood before them.

The seamstress addressed Leila with a small bow. "They will be ready by six o'clock, Lady Tsoukalous."

"Okay, thank you," Leila replied softly, not knowing what was going to be ready, but unused to this type of deference.

Es led her out the shop door and down another hallway past a sign with a large hand and directional finger on it that pointed toward the spa.

"Let's steam first for a while, then we can get waxed and showered, and then a massage before we have our manicures and pedicures." Es said, pulling her into an inner room and removing her robe to wrap an oversized bath-sheet around her perfect body. Leila watched her with envy for a moment and then followed suit. They went into the sauna and Es took an additional bath-sheet to spread over the teak bench and sat down. She patted the bench next to her and as Leila sat down, Es poured water over the heated stones. Steam rose throughout the dry, hot air. Es set a timer for 20 minutes and then relaxed back.

"Es, what does the small council do?" Leila asked, feeling the steam all around her, causing her to relax.

"You are American, correct?" Es asked.

"Yes."

"Well, think of them as a collective congress and president, all wrapped up in one. There are six positions. Two appointments are made by a large council vote, from amongst the members of the large council, but they are supposed to be wholly based on two things. Age and mental stability. These two positions are reserved for vampires older than a century, but younger than four centuries. The other four positions are not subject to vote and reserved for the oldest amongst us."

"What is the large council?" Leila asked, confused.

"It is the oldest 100 vampires in the world. The large council meets every 200 years, and their main function is to vote on the positions of who amongst them will sit on the small council, and any other large issue that could affect the community as a whole that comes before them at the time. Not all the oldest vampires attend either the large or small council assemblies. You are not forced to take a position on either council if you do not care too. But there must be 100 members of the large council, and six on the small council. As you can imagine, meeting every 200 years usually means that the large council members are always different. There are always more than one hundred vampires that arrive during large council gatherings, but only the oldest of the vampires are able to take part in the large council meetings or debates and put forward their votes on whatever the agenda may be. Rarely are back-to-back large councils filled with the same individuals, even with our long lives. Since it is impossible to know who will attend the assemblies for large council selection, it is almost impossible to know how any one vote is going to go.

This, Rom tells me, helps to prevent different factions of our community from aligning together and making power grabs for dominance through the large council structure. The large council just met last year, and this is how we have our new, small council. Due to a vacancy, Rom was invited because of his age to take a place on the small council." Es said, obviously proud of Rom's position.

Okay, Leila thought, *so Nichola is some sort of politician*. She asked instead, "So how often does the small council meet? Is it always all men?"

"Well, the small council makes the day-to-day decisions of community actions. But they officially meet for a week of meetings, four times per year. Though emergency sessions occur occasionally, which is why they are meeting this week. Female vampires are not the majority in our community; there definitely are more males than females. But there is no rule that says that women can't be on the small council. There are always several women on the large council. We have the same rights as our male counterparts, but it doesn't seem like our female elders are interested in serving in a capacity that takes so much of their time for two solid centuries. Maybe if the small council time-frame was shorter, they might be interested."

"Well, if they are only meeting four weeks per year, it doesn't seem like a lot of time." Leila said, thinking out loud. "Wouldn't you like an opportunity to have a voice about how the community is run?"

"Oh, no! You forget, I live with Rom, and he is always doing something or reading something or on a phone conference about something! Or traveling somewhere. It is a full-time job! There seems to be a lot of pressure involved as well. Sometimes decisions of life and death. Too much responsibility for me to want to throw my hat in the ring! If I had known how much time he would spend doing this, I would have encouraged him not to do it."

"Well, what happens when there is an impasse on a decision? There are only six council members. What happens if there is a tie vote on something?" Leila asked, interested.

"Well, not all members just have one vote. The council leader has an additional vote that is cast in the event of a tie and complete veto power over any decision even coming to a vote."

"Wow. That is a lot of power for one individual." Leila said. "So, who chooses the council leader? The large council? Or do all vampires get a vote?" Leila asked, thinking about the presidential election that was held every four years in America.

"No. It always goes to the oldest member of the council. Life experience is highly valued amongst our kind." Leila wasn't really comfortable being lumped into the group with that statement but chose to say nothing. "It is a lot of responsibility and I gather twice the work. That is why Ostrovsky absolutely refused the position again for this term. He had held it for the last two hundred years and Rom told me that Ostrovsky stated that he absolutely would not let it suck up another year of his life. So, it went to the next oldest."

Leila thought to herself, *please don't let her say it, please don't let her say it.*

"Nikolaos."

Leila closed her eyes and breathed out a sigh. *Great,* she thought, *my boyfriend is the King of the Vampires!*

"You did not know this?" Es asked softly, observing her.

"No. I did not. But it explains some things that I have been noticing lately." She looked at Es and realized that she had a worried look on her gorgeous face. "Oh, don't feel bad about telling me, Es. Somebody had to. I am the type of person who likes to face things head on. Thank you for telling me." Reaching over, she patted her hand and Es gave her a blinding smile.

After their session with the esthetician, where both Es and the esthetician had tried to convince her to remove all of her pubic hair, Leila was not in a particularly good mood.

"But he will like it," Es had coaxed, as Leila kept shaking her head no.

"I am very sure that he will not." Leila replied, knowing instinctively that she was correct.

"How about a very small amount, lady?" The esthetician said. "Just to clean up the area. I promise you will be pleased with the effect."

"Just a small amount." Es had said with a smile.

"Fine." Leila said, bowing to the vampire's influence. Even a small amount was painful in her opinion. But she had to admit that she liked the effect, not that she was used to looking at that area of her body.

Unfortunately, the first man that got to see 'the effect' was the massage therapist.

Leila and Es were laying on two massage tables on their stomachs with towels over their rear ends for modesty's sake. Leila had never had a massage before and wasn't sure if she was enjoying it. Her massage therapist was an extremely dark, sexy, human man and his strong hands rubbing sensuously over her body were making her quite nervous and she was finding it hard to relax.

"You are so tense, Bella." He said to her softly in a beautiful Italian accent, as his hands ran over her body, applying tea tree oil to her skin. "I promise you I will be gentle with you."

She didn't say anything to him, just attempted to relax her muscles. She asked Es, who was moaning softly under the ministrations of her equally sexy, but blonde, massage therapist, "Es, is there magic involved with being what you are?"

"Mmmmm. Magic? In what way?" Es asked softly.

"Well, I swear Nichola made me sleep the whole way here." Leila admitted her doubts about last night. "I didn't feel tired at the club we were at and then all of a sudden I did, but only after Nichola told me I was. I think he made me tired, and then put me to sleep."

"It's not magic per se." Es told her quietly. "It's not like we cast spells. We are not witches, after all. It is more like a force of will. He is an elder, you are not. It is perfectly possible for him to have done so. He can make other vampires do as he wants after all, even something that they really don't want to do. Being 'made', I was never a changeling. As a changeling, do you have any kind of abilities or powers at all beyond being able to communicate with your mate?"

"I don't know if I would call them powers. I am able to sense people, like where they are at in location to myself. I can read them also, like their intentions. Sometimes I pick up their direct thoughts. Sometimes I just, I don't know how to describe it, just 'know' something." Leila returned softly, realizing that she liked the massage after all.

"I have similar abilities. But born vampires such as yourself outstrip made vampires in the nature and strength of abilities, especially in the beginning of their lives. As we all get older, we develop more and more abilities, and it also becomes easier to wield those abilities. Many elders have the ability to shape-shift and fly. I on the other hand, probably will never develop those abilities." Es said, rolling over to her back.

Shocked by her statement, Leila automatically did the same and quickly tried to adjust her towel. Her masseuse assisted her with her towel, but not before revealing to her he appreciated the 'effect' of her waxing experience. She blushed at his thoughts and ignored him while he started massaging her feet and ankles.

"Fly? Like superman? Or do they change into a bat?" She asked Es.

Es laughed heartily. "No, not like superman or a bat! You are so humorous, Leila. Most of the movies are based totally on fiction. Flying is more like defying gravity. They also have super speed, but I don't think they could continue either one of them for any great distance. The amount of energy involved would be too great. Rom doesn't have the ability to fly, but he has told me of others who do. He says it is amazing to see."

Leila thought back to the super speed that Nichola exhibited, moving from her bedroom to the living room the night he had returned her memories to her. One second he had been kneeling before her, apologizing in

Greek, then next back into the bedroom. He had moved so fast it was as if he had appeared and disappeared. So that was super speed?

"Es, please forgive me if this is too personal a question." Leila said, pausing.

"Oh, you can ask me anything. But I reserve the right not to tell you if I don't want to." Es turned her head toward Leila with a bright smile.

"Fair enough." Leila said in return. "How old are you?"

"That's too easy!" Es chuckled. "Two hundred and twenty years old. I was born in 1775. I was made a vampire in 1800. I met my Rom and Nikolaos in 1820. How old are you, Leila?" Es asked curiously.

"Twenty-nine," Leila told her in return.

"So young." Es said with a sigh. "So, I understand from Nikolaos that you are part of his bloodline, so your family has had its share of vampires. Did they tell you none of this before you transitioned?" She sat up, wrapping the towel around her.

Leila looked at her masseuse and he smiled, nodding he was finished. She sat up and thankfully wrapped her own towel around her. She had to admit that her skin had never felt so soft and supple before.

"Es, I just started to transition. I had no idea that vampires existed before two weeks ago, so no, I knew none of this. The person who should have told me chose not to for their own selfish reasons." Leila said, realizing that the more she learned, the angrier she was with her father. There was no guarantee that she would be the only one to transition. She had two younger sisters, after all! For him to hide such a secret from them, to put his own interests before those of his daughters was obscene!

"For just learning about our community and beginning your transition, I must tell you that you seem to handle all of this very well! Then you immediately met your mate! That is incredibly lucky indeed." She said in her soft British accent, leading Leila into the outer room to retrieve their robes.

"What do you mean by lucky?" Leila said.

"Well, having a soul mate is wonderful, isn't it? You gather strength from each other, and you will never be alone. Our existence can be very lonely. You bring out the best in each other. As I told you, my life has been so much happier and more interesting since I met my Rom." Es' bright smile lit up her face.

"I am not sure that I do that for Nichola." Leila admitted, thinking of their fight on Thursday night.

"That's not true. I have never seen him happier in all the years that I have known him as he was last night when we greeted him." Es said with conviction. "So, how did you meet? I know that he and Mansuetus keep an eye on those within the Tsoukalous bloodline. Did they find you when you started to transition?"

"No. Nichola has known about me for a number of years." Leila told her. "I just never knew about him."

"What do you mean?" Es asked in astonishment as they made their way into the salon area of the women's spa. They were directed into pedicure chairs.

"Do you know my Aunt Iris?" Leila asked.

"No, but I have heard of her. She hasn't been a vampire awfully long, but she has many of the powers of an elder."

"Yes. Well, when she was going through her change, she was resisting it and the last summer of her human year, I was staying with her. Nichola arrived to tell her to get on with it, basically, to stop fighting the change because she was killing herself. He sensed me in the house and realized that I was his mate. He left shortly after and had Mansuetus keep tabs on me for the next several years until I began my transition." Leila explained quickly and simply. She felt she didn't need to give Es too many details.

Es looked at her in disbelief.

"What?" Leila asked.

Es pointed out a color to a woman that came over to them with a selection of nail colors. "And she will take this color." Es said, picking a blood red color and looking at Leila with a smile.

"I don't usually wear nail polish, Es." Leila said.

"I guarantee you it is going to look fabulous with your new dress tonight." Es said. "Take my word for it. I am exceedingly punctilious about matters of fashion."

"Okay." Leila said, nodding at the nail technician. "Now tell me why you gave me such a look."

"It must have been extraordinarily difficult for Nikolaos to let you go, Leila." Es replied softly to her as their technicians filled the chair basins with warm water and did their pedicures.

"Why? I was a twelve-year-old child at the time. There had been some doubt I would survive if he had made off with me," Leila said simply. To her, it made sense.

"Leila, when a vampire is newly mated, it is almost impossible for them to be separated from their mates. After years, yes. Even Rom and I take occasional breaks from each other. Vacations, as you might call it, but never for any great length of time. But, in the beginning, after we first met, it physically hurt me to be separate from him, and I know it hurt him too because I felt his pain along with my own. It must have taken everything that Nikolaos had to not take you into his own house immediately, even if you were still only a human child. He must have only been able to accomplish such a feat of strength due to his great age." Es said with admiration and some amount of pity. "I am not sure many of us would be able to do that. Even if it was in our mate's best interest. We are selfish beings. Usually, we get more selfish as we get older and more powerful. Sometimes so very selfish it is to our own detriment and to those around us. Rom was considered an elder when we met, but he could never have stepped away from me. He wouldn't have had the strength. Nikolaos must value your happiness and well-being highly."

"Do you guys ever argue?" Leila asked as a woman handed her a loaded Bloody Mary complete with a full course of vegetables. She took it automatically and took a sip. It was spicy and delicious.

"All couples argue, Leila!" Es said with a giggle. "Being soul mates doesn't mean that you give up your individuality. Rom and I are totally different in a great many ways. Still, we are the same in many others. Love helps over time."

"Did you love him immediately?" Leila asked with curiosity.

"No. But I wanted him. With everything that I was. Every breath I took, and every part of my being, I wanted him with me. Love came later as I grew to know him, know him as a person. Now, I love him dearly." Es said softly, remembering.

Leila sipped her drink in thoughtful silence.

"Leila, you are beautiful!" Es said in admiration, looking perfectly ethereal in her own ice blue gown. The material had some sort of silver thread weaved throughout it and when she moved, it was as if fairies were throwing stardust around her.

Leila stared at herself in the full-length mirror in the back of the seamstress's shop as the seamstress fussed around her. It was like a beautiful stranger was looking back at her. Her makeup was perfect, and the stylist had curled and dressed her hair back away from her face, highlighting her high cheekbones, and slightly slanted, large, teal-colored eyes. She had then placed a gold leaf branch, hairband on her head like a crown. But the most beautiful thing that she had seen was the gown that she was now wearing. It was remarkably similar to the gown that she always wore when she had first dream-walked to Nichola. Obviously, he had given the seamstress instructions on what to make. The little woman was chatting to her as she was helping her into the gown.

Upon their return to the seamstress, Leila had been shocked to find herself laced into a white silk corset, which pushed her breasts up high and almost overflowing and wearing real silk stockings that were secured by lace garters. The flimsiest and sheerest silk panties had gone on last over the garters and as the soft fabric of the dress had gently flowed over her head she had been thinking, what have I gotten myself into, surely I look like a porn star, and then when she caught the first glimpse of herself in the mirror her mind was stunned into silence.

"I hope that Lord Tsoukalous does not mind the alterations I have made to his description, my lady." The seamstress was saying, tying the blood-red silk shoulder straps on her shoulders with a simple knot and smoothing the ends of the cloth on either side of her shoulders. The majority of the dress itself was a tea-length white silk that was edged in a gold thread with a single modest slit up the front ending just at her knees to make walking easy. The bodice was low and tight, and the blood red silk sash tied beneath her breasts emphasized their curves. "I find men do not understand how fabric must lie over our under garments and sometimes the difference between a gown and a nightgown." She was saying with a smile as she adjusted the blood-red silk train edged in the same gold thread, which ended at the back of her knees and was attached to the shoulders of the dress. "Does this feel too heavy?" She asked Leila looking at her in the mirror's reflection.

"No. It's beautiful." Leila replied, admiring how the dress looked on her. She had never worn anything so beautiful in her entire life, including her own wedding dress when she had gotten married the first time.

The seamstress' assistant was sliding handmade blood-red silk slippers, with just the smallest hint of a heel, onto her stocking feet and crisscrossing the long silk laces around her calves to tie just below her knees.

It was just past seven o'clock by the time that they were finished in the seamstress shop and were making their way back up to Leila's suite. It was almost as if the hotel were waking up, as they noticed several additional members of the staff hurrying about their duties.

"Leila, let me give you some advice." Es said to her seriously and Leila looked at her. "When we get to the suite, resist Nikolaos."

"What do you mean?" Leila said, bewildered.

"He's going to take one look at you and not want to let you leave the suite for dinner." She said, giggling.

Leila started laughing at her in return, saying, "I don't have to be dressed up for that to occur most times. Besides, I am sure that you are going to have the same problem."

"Men, they can be so naughty!" Es said, chuckling.

Both were laughing as they entered the suite to find Nichola and Rom waiting for them. Both men looked sleek and handsome in their plain black tuxedos and crisp white shirts. They stood up as they entered the room.

Eyes widening in surprise, Nichola walked slowly over to and around Leila, taking in everything about her. "Es, what have you done to my Glykó?" There was wonder in his voice as he looked at a beaming Esmerelda.

Taking Leila's hand, which was encased in a blood-red silk, elbow-length, fingerless glove, he brought it up to caress her fingers with his lips. "You are beautiful, my love." His eyes were warm on her.

Leila noticed Rom looked at Es in much the same manner, as she replied, smiling shyly, "Thank you."

"While I understand nothing would be able to enhance your beauty and you are perfect as you are, I have a gift for you." Nichola walked over to the bar picking up and opening a velvet box, bringing it back to her. She looked inside to see a beautiful heart-shaped diamond and ruby necklace in a yellow gold setting. The diamonds sparkled in the light and the large rubies shone with a flame deep within the gemstones.

"It's beautiful, Nichola." Leila whispered.

"Not as beautiful as you are, glukó mou." He whispered in return as he stepped behind her and brought the necklace over her head to fasten behind her neck. The rubies and diamonds soon warmed to her skin as they lay flat against her, just above her breasts. Feeling his hands caress the soft skin of her upper arms, and the heat of his body against her back, he leaned forward to whisper in her ear. She felt his *voice* throughout her body, "If you are tired from your day, we can always order room service and stay in the room." He placed a small kiss against the side of her neck.

Turning her head toward him, she felt him in her mind, trying to influence her. Pushing back on his mind gently, she looked at him out of the corner of her eye, and thought, *If you wanted to stay in, we should have stayed at home. Since we are not at home, I am choosing to look at this trip as a vacation, so I want to go out.*

Blinking twice in surprise, he replied softly, "As you wish."

Entering the large open dining room on Nichola's arm with Es and Rom following behind them, they were approached by a vampire with light brown hair and brown eyes. "Sir. My lady." Addressing them, he bowed to Leila.

"Leila, this is Nelson. He is the majordomo here at the Château. If you need or desire anything this week, Nelson will make it happen." Nichola introduced him to her.

This week?! Leila thought at Nichola furiously but kept her expression neutral and voice calm as she spoke to Nelson. "A pleasure to meet you, sir."

"You also, my lady." He smiled. "I have arranged for your table to be up front and next to the dance floor." Indicating that they follow him.

As he led them through the room, it was like they became the center of attention, and she could feel several dozen pairs of eyes on them. Holding tightly to Nichola's arm, she didn't like the sensation.

Everyone is staring at us. She thought to him self-consciously.

They are dazzled by your beauty. He thought to her in return as she looked at the people around them, seeing many extremely beautiful women in attendance.

Yeah. Disbelief edged her thought. *I don't think that is it, Nichola.*

I am sure that they all know by now that we are mated, Leila. Gossip runs just as quickly through the vampire community as it does through human communities. Es and Rom usually cause quite a stir at first, though usually not at these functions, where they are well known. There are not too many others besides the council members and their retinues here. He thought, assisting her into a seat so that she could see the orchestra, dance-floor, and a good portion of the dining area. *Mated vampires are fairly rare after all, and of course, none of them knows you. So, your presence at my side must be a curiosity.*

And of course, you are 'the King of the Vampires'! Her thought was snarky, and he met her gaze with surprise. *Did Aunt Iris know you were kidnapping me last night?* Leila thought suddenly and sharply.

I didn't kidnap you and God no! He thought in return. *She would have insisted on coming, and Ostrovsky would have been wholly inattentive in our meetings. We have many things to discuss and decisions to be made this week. You may choose that this is a vacation for yourself, but it isn't for me.* His thoughts were sharp in return.

"Well, you two have caused quite a stir!" Es spoke in her bright and happy voice. "At least the attention is not wholly focused on us for once." She giggled, patting Rom's hand.

Rom smiled, bringing her hand to his lips, "I am sure that you are receiving a good amount of admiration tonight, my dove, as you are looking radiant in that dress."

"Well, she is about to be admired much closer than you want, my friend," Nichola murmured and Rom looked up at someone approaching them, to squint his eyes in irritation.

Charles Peake was greeting one and all as he made his way to the table. "Ladies," his smile was smooth. "I hope to obtain both of your hands for the dancing this evening." His cornflower blue eyes twinkled with excitement and admiration.

"Oh, Charles. I would love to dance with you." Es told him, ignoring Rom's jealous look. "Leila, let me recommend Charles to you. He is an excellent dancer."

"My lady's dance card is full tonight, Peake." Nichola growled. Now he understood why Rom was always irritated with the friendly Brit.

"Nichola! Stop that!" Leila told him in admonishment. "I would, of course, love to dance with you, Mr. Peake." She smiled in return.

"I look forward to it! Ladies, sirs, I will leave you to your dinner." He smiled with a small bow, leaving their table to greet others.

Leila looked over at Nichola, who gave her a highly irritated look. "Do not be rude, Nichola." She said softly then thought at him, *You know who I am going home with tonight.*

He stopped glowering at her and leaned over to place a small kiss on the corner of her mouth. "Stop," she whispered, "or you will end up wearing my lipstick." She reached up to run her finger across his bottom lip.

"I don't care." He whispered in return, kissing the tip of her finger.

Leila moved across the dance floor in a slow waltz in the arms of Aleksei Ostrovsky. The vampire was a graceful dance partner.

"I've been told that you recently gave up leadership of the small council, Mr. Ostrovsky." Leila said.

"Aleksei, please. That is due to your aunt's influence, my child. She has shown me the error of my ways. No more spending my eternity on endless bureaucratic nonsense. I will do my part, of course; my duty as an elder. But the leadership position entails so much more effort and time than just a regular council member. It is better suited to a younger, forward-thinking man such as your Nikolaos." He smiled in Nichola's direction. Nichola and Rom were sitting at their table looking decidedly disgruntled as she and Es, who was dancing and laughing with Charles Peake, were on the dance floor. "He is doing very well in the position."

"So, when did you meet my aunt?" Leila asked curiously.

"Ah, the beauteous Lady Iris! Shortly after, she turned. Nikolaos was a member of the small council and since Iris was part of his household at that time, she would attend him when we would meet. Much the same as you and the Lady Es are doing. She spent her days resting or enjoying the amenities of our location and in the evening she would attend dinner and assembly as we are tonight. Such a gracious and lovely lady! She has quite bewitched me. I am actually expecting her to arrive sometime before dawn." He smiled at Leila.

"You are?" Leila asked, surprised.

"Oh, yes. My human assistant received a phone call from her today while the small council was meeting, requesting me to call her. She and I are," here he paused significantly, "particularly good friends. I spoke with her before I came down to dinner. She heard we had an emergency session this week and as Nikolaos was not answering his phone, to which she is convinced that he was intentionally avoiding her calls, she called me to verify that you were here and safe. She looks on you as a daughter, you know." Leila smiled. "Since she is close, I have sent my car to retrieve her." He said with a smitten smile. "Of course, I have offered my rooms for her use as well." Whispering, his smile turned boyishly devious.

"Aleksei, I am not sure that Nichola will appreciate that." Leila whispered back. "He has just now gotten me all to himself."

"When I was human, I had the experience of a mother-in-law." He told her, chuckling. "The experience will do Nikolaos good." Bowing over her fingers as the music came to a stop. Charles Peake escorted Es back to the table, turning to walk toward them to claim Leila's hand for the next dance. Aleksei whispered, "Just like you dancing with this young man will do him good. After all, a man needs to know that he is not the only one to care about or desire his woman. It keeps him honest." Smiling broadly at her, he placed her hand into Mr. Peake's for another waltz.

Nichola and Leila walked arm and arm slowly along a beautiful garden path just after midnight. The fragrance of the tender exotic plants was heady throughout the night air. The music from the dining room softly serenaded them as stars shone and twinkled like blinking eyes in the sky. "You know I am still angry with you for just bringing me here without asking me." Leila told him in a soft, tired voice.

"I am aware." Nichola replied softly. "I had to be here, and I could not imagine being without you for so long. Thursday was bad enough. This is why I was so bad tempered when you came to me Thursday night." He explained. "That, combined with the subject of our discussion, set me off." He looked at her. "The thought of being without you is...difficult for me. I lived without you for so long, and I've had to share your time not only with the children, but with Iris and Mansuetus. I want you to myself for a few days, and it was also past time to start your education."

"Well, you might as well know Ostrovsky has sent a car for Aunt Iris, and she'll be here by dawn." Leila looked at him sideways to gauge his reaction.

He closed his eyes as if he were counting. "Well, she is not welcome in our suite!" Exclaiming sharply after an emotional battle in which it seemed he had lost.

"Nichola!" Leila replied, shocked.

"I mean it. I intentionally did not tell Iris about the meeting this week. She distracts the hell out of Ostrovsky, and the other council members as well, with the exception of Rom. It's like throwing a bitch in heat amongst the dogs! We have important items to be reviewing, discussing, and solving this week. So, she can stay in her own room, and she can pay her own bills!" He ranted angrily.

"Nichola, stop!" Leila reached down and held his hand, bringing him to a stop on the path. "Ostrovsky says that Iris is going to be staying with him."

"Leila, sometimes your aunt does the most foolish things! Did it never occur to you she might bring the young Dr. Lambert with her? If she does, I can guarantee that Ostrovsky will not want Iris and her lover in his suite. Ostrovsky may seem like a harmless, benevolent gentleman to you, but I guarantee that is not true. He may be civilized now, but that wasn't always the case, and he can be extremely dangerous. Iris's doctor wouldn't last a day before an unfortunate 'accident' occurred. Jealous vampires are nothing to be trifled with, and Ostrovsky is obsessed about Iris." Nichola explained with concern.

"Of course she wouldn't! One, Dr. Lambert has a job. He just can't pick up and go with her. Two, he is human, and I am sorry there is no way that you can look at the people here and not know that there isn't something strange about them. I'm not sure that he could take all of this in so soon after he has realized that Iris is a vampire."

Nichola, who was holding her hands, studying her painted nails curiously, looked into her eyes sharply. "Since when does the good doctor know about vampires?" He demanded.

"Nichola, I think he has known for a while. He planned to tell Iris last night that he knew."

"How do you know this?" Nichola asked softly.

"He and I talked about it. He loves her, I think, and wanted to be honest with her."

"Why didn't you tell me?" His voice was still soft.

"When would I have done that, Nichola? While I was 'sleeping' on the way 'home'? When you were tossing me out of the suite because you had a 'meeting'. I didn't have time to tell you anything." Leila realized he was angry with her.

"Leila, we kill humans who are deemed a threat; to ourselves, to our families, to our community. The good doctor might be dead right now," Nichola told her softly, suddenly pulling her back toward the Château. "I have to call Mansuetus."

"She wouldn't do that, Nichola. Iris is not a killer!" Leila exclaimed with a hint of fear in her voice, skipping to keep up with his longer legs as he gripped her hand tightly, pulling her along.

"Leila, the only vampire in the whole southeast who is not a killer, is you." Nichola said, shaking his head as they hurried back into the Château and to their suite.

Hanging up the phone in their suite, Nichola looked at Leila, who had been watching him from the living room sofa while he spoke with Mansuetus.

"Well?" She asked as he continued looking at her silently. She noticed he was blocking the majority of his thoughts from her. She didn't care! She didn't for one minute believe that Aunt Iris would kill Dene!

"He hasn't seen or heard from her today." Nichola replied softly, thinking.

"Is that good or bad?" Leila asked.

"I don't know." Nichola stated.

"Well, Aleksei said that she'd been trying to call you. Didn't you receive any messages from her?"

"No. What if she was trying to tell me she had, accidentally or otherwise, killed the doctor?"

"She wouldn't." Leila replied tiredly seeing Nichola look at her with sympathy. "I am serious, Nichola. She wouldn't. Aunt Iris really likes Dene. She wouldn't kill him."

"Come." He commanded, holding his hand out to her. "We are going to bed. Do not worry anymore tonight. Mansuetus will go to the doctor's home tomorrow to investigate." Nichola led her into the bedroom, turned her around and started to undress her.

"He can't take the kids to investigate whether Dene is dead! What if he finds his body?" Leila half turned to him in concern.

He turned her back around to finish unfastening her.

"He wouldn't. You forget my team is in town. He will call on them to stay with the children. The boys will love it. It will be like having new visitors to the house." Nichola soothed with confidence, helping her to remove her dress and taking it to hang in the closet.

When he returned, he didn't have his jacket, pants, cuff links or bow tie on and was unbuttoning his shirt when he noticed Leila sitting on the sofa bent over untying and unwinding the long silk laces of one of her red slippers from her calves. His gaze fell on how her breasts were trying to spill over the top of her corset.

Looking up, she came face-to-face with him as he knelt before her, looking at her with eyes that burned into her soul.

"Let me help you." His voice was gentle as he took the laces from her hands to finish removing the slipper from her stockinged foot. Taking her other leg in his hands, he untied those laces as well, while she sat back and reached up to her hair to gently remove the delicate, gold, leaf and branch headband and place it on the end table next to the sofa. He watched her intently as she moved.

Removing her other slipper, he stood to look down on her and finished removing his shirt, pulling it from his body to stand before her in his black silk boxers. Her gaze flowed up his muscled abdomen and chest to look at him. "I am going to need your help with this corset." Leila told him breathlessly.

Reaching down, he took her by the hands, pulling her up against him, holding her lightly as he led her to the bed. Turning towards the bed, presenting her back to him, she expected him to untie her laces, instead she felt his lips on her shoulder and his hands on her hips slipping her panties from her. He slowly bent her forward to rest on the bed, keeping her feet on the floor. She gasped as she felt his lips on her from behind. Suddenly she found herself on her back and he was looking down at her with interest. Flushing with embarrassment, she tried to cover herself with her hands.

He moved her hands out of the way to study her.

"Nichola, stop it!" She whispered, mortified by his interest.

"Did you do this for me?" He asked, simply running a finger against her.

"No!" She gasped out. His touch was intensified against her smooth, almost hairless skin.

"Ah. I see. You did this for yourself." He whispered, stroking her lightly again, causing her to squirm in desire. "Well, let me see if I like it as well." He said, kneeling between her legs to put his mouth on her.

She couldn't. She just couldn't cum anymore. He was killing her.

He climbed up her body to kiss her mouth, and she tasted herself on his lips. He breathed almost as heavily as she did. "Yes, I have decided that I like it also, but mostly I like it when you scream your release." Chuckling softly in her ear, he guided her hand to him. "Make me cum, i psychí mou."

"You still need to help me get out of this corset." She stroked him, causing him to groan.

"I love your corset." He gasped as she continued to stroke him. He rolled her on top of him to straddle his body and sat up with her to kiss the tops of her breasts as she slid down on him. "Mmmmm." He moaned into her skin. "And I love your garters and your stockings, and the silkiness of your skin and how you feel against me."

"You do?" She asked sweetly clasping him to her as she slid up and down the length of him.

"Yes." He gasped, holding her close as she moved. "Oh, god, yes."

"What else, Nichola? What else do you love about me?" She whispered in his ear as she felt herself react to his desire, causing her muscles to grip him tightly.

"I love your scent and I love the way you feel when I am inside you like this," he gasped. "There, Moró. Right there." She threw her head back as she felt him grow harder and continued to ride him. "God, I love how tight you get just before you cum, and I love how you taste." He whispered against her shoulder, and she felt the tips of his fangs on her skin.

Feeling her body squeeze him tightly over and over in orgasm, he suddenly realized that she wanted, no needed, something more from him. He gently pierced her shoulder with his fangs as he came inside of her, and when he felt her bite down on him in response, he was lost.

Nikolaos

CHAPTER THREE

O PENING HER EYES SLOWLY, Leila noticed that somewhere in the night Nichola had removed her corset, garters, and stockings to leave her naked between the sheets. She looked to his side of the bed, panicking when she found it empty.

Hearing the water running in the open bath area where the dual vanities were, she realized he was in there. Obviously, he was not injured since he was up and moving around. Still, she felt the need to check on him, to touch him, to see if he was okay. Sitting up, she looked to see if he had put something on the end of the bed for her to wear; she saw her robe, which looked freshly laundered. Putting it on, she headed into the vanity area to see him shirtless and shaving at the sink.

Watching, she was surprised that he was using an antique, mother-of-pearl handled straight razor to shave with. He saw her in the mirror's reflection, smiled at her, then continued to finish shaving. "Why do you use that to shave with instead of a modern razor?" She asked when he was done.

"I get a closer shave with this; besides, it takes skill to use one of these. I keep it a hell of a lot sharper than a modern razor." Wiping his face with a towel, he cleaned the razor.

Walking closer to him, she saw the small teeth marks still on his shoulder and she closed her eyes in shame. "I am so sorry, Nichola. Are you alright?" She whispered. "Why haven't they healed?"

"I'm not sure why they haven't healed totally. You're new, your saliva probably isn't changed enough yet, or it is affecting my own healing abilities." Calmly looking at her via the mirror. "I could obviously heal them myself with my own saliva, but I have decided to attend the small council meeting shirtless and wear them as a badge of honor." His smile was wicked!

"Nichola, you are not funny!" She exclaimed angrily, but really upset with herself.

"Oh, i psyhí mou! I am a little funny, yes?" He teased, turning too quickly for sight to pull her against him as she turned from him to stomp off in pique. "Glykó, do not be upset. Your fangs are small, and the damage is minimal. Besides, after the initial shock, you know I loved it." He bent, placing little butterfly kisses against her temple; picking her up to sit her on the edge of the granite counter, positioning himself between her legs. "You know, I just realized that I have never made love to you in a bathroom." He groaned huskily capturing her mouth with his and running his hands over her bare legs.

"Leila!" They heard Iris call loudly from the living area, followed by Ostrovsky's murmured response.

"I know you love your aunt Leila, but I really want to kill her right now." He whispered as he stepped back from her so that she could get off the vanity.

Leila was slightly frightened to realize that he did not say this in jest.

"I will find out what she wants." Leila straightened and retied her robe. "Put a shirt on." She threw back over her shoulder as she left the bedroom.

Walking into the living room, Leila heard Ostrovsky say to her aunt, "Moy golub', they are a young couple, you could be disturbing something important."

"I have spent days in the same house with them. I am aware of what they do for most of the day." Iris replied with a sexy smile.

"Aunt Iris!" Leila exclaimed. "What are you doing here?"

"That's an extremely good question." Nichola said irritably following her out of the bedroom, buttoning his shirt. "A better question is, how did you get into this suite?" He asked, fixing Iris with a stern look.

"The front desk knows we are family." Iris replied sweetly, producing a room key. Walking over, Nichola took it from her, slipping it into his pants pocket. "And I am checking on my niece, since you never made it home on Friday night, and no one said anything about a trip." Quickly stepping away from him, Iris gave Leila a hug. "Aleksei tells me that the small council is scheduled for meetings and interviews all day. You and I should enjoy the facilities." Leila saw Iris was wearing a black silk robe and matching slippers that set off her dark beauty and light golden skin.

"That's a good idea, Auntie. Since I didn't pack anything, I have very few things to wear. I didn't have a chance to go to the clothing store here yesterday. Maybe we could stop in there after we have breakfast." Leila led her out the door, turning to look at Nichola and Aleksei. "We will see you gentlemen later. Have a productive day."

Nichola fixed Aleksei with an irritated look. "You know I can resist her nothing, my friend." The older vampire explained with a shrug of his shoulders. "She is staying in my suite, and I have every intention of keeping her occupied when we are not meeting." Nichola continued to stare at him. "I give you my word to remain attentive during our conferences. I am aware of the important nature of our decisions this week." Aleksei smiled.

Nichola finally shook his head, smiling fondly at the old vampire. "Please call down and have something sent up from room service, my friend, while I finish getting dressed, and if you don't mind give Rom a call and see if he can send Es downstairs to keep an eye on Leila and Iris, before Iris leads my mate astray."

"Did you kill Dr. Lambert, Aunt Iris?" Leila whispered as the waiter left to put in their order.

"Why would you ask that?" Iris did not meet her eyes.

"Why aren't you just answering me?" Leila asked loudly in panic, then glanced around as she noticed several robed women looking in their direction. "Are you running away from what you have done?" She whispered, heartbroken.

"Leila, I didn't kill him." Iris's voice was soft. "But I might be running a little bit."

"Aunt Iris, what did you do?" Leila was concerned. "Did you hurt him?" Iris wouldn't look at her. "You need to tell me, Aunt Iris. Mansuetus is going to check on him today. He needs to know what he is going to be walking into."

Iris' eyes filled with tears as she looked down into her lap. "He's not injured, but I bit him very deeply. I also pumped him full of venom. I didn't mean to; I had little control over what I was doing. The situation was so wild. I felt so good and so strong, and he was so delicious." Shaking her head, remembering, as a tear overflowed her eye to roll down her cheek. "I healed the bite. But he was unconscious most of the day. He regained consciousness for a little while last night before I left. But he didn't look good. I am afraid, Leila." Her voice trembled.

"Damn." Leila quietly stood up. "Stay here. I will be back." Looking up, she saw Es approaching the table. "Thank God. Es this is my Aunt Iris. Aunt Iris, this is my friend Es. Es, I have to talk to Nichola. It's an emergency. Please make sure that my aunt gets some blood and stay here with her. I will be back in a moment." She clutched Es' hand. "I am sorry for imposing. Thank you."

"Nonsense. Go." Es waved to the waiter as she sat down next to Iris.

Opening the door to find out who was pounding on it, Nichola was surprised to see Leila.

"Why don't I have a key?" She demanded with panic-stricken eyes.

Pulling the key that he had taken from Iris out of his pocket, he gave it to her.

She gripped it tightly, desperately. "You need to call Mansuetus. He needs to get over to Dene's house right away."

"Come." He told her gently, putting his arm around her to lead her to the bedroom. Leila noticed Rom and Ostrovsky sitting at a table, drinking something out of coffee cups and reading over documents. They glanced up briefly before going back to the papers in front of them. "What has happened?" Nichola asked, closing the door behind them. He picked up the bedroom phone to start dialing.

"Aunt Iris bit him. She says that she bit him bad, but she healed his injury. She says that she injected him with her venom. A lot of it. He barely regained consciousness last night before she left. She's very worried about him."

Closing his eyes briefly Nichola started relaying the message as soon as Mansuetus answered the phone. He paused to listen. "Yes, I am sure that will be fine. I will be in my meeting but will have my cell phone with me. Keep me informed." Hanging up the phone, he looked at Leila. "Your friend Jackie is there. He will leave immediately to check on the doctor. She will watch the children until he is able to return. Where is Iris now?"

"She's in the dining room with Es."

"Fine. Keep her with you and keep her busy. I will connect with you when Mansuetus reports in."

Looking at him in shock, Leila told him, "I am sorry. I didn't even think to contact you that way. I just needed you." Her voice soft as Nichola pulled her into his arms and she held him tightly in return. "Do you think he is okay?" She whispered with a small, frightened catch to her voice.

"Let us pray he is." Nichola replied in a troubled whisper as he gently kissed the top of her head.

Leila got back down to the dining room as her breakfast was arriving. Iris had composed herself and was sipping a small glass of blood while she chatted with Es.

Surprisingly, Iris and Es got along famously. Which is not always the case when extremely beautiful women meet each other for the first time. But they were on the opposite ends of the spectrum of beauty. One light and angelic, the other dark and devilish. As is often the case, opposites attract. Iris was also very curious about soul mates, having only been around Nichola and Leila, and so was asking Es about her experiences.

As the women chatted, Leila silently ate her breakfast. Troubled about Dene and whether or not he was okay, and how her aunt could behave so calmly as if nothing were occurring. She looked up in surprise to see Nelson, the vampire majordomo at the Château approaching their table.

"Lady Tsoukalous, good morning. I have a message from the seamstress that she will need to see you before the morning is out for a final fitting if you would be so kind to drop in at your convenience."

"Oh, thank you, Nelson." Leila replied as he bowed and left.

She looked at the other two women.

"Lady Tsoukalous?" Iris asked with a roll of her eyes.

"He is her mate. She deserves the title." Es, suddenly becoming a very proper British vampire, said simply while she ate her strawberry crepes.

"I didn't even know I had an appointment at the seamstress today." Leila told them, bewildered.

"Nikolaos has probably ordered you a whole trousseau. He is very generous with you." Es replied.

"Yes, I had noticed that." Iris, pointedly looking at Leila's ruby and diamond necklace, which she still wore around her neck, smiled. "That must have put him back a mint."

Blushing in response, Leila touched the beautiful necklace with affection.

Pushing a small plate at Iris, Es said, "Iris, try this ham. It is to die for." Iris glanced at it and made a face. "Iris, eating helps with the blood-lust." Es told her.

"It does?" Iris, who had been clutching her empty glass like a lifeline, asked, looking at Es.

"Oh, yes. For the first twenty years of my vampire existence, I subsisted on nothing but blood. The more I had, the stronger the addiction became. At that time, I drank nothing but human blood, and could never get enough. I was a monster." Es' voice was simple and emotionless, as if she were reading aloud an encyclopedia on a subject that bored her. "When Nichola and Rom found me, they helped me. Eating food helps me maintain control when I do drink blood. It is not like it is going to make us fat," she gave a small laugh, "and besides, the chef here is exceptionally good."

Looking at the ham, Iris picked it up with her fingers, taking a small bite. Closing her eyes, she chewed slowly.

Leila waved the waiter over to the table, smiling at Es gratefully.

The ladies went to the seamstress for Leila's fitting after a breakfast in which Iris tried almost everything on the breakfast menu. Iris decided to also be fitted for a gown. The seamstress looked a little haggard, but her attitude improved when Iris told her to charge it to Ostrovsky's suite, promising that it would be ready by seven. The ladies then went to the spa to use the steam room and shower before heading for massages.

Leila was much more comfortable today with her female masseuse. Iris and Es had the two sexy male masseuses from the previous day. As sometimes happens when more than two women get together, the talk invariably turned to men.

"So how long have you known Ostrovsky, Iris?" Es inquired.

"Since my turn, I know many current and former council members." Iris replied importantly.

"Is Ostrovsky the oldest known vampire?" Leila asked.

"No. But he is the oldest vampire that is interested in participating in the direction of the community. I have heard there are several vampires who are older, though I don't know them personally, that have no interest in being involved, either in the large or small councils. Many find the efforts boring or beneath them." Es replied.

"When I first turned, I was part of Nikolaos' household, so I met all the small council members from the last session. I am also friends with the Prince and Beutel. I was also involved with Gervais Milhaud. It is tragic what occurred to him." Iris said.

"How so? Rom knew Milhaud. He was criminally insane, and most likely had been for several years. He killed over seventeen people, in a two-year span, including a six-year-old and a two-year-old, and that's the ones that are known. He didn't even try to cover up the fact that a vampire was committing the crimes. He not only drained them of their blood, but he also had sex with the corpses, then dismembered and ate the bodies. His actions put the whole community in danger!" Es exclaimed, disgusted.

"I knew him intimately. The community didn't even try to rehabilitate him. He was almost eight hundred years old and a member of the small council at the time! They held a special session in that case as well. I know I was here. He wasn't even in attendance. He didn't even get a chance to defend himself!" Iris said, incensed at the supposed injustice of it.

"There were multiple witnesses to at least half the murders. Not just human witnesses, either! There is no rehabilitating anyone who kills, fucks, and eats children. He was a monster!" Es was vehement.

"What are you talking about?" Leila asked sleepily, totally relaxed under her masseuse's ministrations.

"Gervais Milhaud." Iris replied. "He was a French elder on the small council during the last session. He was very polished, handsome, and brilliant in bed. He survived so much of the world's history. Hell, he even survived the Reign of Terror! But he was found guilty of crimes against the community and summarily executed. There wasn't even a trial! The small council decided on its own."

"He went insane and turned into a serial killer, Leila. The evidence against him was staggering. Our society is different from human society. We do not have a trial by jury. Evidence is presented to the small council, and a vote is taken on guilt or innocence. Much never even reaches to the level of the small council as most transgressions are overlooked or covered up. So, in reality, the vampire community has carte blanche to conduct some really heinous activities, at least up to a point. When the crimes are so serious and public that they put our community at risk, the small council steps in with an investigation and a judgment. These crimes were horrific and human authorities were hunting for a serial killer. The last thing that needed to happen was for them to find out about the existence of vampires! Nikolaos and Rom were finally appointed to hunt him down and execute him in February 1979." Es explained.

"I didn't know that Nikolaos was involved with that." Iris said softly.

"Yes. He investigated the murders on behalf of the small council for three years. Starting in 1976. Rom wasn't on the council at the time but was appointed to assist because he is a well-known hunter. Iris, the evidence, was overwhelming. It was like he wanted to get caught, to expose the community! Why do you think Gervais was the only one who didn't turn up to the emergency session of the small council in February 1979? He knew he would be executed, and he ran. It took them six months to track and catch him, but until they caught him, he continued to leave a trail of bodies in his wake. He was sick and needed to be put down!" Es was adamant.

Focusing on her own thoughts while the two women debated over the details of the murders, Leila knew Nichola had not been in a good place mentally when they met in 1977. Maybe investigating such tragic and brutal slayings that were done by someone that he knew and worked with had taken a toll on him?

"Aunt Iris, how many vampire lovers have you had since you became a vampire?" Leila asked out of the blue to turn the conversation away from something other than the details of the grisly killings which had begun to get more morbid and vivid as the women discussed them.

"Leila! What kind of question is that?" Iris asked in return, giving her a stern, shocked look.

"A direct question, Auntie."

"Quite a few," Iris replied, disgruntled.

"Is that normal for vampires?" Leila asked Es.

"Leila!" Iris exclaimed.

"I am curious, Auntie. I need to know these rules."

"Actually, yes," Es explained, looking at Iris.

"Even for mates?" Leila asked softly.

"Well, sex outside of a mated bond could never be considered overly important, could it? But occasionally it happens. It would be dangerous to conduct sexual congress with your mate in residence, though. Jealous vampires are not anything to be trifled with. I know I would become absolutely murderous if Rom flaunted another woman in my presence." Es responded with a dangerous glint in her eyes.

"Are you thinking of taking a lover, Leila?" Iris asked softly. "Are you not satisfied with Nikolaos?"

Leila burst out laughing. "No, Auntie! I am sure that I cannot handle another man in my life at this point."

"One could hardly blame you, my child, if that were the case. I told you he is decidedly a cold fish!" Iris exclaimed.

Es burst out laughing, and both Leila and Iris looked at her in surprise. "That is the farthest from the truth that I have ever heard! Not that I know from personal experience." She quickly said, holding her hands in the air. "But his reputation is legendary!"

"We cannot be talking about the same person, Es. Nikolaos has been worse than a monk since I have known him and that has been for almost twenty years." Iris stated firmly.

"Hmmm," Es thought. "What happened almost twenty years ago?" She asked softly, looking at Leila pointedly.

"He discovered me." Leila answered.

"Yes. Maybe he chose to save himself for you; to be monogamous to his mate?" Es gave her a small smile.

"I told you he was strange!" Iris groaned out in pleasure as her masseuse pummeled her back.

Es and Leila laughed until they cried.

For Leila, the next two days and nights were filled with enjoying the spa treatments, the indoor pool, the wonderful food, beautiful clothes, dancing, and laughter. Aunt Iris flirted with all the small council members, dancing with them all and laughing and whispering suggestively with each of them. Only Rom was immune to her charms. Nichola was torn by her actions. On the one hand, he was irritated because her outrageous behavior was such a distraction, but on the other, her behavior kept the other vampires focused on her and from trying to manipulate Leila's time.

Ostrovsky always watched her good-naturedly in a self-assured manner. But Nichola was right about one thing. It was like throwing in a bitch in heat amongst the dogs. The Prince, Beutel, and Peake were all over her. But clearly, Ostrovsky had a claim on her, and the other council members gave him a wide berth when he claimed her at the end of each evening to escort her to his suite.

If Leila hadn't known that these creatures were vampires, she wouldn't have seen much difference in their behavior than any other group of people enjoying themselves at a resort. If a person were to look closely, they might notice some strangeness. Like the way they held themselves, sometimes in the most still manner, their utterly graceful way of moving that would put a ballerina to shame, the way they spoke, as if it were in some archaic language, in which they had their own manners, customs, and rules. Which, given everything, she supposed was true. Leila was amazed that they could be so different from humans and yet so much the same.

Making love each night, she woke up each morning in Nichola's arms, feeling more loved than she ever had in her life. Leila strongly resisted the urge to bite him. He, understanding her mood, refrained from tempting her by biting her also, as if they had an unspoken agreement that until she was comfortable with what she was becoming, they wouldn't rush it. The bite marks on his body were healed. The only evidence of their existence left behind were four small round white scars on the tan of his skin.

The small council's business was expected to be completed on Wednesday and Nichola told her they would be driving home as soon as the sun sank. Which, even though she had enjoyed herself, she was happy about. She missed her children and was worried about Dene and upset that Iris didn't seem to be.

According to Mansuetus, Dr. Lambert was alive and 'functioning', but kept showing up every evening to ask when Iris would be returning. Nichola, point blank, told Iris that he expected her to return with them when they left on Wednesday evening. The words were not direct enough to be an order, but both Leila and Iris recognized the authority behind it, and Iris acquiesced to his statement with a slight nod.

On Tuesday afternoon, while she, Es, and Iris lounged around the indoor pool area, Leila felt Nichola in her mind. *Leila, I want to take you on a tour tonight of the Château grounds. Just you and I.*

Do you want me to meet you in the suite? She thought in return.

No. At sunset, meet me in the gazebo in the center of the gardens. I will come to you.

But Nichola, I am in my swimsuit. I will need to change. It might be cold.

I promise you; the night will be beautiful. He thought at her in return. *As long as you come alone.*

So now you control the weather? She thought to him in a disbelieving tone.

Maybe. He thought in return, and she could feel his humor.

It was dark, and the night was warm, as Leila sat in the gazebo wrapped in her robe over her swimsuit, simple leather sandals that she had purchased in the clothing store on her feet. She wondered where Nichola was. Suddenly, the lights amongst the plants in the garden came on and it was as if she was sitting in the middle of a fairy forest. The small lights were of different colors: white and muted yellows, blues, and pinks.

She saw him walking toward her on one of the flagstone paths, dressed in a loose-fitting three-quarter sleeve white shirt and long white pants. Casual brown sandals were on his feet. The white material of the casual outfit stood stark against his tanned skin, and as she watched him walk toward her, she realized how very human he looked this evening.

Standing up, she smiled at him in greeting, meeting him at the entrance to the gazebo.

Pulling her into his arms, he kissed her fiercely, surprising her, as she clung to him in response. He seemed unusually vulnerable this evening as she cuddled him.

When he pulled away, she asked softly, "Did you have a bad day?"

"I don't want to talk about it." He murmured in response. "I just want to be here with you." He kissed her again, this time more gently. When he finally pulled back, her body was responding to him, and her heart was thundering in her chest. Smiling knowingly at her, he took her hand, pulling her out of the gazebo and down another path.

After the third turn, she laughed. "This is like a maze. I am not sure that I could find my way back out."

He smiled at her. "As long as you are with me, you will never be lost."

They came upon a side path which opened up to a private alcove in the plants. The alcove was dimly lit, and there was a small table set with food and wine.

"Nichola, this is so beautiful!" Leila exclaimed as she suddenly realized that the alcove was set in glass panels and behind the panels were more of the tiny lights.

Holding her chair for her as she sat down, he stroked his hand over her shoulder before he took his own seat. Reaching into a basket next to the table, he came up holding a single long-stem red rose. Presenting it to her, he murmured gently, "It isn't as beautiful as you are, but it is beautiful nonetheless."

"It is beautiful, thank you, Nichola." Smiling as she took it from him to breathe deep of its heady fragrance. "I thought vampires were supposed to be repelled by roses?"

"There are so many superstitions about us. Foolish superstitions made up by humans over the centuries, hoping to ward us away. Could you imagine the panic if they realized that little to nothing that they thought protected them truly did?" He started putting food onto her plate. Cold shredded chicken, red seedless grapes, tangerines, sliced beets. Picking up a grape, he popped it into his mouth.

Surprised by his action, she watched him as she started to eat. "Well, I know now that some of you do eat. Es eats all the time, and she says that Rom is mad about chocolate."

"Yes. I don't know what about it drives him to crave it; I personally don't have a taste for it."

"Es has convinced Aunt Iris to eat. She told her it helps with the blood-lust. Aunt Iris has been eating everything in sight ever since."

"Iris shouldn't be on her own yet. She is powerful, but uncontrolled. She is going to have to move back into my household. She just doesn't know it yet. She needs to be around an elder to learn to harness her darker nature." He said, eating a tangerine slice.

"Does it help with the blood-lust?" She asked softly watching him carefully. He never ate when it was just the two of them together. Knowing something was off, but unsure what it was, she realized she was wholly unable to read him.

"Some," He replied, picking up and eating some of the shredded chicken with his fingers.

"Well, I know the mirror thing isn't true either." Nervous, she tried to change the subject.

"No. But the film is. At least for some of us. I can be filmed. Which is important why I never should be. Could you imagine the problems if someone saw pictures of me from one hundred years ago? But made vampires like Es are unable to be filmed. At least clearly. A picture of her would be blurred or unfocused." He poured her some sweet wine.

"Do you know why?"

"Because she wasn't born to be a vampire." Looking at Leila's raised, inquiring eyebrow, he continued. "We and others of our bloodline, and several bloodlines the world over, are born to be vampires. We are essentially a different branch of humanity. If humans are homo sapiens-sapiens, maybe we would be termed homo sapiens vampiris? Es is a human who has had her DNA altered, or overwritten, by vampire DNA.

Sticklers, like someone I once knew who is no longer alive, considered made vampires to be mutts of our species, barely vampire at all, and worthy of killing. Of course, that is a ridiculous and prejudicial way of thinking. Es is every bit a vampire and just as dangerous as Iris is." He ate more chicken. "But I believe that the reason why made vampires are unable to be clearly filmed is because their cells are not truly frozen in time, the way yours and mine are. Es has changed over the years, quite a bit actually. Not older per se, but different physically. I have changed truly little. It has taken me almost a thousand years to have a bit of creases around my eyes when I laugh." He smiled, eating another grape.

"So, are you saying that you don't think that Es is immortal like a born vampire?"

"No. I am not saying that. I say that I don't know. But I suspect that her lifespan may not be as long as ours."

"Well, who's to say, right? Who's to say that born vampires are immortal? What is immortal anyway? Vampires die. They can be killed." Leila stated.

"That is true." He expressed soberly, eating another piece of tangerine, obviously thinking about something that bothered him.

She watched him intently. "So, what else?" He focused on her. "What else is superstition? Aunt Iris says that a stake through the heart is not superstition. But garlic is just a superstition."

"Yes. Most things die with a stake through their heart. Just as beheading kills all things." He agreed, looking at her.

She suddenly saw something move awfully close to the glass. She turned her head to come eye to golden eye with a large black panther. "Oh, my gosh." She whispered in wonder as the big cat put its nose against the glass, fogging it slightly as it breathed out.

"I wondered if he would make an appearance tonight." Nichola said softly. "This is Samson. He is the menagerie's black jaguar."

"He's magnificent." Leila whispered, placing her hand on the glass and the big cat rubbed his head against the glass as if he wanted her to pet him. "Oh. He's like an overgrown Gladiator." She smiled.

"Hardly." Nichola said. "I am sure that your cat would never try to eat you. I can't say the same about Samson. No matter how tame he looks. That's why he is on the other side of the glass. Looks can deceive, it is a lesson you must always remember."

"I know that Nichola." She told him, pointedly looking at him.

He cleared his throat. "Come. Let's walk to the beach." He stood, holding out his hand to her.

Holding hands, they walked down the path. "How many vampire sanctuaries are there? How many do you own?"

"You think that this is a sanctuary?" He asked, looking down at her.

"Isn't it? It caters to vampires and the humans that work here know about vampires. Isn't that what you intend it to be?" Leila asked. "Did you not want me to know?"

"It's one of my business ventures. Not all of my business ventures cater to vampires." He explained.

"Is this the only hotel that you own?"

"No. I have one in London, Greece, near to my ancestral home, Egypt, and India, close to the Burmese border. I am sorry, Myanmar. But, frankly, it will always be known as Burma to me, and another in Bangkok. I have plans to open another in Peru in the next two years."

"I didn't realize that there would be so many," Leila mused.

"There was no reason for you to." He said simply. "They run themselves without much interference from myself. They have exceptionally good majordomos in charge of each one. All of them are part of our bloodline. We rotate the small council meetings between them. So, I am in attendance for at least a week most years. Emergency meetings such as this one are usually held wherever I am closest. That is why we are here in Ponce Inlet this week."

"Nelson is a relative?" Leila asked.

"An English cousin." Nichola stated, "and one of my first 'projects'." He smiled.

"What does that mean?"

"You know, Mansuetus has been tracing our bloodline and keeping track of potential vampires. Nelson was one of the first that Mansuetus found. He lived in England and turned two hundred and fifty years ago. I was practicing medicine in England at the time."

"So, what is it like to be King of the Vampires?" She laughed, and he did not look amused.

"You said that to me the other night and I can only tell you it isn't true! I simply lead the small council. I am no King! I would not wish to be a King." He said, irritated.

"Oh, Nichola." Leila giggled, hugging his arm. "I am just teasing you."

"Leading the small council is a pain in the ass!" He voiced with irritation.

"Nichola!" Leila was surprised. He rarely cussed unless he was throwing her own words back at her in an argument.

"Seriously, Glykó. I totally understand why Ostrovsky stepped down. Beutel is power hungry, and Peake is just a puffed-up idiot. The Prince, though he is considered an elder, is a dilettante. Rom and I end up doing the bloody work, just like last session!" He growled in genuine anger.

"Like with Gervais Milhaud?" She asked softly.

He looked sharply at her. "Who told you about Gervais?"

"It was a topic of discussion between Es and Aunt Iris."

He sighed.

Walking around a hedge corner, they came to a small stretch of beach that was no more than seventy-five yards wide and protected from prying eyes by large rock formations on either side. The moonlight flashed off the waves of the ocean. Nelson was there, had a small fire built and lounge chairs set up, and another basket.

"Hello, Nelson." Leila smiled in greeting.

"My lady, sir." Nelson smiled in return. "Unless you require anything else, I will check on our guests."

"Nelson, would you see that this makes its way back to our suite, please?" Leila held out her rose to him.

"Absolutely, my lady." He took it from her.

"Thank you, Nelson." Nichola sat down in a chair to rummage in the basket.

Leila sat next to him. "So, tell me about Gervais." Her voice was gentle.

Nichola busied himself with opening another bottle of wine. "We were friends for over four hundred years." He stated quietly. "He was funny, fearless, highly intelligent and very reckless. Women loved him. Your aunt adored him!"

"She said as much. She defended him and was outraged about his sentence by the council."

"Iris can be a fool. There is no defending what Gervais had become." Nichola poured her a glass of wine and drank from the bottle.

Leila was shocked to see him like this. "What happened?" Leila asked.

"About 50 years ago, Gervais met a young human girl. No more than thirteen. He knew right away, like I did with you, that she was his mate.

Unlike myself, he chose to take her away in the night." He stopped talking to stare into the flames of the fire. "I can't describe to you the need, the desire, the blood-lust that I felt for you the first time that I held you in my arms. There are no words. My blood boiled with an insanity to become one with you. If it hadn't been for Mansuetus, I would have taken your small body in more ways than just sexual. I wouldn't have intended to hurt you, but it definitely would have been rape. As you know, I prayed to God to stop me. That you understood my prayer made me pause, but still my control was all but shredded when Mansuetus arrived. If not for him, our fate may have been the same as Gervais and his mate."

"He killed her?" Leila gasped.

"Oh, no. Not directly. She was a child. Like you were. Children are not meant to be taken in such a way. Nor drank from. Nor kidnapped and removed from their family. She was much like you and totally un-aware of the vampire world. She was terrified. The thing that separated you and she was that when I discovered you, I originally thought that you were a vampire. You had abilities that were vampire-like. You were able to read me, you felt my emotions, you knew what I was thinking, you understood me regardless of language. I can't tell you how unusual that is for a human, mate or not. Gervais' mate, being wholly human and so far away from even beginning to transition, did not recognize him. So, while he recognized her, and wanted her and needed her with everything that he was, he also terrified her. Her fear of him did not sway him. He was not patient with her."

"How could he not be? You are extremely patient with me," Leila whispered.

"I have been watching you for seventeen years, Leila. I know you. Even though I am still relatively a stranger to you, I know you very well. It is sometimes difficult, but I want to be patient with you. I want to spoil you because I love you." He paused in realization. Looking at her with soft amber eyes, "I psychí mou, my soul, I love you," he declared, pausing again almost surprised with his sudden revelation, "I haven't said that to a woman in over 900 years, and I have never meant it as I do now." He bent his head and possessed her lips tenderly. Looking at her as she remained mute, surprised at his intensity and sincerity, unsure of what to say to him. He smiled at her in understanding.

"But in the beginning, it wasn't love," he continued. "It was want, need, desire, blood-lust, only much more than all of that. Much how you feel about me." Here she blushed. "None of those feelings includes patience, does it?" She shook her head no. "Gervais was not patient either with his human mate. Instead of allowing her to grow to know him, or mature, he forced himself on her day after day, and though he tried extremely hard not to bite her, when her monthly menses came he could not help himself and he fed on her."

"How do you know all of this?" Leila asked.

"I was his friend Leila, and after his mate took her own life, his confessor."

Leila put her hand over her mouth in shock. "Oh, no! She killed herself!"

"Unfortunately, yes. I think he had her with him for almost six months before she found a way to end what to her must have been torture, being trapped with a creature, a creature out of her nightmares, who she didn't understand and who didn't care enough for her to understand how frightened she was of him. Someone who would rape her day after day, and drink of her every month. A creature that she could find no escape from."

"Is this what made him into a killer?" Leila asked.

"He was already a killer a thousand times over before he met his mate, Leila. I keep telling you that you are the only vampire, probably in this hemisphere, that isn't a killer. That includes me and your aunt." His voice was sharp. She looked at him with wide, frightened eyes and he sighed deeply, continuing in a softer tone. "I am sorry. Her death set Gervais on a course to madness. He was looking at an eternity of being alone. We only have one mate, Leila, ever. Not only was Gervais' mate dead, but she was dead by her own hand in order to escape from him because he could not wait for her to mature and to come to him in her own time. He didn't protect her, even from himself." He stared into the fire again. "He let his guilt and shame drive him insane."

"And he killed seventeen people." Leila whispered.

Nichola laughed bitterly. "That's what the community knows, Leila. He killed well over five hundred people and other vampires throughout many countries from 1944 until 1979, before we sentenced him to death."

"What?!" She exclaimed appalled.

"Gervais was an elder of the community, a member of the small council. Much of what he did was covered up." He told her, looking at her seemingly without guilt or shame.

"The small council covered up his crimes? Why?" She asked outraged.

"Because as individuals, vampires are autocratic. We usually take no account of other people's wishes, opinions, or rules in our day-to-day activities. Humans mean little to nothing other than a food source for most of our kind. Things get complicated and bloody when disputes occur between vampires and in order to keep conflict from arising between our kind and bringing it to the notice of the human authorities, the large, and small councils were created. There are minor rules and laws that we have created for self-governance and control over our baser emotions, and minor punishments, which usually include fines. But as a community, we have one cardinal rule. A vampire's actions will not put the community at risk of discovery. A vampire who continuously breaks this rule faces death.

Gervais made several mistakes, he got sloppy in his killings of humans, there was no attempt to cover-up that the killings were committed by a vampire, it attracted the attention of federal agencies and Interpol. Then he killed young, unprotected vampires, made vampires at first, but then even born vampires were not spared. Actually, your aunt is probably lucky to have escaped Gervais when I think about it. She was probably spared because she was part of my household when they met and conducted their activities. She was never truly on her own with him. I was always in residence. He also liked her very much. She seems to have a knack for bringing out the best in others, at least vampires. He seemed better around her; less mad. I am also sure that he knew if he would have harmed one of my fledglings under my protection, I would have killed him outright, without sanction of the small council, as would have been my right to do so.

But, then he started to kill children. We don't kill children. Since the knowledge of how we become what we are, through bloodlines, is widely known throughout the community, we would never know if we were killing off our future. Unlike adults, children are innocent of offense. We do not kill children. This is sacrosanct amongst our community."

"But he did horrible things to people. Es said that he drained his victims, had sex with their corpses and then ate them! You guys just let him go on doing that until he killed children?" Leila interrupted, appalled that the community had let him go on for so long.

"The savagery of his actions was not considered in his sentence of death. He had exposed the community one time too many, had tried to thin our ranks through his actions of genocide, and had killed children. This brought him a death sentence." Nichola said sharply, drinking deep from the bottle.

"And you and Rom killed him?" Leila asked softly, knowing he would hear her over the crashing waves.

"Rom and I hunted him for six months. He knew what was coming. It's why he didn't show up to the emergency session of the council. Following the trail of corpses that he left, we caught up to him in Istanbul. It was the last leg of his game." Nichola finished the bottle and reached for another.

"His game?"

"He wanted us to catch him. He wanted us to kill him. He had been increasing his atrocities for a decade, trying to get us to sentence him to death. He felt he deserved it. In the end, he was right, he did." Nichola opened the bottle of wine and drank deep. "So, I killed my friend. I cut his head off and burned his body to cover up the murder. But, in the end, it was a mercy killing."

Leila kneeled before him and tried to take the bottle out of his hand.

He just moved it to his other hand and pulled her against him.

"You know this won't do you any good." She said, indicating the bottle.

"It won't do me any harm, either. It won't make me drunk much, anyway." He said, nuzzling her cheek with a soft kiss.

"Really?" Doubt in her voice. "Then continue on with my education on vampires." He rolled his eyes. "If mirrors, roses, garlic, and holy water don't work, how does a human tell if we are a vampire?" Leila asked.

"When we feed on them?" He chuckled as if he were answering a riddle, drinking deeply from the bottle again.

"Nichola! I am serious. Es says that elders have super speed, can shape-shift, and can fly. I have seen how fast you are. Can you shape-shift? Can you fly?" She asked, taking his face in her hands to get him to pay attention to her.

He focused on her; his eyes were tinged with red.

"Shape-shifting is difficult for us all. When I change, I can't make myself smaller or larger than I already am, size wise in any case."

357

"What do you mean?"

"Well, I weigh approximately one hundred and eighty pounds. So, I shift into a wolf, but it is a one-hundred-and-eighty-pound wolf. That is an exceptionally large wolf and would be quite noticeable."

"Oh. Do you know what you are doing when you become an animal?" She asked him curiously as he finished off the bottle of wine.

"Do you mean, do I retain my highly intelligent vampire mind while in animal form?" She looked at him skeptically at his tone. "The answer would be yes." He reached into the basket again, coming up with a third bottle. She looked in the basket next to him to see three more bottles. "Would you like me to take off my clothes and transform into a wolf?" He asked, opening the bottle to drink some more. "Are you looking for something bestial tonight?" His tone was suggestive.

"Don't be ridiculous." She stated, taking the bottle. He gave her an irritated look, but didn't try to fight her for it. "Can you fly?" She asked him, leaning on his legs as he sat back in his chair to look at her.

"Yes. When you refused to move into my house, that is how I got back and forth between our two houses. I would come and watch you sleep." He said softly leaning forward to put his forehead against hers. "Except for the first night, you never knew that I was there. I could have done so many things to you if I were inclined to do so, my sweet changeling." He touched her face tenderly. "I will fly for you in exchange for..." He paused, considering.

"In exchange for what?" She asked excitedly.

"That you then allow me to change into a wolf and let me have my wolfy way with you?" He threw his head back, laughing.

"Nichola! What is wrong with you tonight?" She asked, aghast.

"I psychí mou. After almost a thousand years, there are not many things that I haven't done. Having sex in my animal form is one of them. You can be my first. I believe you would enjoy it. My tongue in wolf form is exceptionally long." He told her, trying to be persuasive only to end up laughing and holding her tightly as she made a noise of outrage and hit him on the arm. He sighed deeply as if disappointed. "So, virginal, tsk, tsk."

"What is wrong with you tonight?" She repeated after a moment as he held her close to him.

"The council is going to vote tomorrow on an order of execution. It is going to pass. It needs to pass. Then I am going to have to execute another one of our people. I am only tired of being the executioner." He rested his head on her shoulder, despondent.

"Then make one of the others do it. Have Beutel do it. You don't like him, anyway." She said simply.

"He would probably get himself killed." He murmured against her, stroking her back.

"Better him than you. Besides, you don't like him, good riddance." She whispered in his ear.

"You are so bloodthirsty and wicked, agápi mou." He chuckled lightly.

"Not wicked enough to have sex with you in your wolf form. Just remember that." She giggled softly, holding him and running her fingers through his hair, trying to comfort him.

"More's the pity." He whispered, as if extremely disappointed. "But we will be together for a long time, so there is always hope that you will change your mind."

"You are so bad." She whispered with a giggle.

"I am better with you in my life, Leila." He stood, pulling her up with him and picked her up in his arms, holding her up high.

She wrapped her arms around his neck. "What are you doing?"

"Hold on tight." He said, then they were up in the air, and she was clutching him tightly. They glided over the beautifully lit gardens and the animal menagerie, but she didn't take the time to enjoy the view, so fearful was she that he would somehow drop her. They came to a soft landing on the lawn behind the hotel. Setting her on her feet, Nichola pulled her along to a glass door that was mostly hidden behind some tall foliage and entered a combination keycode to open the door. They entered through more foliage into the garden area of their suite.

"I didn't even know that door was there!" Leila exclaimed, surprised.

"That's the idea. This is my personal suite. No one else uses it whether or not I am in residence. That is my personal security entrance." He told her. He seemed to have shaken off his drunken mood. "So, did you like it?" He asked, walking into the living room to pick up the hotel phone.

"It was terrifying! Obviously, I have issues with heights!" She disclosed in a squeaky voice.

He chuckled, then said into the receiver, "Nelson, we are back." He looked around. "Yes, it is here. Thank you. Good night."

Leila saw another basket sitting on the table in the living room. Nichola went over, opened it and pulled out another bottle of wine and a bunch of red seedless grapes. He opened the bottle while throwing two grapes in his mouth. Leila went over to him, and he handed her a glass of wine, which she took, and then sat down on the table. She then took the bottle of wine out of his hand. He looked at her.

"Nichola, come here." Taking him by the hand, he resisted her pull.

"Where are we going?"

"Just come." She pulled him into the bedroom, closed the door behind them, and then pulled him into the bathroom, turning on the shower. "Nichola, you seem very stressed out." He rolled his eyes at her observation. "Do you know what I do when I am stressed out?"

"What?" He asked as she started unbuttoning his shirt.

"I take a nice, long, hot shower." She looked up into his eyes.

"And that helps?" He asked doubtfully looking down at her.

"Oh, yes. It helps immensely." She told him positively, pulling his shirt off of him to reach inside of his waistband to untie his loose pants. Pushing them down over his hips and legs, his eyes started to gleam at her. "That's interesting." She whispered to him, and he raised his eyebrows in inquiry. "Commando." She said with a small laugh.

"What's that?" He asked as he untied her robe.

"I'll explain later." She told him, pulling from his grasp to lead him over to the shower and push him inside, closing the glass door behind him.

"It is very hot." He told her as she left the bathroom.

"It is supposed to be." She answered.

"I am not feeling any better." He complained.

"Be patient."

"I am patient all the time. I am tired of being patient." She heard him say to himself, but she could tell from the noise that he was standing under the water.

She opened the door and stepped inside the shower with him. He turned around with a smile to face her. "Oh, no. Turn around." She turned him as he huffed in irritation.

"I am still not liking this," he said, standing under the hot water facing away from her.

"Be quiet, stubborn vampire, and try to relax." She took the liquid soap and poured some in her hands, rubbing it over his back. He reached behind him to touch her. "No, sir! Place your hands on the wall in front of you." She ordered, and he complied with a sigh. She washed and rubbed his back and she felt his tense muscles start to relax. "You have a luxurious full spa here for your customers. Don't you ever use it for yourself?" She asked, working her soapy hands over his ass and legs. She reached between his legs to wash him from behind. He responded with a moan as she noticed his fingers were curled against the wall in front of him. She wrapped her arms around him, bringing her body against his back and her hands around his front to wash and massage his chest and abdomen, eliciting another small moan. She continued washing him and then took his cock in her hands to wash and he immediately went fully erect, throwing his head back. She quickly finished and removed her hands and said, "Now we rinse."

"What? Rinse?" He asked, bewildered and disappointed.

"Yes." She turned him around under the water and his wet hair hung over his forehead and into his eyes. He looked at her hungrily through the water trickling down his face and strands of hair with red eyes. She ignored his look and rinsed the soap from him.

"I am not feeling less stressed at this moment, Leila." He told her, his voice gravelly.

"Sit." She said, pointing to the shower seat. He sat and wrapped his arms around her, pulling her in between his legs and nuzzling her breasts. "Stop." She told him, as she poured some shampoo into her hand and washed his hair.

"You cannot expect me to ignore such sweet treats when they are right before me, agápi mou." He murmured against her. He moaned slightly as she massaged his scalp. "Though I admit that this feels good."

After a minute or two, where he continued to nuzzle her, she stopped washing his hair and rinsed herself off. Looking at him as she stepped out of the shower, she said softly. "Rinse your hair and meet me in the bedroom." He grinned at her in return and did as he was told.

When he stepped into the bedroom, he had a towel wrapped low around his waist and was towel drying his hair with another as he looked at her. She sat on the bed wrapped in her own towel, looking at him admiring his tanned, muscled chest and abdomen. "Do you feel better?" She asked him with a small smile.

"Marginally." He smirked.

"I thought you might say something like that." She told him. "Come over here and lie on the bed."

"But I am not tired." He teased. His eyes were back to their normal playful amber color.

"Good things happen to those who are not stubborn." Leila told him with a lift of her brow, patting the bed. "Towels off."

"This is definitely much better." He said, dropping the towel in his hands and from his waist and climbing onto the bed.

She stood up and danced out of his reach.

"Where are you going?" He asked, irritated again.

"Nowhere." She giggled, walking over and turning off the main light in the room. The bedroom was now only illuminated by the light in the bathroom. She walked to the end of the bed, still wrapped in her towel. He had his arms crossed over his chest in irritation. "Put your hands behind your head." She said to him softly.

"Why?" He asked.

He could tell that she considered several things before answering him, "Because I like the way your body looks when you are stretched out like that." And as if her words were magic, he did as he was told.

She dropped the towel to the floor that she had on, and for a few seconds, just looked at him. She then started climbing up on the bed in between his legs. He watched her intently.

"Leila, your eyes are slightly pink." He said in wonder.

"Are they?" She laughed softly, seductively, running her hands over his legs, hips, and abdomen as she kneeled in between his legs. His cock was erect again, and twitched in response to her touching him, as if it were jealous and begging for its own attention. She leaned over and ran her lips up his length.

His body quivered in response.

"O Theé mou." He whispered, groaning deeply, and closing his eyes as he felt her small soft hands pull him up away from his body and her hot, wet tongue encircle the head of his cock. He felt one of her small, sharp fangs graze him gently as she took him inside her mouth. "You wouldn't bite me, would you, Moró?" He asked tensing, lifting his head to look down at her.

She looked up at him, her mouth around him, with deep blood-red eyes and chuckled in her throat darkly and he damn near climaxed in both fear and desire.

I promise to be gentle with you, Nichola. He heard her in his head, thinking to himself that was not quite the answer he wanted, and then she sucked him into her throat, causing him to stop thinking at all.

"Oh, God." He said softly, breathing heavily. "Oh, God."

"Do you feel better now? Are you relaxed?" She whispered into his ear with a small laugh as she slide up his body to lay next to him, her arm draped over his chest.

"Yes." He whispered back, closing his eyes.

"Then sleep." She said, kissing the side of his neck softly snuggling against him.

The room was in total darkness when she woke to feel him pull her underneath him and settle himself in between her legs. She wrapped her arms around him and ran her fingers through his still damp hair, which told her that not too much time had elapsed.

He plundered her lips softly tasting himself on her tongue as he ran his hands down her body. She smelled faintly of blood, and he breathed deep of her skin, feeling irresistibly drawn to her. She moaned underneath him, squirming under his hands as he breathed his way down her body. He knew exactly what had occurred when he tasted the blood in between her legs and he moaned in ecstasy, using his shoulders to open her legs wide, holding her tight and sucking on her hard, barely registering her moans and cries of passion as he became intoxicated by her blood.

Each of her orgasms caused contractions that sent more of her blood to him to drink. He did not know how long he had her like this or how many times she came for him. He was barely rational when he heard her gasping and begging for him to stop. He slowly, reluctantly, released her hips to crawl up her body. He was painfully engorged and aching for release. He slid as gently as possible into her, moaning loudly as she surrounded him. She was making so many sounds; he wasn't sure if they were pain or pleasure. He moved within her, and the smell of her blood was overwhelming. He held her tightly and stroked in and out of her body and then sank his fangs deep into the curve of her neck as she arched against him, whether in pleasure or to stop him he didn't know, and at that point didn't care.

Leila lay in the bathtub, soaking her aching body.

About a half hour before, after he had had his way with her, Nichola had quickly gotten dressed and left the room.

She got out of bed right after she heard the door to the suite close. Once she had realized that she had started her period, she knew what had happened. She figured he had run off to fixate on what had occurred, but since her whole body felt sore, she wasn't in a charitable mood towards him, so didn't particularly care, as she turned on the water in the tub.

After another quarter hour, she heard the bedroom door open, and his footsteps enter the bathroom. She looked up, and he was leaning in the doorway looking guilty and positively strung out. He had a box of tampons in his hands.

"I brought you these." He said, looking at her and sat down on the edge of the toilet.

"How did you know what to get?" She asked.

"I asked the man at the all-night grocery."

"That must have been some conversation." She said, holding back laughter.

"Well, I am sure he knew I wasn't going to eat them." He said grouchily.

She couldn't help it, she burst out laughing.

"Don't laugh at me, Leila. I am so angry with myself. I haven't lost control like that in seven hundred years." He said, closing his eyes in self-loathing.

"Nichola, I am sure that this happens." She said, leaning her head back against the tub.

"It doesn't to me, Leila. I don't involve myself with humans sexually, and I keep forgetting that you are just a changeling, neither fully vampire nor fully human. I should have been prepared for this."

"Oh, please!" She told him in astonishment. "This is not the end of the world and quit trying to carry it all on your shoulders! I am a little sore, but basically fine." She then looked at him mischievously. "You should be thankful, because all this really means is that you haven't knocked me up and won't be trapped into a marriage of necessity." She said giggling and then laughed loudly as he sat the box of tampons down on the back of the toilet and stomped out of the bathroom in annoyance.

Later, when she walked out of the bathroom wrapped in her robe, he was sitting on the side of the bed, still obviously upset. She walked over to him and sat on his lap, wrapping her arm around his shoulders, surprising him.

He held her gently to him. "Did it fit?" He asked her.

She gave a little snort of laughter. "Yes, it fits."

"I could have hurt you, Leila." His voice ached as if she were the most precious thing in the whole world, and he rested his forehead against hers.

"You would never hurt me, baby." She reassured him, touching the soft stubble of his beard.

Nichola ordered her to stay in the bedroom Wednesday morning; to watch television, to pack, to sleep, whatever she wanted to do, but to stay in the bedroom. He called room service to get her something to eat.

She had protested, loudly.

"Leila, do not argue with me today." He told her in his *voice*, attempting to influence her behavior. "I have enough going on without worrying about what is happening to you and whether you are in danger."

"You know that your voice thing doesn't really work on me if I actively try to resist it." She told him with a level look.

"Cut me some slack, please, and follow my guidance. It will make me feel better." He said, combing his hair, trying a different approach with her, as she stood watching him with crossed arms.

"Only if you promise me something." She told him.

"What is it you require?" Nichola asked, looking at her reflection in the bathroom mirror.

"Promise me you will let someone else do this...job." She told him. He looked at her steadily. "I am serious. Give it to Beutel, it will make him feel important. Have the Prince assist him as a supervising elder to gain experience. Let them carry this. It doesn't have to always fall on your and Rom's shoulders."

"So, this is for Rom, too, i psychí mou?" He smiled, turning to face her, buttoning his shirt.

"No. It is for me and Es. She worries about Rom too. If you do not want me to make you worry, you should do the same for me, and you should do it for Es as well."

He walked over to her, bent down, and kissed her gently on the lips. "I promise."

"You do?" She asked, surprised as she heard someone knock on the door of the suite.

"Yes. It is sound advice you are providing. We will see how they work out. If Rom and I continue to do all the difficult work, the other members of the council will never develop to their fullest potential." He told her reasonably walking out to open the door for room service.

He allowed her to briefly say goodbye to Es, Rom and Ostrovsky before loading her and Iris into the car at sunset.

As she gave Es a hug goodbye, she heard Ostrovsky speaking to Iris.

"Moy golub', our time here has been so short. Come and visit me in June at my villa in the Riviera. Stay for the summer. It is beautiful and relaxing.

The beaches, food, and shopping are wonderful. I promise you will enjoy yourself immensely." He told her lovingly as he kissed her softly on the cheek. Iris surprisingly blushed and told him she would call him.

One of the attendants at the hotel had put the top down on the Mustang, and both she and Iris wrapped scarves around their heads to keep their hair from blowing all over. Having the top down precluded having any lengthy conversations, which is probably just as Nichola had planned it, and Leila settled back to nap. She woke up when they were pulling into the driveway at the London Hill House.

"Nichola," she said sleepily to him as he opened her door. "I want to see the boys. Please take me to my house."

He helped her out of the car and pushed the seat up for Iris, and helped her out as well. He wrapped his arm around Leila as Iris walked up the front stairs to the house. "Mansuetus has the boys sleeping here tonight. Spend the night with me. He will take you all home tomorrow, if that is what you wish."

"Are you planning on biting me again?" She asked him sleepily.

He made a small noise, which she took as a sound of humor. "I suppose it is always possible." He said, looking at her with amber eyes. "But to tell you the truth, I just want you in my bed, wrapped in my arms tonight." He kissed her gently picking her up to carry her up the stairs and through the front door.

Hunted: Self-Defense or Murder?

NEITHER LEILA NOR THE boys left the next day. Mansuetus went to take care of Pepper and Gladiator and ended up bringing them both back to the London Hill House, and extra clothes and toys for the boys. Pepper loved the large, fenced property and leaped into the pool to join Mansuetus and the boys, making Leila and Iris, who were sitting poolside, laugh. Gladiator surprised everyone by leaping up into Iris' lap to settle down for a nap.

Iris smiled at Leila with unshed tears in her eyes as she gently stroked his soft fur.

Nichola spent most of the day on the phone conducting business, while keeping an indulgent eye on them all from inside the French doors in the basement. Leila knew that Beutel and Prince Khaldun were keeping in constant contact. As Nichola had held her in his arms the night before, he had told her of their meeting.

"Once the order for execution was passed unanimously, no one was more surprised than Rom of my decision to assign the execution to them." He said, kissing her temple softly.

"Why?"

He chuckled before replying. "Well, for almost two centuries, all executions had been conducted by him and I. He assumed we would continue on in the same mode this session, and frankly so did the rest of the council. So, when I assigned the others as field operatives, it was a surprise, but I know him well enough to believe that it was a welcome surprise. Beutel, who constantly complains and undermines my decisions, was shocked, to say the least. Frightened was more like it, though he had no choice but to accept." His chuckle had a slight tinge of evil glee to it, which made Leila smile. "The Prince was surprised, but I would say eager, to fulfill a larger role as lead elder.

He at least is capable. Peake, I think, was disappointed to be left out, so I assigned him logistic support. He deals in information and has an extensive network worldwide. But, in the end the decision was mine as council leader. It is one of the areas that the decision is wholly mine without input from the others."

"So, it is good to be King?" Leila giggled.

He snorted at her laughter. "I think Ostrovsky was pleased with the decision." His voice soft.

"His opinion is important to you, isn't it?"

"He is incredibly wise. If anyone could be king, it would be him. But he doesn't want it any more than I do. He's seen and learned so much. He is old. No one knows for sure how old. But it has been speculated that he became a vampire before Christ walked the earth." He mused.

Thinking about their conversation, Leila watched Iris lovingly stroking Gladiator as he purred in her lap. "So, did you have a good time with Aleksei?"

"I always have a good time with Aleksei." Iris smiled. "He has a calming effect on me."

"He likes you very much, Auntie. He says that you have stolen his heart." Leila said with a small smile.

"He is quite a rogue. I am sure that he says that about many women." Iris gave a small twist of her lips.

"Auntie, you know Dene will show up here sooner or later. When he finds no one at my house, you know he will come here. What are you going to say to him?" Leila asked kindly.

"I don't know. Mansuetus won't tell me any details about how he is. I know. I asked him repeatedly last night. The only answer he gives me is that he is 'functioning', and then he fixes me with that look of disappointment." She frowned. "Leila, I am sorry to have harmed him. We are complex and driven creatures, with strong and sometimes uncontrolled urges. Young vampires are often in need of the calming influence of an elder. Just being around them seems to help." Iris fixed Leila with a steady look. "Listen, I know I messed up. I have been thinking about it, and I am going to talk to Nikolaos about coming back to live with him, permanently, at least for the foreseeable future. And Leila, you need to live with him, too."

"Aunt Iris, I have other considerations besides myself." Leila explained, looking at the boys and Mansuetus floating around in the pool. "I'm not convinced that raising my sons in a vampire household is the best thing for them. I didn't even tell Es that I have children, because I don't want the vampire community at large to know that I do, Auntie, and despite everyone's well-mannered behavior at the Château, I'm not a fool. Vampires are dangerous. I'm not sure that raising human children amongst the vampire community is wise or safe. Though our small family here may be safe, Nichola interacts with a great many people. I can't say that *they* are safe, and the community in general looks down on humans as less than nothing, simply as a food source. Nichola says that the harming of a child is a major crime. But you and I both know that it still happens." Focusing her attention back on Iris, her voice hard as diamonds. "And Auntie, as long as I am not a danger to them, I won't give them up. I will never give them up."

Iris reached over to hold her hand. "Oh, my darling child. I would never want you to give them up. I understand."

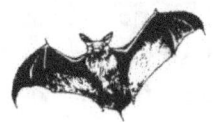

While the kids took a nap, Leila and Iris were in the living room, reading. They had raided the books that were in Nichola's study, left from the previous owners, and much to Nichola's disgust, they had found more than a dozen of what Iris referred to as 'bodice ripper' romances. "Take them," he had told them. "Take them all."

Focused on a financial portfolio, they were bothering him by invading his space. As they headed out the door, they heard him call after them, "You realize they aren't historically accurate!"

They both started laughing, and Leila called back to him, "Honey, that's not the point of reading them!"

Engrossed in their books, they heard a knock on the door.

Leila got up to answer it, and Mansuetus was there before her.

"No." He shook his head. Looking behind her, she noticed Nichola standing in the doorway to his study.

Mansuetus opened the door to a disheveled Dene, who looked at him asking, "Is she here?"

"Yes." Mansuetus told him not unsympathetically. "Come in."

Dene saw Leila standing there and stepped forward. "Hi."

"Dene, are you okay?" Leila asked, taking him by the hand, then realized that Nichola had moved with lightning speed to stand directly behind her, startling both her and Dene.

"Can I speak with Iris?" Dene asked her and looked at Nichola, who was watching him coolly.

"Are you here to harm my family, Doctor?" Nichola asked him quietly and Leila suddenly saw Mansuetus behind Dene's shoulder blocking the front door and realized that Nichola was preparing to kill him, though the doctor had no inkling of the danger that he was in.

"God, no, Nick. I never would." Dene told him; his ice-blue eyes sincere.

Iris walked out of the living room, and Dene gave her a look of yearning. "Iris, are you all right?" He asked, stepping around Leila and Nichola, walking toward her slowly as if she might run from him. He reached out, taking her hand, holding her gaze. "I am sorry that I scared you. Everything is okay."

Making a small sound of despair, Iris was suddenly in his arms, sobbing uncontrollably as he shushed her. "Everything is okay now, baby. We are okay." He told her, gently holding her tightly as Nichola and Mansuetus exchanged inscrutable looks.

Flashing them a stern look of warning, they dropped their eyes, refusing to meet Leila's. Both of them blocked her from seeing their thoughts. Whatever they were thinking didn't bode well for the doctor.

Leila ran interference between Dene and Iris, and Mansuetus and Nichola. She knew that neither of them would attempt anything against the doctor in her presence; the problem was that meant she had to stay with Dene and Iris at all times. Mansuetus and Nichola finally left the living room together after silently determining that he posed no immediate threat. But she had had enough of their silent, glowering presence. She finally left Dene and Iris alone together in the living room, huddled in each other's arms on the couch, not talking, just holding each other. She could read that Iris knew he was in danger, and she was sick over it, and Dene thought Iris was in trouble and wanted to protect her. She frankly thought the pair of them were pitiful.

She stuck her head into the study to see Nichola and Mansuetus with their heads together, barely speaking above the sound of a breath. They had been so intent on their own conversation, and she had tried so ridiculously hard for stealth as she had made her way down the hall, that her entrance was a surprise, and they broke guiltily apart when she walked in glaring at them with her hands upon her hips. Turning around, she quietly closed the door and then walked to where they were sitting on either side of the desk.

Leaning down, she placed both hands upon the end of the desk, then proceeded to fix her gaze harshly on both of them with a glare.

"I will not have it!" Growling low, she felt her face change in her anger. "Do you hear me? I will not! Neither one of you is to harm one hair on his body!"

Mansuetus did not meet her eyes, but Nichola gave her a deadly steely-eyed glare. "I will not allow him to harm my family, Leila."

"This is my family too, Nichola, and he has no intention of harming any of us." She whispered sternly.

"You don't know that i psychí mou. He is not behaving as he should behave after everything that has happened to him." He told her, frustrated. "You don't have the experience to understand this."

"Then make me understand, goddamn it!" Her voice was diamond hard and challenging.

He glared, growling dangerously in return. "Leila, you will be guided by me in this—"

"The hell if I will, Nichola!" Hissing at him dangerously, she felt her teeth lengthen in anger.

"Kyría," Mansuetus interrupted softly, and she instantly fixed him with a glare. He held his hands up to show that he was not a threat to her, continuing in a soft reasonable tone, "Iris injected him with enough venom to kill him or make him her slave. What vampires call companions. So much venom I could smell it coming out of his pores almost two days later. He's surprisingly alive, but is not acting like a companion.

Companions are subservient to vampires, but most especially to their maker. They are bewildered and lost without them, without their guidance or direction. He has been working at the hospital, just like he normally does. Regardless of his unkempt appearance, he is not acting much differently than he always acts, except for his excessive worry about Iris. There is something strange...something off about him. He is not acting like a normal companion. This makes him dangerous."

"Well, neither do you, Mansuetus!" She looked at him intensely.

"What do you mean, Kyría?" He Asked, bewildered.

"You don't act like a normal companion either!" She told him quietly. "You live and function very well without Nichola around giving you constant direction." Looking at Nichola, who blinked at her in surprise, she focused her attention back on Mansuetus. "Do you think, maybe, it's because Nichola didn't 'glamour' or 'mesmerize' you? Well, Iris didn't enthrall Dene Friday night either. She didn't have to. He knew what she was and still wanted to be with her. Because he loves her."

Whirling to face Nichola, an irrational fury coming off of her in waves, she pointed her finger at him. "You!" She growled.

"Me?!" He exclaimed surprised.

"Yes, you! You claim you love me."

"I do. More than my own life." He said earnestly, his amber eyes met her red angry eyes in sincerity.

"Then how can you not recognize it in someone else?" She asked him gently. "He loves her, and she loves him. He's no threat to any of us. The only threatening things in this house are you two." Turning away from them, she started walking to the door.

"You are not queen of this house." She heard Nichola's voice say quietly.

Turning to face him, he met her furious red gaze calmly as her eyes glittered dangerously. "Excuse me? What did you say?" She asked, her voice pitched low.

"This is my house, which makes me king. The decisions that are made here are made by me." He told her, standing and walking over to face her, looking down into her eyes. "This is my house. Which you refuse to be a part of. If you want an equal share, any share, in the decisions of the running of this household, and of this family, you will have to become a part of it."

"So, in order to keep Dene from being killed, I have to place myself and my children under your authority? Under your control? This is what you are telling me?" Her hands started to ache almost as much as her teeth did. Looking down, she realized her fingers were bloody, and that she had grown claws. She saw Mansuetus stand to look at her worriedly.

Looking down at her hands also Nichola then met her eyes, his amber eyes calm and unimpressed by her anger. "Becoming a part of my household does not mean that you are acquiescing to my authority any more than you already do now, i psychí mou. It just means that you are actively, equally, taking part in the direction and protection of this family as my mate."

"I will not let you control or manipulate me, Nichola!" She warned in a throaty voice.

"Being part of my household is not about me controlling you, Leila. It is about protecting you and the children. From others and from yourself." He looked pointedly at her clawed hands, slowly moving to gently take them in his own.

She flinched as the ache in them suddenly flared painfully up her arms, then subsided the longer he held them.

"Young vampires benefit from being a part of an elder's household. Our very presence brings self-control and peace. I have already told you I am better when you are with me. Leila, when will you accept you are better when I am with you?" Nichola's voice was soft and persuasive.

She swayed slightly as she felt her body gradually return to normal.

He gently enfolded her in his arms, steadying her.

"Don't kill Dr. Lambert, Nichola. He doesn't deserve it. He's not a threat." She whispered.

"Do you want this to be my decision?" He asked softly into the top of her head, which now rested on his chest.

"I want it to be our decision." She answered just as quietly and felt him kiss the top of her head as she leaned into him, suddenly exhausted and barely able to stand.

"If that is your wish." Picking her up, he sat with her on the leather sofa, cradling her in his lap, holding her tenderly against him, as Mansuetus left the study quietly, closing the door.

The rest of Thursday evening was uneventful. Leila invited Dr. Lambert to eat dinner with them, since she suspected he hadn't been eating much since they had been gone. Mansuetus made a roast with carrots and potatoes, and creamed peas, as well as a tossed salad.

"You made a ton of food, Mansuetus." Leila remarked quietly to him as she helped him set the table.

"Everyone needs to eat," he replied to her just as quietly.

Watching Iris eat heartily she was surprised that Nichola was eating heartily as well. She figured he wouldn't bother, since Dene realized they were all vampires. Of course, she had no idea what he thought Mansuetus was. Then she remembered she was still on her period. Watching Nichola closely, she fed Devin some potatoes. Feeling her gaze on him, he looked up to meet her gaze steadily as he cut his roast and took a bite; she understood what Mansuetus had meant.

Obviously, everyone was a little on edge.

Dene's beeper went off. Glancing at the number, anger radiated from him; more anger than she had ever felt from him. Leila looked at him with concern. "I'm sorry," he told her, in quiet embarrassment. "She has been beeping me several times a day since last Friday. She even showed up at the hospital on Tuesday demanding to see me. It was embarrassing. I had security throw her out and ban her from entering unless it is an official health emergency."

"Didn't you talk with her?" Leila demanded.

"Yes. He made it clear to her Friday before we left the parking lot," Iris said coolly. "She understood his feelings, and he definitely understood hers." She flashed Dene a half smile here, to which he looked even more embarrassed. "There should have been nothing left to be said."

"I explained this to Iris. But it should have never really been an issue. She and I were not exclusive. I was not the only guy that she was..." here he paused to look at Zachary, who was chatting at Mansuetus as he ate his vegetables, "involved with." He finished in a hushed voice.

"I can attest to that," Nichola agreed, drinking his wine. He looked around the table when silence greeted his statement to find the men staring at him and both Leila and Iris glaring holes through him. Finishing his wine in a gulp, he quickly refilled his glass. "I am just saying that she made herself readily available to me quite easily..." his voice trailed off as Leila continued to glare at him.

"Stop digging that hole," Mansuetus said to him under his breath. "Yes, Master Zachary, if you eat all of your carrots, you will have eyes just like a hawk." Mansuetus smiled indulgently as Zachary ate another carrot.

"Hawk Eyes!" Zachary yelled loudly, and the men chuckled self-consciously, thankful to move on to another conversation.

Iris walked Dene to his car around nine o'clock, as he had to work early the next morning. Looking like he had not slept for a week, she was worried about him.

"I am so glad you came back, Iris." He told her, kissing her softly before getting into his car. "Everything is going to be okay now, you'll see."

Walking up the front steps as he pulled out of the driveway, she sadly watched his taillights down the dark road. Walking in the door to see Leila and Nichola waiting for her in the foyer, she hugged her niece tightly as she looked up, fixing Nichola with her sad eyes.

"He lives for now." Nichola said simply, as Leila and Iris both smiled at him. "But if he shows signs of madness, you know what we must do." He told Iris directly. She nodded once.

Leila hugged him. "He won't, baby. He's just in love. He's going to be fine."

By 11:00 pm, the boys and Mansuetus were in bed and Iris was in her room with several of the 'bodice ripper' romance novels. Leila, wearing the thin satin robe that she had gotten at the Château, headed to the study. She had lain in bed for almost an hour waiting for Nichola to come in; obviously, he wasn't in any hurry. She was unable to read him, and she had gotten tired of waiting for him. Walking into the study, she found him reading another business portfolio, an opened bottle of wine next to him on the desk.

"You're drinking and you're avoiding me." She told him matter-of-factly.

"You are correct."

"Why?"

"You know why. I now understand Gervais' madness toward his mate. After conquering my blood-lust for centuries, it is humbling to know the levels of need that I can still sink to."

"Don't be ridiculous. I am not even flowing that heavily. Me being on my period didn't make any of the other vampires wig out." She started to tell him moving forward. "You cuddled me last night with no problem."

He held up a hand to stop her. "Your transformation sparked a response in me today that was extremely difficult for me to overcome, and now that I haven't made love to you in two days, I find I want too very badly. The scent of just one drop of your blood makes me want you even more. I don't trust myself. I might hurt you."

"Do you want to hurt me?" She asked, not moving forward anymore.

"Of course not." He glanced at her. "And I won't be able to if I keep my distance."

"So, you are horny?" He gave her a sharp look. "Yeah, yeah, I know you don't like that language when it comes to us. But it is the truth. Well, I have needs too. So, you are going to torture us both on the off-chance that you are going to 'hurt' me? You know you basically lost it the other night, and you didn't hurt me then! If you were going to hurt me, you would have done it the other night!" She paused, thinking. "I didn't think that it did, but if it freaked you out to have sex with me while I am on my period, just say so. It won't hurt my feelings, and I won't make any demands on you if that is the case." She said to him gently.

He scoffed at her. "A warrior does not fear getting his sword bloody."

"Wow! That was quite crude! And you chide me for my language! So, you will not come to bed with me until my period is over?" She asked, crossing her arms over her chest as if she was clarifying something.

He looked at her calmly and stated, "That is my decision."

"That's your decision?" She inquired with an arched brow; he met her gaze steadily. "Fine. It's not like I haven't been here in my life before. I will go take care of myself." She turned around, heading for the door.

"What does that mean?" He asked her, slightly bewildered by her nonchalant attitude.

"Never-you-mind, just go back to your work," she calmly said over her shoulder, walking out the door.

He sat there for a few minutes, trying to concentrate on the papers before him, failing miserably. He already knew that the prospectus in front of him was a good investment. *What the hell did she mean by that?* He asked himself, taking another drink from the wine bottle.

He felt a fissure of pleasure pulse through him, just before he heard her soft moan in his mind, causing him to grow half erect. He immediately got up to walk to the master bedroom at the back of the house. Opening the door slowly and quietly, her scent that he always found so intoxicating mixed with the faint scent of her blood, overcame his senses, causing his fangs to grow.

Quickly pulling his clothes from his body, he walked silently to the bed to watch her. She had one hand in between her legs, rubbing gently, while the other was softly squeezing one of her rock-hard nipples. Her head was tilted back, and her mouth was open, revealing her small fangs. He had never seen anything look so erotic as he watched her pleasure herself. His erection was painful when he finally reached out a hand to stop her.

"I psychí mou, stop, you are killing me. Giving you pleasure is my duty." He said quietly as he lay down beside her, his hand stroking up and down her bare stomach gently. "I will do my best to fulfill my duty without harming you."

"Silly vampire," she declared with a small, soft laugh as he brought her hand to his mouth to gently suck the blood from her fingers; he let out a soft moan. "Making love to me isn't your job. It's *our* pleasure. If you don't want to hurt me. Just don't do anything that you don't want to do, and you won't." She kissed him softly on the lips. "Make me cum, Nichola." She commanded quietly in a husky whisper, as he gave her a half smile before he proceeded to kiss and lick his way down her body.

Walking into the kitchen the next morning, she found Zachary at the kitchen table coloring and Devin roaming around the kitchen in his walker. Mansuetus was feeding the dog and the cat and making breakfast.

"Mansuetus, you know you are eventually going to have to take them back to daycare."

He ignored her.

"Playing with other children is beneficial to their development. It helps them learn cooperation skills." She told him.

"They pick up bad behavior from other children." He stated, taking Devin out of his walker and putting him in his highchair. "They are better taken care of when they are with me."

"I won't disagree with you there. You take exceptionally good care of them. But they need to learn how to stand on their own with children their own age." She said, getting herself a cup of coffee. "Besides, wouldn't you like a little bit of a break? Maybe to take Jackie to lunch?" She said, smiling.

He gave her a funny little smile in return and proceeded to feed the kids breakfast.

"If we take them to daycare, you and I can go to the grocery store. You know you enjoy that." She popped a grape into her mouth and popped a piece of sliced banana in Devin's mouth, who had been looking at her with an open mouth like a small bird waiting to be fed.

Smiling at her with a wrinkled nose, he chewed.

She wrinkled her nose back at him and he waved his arms around cheerfully. "I will even wear that atrocious looking hat and sunglasses that Aunt Iris bought for me."

"That is not true! That is a beautiful hat and sunglasses, Leila!" Iris said, coming in to sit down at the table with her book in her hand.

"Yeah, if you are Elton John!" Leila snickered at her.

"Are you bored, i psychí mou?" Nichola asked smoothly, walking into the kitchen.

"I am not much one for being cooped up." She told him, taking a sip of her coffee.

"Yes, the daylight hours can be confining." He agreed. "You will get used to it."

"I don't believe I will." She told him firmly.

"Well, we can meet Dene at the state park this evening to go for a walk if you like," Iris told her. "He gets off of work at seven and sunset is around eight. We can even take the kids with us. I am sure that they would enjoy it."

"Nichola, may I borrow the keys to the mustang?" Leila asked sweetly with a twinkle in her eye.

"Absolutely not!" He said in return, appalled at the thought of her driving his precious car.

"What say you, Mansuetus, protector of women and children? May I borrow the keys to the limo?" She asked him just as sweetly.

"No, but I will take you, Kyría." Mansuetus told her with a smile.

"Fine. I will go as well." Nichola said grumpily.

"I don't believe that you were invited. Did you invite him, Auntie?" Leila asked with an impish look.

"No." Iris said, smiling.

Leila looked at him, continuing to smile.

He glared back at her. "I am going."

"Fine, if that's what you wish." She said, taking a sip of her coffee.

The evening was cool with the river breezes on the trail of the Crooked River State Park.

Leila had been wanting to bring the kids out here for a while now, but Michael was never interested and couldn't be bothered. It was a large task to bring the children and all of their 'equipment' for just one person, so she had never attempted it on her own; and if she had ever gone without him, Michael would have immediately thought that she was 'up' to something. That was the way it had been for her the last several years, living and operating as a single parent, but never really being single and enjoying making decisions on her own without harassment from someone else. Having someone to help with one of the children while she was getting the other readied was an enormous benefit, and she knew she would be eternally grateful to Mansuetus for all of his support and love for the boys.

Pushing the stroller over the fairly flat and wide trail, Mansuetus, and the boys, seemed to be having a fairly good time looking at the woods on either side of the trail in the fading light.

Leila and Nichola followed hand-in-hand a couple of paces behind, and Leila held a small flashlight in her hand.

Dene, who was walking with Iris about ten yards in front of them, had another flashlight.

Of course, Nichola and Iris had no need of flashlights and Leila still wasn't sure how many vampire benefits Mansuetus had, but he had never seemed to be unsure of himself in the dark.

"Is this better, agápi mou?" Nichola asked, quietly swinging her hand gently.

"Much better than being stuck in the house, absolutely." She told him sincerely.

"It might be easier to bear if you were to start changing your schedule to rest during the daylight hours. It will feel more normal to you then, and you will not feel so confined."

"Then when am I supposed to see the kids? Just a few hours per day? I don't think so. I need to keep to the hours that I am keeping. You don't care, anyway; you don't really sleep."

"I sleep more now than I have in years. You exhaust me, Panemorfi." He said with a sexy smile.

"Are you complaining?" She asked softly with a giggle, stroking the arm that held her hand firmly.

"Never."

Up the trail, they heard running footsteps and then there was a commotion, like two people had collided.

"What the fuck are you doing here?" Dene yelled.

"Did you really think that I would let you use me, Doc? Is that what you think? I am just a piece of garbage to be thrown away for some old whore?" They heard a woman's voice say in the darkness.

Leila shined her light on the backs of Iris and Dene, and in front of them on the trail blocking their path was Bobby Rebekah.

"How the fuck did you even know I was here?"

"I followed you from the hospital, you idiot! You were so intent on getting here to see *her*," she said, screeching with loathing, motioning to Iris, "you didn't even notice, and you think that you're such a genius!"

Leila looked around to see if anyone else was on the trail. It looked like they had this section of the park to themselves.

Just great! She thought, turning loose of Nichola's hand to head forward, grabbing Mansuetus' arm to halt him as he moved forward as well. "Stay with the boys, Mansuetus." She walked into the fray.

"Bobby, just go away. These people don't need to be exposed to this; we've got kids here for Christ's sake. It was just sex between us, and you and I both know I wasn't the only one! We didn't even date. You are acting crazy. I was never that important! Just go away." He told her calmly, trying to be reasonable.

"I am not going away! You care about me!" She continued to yell.

"I never did, and you never heard me say anything of the sort. If I had, do you think I would have tolerated you fucking everyone else? Hell, Bobby, it was getting old before I ever met Iris. We were just having a good time; it wasn't anything serious on my part." He told her coldly.

"It is for me, and I know it was for you too, until she came along." She told him, coming closer to him and her voice trembled with barely controlled rage.

"Well, you are wrong. It never was for me." He, too, was angry. "Just go away. You are just embarrassing yourself!"

"So now I am an embarrassment? Well, don't worry Doc, I will never embarrass you again, because if you aren't with me I will stop the air that you breathe!" Bobby Rebekah screeched raising her arm high gripping a hunting knife tightly in her hand, its blade gleamed in the light from Leila's flashlight.

Watching it all happen as if in slow motion, Leila rushed to get there to stop her, to push Dene out of the way.

Iris, closer and faster, was there before her to step in front of Dene, and Bobby's downward arc of her arm buried the knife to its hilt through her chest just above her heart. Iris slumped to the ground as Bobby's mouth dropped open in fright and she ran into the trees.

Both boys started screaming and crying.

Dene and Leila kneeled next to Iris, who moaned slightly as her eyelids fluttered open. "Are you okay?" She gasped, looking at Dene.

Leila reached for the knife and Dene grabbed her hand quickly. "No, don't! She'll bleed out!" His voice was sharp in fear. "We've got to get her to the hospital." Dene said, as Leila heard the barely concealed panic in his voice as he tried to move Iris.

She made a small cry of pain that they barely heard over the screaming of the children.

"No hospitals." Nichola growled, his teeth long and bared. Moving forward, he had Bobby Rebekah, whose own screams added to those of the children. One of her arms was pinned high behind her back and his other hand was fisted in her platinum hair, her head pulled back. He pushed her to kneel on the ground, holding her over to Iris. "Drink." He commanded.

"No! I won't do it, Nichola!" Iris yelled, her teeth growing in agony, a cry of pain escaping her lips.

"Just a little, Auntie." Leila coaxed softly. "Then we can remove the knife and you can start to heal."

"A little is not going to do it, and she knows it, Leila." Nichola barked, cruelly shaking Bobby Rebekah over Iris ever closer to her face as Bobby fought his superior strength futilely, yelling for all that she was worth. "Drink, Iris!" He commanded and Leila could feel the raw power in his command, as her own mouth started to ache as her small fangs started to descend. "Drink!"

"I promised myself I would never kill another person again! I won't do it, no matter what!" Iris wailed, then gasped and coughed sharply, bringing up blood to pour out of her mouth and over the side of her face.

"God damn it, Iris! I won't lose another member of my family to a fucking human!" Nichola roared in fury, pulling Bobby Rebekah's head back on her neck almost to the snapping point, and her eyes rolled in terror as her yells ceased in horror to the transformation she was witnessing of the people around her.

Leila knew in that moment that Nichola was going to rip open the woman's throat and she also knew that she couldn't watch her aunt die, she wouldn't lose her again. She met Dene's eyes and as she started to reach for the knife Dene beat her to it and pulled it free of Iris' body with a sickening sucking noise, causing Iris to give an open-mouthed gasp of pain and her eyes to go wide in shock.

In one smooth move, he deeply cut Bobby Rebekah's throat from ear-to-ear and her blood spurted all over Iris' face and into her mouth in a waterfall. Dene held Iris down and Leila held Iris' head, forcing her to drink, as blood splashed over them all. She felt her own teeth fully descend in response, as Nichola lowered Bobby Rebekah's spasming body over Iris' face.

Iris finally stopped fighting them, proceeding to drink deep, gulp after gulp, as the children screamed on and on.

The ride back was in almost total silence save for Zachary's quiet hiccupping sobs into Leila's blood-covered shoulder as she held him tightly. Devin sat secured in his car seat, intently, but silently, staring wide-eyed at Iris' blood-soaked body, gasping in pain on the opposite seat in the back of the limo.

Dene drove like a maniac out of the park at nine-thirty and Leila said, using her *voice*, "Slow the fuck down, Dene. You are going to get us pulled over."

He silently complied, going no faster than the speed limit, until they got to the London Hill House to pull into the garage.

Leila unhooked Devin, scooping him up into her arms, taking Zachary securely by the hand. She sat them down against the wall of the garage. Wrapping Zachary's arms around his brother, she used her *voice* to tell them, "Don't move. Stay right here." They nodded, silent and wide-eyed. She then grabbed a black trash bag out of a box on a garage shelf and told Dene as he climbed into the back seat, "Get Iris out of those clothes." Dene stripped Iris, as Leila asked, "How's the wound?"

"It's not healed, but it isn't bleeding anymore. I think it is knitting." He examined Iris as Leila took her clothes from him and put them in the trash bag.

"Take your clothes off, Dene, you are covered too. Then take Iris into the bathroom down here off of the rec room and let's get cleaned up. Be careful. We cannot leave any traces of blood in the house." She told him detachedly. She then started to take off her and the boys' clothes to add to the trash bag.

Dene looked at her, surprised by her calm and cold behavior, and then proceeded to strip. They moved into the house, Dene supporting Iris, crossed the rec room and into the bathroom.

Thankfully, the boys had only gotten a small amount of blood on them by being handled by their mother, so were quickly cleaned. In shock by what they had witnessed, they were noticeably quiet throughout the whole process and sat wrapped in a towel, huddled together in a corner of the bathroom afterwards, while the adults who supported Iris between them showered.

Leila wrapped herself in a towel and walked back to the garage, looking for any traces of blood in the house as she went to retrieve the diaper bag from the trunk of the limousine. She walked back in to find Dene with a towel wrapped around his waist, helping Iris over to the couch.

"Wait!" Leila commanded and then ran to grab an additional towel to lay it on the couch.

"She's not bleeding anymore, Leila." Dene said softly.

"I don't care. Watch." Leila said and her voice sounded alien even to her own ears.

Taking her own towel from around her body, surprisingly unembarrassed, she proceeded to gently dry Iris' hair. The towel came away slightly pink.

"I can smell it." Leila said to him as he sat next to Iris to dry her off. She watched him for a few heartbeats and then went into the bedroom to take care of the children.

They looked at her, quiet as church mice, as she tucked them into the bed in the rec-room bedroom. Zachary kept his arms around Devin, who was silent, his cognac-colored eyes wide and frightened. She smoothed their hair away from their foreheads, bending forward to kiss them both gently. They kissed her back. "It's okay, guys. I promise, it's going to be okay."

"Iris okay?" Zachary asked in a scared little voice.

"She's going to be fine, honey." Leila choked out quickly falling silent on a sob.

"You okay?" Zachary asked her.

"Yes, baby, I am okay. I promise I am okay." She held his little hand in hers gently.

"I want Daddy." He said softly as a tear rolled down his cheek.

"He's going to be home soon. I promise. Until he is, you guys are going to be safe with Mommy. Okay?" She told him in a whisper. "Mommy has to take care of some things, so I need you guys to go to sleep. *You go to sleep and dream nice things.*" She used her voice as they both closed their eyes and she felt them relax under her hands.

Leaving the light on in the bathroom and the bedroom door slightly ajar she made her way upstairs to throw on a pair of shorts and one of Nichola's t-shirts, putting on a pair of canvas tennis shoes that Mansuetus had brought from her house. Looking around, she realized that he had moved most of her clothing to this house, and vaguely wondered when he had done that. She walked back downstairs to see Iris laying on the towels on the couch, eyes closed, breathing shallowly, and Dene sitting next to her on a chair that he had pulled over from the card table, gripping one of her hands tightly.

"Put these on." She told him, putting a pair of Nichola's jeans and a t-shirt on the table.

She then went and gathered up the towels that were in the bathroom, briefly checking on the boys who were huddled together and sleeping deeply in the bed, and then went to retrieve the towel that Dene had been using.

He glanced at her in silence as he pulled the shirt on over his head.

She, too, remained silent.

She took the towels to the garage and added them to the trash bag, grabbed the lighter fluid for the grill that Mansuetus had bought and a box of wooden matches from a shelf, pulled the bag over her shoulder and headed out the back toward the marsh. Though there wasn't much light amongst the trees, she realized she didn't have any difficulty seeing as she headed for the fire-pit and seating area that was situated on the property about thirty feet from the marsh. Sitting everything down on one of the benches, she walked among the trees, gathering sticks and pieces of wood for the pit.

Leila's mind was totally devoid of feeling as she gathered what she need-ed. She realized she wasn't sad, scared, angry...she wasn't anything except determined to do what needed to be done.

Working assiduously to start a fire, it was like she was out of her body looking down on herself; watching herself pour the lighter fluid over the wood. Striking a wooden match, she threw it in the pit to watch the flames eat up the fluid and spread throughout the wood, catching it ablaze. When the flames were high, one by one she added items from the trash bag to the fire, watching the greedy flames lick and consume each item.

Distracted briefly by headlights pulling through the gates at the front of the property, she felt a presence behind her. She glanced over her shoulder to see Nichola.

He was covered in bloody gore from head to foot and smelled like a slaughterhouse. He held a large bundle of clothes in his hands.

"Go. I will finish this," He told her quietly.

She walked back to the house.

Mansuetus was naked and wiping the inside of Dene's car down with a wet towel and cleaner.

She looked at him in inquiry.

"It should be fine." He stated. "I stripped before I got in it. How are the children?"

"Sleeping." Leila responded, heading into the garage to walk into the house. Sitting at the table, she looked at Dene, who still sat next to Iris, holding her hand in his.

"She seems to be doing better, and the wound is knitting." He told her, though, his eyes were haunted with worry. Leila nodded to him, remaining silent. "This is my fault," he whispered to the silent room, his eyes locked on Iris.

"Is it?" Leila inquired without emotion.

"Iris would have never been hurt, if it wasn't for me." He bent his head over her hand as if in prayer.

"I think that there is enough blame to go around, Dene." Leila told him; her voice and body were exhausted. "If I had known what to look for during my transition, maybe I would have never went to the hospital. If I had never gone to the hospital, Aunt Iris would have never met you, and she wouldn't have bitten you. You definitely wouldn't have been on the radar." She sighed deeply. "It's no more my fault for being uninformed about my vampire physiology than it is your fault for getting bitten for trying to help me or your fault that Bobby Rebekah was obviously a deranged stalker."

He never moved his head from his prayerful stance over Iris' hand. "I killed her. I am at fault for that." His voice was low and despairing.

"Bobby Rebekah's fate was written when she plunged that knife into my aunt. If you hadn't done it, I would have. If neither of us had acted, Nichola would have. The three of us would not allow Iris to die; in reality, we all killed her." Leila's voice was soft and emotionless, facing Dene and Iris with unfocused eyes, reliving those moments in her mind where Bobby Rebekah's blood had pumped out of her dying body and drenched them all. "But it would not have happened if Bobby had at all been stable."

"What do you think they did with her?" Dene whispered.

"We ripped her body apart and fed her to the alligators in the marsh." A stern, cold voice came from the doorway.

Turning to look, Nichola stood there naked. He had obviously wiped himself down, but still was stained with blood throughout his entire body. His hair was wet with it, making it dark and matted.

"We are showering down here." Leila told him, and he walked into the bedroom off the rec room. Leila went upstairs to get him and Mansuetus clothes, leaving Dene with Iris.

When she returned, Nichola was standing next to Dene, with a towel wrapped around his waist, looking down at Iris critically with a worried look on his face. She gave him his clothes, and he quickly put them on. She took his towel and headed into the bathroom to where Mansuetus was showering and put it and his clothes on the toilet for him.

When she came back to the rec room, Nichola and Dene had Iris sitting up, looking weak and in pain.

Nichola was looking at the wound. "She needs more blood." He said, looking at Dene.

Dene immediately sat next to her, holding out his arm to Iris. "Iris, honey, I want you to take a drink." She turned her head up and away from him.

"No." She told him quietly.

"Auntie, you must," Leila said, kneeling in front of her, holding her legs. "You have to in order to get well."

"Iris! Do not make me hurt Dene in order for you to drink from him!" Nichola said sharply startling both Leila and Iris. Dene just looked resigned at his words.

Iris looked at Nichola with haunted eyes. "I don't want to hurt him."

"We will not let you," Nichola told her gently. "But you must drink."

Iris slowly took a hold of Dene's arm with both of her hands and opened her mouth wide, her fangs descending like a snake, to bite down on his wrist. Dene took a sharp intake of breath and put his arm around her to hold her tenderly as she sucked at his arm gently.

Mansuetus came in as Nichola and Leila watched them intently, and after a few minutes, Nichola placed his hand on Iris' shoulder and said, "That's enough."

Iris lifted her head, sealing the bites with her tongue. She looked at Dene, who looked pale.

He nodded at her. "I am okay."

Nichola fixed Dene with a commanding stare. "You will stay here for the next several days. Go to work from here, return here every evening. Everyone must be able to say convincingly that we were all together tonight. Once the bartender is reported missing, the first people that will be questioned will be you and Iris. The breakup has been too violent and too public for that not to happen. Our story is that we have all been together. Not one of us has been on their own. You have either been here, or at the hospital, and will remain here with your new girlfriend. That is our story." He included Iris, Leila, and Mansuetus in his gaze. "We are going to keep this family safe at all costs. Is this understood?" All four of them nodded yes as he stood up. "I am going back to the park to move her car to the waterfront and then I will return."

"Is that safe?" Leila asked, frightened.

"Safer than leaving it there. There is no doubt someone noticed the limousine parked there earlier, but fewer odds that anyone would have noticed her car."

"It wasn't in the parking lot when we left." Dene said.

"That is even better. It will be on one of the less traveled side roads leading to the trail. I have her scent. I will find it." Nichola told him, heading for the garage.

"How will you start it?" Leila asked, following him, skipping to keep up, growing more nervous with each of his steps. "Will you have to hot-wire it?"

"Her keys were in her clothes. I have them. Do not worry, Glykó." He turned, briefly cupping her face to give her a quick kiss on the lips. "I will be careful, I promise. I will not let my family down." He told her as he walked out of the garage and took flight, quickly disappearing from her sight.

Mansuetus and Leila put the children in their own beds, and then Mansuetus carried Iris to her bed.

Dene stood up to follow, stumbling.

Leila quickly caught him, supporting him as they made their way to Iris' room.

Dene lay next to her, wrapping her in his arms, both of them closing their eyes in exhaustion.

Leila sat in the living room, waiting for Nichola to return. After more than an hour, Mansuetus joined her.

"Where were you?" She asked tiredly.

"Burning the rest of the towels and cleaning the interior of the limousine and the downstairs. When the ashes are cool, Kýrios will gather and spread them out over the water." His voice was deeply tired as well.

"It seems you and Nichola have done this before." She stated, her heart aching with the knowledge.

"I would like to tell you it hasn't been often, but often is a relative word, so I cannot. One time could be considered too often. Suffice to say that it has happened often enough over the centuries that we know what to do." He, too, sounded heartbroken. "You have handled yourself well in this crisis, Kýría." He looked at her with pity, though his words were proud.

"What does that say about me?" She asked him with a haunted look.

"That you love your family and will do whatever it takes to insure their survival."

"Yes, I love my family. I also love my children. I can't raise them here, Mansuetus." She told him, her soft voice breaking as she looked at him with tear-filled eyes.

He looked at her, clearly torn and swallowed hard, his eyes too filling with tears. "I know, Kýría. When this crisis is past, I will support your decision, whatever it may be."

She stood up and put a comforting hand to his shoulder and then walked down the hall to go lay down, though she didn't expect to find sleep anytime soon.

Surviving Guilt

S ATURDAY PASSED UNEVENTFULLY.

Dene went into the hospital in the morning, Mansuetus went to the grocery store after breakfast and then returned to join Leila, who played with the children. Both boys, who at first seemed abnormally subdued, rallied later in the day, and were behaving almost normally as evening approached.

Iris rested throughout the day in her room, and Leila frequently brought her warm cow's blood to drink. Her wound was still present, but healing slowly.

Nichola closeted himself in his study and stayed on the phone, coordinating with other members of the council.

After Dene returned in the evening, they helped Iris, who was still weak, into the living room to watch television.

Both boys latched onto her in relief and sat on either side of her throughout the evening.

Leila was unusually quiet and absorbed with her own thoughts and fears.

Nichola watched her with concern during the infrequent times that he was present. He knew she was worried and was more concerned with her abnormal silence than anything else. He had expected her to question him when he had returned at almost two o'clock in the morning, but instead found her in bed curled up on herself, pretending to be asleep. He didn't push her or confront her; he just had spooned himself around her and held her, pillowing her head on his arm, trying to comfort her. Eventually, she relaxed and fell into an exhausted sleep.

That she continued to be so silent and non-confrontational throughout the day worried him more than he wanted to admit to himself. Uncharacteristically, he would have rather that she barge into his study with a myriad of questions demanding answers. This silence of hers disturbed him greatly.

391

She went to bed without trying to retrieve him from the study, and he went into check on her around midnight. She once again was curled up on herself, but at least this time, she was sleeping soundly.

He returned to his study, allowing her to rest.

Sunday was a replica of Saturday. Leila spent time with Iris in her room. Iris was better physically though still weak, but mentally she was despondent. Leila was in Iris' bathroom, helping her curl her hair.

"Auntie, you know that nothing that has happened has been your fault." Leila told her sympathetically.

"Leila, if I hadn't bitten Dene in the first place, you would have just been another patient. He would have never tracked us down and I wouldn't have gotten involved with him. I could have influenced him without biting him. I chose not to. I wanted to bite him. I freely admit that." Iris said sadly.

"Aunt Iris, it's like I told Dene. There is plenty of blame for this situation. We can even blame my dad for not doing his job and educating me or my sisters on what the future could hold for us as vampires. I could have then maybe recognized the signs and avoided this whole mess of going to the hospital to begin with."

"Does he blame me, too?" Iris asked.

"Hell, no. He blames himself for killing her. Ridiculous really. As I explained to him, we would not let you die. He just did it before Nichola, or I did."

"Would you really have killed her, Leila? Could you have done that?" Iris asked, shocked.

"Yes, Auntie. We were both reaching for the knife. Dene just got to the knife before I did. It's really as simple as that."

"Leila! You can't become a murderer just because you are becoming a vampire!" Iris told her, horrified.

"It has nothing to do with my becoming a vampire. This is based purely on being human. I won't lose you again, Aunt Iris. I won't. Especially not because of some crazy woman." Leila told her calmly and emotionlessly as she arranged Iris' shiny black curls on top of her head.

They heard the front door open, sensing Dene and two other people walk in the door.

Pepper started barking loudly.

Leila and Iris stepped into the hallway as Mansuetus took her by the collar and told her to sit.

Dene and two uniformed police officers were standing in the foyer.

"Hi Dene!" Leila said, stepping forward as Devin came down the hallway in his walker and Zachary followed to look up at the police officers. "What's going on?"

The police officers took in her small form, the presence of the children, and relaxed their posture.

Nichola stepped out of the study to stroll into the foyer, looking at the police officers with composure, and picked up Zachary, saying to the officers calmly, "My name is Dr. Nick Tsoukalous, I am the homeowner, how may I help you officers?"

"Dr. Tsoukalous, my name is Sheriff Roy Jenkins, and this is Deputy Matt Holmes. May we speak with you and Dr. Lambert for a few minutes?"

"Absolutely, Sheriff. If you would care to step into the living room? Honey, would you take Zachary for me?" Leila stepped forward and took Zachary.

"Sheriff, would you and Deputy Holmes care for something to drink? Some Lemonade or Sweet Tea, perhaps?" Leila asked him politely with a bit of southern twang in her voice.

Both of them remembered their manners all of a sudden and removed their hats. "Thank you, Ma'am! Lemonade would be appreciated!" He gave her a warm smile, which she returned.

Leila, Iris, and Mansuetus, who scooped up Devin and the walker, headed for the kitchen, while Nichola ushered Dene, Sheriff Jenkins, and Deputy Holmes into the living room.

"Please have a seat, gentlemen." He said, sitting down in a wing-backed chair. Dene took the other opposite him, and the Sheriff and the Deputy sat on the sofa adjusting their gun belts. "Now, how may I be of assistance?"

"Well, Dr. Tsoukalous, my deputy and I followed Dr. Lambert on his way here this afternoon. We have had a missing person's report of a Bobby Rebekah Patterson, an...associate of Dr. Lambert's."

"I explained that I have not seen her since Tuesday." Dene began.

Nichola cut him off. "I have not had the pleasure of meeting Ms. Patterson, gentlemen. I am at a loss of how I can help you." He told them softly.

"Dr. Lambert here has told us he has been staying here with you for the last several days." Sheriff Jenkins said.

"That is true." Nichola told him.

"May I ask why?" The Sheriff asked him.

Leila walked into the living room, balancing a tray with a pitcher of lemonade and four glasses of ice. The men stood up as she entered the room and she smiled brightly at them, placing the tray down on the coffee table and poured them glasses. "Please sit down, gentlemen." She said happily. "I can answer that, Sheriff. Dene and my Aunt Iris are courting." The southern twang was back in her voice.

"Really?" The Sheriff looked at her with a smile.

"Oh, yes! For a number of weeks now." She said brightly.

"Yes." Nichola agreed. "I have also been consulting with Dr. Lambert on a medical case." He said, taking a glass from Leila and taking a sip.

"Is your aunt here, Ms. ...?" Deputy Holmes asked, a notepad and pencil in his hands.

"Sutton. Leila Sutton." She said, smiling sweetly. "Yes. Would you like to meet her?" She inquired.

"Please." He said to her, responding to her smile with one of his own.

Leila left the room.

"Do you have reason to believe there is foul play in Ms. Patterson's disappearance?" Nichola asked worriedly.

"Well, no, not at this point, doctor, but..." he stopped pointedly as Leila and a brightly smiling Iris walked back into the room. The gentlemen stood as they entered, and both the Sheriff and deputy were struck by Iris' beauty.

"Sheriff?" Iris smiled softly at Sheriff Jenkins and extended her hand, which he instinctively took. "I am Iris Gauche. How may I help you?"

"Miss Gauche, we are here investigating a missing person's report on a Miss Bobby Rebekah Patterson." He told her, being captured by her dark eyes.

"I am sorry, I don't know, Miss Patterson." Iris said sincerely.

"Dr. Lambert is acquainted with her." The Sheriff said, intently watching her reaction.

Iris looked puzzled for a few seconds, then looked at Dene. "Is that her name?" She asked him. He nodded his head. "Well, I have seen her then." She told the Sheriff.

"You have?" The deputy spoke up. "When?"

"A week ago, Friday in the parking lot of The Sound House at about one a.m., I guess that would make it Saturday morning." She told him calmly.

"What were you doing there? What was she doing?" The deputy asked her.

"Well, Dene and I were leaving after we had spent the evening in the Sound House enjoying the band. I was in the car, and she was speaking with Dene. One of the waitresses called to her from the entrance and she went back into the club and then we went home," Iris said simply, giving Dene a loving smile, which he returned.

"What were she and Dr. Lambert speaking about?" The deputy asked her as if he had scented blood.

"I do not know exactly as the window was up, but I gather she was angry with him." Iris told him.

"Why do you think that?" The deputy asked, looking at Dr. Lambert.

"Because she slapped him. She is not a well woman." Iris told him, looking sympathetically at Dene.

He smiled softly as if appreciating her understanding.

"Exactly as I told you," Dene told the Sheriff.

"Thank you, ladies." The Sheriff said, effectively dismissing them.

"Let us know if you need anything else," Leila told them as she and Iris left.

The Sheriff turned to Dene, saying in a soft voice so as not to carry outside of the room, "Dr. Lambert, we know you were sleeping with Bobby Rebekah. We know that there has been some conflict between the two of you, but we are not accusing you of anything. We are inquiring about your knowledge of her whereabouts."

"Sheriff, I don't know where she is." Dene told him, his voice ringing with honesty. "There was never a conflict on my part with her. We never dated, never had a relationship, it was strictly sex and I have not been sleeping with her for weeks. I believe that we both," here he looked pointedly at the Sheriff, "know that I wasn't the only one in town who she had been keeping company with." He looked at both the Sheriff and Deputy Holmes pointedly, who, despite both wearing wedding rings, shifted guiltily. "Besides, I was trying to help her, mostly." Dene continued.

"What do you mean?" Sheriff Jenkins asked.

"Have you checked out Stevie Tyler? That's her ex. He was always harassing her. She told me herself that she was afraid of him because he was dealing methamphetamines." Dene told them with worry in his voice. Sheriff Jenkins and Deputy Holmes exchanged looks. "She's been acting erratic for a while now. Check with the guard at the hospital! I had to have her banned from entering the hospital after that stunt she pulled on Tuesday; she definitely acted like she was on something. I've been avoiding going home ever since because I didn't want to have to call you and press charges. She has enough problems as it is."

"Dene has been with my family or at the hospital for the last several days, Sheriff. It is harder for anyone to harass him here as the neighborhood is secured in addition to the property gates." Nichola said to the Sheriff. "Normally, I wouldn't offer my home, but Dene is a friend to my family, attached to my cousin, and Leila's physician." He told them, sounding grateful to have Dene as part of his family. "When was Ms. Patterson reported missing?" He inquired.

"Well, as far as we have been able to gather, the last time anyone saw her was Friday morning when she was working the lunch shift at The Sound House. She was supposed to return at 8:00 that night to bar tend and never showed. She was reported missing by the manager, Marcus Tyler, after she didn't report in for her Saturday shift. He ran out to her place after several phone calls to check up on her and she wasn't home."

"Is Marcus Tyler any relation to Stevie Tyler?" Dene asked.

Sheriff Jenkins and Deputy Holmes exchanged looks and stood without answering the question.

The Sheriff offered his hand to both Dene and Nichola. "Thank you doctors. We appreciate the assistance."

"Absolutely." Nichola replied. "Anything we can do to help."

"Was any of that true?" Leila asked Dene, watching the Sheriff's cars leave from the front window.

"About the Tyler's? Yes, almost all of it. Stevie Tyler is Bobby's ex. He deals drugs, his brother Marcus is the manager at The Sound House, and Marcus moves those drugs through the bar occasionally. The police are aware of what is going on in town. The sheriff is a county official, but I would be surprised if he doesn't know exactly what goes on in town as well. They will have something to pursue now and will chalk her disappearance down to something drug related." He told her emotionlessly turning to help her gather the glasses of half drank lemonade. "I hate this," he whispered to her softly, guiltily.

"As do I. But we both need to get over it." Leila replied just as softly taking the tray from him.

Nichola left his study at midnight that night and the house was quiet. Scanning the property, he realized Leila was in the pool area. Downstairs he saw that the only lights on in the solarium were the pool lights casting a ghostly glow as she floated on her back, eyes closed, hands moving slowly in through the water.

Leila was attempting to clear her mind of the worry that had taken hold since the murder of Bobby Rebekah and now the arrival of the Sheriff on their doorstep. The boys didn't seem to have any lasting effects after witnessing so much and she hoped it stayed that way; that they hadn't been able to see much on that dark trail, that because of their young age, much of what they did see would eventually fade. She also hoped that the Sheriff was satisfied with Dene and Nichola's performance and that would be the end of it!

Suddenly, hands grabbed her around the waist and pulled her under the water to then release her. Pushing herself to the surface, sputtering and spitting water, she yelled, "What the hell?!"

Seeing Nichola treading water about six feet from her, he told her coldly, "You have been avoiding me."

"I'm not avoiding you." She swam to the side of the pool.

Suddenly he was right in front of her, in between her and the side. He moved so fast through the water that he caused small swells throughout the surface of the pool. "You would lie to me? You are avoiding me." His words were angry as he glared at her.

"I am tired, Nichola. Just leave me alone." Turning to swim to the other side, he appeared in front of her, just as quickly as before, to block her, causing more small waves, giving her a fierce angry look. "Stop it, Nichola! I'm not as strong a swimmer as you are. I can't tread water here all night!"

She found herself wrapped in his arms and pushed against the side of the pool.

Water rippled around them as he looked hard at her. "You will speak to me about what you are feeling, i allagí mou. Or I can come inside of your mind and pull it out of you."

Though she had always been aware that he had the power to do so, it was the first time he had threatened such a thing.

She guiltily realized that she had been shutting him out. Wrapping her arms around his neck, she buried her face against him, bursting into frightened and worried tears.

He held her close and, like magic; they were standing beside the pool, and he was holding her wet shaking body against his naked one. He looked bewildered as she started sobbing and laughing hysterically at the same time.

"I knew it." She laughed and cried. "I knew you preferred to swim naked." Breaking out into another round of hysterical sobs.

He shook his head at her, confusion written all over his face. He removed her swimsuit, wrapping her in a towel, and picked her sobbing body up in his arms. He laid her shivering and sobbing form on the bed in the bedroom off the rec room, joined her there and covered them with the blankets. Holding her tightly against him, sharing his body heat, he shushed her tenderly as she sobbed louder.

Soon her eyes were red and puffy, and she was almost cried out.

"Why didn't you take me upstairs?" She asked him quietly tears still in her voice.

"You were crying so loudly you would have woken up the whole house." He said dryly.

"You don't understand, Nichola!" She exclaimed with a sob.

"I understand more than you realize, my love." He whispered against her temple mournfully.

"What we have done is so horrible!" She said hiccupping.

"Yes." He agreed.

"There is nothing we can do that can fix this." She wailed, more tears coming.

"No." Shushing her as she shivered in reaction.

"I feel so terrible and so frightened." She cried softly holding him tight.

"Yes. But, after a certain point, what choice did we have? It was either her life or Iris' life. We could not let Iris die." Nichola told her in a soft, sorrowful tone. "Sometimes we do what we must in order for ourselves and our family to survive. We should always try to avoid conflict, but when it is visited upon us, we must never be afraid to do what it takes to survive or to protect our family." He stroked her back soothingly.

Holding him made her feel better. It didn't eradicate her worry or her fear, but it did help lessen it. "What if someone finds out what we have done?" She whispered fearfully.

He took her chin in his hand and softly kissed her lips. "I will let nothing happen to you, i psychí mou. I will always protect you and the children. You are my mate, and I will always love and protect you, and give whatever it takes to keep you safe. Just as you have my heart and soul, you have my promise." He opened her towel to hold her to him, skin to skin, running his hand down her body.

"No..." she whispered softly, though her body responded to his touch.

"I psychí mou, you need me. You need my strength to keep from being crushed by this grief. Let me make you feel better." He whispered, kissing her throat and stroking her gently.

"It won't change anything." She whispered, shaking her head slightly.

"No. But it will make you feel better and will give you the strength to carry on. You need to be strong, for me, for the children, for your family, for yourself." He told her as one of his knees parted her legs.

"Please." She resisted lightly, putting her arms against his warm chest.

"Thélo na eímai mésa sou, Glykó; I want to be inside of you, sweet one." He moved against her, stroking his erection against her curls. "Wrap your arms around me, Leila." He commanded in his *voice*, whispering in her ear, stroking against her once again, settling himself between her legs.

"Nichola, please don't." She whispered, but wrapped her arms around him and he covered her breasts with his warm chest.

As he braced himself on his forearms on each side of her, she was enveloped by his scent: cinnamon, ginger, and sandalwood.

"Oh, please, no," she groaned out softly as he placed small butterfly kisses all over her face and moved to suck softly at her throat, gently stroking himself against her. Her body betrayed her wishes, and she felt the familiar melting heat between her legs.

"You are mine, agápi mou." He whispered against her throat, stroking against her sex, making her groan softly. "Fíla me; kiss me." He commanded in his *voice* and took her lips with his, passionately dipping his tongue into her mouth, and she returned his kiss, her tongue playing against his as she ran her hands over his back. "We belong to each other. Resistance is pointless." He whispered against her now swollen lips, nipping her bottom lip gently as he slid into her unresisting body, causing her to cry out softly as her traitorous body arched against him.

He took his time, stroking in and out of her slowly, telling her how beautiful and strong that she was, how much he loved her, swallowing her small cries of passion with his lips, as he continued to slowly plunder her body; deliberately stoking her passion, warming her with his hands and his mouth as she held him tightly, arching to meet him every time he stroked into her with that roll of his hips. Gently she wrapped her legs around his, feeling that familiar tension take hold of her.

"Yes, glukó mou, my sweet. You like that, don't you? I love to stroke into your tight, wet pussy." She groaned in response, thrilling to his words, bringing her closer to the edge. "I love to feel you hold me tightly within you. You are so beautiful in your passion." He was using his *voice* to speak to her, and her breathing deepened, coming in a low moan and an ache was building in her body; she could feel her fangs lengthen. "That's it, my lover. Don't hold back. I want you to take me as I am now taking you." She tried to fight him, tried to resist the pull of his *voice*. "No, lover. Not tonight. You need this and so do I." He stroked her slightly faster, and the ache in her body intensified. He held her tightly to him so that the curve of his neck and shoulder were right against her face.

She ran her tongue over him as the tightness in her body increased around him.

"Yes, baby. You are close, so close to coming. You are almost there." She felt his own fangs against the curve of her shoulder as he whispered, and his *voice* was bringing her to the edge.

She felt the edge of her orgasm, as did he, and as they sank their fangs into each other simultaneously as her body exploded in pleasure. His blood tasted of spice and power, and she drank him in.

Love and Duty

WAKING UP THE NEXT morning to an empty bed in the master bedroom, Leila remembered waking briefly in the night to Nichola, carrying her to their room and joining her to sleep the rest of the night away. The filtered light coming in the UV film covered windows told her it was still morning, but it wasn't early morning. Glancing at the clock on the nightstand, she saw that it was past ten and knew that Mansuetus had things to do today, so had already taken the boys to daycare.

Closing her eyes briefly, she was disgusted with herself that she hadn't woken up in time to see the children off. Getting up and quickly showering, she wrapped a towel around her as she took a long hard look at herself in the mirror. Her eyes were turning a lighter shade of teal, and the freckles stood out starkly on her pale skin. Light circles were under her eyes. She had lost weight, and it was showing, especially along her jawline and her collarbones, which stood out.

Shaking her head worriedly she looked critically at herself. *So, this is what worry and stress look like?* She thought. *How stupid could I be to think that I had stress before this all started?*

Getting dressed, she wandered out into the house. The kitchen was empty, and she knew Dene had a shift at the hospital today, but Iris and Nichola had to be somewhere. She was sure that they weren't out running around in the sunshine. Noticing that the door to the study was ajar, she heard muted voices. Making sure to concentrate on keeping her presence blocked, she silently approached to listen at the door.

"You realize, cousin, that a decision has to be made about the good doctor." Nichola told Iris while he sat behind his desk looking across at her. His tone had a touch of the arctic in it and could have frozen water.

Surprised, Leila suddenly realized that he had never spoken to her or Iris with this tone before, at least in her presence. It was like a stranger was speaking.

"Yes, Nikolaos." Iris replied quietly.

"He knows too much about us all to remain here as a human." Nichola continued in his frozen tone. "That makes him supremely dangerous to us all." He fixed Iris with a hard, amber-eyed look.

"I realize I am responsible for him." Iris replied. "I started this, and I will take care of it." Iris continued. "I would like to remain in your household, for a while at least." She whispered.

"My household is normally quiet and orderly, Iris." He told her coldly.

"Until Leila arrived and consequently me at any rate."

"Leila is still just a changeling. Her transition is occurring slowly. But, as a changeling, I expect disruption from her and as my mate, I am more inclined to tolerate it. From you I am not. I have not been involved in murdering a human for many years." Nichola said smoothly, coldly. "We had discussed what could happen with your continued and escalating involvement with Dr. Lambert. But you did not heed my words."

Iris looked down at the hands clasped in her lap. "I know. I am sorry. I am wholly to blame for this whole situation."

"His presence will be missed, Iris. As such, his disappearance must be managed well. There is too much human focus on us as it is." Nichola told her abruptly.

"I know. I will not kill him, Nikolaos. I can't. I care about him." Iris replied nervously.

"Then what are you going to do?" Nichola's voice was sharp. "Do you expect me to take care of this situation?"

"No, Nikolaos. I am going to take care of this. I am going to keep him as my companion."

Leila listened to the long silence, stunned by her aunt's announcement.

"In my house?" Nichola asked.

"Yes. If you will allow it."

"He is under contract with the government. Taking him out of the country is out of the question. Do you think they wouldn't attempt to track him down if he disappeared? I have responsibilities and duties that I must fulfill. My residence here is not indefinite, and this property is not as protected as my estate in Canada, or any of my other residences, for that matter. You cannot expect me to leave you here in this residence to create anymore havoc in this township with the young doctor. Nor should you expect me to stay here indefinitely. Staying in this area with my mate is dangerous in its own way." Nichola's voice was icy, sharp, and scary.

Leila couldn't believe that it belonged to the man that held her in his arms last night.

"You can buy him out of his contract, Nikolaos." Iris said desperately. "He can be useful to you. You can give him a job."

"Doing what exactly?" Nichola asked brutally.

"You are building a hospital now in Toronto. You could use him on your staff. You'll need at least one doctor in addition to yourself. A medical doctor, in any case. Dene's brilliant, Nikolaos. You don't know how brilliant. He can study us. He can study our blood and our genetics. We know it is a gene that makes us different, but which one and why? If it is based purely on genes, how are we able to create made vampires? There are so many questions to be answered and Dene could help us answer them! He dreams of being a researcher." Iris exclaimed excitedly.

There was a long silence, and Leila knew Nichola was pondering her words. "I suppose his research could help us overcome our frailties, few though they are." He muttered out loud. "Fine. But you should pay his debt. He is your companion. What is the going rate for an indentured servant in this century?" He asked forcefully, with a cruel tone to his voice, knowing what her answer was sure to be.

"Nikolaos! I cannot. My wealth is nothing compared to yours! His debt is great. But an amount that you won't even miss." Iris told him.

"Humph! Fine. But your time here is limited. There is too much exposure on both you and the good doctor due to the 'disappearance' of that young woman. You both will need to leave as soon as possible without exposing this family to too much interest from the local authorities. As soon as the attention dies down, you both need to fly to Toronto and stay there." The order was delivered in an ice-cold voice.

"But what about my niece? I don't wish to leave her here!" Iris said, raising her voice.

"She is mine. That makes her my responsibility." Nichola warned. "In any case, we will not linger here for long. She needs to be in a secure environment when her change manifests itself. We will go to Toronto as soon as the husband comes back, and she can leave the children with him." Leila gasped softly at his words, then she heard, "Isn't that right, Leila?"

She walked into the study to face him as Iris whirled around to look at her, surprised. "How long have you known that I was out there?" She asked.

"Not long, I suspect." He replied. "You are becoming stealthy, i psychí mou." Amber eyes met her teal ones. "I assume you are in agreement that the children shouldn't be raised in a vampire household."

With those words, she knew he had read her thoughts from yesterday.

"My children shouldn't be raised in a vampire household." She confirmed coldly. She could feel him trying to probe her mind, and with supreme will power she shut him out.

He gave her an ironic half smile, his eyes hard. "Keep your secrets if you wish, my darling. We have all the time in the world to reveal them."

Leila avoided Nichola for the rest of the day, only coming out of hiding when Mansuetus brought the children home in the afternoon. The tension between them was obvious to all the adults around the table during dinner, making the conversation stilted.

Dene and Iris were abnormally quiet during the meal, and Nichola drank large amounts of wine. Beside the general inquiries into Dene's day at the hospital and Zachary's conversation with Mansuetus about why Bart the Dragon liked goats above anything else, the table was mostly silent.

"I would speak with you, i psychí mou." Nichola commanded coldly, moving behind her to head to his study as she was helping Mansuetus clean the kitchen after dinner.

Exchanging glances with Mansuetus, who looked worried, she followed Nichola into the room.

He held the door for her, softly closing it behind her.

She heard the lock click into place. Turning around, she looked at him bravely. "Do you plan violence against me?" She demanded.

"I never plan violence against you, Leila. That doesn't mean that it won't occur. I am quite experienced in dealing with young vampires and hard conversations." He rationalized and his tone was entirely reasonable as he walked past her to sit in the chair behind his desk. "Sit." He commanded, motioning to the chair across from him.

She looked at him briefly and complied.

"What would you like to talk about?" Leila asked, unsuccessfully trying for a reasonable tone.

"Why were you spying on your aunt and I this morning?" He asked bluntly.

"I wouldn't call it spying necessarily. But I must admit, it was educational." She looked at him calmly. "Why did you feel it was necessary to hide your true personality from me?"

"What personality would that be, Leila?" He was just as calm as she was.

"That you are a harsh, overbearing prick!" She accused quietly with passion.

His eyes glittered darkly in anger, but his voice remained calm. "I deal with you differently than I do with Iris. It's quite simple, really."

"Simple? Is that why you invade my thoughts? If you had ever talked down to me like you did to her today, I would have told you to go fuck yourself. She asked you for your help and you were cold and cruel and basically made her beg," Leila told him furiously.

"Cold and cruel?" He asked, laughing harshly. "You malign me, Leila. I had several conversations with Iris advising her on her conduct and she willfully ignored every single one, resulting in the death of one human, and the altering of another human forever! Now, I am expected to go along happily with having to take her into my house as a permanent resident and her mistake as well? Not to mention paying an exorbitant amount of money for that privilege! That is too much to ask without showing my anger over the situation, even someone of my age and patience; any other elder would have killed them both! One for disobeying and risking our discovery by the authorities, and the other for being a mistake! She got off lightly due to the love I have for my family; your aunt knows this, and if you don't believe me, ask her!" His tone was a low, hot growl as he glared at her. "You are my mate. I give you leeway as such, but do not interfere with this. We have a hierarchy

406

to our society and as the elder of our bloodline, it begins and stops with me." He snarled at her for challenging him.

"So, basically you are King of us all and we need to bow and scrape for your approval? I don't think so!" She spat out, leaped from the chair and turned on her heel to head to the door only to run right into his chest.

She felt him grip her upper arms tightly and give her a small shake, forcing her to look up into his eyes, which blazed angrily into hers. She surprised him by not shrinking at his fury.

"I am not your king, Leila!" He said softly, dangerously. "I am your elder and your mate. You will respect my experience and the fact that I have survived nearly a thousand years. When I tell you to do something, it is with your survival and the survival of this family in mind. This is a lesson that you must learn." He gave her another small shake as she mutely glared back at him. "Besides, your actual anger is not for your aunt but for some imagined slight against yourself."

"You have no business plucking thoughts from my mind, Nichola. I have a right to the privacy of my thoughts!" She told him, trying to remain cold and calm, though she was seething inside.

Shaking his head at her, he gave her a small push, backing her further into the study, causing her to stumble slightly, but the small distance between them kept his hands off of her.

So, we come to it. You are my mate; your thoughts are not private from me. He thought at her as she struggled to push him from her mind.

She did so, but only with supreme effort. "Get out of my head!" She yelled at him.

"In deference to your wishes, I am rarely in your head." His tone was cruel. "Though it would take me little effort to force my way in. I am mostly gentle with you, Leila. Though you do not appreciate it."

She scoffed in disgust at him, giving him a contemptuous roll of her eyes.

He snarled softly at her, and his eyes blazed in fury at her reaction. "You hide many things from me and fight me at every opportunity. You willfully refuse to learn our ways and our rules."

Closing the distance between them, he grabbed her by the arms again to give her another small shake, his movements too fast for her eyes to see him.

Feeling him once again in her mind, he overpowered her. *I am tired of it.* Hearing his voice once more in her head, she fought him as he laid open her thoughts, reading her quickly. *If you think I would allow a transitioning vampire of my line out into the world, my mate no less, with no safeguards and no elder protection, you are deceiving yourself.*

Feeling him move easily through her thoughts, she battled him. *Yes, your father.* His thought was derisive. *If he stepped one toe over the line, I would kill him in an instant and he knows it.* Her mouth went dry in terror. *Unfortunately for you, everyone lies to you, my love, except myself. Yet, I am the only one that you distrust and fight with. He has met me and knows me. His current existence is only tolerated because he is your father, otherwise I would have forced him to face his nature or die long ago. I am tempted to kill him in any case for intentionally failing to do his duty by you, as we had agreed upon.*

Shocked at his thoughts, she tried to battle him for control and failed miserably as he delved deeper into her mind while she physically tried to pull away from him.

Yes, your husband. This guilt, shame, and duty you feel towards him is highly misplaced to be given to a man who puts you and your children second to himself and his desires. What makes you think he would even want you after you have been in my bed, and I have taken you in every way possible? He questioned in her mind, as she felt the rage and jealousy pouring off of him like lava out of a volcano.

Finally able to break free of his grip, she struck out, slapping him hard across the face. He paused briefly and because their minds were still connected; she knew he was tempted to strike her in return.

Instead, he pushed her harder this time, and she stumbled to fall back against the leather sofa, twisting around to grip the back of the couch hard, to keep from falling to the ground.

She felt him grip the back of her t-shirt hard and he tore it from her body, and she yelled obscenities at him, trying to fight his superior strength.

He gripped her around her throat from behind, and she realized his hands were tipped with lethal claws. *Scream away, Leila. If that is what you wish, I do not care.* He told her in her mind as she went silent. *You will only upset your children, and there is no one here who will come to your aid in any case. Both Iris and Mansuetus know I won't kill you and will stay out of our battles. You are my mate, and they know our rules and respect them and my place, unlike you!*

His claws made short work of her bra and the metal clasp released with a snap dragging across the skin of her back, scratching her and she gasped in pain as she smelled her own blood. His long tongue was on her back in an instant licking her as he grasped her breasts tightly and painfully in his hands, pulling her back roughly against his chest he unceremoniously sank his fangs into her shoulder as she cried out, tears escaping from her eyes, against the burning pain of his bite. *You are mine, Leila. No one else's but mine. Never forget that again!* His voice was harsh and angry in her mind as he drank deeply from her.

It was over in less than a minute.

She felt him run his tongue over the bite marks and then he roughly pushed her limp body to fall onto the sofa, walking to the door of the study slamming it open, almost tearing it from its hinges, he walked out. Seconds later, she heard the front door slam shut.

She curled up on the sofa, her knees to her chest, and sobbed.

After a minute or two, Iris came into the study to wrap her in her arms and hold her, rocking her sobbing body as she tried to shush her. "Don't cry, baby, the children will hear, and you will upset them. Come, let me help you to the bedroom." Iris supported her body as she could barely stand or walk, and got her into the bedroom, helping her to the bed.

Nichola returned to the house before midnight, finding himself in their bedroom, looking down on her sleeping form.

He was ashamed of himself for treating her so harshly and cruelly. Though he had only spoken the truth to her earlier. What should it matter to him that she knows her father had sold his care of her for his freedom and a puny human-like existence? Why should he point out to her that her selfish husband wouldn't welcome her back after she had so fully and eagerly given herself to him? Both things were true, but there had been no need for him to enlighten her of them so cruelly.

He used the truth to hurt her because her plans of escaping cut him deeply.

Suddenly, her eyes flew open to meet his, and she quickly scrambled away from him to cower like a beaten dog against the headboard, her arms wrapped around her naked breasts and her knees pulled in tightly against her body. He noticed she was still wearing the shorts that she had on earlier; either Iris or Mansuetus had put her in the bed obviously.

"Don't be frightened, i psychí mou. I am not here to beat you." He told her softly, sorrowfully.

"Why not?" She whispered fearfully. "You mind raped me, bit me, and considered doing more. Beating me would be nothing at this point."

"I am sorry, i psychí mou. I am terribly sorry and ashamed of my actions. Fury overtook me at your plans to leave me. I have no other excuse." He slowly sat on the edge of the bed, as she cowered more into the headboard, trying to put more distance between them. "Please don't be afraid of me, Glykó. I love you."

"Well, you have a strange way of showing it." She told him with sharp, angry eyes.

He almost breathed a sigh of relief.

In his opinion, anger was better than fear. He would rather have her angry at him than afraid of him. "You can't leave me, Glykó. Young vampires rarely survive in the wild in these modern times. You would also be dangerous to your children without my influence. You don't understand this because you have been lucky enough to be with an elder almost nonstop since the start of your transition. If you were to leave on your own, only disaster would follow. I would be lost if you were killed or ended up killing yourself because you harmed one of your children and many people, our family, depend on me. I wouldn't survive it, Leila." He told her softly, but sincerely. "God, help me, I wouldn't." He said and his voice broke.

"Nichola, I cannot raise my children here. They cannot be a witness to murder and death and grow up to be sane and well-adjusted people." She whispered to him in a pained voice. "It's too dangerous for them, and Mansuetus, me nor you, or all of us combined, can protect them. That is too obvious now."

"Mansuetus and I had hoped that we could, i psychí mou. Our lives are usually not this dangerous. But you are correct. Our existence is still too dangerous for them." His words were softly spoken. "On the other hand, you cannot raise them on your own either. Your existence will only become harder as you transition into a full vampire. They would be in a more dangerous situation if that were to occur, especially without the presence of an elder for their own protection." His pained whisper rang with honesty.

She tried swallowing the tears in her throat as pain spread throughout her chest at his words. "I can't. I can't give them up." She lowered her head to her knees and sobbed. She felt him pull her to him and wrap her shaking body in his arms.

"I am so sorry, Leila." Nichola whispered against her hair and his heart broke as he witnessed her soul-wrenching heartbreak. "I'm so sorry."

He held her tenderly against him as she sobbed herself to sleep. There was nothing he could do or say that would stop the pain that she was feeling.

There was a soft knock on the bedroom door, and he laid her down on the bed and covered her sleeping body with the blankets as he went to answer it.

Mansuetus was there in the dim hallway, his cell phone clutched in his hand.

Nichola stepped out of the bedroom, closing the door behind him.

"What is it?" He asked softly and Mansuetus handed him the phone with a worried look.

"Hello?"

"Tsoukalous, this is Beutel. We need your assistance. The Prince has been injured." Nichola heard the panic in Beutel's voice.

"What is his condition?" He asked coldly and calmly to counter the other vampire's panic.

"That damned rogue skewered him through the chest and damn near sliced his arm off, though for now, it looks like he should survive." Beutel's voice was laced with fear.

"Where are you?" Nichola asked calmly.

Nichola glanced at the clock on his desk: two a.m., as he handed Mansuetus the phone. "Call Rom. He should still be at Château les Ténèbres. Explain to him the situation. I need him to be here by dawn. Then prepare the downstairs bedroom for his use. He and I will leave here tomorrow evening to take care of this rogue once and for all."

"Yes, Kýrios." Mansuetus nodded.

"You know your duty to this family while I am away." Nichola stated, standing and heading for the study door.

"I do, Kýrios." Mansuetus replied with a bow of his head.

"I trust you with their lives, my friend," Nichola spoke softly, looking grateful.

"I am honored, Kýrios. My life for theirs."

Nichola climbed into the bed, naked, to lie beside Leila's sleeping body. He removed the rest of her clothes gently and ran his hands up and down her body and place small butterfly kisses on her skin.

Waking up, she said firmly to him, "You have got to be kidding me, right? After what you did to me tonight, you think you are going to get laid?" She pushed his hands from her, disgusted.

"Leila," he whispered, wrapping his arms around her tightly. "I know you are angry with me, and you have every right to be. I was a bastard," he stated bluntly. "I would allow you to torture me by denying me your body under normal circumstances, but I am leaving tomorrow night and I don't have any idea of when I will return. I cannot leave you weak. Without my presence giving you strength, things can go wrong with your transition, or they could speed up very quickly and you could become out of control."

She rolled out of his arms and onto her side, presenting her back to him. "The excuses men use to get laid have never ceased to amaze me." But even she noticed that her voice lacked strength. Rallying herself, she said firmly and sarcastically, "Truly, it's one of the best lines I have heard in years, 'Baby, my dick is medicinal! Let me fuck you and make you feel better!'"

"Willful and foul-mouthed!" He growled into the nape of her neck as he spooned against her back, plunging his hand in between her legs. "Any other man would have beaten you a half dozen times by now."

She bucked, squirming in his arms. As her body started to heat up and betray her mind, she felt his erection against her ass. "Stop it!" She started to yell, and he quickly covered her mouth with his other hand.

Leila, I don't want to overpower you! She heard his voice in her mind. *I don't deserve you to participate giving me pleasure in return, just still yourself and absorb my strength and power. You've known from the beginning that as my mate, this is how it must be for you to take my strength.* He thought somberly.

In other words, just lay there and take it, bitch! She thought in return, furiously struggling against him.

I love you, Leila. It isn't like that at all. I am going to do whatever it takes to keep you safe, even if you are angry about it. He thought as he pushed her struggling body to her back as gently as he could, covering her mouth with his own before she had the chance to yell out her anger again. He forced her legs apart with his own, settling his heavier body onto hers, pinning her to the mattress.

I hate you; she thought with a sob as he plundered her mouth, and she felt the familiar wetness in between her legs as he rubbed the head of his cock against her entrance.

I love you, i psychí mou. I love you. His return thought was a whisper full of desire and sadness as he slowly entered her tightness.

Leila woke just before dawn to noises in the hallway. She got up, throwing on her robe and left the bedroom, seeing a chauffeur taking a couple of bags down the hallway following Mansuetus. She followed also and as they passed through the kitchen; she saw Es, beautiful and angelic as ever, sitting at the kitchen table with a cup of coffee in front of her.

She came over to embrace her quickly and exclaimed happily, "Es what are you doing here? Where's Rom?"

"He's in the office with Nikolaos." Es told her warmly returning her embrace. "Beutel and the Prince have run into some trouble on their hunt. Rom tells me that the Prince has been severely injured and Beutel called last night to request assistance from Nikolaos. They are leaving tonight for Prague to join them. Do you mind if I stay with you? Just overnight. I need to return to our home in Utah tomorrow."

"No, Es! Of course, you are always welcome!" Leila told her. She could tell that something was bothering her. She sat next to her at the kitchen table and held her hand. "What's wrong? You seem worried."

"This hunt. They weren't even supposed to go. Now the Prince is injured? What in the world could have happened?" She asked Leila.

"I don't know Es; this is the first I am hearing about it..." Leila told her bewildered.

Suddenly Rom and Nichola came walking into the kitchen. Rom spoke sharply, "Beutel is a complete idiot, is most likely what happened. Probably abandoned the Prince at the first sign of danger, the coward!" He turned toward the coffeepot, grabbing a cup from the counter. "There is a damn skill to assassination after all. It can be dangerous! In either case, they were both reckless, otherwise the Prince wouldn't be hurt right now. Most likely a complete lack of planning." He told them pouring his coffee, he turned, noticing their scared expressions in surprise. "No need for you ladies to worry yourselves." He said smoothly.

"So, you think that it's a good idea for you to be putting yourselves in danger?" Leila questioned sharply, encompassing both Rom and Nichola.

"This is our duty, i psychí mou. We will help them take care of this situation. We will meet Ostrovsky in Prague tonight and we will pick up the trail. We will not lack resources or personnel, agápi mou. I assure you we will take precautions; we will be safe." Nichola told her, warmed by the concern that he felt coming from her.

"Who are you hunting that is so dangerous that they would be able to harm the Prince?" Es demanded.

"It's Earle." Rom told her quietly and Es gasped.

"What happened to cause that?" Es asked.

"Who's Earl?" Leila asked.

"It's Earle." Nichola told her quietly, but Leila could hear little difference.

"Professor Randall Earle." Es told her. "What did he do? He always seemed so polite and quiet. I can't imagine him doing anything atrocious." She directed at Rom.

"Well, you imagined wrong!" Rom told her irritably and she gave him a sharp look at his tone. He looked away from her in bad humor.

Nichola smoothly cut in, "Professor Randall Earle is a two-hundred-year-old made vampire originally from Australia, Leila." He sat down at the table with them a cup of coffee in his hands. Looking at Leila, he said, "When he was turned, he was a professor at Oxford. He specializes in human anatomy. He is highly intelligent by all accounts, and extremely skilled with a blade." Here he looked at Es, "Unfortunately, for the world at large, for the last several decades the professor has fancied himself as another Ripper." Es gasped in shock. "Fortunately for him, he never hunted more than once or twice in the same city and avoided any major detection."

"So, he goes after prostitutes like Jack the Ripper?" Leila questioned.

Rom answered with disgust, "Yes. He gets off on kidnapping, repeatedly raping, torturing, and then dismembering prostitutes. He's a sick bastard."

"Well, how did the council discover he has been doing this and what caused their change in attitude?" Leila's voice was calm and cool, but her heart hammered in her chest in fear.

Nichola looked at her sympathetically. "As you and I have discussed, as long as our population doesn't bring undue attention to our community, we will warn, but not interfere. The small council has known of his activities for a few years. He himself was warned a few times."

"The crazy bastard has finally crossed the line this time!" Rom said with a growl, and Leila could tell he was incensed. "He kidnapped a teenage girl in Paris two months ago, mistaking her for a prostitute. He didn't realize his mistake until after he raped her, and she turned out to be a virgin. He had done major damage to her body and tried to heal or turn her; frankly, we are unsure of his intentions. Probably due to the fact that he's a relatively young, made vampire, it didn't quite work. She must have escaped him because she was picked up by the Paris police. She's in a mental institution now and when she isn't screaming her bloody head off, she is telling everyone about her 'vampire' rapist. The French papers are calling him Le Violeur Vampire Déchirant."

"What does that mean?" Leila asked.

"The Ripping Vampire Rapist. The girl was able to lead them back to the place that he had been keeping her, where there were three dead prostitutes in various phases of dismemberment. A veritable slaughterhouse! We think he was draining them to get the girl to drink their blood, but it is really unknown what he was doing. It makes no difference in any case, the line's been crossed and after his warnings there is no going back. He is done." Rom said with some satisfaction.

"Will the little girl live?" Leila asked him, quietly horrified.

Nichola answered, "Yes. But mentally, who knows if she will ever lead a productive life."

"This is why we need to pass that resolution," Rom said quietly, and Nichola gave him a look.

"What resolution?" Es asked.

"Romulus put forth a resolution that would allow teenagers to be fully classified as children and not allowed to be harmed or fed from. Unfortunately, it did not pass the council." Nichola said with a sigh.

"Backwards bastards." Rom muttered.

"Didn't you vote for it?" Leila asked Nichola.

"Of course, I did!" He told her. "But the rest of them voted against it, making it a 2-4 vote. They don't consider teenagers to be too young for either feeding or sex," Nichola said simply.

"Perverts!" Es said, shocked.

"Exactly!" Rom said. "Thirteen and above, it's open season to feed from or fuck them. Freaking amazing." He said in disgust.

"There was a modification, Rom." Nichola said reasonably. "There is no killing them unless it is in self-defense, and they must be willing for both feeding and sex. It was something, if not everything. Change takes time, and time is something that we have plenty of, my friend."

Just then Zachary, still wearing his pajamas, ran into the kitchen to come to a screeching halt, looking up at Rom in surprise.

Rom looked at him in total shock.

"Who you? You a pirate?" Zachary asked him wide-eyed, which didn't surprise Leila much and she smiled since Romulus definitely looked like a pirate dressed in his long-sleeved, loose-fitting, white shirt, tight black pants, and knee boots, his dark skin was a stark contrast against the white of his shirt, his long black hair was pulled back and he wore a large diamond stud in his right ear. Zachary then noticed her sitting at the table and ran to her with a "Mommy!" She helped him up on her lap as Iris came into the kitchen

416

holding Devin. Zachary looked at Es' shocked expression and yelled, "You pretty!" Turning to Nichola, he said, "Hi Nick!".

Nichola smiled at him, saying, "Good morning, Zachary."

Devin squirmed and started squawking, reaching out for Nichola and Iris handed him over. He sat him down on his lap as Devin started yelling, "Da, da, da, da, da," looking in Leila's direction.

Romulus sat down at the table in shock, looking closely at Devin, who turned and gave him a sharp, calculating look. "He thinks you are his father?" He asked Nichola softly.

"No, that's his name for me." Leila told him, smiling.

"They are your children?" Rom asked her in awe.

"Yes. They are." She responded by giving Zachary a kiss on the head. Standing up and putting Zachary in his booster seat next to Es, she headed to the refrigerator to fix them breakfast.

"They are your bloodline?" He asked Nichola in wonder.

"They are." Nichola nodded, giving him an amused look.

"You didn't tell me you had children." Es said quietly to Leila as she returned to the table with sippy-cups full of milk for the boys.

"I am kind of keeping it a secret. So, please don't tell anyone else." Leila requested quietly.

"Oh, no! I understand. You would want to protect them at all costs." Smiling at Zachary next to her.

He took a drink from his cup asking her, "What your name?"

"My name is Es; I am a friend of your mother's." She gave him a bright smile.

"Ezzzzz." Zachary smiled.

"Yes." She encouraged him, smiling in return.

"Are you swim with us, Ezzzzz?" He asked.

Es looked at Leila questioning.

Leila looked at him, "Well, I suppose you guys can stay home today and we can go swimming."

"This is good." She heard Mansuetus say as he came into the kitchen and started to make breakfast.

Rom was still looking at Devin, sitting on Nichola's lap in wonder.

Devin was making faces at him.

Rom suddenly smiled and Devin gave him a big, mischievous grin.

Zachary leaned over the table, saying to Rom, "Devin bites!" Which caused Rom to burst out laughing.

"He is your companion, Iris?" Es asked poolside as they watched Man-suetus and Dene playing with the boys in the pool. Rom and Nichola were closeted in the office on a conference call with the other members of the small council.

"Yes." Iris replied. "It's new."

"He's very handsome." Es observed, smiling.

"He's very nice as well." Leila said, smiling.

Iris smiled at them and then asked Es in a serious tone. "So, how do you think that Randall Earle was able to injure Khaldun?"

"I do not know. Nikolaos is right. From everything I know about him, he is highly intelligent. He had to have known that the small council would send someone after him to end his life. I am sure that he has prepared for it. I know it sounds terrible, but I am just thankful that it wasn't Rom or Nikolaos that was injured. From what Rom has told me, the Prince is lucky to be alive." Es said with a shudder.

"Has anyone ever considered that the community should start policing actions sooner? Why let situations get out of control? Why take these risks at all? There should be hard and fast rules about actions that constitute the needless death of humans! He was killing them for sport, not for survival or self-defense!" Leila spoke up passionately. "These endless games are ridiculous and dangerous! He was 'warned' several times for his actions? What does that exactly mean? Obviously, the warnings didn't faze him in the slightest! This was coming. Everyone on the council saw it, yet no action was taken to stop it before it occurred."

"I agree." Iris said. "The system is archaic!"

"That's what happens when the system is run by archaic beings." Es replied. "Just like the resolution that was voted down in this last session about teenagers. I am sure that all of them, Rom and Nikolaos included, have had teenagers in their beds at one point or another throughout the centuries." Es said, making a face of disgust.

"Well, a seventeen-year-old is different from a thirteen-year-old, after all." Leila told her, much to Es' surprise. "Where are you going to draw the line when sixteen-year-olds can marry right now in this state? It is a more complicated issue than just having a law that says that vampires can't indiscriminately kill humans. There have to be rules for justifiable homicide." She thought for a moment and then continued in a lower voice. "Besides, I was seventeen when I graduated from high school. I have thought a lot over the last couple of weeks about how much less complicated my life would be right now if Nichola had just come and collected me after I graduated."

"Oh, honey, don't say that!" Iris stopped petting Gladiator, who had settled himself for a nap on her lap and gripped Leila's hand hard.

"I don't regret my babies, Auntie! Truly, I don't. But I fear for them every day." Leila said sadly. "And it is just a terror that keeps building."

"I would have given anything to have a child of my own." Es said wistfully. "I totally understand your fear. Our community is not without violence, and violence that is tolerated at that. All for some idea to keep us from fighting each other so that we aren't discovered and exterminated. But, from my sight, you are so lucky to have what you have, Leila. I have never seen a vampire household more like a human household in my entire existence. There is love, and children, and pets. I am surprised that Nikolaos of all people is living like this. I was astonished to watch him hold and feed your youngest son this morning, and actually enjoy it. I could tell that Rom envied him. You, and your children, have influenced Nikolaos greatly and let me tell you, it has been for the better. I have never seen him happier."

"He's still a vampire elder, Es." Leila said bitterly, remembering their encounter from yesterday. "And acts as such, often."

"I am sure that is true, and it must make life difficult. It is hard for us to go against our very natures, no matter how civilized we try to be," Es told her, nodding her head in agreement.

Nichola held her tightly that evening as Mansuetus loaded the Mustang with his and Rom's bags. "I am sorry it has been difficult between us over the last few days, i psychí mou." He whispered, gently placing butterfly kisses against her temple. "I regret it. I'll miss you terribly. Hopefully, we are able to return soon."

"Be careful, Nichola. Take care of each other and don't take any unnecessary risks." Leila told him, glancing over at Rom, who was also holding Es close to him.

"I promise, we always do. Mansuetus will keep you and the boys safe, Leila. He has my complete trust in keeping you safe or I wouldn't leave you for anything." He whispered against her lips, kissing her tenderly.

"Just keep us informed. Not knowing what's going on is the worst part of all of this." She told him.

"I promise, I will. I love you, Leila." He told her, looking down into her worried teal eyes as he cupped her face gently.

She held his hand tightly to her face, feeling his lightly calloused fingers against her skin.

"Ready?" Rom said from the passenger side of the car.

Nichola kissed her deeply, then lifted his head, saying to him, "Yes."

Es and Leila spent an uneventful evening and the next day with the children, Iris and Mansuetus. Just after dark, Mansuetus loaded Es' bags in the limousine to take her to the airport. Nichola had sent his private jet back to her for her use in returning to Utah. Ostrovsky had offered the use of his jet while they were all hunting together, as Nichola wanted to make sure that his family had air transportation if it was needed.

While Mansuetus loaded the bags, Leila and Es held each other's hands and spoke quietly. "Take care of them, Leila. You have such a blessing. Do whatever it takes to keep your beautiful children safe."

The two women hugged each other. "I will Es, I promise. No matter what, I will keep them safe."

"Goodbye, my friend," Es whispered. "Take care of yourself." She gave her one long-lasting look before getting in the back seat of the limousine where Mansuetus held the door.

The next morning, Leila walked out into the garage with Dene and Mansuetus. They waved goodbye to Dene as he pulled out of the driveway to go to the hospital, and she helped Mansuetus buckle the kids into their car seats to go to daycare.

"Did you remember the grocery list?" She asked him with a smile.

"Yes, Kyría." He said grumpily.

"They were here two days in a row, you know." She smiled. "Don't forget the spinach, broccoli, and pomegranate and apple juice. We are all out."

"Okay." He answered.

She waved goodbye as he pulled out of the driveway. As soon as he was out of sight, she ran into the recreation room, quickly put on her bathing suit and ran behind the bar to pull a basket of pool accessories out. She had noticed the basket of sunscreens when they had explored the house the first time they had brought the kids out to swim. Of course, it had remained untouched. Going into the bathroom, she lathered sunscreen all over every inch of exposed skin, rubbing it in well. She then headed back into the garage.

The sun was now above the horizon.

Breathing deeply to calm herself, she intentionally blocked herself from Nichola, trying to put up walls of steel around her mind. Putting her dark rhinestone sunglasses and floppy brimmed hat on, she walked out of the garage doors and into the driveway, which was still mostly in shadow.

Making her way slowly to the edge of the parking pad, she stood in the shadow to extend one of her arms out into the sunshine.

The light tingled against her skin, slightly burning, but the pain was nowhere near as bad as it was several weeks ago. Slowly, reaching forward with both hands, testing her pain threshold, she slowly walked into the sunlight.

Mansuetus was just through the checkout line at the grocery when his cell phone rang.

"Yes?" He answered.

"What the hell is going on there?" Came Nichola's stern voice.

"What do you mean, Kýrios?" Mansuetus questioned, puzzled.

"I feel something. Something from Leila. Something is not right!" Nichola told him.

"I am in the grocery parking lot. I will call the house immediately and will call you back."

Mansuetus looked at the phone with concern and dialed the house.

"Hello?" Iris' voice rang out cheerily.

"Iris! What is going on? Where's Leila?" He demanded.

"I don't know. She is here somewhere." Iris responded.

He could hear her calling throughout the house for Leila. She got back on the phone. "She's taking a bath."

"Is she alright? Is anything wrong?" He asked, then he heard Iris speaking and heard a muffled reply.

"Nothing's wrong. She's fine." Iris told him. "What's going on?"

"Go into the bathroom and see if she is okay." He demanded.

He heard her open the door and then Leila's voice, "Auntie, I am taking a bath! What do you want?"

"Mansuetus is on the phone. He wants to know if you are okay." Came Iris' muffled voice.

"Of course I am okay. Why does he think something is wrong?" He heard Leila ask her.

"She's fine Mansuetus! What's the problem?" Iris spoke into the receiver, concerned.

"Kýrios called, concerned. He says he felt something." Mansuetus explained in bewilderment, putting the groceries in the trunk. "I am on my way home."

"Okay. We will be here." Iris said snootily as if put out, disconnecting the line.

Humphing in irritation, he got into the car, dialing Nichola.

"Well?" Nichola demanded, sounding worried.

"She is fine. She is taking a bath." Mansuetus told him. "What made you think that something was wrong?"

"It felt wrong. Something felt wrong." Nichola replied, and it sounded like he was at a loss for words over the feeling that he had experienced. "You are sure she is okay?"

"Yes, I even made Iris go into the bathroom to check on her. That did not make her happy!" He told him sympathetically. "She is fine. Irritated, but fine."

"Maybe it is the distance between us?" Nichola questioned, but Mansuetus could tell he didn't need a response. "Thank you, Mansuetus. I apologize for interrupting you."

"Not at all, Kýrios. I will keep an eye on them."

"Thank you, I know you will." Nichola hung up.

Mansuetus drove straight home, a puzzled expression on his face.

Adapting

CHAPTER ONE

"MANSUETUS, WOULD YOU TAKE me to get my car this evening?" Leila asked Mansuetus after dinner.

"Why Kyría?" He asked, drying the plate that she had put in the dish rack.

"Because I want it! Am I a prisoner?" She demanded.

"Well, no, of course not, Kyría!" He told her surprised by her tone.

"I want the windows of my car to be outfitted with the UV film, like the windows here at the house have." She told him, trying to remain calm. "I should be able to take a drive if I want to without worrying about what time it is! I am tired of being tied down here every day; I feel like I am in prison!"

"Of course, Kyría. I can do that for you." He told her meekly.

"Thank you." She said softly, regretting her tone.

She and Mansuetus pulled up to the house to find Michael's truck in the driveway.

She sighed deeply. *That's just great!* She thought getting out of the car.

They went into the house and Michael came walking out of the bedroom. "Where the hell have you been? Where's the kids and the animals?" He asked her, ignoring Mansuetus. "I called your parents to find out where you were. Your Dad is really worried!"

"When did you get in?" She asked him.

"Early this morning. I came home, and you guys weren't here! What the hell? You couldn't have left a note?" He asked, irritated. "Why is your Dad so freaked out?"

"I didn't know that you were going to be here, Michael." Leila told him coldly.

"We came in early. I tried calling several times, but you haven't been here." He answered softly in a pained voice.

"I am sorry. It wasn't planned. It's complicated." She said softly as she took her keys out of her purse. "I am just here to get my car."

"Woah! Oh, no way! You are leaving me? Where are the kids?" He asked her, shocked, and she heard the raw pain in his voice.

"Mansuetus, would you run and get the kids and the animals? Bring Aunt Iris back with you too, please?" Mansuetus gave her a sharp look, shaking his head no. "Please, Mansuetus?" She looked at him pleadingly.

He gave her a stony-eyed look and left the house.

"Is he going to get them?" Michael asked, bewildered at the big man's behavior.

"I don't know. Probably." She replied honestly walking into the living room to sit down.

"You've lost a lot of weight." Michael observed as he sat next to her on the couch.

"Yeah, I guess." Her tone ambiguous.

"Listen to me. I am sorry about everything." He began reaching over to hold her hand.

"So, am I." She removed her hand. She was tired and weak from her experience in the sun that morning, and his touch made her feel things that she didn't want to examine too closely.

"Your Dad was losing it when I called them to find out if they knew where you were. I told him that the new doctor had arrived a couple of weeks ago and he just lost it. He was saying a lot of things that didn't make sense. Something about how you promised him you would try. He kept talking about how you haven't even given it a chance. He was acting more squirrely than normal." Michael was saying.

She looked at him sharply. "That's because he bears a lot of guilt over this. I never promised him a thing, but he wouldn't know a promise if it hit him in the face! That's what happens when you are a liar."

Michael faced her, looking puzzled and shocked. He'd never heard her say a bad thing about her father before. "What do you mean?"

"Michael, I can't explain it to you in words. You just won't believe me. I am going to have to show you. I can't do that by myself. Aunt Iris will be here in a little bit. Then I promise I will tell you everything." She sighed tiredly.

"How are the kids?" He asked quietly, confused, but trying not to push her.

"They're really good. Zachary has grown some. He is getting really good at coloring. Devin isn't walking yet, but he's close. He's getting better about being around strangers. He has been learning to swim. They have been eating well." She told him, getting choked up.

"Leila, please tell me what's wrong." Michael pleaded, and she hadn't heard him this patient in years. "You are scaring the hell out of me."

She sighed, struggling to regain control of her emotions. She took a deep breath, held it for a few seconds to let it out slowly. "I have gone through a lot of changes lately. It's been hard and scary..." Her voice faded away as she heard the front door open.

Iris, Dene, the boys, and the animals walked into the living room.

Mansuetus closed the door and stood in the entrance behind them and met Leila's eyes.

She closed her eyes against the sight of his pain.

"What do you mean, vampire?" Michael asked, disbelievingly.

"As far as I can tell, it's a physical change. A different species of human, maybe. But scientifically, I am just not sure. I am going to be researching it." Dene told him gently, calmly, while Leila and Iris sat still and quiet.

"What kind of bullshit is this, Leila?" He glared at her, ignoring Dene and Iris. Mansuetus had taken the boys into the bedroom to put them to bed. "Where the hell is the other doctor?" Glancing Dene's way like he was crazy.

"He's out of town and he's the last person in the world that you need to meet," Leila said sharply and he returned a look distraught with confusion. "I told you that telling you wouldn't work. I told you that you wouldn't believe me." She said firmly. "Aunt Iris, please show him." Iris gave her a reluctant glance. "Please." She begged. "I don't want this conversation to go on any longer than necessary. He needs to know, and he needs to believe."

Iris left the loveseat to sit next to Michael on the couch.

He looked at her suspiciously.

She breathed deep and opened her mouth and her fangs started to descend.

Michael leaped from the couch, tripping over the coffee table, and yelled, "The fuck!"

Mansuetus came to stand in the entrance of the living room. "The children are asleep." He told them all coldly. "We will handle this conversation like adults!" They all could feel the fury coming from him.

"Were you bitten?" Michael demanded, standing in front of the fireplace with his arms crossed. "Did she bite you?" Glaring at Iris; she rolled her eyes at him.

"No. I was born this way. Just like Iris was. Just like my Dad." Leila told him in a calm voice. "Now you know why he was freaking out."

"Did you know about this? Did you know that this could happen to you?" Michael accused her.

"Hell, no! But Dad had made a deal. In exchange for his freedom, he promised to take care of me and to raise me. He promised to tell me when I got older. He didn't. Now you know why he's a liar." Iris looked at her in shock. "I know you didn't know, Auntie." She glanced at Mansuetus, meeting his eyes calmly. "But, you knew, didn't you Mansuetus? You knew about the deal he made with Nichola."

"Yes, Kyría. I was there when the agreement was made."

"Of course you were." She whispered.

"It was a good agreement. Your father got what he wanted, and it protected you as a human." He said unashamedly.

"For a while, maybe. But it just ended up dumping it all on me at once, and I have exposed my children through my lack of knowledge!" She said sharply. "It would have been better to have just been taken when I was a child!"

"No, it wouldn't have been, Kyría. Believe me, it wouldn't." Mansuetus told her sincerely.

"The fuck, Leila!" Michael interrupted. "This is fucked up! Royally fucked up!"

"I am not asking anything from you except that you take care of your children! Unless you don't want them?" She asked.

"You are fucking leaving me?" He said incredulously, going from outrage to disbelief in two seconds. "We can deal with this! Your dad deals with this! We can deal with this too! I love you, Leila! I don't want you to leave." Taking her hand in his, her eyes filled with tears and her breath caught in her throat.

She swallowed heavily. "Being a vampire is not something that can be undone. It is complicated, and I can't undo it."

"I don't care! I love you and we will deal with it!" Michael told her, hugging her to him.

She swallowed heavily trying to remain calm as she breathed him in. His scent was making her feel desires that had nothing to do with sex, and she was starting to panic.

Needing to get away from him, she blurted out, struggling to pull away. "I have a vampire mate, Michael!"

He pulled back from her, looking at her with puzzled eyes. "What does that mean?"

"It means that I have been unfaithful to you." She told him sharply and he flinched as if slapped.

Standing, he looked down at her, his dark brown eyes reflecting his pain. "So, you are fucking somebody else? Is it Mansuetus?" He accused, looking at Mansuetus like he might launch himself at him.

"Don't!" Leila warned him quickly with a hard hand on his arm. "Mansuetus isn't even a vampire!"

"That's bullshit! He's something!" Michael said in fury.

"I don't have a choice in this, Michael!" Telling him with a sob. "Vampires don't choose their mates. It just happens."

"Where the fuck is he, then? He's letting you do this by yourself?" He glared at her, his pain lancing her soul as he backed away from her. Looking at her angrily, he turned on his heel, walking out of the house.

They all heard him get in his truck and speed off down the road.

Leila put her face in her hands and Iris said to no one in particular, "Well, that didn't go very well."

"Shut up, Iris." Dene told her softly, looking at Leila with sympathy.

After about twenty minutes of silence, Dene asked, "Do you think he will come back?"

Mansuetus, who had sat on the fireplace hearth, responded softly. "He never left the neighborhood." It looked like he was talking to the floor as he had placed his forehead against his fisted hands and arms that were resting on his bent knees. "He's just been driving around."

"You can hear him?" Dene asked, impressed.

"You are new. You also will be able to do so in time."

Dene looked like he didn't know how to answer that, nor whether or not he wanted that ability.

A few minutes later, they heard the door from the garage open and close, and Michael walked into the living room. "May I have a few minutes alone with my wife, please?" He asked softly, calmly.

Mansuetus shook his head no, even as Iris and Dene stood up.

Leila looked at him and said, "Mansuetus, please. He doesn't have any intention of harming me. Do you?" She looked at Michael.

"Of course not!" He told her as if she was being ridiculous.

Mansuetus stood up, gave him a look of warning, then left through the front door with the others.

"Leila, I can't even begin to understand what you have been going through, and I am sorry that I wasn't here for you. But I am here now. I don't care what has happened. I want you to leave him and come home. I love you and I want you to come home." He told her, his voice gentle. "Don't go back to him."

"He's not even here, and it isn't about him." She looked at him sadly. "I am trying to fix this. I am working to regain some of what I have lost. I started today. I think I did well. But I can't make you any promises. This is not an illness. This is what I am. All I can do is try to control it. But right now, I am not safe to be around. Not here. Not where I could harm you or the kids."

"Do you love him, Leila?" He asked gently.

"He makes me strong. He keeps me under control. He is not bad, or exceptionally good for that matter. He just *is*. He is my elder and so much stronger than I am. I am drawn to him. I *know* him. He is my other half. He is my mate." She paused, looking directly at him. "I can't explain it to you any better than that. It isn't something that, as a human, you will ever be able to understand."

"I can't believe that you allowed the kids around them!" His tone was harsh.

She glanced at him sharply, "Like I had a choice! You left remember? Besides, they would *never* hurt them. Those kids are part of their family. Family is important, in fact it is everything! The kids were never in any danger around them. Vampires are not allowed to harm children."

"Then why give them to me if they are so safe?" Michael asked her sarcastically.

"Because they aren't safe. Not all vampires are my family, and not all vampires follow the rules. They won't grow up to be normal kids if they stay with me. They will grow up isolated. Protected from everything and everyone. They would grow up in a gilded cage, but a cage nonetheless." She told him quietly. "They may never become vampires. Most people in my family never do. I can't do that to them. They have to have a normal life. It's the best that I can do for them right now." She told him and her voice became choked up.

Blinking her eyes rapidly to hold the tears back, she stood.

"Don't leave." He pleaded, wrapping his arms around her.

"I can't stay. I am trying to make it better. I am trying to...I am trying." She whispered against him, holding herself rigid, fighting for control as his nearness created a hunger within her. "I put the phone number to the house where we are living on the counter. Call me if anything happens with the kids, otherwise, I will try to come over this weekend to see them. Just believe that I am working on this."

"Do you want me to give your Dad the number?" Michael asked.

"No, he's done enough damage for the time being." She shook her head with rage.

"He was talking about getting a flight down here." Michael told her.

"Call him back. He needs to stay in Iowa. There are many people who are angry with him right now and he could be in danger. I don't need him here;

he would only make things worse." Leila backed out of Michael's arms and looked up at him. "I am sorry."

"It's not your fault. I love you, and I am not giving up on you!" He told her with determination.

"I am not giving up on me yet, either." She whispered to him with a small smile, walking into the garage and got into her car to back down to the end of the driveway.

She got out and helped Mansuetus take the car seats out of the limousine and put them into the garage.

Sitting in her car, she looked at the house before she backed out of the driveway. Michael was looking at her out the front window, and she sensed his shock and anguish.

She closed herself against his thoughts before they could crush her already broken heart and left, following the limousine down the road.

It was abnormally quiet like the soul of the house had died without the sustaining presence of the children.

Everyone gave Mansuetus a wide berth as he entered the house, walking down the hallway and entering the study, presumably to call Nichola.

They felt the fury coming off him in waves. Leila knew that his fury centered on her.

He was furious because she gave the children to Michael, he was furious because she had revealed their secret to Michael, he was furious because he felt responsible for them and now he was going to have to tell Nichola about what had transpired.

Looking at Iris, Leila asked, "Would you come for a walk with me?"

Nodding her head, Iris walked to the front door with her. Dene started to follow them.

"No," Iris commanded. "Stay here with Mansuetus."

"You are joking, right? He doesn't even feel safe to be around at this moment." Dene said quietly, fearfully, following them both out the front door.

"Well, then sit on the front porch and wait for us. Odds are that he will not attack you on the front porch, especially since he is angry at Leila." Iris said with a twisted smile.

Dene sat on the porch steps, saying to her in a serious tone, "You aren't funny, Iris."

"Actually, I am very funny, Dene." She said, giving him a quick kiss, following Leila out the gate.

"We are going to have to leave soon." Iris told her after they had made it down the dark road and couldn't see the house anymore.

"What do you mean?"

"Dene and me. As soon as Nikolaos is finished paying his accounts, Dene will be able to quit the hospital and we will go to Toronto." Iris' voice was quiet and soft.

"When?" Leila asked, facing forward.

"A couple of weeks, maybe. I am sorry that I won't be able to help you more."

"Good. Not too soon then. I am going to go back to work on Monday, and I would like for you to stay as long as possible."

"What?" Iris exclaimed.

"Yeah. I can do this, Auntie. I am going to try to make it work."

"I don't think that is possible, honey."

"I was out in the sun this morning for almost a half hour." Leila's voice was quiet.

"How did you manage it?" Iris asked, surprised. "Is that why Nikolaos was freaking out this morning?"

"Probably. Though I was able to block him out until after I had got back to the bathroom. He doesn't know. It is better that way. As to how? I am using sunscreen and limiting the amount of time. I wore my hat and sunglasses that you bought me." She threw a smile in her direction. "I still look stupid, but they did help." Iris smiled in return. "I am going to go out and do it again tomorrow morning, and every day after that. I am going to try to build up some resistance. If I can build up resistance to short amounts of time in the sun, I can do this. I work in an office after all. I am not exposed to a ton of sunlight."

"Then what's the plan, honey? Nikolaos will not tolerate that. If you are working and driving your car, he won't be able to keep a constant eye on you. He won't live here forever, and he will not allow you to live here either if he isn't living here."

"I won't be his prisoner for eternity, Iris." Leila said bluntly. "I am my own person, and I won't allow him to be my jailer. Nichola's going to have to accept me for who I am and what's important to me, or he's going to have to move on."

"Honey, he will not do any of that." Iris told her quietly in concern.

"He gave himself away the other night." Leila revealed.

"What do you mean?"

"He won't kill me. Punish me? That's fine, I can take it if it means being a part of the lives of my children. But he won't kill me," Leila responded.

"No, he won't. But you are going to have to make your choice soon, Leila. Don't let yourself grow weak. With weakness comes risk. Look at me and Dene. I wasn't ready to be responsible for another person, to have a companion. I don't know how long it will last or how long he will live. All I truly know is that my weakness caused it. So, if this is your choice, you will have to work on surviving it with everything that you are. If you don't give everything to succeed, the choice will be taken from you." Iris stopped her in the street. Pulling her into her arms. "I love you, Leila. You are one of the few people I would willingly give my life for. If this is what you need to do to be with your children, I will accept it. I will do whatever it takes to help you."

Adapting

CHAPTER TWO

I T FELT STRANGE WALKING back into work after being away for so long.

The past several days working to build up a resistance to the sun had been extremely difficult and painful, but she had never pushed it past the point of endurance. Dodging Mansuetus while she exposed herself to the sun wasn't as difficult as she had expected.

Of course, she had Iris to thank for that. Iris would distract him with any number of excuses why she would need his assistance, and he often avoided Leila's presence in any case, as he was still angry and upset with her over leaving the boys with Michael. During the exposure she was always incredibly careful to concentrate on blocking Nichola from her mind and she felt sure that the extra effort had actually helped her to focus on lengthening the period that she could stand the sun.

After that first time, Nichola had not called again to check on her, so she had to believe that he was not aware of what she was doing. She worked her way up to forty-five minutes of morning sun exposure in just a few short days and was proud of her progress so far. She wasn't sure if she could survive such a long time in the stronger afternoon sun, but was sure that she would be able to tolerate some exposure; and some was all she felt she needed.

She had left the house this morning before dawn, driving her own car. She had been lucky to avoid Mansuetus. He had been sleeping later since the boys were no longer living in the house with them. She had on her hat, sunglasses, and wore a pair of black slacks, black flats, a teal short-sleeved shirt, and a black suit jacket. She was ready to get back to work. She had left a note and a phone number on the kitchen counter for him.

It would be just one more thing for Mansuetus to be angry about.

Waving at the few other people who worked the seven o'clock shift who were getting their coffee and starting their workdays, she walked back to her cubicle. As she was putting her purse in her desk drawer, the phone rang on her desk.

She answered, "IT Security, this is Leila speaking."

"Kyría! What are you doing?" Mansuetus' voice was surprisingly calm.

"I see you got my note." She replied.

"Kyría, you cannot do this." He began.

"Mansuetus, I am doing this." She said, cutting him off sharply. "I love my job. I am not giving it up. I made it here okay." Turning on her computer, she continued. "You can't call me all day checking on me. It is only going to make me angry. I'm fine here. I have a cubicle against the wall. I am not exposed to any sunlight from the windows. I'm okay. Let me do this without taking any flak from you, please."

After a deafening silence, he finally asked her, "When does your work-day end?"

"I get off at four. I have planned this out, Mansuetus. I have my hat, sunglasses, and an umbrella. Because I arrive early, I always get a remarkably close parking spot to the building. Now that you have the car outfitted with the UV film, I will run to the car and drive straight home. I promise."

"Do you get a lunch break?"

"I do."

"Did you bring anything for lunch?" He asked.

"I will get something from the cafeteria downstairs." She replied.

"If you are going to attempt this, Kyría, do it right! I will bring you your lunch. When is your break?" His voice was firm.

She sighed, replying, "Eleven-thirty."

"I will be there."

"Oh, my God! You're back!" Jackie said loudly at the entrance to her cubicle around eight o'clock. She gave Leila a hug, stepping back. "You look terrible!"

"Wow! Thanks, Jackie!" Leila laughed, rolling her eyes.

"I didn't mean that the way it sounded!" Jackie said apologetically. "You have lost so much weight! Mansuetus said that Nick took you to a health spa. Did that help?"

"Yeah, a bit. It was mostly relaxing." Leila smiled.

"What did you do?" Jackie asked, perching herself against her desk.

"Massages, facials, food, that sort of thing. Lots of luxury pampering. It was beautiful there." Leila told her, smiling in remembrance.

"How's things on the home front?" Jackie asked in a whisper.

"Well, Michael is back home. But I am not. I dropped the kids off with him on Thursday." Leila's voice quivered in sorrow.

"Why?" Jackie asked, reaching over to hold her hand.

"It's better for them for the time being until I am fully recovered. Neither my health nor the kids need us at each other's throats. We'll see how it works out when I am better." Leila explained quietly.

"What's Michael thinking about that?"

"Well, he's not happy. He wants me to come home. But right now, it's not about him, it's about my condition and what's best for the boys."

Jackie leaned over and whispered into her ear, "How's Nick feel about that?"

"He's out of town on business and doesn't know when he will be returning, so right now he doesn't know what's going on. It's okay though, he isn't part of the equation." Leila whispered in return.

"Girl, that's cold." Jackie whispered with her eyebrows raised.

"Not really. The kids have got to come first, before any other consideration. Whether it's his, mine or Michael's. They come first. It has got to be whatever is best for them." Leila explained gently.

"No matter how you feel?" Jackie asked in a sad whisper.

"No matter how I feel," Leila whispered back with a small, poignant smile, patting her hand. "Have you seen Bart yet this morning?" She asked.

"You don't look great." Bart Crispin told her as he looked at her across his desk in his office.

"Thanks, Bart. You and Jackie both!"

"You know what I mean. You have lost a lot of weight." He replied.

"Heck of a way to diet, isn't it?" She asked rhetorically.

"Are you sure that you should come back?" He asked worriedly.

"Bart, if I stay at home any longer, I am going to go stir crazy! My brain is calcifying!" She told him with an influencing smile.

He smiled in return. "Okay. But take it easy for the time being. Support role. Not lead!"

"That works for now. I want to talk to you about my schedule, though. I would like to start a flex schedule starting next week. We still do that, right?" She asked.

"Yes. We are. What are you thinking?" He asked guardedly. Because he was a department head, he was required to be there Monday through Friday and, as such, he hated the flexible schedule system the base had put in place the previous year to improve civilian employee morale.

She pitched her voice softly and sweetly. "I think I would like to work ten-hour days, four days per week. I am thinking seven to five-thirty, Monday through Thursday, with Fridays off. Reduce my one-hour lunch time to thirty minutes."

It was a schedule that she had always wanted and had requested in the past. Of course, Bart had total control over his employee's schedules, and was usually flexible and easygoing about it. But, with Leila, he always depended on her to pick up everyone's slack. She also assisted him with his own reports, especially the department finance reports, which he found difficult and tedious, so he had never agreed to a flex schedule for her. Preferring her around anytime he needed her. Of course, he hadn't promoted her either. She had decided it was time to get something for doing hers and everyone else's job.

"You know, I really need you around here." He told her, but his voice was weak.

"I will still be able to do everything I do now and work on your reports, Bart. With me here so late, I will be able to be here after you leave. You might even change your own schedule and work the same hours as Madge now and get off earlier if I am here till five-thirty every night. Fridays are easily covered. As you know, it is the most requested day off for the rest of the department and it is always like a ghost town on Friday afternoon." She had pitched her voice soft and low, influencing him with her mind.

"You know that would be nice. Nothing ever happens around here after four, anyway." He mused out loud, justifying it to himself. "Madge and I could carpool if I worked from seven to four." Madge was Bart's wife and she worked at the base medical building.

He constantly complained about them having to drive two cars to work every day because he worked from eight to five to cover the majority of his employees shifts when she had to be at the base a full hour earlier and got off of work a full hour before he did. He often had to come in early to meet with the commanding officer on network issues, so he felt like he was at work all the time. As Department Head, just because he came in early didn't mean he could leave early when he needed to be there to supervise the majority of his people in the afternoon.

"Yeah, it will work out for both of us, Bart." She agreed, still influencing, knowing she had him hooked.

"That sounds really good, Leila. It's a great idea!" He told her enthusiastically, as if he was the one to have thought of it. "Do up the paperwork, I'll sign it, then you can take it to human resources."

"I got it right here, Boss." Smiling, handing him the request form that she had brought with her. *This mind control thing just might work out,* she thought.

Leila was reading through the draft documents for the basic PC Literacy course that the department was developing for employee training when her phone rang. She answered it, still engrossed in how detailed the section of how to get to and how to use the MS-DOS command prompt was. Thinking to herself, *I don't think so,* as she marked through the document with her red pen automatically speaking into the phone, "IT Security, this is Leila."

"Hey," a deep voice came through the handset.

She paused in shock and returned, "Hey."

"I didn't know that you were starting back to work today." Michael told her.

"I decided to try to come back a little early." She said quietly. "How did you find out that I was here?"

"Your aunt told me when I called."

"Are the kids okay?" She questioned.

"Yeah. I just was calling to find out if you were okay and to ask you if you wanted to stop by later tonight, or this week sometime, to see the kids. They haven't seen you since Saturday, and Zachary was asking for you this morning." His voice was gentle. "We all miss you."

She closed her eyes briefly feeling a sharp pain in her chest. "Yeah, I can do that. If I am not too wiped out when I get off of work, I will stop by this evening."

"Did Mansuetus drive you to work?" Michael asked her.

"No. I drove myself. He tinted my car windows for me, and I don't think that I will have a problem going home this afternoon."

"I am surprised that he let you do that." He replied.

"He didn't know about it. I just did it." She stated.

"Hey, I can come and pick you up for lunch if you want." He said out of the blue.

He hadn't asked her out to lunch in at least a year, even though they worked less than a mile away from each other, and the question surprised her.

"No, I don't want to expose myself to any additional sunlight today if I don't have to. Besides, Mansuetus is bringing me something to eat."

"Do you still eat regular food?" He suddenly asked sharply.

"Of course, I do." She replied dryly pursing her lips in irritation at his mercurial temperament. "I am sure that you have many questions, unfortunately it's not a good time for me to get into the details. I am due in a meeting in five minutes." She told him bluntly.

"Sorry." He apologized and his voice was sincere. "Please try to come over tonight."

"I will plan on it and will call you if anything changes or if I am feeling...unwell. I have got to go." She said in an emotionless voice.

"Okay."

439

"Oh, my lord, you're back!" Leila was greeted by Linda's deeply southern lady-like voice as she walked into the conference room. Linda got up to embrace her and Leila held herself still, returning the embrace gently, working to remain in control of her vampiric urges, as she smiled wryly at her colleagues around the conference table.

"Wow! You look..."

"Don't say it!" She warned the handsome geeky Eric who was her partner in crime in most of the escapades that went on in the IT Security Division.

"How are you feeling?" Neil asked her, looking around everywhere but at her.

She had never before noticed how nervous and paranoid he acted before her change began. She worked to block his thoughts, instinctively knowing that she wouldn't like what she found there.

"I am better." She maintained her smile with difficulty. The various emotions of the room were hard to keep up with.

"Well, let's get to it," Bart said, sitting down at the head of the table.

"...from a security perspective, it is not a good idea to include directions to the command prompt in the PC Literacy training. After all, what is the ultimate purpose of the training course and who is our target student?" Leila asked, looking around the table.

"No fear!" Eric said with a laugh.

"Exactly. No fear. The whole concept of the course is to introduce the lowest-level computer users to a desktop PC. Remember, these are people who, if they have any experience at all, have dealt with only mainframe systems. The class should make them understand that the PC, though more powerful, is not complicated, and a great tool to help them do the job better, faster, and easier. Showing them the command prompt only encourages them to experiment. It will become a situation where calls increase because people started messing around at the command prompt. Nobody wants to do more trouble tickets than necessary, especially our already overloaded help-desk. My recommendation would be to give them a history of operating systems from DOS to graphical user interfaces like Windows and explain how the PC itself came about. A history lesson is better knowledge to still any fears that they may have about using these machines than trying to teach them where the command prompt is. The only people that should be at the command prompt are those of us who are in IT."

"I agree with that." Came a deep southern voice from the other end of the table. It was Bo Cannon, known to all as B.C. He was the department Oracle programmer. Anti-social to the extreme, basically, B.C. was the department asshole who rarely agreed with anyone on anything. Normally rude and nasty to all and wide, including Bart and their customers, he consistently had the attitude that he was above them all.

She was picking up warm and friendly vibes from him directed at her, which she found quite disturbing, as she had always felt that if anyone in the department was a borderline serial killer, it definitely was B.C.

Surprised, Bart looked at Leila and B.C. and said, "Well, then we cut it and replace it with a history lesson designed to increase familiarity instead. Any other items for discussion?" He glanced around the table as everyone shook their heads. "Okay. Just to let everyone know, I am changing my hours from seven to four starting Monday. Leila will change her hours as well. She is going to be working from seven to five-thirty, Monday through Thursday, so will cover anything after I leave."

Thanks, Bart! Leila thought to herself as she felt jealousy from almost everyone at the table except for B.C. who worked that schedule already, which had bothered no one else because they were happy that they only had to put up with him for four days per week. He actually seemed pleased that she would be working on it as well.

They all filed out of the conference room and Leila headed for her cubicle.

"Leila!" Jackie called to her as she noticed everyone walking down the outside of the cubicle bays. Leila headed towards her desk and saw Mansuetus perched on the desk beside Jackie's chair in her cubicle. "Look who's here!"

"Hi Mansuetus. Our meeting ran a little over, sorry." She told him as she realized that it was ten to noon.

"Not at all, Kyría." Mansuetus said in his smooth, deep voice. He stood up and took Jackie's hand in his and bowed over it, murmuring "Goddess," warmly to her, as she blushed. Leila smiled at her and gave her a little wave as Mansuetus picked up the bag that he had with him and motioned for her to lead the way.

As they headed downstairs to the cafeteria, he murmured to her, "If you are going to do this, you must eat properly, or you will fail."

"Are you supporting me, then?" She asked.

"No. I am not. I am advising you on the proper course of action to take, since you are insistent on this path." He told her in a soft, disapproving voice.

Leila was tired when she pulled into the garage at 4:30 p.m. She got out of the car and immediately headed into the house, intending to take a nap for a while. Her brain actually hurt! By the time she left work, she was totally focused on keeping the thoughts of her co-workers out of her head.

The things that she had learned!

Neil was paranoid and felt that the government was listening to him on his desk phone and trying to control his mind.

Mike was fighting a desperate desire to expose himself to the women in the office.

Linda was a closet dominatrix and the thought of her and her husband Austin, who were both in their fifties and at least fifty pounds overweight, was an image that she wanted so badly to forget!

Not discounting the fact that her buddy Eric had slept with almost all the single women in the office and a few of the married ones, too.

The only normal one seemed to be B.C., whom everyone hated. He was not a serial killer, but he did have a slight crush on her!

Two months ago, she would have been shocked. Now, she was just wanting to get away from it all!

She popped her head into the kitchen to say *hello* to Iris and Mansuetus. "I am going to lie down for a while. Please don't let me sleep past six. I want to go to see the kids later this evening." Mansuetus looked at her hopefully. "You can come too, if you want." He smiled broadly and she smiled at him in return, heading for the bedroom.

At a little after seven, Mansuetus pulled up in the driveway and Leila pulled up next to him in her car. He was not happy that she had insisted on driving her own car and had thrown a small fit when she told him she was driving herself. She calmly informed him she would decide when she would come home and that if he didn't like it, then he didn't have to come with her. He had given her a hurt look before closing his mouth and accepting her decision.

With the sun still up, she was careful to have her hat and sunglasses on and quickly ran to the covered porch to avoid the light. She rang the doorbell, though felt a little foolish doing so.

Michael opened the door, "Leila, this is your house too. You don't have to ring the doorbell or knock." He said to her. "I am happy to see you." He ignored Mansuetus' presence entirely.

She walked into the house and Zachary screamed, "Mommy!" and ran to hug her legs. She picked him up and walked into the house, looking around. Devin was in his walker and looked at her sternly. She gave him a smile. After a moment, he returned her smile, showing all four of his sharp little teeth. Then the boys saw Mansuetus, and both screamed, "Man!" and she had to dodge Devin as he quickly moved to Mansuetus. She put Zachary down and he ran to the big man, who looked overjoyed at seeing them.

"Man, the alligator is eating our baby ducks again!" Zachary told him.

"Is he?" Mansuetus smiled down at him, now holding Devin in his arms, who was hugging him tightly.

"Yes. You should shoot him! Pow! Pow!" Zachary demanded.

Leila looked at Michael in curiosity.

"Some of the neighbors were taking pot-shots at the alligator while it was swimming in the pond on Sunday, and somebody called the Sheriff about it." He explained.

"Oh." Leila said, smiling. "You weren't involved, were you?" She asked, knowing that it wasn't outside the realm of possibility.

"Hell, no! They are damn lucky no one actually shot him. It's illegal to hunt them. The Sheriff gave them a warning."

"I cannot break the law, Young Master." Mansuetus said solemnly, looking down on Zachary.

"Aww!" Zachary said.

Leila came in and sat down on the couch as Gladiator and Pepper jumped up next to her. She petted and hugged them, watching the boys with Mansuetus who had sat down on the loveseat with them. Her heart was aching.

Michael sat next to her and took her hand in his, surprising her. He looked at her, continuing to ignore Mansuetus. "I want you to come home." He told her softly.

Mansuetus looked sternly at him. "You do not know what you are asking, and this discussion shouldn't happen in front of these children!"

"I am not talking to you." Michael glared at him.

Leila pulled her hand out of Michael's grasp. "Stop it, both of you!" She said sharply, standing. "Come with me, Michael."

"Kyría..." Mansuetus began worriedly.

"I have been in control all day; I will not lose it now." She whispered to him.

She paced in the garage where her car was usually parked with her arms crossed over her chest. She looked at Michael as he leaned against his truck. "I want to be spending my time here with the kids, not fighting with you, Michael." She told him.

He crossed his arms over his chest. "I want you to come home."

"I can't. I am not totally safe to be around right now." She looked at him directly feeling her emotions stir. "I could hurt you." She stated simply.

"Are you a danger to the kids?" He asked her.

"Of course not! Though I have been warned that I could be if I am not careful." She said quietly.

"Really? Do you really think that you would ever hurt our kids, Leila?" He asked, demanding an answer.

"No, I can never imagine even wanting to hurt them." She told him honestly.

He came over and wrapped her in his arms, hugging her to him. "Then this is all bullshit! Come home. Be with me and the kids."

Leila breathed in the scent of his body and tried to relax in his arms. He felt warm against her as she felt him stroking her back and the small hairs on her arms stood up in goosebumps. She felt him softly kiss her temple and then put his hand under her chin to lovingly kiss her lips. Hearing his heart beating strongly she wrapped her arms around his waist, hugging him closer. He responded by spinning her around and leaning her against his truck, never breaking contact with her lips.

He gripped her ass hard with both hands, rubbing his erection against her, and she felt a surge of power run through her veins as he started kissing and sucking on her neck. She reached in between them to run her hand over him, stroking him through his jeans, and he moaned into her mouth. "Jesus, Leila. Baby, that feels great. Oh, God, don't stop."

She saw images flash through her mind from him, reading him. She was seeing him as she rode him in the hot tub; the water swirling around them. She was watching him as he slid into her, ever faster as he held her pinned to their bed. The images made her feel desire and something more. A deep, overwhelming hunger and an ache spread throughout her body.

She felt him move one of his hands to her breast as she slid her hand into his jeans, which were now open. She hadn't realized that she had unfastened them, and obviously neither had he when she felt him stiffen and gasp as she gripped his naked cock.

She suddenly spun him around and he found himself half in and half out of the backseat of his truck, with his jeans pulled down around his knees.

He hadn't even realized that she had opened the back door of the truck at all and was surprised to be there and then it didn't matter as her lips fastened to his with a groan of hunger and her hand once more gripped his cock. He moaned as she stroked him, and he felt her hold him tightly by the shoulders with her other arm as she brought her mouth to the side of his neck to lick and suck at him, almost in a frenzy.

Leila could feel her teeth descend as the need grew expanding throughout her body and she could feel his body stiffen in anticipation as she stroked him closer to orgasm. She licked his throat and could feel his carotid artery pulsating beneath the muscle of her tongue, causing her to salivate, and she swallowed in anticipation.

Michael couldn't believe how good this felt. She had never done a great job of jerking him off before, never quite getting the hang of the rhythm he wanted. Now, it was like the simplest touch of her hand was making him want to come. As she ran her tongue over his skin on the side of his throat, he breathed in her scent, becoming intoxicated with desire.

He panted at her as the strokes of her hand became faster and firmer. "Oh, God, Leila! Oh, Jesus, baby, yes. You smell so good! Don't stop I am going to cum!" He felt her hesitate just briefly but then she continued to stroke him, and he felt his balls tighten against his body as his hips involuntarily arched forward and he rode the edge of a powerful orgasm for a handful of seconds. He crashed over the edge of the precipice, shooting his cum all over the truck, and cried out in orgasm.

Leila covered his mouth with her own to swallow the sound, holding him gently as he shook in the after throws of his orgasm in her arms. After a few long seconds, his gasps slowed, and she withdrew her mouth from his.

"Look at me." She commanded him and his eyes flew open, and he gasped at her transformation. Her eyes were red, and he could just glimpse the whiteness of her upper fangs as her cherry red lips were parted and she was breathing heavily. "You are so close to being bitten. You do not know how close. I never want to feed from you. This is why I am not living here."

She made her way through the living room, heading for the front door.

Mansuetus, who was sitting in the living room with the boys, took one look at her and asked, "Is he dead?"

She looked at him with disgust. "He's not even bitten. But I need to leave now." She started heading to the door and Zachary ran to her, grabbing her by the leg.

"Don't leave us Mommy!" He yelled.

She touched him gently on the head, running her fingers through his silky golden curls. "Mommy has to go, buddy. Mansuetus will stay here with you for a while until your Daddy comes in."

Devin, who was standing on Mansuetus' lap gripping his hands, fixed her with his clove-colored eyes and yelled at her, "Momma!"

She gasped softly and took him in her arms, clutching him against her body. As he hugged her tightly in return, she sat on the couch and started sobbing against him.

Zachary climbed up on the couch to stand next to her and hugged them both, saying, "Don't cry, Mommy, don't cry."

Adapting

DUTY OVER LOVE

D RIVING HOME AFTER FINISHING the first week of her four-day flex
schedule, Leila was pleased with how her second week back to work
had gone. Finding that she tolerated her exposure to late afternoon sunlight
at 5:30 p.m. much easier than the sunlight at 4:00 p.m. hadn't stopped her
from spending as much time exposed to the sun as possible. The more time
spent in the sunshine, the less her desire to drink blood. At least with a very
few exceptions. Blocking out the thoughts and desires of her co-workers
remained challenging, but with each passing day, it grew easier, resembling a
series of small victories as time went on.

This week she returned to teaching security classes. Using her vampire
influence, she improved her instructor ratings and increased the department's requests for additional training, making her proud of how well she
was adapting.

She established a routine for herself. After eating dinner to make sure that
she had curbed her blood-lust, she visited the kids nightly, with Mansuetus
accompanying her each time. Unsure if he were there to prevent her from
making a huge mistake or just to see the boys; she suspected it was a bit of
both.

After her close call with Michael, she kept a physical distance; not that he
didn't try to touch her, he often did, asking her every night to come home,
but she never allowed herself to be alone with him again.

Being around Michael was the most difficult part of her day. She didn't
want to hurt him, but he was an open book, and she knew he wanted her.
He didn't even try to disguise his thoughts, and his desire made her hunger
for him. Unlike him, her hunger wasn't sexual. Since Mansuetus acted as
her chaperone, she avoided him for the most part. The major problem was
that he was totally unafraid of her, as he made every effort to invade her

personal space, making it agonizingly difficult and dangerous to be around him. Though foolish on his part, he had convinced himself that she wouldn't hurt him.

Michael asked her as she was leaving last night, "Why do you insist on bringing *him* with you every night?" He nodded toward Mansuetus, who was walking down the driveway to the limousine.

"He is here to protect me." She replied softly.

He ran his hand over her arm to the end, holding her hand, keeping her from walking through the front door.

She felt the tightness in her chest expand painfully.

"I would never hurt you, Leila." He said, stepping close to murmur against her temple.

"Don't be stupid." Telling him sharply, trying to pull away as need arose in her, and she battled to keep it inside. "He's here to protect me against myself."

"You know you would never hurt me, Leila." He whispered.

She wished she had as much confidence in herself as he did her, but she knew better than to trust herself. "I wish you would understand how hard this is." She whispered in return.

"Make me understand." He murmured, running his hand down her spine.

"Being around you, being close to you, is like putting an alcoholic in their favorite bar, on their favorite stool, with their favorite beverage on every shelf. You can smell the alcohol, taste it in the air across your tongue, and it causes you to shake and shiver with need. To want that taste, to get that high. But, you also know if you take that first sip, it will all fall apart, and you will find yourself on a month-long bender that will only end in pain and disaster for everything that is important in your life." She looked up at him. "Your scent is that alcohol, and it is torturous."

"Is there a twelve-step program or a vampire's anonymous?" He laughed softly against her hair.

"You need to take this seriously." She pulled away from him, trying to get out the door.

"I do, and I don't care about you being a vampire. I love you." He pulled her against him. "I have loved you since the first time I laid eyes on you. You are my wife and the mother of my children and the strongest person I know.

I took for granted that you would always be here with me, and I am sorry for that. You are the most important person in the world to me, and I know I don't deserve you, but I am getting my shit together. I can't lose you. I won't lose you." He whispered, holding her close.

Leila breathed deep, fighting for control, and she could smell the blood under his skin.

"I smell you again, Leila." He whispered huskily and she felt his body react to her scent.

"That's a warning sign." She whispered, stepping away from him. "I have to go."

Suddenly grabbing her by the shoulders, he kissed her lips.

She stiffened, fighting herself, wanting desperately to drink from him.

"We will figure this out, baby." He told her as he let her go and she looked at him in despair, bolting from the house.

Shaking her head to rid herself of last night's memories, she pulled into the garage at six o'clock. Nichola's mustang in the bay next to her shocked her. Surprised that she hadn't sensed that he was in the house when she pulled into the property, she sat in the car for a full two minutes clutching the steering wheel; breathing deeply, slowly in and out; trying to control her rapidly beating heart.

Knowing that he must be furious with her for going back to work, she hoped Mansuetus was safe. Fairly certain that he wouldn't hurt him, she knew he definitely would blame him for her actions. Trying to sense him just to see if she could read his mood, she failed utterly, realizing that he was easily blocking her.

Breathing deeply one last time, she bravely opened the door to get out of the car.

Stepping off of the elevator and walking into the kitchen, she realized that there was a flurry of ongoing activity in the house. Turning, she saw Iris, who quickly hugged her tightly.

"Auntie, what's wrong." Leila asked bewildered, seeing the lawyer's assistants carrying through bags and suitcases.

"Dene and I are leaving for Toronto tonight." Iris said, sniffing back tears.

"Why? Why so soon?" Leila hugged Iris to her.

"Because it is time for them to go, Leila." Nichola's cold voice came from the entrance to the kitchen. He glared at her as Dene moved past Leila with a suitcase to get onto the elevator, avoiding her eyes.

"But what about Dene's job at the hospital?" She asked, perplexed, as the elevator doors closed after Dene.

"His debt is paid, and he now is indebted to me. I want him in Toronto to oversee the preparations for the hospital there." Nichola's voice could freeze water. "It is time for you to pack, as well."

"I am not going anywhere, Nichola." She responded calmly, walking past him to the master bedroom to change out of her work clothes; while Iris looked at him fearfully and scurried to her bedroom.

"No words of welcome for your returned lover?" Following her down the hallway, Nichola's question dripped with sarcasm.

So, we are going to get right into it, are we? Sighing under her breath in resignation, she continued in a normal voice, "I guess that your business is complete? That one more vampire is now dead at your hands." She threw him a cold angry look, feeling resentment at his tone, walking into the closet to change.

"Yes. One more maniac has been put down." Watching her from the doorway of the closet, she started to change ignoring his presence.

"I guess you are okay. You look okay. How is the prince? Was anyone else harmed?" She asked after a few seconds, feeling his furious gaze on her like a physical thing.

"The prince is recovered and there were no other serious injuries to the rest of the hunting party." He told her calmly, coldly, and politely.

Despite his tone, she could feel the fury pulsating off of him.

"That is a relief." Sighing, her back to him, she pulled off her shirt, quickly pulling a t-shirt on over her head, then stripped off her dress slacks. "So, let me take a wild guess at this, then. You're pissed because I went back to work?" Asking as she pulled on her jeans, buttoning them.

"Not at all. I trust you won't become homicidal in your office environment. Your control exceeds the majority of young vampires." His voice was matter-of-fact, which didn't stop her from feeling the waves of fury radiating from him.

"Well, you are furious about something." Sensing him behind her, she turned to face him, looking directly into his red eyes. "You can block me out all you want, but even you can't block out the fact that you are brimming over with fury."

His lips twitched and rose in a twisted half smile as his red gaze narrowed on her. "Maybe it is different for you? But do you expect me to rejoice in the fact that my mate is fucking another man when I am gone?"

"What the fuck are you talking about?" She asked incredulously.

"Did you really think that I wouldn't be able to feel it? Your desire? Your need? I shut our connection down before you completed the act, as I was in the middle of trying to survive." Disgust and fury dripped from his words. "The last thing I needed was to feel your orgasm across the Atlantic, which would have sent me into a murderous rampage." Moving swiftly as he spoke, he now had a brutal, bruising grip on her upper arms. He pushed her against the back wall of the closet.

She tried to hold him back with her outstretched arms, her hands against his chest, as he bounced her against the wall. "I didn't!" She screamed.

"Don't lie to me!" He growled, pulling her close, nose-to-nose with her, his fangs distended, his clawed hands digging into her arms.

Crying out in pain, she pushed against him with everything that she had. "I didn't! Ask Mansuetus! He was with me every time I went out," yelling at him while he continued to grip and shake her with ferocity.

Rage overtook her at the injustice of his accusations, especially since she had struggled so valiantly to control her vampire nature. Losing control, she dug her own claws deeply into the muscles of his chest as she pulled him sharply towards her, leveraging his body weight as she drove her knee into his groin as hard as she could.

Gasping in pain, his eyes widened in shock as he dropped to the floor of the closet, clutching himself.

As if hellhounds were in hot pursuit, she ran as fast as she could, figuring she had minutes before that became a reality. Sprinting down the hallway through the front door, past Mansuetus, who was loading the limousine, then into the garage, she jumped in her car. Starting it, she threw it into reverse to exit the garage, and sped out of the gate towards Harriet's Bluff Road.

Watching her in confusion, Mansuetus' eyes widened in concern as he glanced back at the house. Running up the front steps and into the house, he paused just inside the front door as if searching for something, then he ran into the master bedroom to stand in the open doorway of the closet. Nichola was sitting up, leaning against the back wall of the closet, holding himself and grimacing in pain.

"What happened?" Mansuetus said in concern.

"I am an idiot, that's what happened," came Nichola's painful groan, laced liberally with self-disgust.

"Kýrios, usually when a couple has been apart for several weeks, they fall into each other's arms and then into bed. They don't normally bludgeon each other." Mansuetus held out his hand to help him up off of the floor of the closet.

Standing up slowly with Mansuetus's help, Nichola groaned out, "I told you I was an idiot!" As he stood, he paused to get his bearings before trying to move forward, still almost doubled over in pain. Putting his arm around his waist, Mansuetus securely took Nichola's arm. "I felt her Mansuetus. I felt her desire and her need. It was maddening." His voice was soft in pain and despair as they slowly made their way out of the closet. "I accused her of having sex with him." Whispering, he groaned as Mansuetus helped him to sit in one of the armchairs in front of the fireplace.

"She didn't." Mansuetus stated simply.

"I have come to realize that." Nichola cried out softly, as he leaned forward, trying to alleviate his discomfort.

"She did almost tear his throat out. Knowing young vampires like I do; I am surprised that she didn't. Pleased at her control, but surprised nonetheless." Mansuetus told him. "I have been with her whenever she visits the children. She hasn't really been alone with him since. Not for lack of trying on his part." Mansuetus looked at Nichola sharply. "And if she had sex with him?"

Nichola returned his look. "I would be furious. But I would never truly harm her over such a thing. I love her. Though it doesn't look like it from my actions, I really do love her."

"Exactly. You are behaving like a human." Mansuetus said in irritation and sat on the couch across from him. "You know that once she starts to feed, she will end up feeding and fucking on occasion. Sex and blood go hand in hand in most cases." He fixed Nichola with a stern look. "You know this to be true. You remember what it was like for yourself?"

"I am aware, it doesn't mean that I have to like it." Nichola's growl transformed into a pained groan. "Most especially not with him."

"What makes him special? He's not overly remarkable." Mansuetus's antipathy dripped from his words.

"He's her husband. But, mostly, he's the father of her children. They take priority over everything else. You know that," Nichola breathed out slowly.

"As well, they should." Mansuetus stated firmly.

"Yes." Nichola looked up at him. "Where is she?"

"Gone. Probably to see them. They bring her comfort. But she hasn't eaten. That will give her a dangerous edge." Mansuetus stood up. "Are you injured? Or are you just hurt?"

"If I were a human, my days of procreation would now be over. But I am healing quickly, so now I am just hurt." Nichola said with a smaller grimace of pain. "Let's go get my mate."

Leila walked into her house, feeling exhausted. Zachary was sitting at the kitchen table and Devin was in his highchair. Michael was fixing them dinner. He took one look at her, seeing that Mansuetus wasn't with her and said, "I wasn't expecting you so early. Have a seat. I made plenty."

She sat down at the table after giving both boys a kiss and closed her eyes in exhaustion. Michael sat a plate down in front of her that had a pork chop, mixed vegetables, and macaroni and cheese. She thanked him with a smile.

"You look a little messed up." Concerned, he sat down at the table with his own plate. "Are you okay?"

"Yeah. I am okay." Leila told him, eating her food, not meeting his eyes. "How did it go at daycare today? How was your day?" She questioned, trying to shift the conversation away from herself.

"It was good. I had a meeting with the Director at childcare earlier this week about the condition that the kids were coming home in, and they have been doing better." He looked at the boys, who were eating.

She looked at the kids and noticed that they were cleaner than they normally were right after daycare. "I am glad that you did, since she never listened to me about it. They look good." She smiled at Devin, who gave her a big smile, his mouth full of macaroni and cheese.

"They said that Devin is really trying to walk." He told her, his look of concern for her not decreasing.

"That's going to be fun when he is totally mobile!" A small but apprehensive laugh escaped her.

"So, where's Mansuetus?"

"He's busy right now. I am sure that he will be here later." Concentrating on her food, she missed the gleam in his eye.

"Well, I am glad he's not here. We really need to talk about what we're going to do about this situation."

She looked up from her plate to meet his eyes. "I am doing everything I can to—"

"To what? I don't see what you're doing other than not being with us." His tone resentful.

"Right now, Michael, I am just trying to be normal. To be human. To be a part of my kid's lives."

"Then move home!" He told her as she stood, picking up her plate.

Not looking at him, she picked up the kid's plates and took them to the sink to rinse them off. Concentrating on clearing her jumbled thoughts, she didn't feel him approach her from behind until he had wrapped his arms around her and bent to kiss her shoulder.

"Do you love me, Leila?"

She choked back tears. "If you would have asked me that a few months ago, my response would've been an unequivocal 'yes'. Today, I don't even know what the word love means anymore. Now I would be satisfied with just having an honest relationship with you. One where I don't end up killing you."

"Well, I can tell you unequivocally that I love you, Leila. It took me losing you to make me realize how much I love you, how bad of a husband I have been to you, and how lucky I was to have your love. I want to make it right between us, but I can't do that if you aren't here with me. You aren't giving me a chance, and frankly, you aren't giving yourself or our kids a chance. They need you to be more than a part-time mom."

Leila turned, wrapping her arms around his waist to place her head on his chest, realizing that she just wanted to hold him until she wasn't afraid anymore. Closing her eyes, she hid her face against him.

Holding her close to him, Michael ran his fingers through her thick curls, trying to comfort her, knowing that she needed him to hold her, to be there for her. "Leila, we have been through so much. I am sorry about all of these years. I know I am mostly at fault because I have been impatient and selfish. I have been jealous of everything, your job, the kids, your family. I understand now, and I know how hard you have tried to make our family and me happy and how determined that I have been to find fault with you." Kissing the top of her head, he continued. "I have been so angry for most of our marriage, but I am not going to be that way anymore. I want to be here with you, together with our family. There is nothing more important to me. Nothing! I don't know what our future is going to be like, but I will never stop wanting to hold you until I die."

Reading the truth and sincerity of his words, she held him tightly. His understanding cooled the flames of her addiction, like a cool desert wind blowing the heat away. Relaxing in his arms, the tightly held blood-lust evaporated from the back of her throat and she closed her eyes in exhaustion pillowing her head on his chest.

"Listen, Leila. I will do whatever it takes to keep us together, to keep our family together. I know you are afraid that you will hurt me. I will move into the spare bedroom if that's what you want. We can take this slow, so that you won't have to be afraid. I know we can make this work. I love you. Just come home." He held her tightly to him, kissing the top of her head gently.

Don't make me come in, i psychí mou.

Leila froze in Michael's arms, giving him a terrified look.

"What's wrong?" Michael asked, noticing the change in her body.

"I have to go." Starting at the sound of the doorbell, disengaging herself from Michael, she walked to the front door. Fear ran through her veins, and she was sure that her heart was going to beat right out of her chest as she took a deep breath, trying to still her emotions.

"Where are you going?" Michael asked, putting his hand against the door to prevent her from opening it.

"Don't Michael!" Her voice panicked. "I have to go." Grabbing the doorknob and pulling open the door with one hand, she easily moved him from in front of the door with the other.

Mansuetus looked at her from the front porch and she looked around him but didn't see anyone else, though she sensed Nichola nearby.

Come to your car, pio agapiméni mou. Mansuetus would like to visit the children.

Leila gave Mansuetus a stern look. "You would never betray my rules in my house, would you, Mansuetus?"

"No, Kyría. I would never do harm under your roof. You are still Queen here. I can't make that guarantee about anyone else." Mansuetus' deep voice was soft, sincere, and sad.

"I am trusting you to protect *all* of them, Mansuetus."

"I will do so to the best of my ability, but if it comes to a fight, I will lose. I will fight for you, Kyría, but I will lose." He looked into her eyes as she nodded her head in understanding.

Looking at Michael, she quickly grabbed him by the back of the neck, bringing him down to her eye level. "Let Mansuetus in. I need to leave now."

Michael opened his mouth. Giving him a stern look, she used her *voice*. "Don't argue. Just do what I ask."

The Choice

A BARGAIN

WALKING OUT TO HER car, she got in to see Nichola sitting in the passenger seat.

"I am glad that you came of your own accord." His beautiful voice was soft, his eyes were warm.

"Did I?" Starting the car, she asked, "Where would you like to go?"

"Back to the house." Neither of them said a word while she drove.

Pulling into the garage, she turned off the car and looked at him.

"Come for a walk around the property with me, Leila."

She got out of the car, sensing that no one was in the house. "Where are Iris and Dene?"

"Most likely boarding my jet to go to Toronto."

"But I didn't get to say goodbye!" Leila complained sadly.

"Iris will call you when they land. I am not interested in separating you from your aunt Leila." He murmured, walking toward the back of the property.

Following slowly, dreading another confrontation, she watched him sit on a bench in front of the fire-pit. Her mind flashed back to the night that they had burned the bloody clothing of the now very dead Bobby Rebekah. It seemed like it had been forever since that night.

Waving his hand at the fire-pit, the wood caught fire, blazing high, surprising her. "Didn't you tell me we don't have any magic?"

"Maybe we have a little 'magic'." Giving her a soft teasing half smile. "You know that we have psychic abilities. You and I communicate psychically all the time. Pyrokinesis is just another form of psychic ability. Our brains are more advanced than humans. Advanced brains give us advanced abilities, but they don't make us magical."

"Can you move things with your mind also?"

"I can do a lot of things, Leila." He looked at her warmly.

"Why haven't you told me about them? Why do I always seem like I am the last to know?" Her voice was angry, like he had betrayed her.

"I have been trying to transition you slowly, Leila. If you remember, it wasn't too long ago that you thought you were going insane. I didn't want to overload you. The knowledge and physical changes that you have endured have upset your life enough, don't you think? You've plenty of time to learn about what you are. You are not alone." He patted his hand on the concrete bench next to him. "Sit with me." His tone made it clear that it wasn't a request.

Her heart skipped a little in fear, but she did as he commanded, facing forward, not meeting his eyes.

Sighing deeply, he looked at her profile. "I would not have you be afraid of me, i psyhí mou." He studied her impish face, with its pointed chin and pert nose, as she looked deeply into the burning fire.

"You've not been very balanced the last couple of times I've been around you, Nichola. You've been terribly angry, and I don't want to fight with you. I don't want you to hurt me or anyone that I care about." Her words were strong, though her voice was calm as she continued to look into the fire.

Looking deeply into the fire with a reflective look, he finally responded to her. "Mansuetus accused me of behaving like a human. I'm sorry to say that he is correct." His voice was soft as he turned to look at her, and she met his amber gaze calmly. "It is because you have awakened emotions inside of me that have been sleeping for centuries."

"So, this is my fault? That you are angry?" She looked at him incredulously.

"No. I am the elder. It is absolutely my fault." He picked up her hand from the bench, causing her to flinch, and he sighed. "I will not hurt you, Leila. Even if you cause me to feel anger. I give you my word. I will not hurt you again. I love that your presence makes me feel again, but I can control myself."

"You can shut off your emotions?" She asked softly.

"Well, it isn't as if I am heartless, agápi mou, but I can control my reaction to them. I can put them into a box, so to speak. After all, I had done so for many centuries before you entered my life." He smiled bitterly. "I admit, I do like the way I feel when you are around; even the baser emotions such as anger and fear send thrills through me. I know I am alive. It is much better than the logical, robotic, emotionless existence that I had been enduring before I met you."

"Aunt Iris always says that you are a 'cold fish'." She told him delicately.

He laughed in return, his voice quiet. "I am sure that she sees me that way. To be honest, I don't really have strong emotions toward Iris. Our relationship is elder and young vampire. When she makes me angry, and she does, I do not feel the need to murder her; only to continue to instruct and guide her."

He'd been blocking himself since she had got into the car, and she was unable to read the meaning of his words. Her voice trembled. "Do you want to murder me?"

"No." His calm voice hinted at more laughter. "I want to throttle you and fuck you silly at the same time." She met his lustful gaze with shock. "We are vampires, and we are soul mates. Despite my age, your presence makes me feel powerful emotions. As strong as those that I felt since I was a young uncontrolled vampire. Young vampires are overwrought with emotions, elders are more controlled. It is time that I behave like the elder vampire that I am instead of a love-struck fool."

"Nichola, I don't want you to stop loving me." She told him sincerely.

"Leila, even if I wanted to, which I don't, I could never stop loving you." He gently stroked her jaw, leaning forward to kiss her tenderly.

"Nichola, I don't want to be a vampire." Leila looked at him sadly. "I don't want this existence."

"You really don't have a choice." His voice was not unkind despite his words.

"My children need me, and I am no good to them like this. I also care for my husband." Her eyes met his, and she saw the anger there. Rushing, she continued, "You once asked me what is being a human wife compared to being your soul mate. The answer is nothing. But, if it means that I must spend my life without my children, it is everything!" He turned to look back into the fire as she spoke quickly, willing him to understand her. "You helped my father when you made a bargain with him for my care and education. Why won't you help me? I know you can."

Breathing deeply to control himself, he answered her just as quietly, "Your father wasn't as far along in his transition as you are. He never grew fangs;

never transformed in any way. Look at your arms where I marked you earlier." He held her arm up and they both looked. Her arms were fully healed and clear of any scratches or bruising. "You are more vampire now than your father ever was."

"Oh, Nichola!" She reached out her hand to hold his face, forcing him to look at her. "You are so strong. You can help me; I know you can."

Frustrated, he stood up quickly putting some distance between them.

Turning, he demanded harshly, "Who told you I helped him at all?"

"No one, Nichola. I didn't know it for sure until just now. I know you. You would do whatever it took to make sure that I was safe and happy." Her teal eyes gleamed at him with hope.

Angry, he turned from her to avoid her gaze. Gritting his teeth, he asked, "Who says that I want to help you?" Turning to look at her, she was overwhelmed by his anger and grief. "Leila, I am many things, good and bad, and I love you more than my own life, but I am not a martyr! Why, after searching for centuries, would I want to lose my soulmate forever? Your need to be a human mother notwithstanding, I would never agree to that! Hate me if you must, but I will never give you up!"

"It won't be forever!" Her voice rang with hope and sincerity. "Only until they don't need me. What is time to you, after all, Nichola?"

He glared at her, walking past her heading toward the house.

Following him through the garage and into the recreational room, Leila made to follow him as he stepped onto the elevator.

"No!" His voice was sharp with warning as he pointed his finger at her. "Don't get into this box with me." The elevator doors closed between them.

Turning, she ran up the back stairs. She walked into the kitchen to see him pouring himself a glass of wine. "Nichola, you love the boys just as much as I do, and you love me. Please. Give me this. Give me this time." She begged. "I never asked for my childhood, but I am asking for this. For me to be able to be a mother to my children. A real mother."

He drank the wine down, looking at her. "It's not fair that you ask this of me, Leila. I searched for you for so long and I waited for you after I found you. Your body is telling you it is time. That you are ready."

"That's just it! I'm not ready, Nichola! I need to be with my children, to raise them, to educate them on the possibilities. I can't abandon them only to see them struggle with this as I have. I don't want them to question their

461

very existence! If I have to leave them now, it will break me. I can't live with that. They have no one who can teach them to be the best of men. They have no one but me to teach them about their bloodline."

"So, your choice is to turn your back on who and what you are? To leave me to a bleak and lonely future? To abandon your other half?" His look was pained, and he clutched the granite countertop as if he were trying to prevent laying his hands upon her.

Tears escaped her eyes and her chest ached. "No, Nichola. My choice is only to wait. Just to wait. I will stay human while they need me. When they no longer need me, when that time comes, I will no longer fight it. I will accept and embrace what I am. I will embrace you." She slowly approached him, wrapping her arms around his body, which stiffened in response. After several seconds, he held her tightly to him. "I will love you and spend eternity with you. I will be everything that you want me to be. Forever is only the beginning." Looking up to meet his eyes, she saw they were red with unshed tears. "I am not my father, Nichola. I can't lie to you; you would know it. Please help me be what I need to be. I promise I will be a vampire one day, your vampire, just not yet."

"Don't you love me at all, i psychí mou?" His soft, beautiful voice was filled with pain and heartache.

"Oh, Nichola." Her tears spilled over unabated. "You are the one that I love and still I have to do this."

He pulled away from her and instantly he was gone. Seconds later, she heard the Mustang in the driveway and ran to a window to watch him pull out of the gate.

"Who the hell are you?" Michael asked in surprise.

Nichola looked around the living room as Zachary came running up to him to hug his leg, yelling in delight, "Nick!" He reached down, stroking Zachary's soft curls gently.

Devin, who was standing on Mansuetus' lap, called, "Neh! Neh!" holding his arms out for him.

Taking him from Mansuetus, he held him close, breathing in his clean scent, as he kissed him gently. "I am Nikolaos Tsoukalous." Looking at Leila's husband, he was unimpressed, and it showed in his tone. "I would speak to you."

"About what?" Michael asked. "Who the hell do you think you are walking into my house like you own it?" He asked the stranger, who was lovingly holding his temperamental youngest son, who beamed at him like he had found his best friend.

"About my soul mate." His voice was sharp and cruel, twisting the knife. "Your wife."

Mansuetus was between them instantly as Michael tried to launch himself at Nichola.

"Don't!" He commanded Michael as he held them apart, though Nichola wasn't trying to approach the human. "Not in front of these children. Do you want your children to see you die?" His voice was low. Looking at Nichola, he told him bluntly, "Kyría would not want this!"

"Kyría doesn't make all the decisions, Mansuetus." Nichola's voice was sharp with anger. He visibly controlled himself. "I am only here to talk." The look he gave Michael was cold, but his whole demeanor softened when he looked down at Zachary, who was looking up at him with worry, as he once again clutched his leg. He smiled gently running his long fingers through Zachary's soft curls again. "Would you like Mansuetus to tell you another story about Bart the Dragon?"

"Yeah!" Zachary yelled, smiling.

Mansuetus bent down to scoop Zachary up in one of his arms.

Nichola gave Devin another gentle kiss and handed him to Mansuetus. Nichola met Mansuetus' harsh look passively as Mansuetus reluctantly left the living room with the children.

"I love them as if they are my own." Nichola told Michael, looking briefly at him as he walked over to the loveseat and sat down uninvited.

Michael stood looking at him in outrage. "Well, they're not! They're mine!"

"Calm yourself, human. We can fight each other and trash your living room if you would like. You would lose. I am both faster and stronger than you are. But it wouldn't be very satisfying for me since I am not allowed to kill you, as that would hurt my mate." His tone was reasonable despite his words. "Sit." He ordered, and Michael sat on his own couch, unable to refuse.

Michael glared at him, taking in his good looks and otherworldly attitude as Nichola crossed his legs and sat back on the loveseat. As jealousy flowed through him, Michael fought to banish the imaginings of Leila making love to this man from his mind. "What do you want?" His voice was laced with hatred.

"I want it all, of course. Just like anyone else." Nichola mocked. "Why are you determined to have her back, human?"

"She's my wife!" Michael grumbled, struggling to launch himself at this monster but finding that he was frozen in place.

"So? These things are easily dissolved today." Nichola watched him battle to move. "I was surprised when Mansuetus told me you wanted her to come back. You realize she is a vampire, don't you?" His tone indicated that Michael might be dense.

"Of course, I do!"

"You do also realize that she has spent much of her time over the past several weeks in my bed," Nichola gloated with a cruel gleam in his eyes.

Michael flinched as the thought cut through him. "Let me go!" He ground out, struggling against invisible bonds.

"Why should I? I would then be forced to hurt you, and Leila would not be happy about that. I am sure that I would also have to endure Mansuetus' long-suffering silences and disappointed looks." Nichola sneered. "After knowing that she was a willing and eager participant, why do you want her back? It is a simple question."

"Because I love her!" Michael's voice rang true as he snarled at him in frustration, fighting to move.

"Yes." Nichola mused. "We both do." He looked at the human in speculation.

Michael was instantly able to move and launched himself at Nichola. His hands extended toward his throat, only to clutch the back of the empty loveseat. He looked around and Nichola stood behind the couch, looking at him in amusement. "You are too slow, human. If you continue in this folly, you will only end up being hurt. Is that what you are looking for from her? Sympathy?"

Michael closed his eyes, his shoulders sagging in defeat as he sat on the loveseat, his face in his hands. "Just go away. Just leave."

"Not until you answer my questions."

Not understanding his tone, Michael looked at him in curiosity.

"Why would you do that?" Michael asked.

"How could you ask that question? Because I love her, and I love the children. You say that you love her as well. Would you not put their welfare before your own?" Nichola asked calmly.

Michael couldn't answer him and he felt him in his mind, wincing at the sensation.

"I see. Well, if you want to live well, you will do so. If I find that you have mistreated them, or not cherished them like they deserve to be cherished, I will collect them all. Regardless of her wishes. The dangers of living with me would not outweigh being mistreated at your hands."

"I would never! I will always take care of them. They are my family." Michael said heatedly.

"See that you do. We will be watching." Nichola's voice was threatening.

"Does she know you came here?" Michael asked the vampire as he followed him out the front door and to the driveway, looking appreciatively at the classic Mustang as Nichola opened the driver's door.

"No. She does not require that knowledge. Remember what we have discussed, and do not make me hunt you down and kill you, human." Nichola looked at Michael, his eyes flashing red.

"I hate you. You realize that, right?" Michael glared at him.

"I don't particularly like you either, but this isn't about us, is it?" Nichola got into the Mustang and drove away.

"Where have you been?" Leila demanded as soon as he stepped off the elevator.

He pulled her close, wrapping his hand behind her neck to capture her lips passionately with his own. After a time, he pulled away to look into her eyes that shown neon teal in desire. "Out." His voice was mild.

Her gaze was bewildered as he released her, moving past her to walk through the kitchen and down the hallway into the master bedroom. Following him quickly she watched him curiously as he sat down and took his boots off.

"You were gone a long time." Her voice quiet with apprehension.

"Mmmmm." He stood and started unbuttoning his shirt, pulling it from his jeans, causing her mouth to go dry with desire as she viewed his tanned chest. He smiled at her as her desire washed over him. "Do you still wish for me to help you, lígo vampír?" He questioned softly as he unbuttoned the cuffs at his wrists and fear coursed through her.

"Can you? Would you?" Tears filled her eyes as multiple emotions crashed together: fear, need, desire, and hope.

"I would give you what you desire if I can. But my help comes with conditions." He gazed into her eyes.

"What conditions?" She squeaked.

"One, you must never reveal to another human what you are. Your existence among them must be kept secret, for your protection as well as for others. If it is found that you have done so, I will remove you to one of my estates." Moving to hold her upper arms in his warm, calloused hands, he realized she was trembling.

"I can do that." She told him, her voice brave as she looked into his red eyes.

"You will give yourself to me everything that you are over the next several days. Without reservation." His gaze bore into hers.

"I..." she started, unsure what he was asking of her.

"Without reservation." As his warm hands gently caressed her arms, she nodded mutely, staring at him in fear.

"What are you going to do?"

"I am going to introduce my venom into your bloodstream. I hope that, as an elder, my venom will help you maintain control over your blood lust, if not eliminate it for a time. It should help you gain enough control to block human thoughts easily, so that they do not overwhelm you. I make no guarantees on how long I can give you relief from your vampiric deficiencies or if you will be able to lead a fully human existence. You are so far advanced that it may not work as well as you would like." His voice was matter-of-fact. Then it softened. "But I will do what I can, mikró." He gazed at her with sorrowful eyes.

"Why?" Her voice was a whisper laced with hope.

"Because I love your sons as my own; almost as much as I love you. Leila, I was a good man before I was a vampire and though many centuries have passed, I still remember what it is like to be human. I know children need their mother. I am putting their needs before mine, if ever so briefly, no matter how much it pains me, because I love them, and I love you."

"Do you think it will work?" Apprehension laced her words.

"When vampires fight without weapons, they bite each other and infect their enemy with venom. This severely weakens the abilities of the vampire who is bitten. It takes time, but eventually the vampire recovers. With you only being marginally a fledgling, and I an elder, I hope that the effect is more pronounced and longer lasting." He turned his back to her and walked a few steps away. He removed his shirt. "Let's call it an educated guess."

She watched the muscles of his back ripple as he tossed the shirt on the floor. Walking to him to stroke his back gently, she wrapped her arms around him, hugging herself to him, laying her cheek against his back. "Thank you, Nichola."

"I don't want your thanks, Leila." His voice was bitter as he placed his hand on her folded ones across his abdomen.

"I know, but you have them anyway."

"You understand I cannot stay after this process is complete."

"What? Why?" She moved around to look up at him. "Why not? You own this house!"

"I will continue to own this house. It will always be here as a refuge for your use if you find you are having a difficult time and need to be alone."

"I don't understand, Nichola." Confusion flooded her mind.

"A human life and family cannot include me, Leila. I am not human. I respect and understand your decision to remain human, but I cannot stay and not have you with me. It would be dangerous to both of us, and more than just us vampires. I will not share you, and as a human, I cannot have you. My presence and my duties on the small council require me to be available to other vampires. Your attachment to me will invite scrutiny from other vampires for yourself, your children and, eventually, your human family. While you are raising your children, we must remain far apart." He explained.

She looked at him, stricken. "I..."

"Don't tell me you didn't think this through, agapitós?" Nichola's voice was sharp. "As a vampire, you cannot remain with your children. If you live as a human, I cannot remain with you. I will not live here without you, waiting for a crumb of your attention. It would drive me mad. I will not have you so near and not be able to live with you. It is not rational of you to ask that I should." Looking at her heartbroken eyes with clear amber eyes, he jerked her against him and kissed her wildly as if he never wanted to let her go.

He scooped her up into his arms effortlessly and carried her to the bed, swiftly removing her clothes to gaze down at her naked body. His eyes were hot as he stood next to the bed, slowly removing his belt and jeans, his gaze locked on hers in promise.

How she wanted him! Exploring his body with her eyes as she lay on the bed, she marveled at his ethereal beauty, which glowed in the semi-dark bedroom. Liquid desire flowed through her veins as he reached out his calloused hand to gently run his fingers from the hollow of her throat down between her breasts and over her stomach to gently caress her curls between her legs; his touch burning on her skin.

"If you don't stop looking at me that way, i psychí mou, I will not be able to control myself for you." He teased her with a small chuckle, and she reached out to grasp his hard cock, running her fingers over him as he threw his head back in pleasure giving a soft moan. She quickly rolled to him, taking him into her mouth to taste him as he stood next to the bed. A sensual groan escaped him, and he ran his fingers through the curls on her head.

Pulling away from her grasping mouth, he pushed her to lie back on the bed and joined her there. "Glukó mou, my sweet." Nichola ran his tongue along the silky skin of her throat, tasting the peppermint and licorice of her skin and breathing in her jasmine scent. His tongue ran over the rapid pulse of her carotid and his fangs descended. He felt her stiffen in his arms as he gently grazed his fangs along her artery. "Fear me not, pio agapiméni mou, my most beloved one. This night is for us." He moved down her body with butterfly kisses to fasten his mouth on her nipple, reveling when she arched her back pushing herself into him and he felt her small delicate hands run her fingers through the golden waves of his hair as she held him to her breast with a small moan of pleasure.

Moving to cover her body with his own, he parted her legs and thrust himself into her tight wetness, not wanting to wait to feel the pleasure of her surrounding him any longer. He straightened, thrusting deeper and captured her lips with his own as she gave a small gasp of joy.

As he slowly thrust into her body, his mental wall collapsed and she was awash in him; his emotions flowed through her body like physical things. Leila felt his anguish, heartache, desire, and steadfast love. "Oh, Nichola. I love you so." She moaned as her body tightened around him in orgasm.

She stood with him outside of the small hangar at the St. Mary's airport Sunday night while his small jet taxied over to them.

"I can't do this." She told him tearfully, clutching at him as he held her close against his body and she sobbed into his chest.

"You know how to reach me if you have need of me." He murmured into the top of her head as he held her tightly. "I will always be a phone call away. When you are ready, you will call me to you."

"I can't feel you anymore." She cried as she clutched him to her.

Since his last bite of venom last night, it was as if a black hole had opened in her soul and she was numb. She had never felt alone when she was with him, not since she had met him, and it was breaking her.

"I can feel you, i psychí mou. I can still feel you. I will always be able to feel you." His soft tenor voice was filled with heartache as he held her. "Will you miss me a little?"

"Nichola, I will miss you every moment we are apart!" She sobbed. "I can't do this!" She grasped him tightly.

"Shh. Glykó, remember why we are doing this? The boys deserve their mother with them. What we have is timeless and my love for you is endless." He looked down into her distraught, dark teal human eyes.

"I still need you! I still want you! I still love you! Please don't leave me! The thought of you gone makes everything wrong in my life. It makes it all feel so wrong." She begged him.

He bent down kissing her wildly, passionately, not caring who saw them. "I swear to love you all my life, Leila." He vowed against her lips. "I am not your first love, i psychí mou, but I will be your last. I'll reach my hands out in the dark and wait for yours to interlock. I will wait for you." He felt her love and pain. He felt her terror that she could no longer read him. His gaze bore down into hers, willing her to believe him. "I love you more than you will ever know. I will always be yours, and as long as I am with you in the end, I will give you and the boys this chance. I waited centuries to find you. I can wait a little more. I'll wait for you because I know you will find your way back to me. You are worth the wait. My soul will be with you, no matter where you go or what you do. You will always have me waiting for you in your dreams."

Epilogue One

DECEMBER 1995

THANKFULLY OVERCAST, THE HARSH glare of the sun barely breaking through the clouds, she drove to the bank; now used to the faint itching, crawling pain under her skin, the day could be described as tolerable.

The air conditioner was running and the coolness against her welcoming as she merged with traffic; the thoughts of the other drivers occasionally entering her brain, but even this was more controllable than before.

Everything in her life seemed easier to do with her choice made. Her venom laced veins controlling the largest parts of this addiction, she learned to appreciate many things in her life. She was more appreciative of the people around her, and they seemed to appreciate her and her talents more also; especially at work, where she had finally been promoted to her own management position. It was challenging, interesting and exciting all at once. It also proved to be a needed distraction and a place to focus her attention, other than the changes occurring in her body. Strangely, the added responsibility and pressure helped her with her control.

Who knew that she was this strong and able to thrive in a high-pressure environment?

Nichola had, and it was the reason that he himself strived to do all he did in his life. What's more was that he trusted her. He trusted her to conquer herself and sacrificed his time with her to give her and the boys the best life possible. Lending her his strength, he had kept her from fully changing and helped her keep her control in place.

That decision embodied true love and respect, despite its difficulty. Difficult for them both.

Mansuetus stayed with her, helping her for a long time. Even after a few months when she had finally moved back into her own house, he had stayed in the house at London Hill Bluff. He frequently visited the boys and helped out with them despite Michael hating it, as he was a reminder of Leila's time that she had spent with Nichola. He had left the first of November after taking the boys trick-or-treating on Halloween. They took turns calling each other weekly to talk about the boys. She knew he missed them terribly and knew that he would visit as often as he could.

She thought about Michael. They still shared separate bedrooms, but both were working extremely hard on being good parents and spouses. Sometimes it was tough for them. They were both working through the process of forgiving each other. Still, both had come together to provide a solid base for their children and, in the process, learned that they still cared deeply for each other. More than either realized.

Would he ever come to appreciate the gifts that she had? Musing on this, she found that it wasn't necessary that he appreciate her vampire gifts or not. After all, that wasn't really what she wanted. Her remaining vampire gifts should never be the most important to him; she only really wanted to be important to him for herself, for their family. She wasn't sure yet if it would work for them. But she had hope.

The most important people in her life were her sons. Everything that she did, everything that she had, was for her sons. She would never forget that, and with that knowledge, she would conquer anything and sacrifice what she desired most, to be there for them. To help them be better men or in time vampires until they didn't need her.

She wasn't sure, but she felt that Zachary and Devin could both be in line for what she was going through. Now that she knew what to look for, as she journeyed through this life, day by day, night by night, she was almost certain that both would come to a point in their lives where the changes would occur. There was too much intelligence flashing behind their little eyes. Too much sentience in their actions, their speech. Yes, they were the important ones.

She would do everything in her power to make sure that she was there for them when their times of change came. Their transitions would be easier for them because they would have someone who accepted the possibilities; not someone who hid from them.

She was going to make sure of that.

Her actions were automatic as she drove. Her eyes flicked to check mirrors, one hand resting lightly on the steering wheel. The other hand slowly pushed buttons on the radio, pausing as a hauntingly familiar tune flowed from the speakers.

Nichola. A sharp, sweet longing pierced her chest. It had been surprisingly simple to make her peace with him; though exquisitely painful for her to watch him leave. But for him? He left for her. After all, what was a few decades to a creature so ancient? His love for her children took him by surprise. Her need to protect them above herself, above the needs in her young vampire body, her willingness to give up everything for them, only enhanced his feeling of the incredible power she housed within her soul.

Once he came to this realization, The Bargain was made. Difficult and heartbreaking as it was, she would stay with them. Raising her children, nurturing them, teaching them until the day came that they no longer needed her. She wouldn't neglect them and withhold knowledge from them like her father had. Once they no longer needed her, she would be Nichola's. Until then, he would have no contact with her.

With her decision to stay and be a wife and mother, living out the remainder of her human life, he had to leave. He was vampire after all and knew he had no place in her human life. She was truly his soulmate. To him, to both of them, what they had together and what they meant to each other, would always be much more than just being a human wife. For her children, their children, they would endure the pain of separation.

Turning the corner, she found a parking space, surprised that there were so many cars in the lot. But as she looked around, she realized it was payday. Not so unusual, after all.

Getting out of the car, she straightened the gray rayon of her skirt and suit jacket, the blue piping on the jacket pulling the blue out in her teal-colored eyes. Clutching the manuscript to her chest as the wind picked up roughly, blowing through her short auburn curls that framed her face and neck, causing her to hold her hat in place.

Safely nestled within the large yellow envelope, it held immense importance.

If she failed, if she faltered even once in her control, she would have to leave; and the manuscript would be the only thing to guide her children. The only thing she could give them to ease their way; to make sure that they would have the knowledge to help them succeed where she didn't.

Looking at the gray concrete exterior of her local bank, she entered, noticing the long line of people at the teller's windows. She moved to the right of the lobby into the customer service area. A petite, pretty, blonde woman looked up in recognition, a smile upon her lips.

"Mrs. Sutton, it's so nice to see you again. How may I help you today?"

Always amazed at this young woman, Leila was impressed at the kind, warm way she served the customers of the bank. It was always nice to encounter someone who liked their job.

"I need to place something in my safe deposit box, please." The answering smile on her lips was sincere.

"Of course. Right this way." Standing, she proceeded to lead Leila to a vault containing rows of boxes and alcoves for privacy.

Leila handed the woman her driver's license, bank card stating box number forty-seven, and her key.

The pleasant young woman had the guard retrieve the box and bring it to the alcove that she led Leila to.

Smiling, ever helpful, the young woman said, "When you are through, Mrs. Sutton, just let the guard know and he will replace the box for you. If I can be of any more assistance, you just let me know." She then left Leila to her thoughts.

Leila thanked her warmly, then sat looking at the box number engraved on the plate. She took a deep breath, took her key, and unlocked it.

She removed her diamond and ruby necklace. The stones brightly reflecting the lights of the vault. The gems exquisitely heart shaped. She smiled as she touched the sparkling stones and remembered that wondrous night.

She remembered the now dried rose and pulled it from the box. The redness of the petals was almost black now. Heat rose in her body. Nichola's amber eyes floated in her mind. "I psychí mou, my soul, I love you" he declared, pausing again almost surprised with his sudden revelation, "I haven't said that to a woman in more than 900 years, and I have never meant it as I do now." He bent his head and possessed her lips tenderly.

She shook her head abruptly banishing the images flashing through her mind. These thoughts didn't help her control. Laying the rose to the side with the necklace, she removed some pictures. Her father and mother, arms wrapped around each other, so much in love.

"I wish you would have told me sooner, Dad." She whispered into the silence of the vault. "Will we ever be able to look at each other the same way again? With that same affection? Well, you made your choice, Daddy, and I at least understand it now." She placed the picture with the other items.

She touched the picture of Iris and Dene. It had been a shock to find it amongst the pictures that Mansuetus had left for her. Their gorgeous dark looks complimenting each other as they smiled into the camera, his arm around her slim waist. Iris made it a habit to call her at least every other week to check-in with her. She still missed the old harridan terribly.

She now looked at the photo of Zachary and Devin. Zachary's curly, golden hair shining damply in the basement room of the London Hill house, little arms wrapped around Devin from behind. Little teeth showing with his smile. Blue eyes shining. Eyes like his grandfather, like hers were at times. Devin's toothy smile, light brown hair just starting to curl. Clove-colored eyes, his father's eyes, flashing.

Little cherubs glowing for the camera.

As her eyes filled with tears, her fingertips barely touching the photograph, she whispered, "I hope you realize when the time comes just how much I love you. Love you both, so very much." Leila then placed this photograph with the rest of the items.

She lifted the manuscript, placing it in the box. Feeling a burden lift from her as she did so. Knowledge that she was doing the right thing rushing through her veins.

Replacing the other articles on top of the manuscript, she locked the box and waved and called to the guard. Watching as he removed the box from in front of her, replacing it in its spot in the wall, securing it in place and giving her the key.

Stopping by the customer service desk, she thanked the little blonde woman for her help and walked through the doors of the bank, putting her black Raybans on to protect her sensitive eyes from the sunlight, straightening her gray sunhat.

Her thoughts were unfocused and wandering as she walked to her car. She looked up and, leaning against the back of her Honda, was Michael. Her footsteps faltered in surprise, but she continued toward him.

She stopped in front of him, looking up into his large brown eyes, thinking how handsome he was in his khaki uniform. She didn't even bother trying to read him. With the venom coursing through her veins, she never seemed to be able to see his thoughts clearly now. There was too much emotion on her part for that to work: too much honesty, too much pride, too much fear, too much tenderness.

He slowly reached out, cupping her face with his large hand to look deeply into her shaded eyes.

"I love you; I have always loved you. I will love you no matter what happens." His words a statement of conviction as he bent and placed his warm lips on hers. She wrapped her arms around his body, rubbing her palms up his back. He wrapped his arms around her, pulling her tightly into his body. His love and humanity anchoring her to her chosen life.

As the sun's rays broke through the clouds shining down on them, she didn't feel any pain at all.

Epilogue Two

FEBRUARY 2019

A S THE FEVER RAGED through me, I knew I was slipping into un-consciousness, and I was reluctant to let go of my control. It's been a long, long time since I felt the need to break free from this cocoon, this prison that I had voluntarily placed myself in. Control has become my second nature and as much a part of me as breathing.

Amazed and frustrated, I just can't understand why I can't shake this fever! Why, when I began to feel better, I would 'relapse'? It's been coming and going for months now, wearing on my patience and my strength!

Why can't I shake this virus? It wasn't the vampire gene that infected my DNA, the one that I'd lived with for almost 25 years with rarely an ill day since. I knew that. Because, according to the doctors and all their tests, it was just a virus. Virus or other, it was a mystery. To one and all.

They had no clue what it was and frighteningly, neither did I. I seemed to get weaker and weaker, and the symptoms were all over the place. Chest pains, sometimes as strong as a heart attack! Headaches, so strong that I had to be in a silent, darkened room! Problems breathing where the slightest scent would take my breath from my lungs and leave me gasping on the floor. Fevers and chills, like a flu, gone rampant! Multiple trips to the doctor, and even being rushed once to the emergency room by Devin. Having every test under the sun performed, only to have several medical 'professionals' tell me, 'It's a virus of some sort and will have to run its course.'

Thank God, none of them are driven geniuses like Dr. Dene Lambert, or I might be in real trouble. But work ethics in 2019 weren't what they were in 1995. If they didn't know what it was, they threw antibiotics at it and told you to see them in a few days if it didn't go away. Still, at times I felt like I was dying, and almost, *almost* welcomed it.

I couldn't shake the feeling that it was something man-made, something unusual, something not natural, and something unique. After all, it had to be to affect *me* this way.

All of a sudden, I felt a slight cooling of my fever and opened my eyes. Instead of finding myself in my bedroom in Texas, where Michael and I had lived for about six years now, I found myself, still in my own turquoise green nightgown, standing barefoot on a damp sidewalk outside of a large mansion. It was night. But I wasn't bothered by that, it was night where I should have been too!

Not understanding where I was, I was confused and pissed off. Where the hell could I be? The lights around the mansion beckoned to me, and I felt the need to move. Before I realized what was occurring, I marched up the front steps, looking at enormous, black-iron, double front doors. Reaching out to touch them, they opened of their own accord.

Feeling ghost-like, I noticed the dark stained wood floors that shone with muted light coming from above my head. Looking up, I realized I was in a foyer and the chandelier, instead of being sparkling crystal, was ancient, iron and very masculine.

Where the hell am I? Now I'm hallucinating! Oh, this has got to stop! I thought to myself seeing yet *another* trip to the doctor in my future, that is, if I were ever able to get out of my bed!

The doors automatically closed behind me as I walked farther into the foyer. A large open doorway to the left emitted more muted light. It came from a large fire in an enormous fireplace surrounded by an ornate flagstone hearth.

This feels so surreal! Where on earth am I? I thought.

Approaching the fireplace, I moved past the old-fashioned furniture; the rich red velvet of the sofa and the gold and green pattern of the armchairs were distinctly familiar and touchable, and unable to stop myself, I ran my hand along the backs as I walked to stand before the fire, staring hard into its depths. Feeling outside of myself, in an unusual state of being, was foreign.

With my vampiric condition constantly under control and held at bay, this intense confusion, and bewilderment, was disturbing, to say the least.

With a start, my memory returned, and I knew where I was; I had just never entered from the front entrance before. Looking around, I could see that there were very few changes in the room. Maybe a picture here or there.

But the furniture and carpet still looked immaculate, rich, and sumptuous. Much like the creature that lived there. Though, I am surprised that he would break our agreement after all this time.

I felt him, before I heard him; sensed him before he spoke.

"Are you really here? Or is this just another one of my dreams? Are you ready?" His melodious voice made my heart ache.

Turning to face him, I saw him lounging in a huge red and gold high-backed velvet chair, which was new to me at least. His legs and bare feet stretched out upon a matching velvet ottoman, a large old book in his lap; dressed in a comfortable looking white silk, collarless, long-sleeved shirt, and black pants. The material of the pants escapes me, but they look oh, so soft and touchable.

The chair was throne-like, and I thought, smiling, *That is so like you, Nichola, my soul mate.*

Instead, I spoke, "I'm not ready. Of course, I'm not ready. How am I here?" Looking him straight in his amber eyes, taking in his golden wavy hair, so like a Greek god, I thought to myself, *Why am I not ready?*

"You must be in distress. This feels different from when we met here, a long time ago. I sense you, see you, and realize that you may be close. But you are weak, less solid than before." He told me, and his confusion rivaled mine.

"I'm sick. I've been to several doctors, and they continuously give me medicine, but nothing seems to work. They don't know what is wrong with me. This wasn't part of our agreement." I accused, wanting to blame someone for my mystery illness.

"This is not your vampirism causing these issues. You already know this. You should be healthy until the day you choose to embrace your true nature. Or it ultimately chooses for you. I think you're coming to see me now because you may have made that decision. Even if subconsciously," he theorized softly, with a note of hope in his voice.

"No." I was firm, gesturing with a sweep of my hand. "I am not ready for that. I am not ready for this. I am not ready to leave my family. I am still needed." I told him with conviction.

"Then you're not ready." He said simply, without accusation or anger, his trust in me complete. "You must be missing me. Since you are dream-walking to me." He smiled softly, teasingly, reminding me of how I viewed our souls communing in the beginning.

"I always miss you, Nichola. Every day. Though this is the first time I have felt you in many years." I smiled softly in return, glad to have the feeling of him back in my soul.

"Time is returning some of your abilities to you." He told me simply. "Though distressing to you, this illness will pass. You will come to me when you are ready to be totally mine."

"I'm frightened. I don't know what could cause me to be ill like this." I tried to control the catch in my voice.

"Your aunt's friend, Dr. Lambert, has learned much about us. A virus is just a virus. Sometimes viruses can interfere with who and what you are. But in the end, even the plague could never *overcome* your DNA. So far, and he has experimented with a great many, viruses are unable to change vampiric DNA, and he has yet to find either 'a cure', or 'a repellent'." His voice was convinced, steady. To calm my fears, he held his hand out to me. "Besides, we both know that Dr. Lambert can be an emotional fool on occasion. After all, we are Vampire. I have always known that condition to be beyond any virus. Even without all his experiments." Nichola told me, smiling softly, happy to see me.

Putting his book aside, he extended his hand further, curling his fingers, beckoning me to him.

Approaching him, it felt like I was gliding instead of walking on my feet. He was right. This was different. Less solid than in the past, weaker. "If not by you, Nichola, how am I here? How can I be here? How am I here?" Confusion and exhaustion were taking its toll on me as I moved toward him.

"We are meeting with our minds, with our souls. You know soulmates can meet with each other's minds, communicate, take strength from each other, even across great distances, especially in times of great stress. You must be extremely ill, and worried, indeed. Or at least you think you are. You must believe you need me." His voice held no worry.

I reached out my hand, taking his slightly calloused hand in mine, and he felt solid. He felt real and warm. I smelled the cinnamon, ginger and sandalwood that was his scent. It soothed my worry. *He* soothed my worries, and as I touched him, I felt my strength slowly returning. Though I didn't feel quite normal, I did feel better. I intertwined my fingers with his as he pulled me to curl up like a child into his lap. I rested my head on his shoulder, taking strength from his very presence, taking strength from his soul.

Feeling his lips gently touch the top of my head, I felt his whisper against my hair. "I have missed you so much, agapoula mou, my little love,"

"I've missed you too, my love, my soul."

"How are the boys?" he asked quietly, as if he didn't know, which we both knew was untrue. After all, Mansuetus kept him well-informed.

"They're adults now. Zachary's out on his own, and I am having doubts he will become a vampire. I'm not sure how I feel about that. After all, it'll be much simpler for him if he doesn't. But then I will lose him, eventually. The thought of that pains me to the core. Devin still lives with us. He's going to law school soon. There's no doubt in my mind that he'll suffer the change." I told him, a little sadly. "He will need your help. He is strong, and smart, and headstrong." I told him with a small smile resting against him and listening to the sound of his slow, strong heartbeat.

"Of course he is. He takes after his mother. He will make a fine vampire." His voice quiet as he ran his hand lightly and gently up and down my arm; trailing warmth in his touch, moving to softly cup my breast. Rubbing his thumb over my nipple, quickly bringing it to a peak. "I always knew that this, in some small part, was part of your denial about who you are and why you didn't come with me." His voice was exasperated, as I flinched slightly at his sensual stroking, but oh, so slight was my resistance.

I placed my hand over his. Pressing his hand to me. Wanting to reassure him. Wanting him to touch me.

"You know why I made the choice I made, and wanting you was never part of it. Besides, you agree with my decision. As painful as it still is, it was the right decision, and I wouldn't have been able to do it without your help." I told him quickly, looking up and placing my hand on his cheek, feeling the stubble of his shadowy beard. "I am just not used to being touched like that, and it has been a long time since I have seen you."

"Another of my regrets. Forgive me. I am lonely without you." His melodic vampire *voice* soft.

I felt his pull and had enough strength to resist it for the moment.

"I'm not sure how we're meeting this way. You said we would never meet again until I was ready to let go of my mortal life and embrace my vampire future."

"You always have questions." Smiling, he shook his head. "I have been and will always be open to meeting with you if you so wish it. Until now, you haven't been strong enough to seek me in this manner, and having you here, I realize I have only punished myself by not seeing you in this way. But, right now, in this moment, you need me to give you strength." Placing his fingers underneath my chin, he lifted my face to look into my eyes as he brought his lips closer to mine.

"I always need your strength, Nichola. Even when you aren't with me, I still want you; I still need you. I still love you." Whispering to him, willing him to read my heart.

He kissed me softly, building deeper and deeper and with more passion.

As his lips met mine, I suddenly knew that I had come to him, that in my hour of need he was the one I would always come to, no matter that my body was not with him. That he would always welcome me, that he would always love me. I knew I couldn't physically be with him at this moment, but I could still feel him on this plane, in our minds. He dipped his tongue through my lips as he plundered my mouth, and I welcomed him.

He lifted his head to look me in the eyes. "You are my mate. I will always give you everything that I have. Everything that I am belongs to you. Take of me my strength and as you do, take of my blood and my soul to bring you through this illness. I will wait a little longer for you to come to me permanently. I will wait until you are ready. But I am hungry and lonely for you."

Noticing our reflection in a vast mirror on the opposite wall, shock flooded my soul. I looked exactly like I did the day he left me, almost 25 years ago.

How could that be? How could I look so young? Time and age had taken its toll on my human body. With vampire venom coursing through my veins, I indeed looked young for someone of fifty-four, but I did not look like I was twenty-nine. Were he and I really communicating? Or was this just a fever induced hallucination? A fervent, feverish wish to be with him?

"This is the way you will look when you finally come to me. Your change started at this age. Because I drank from you and injected my own venom to help give you strength to halt your condition, when I did so, your soul stopped aging. Your body will revert to this age when you fully accept your vampire state, and then your soul will continue on its journey to immortality." He told me softly.

"You still know what I am thinking?" I asked, looking from our bodies wrapped together in the large chair in the mirror, into the amber of his eyes.

"Remember, Panemorfi. We are true soulmates. It isn't just words. I'll always sense you. I'll always know when you are near or far. And I'll always know how you feel; even if I cannot read your exact words; I will always understand how you feel. Knowing how you feel gets me through the loneliness of my life without you. Knowing that you miss me every day. Knowing that your sacrifice has been as great as mine." He looked deep into my eyes and his honesty burned my loneliness away.

Feeling his heart beneath my hand, I felt the love coming from his soul. By partitioning what I was, it was as if I had forgotten what it felt like to be here with him; what it felt like to know another person as completely as I knew myself. He would never lie to me, could never lie to me. We, in a sense, were one.

He slowly pushed the nightgown off my shoulders to touch the skin of my chest. Even with the true realization that this wasn't a dream, but our souls touching, it felt so strange and otherworldly to have him touch me when I knew I wasn't physically there with him. So strange to feel the warmth and pressure of his lightly calloused hands and fingers.

On the other hand, if this was a fever-induced hallucination, I wasn't willing to let it go just yet; and as such, it made me bold.

I heard his voice in my mind. *Make love to me, my sweet one. Always love me, always need me, for you are my heart, my life, my soul. There's never been and never will be anyone else who completes me the way you do.*

As I moved to straddle him, he slowly ran his hands up the outside of my legs, pushing the nightgown up and over my head, running his fingers softly, gently over the tips of my breasts around to my back.

I ran my fingers through his silky, wavy golden hair. Slightly rising to gently touch my lips to his forehead, I ran my fingers gently over his high cheekbones and down through the sparse golden hair on his chest, pushing his white silk shirt open wide. I pulled the shirt from his pants over his shoulders and reached to undo the button of his pants. As I did so, he ran his hands down over my hips and brought me close to him to nuzzle at my breasts, as I rested my face against the softness of his wavy hair.

His soft lips trailed kisses over my nipples as I freed his cock and worked the tight fabric of his pants down over his hips, and with his help, from his legs, adjusting our bodies as I did so. I was feeling a frenzy building inside of me.

"Slow, my love. I have missed you so much and I won't rush this. We have all the time in the world, and we always will." He slowly ran his fingertips over my shoulders and my shoulder blades, and softly kissed the hollow of my throat.

"It's been so long," I panted. "It's been so long for me."

"I know, I as well. But I am here; I am always going to be here for you." He said, running his hands over the curve of my spine, down around my ass cheeks and in through the cleft to stroke and tentatively enter me from behind my back.

I arched my back, feeling my juices slick his fingers, as he rubbed at the crease of my pussy, and I claimed his mouth with my own. I needed him, needed him to fill me, needed him to fill the void of my soul; more so than I ever realized.

I could feel the pressure inside me building. Building toward a quick orgasm.

"Nichola, I am ready!" I half shrieked, nipping at his shoulder.

"Not yet," he murmured against my nipple, and removed his hand.

I almost cried in frustration as I felt the pressure drop.

He moved with vampiric speed, scooping me into his arms and stood holding my naked body high against his chest.

My breath caught in my throat. Wrapped in the days of my human existence, I had forgotten his speed and his strength.

Walking the few steps to the large red and gold sofa, he placed me to sit on the soft velvet of its cushions as he knelt before me. Looking deeply into my eyes, he took one ankle into each of his hands and slowly spread my legs.

I looked at him silhouetted and dark against the flames in the fireplace, his amber eyes shining like lights in the darkness, like two gold rings into mine as he bent his head to place his mouth against the curls of my pussy for a soft kiss. My mouth went dry with desire as his hands moved up from my ankles over the inside of my legs and thighs, spreading me ever wider as his thumbs moved to spread my nether-lips to expose my clitoris, which was engorged with need.

Looking up at me, he gently, softly, slowly, ran the tip of his long tongue over the folds of my pussy, to end not quite touching, but encircling my clitoris.

A deep guttural moan of desire escaped my lips, as I felt the pressure of craving build in me again. I reached for his shoulders, but he moved my hands to either side of my body, so I dug my nails into the cushions of the couch as he again ran his tongue over me and around my clitoris, which was swollen and engorged with my blood. I could feel his magic, his force of will, making my body react, and was shrouded in his scent. I shivered uncontrollably with need.

"Oh, please, Nichola, my love. Please." I begged him for release. As I begged, he sucked my clitoris into his mouth and worked his tongue slowly up and down its swollen length. My hips bucked involuntarily, and my head hit the cushion of the back of the couch as his hands gripped me to hold me in place.

His broad shoulders kept my legs parted wide and open to his mouth and tongue.

My whole body was taut with tension, and I was almost there, when he removed his mouth from my clitoris, whispered, "Not yet," and pierced my inner thigh with his fangs.

I let out a cry of surprise and passion, and before I even had a chance to fully register his actions, or feel him take a sip of my blood, he was sealing the bite mark with his saliva and pushing a long finger into my pussy and rubbing his thumb on my clitoris. I looked into his now glowing, teasing, red eyes and saw a drop of my blood at the corner of his mouth which he slowly dabbed with his long tongue as he knelt between my legs and felt his magic once more surround me bringing me closer to the edge. I could feel perspiration breaking out all over my body, as the fever inside me broke, and I drew ever closer to completion.

As I grew tighter around his thrusting finger, he suddenly withdrew it from my body and whispered, "Not yet," one more time.

I was desperate for release now, and my breath came in small gasps, "Nichola!" I all but wailed as he stood; his pale tan cock was large, swollen, and rampant before me. Reaching out to encircle him, stroking him intently, I brought forth a sharp groan from him. Moving forward, I opened my mouth wide and took him inside. His skin was like the softest velvet over the hardest muscle. I ran my tongue over the ridge on the underside of his cock and his hips moved involuntarily as I heard him gasp.

He ran his fingers into my hair, gripping me to him as I loved him with my mouth, running one of my hands up his hard muscled abdomen and chest. "Agapi mou, my love," he whispered with a groan of pleasure.

Soon, I could feel the skin of his balls where I held them tighten, and he quickly pulled my head and my mouth away from him. He sat down on the couch, lifting me to straddle him, as I had done in the chair; except this time there was no intent to separate us.

I held his face between my hands, kissing him tenderly, looking into his red eyes, as he held himself and rubbed the velvet head of his cock against the lips of my pussy, parting them.

"Slowly," he instructed me, as I slid down his length, while he stayed still, his hands gripping my hips, centimeter by centimeter.

I occasionally slid back up his length as I adjusted to the size of him. Two steps forward, one step back; until I had his full length filling me, stretching me.

Then we moved together: thrusting, reaching, touching, kissing. I felt the pressure once again building inside of me. I could feel his cock expand also, and he held back his own release with a small moan as I built toward mine.

He held my face with one hand, setting off memories in my soul, as he ran his other hand up and down my spine and over my ass, as I slowly rode him. I remembered the first time he had ever touched my face in such a way, when the realization of being his soulmate was new, and I was but a child.

Sliding up and down his length, I opened my eyes, and his met mine.

He reached up to his collarbone and sliced open a small wound with one sharp nail, his voice in my mind. *Drink of me, i psychí mou. Drink of my strength and heal yourself.*

I kissed his lips softly, my hips ever thrusting against his own, building toward my pinnacle, and quickly fastened my mouth to his collarbone, drawing his spicy blood into my mouth to swirl on my tongue and swallow deeply. As I did so, I could feel my muscles contract around him in orgasm as I moaned loudly in pleasure; in turn, I could feel his cock expand and hear his shout of release, as I took another deep drink from his veins.

As the unbridled lust took us to another plane of existence, I rode him hard in an out-of-control orgasm I didn't want to end.

"Soon, my love. We will be together soon." I heard Nichola's beautiful tenor voice whisper to me as I lost consciousness wrapped tightly in his muscled arms.

I woke feeling stronger and healthier than I had in months.

'Soon,' he had said.

Yes, for Nichola, my soul mate, the ancient creature that he was, twenty years could be soon. But, as he had reminded me several times this evening, *NOT YET*.

Foreign Language Glossary

agápi mou - my love
   i allagí mou – my changeling
   allaxiéra – changeling
   ángixe me – touch me
   agapitós - beloved
   áse me na se agapíso – let me love you
   áse me na se agapó gia pánta – let me love you forever
   Château les Ténèbres – Dark Castle
   Despótis: Lord or Master
   Déspoina: lady or mistress
   efcharistó – thank you
   efcharistó, glykó mou, Se agapó – thank you, my sweet, I love you
   éla gia ména – come for me
   éla na to párei – come on pick it up
   epitrépste mou na sas dóso efcharístisi – allow me to give you pleasure
   fíla me – kiss me
   glukó mou- my sweet
   Glykó – sweet one
   i psychí mou – my soul
   i theá tis omorfiás mou – my goddess of beauty
   Kyría: Lady, madam, mistress
   Kýrios: mister, main, lord, master, sir
   Le violeur vampire déchirant – The Ripping Vampire Rapist
   lígo vampír – little vampire
   mikró – little one
   moró – baby
   moy golub' – my dove

THE CHOICE

Naí – yes

nóstimo – delicious

Ochi agápi mou – no my love

o ómorfos ángelos mou - my beautiful angel

O Theé mou – Oh God

Panemorfi – beautiful

Parakaló agápi mou, Lypámai – Please my love, I am sorry.

páre me sto glykó sou sóma – take me into your sweet body

pio agapiméni mou – my most beloved one

Prépei na eímai mésa sou me ton éna í ton állo trópo - I need to be inside of you one way or the other.

Se agapó – I love you

se parakaló agápi mou – please my love

Se parakaló voíthisé me – please help me

sýnchrones gynaíkes – modern women

thélo na eímai mésa sou – I want to be inside of you

Ypóschomai – I promise

Author Bio

V.P. NIGHTSHADE'S LIFE IN Texas is anything but ordinary; her grumpy old husband, two hormonal sons, an Alien Dog, a Cairn Terrier Princess who's very opinionated and talks, and new to the family in August 2023, a Cairn Terrier who Tangos – All makes for an eclectic, and occasionally, chaotic family. V.P. loves her family!

She is both a reader and a writer. She loves reading about all things that go bump in the night, aliens who fly through the skies, and steamy romance novels. In her writing, she masterfully combines her favorite elements to create angsty paranormal romance stories that will keep you on the edge of your seat until the happily ever after.

If you see her in a coffee shop, chances are you'll discover V.P. in the corner, daydreaming about her characters and their stories.

If you enjoy the suspenseful twists, turns, or steaminess of authors like Sarah J. Maas, Stephenie Meyer, H.P. Mallory, Ruby Dixon, or Amber Foy, you'll fall in love with V.P. Nightshade's books!

Please don't wait; production and print costs are always going up, buy them now before the price changes!

Contact V. P. at: https://www.facebook.com/VPNightshade.Author

Follow V. P. on Goodreads at: https://www.goodreads.com/author/show/21223301.V_P_Nightshade

Follow V. P. on her Amazon Author Page to see all of her books at: https://www.amazon.com/author/vpnightshade

Subscribe to V. P.'s YouTube at: https://www.youtube.com/@v.p.nightshade

Twitter: https://twitter.com/VPN_Writes

Want to stay in the loop on upcoming releases, get special reader benefits, and ask V. P. questions directly about her characters and books? Join the reader group by copying and pasting the link below!!

https://www.facebook.com/groups/nightshadesafterdarkdarlings